The Mantis Pact

by
Phillip Malcolm

CepenPark Publishing Ltd
57 Vallis Road
Frome
BA11 3EG
email: publishing@cepenpark.co.uk

CEPENPARK PUBLISHING LTD

First Published in Great Britain in 2012 by CepenPark Publishing Ltd

© 2012 Phillip Malcolm

The author asserts the moral right to be identified as the author of this work. All rights reserved. No part of this publication may be reproduced, stored in a retrieval system, or transmitted, in any form or by any means, electronic, mechanical, photocopying, recording, or otherwise, without the prior written permission of the publishers.

This is a work of fiction. Any references to real people, living or dead, real events, businesses, organisations and localities are intended only to give the fiction a sense of reality and authenticity. All names characters, places and incidents either are the product of the author's imagination or are used fictitiously, and their resemblance, if any, to real life counterparts is entirely coincidental.

www.themantispact.com

A catalogue record of this book is available from the British Library

ISBN 978 0 9564230 2 3
Printed in Great Britain by
TJ International,
Trecerus Industrial Estate,
Padstow, Cornwall, PL28 8RW

For
Absent Friends

Acknowledgements

Writing this, my first novel, has been an interesting journey. It is not the first book I have written, neither have I come recently to authorship having been a Technical Author for nearly four decades, during which time I cannot imagine how many pages of text were produced for numerous customers.

All of those pages described complex machines, procedures and events from the past. The difference, this time, is that none of what you are about to read came from a drawing, or a technical specification, or a recording of a conversation. In fact, I have no real concept of where it all came from, the characters all being fictional and, to my surprise when I reread the completed novel, not based upon anybody I have known, or met for more than a fleeting moment.

I have, of course, been to many of the places described, most of which do exist. The main setting for the story is a place where we lived and worked for periods over the time around which the story is set, and is still one of my favourite places because of the pace of life it provided at a time when my home country seemed to have become way too hectic. So I first want to thank all those people in Wichita who made us so welcome back then, helped us in our work and entertained us in between.

Next, eternal thanks to Jim and Jenny for organising that wonderful fortnight's holiday in Alcudia at a time when my life was changing from being the frantic globetrotter to the retired homeworker. It was during that relaxed break that the genesis of this novel was allowed to form, and although it took several years to acquire the momentum to be completed, that was the spark to ignite the flame that burned within me to see it to fruition.

I would also like to thank my reading panel, Andy, Emma, Richard, Mary, Paul and Leanne who all kindly agreed to read this story, for showing such continued enthusiasm to do so during its long gestation and despite having no idea how good or bad it might be. But particularly for being honest with me when I had finished the draft. I hope you approve of the changes. Then to Holly and Dan for receiving my own efforts at cover design with such disdain that inspired them to visualise this one instead, and then for finding Kevin who turned those ideas into the finished product.

Finally, to my family and closest friends all the thanks in the world for being there all of the time, in particular my wonderful wife Kathy who has suffered me for nearly forty-five years, and still puts-up with my many foibles. I couldn't have finished this without you.

prologue

There was no mistaking the familiar gait of the figure walking down the sloping corridor from the arrivals hall towards her. The body looked leaner and fitter than she remembered, the fair hair a lot shorter, but despite the eight long years since they last met in 1995, the adrenaline rush that the image produced was undeniable. The two met in an ecstatic embrace not unfamiliar for such occasions. Her visitor had no hold luggage to collect, and so, already in deep conversation, they walked through the doors and out into the rapidly-fading sunlight of another Midwest blue-sky day.

The couple chattered incessantly as they crossed the approach road towards the short-term car park. She popped the central locking before slipping into the driver's seat of the silver Boxster, while her passenger deposited a small shoulder bag in the back before jumping-in beside her. The chattering continued unabated as the barrier rose to release them towards I-54. Neither took any note of the depressingly ubiquitous commercial landmarks along the flat expanse around Kellogg, or the few high-rises that came into view to their left as they passed over Main before sweeping south onto I-15.

Ten minutes later, the garage door rose by command of the remote fob to allow them to glide into the double garage of the small simplex, before automatically closing behind as the car stopped clear of the security beam. The couple stopped jabbering for the first time in nearly half an hour; they paused as they released their seatbelts, looking deeply into each other's eyes before instinctively flying into another embrace across the centre console. Had it really been all those years since they had held each other so close?

Up in the comfortable lounge, Martinis were poured, and more history swapped until the doorbell suddenly broke the spell.

"Ah, Dinner!" she exclaimed, her eyes lighting-up with anticipation.

She rose and went to open the front door, revealing a delivery boy armed with take-out from Kwan Court, the best Chinese in Wichita. No cash changed hands as the boy was familiar with this regular account customer. She thanked him and he bowed politely before turning away into the night as the door quietly closed.

Dinner passed in the glint of a candlelit wine glass that had been replenished several times from the two bottles of the finest Californian Grenache, when both suddenly fell silent gazing intently at each other. She slowly rose, walked around the table and gently took her guest's hand before leading the way into the master bedroom.

A passionate hour followed, during which she became somewhat overwhelmed by her guest's surprising technique. She had not experienced this before, as they had never allowed themselves the pleasure, despite the obvious desire on both sides; this had been due to her close and long-term relationship with another of their circle. That relationship had long-since dissolved into permanent friendship, and another, more final, was due to be solemnised within weeks. When what might be the final opportunity to satisfy her curiosity had arisen through the unexpected telephone contact days earlier, she surrendered to her desires without a second thought.

In the afterglow, her emotions were mixed as her guest led her to the bathroom where her body was gently pampered for another half an hour before her consciousness submitted to the combined indulgences of the preceding part of the evening.

She was carried back into the bedroom and gently laid on the bed, her bearer making sure that her position was comfortable. Her guest stood and looked at her whilst slowly dressing, not being one for the tension of pancakes and bacon following a one-night stand, which was all this could ever be. That had been another reason why it had never happened years earlier, but it had been good, better than ever had been anticipated; and there it would stay, an everlasting memory of something wonderful.

Picking-up the shoulder bag, the visitor took one last lingering mental snapshot of the serene form on the bed, so peacefully-unaware of the departure, then slipped quietly through the side door into the night.

a discovery is made

One

The telegraph poles between I-15 and the railway seemed frozen in the side window of Paul Kleberson's Squad Car, as if the red beacon on the roof of the car was acting as a strobe light. At three a.m. the junction with Forty-Seventh Street South was eerily quiet as he sped across it against the lights. Minutes later he turned left on Sixty-Ninth, heading for the northern outskirts of Derby.

Kleberson had been in charge of the Homicide Squad in Wichita for nearly five years, during which time his department had dealt with an average of no more than a couple of dozen cases a year. The majority of those occurred within an area on the north-east side dubbed 'the badlands' by local police, so it would not have been unusual for his Squad to be answering a homicide call to the north of I-54. But all the way down south in Derby it was almost unheard of.

The only cases of any note outside the badlands during his time in the department had been a crime spree by a couple of crackheads that had concluded with the brutal assassination of four friends on a school football field. That case, although quickly and easily solved, produced a subsequent show trial that had been the focus of the local media for two years. From the scant information he had already received, Kleberson was already dreading the thought that the case unfolding in this quiet suburb might create a similar media circus, but for totally different reasons.

His fears were confirmed the minute he turned into Plainlands View. There, outside of one of the neat simplexes, were half a dozen Police Cruisers and the KNKW outside broadcast truck. Heading straight for him as he drew-up at the kerb, microphone in hand, was the familiar figure of Marjoree Rolles, the star link for the station.

'How the hell did she get here so quick', he thought, but before he could think further his door was opened and the offending microphone thrust under his nose.

In the seamless manner of the consummate professional she had become, Marjoree Rolles was finishing the live link she had started as she began walking towards the car: "... and just arrived is the head of the local homicide unit, Lieutenant Paul Kleberson. Lieutenant, can you confirm that the body discovered here this morning is that of Hilary Nicholson?"

Marjoree was the rising star of Midwest media. Her local station was syndicated and it was only a matter of time before she made the inevitable career move to the national network. Although not easily deflected, she was an accomplished and experienced journalist who would respect police requests to give them space if they needed it, although in doing so she drove a hard bargain, a bargain that nearly always resulted in the exclusive that gave her career just that little bit more State-wide coverage, and the resultant occasional national exposure.

Kleberson batted the question in an equally professional manner, looking directly into the camera he responded: "I can neither confirm nor deny any such thing, as you well know Ms Rolles."

He stared through the camera lens towards the person holding it. It was an instrument he would dearly have loved to push firmly into one of darker recesses of that cameraman's body.

Kleberson hated Tom Cochrane; he hated his propensity for invading crime scenes in a virtual way with his intrusive zoom lens, revealing facts live to the TV Station before the Squad had a chance to assess their significance, if any. Oh yes, Cochrane was good at what he did, but it often caused an unnecessary extension of the case.

On the other hand, he quite liked Marjoree, although he couldn't abide the way she spelled her christian name. A keen English student since his youth, the use of misspelling or mispronunciation purely for status or effect was not to his taste. Every time he saw the caption under her name on a TV bulletin he would shudder spontaneously.

Kleberson braced himself for two or three more quick-fire questions before he could reach the sanctuary of the police tape cordoning-off the scene. However, the questioning immediately stopped and Marjoree faced the camera passing her microphone hand across her throat to signal Cochrane to stop the camera. Cochrane's head shot out from behind the viewfinder glaring at her, his face etched with an angry, questioning expression: "what?" he mouthed. She just focussed on him and repeated the gesture, this time with more force.

Cochrane lowered the camera and shrugged with disgust. The promise in his own career had risen inexorably as he accompanied Marjoree on most of her 'scoops', and he expected to 'go national' with her very soon. This unusual compassion for the police had obviously taken Cochrane completely by surprise.

It also caused Kleberson to stop momentarily in his tracks. He centred Marjoree in his gaze as she turned back towards him, microphone at her side. It was then that he noticed the tears welling in her eyes.

"Is it Hilary?" The question emerged in a breaking voice, emotion was melting the media ice-woman.

"You know I can't say right now," he replied gently.

"Off the record," she pleaded, "please …"

Kleberson maintained his professional distance: "you know Hilary Nicholson?"

"Since college … we were room-mates for three years."

"If I say anything off the record, Ms Rolles, it will be you that owes me the exclusive."

"It's a deal," came the tearful reply.

Two

Kleberson entered the house through the front door, which opened straight into the main lounge area, a neat room with light furniture, white leather sofas and a large fish tank in the far corner creating a shimmering blue haze.

The house was a zoo; there must have been twenty people in there, mainly patrolmen searching rooms and the garden, plus three of his Detectives, including his second in command, Chris McKinley, who was briefing two other Homicide Squad members, Moreno and Capaldi.

He spotted Kleberson and beckoned him over: "scene's in the master bedroom Paul. No sign of forced entry, looks like Ms Nicholson knew her killer."

"So we've already decided it's a homicide have we?" Kleberson replied.

"When you see it I think you'll agree. M.E. wants to move the body, wouldn't let her until you'd seen it. CSI have photo'd everything."

"That's quick work Chris."

"Yeah, the Chief ordered it all by cellphone, he started back from Topeka soon as he heard."

"Topeka?"

"Charity bash."

"Oh great! So he'll be bustin' our balls within the hour, huh?"

"You got it Paul."

"Well if he's gonna do that, get everyone out of here except the techies while we still have the remains of a crime scene left for them, shall we?"

"Sure thing." McKinley nodded to the other two: "organise it guys will ya." Moreno and Capaldi started moving around clearing out patrolmen.

"We sure it's Hilary Nicholson?" Kleberson enquired.

"Can't mistake the face of 'The Prodigal's Saviour', even in the circumstances the rest of her's in."

Three

The reference was to a headline in the 'National Enquirer' the previous year when Hilary Nicholson, accountant to the Kendrick empire, announced her engagement to Jackson Kendrick III, heir to the Kendrick family fortune.

This had happened shortly after the previously-estranged groom-to-be had been welcomed back into the fold of one of the most wealthy and powerful families in the State. The family-owned Kendrick Corporation was the holding company of a huge multi-national conglomerate with businesses engaged in everything from real estate to entertainment. The current president of the corporation was Jackson Kendrick Junior.

The family was very much new-money, because the company had only been founded in the nineteen-forties by Junior's father. Jackson Kendrick Senior was a hard businessman; he had to be, having been an 'Okie', a dirt-farmer from Oklahoma who lost everything during the Dust Bowl period of the mid-thirties, including his wife and children to malnutritional diseases. Other than that fact, details of which he would freely offer to anybody willing to listen, little was known of what happened to him in the dozen-or-so years following those events, up to and including the second world war, a period on which he avoided discussion throughout the rest of his life.

He emerged in eastern Kansas in 1946 with a second wife, a young son and several thousand acres of farmland. Authorised biographers attributed the acquisition of this wealth to inheritances received by his second wife; unauthorised accounts hinted at more dubious methods during the war years. Whatever the truth, it was what he did with those assets that forged the future. During the next ten years, the land was developed and the profits used to acquire failing companies, which he generally turned-around into thriving businesses.

By the early 'sixties, he was a multi-billionaire approaching his seventieth year and had turned his mind to philanthropy. This aspect of his life was mainly-attributed to his second wife, twenty-five years his junior and a lady of deeply-religious upbringing. She ran all of the many charitable-foundations that were set-up by her husband, and continued to do so after his sudden death in 1964, right up until her own demise on millennium night just two weeks short of her eightieth birthday.

On the death of his father, and as the only child of the second marriage, Jackson Kendrick Junior had been thrust in charge of the conglomerate at the age of just twenty-three. Although Junior, as he had always been known, was barely out of university, he took to this new responsibility like a duck to water. Through the ensuing near-forty years, he had multiplied the size of the already large organisation by a factor of hundreds, maybe even thousands. Nobody really knew quite how large the corporation actually was, except Junior himself and, perhaps, Emil Friedmann, the ambitious young lawyer who had snared the hand of Junior's teenage elder-daughter twelve years earlier. Such was the success of Friedmann's offshore activities, that even Forbes Magazine was unsure of where exactly Jackson Kendrick Junior should figure in its annual list of the world's richest people.

Three years after taking the reins, Junior married Estelle Gray, an East Coast socialite from an old-money family that had fallen on difficult times and was in need of an injection of new-money status. To all intents and purposes the marriage was a huge success; two years in, she produced their daughter, Gloria, and three years after that, the son and heir - Jackson Kendrick III. There had never been any hint of impropriety on either side of the marriage, both regularly appearing arm-in-arm at business and society functions.

The truth was that, although very close, they essentially never had time for dalliances. There was simply too much money in this world that was not already under Junior's direct control, so he simply devoted almost all of his waking hours to acquiring as much of the rest of it as he could. Having always been a member of East Coast 'royalty', Estelle was constantly busy on the national social circuit. When she wasn't, she was either at home being a devoted mother and grandmother, or busy running the family's many Foundations, a role she had officially inherited on the death of her mother-in-law, but in reality had been covering behind the scenes for many years previously.

Junior had always intended to devote more time to the Foundations himself. As he grew older and retirement age beckoned, he had planned to pass the company reins gradually to his son. But this had proved impossible due to a lack of apparent fiscal responsibility in his male offspring, who also acquired a history of high-profile run-ins with police forces all over the country through drunkenness and womanising that eventually developed into drug-abuse. Junior had been constantly busy behind the scenes keeping his son out of the criminal courts, and the almost-definite subsequent jail.

Millennium year proved a major watershed for the family in several aspects. One was the receipt by Junior of a private warning from senior Senators that his influence would no longer save his son should he fall-foul of the authorities again, wherever that may occur. As a result, Jackson Kendrick III was publically disowned and disinherited by his father.

Following this humiliation, and stripped of the greedy attention of the host of human detritus that such a tabloid figure accumulates through little effort, but great expense, 'The Turd', as the son had become referred to colloquially by the gutter press, and privately in police forces across several States, achieved something of a turnaround in his public image. Three years on, and engaged to one of the most respected young businesswomen in the Midwest, he was considered by the family, in public at least, as something of a saved soul. The quality press rejoiced in the reconciliation to virtually the same sickening excess to which the tabloids had previously charted the long descent into depravity.

However, those closer to events were well-aware that his behaviour in private had not changed; it was the public-relations aspect that had become much better-managed. There were two reasons for this. Firstly he had restricted the majority of his excesses to within his home State borders, where Junior's influence was still strong enough to ensure that blind-eyes were turned whenever necessary, hence the disdain with which his name was treated by the foot-soldiers in law-enforcement. Secondly, the PR was firmly in the control of Emil Friedmann, brother-in-law to 'The Turd', father of Junior's two young grandsons and chief lawyer to the Kendrick empire.

Friedmann had been tireless in his efforts to keep his relative-by-marriage out of the headlines, coaching him in his public responsibilities and, wherever necessary, persuading injured-parties to 'be reasonable' by whatever method necessary. Although public-opinion was divided on the motives behind Friedmann's actions, and at what cost to the empire's coffers they had been achieved, there was no division of opinion about how successful he had been.

This night's turn of events undoubtedly had the potential to bring that particular house of cards crashing around Friedmann's ears.

Four

Kleberson and McKinley walked slowly down the corridor and into a bedroom that looked remarkably normal, given the circumstances, other than for the form laying on the bed. The bedside lights were on, providing a demure light that was only disturbed by the neon light beaming from the wide-open bathroom door, through which two white-overalled CSI Techs could be seen carefully swabbing exposed surfaces.

On the queen-size bed was the naked body of an attractive woman in her thirties, led face-up. Her head, which was resting on a pillow plumped-up against the headboard, was completely shaven; the facial expression was totally peaceful. Her smallish-breasts were firm and perfectly round, as if they had some form of enhancement, but there was no evidence of any surgery. Her arms were laid straight out at right angles to her body, spreading across towards both sides of the bed, hands palm-up with the index finger of the right hand pointing slightly upwards. Strangely, both thumbs were folded along the line of their respective middle fingers.

Both legs were spread to an angle of about sixty degrees, fully-revealing her vagina which showed signs of recent sexual activity. Her right foot was pointed at the ceiling, her left pointed outwards resting on the bed. There was no pubic hair; in fact the entire body appeared to have no hair at all, as if recently-waxed. Kleberson thought it had something of a sheen to it, but dismissed the thought as a trick of the ambient lighting.

"Who called it in?" Kleberson asked.

McKinley replied: "nine-one-one call, anonymous, just after midnight"

"Great! Nobody here then."

"No. Caller said there was a break-in, patrol was despatched and found the house unsecured. They entered and found everything looking normal, radio on, no obvious point of entry, but nobody answered their calls, so they started to search and found the body."

"Who did?"

"Officer Pendleton."

"Don't know him do I?

"Two months out of academy, only issued a few speeding tickets up to now, ran out in the garden and threw-up all over the place. He's out there now sobbing his heart out."

"It just gets better! Now just tell me how many head of cattle were stampeded through here as well will ya, just for the record."

Mary Jourdain, the County Medical Examiner, emerged from the bathroom: "hey Paul," she greeted him, somewhat sadly.

Kleberson acknowledged with a nod and a faint smile: "Mary."

She looked at the bed: "bit weird doncha think?"

"I assume we have eliminated some form of ritual-suicide, shaving her hair to indicate her loss of self, then writing a note saying how she couldn't face the rest of her life with that sonofabitch Kendrick-from-hell, before emptying the entire bathroom cabinet of barbiturates?"

Mary Jourdain turned and gave her normal look of disdain that Kleberson had become used to over the years they had worked cases together. She started narrating her notes: "female, early/mid-thirties, no obvious wounds from what I can see from how she is laying there, so I would like to move her and check the rest of the body while you're here, if that's OK."

Kleberson turned to McKinley: "we don't need anything else here do we?"

"No Paul, like I said whole scene's been photographed."

"OK Mary, off you go."

She called to one of her overalled assistants: "give me a hand here would you."

The body was turned over on the bed. There appeared to be some bruising across the back, but Mary Jourdain quickly dismissed it as she conducted an initial cursory examination, commentating as she went: "minor bruising to the back and rear of the legs caused by the time the body has lain in that position post-mortem. No other pre-mortem injuries, so no obvious struggle ... hold on ..."

Kleberson stepped forward: "what have you found?"

"Hmm - small needle puncture at the back of the neck. That changes everything Paul. You don't self-medicate in that location and because there are no signs of a struggle, we're almost definitely looking at an additional party here. I'd say she was either asleep or in someone's arms."

"Or drugged?"

"I can only tell you that when I get her back to the morgue. She's been shaved, then washed-down completely, my guess would be in the shower as the bath drain looks completely dry, although it would be far more difficult to do in the shower if she was already dead, so that would suggest pre-mortem complicity of some sort. I'd say there's little chance of finding anything helpful on the body. If the killer's been as efficient as I think, there'll be no fluids or alien body hair either."

"Alien body hair - what's this an X-File now?"

She gave him another look of disdain, this time showing some signs of annoyance. Kleberson tilted his head slightly and shrugged. She returned to the examination: "as you probably saw from her original position, there's been obvious sexual activity ... I couldn't tell exactly with the body in that position, but ..." her voice faded away.

"But?" Kleberson prompted.

Mary Jourdain rounded on him, eyes unusually wide, her growing anger showing clearly in the answer: "you're asking me to make a prejudgement - you know I don't guess, but you always ask me to guess."

Kleberson was also becoming a little agitated: "which you always want to don't you? But you won't until I issue a disclaimer just in case, which is a waste of time because you're always right. So let's just cut to the chase, take it as read that I won't quote you like I never do - just tell me what you think."

"The intercourse may have been post-mortem, front and back. There you go, I wasn't being coy, I just didn't want to say it. Now can I take her to the morgue?"

Kleberson saw the anguish in her eyes, something he didn't see often and he felt dreadful. It was as if he had inflicted a similar, but mental, violation on his colleague and friend to that which had been inflicted physically on the actual victim.

"Of course - and Mary, I'm sorry, OK?"

"OK."

"One last thing - time of death?"

"Best I can tell here, between eight p.m. and midnight - and I'm sorry as well, Paul." She managed a weak smile.

Kleberson looked at her with compassion in his eyes. They both knew what was meant and, had this not been a crime scene, they would probably both have hugged, because they knew instinctively that this was only the beginning of what was going to be a very protracted case.

Five

Kleberson and McKinley walked back into the lounge area, which was finally empty. Kleberson could just make-out, through the french doors at the rear, the figure of a patrolman outside, slumped in a patio chair, head in his hands: "I thought I said get all the foot soldiers out Chris."

"That's Pendleton. Thought you might want to speak to him. His partner's outside in the Cruiser waiting for him."

Kleberson stood still, hands on hips and breathed a long, deep sigh: "let's just summarise here a minute shall we Chris? Our victim most likely was asleep when she was killed, maybe on the bed in there, maybe raped as well; but the killer didn't break-in. The body was taken into the shower, shaved and washed. Then most likely the killer did the housekeeping, called nine-one-one and vanished. Our newest-finest out there rolls-up with his buddy, tramples through the house, then back again before depositing his dinner on the lawn out back. They call it in, Chief gets alerted because of who the victim is, but as he's a hundred miles away, he immediately invites the entire population of Wichita to view the scene, ensuring that anything our rookie out there hasn't already

A Discovery is Made

disturbed is definitely contaminated. Now the Chief's less than half an hour out, expecting a fully-solved crime, perp in custody, on arrival."

"Guess that about sums it up."

Kleberson looked at the ceiling: "beam me up Scotty!" He held the pose for a split second, then dropped his shoulders and looked briefly at the floor before turning to McKinley, fixing him momentarily with a focussed stare. His face relaxed again as he began his instructions: "OK Chris, lock it all down, don't let anyone in the place, including the Chief, until Mary's boys have been over it with a fine-tooth comb. Then when they've done that, get them to do it again with a finer-tooth comb. We're looking for anything that doesn't fit - get that, anything!"

"Sure thing Paul."

"And no, I don't need to speak to Pendleton, just let him write it up when he gets back to City Hall, via the side entrance please. I'm going down to the garage, maybe we can use that for a bit of privacy. Who else have we got here?"

"Just Moreno and Capaldi at the moment."

"Tell them to meet me in the garage. Then you meet 'n greet the Chief outside and bring him to me in there as well."

Kleberson made his way to the garage via the basement and checked the side-door; it was unlocked, as he suspected it might be.

Capaldi came down the stairs. Kleberson turned to him: "get someone down here to check and print this door, can you?"

"Sure Boss," came the reply, as Capaldi turned and sprinted back up the stairs.

Kleberson looked around. A silver Porsche Boxster stood in the centre of the garage, hood down. He moved to the rear of the car and dropped down by the rear bumper. He reached under and touched the exhaust - it was still slightly warm to the touch; the car hadn't been there many hours.

A CSI technician appeared at the bottom of the stairs and walked over to the side door. Kleberson spoke to him: "open it and leave it open when you've finished, then photograph everything outside."

"OK Lieutenant, came the reply."

Capaldi came back down the stairs, this time accompanied by Moreno. Kleberson issued their instructions: "OK you two, house-to-house, find out if anyone saw anyone coming and going, you know the deal."

Moreno was the more outspoken of the pair: "it's four a.m. Boss, they're all asleep."

"Sure they are, with a police and media convention going on outside! If they are, then wake 'em up. Then when you've done with that, find-out whose house this is, 'cos it sure as hell ain't Ms Nicholson's. Then contact the owner and find-out what their connection is to Wichita's most famous accountant and why she is all the way across town here sleeping in someone else's house with her car in the garage, instead of being safely tucked-up in her million-dollar security-guarded home in Eastborough."

"And then what should we do to fill the spare hours until breakfast?" quipped Moreno.

"Well you could always humour the Chief for me."

"Humour me yourself Kleberson …" The booming voice came from the side door where Chief of Police Stanton stood, filling the portal with his huge frame; Kleberson could just make-out McKinley standing behind him.

"… 'cos you see, I could really do with a little humour right now, having to just run the gauntlet of that rottweiler Cochrane trying to interview me. How'd he get here so quick, and without the lovely Ms Rolles?"

"She's not out there?" Kleberson asked.

"She's sat in her car Paul," McKinley interrupted.

"What the hell are we discussing that bitch for anyway?" Stanton bellowed: "we got a murder here and one that's gonna put a millstone round our necks quick enough without her damned help!"

Kleberson rounded on the massive frame standing inside the doorway: "she knows the victim and I suspect a whole lot more, but before I can get to that, I need to secure what little I have left here."

McKinley backed out of the doorway. He knew the signs well enough of when a bomb was about to go off between his two bosses, and ground zero was not the place to be when it did. So did Moreno and Capaldi, who quickly exited stage right up the stairs. The CSI tech needed no prompting to follow McKinley outside and carry-on his work.

Stanton and Kleberson had a strained professional respect for each other. Stanton knew Kleberson was the best detective he had and that the department had been lucky to get him from the Feds. Kleberson knew Stanton was an ace politician and would keep the elite from falling on his Squad from a great height in situations like this. So both needed to keep their professional relationship onside, despite neither approving of the other's methods. Kleberson fired the first volley: "this is your handiwork isn't it Chief?"

"Don't you start on me …" Stanton was cut-off in mid-sentence, Kleberson unloading his ire on his newest visitor.

"Shut the fuck up Chief, you started this three-ring circus. How did Cochrane get here? You sent him here, or rather the Mayor did after you got him out of bed at two a.m. no doubt. And Why? 'Cos we have a high-profile murder here and someone wants it cleared-up, covered over and out of the headlines before Election Day!"

"Now just a cotton-picking minute …" Stanton tried to stem the flow.

But Kleberson was off and running: "when I got here, the whole crime scene has heaving with maggots 'looking for clues' - destroying them more like - and you put 'em here. How the fuck am I supposed to close this with no evidence, huh? Or am I not supposed to, is that it? Don't tell me - one of the Kendricks rang you, or were they at the function and got a call? Well which was it?"

Stanton could see that he was going to have the facts dragged out of him, Kleberson was too damned good in this type of scenario for them not to be. So he switched tack, in order to try and take the heat out of the situation: "Junior got a call from Friedmann and came across to my table, but I had already been briefed by …"

"So where was the son?"

"I don't know."

"So he wasn't there with good old pappy then?"

"Hell no, he …"

"So Junior gets a call from Friedmann telling him that his son's betrothed is lying dead in someone else's house in Derby, at the same time that you're getting a heads-up from control. The son's nowhere to be seen, but instead of you thinking 'hold-on a minute, where's the boyfriend in this?' you send in the cavalry to destroy any evidence, quite legally of course, that might connect the State's darling first family to any wrong-doing. Then you round-up the local media, whose lead reporter is an old friend of the victim, just for good measure. Well, I think I know who my perp most likely is, so while I'm down at the Judge's office swearing-out an arrest warrant, why don't I just get one to serve on you for good measure. How does accessory after the fact grab you, huh Chief?"

Throughout this tirade, Stanton had been reaching boiling point. Finally it was his turn: "right, now you listen-up here, you got nothing on any member of the Kendrick family, not even circumstantial, so don't even think of going there. As for Junior, course he's gonna hit on me, this was his future daughter-in-law, the mother for his grandchildren-to-be, why wouldn't he demand action?"

"Tell it to the electorate Chief, in the meantime get the fuck out of my crime-scene and pray I don't find any probable cause to swear-out that warrant."

"You won't have time, sonny-boy, ten a.m. press conference and you'd better have something to say."

Stanton stormed out of the side door and across the lawn towards his car. Cochrane made a move to get another quote, but only met the lowered shoulder of the two-eighty-pound former KSU linebacker as he ducked under the police tape. Stanton would later apologise for the 'accident' that Cochrane clearly knew was anything but.

Six

"Elvis has left the Building," McKinley quipped as he re-entered the side door.

"Idiot," Kleberson snapped.

"You always say that."

"Not him Chris, you! How could you let the scene get so far out of control?"

McKinley tensed as he reacted to this unexpected accusation: "it was like this when I got here Paul. Good grief! I was only a couple of minutes ahead of you. The Chief, however, had been phoning everybody at two-minute intervals from his car, trying to gather information."

"Yeah, probably had Junior on the cellphone feeding it back too. Sorry Chris, it's just that family always seems to have the drop on us."

"You're convinced it's 'The Turd' aren't you?"

"Well tell me Chris, you got any alternatives right now, 'cos if you have lets get 'em in now before the Chief railroads some poor unsuspecting Hispanic from bandit country just in time for the press conference!"

"There ain't anything Paul, nothing obvious anyway."

"Then find out where 'The Turd' is. No doubt he's sleeping off whatever last night's indulgence was somewhere, 'cos he sure as hell ain't here bustin' my balls like any normal bereaved husband-to-be would be, is he? When you've found him, call me. Don't interview him, leave that to me; you can bet your boots Friedmann's with him in any case. But first, on your way out, see if the delectable Ms Rolles is still in her car. If she is, make sure Cochrane's out of earshot, then ask her to meet me alone in Glenda's at Topeka and Kellogg in half an hour. I'll meet you back at base. Let's have a sitrep at six a.m. Oh, and while you're at it, cancel everyone's weekend."

Seven

Kleberson's maroon Chevy dropped off the ramp from I-54 and through the green lights on Topeka. He pulled onto the forecourt of Glenda's where there was just one other car parked, a dark green Chrysler 300M. Marjoree Rolles was sat at a table in the window behind the car, holding a scrunched-up napkin in her hand. It was 4.45 a.m. and the restaurant was empty apart from the night boy.

Marjoree's eyes were red from the tears that still dampened her pronounced cheekbones. Kleberson offered to get her a drink, but she just shrugged. He ordered a black coffee, then gestured to her to join him at a table away from the window. She slid into the stall opposite him and gave him an intensive stare: "is it Hilary?" she asked

"No positive ID yet, but totally off the record?" She nodded, her look more fearful. Kleberson continued: "I never actually met the lady in life, but I would be as sure as I can be that it was her."

Marjoree slumped forward onto the table, buried her head in her arms and quietly sighed: "the bastard."

"Who is?"

"Jackson Kendrick the Third, or should I say 'The Turd' as you guys prefer to call him."

"And you guys as well, huh?"

"It does seem an apt soubriquet doesn't it, although I never expected him to plumb these depths." Her head raised again, exposing the damp patch on her sleeve where the fresh tears had fallen.

Kleberson prompted her: "tell me what you know, and what it's going to cost me."

"Let's call it a charitable donation in memory of a dear friend."

"What no exclusive?"

Her eyes narrowed angrily: "cut the cynicism Lieutenant, it really doesn't suit you. If it makes you feel better, you can match my generosity with whatever you think is appropriate when the time comes, OK?"

"Fine, I'm all ears."

"Hilary and I met at USC; we had rooms on the same landing. Within months we were inseparable, and by our second year we had moved-in together …"

"Just a minute," interrupted Kleberson, "are you saying you were an item?"

"What's the matter Lieutenant, you shocked? Or are you getting a hard on?" She smiled a wicked smile.

"Ms Nicholson was ac/dc - that what you're telling me?"

"I'll talk, you scribble - alright? Like I said, we were together for the next two years. Then, when I moved home to Salina, Hilary came too. She was much more clever than me, got a job very quickly with Ernst & Young in Kansas City while I got a break at the Wichita Mail. So, she moved to KC and I moved down here. For the next couple of years we alternated weekends at each other's places, then I landed KNKW and the hours went haywire. S'pose we just drifted apart, from the commitment point of view, but we remained the very best of friends."

"So, when she moved here, what, three years ago, you took-up again?"

"No, like I said, really good friends, almost sisters really, but not enough common time for anything else."

"What, not even one-night stands?"

"Watch your hormones Lieutenant, I'm not answering that 'cos it ain't relevant! She had the odd fling, mainly people she met out-of-town whilst on business, but nothing either significant or important."

"How do you know that?"

"I told you Lieutenant, like sisters."

Kleberson realised there was a lot more here, but he would have to settle for what he got voluntarily, for the time being at least. But he pushed a bit more - he needed a break: "so, no weirdo's then?"

"Hilary wasn't into anything kinky, neither am I and neither was anybody else she took-up with. It was as much companionship with her as anything. When there was sex, it was always gentle and meaningful and the infrequency made it all the sweeter."

"So if anyone cut-up rough, she would have dropped them?"

"Literally on the spot Lieutenant, she was sixth dan karate blackbelt, knew all the pressure points, nobody could have got close enough to attack her. Only a gun would have killed her."

"A gun? What type of gun?"

"She was shot, right?"

"No details, my call on the donation remember?"

"But she must have been shot. Nobody would have been allowed any closer - I'm telling you!" The tears welled-up again as a look of fear crossed her face.

"OK, OK, she was shot. But you quote me on that and I'll lock you up and throw away the key."

Marjoree calmed down. Kleberson continued: "so, nobody out there that you wouldn't be aware of?"

"Absolutely not and no men either, not that I know of, until that slimeball came along."

"I'm glad we got to him. How do you explain it?"

"Oh that's easy, it was a marriage of convenience, or at least a marriage-to-be. You see the one thing Hilary wanted was a child - not adopted, her own. But she didn't want anything else, just one roll in the hay, perfectly timed and hey presto! Offspring, with no attached subsequent sexual commitment."

"But 'The Turd' would never have gone for that, he's testosterone-supercharged. How would he possibly survive? It's like making a pact with a female Mantis. One jump and you're dead!"

"That's where it was prefect. They drew-up a pre-nup. He got her once, or as many times as necessary at her instigation only, from which she delivered an heir to the dynasty. He would leave her to bring-up the child and could carry-on with his 'private life' as if nothing had happened. She would be the doting wife and mother, whilst being allowed her own 'friends'."

"But what about when he finally got caught-out? After all, he's hardly Mr Subtlety is he?"

"That was the coup-de-grace - he mustn't, otherwise the entire Kendrick fortune went to the child in trust. If he got caught, he lost everything."

"So what did Junior think of all this?"

"He didn't know, Friedmann drew it all up."

"Friedmann? But he's Junior's right hand."

"That's what Junior thinks, but 'The Turd' has been in Friedmann's pocket since the banishment, and heavily into sweeteners to keep Friedmann quiet."

"So that's it then, 'The Turd' realises he'll never keep his end of the bargain, wants out, she refuses, he kills her."

"Good try Lieutenant, but no-sale. Hilary would have torn-up the agreement at anytime. You see, she wanted the child, nothing more. She just needed to be sure that the kid would be provided for and, as you say, 'The Turd' could never have kept his end of the bargain, so she was home and hosed, but only after the kid came along. If 'The Turd' wanted out, she would have let him go, then waited for another stud with the right credentials to come along."

"But he ain't that intelligent, he wouldn't be able to accept that someone would let him off scot-free."

"You might think that, but I witnessed the agreement. Anyway, if he started any funny stuff, I've got enough unused garbage on him to bury him ten times over; he wouldn't have kept Junior's blessing for anything once I'd done that."

"OK, OK, so if it's not him, and I ain't letting him off that easy, then who?"

"That's it, I have no idea, not an inkling. She was in her safehouse, nobody else had a key. The alarms would have been set …"

"Wait, wait, wait! SAFEHOUSE?"

islands

Eight

Paul Kleberson had lived in Wichita for over ten years. He was born in California into a military family; his father, Walter, had been a high-flyer in the US Air Force, literally, piloting a U2. Walter had been part of the select unit operating out of Florida in the early 'sixties to photograph the Soviet missile bases in Cuba, after which he rose steadily through the ranks.

Paul was born in 1969 in the base hospital at Davis-Monthan Air Force base in Tucson, Arizona, where his father was stationed at the time. In the midseventies, the family moved to California when his father's unit was transferred to its new home at Beale Air Force Base, near Marysville in Yuba County. Paul's mother, Margie, loved the area and would have happily stayed there with Paul, his younger brother and sister when, in 1983, Colonel Walter T Kleberson was transferred to RAF Alconbury in England, to command the newly reactivated Seventeenth Reconnaissance Wing. However, Walter wouldn't hear of it.

So the entire family decamped to the flat Cambridgeshire countryside. Walter was keen for his family to get the most from this experience and organised family life so that they lived off-base, becoming part of the local community. They rented a house in Godmanchester where Paul's younger siblings were enrolled in the town's primary school, a short walk from their home in Post Street. Being the eldest, Paul attended secondary school, his father selecting Hinchingbrooke School on the outskirts of Huntingdon, which was a local authority school based in the grounds of the historic sixteenth century Hinchingbrooke House, which itself formed the base for the school's sixth form centre.

Paul loved everything about the area, especially the history of the town, which dated back to Roman times. He had always been fascinated by history. Backhome he had often spent entire days in Marysville Museum, where they documented the history of the Gold Rush, the spark that ignited the development of the city into, at that time, one of the three largest in California. To an eight-year-old, a hundred and fifty years ago seemed like an almost incomprehensibly distant past, yet he could view, and actually touch, buildings and artefacts that had been there for twenty-times his short lifespan.

But, following the move to England aged thirteen, he could then walk along London Road in Godmanchester, knowing that he was on the same pathway that two-thousand years earlier had been called Ermine Street, the Roman road that linked the important port of Londinium in the south to Eburacum, the capital city of Brittania Inferior in the north. Back then, Godmanchester was called Durovigatum, parts of which re-emerged regularly whenever a building site was excavated in the town.

When visiting this town's small museum, he was not touching a one-hundred-year-old building, but one that was more than four-times as old, originally a school given letters-patent by Queen Elizabeth the First over twenty years before Sir Walter Raleigh's expedition had laid claim to Virginia. Not only that, in the grounds that he walked every schoolday was the ancestral home of the Cromwell family, sponsors of the Pilgrim Fathers and, more infamously, of a civil war against their King. Paul no longer needed to content himself with looking at remnants of his own country's short history; in Cambridgeshire he could visit the very places where its destiny was forged.

Paul quickly settled into English life, helped by the fact that some of his classmates also lived in the town and were more than happy to entertain their new-found friend of the weird accent, dubious spelling and unusual definitions of everyday words. Although the latter regularly generated misunderstandings proving, as Shaw observed, that here were two nations divided by a common language, more often than not they simply caused the gathering to descend into immense giggling fits.

However, Paul quickly learned that such hilarity was best enjoyed just within his circle of English friends, after his father grounded him instantly for calmly announcing, on the way home one Friday evening, that he had seen one of the sixth formers trying to 'bum a fag' that lunchtime. Walter was all ready to launch a full-on pre-emptive strike on the school's headmaster first thing on Monday morning for condoning such behaviour, but luckily, at a drinks party that weekend, one of their neighbours managed to convince him that the local meaning of the phrase, the action of cadging a cigarette, was far more innocent than any potential American connotation might suggest. This caused much amusement amongst other nearby guests, but unfortunately not to Walter, who found the entire episode somewhat embarrassing.

Embarrassment was something that seemed, to Paul, to affect the average Brit far less than most Americans, the latter going to incredible lengths to avoid causing, let alone experiencing, it. Paul quickly encountered the nature of his new classmates' locker-room banter, where they would utilise a natural wit in order to diffuse a potentially confrontational scenario.

This contrasted totally with something he had witnessed shortly before leaving his previous school in the 'States, where what had started as a bit of innocent teasing among classmates quickly developed into a nasty bout of venomous mockery of one specific child by a group of emergent bullies, egged-on by their formative alpha-male. At that place and time, Paul had felt helpless to do anything about the situation. Although he didn't consciously realise it, his new environment was equipping him with a completely different set of social tools to those of his peers across the water, tools he would eventually use regularly during his career as a senior detective policeman.

Paul had already developed a good basic sense of humour and loved comedy in any form. Back home, he would watch TV sitcoms with the family and, although he was too young at the time to realise that they often had an underlying moral message in each episode, there was always an easy familiarity about them. The only British television programme he had ever seen before arriving in the UK was 'The Benny Hill Show' and, like most of his countrymen, he found the visual gags in it hilarious. He had anticipated that British TV would contain more of the same.

At first the family did not watch as much television as they did at home. For a start, daytime TV in the Britain of the early 'eighties was not as prevalent as in the 'States and, as it was summertime when they arrived, Walter preferred to get his family out and about, exploring their new environment and meeting new people, both on and off-base. When they did start spending more time at home, as the unexpectedly chilly autumn evenings drew-in, Walter and Margie tended to look in the schedules for the American series that provided a link to their homeland back across the pond. This same pattern was repeated when they visited the homes of other service families, where the kids were packed-off to a child's bedroom to watch, while the grown-ups in the lounge debated the latest news from America. British families usually owned just one TV set; when they had visitors, that generally remained off, it being considered bad form to leave it on when guests were being entertained. So, it wasn't until Paul began sleeping-over at schoolfriends' houses that he encountered the real UK comedy of the day, which he found both fascinating and entertaining.

As an adolescent, he was already beginning to experience the edginess of the rebellion that swells within all boys in their teenage years, but whereas in his homeland this was tempered by the calm suppression of society in general, in this new environment he found no such restrictions. Back home, they used puppets to educate pre-school kids on daytime TV; in this foreign, yet strangely familiar, land they were used to lampoon politicians at prime-time.

TV comedy in the UK was more observant; not only did it expose the pomposity of the establishment to ridicule and scorn, it showed that the British were also quite prepared to show the humour in their own failings. In the 'States, the theme of a sitcom may amusingly lead to a moral lesson to be learned. In England, there was a loud message in every comedy situation, which was - if you watch anybody for long enough, they will do something stupid or amusing, occasionally both. But more importantly you, the erstwhile observer, were not immune to observation yourself; British comedy held the mirror up to your face, and if you didn't like what you saw, then tough!

Paul's first real encounter with this new, edgy comedy was when he was invited to a friend's house to watch the first episode in a new series of 'The Young Ones'. This was a highly-popular and radical sitcom about four students living together in an off-campus house. The four characters were a suicidal hippy, a pompous anarchist, a 'Mr Cool' and a punk - Paul had never encountered a punk before he came to the UK. When he tried to find out more about the basic storyline, his friends were a bit reluctant to explain. Eventually, one of them said to him: "look Paul, you like Benny Hill don't you?"

"Yes," Paul had replied.

"Well it's like that," his friend had concluded. The others had all laughed, alerting Paul that he was probably being set-up.

That evening they gathered round his friend's TV to watch the show. Paul was fascinated by the characters and the mayhem they produced, but most particularly by the violent punk character, Vyvyan, who at one point leant out of the window of a moving train to be decapitated by another train travelling in the opposite direction. In the next scene, his headless body was seen staggering back down the line towards the head that was laying beside the tracks, shouting directions at the headless body so that it could be located. When the body finally got to it, the head shouted to be picked-up, at which point the body kicked the head further down the tracks and set off again in pursuit.

As he rocked with laughter along with his friends, Paul thought to himself: *'shit, if this is supposed to be like Benny Hill, someone must've slipped something into the scriptwriters' tea!'*

Nine

For Paul, the next five years were a ball, apart from the regular vacation trips back to the 'States that more often than not involved visits to relatives and, occasionally, the inevitable family funeral. A serviceman's family never really developed roots; as soon as they thought they may be settled, a posting moved them on. Because of that, career servicemen rarely bought a family home until they knew they would no longer be moving prior to their retirement.

Walter's family were in the East, Margie's near the Mexican border, so it was rare that they could combine visiting both in the same trip. If they did it was normally because Walter had Military business to conduct as well, meaning that he was not with the rest of the family for the entire vacation. Through the resultant family diaspora, each member had come to view different locations as their 'home'.

For Walter it was New England, specifically his family home in Foxborough thirty miles south of Boston, where Paul's grandfather Bill lived alone or, as Walter termed it, rattled-around in the huge turn-of-the-century colonial house where Walter was raised. Bill had been a successful realtor in Foxborough, which had meant that he had always been able to pick-up the best properties when they were in need of a quick-sell, his house on Central having been one of those cases.

At one point it had been speculated that he owned about a quarter of the town and, although this was an exaggeration, he had become a very wealthy man by the time that Walter and Margie were married. Not long after, Liz, Paul's grandmother, had caught Bill 'in flagrante delicto' with his latest bimbo secretary whilst working late at the office. The settlement for the resultant quiet divorce considerably reduced Bill's real estate portfolio, but set Liz up for life in a palatial Palm Beach mansion. Neither Bill nor Liz had ever remarried, although

Paul had met plenty of new 'Uncles' or 'Aunties' on family vacation visits over the following years.

Rick, Paul's younger brother, also loved New England and his Grandpa. Bill doted on Rick, who was always guaranteed the best tickets in the house for Red Sox or Patriots' games when he visited, dependent on the time of year. Rick made no bones of his ambition, when the time came, to go to Harvard and to live with Grandpa Bill, although Grandpa Bill himself was somewhat lukewarm about the proposal, often suggesting Brown, which was further away and less likely to curtail his own activities by having some young whippersnapper arriving home unannounced at an inconvenient moment. Whichever it was to be, it would be in Grandpa's gift, as Walter had no intention of paying for the privilege.

Maisie, Paul's sister and the youngest of the three children, was most at home with her grandmother in Palm Beach, mainly because of the luxury lifestyle afforded by the army of servants Liz maintained in her mansion.

Paul's mother Margie, on the other hand, just wanted to return to Yuba County, in the shadow of the Sierra Nevada and where, on average, less people lived within a square mile than lived in the street containing their house in Godmanchester. She was born in 1951 in Bisbee, a small Arizona mining town just north of the Mexican border, the youngest of five children. Her father, also called Walter but preferring the shortened form of Walt, worked in the copper mines; he was also a highly-skilled amateur carpenter, having acquired his skills as a boy helping his cabinet-maker father. When Walt's father died, he had inherited all of the woodworking tools, using them to turn his own basement into a workshop where he took-up restoring antique furniture to bring-in additional income to the family for those little extras that life often demanded.

It was not unusual to hear the flat-head in the family's ancient F100 fire-up before dawn on a Saturday morning as Walt set-out on one of his regular expeditions to a house-clearance sale up in the mountains, returning near dusk with something in the back looking more akin to pieces of driftwood. A few weeks later the debris would emerge again from his workshop intact and polished, to be put in the back of the truck, covered with a tarpaulin and trundled up to an antique dealer in Tucson or, if it was a really choice piece, to a saleroom in Phoenix.

By the time Margie was in her early teens, the town of Bisbee and the mines around it were in decline. One day, Walt returned from a delivery run to Phoenix to announce that the family were moving to Tucson; he had decided not to wait for the inevitable mine closures and had been offered work restoring furniture for one of the dealers that he had supplied over the years. His eldest daughter Patty and her husband Jonas, also a miner, stayed and took over the family house; in the fall of 1965, the rest of the Arnold family moved to the city.

Walt rented a run-down house south of Downtown, with enough room for the family and his workshop. Although it was across town from the upmarket shopping areas where his work would come from, it was all they could afford, an added bonus being that he also picked-up a lot of carpentry work from local landlords patching-up the properties they were renting-out in the largely Hispanic areas between Twelfth Street and the Airport.

Margie hated it. Bisbee had been a small community where everyone knew everyone else and, although it was a basic life, it was wholesome, clean and safe. In Tucson some of her school class barely spoke any English, while others were from broken homes with self-discipline to match, having regular brushes with authority both within and outside of school. She managed to make a few acquaintances, of which the one that became her closest, and ultimately life-long, friend was Linda Kennedy.

Linda lived two streets away and walked to school along the same route as Margie. She came from an Irish-American family and her father was a security guard, a massive bear of a man with the most easy-going manner, plus probably the warmest smile Margie had ever seen. Nobody messed with Donal Kennedy and, as a consequence, nobody messed with his kids or their friends. So Margie was able to live in the secure bubble that surrounded the Kennedy family and their circle, a grouping that grew to include the whole Arnold family as Donal, Walt and their wives all became good friends, often organising joint family celebrations at Thanksgiving or St Patrick's Day.

It was Donal who got his daughter and her friend the tickets when The Doors played Hi Corbett Field in the summer of 1968. Hi Corbett was a small disused baseball stadium on the edge of Gene Reid Park, just a few blocks from where they lived and, being well-known to the promoters, Donal had been roped-in to help with additional security for the concert, needed because the band were building a bit of a rabble-rousing reputation. Linda had a massive poster of a brooding Jim Morrison on her bedroom wall, so Donal knew that he would never be forgiven for not getting tickets for her. He also recognised that, as she knew her father would be somewhere around, Linda would not misbehave. But just for insurance, clean-cut Margie would act as a steadying influence on his daughter if he became 'distracted' by certain events during the evening, as he inevitably would at some time.

So it was, on a hot and sultry evening in late May, that Margie and Linda were crammed into the stadium with what seemed like half the local population, focussing expectantly on the stage when suddenly, literally out of right-field, three figures appeared and started to play the intro for the first song. The crowd started to cheer, but Linda became agitated: "where's Jim?" she shouted to Margie, "he's not there! Oh my God, no, he can't not be there!"

Then, after about thirty seconds of intro, the crowd went wild as they saw a dishevelled looking figure in black leather stumble across the stage towards the microphone; it was Jim Morrison. Upon this recognition, Linda began to scream at the top of her voice, along with almost every other female in the stadium. The figure grabbed the microphone stand, stared at the front row and asked: "hasn't anyone got a cigarette for me?"

Within seconds, hundreds of lit cigarettes rained down on the front of the stage and on the security guards, including Donal, who was not impressed. Jim studied the array of glowing white sticks before picking one up, taking a long drag and flicking it back towards the audience. Immediately he launched into the first line of the opening song.

The following lyrics were subsumed by the combined decibel count of ten thousand fans and hundreds of watts of PA, at which point the stadium power failed and everything went-out; sound, lighting, the lot. Some of the crowd began to panic and move in different directions, blinded by the sudden blackness and disorientated by the sound of just a drum set beating-out a rhythm in the distance. As the jostling became frantic, Margie felt herself bump into a large body, whose arms instinctively wrapped around her and held her tight; at exactly that moment the power came back on and the sound deafened once again. Unreliable power supplies were a regular occupational hazard of stadium gigs in the 'sixties, so the band had carried-on playing in anticipation of the restoration. A few seconds later there was light, but just one main spotlight as the rest had fused. The stark beam picked-out the leather-clad figure at the microphone, still singing perfectly in tune with the backing.

Margie realised that she had turned her back to the stage and was looking at the outline of her shadow against the chest of a uniform - an Airforce uniform being worn by somebody considerably taller than her. This somebody also had their arms around her. Across the PA came the words of a line that perfectly summed -up the moment as she looked up to see a pair of smiling bright blue eyes gazing down at her.

And from the lips holding the broad beaming smile below those clear blue eyes, came the perfectly complementing phrase: "looks like you've just found an island of your own, little lady." The words, arms and eyes all belonged to Major Walter T Kleberson and, in that moment, Paul's future was defined.

Ten

Walter was twenty-eight, Margie just sixteen, yet somehow they hit it off immediately. Walter, recognising Margie's embarrassment at having his arms around her, but not realising that he was the first man to receive that privilege outside of her family, let her go and apologised, at the same time adding that had he realised how pretty the body was that he was saving from falling underfoot, he would have taken it into his care much earlier. Margie immediately lost interest in the sex symbol smouldering on the stage.

She assured Walter that it was fine - really - adding her thanks for his assistance, at which she turned back towards the stage before allowing her own beaming smile to engulf her face, momentarily forgetting who she had gone to the show with. Once that recognition dawned upon her, she looked around and realised that Linda was no longer beside her. Margie became agitated, craning her neck to see over the crowd, but as she was only five feet two, it was impossible to see beyond the human barricade that surrounded her.

"What's the matter little lady?" came that same warm voice from behind her. She turned back to see Walter's friendly eyes still anchored on her.

"Linda, she's gone. Did you see her?" Margie replied.

"What does she look like?"

"She's blonde, about five-five, with a white polkadot dress and a pony-tail."

Walter drew himself up to his full six feet three and surveyed the crowd as best he could in the reflected light from the one spotlight: "I think I see her, she's about five rows in front, but she doesn't seem to be missing you right now, I think Jim has her mesmerised."

"I have to get to her," panicked Margie.

"I don't think that's a great idea little lady. But I'll tell you what, you stay there and I'll keep an eye on her for you from up here. Then when the show's over, I'll get you to her - how's that?"

Margie thought it was a great idea, but just allowed herself a relatively non-committal: "OK, if you're sure you don't mind."

"Not a bit little lady, now enjoy the band, they're the best around you know."

As the Doors launched into their finale, Jim Morrison called out to the crowd to join him on the stage. The main body of people began to press forward, causing the front rows to crush-up. Donal and his colleagues did their best to hold back the tide, but quickly recognised the inevitable and took a fall-back position on the stage, surrounding the band. As the crowd surged towards the stage, Linda was swept-along with them, but Walter gently took hold of both of Margie's arms and told her to stay with him.

He then gave a running commentary on where Linda was, until Margie herself saw Linda jump-up onto the front of the stage, just a few feet from her beloved rock-star. She also saw that most of that few feet was occupied by Linda's father. The minute Donal saw Linda, he grabbed her in a huge bear-hug with one arm, holding her clear of the rabble, who he continued to hold away from Jim Morrison with the other.

"Oh dear, that security guy's got her!" said Walter.

"It's OK, that's her Father," replied Margie.

"Really?"

"Yep, he got us the tickets."

"Is she in trouble then?"

"Only once he realises that she's lost me!"

"We'd better get you to them as quick as we can then."

As the band finished and left the stage to tumultuous applause, Walter helped Margie through the crowd towards the right-hand side of the stage. He could see Donal was guiding Linda to the same area, whilst looking-out into the blackness shading his eyes from the spotlight's glare to see if he could spot Margie amongst the sea of humanity calling Jim Morrison back for more.

Donal knew the band weren't coming back, as the local police had insisted that they be escorted away before the crowd realised that the concert had ended. As Donal and Linda reached the top of the steep steps leading down from the side of the stage, Walter and Margie appeared at the foot of them; Donal guided Linda down. As they hit terra firma Walter, wearing a generous smile, outstretched his hand in greeting towards Donal and shouted above the commotion: "how do you do Sir, I am Major Walter Kleberson, Hundredth Air Wing, United States Air Force. I believe I have found somebody you may have mislaid."

Donal, who previously was ready to explode into full celtic rage, was completely disarmed by this charming approach amid such chaos. Instinctively he took Walter's hand within his copious mitt, shaking it firmly: "Major Kleberson, you have saved me some considerable additional trouble to that which I am already dealing with, as you can see. Thank you so much for your help."

"No trouble at all Sir, in fact if I may be so bold, I can see that you have enough on your plate at the moment, so as I have my car parked at the other side of the park, it would be no problem for me to escort these two young ladies home for you, if that would be of any further assistance."

Donal could see that the crowd were becoming restive at the lack of re-appearance by the band; he knew where he was needed. He also realised that he could entrust his charges to this upright airman standing before him. He made a mental note to light a candle at Saint Augustine's on Sunday in thanks for this divine intervention: "if you're sure it's no trouble, we live just off South Stone and little Margie here is a couple of streets further over."

"I can take that route back to base Sir, so it would be a pleasure to assist."

"Why thank you. Now girls, Major Kleberson will drive you home; and Linda, you be sure you stay right there until I get back, you hear?"

"Yes Father," came Linda's resigned response. She knew she was in line for a potential grounding later that evening, but it had been worth it to get within feet of her idol. Walter detected the atmosphere between father and daughter and thought about putting in a good word, but decided to hold his counsel at that point. Instead he escorted the girls across Gene Reid Park to where his car was parked on South Lakeshore.

All the way, Linda was immersed in an excited teenage monologue about the evening, but somehow Margie only heard parts of it, interjecting the odd "Oh Yeah!" when Linda occasionally paused to grab enough air into her lungs to embark on the next section. Instead, Margie was preoccupied by their temporary guardian and would occasionally turn around to check that Walter was still there, giving a slight shrug of apology in his direction, to which he would just smile that incredible smile back at her.

Eventually, the now-familiar voice came from behind them: "here we are then ladies." Margie span around to see Walter holding the door open on a bright red '66 Mustang Convertible. She was also aware of Linda's voice fading away slightly and, turning back, she saw her friend gabbling off into the distance blissfully unaware that her companions had stopped walking.

"Linda!" Margie called somewhat tersely. Linda spun around to realise that she had almost done it again, so lost was she in her thoughts of the concert and, specifically, Jim Morrison. Linda trotted back full of apologies and slid into the middle of the white front bench seat, still jabbering away. Margie got in beside her and Walter shut the door, then walked around to get into the driver's seat.

At this point, Margie realised that Linda had unwittingly separated her from Walter and began to feel an animosity welling within her that she had never felt towards her friend previously - ever. She found that to be a strange sensation, but Walter soon unwittingly put a stop to it as he asked for each address, then calmly announced that he would drop Linda first as her house was the nearest to the park. As they swung out onto Twenty-Second Street, Margie realised that she would have a few precious minutes alone with this handsome airman as they drove between Linda's house and her own. Despite Linda's incessant chatter, it was the only thought in her mind.

When they arrived outside of Linda's house, Walter insisted that he escort Linda inside, so Margie decided that she would also do so, as she didn't want her chauffer being hijacked before he had the chance to drive her home. When they got inside, Walter explained to Linda's mother why it was he that had brought them home, making sure that he absolved Linda from as much responsibility as he could for what he termed the forced separation of the two girls in the confusion of the darkness imposed upon the stadium. His manner was so reassuring that Linda's mother was also finding herself thinking of lighting candles of thanksgiving, but instead offered Walter some supper for his trouble which, much to Margie's excitement, he politely declined explaining that he had to get back to base as he had a briefing early the following morning.

So Margie got her few minutes alone with Walter, during which he quietly quizzed her on her background without causing her either to be flustered, or to suffer the teenage embarrassment of not knowing how to initiate part of a conversation. When they arrived at Margie's house, again Walter escorted his charge indoors and explained to her parents the circumstances of his involvement in the evening. Margie's mother, as captivated with this handsome visitor as had Linda's been ten minutes earlier, offered refreshment and, to Margie's surprise and delight, Walter accepted the offer of coffee. Margie's instinct was to ask *'why here and not at Linda's house'*, but she sacrificed that curiosity for a few more minutes in the company of this unexpected and fascinating companion.

Margie's father began to quiz his guest about his role at the base, but soon found himself unwittingly redirected into giving the Major his own life history. As they sipped away at their coffees, Margie discovered hitherto unknown facts about her parents' lives and, at the same time, how charmingly well-versed their guest was in the art of quiet interrogation. She had become captivated and there was little she could do about it.

When Walter made his farewells, Margie suddenly realised that she might never meet him again. The parting was made worse by the delicate way that he shook her by the hand and thanked her for her charming company that evening. She could not think of the words she needed to say to create a reason for him to return, someday, any day! But then her mother, ever the friendly hostess, gave Walter an open invitation: "now if you ever find yourself bored by that same old fast food they serve you at the base canteen, you be sure to come over here for a bit of good old-fashioned home cooking."

"Thank you Ma'am," Walter responded, "you're very kind, I may just do that."

"You be sure that you do, young man, it's the least I can do to thank you for keeping our little girl here safe from harm tonight."

And with that Major Walter T Kleberson drove off into the sunset, taking with him a borrowed piece of Margie's young heart, which had been replaced by an ache in the pit of her stomach at the dread of never having it returned.

Eleven

Margie barely slept that Friday night. When the sunshine of the morning broke through the blinds and she could bear the waiting no longer, she got out of bed, put on her wrap and went downstairs to the kitchen to make some coffee; it was 5.50 a.m. As she sipped at the cup, staring skywards out of the kitchen window, she heard the distant sound of a jet engine and became aware of a single-engined aircraft with wide, slim wings lifting into the blue sky above the Davis-Monthan Air Force base, about two miles east of the house. She wondered if a certain Major was seated at its controls; maybe the reason why he had to be back the previous evening was this early-morning flight. What could its destination be? Was it ever coming back? Or was her dashing airman leaving the base forever? She groaned at the return of that ache in her stomach.

She could hear her father bumping around in the workshop. It was Saturday morning and he was gathering a few things together ready for another foray out into the desert to a remote house-sale. She padded out into the workshop: "hi Pop, want some coffee?"

"My, we're up early this morning" he remarked, looking at his watch: "why not, I've got a few minutes before I have to set-off."

Margie went back into the kitchen and poured her father a mug of coffee. He followed her into the room a few seconds later and sat at the table: "an interesting guest you brought home last night, don't often get to meet many of them fly-boys."

There was no reply. He glanced at her face as she lifted the coffee over to him; it looked flushed but sad. He had seen this many times over the years with his other daughters and knew that it was the first sign of another fledgling reaching the potential point ready to fly the nest. He made an offer: "I guess, if you're as wide awake as you look, you might like a bit of desert air. Want to come to the sale with me this morning?"

It had been years since this invitation had been offered and the memories of those previous trips where she got a day alone with her beloved father welled within her, lifting her spirits: "why not, Pop, where is it today?"

"Tombstone," came the reply.

Margie knew this was only about twenty miles from Bisbee; she also knew that her father normally took the opportunity to call-in on her sister when he was out that way. Before she could reply, Walt added: "and if the sale's no good, we can just mosey on down to see Patty."

"Great Pop," Margie replied, "give me ten minutes and I'll be ready"

As it turned-out, they did both. The sale was full of junk, apart from a very dilapidated old chest of drawers. The locals thought Walt was mad even bidding on it, ribbing him, as he and Margie loaded it into the back of the old F100, that the six bucks he had paid was the most expensive firewood they had seen for years. What they didn't realise, but Walt knew, was that beneath all the grime and faded lime green gloss paint, was a genuine late eighteenth-century tiger maple New England tall chest that, after a few weeks of his own careful brand of TLC, would add a couple of zeros to his outlay in one of the more fashionable Phoenix auction houses.

With his prize securely tarped-down in the truck bed, they headed south through the midday sunshine to their old house in Bisbee, where Patty was preparing lunch. Half an hour later, they were all sat at the table on the rear deck with Jonas and the kids, just like the old days when Margie had been the same age as the nieces and nephews sat across from her, devouring their food.

Walt couldn't help but relate the events of the previous evening and whereas Patty's eldest daughter Nancy, who was only three years younger than Margie, wouldn't stop asking about Jim Morrison, Jonas was more interested in the dashing Major that had rescued his wife's kid sister from the crowd. Afterwards, while they were washing-up together, Patty reminisced about the day she first set eyes on Jonas and, although it was done purely in sisterly innocence, Margie began to realise that what her sister was saying about her own emotions at that time was not far different from what she was now experiencing herself.

On the way home, Walt chattered away more than was usual for him at the end of a long day. Although he didn't ask Margie any direct questions about her feelings, his ramblings were not completely without an agenda, particularly the parts where he related how the ten-year gap in ages between himself and Margie's mother had never been a problem to them. By the time they arrived back at the house in Simpson Street, it was approaching supper time and Margie had made a realisation; she was probably in love for the very first time.

The excitement of this new awareness, however, was still tinged with the recognition that this love, like many first loves throughout history, may ultimately remain unrequited. If not just for the thought that the plane she had seen soaring into the heavens that morning may have been carrying her love away forever, there was also the gulf between them, not only in age, but in worldly experience. Whatever could a USAF Major possibly see in a giggling schoolgirl?

Her melancholy stayed with her as the family sat down for supper. Noticing this, her mother looked towards her father with a knowing smile, then said to Margie: "you had a visitor while you were out."

"A visitor?" replied Margie, quizzically.

"A certain military man."

Margie's jaw dropped open and stayed there. She was genuinely shocked.

"Careful girl, you'll be catching flies in there if you're not careful," quipped her father, barely concealing his amusement, having already been tipped-off by his wife before they sat down.

"But … what … did …?" Margie spluttered.

As Margie's elder siblings were beginning to giggle at her embarrassment, her mother intervened to spare her that indignity: "he said there was a dance over at the base a week next Saturday and wondered if you and Linda might want to go."

"And you told him …?"

"I told him you were both probably way too busy at the moment, what with school being out in a couple of weeks an' all. So he just apologised for his intrusion and drove away."

"And you let him go? Just like that?" Margie's voice was rising and she had a look of sheer horror on her face: "no message, nothing else?"

Margie had no idea why she was shouting at her mother. She never shouted at her mother. Why did she feel like this? It was as if all her wishes had been answered in a moment, then instantaneously smashed into a million pieces. He hadn't flown away, he had come back! And what's more, he had come back to see her, only to be sent packing again into the sunset. She could feel tears welling: *'how could life be so cruel?'* she thought, *'life rarely gives second chances, let alone thirds!'*

Her mother calmly replied to the strident question: "no dear, but I may have just mentioned that he might like to ask you himself when he comes over for Memorial Day dinner on Thursday."

Margie looked across the table at her mother, who was wearing her broadest, kindest smile. Margie burst into tears; this time they were tears of joy.

"I think we already know what the answer may be," observed Walt as Margie got up from the table and threw herself into her mother's arms. She didn't notice the tears in her mother's eyes - tears of resignation for the imminent departure of another daughter.

So it was that Margie left school in the summer of '68, that same December becoming the wife of a United States Air Force U2 Pilot, at the tender age of seventeen. They set-up home on the base and Margie got a job at the BX. A year later their first child, a son christened Paul, arrived on December eighth which, in one of those strange quirks of fate, was also Jim Morrison's twenty-sixth birthday.

the bitch had to die

Twelve

It was 6.05 a.m. and Kleberson was late. This was not unusual; in the six years that Chris McKinley had worked with Kleberson, first in Narcotics, then in Homicide, his boss had barely ever kept an appointment exactly to time. There was always a good case-related reason, he just followed any live-lead that lit-up the board without considering the consequences.

That was what was mildly infuriating. Kleberson expected, nay demanded, total obedience during an investigation, which often meant periods waiting around for him to show, minutes that became parts of hours, all of which added into dozens of man-hours wasted during an investigation. A wry grin pulsed across McKinley's face as he thought that such an admonition, even unspoken, probably meant he was more likely than his boss to rise to the position of chief of police, as Kleberson had no time for bureaucratic whinges such as these.

McKinley looked around the dim Squad Room. There were Moreno and Capaldi, the latter throttling a plastic cup of coffee with his large hand as always, both thinking similar thoughts along the lines of: *'if we'd only known he was gonna be late, we could have banged another door or two.'* They could never help thinking that a bit more time may have helped them come up with a lead that might draw faint praise, instead of the hawkish looks their empty answers would receive even at this early stage in the investigation.

Also in the room were Dean and Holdsworth, the other two members of the Squad. Jerry Dean was the elder statesman, gnarled and wounded by over twenty years of zero promotion and multiple drive-bys. Scott Holdsworth was the rookie, assigned to the old lag for both protection and cynicism-training, the latter a necessity in Homicide if one was to remain remotely human into one's early-thirties.

And there also, in the most shadowy corner by choice, was Lieutenant Morley, slumped on a desk, his only sign of life the rhythmic pulsation of a cigarette end as it lit up his face like the red light on a whorehouse. Morley headed, no - Morley was, Internal Affairs and, therefore, a pariah in this company. He was also Stanton's lackey, his mouthpiece and messenger when not going about the duties in his job description, which was actually most of the time in a Midwest town like Wichita.

There had been a time around his appointment when questions were asked at City Hall as to why a dedicated IAD officer was needed when, on average, there were only a handful of complaints against police officers in any given year. Then the quadruple-homicide had occurred and everyone blamed everyone else.

Stanton, consummate politician that he was, used the excuse of needing IAD locally, rather than calling-in State Police from Kansas City, thus elevating his puppet into an untouchable position that allowed him to snoop wherever and on whoever he liked, thereby limiting the possibilities of any challenge to the Chief's authority.

Morley was, therefore, rightly despised by all, the sole unifying subject of conversation within the entire Police Department; and he revelled in it. Kleberson had once observed, at a civil reception and within Stanton's earshot, that Morley had all the wit and charm of a great white shark and, as Stanton tried to wither him on the spot with a glare that would have melted titanium, continued with a smile to observe that was exactly what was required of an IAD man. This had left the tittering ladies gathered around Kleberson admiring his utter loyalty to the cause, and Stanton in no doubt as to where his potential nemesis was located.

At 6.11 a.m. Kleberson breezed into the room and without even looking into the dim corner behind the door he began: "well, what a completely unsurprising and dubious honour it is to have you with us this morning Lieutenant Morley. Please pass my humble thanks to the Chief for releasing you from your normal onerous duties in order to help us on this high-profile investigation of ours. As you can see we are already hot on the trail of our perp and expect to make an arrest sometime between now and ten a.m. Can't release the full details right now, but likely to be an Hispanic male, early twenties with an unusual name like Gimenes or Garcia. Of course, he will have an airtight alibi, as he was at home at the time of the murder shooting all sorts of illegal substances into his veins in full view of half the neighbourhood, who will doubtless also attest to the fact that those ugly bruises on his face were the result of the usual police brutality used during the arrest, what you would otherwise doubtless be investigating on his behalf had you not been otherwise assigned by your master."

"In other words," observed Morley, "you're fucking nowhere as usual. What a surprise Kleberson."

"Well seeing as you think that Morley, old friend, you won't need to hang around here to witness our collective embarrassment. So tell you what, as you are going to be part of this team for at least as long as it will take to become partially humanised by our warm and affectionate company, perhaps you would like to pop-along to the morgue and get the preliminary report from the M.E, who should have completed the less-digestible parts of the post-mortem process that are known to cause you some degree of personal embarrassment."

"Go fuck yourself Kleberson ..." Morley responded, but the words had barely fallen from his mouth before Kleberson rounded on him and fixed him with a laser stare that penetrated the gloom of his chosen hiding place.

"Oh dear! Was that a 'no' Lieutenant Morley? To a specific request from the senior officer in charge of the investigation to which you have been assigned? Now what do Disciplinary Procedures say about insubordination by an IAD officer. Something about surrendering yourself to the Police Chief I believe -

can't quite remember. So let's just say that's a NOW shall we - immediately, with all haste and without further ado as Shakespeare might put it."

Morley catapulted himself from his lair to within half an inch of Kleberson's face: "seeing your ass on parking duties will be a pleasure, and I have a feeling it won't be long."

Kleberson didn't even flinch, instead calmly directing his adversary: "that's the ticket Mr Morley, now run along would you, like the good obedient little mutt that you are."

Morley slammed out of the room as the rest of the assembly erupted with mirth, the door rebounding with a shudder from the doorframe back to the fully-open position it had previously occupied.

"Problem is gentlemen," observed Kleberson, "he's right I believe in that we currently have jack shit, unless one of you is about to pleasantly surprise me." The mirth immediately evaporated and an icy silence filled the room. Kleberson broke it: "OK, close the door, there's something you all need to know before the lapdog returns." He nodded at Holdsworth, who quickly obliged by shutting the door that momentarily before had refused to occupy the position under Morley's forceful exit.

Kleberson continued: "alright then, here's a brief overview. Our victim is Hilary Nicholson, high-profile accountant, betrothed to our star citizen, one Jackson Kendrick the Third, so future mother of the grandchildren of Jackson Kendrick Junior, and an old friend of our very own media rising star Marjoree Rolles."

"Holy shit," exhaled Dean, immediately aware of the politics already in play.

"Exactly, hence the close involvement of our most popular colleague, the ever-joyous Lieutenant Morley and his need to keep the Chief fully informed of our speedy progress so that he, in turn, can pacify the aforesaid Junior who is already all over this like a rash and will continue to be so until someone, anyone, can be locked-up, or preferably lynched before trial in order to keep a lid on their perfect world before its soft underbelly is exposed for all to see. In which case, we will run the show so that everything, without exception, goes to Chris first; he will tell you what you can release to Morley and you sit on everything else, no matter what Morley threatens you with - are we clear Holdsworth?"

"Sure are Skip," the rookie responded brightly.

"No, really Holdsworth, Morley will use anything and everything to make you talk, even kidnapping your grandmother - everything! We know how to handle him, you don't, so stick close to Dean and follow his advice to the letter."

"No problem, my Gran's dead these two years anyway," Holdsworth observed trying to maintain a little brevity in the situation.

But it didn't cut any ice with Kleberson: "then Morley will take out an exhumation order and charge the corpse with every unsolved case from before the funeral - anything and everything, you understand?" Holdsworth nodded sheepishly and focussed his gaze on his shoes.

"Chris will be a one-way feed to me. He knows how to keep the investigation files open enough for Morley's benefit but closed enough for me. I'm the only one to brief the Chief, all media comment is 'no comment' and, if that doesn't work, use the 'three billy-goats gruff' technique."

He turned to Chris McKinley: "one thing we do have on our side is Marjoree Rolles. She'll give you a full statement later this morning at her home. Take Dean, be as thorough as you always are. Holdsworth, you're with me; we'll be interviewing 'The Turd'. Watch him closely when we do, don't be distracted by Friedmann, I'll deal with him."

"We haven't found him yet," Moreno chipped-in.

"Don't worry, daddy will, then he'll find us I'm sure. Anything on house-to-house yet?"

"Three monkeys," said Capaldi.

"Thought so, keep on it, something will break. Sit on CSI as well, there has to be something there. Moreno you concentrate on the full M.E. report."

"Thought Morley was getting that," Moreno responded.

"So does he, but it's just a preliminary, you'll get the full report later today."

"Sorry," Holdsworth piped-up, "but are you saying we're running two investigations here, one for us and one for the Chief? I'm not sure I'm comfortable with that."

"Now listen up you naive dumb fuck!" Dean had rounded on his young charge and was turning purple: "haven't you got it yet? This damned family owns half of Kansas and runs everything how it wants, including the Chief. You may not have figured it yet, but 'The Turd' has to be suspect numero uno, a fact that won't be lost on daddio who probably has all his muscle out, right now, trying to find his son and disinfect him before we get a warm trail, just in case. Capaldi and Moreno have told you how the Chief fucked-up the crime scene before we could seal it, so before your devotion to duty gets the better of you, just think of our proffered prime suspect, Mr Garcia, who doesn't even know he's the scapegoat yet. Like the Lieutenant said, watch and learn boy, but most important, don't tell no-one nothing except him or Chris - you got that, no-one!"

Thirteen

The commotion outside of City Hall was building. There were half a dozen outside broadcast trucks from various networks brought there to beam the press conference live. News of the demise of Hilary Nicholson had been top story on every local station, plus breaking news on some national breakfast shows between eight and nine a.m. She had become a celebrity, of sorts, when linked to Jackson Kendrick III who was a gossip-columnist's dream. She had just become all the more famous for dying obtrusively.

Tom Cochrane had pitched the best spot at the foot of the steps. This time he was in front of the camera, as his immediate boss was 'unavoidably indisposed'. He knew that Marjoree and Hilary had been close for many years, but did not know the full reason for her absence, which was why his usual place was behind the camera - he was neither a trained journalist, nor an instinctive one. But this was a once-in-a-lifetime opportunity and Cochrane was going to take it.

He had almost come to blows with Pete Christensen from KNSZ who had tried to usurp the space having heard that Ms Rolles would not be using it, as was normally the case. Cochrane suffered some cheap jibes from the KNSZ crew for his pains, but he had stood his ground causing the somewhat effeminate Christensen to cave-in rather than risk anything quite as dreadful as fisticuffs.

Cochrane and his crew had broadcast live links at quarter-hour intervals from seven through to nine a.m, in between which they did recorded links for possible syndication, followed by some curious rehearsals between nine and nine-thirty, or at least curious to their rivals who were sipping coffee and double-checking equipment in preparation for the main show at the top of the steps at ten a.m.

At nine-forty, Christensen could stand it no longer. He approached Cochrane: "better take our seats I s'pose, get the best ones before the press guys do. I'll take the one next to you as you'll be getting the first question, huh Cochrane?"

"That's OK Christensen," Cochrane smiled calmly, "you go on ahead. If I'm getting pole position, they'll find me wherever I am."

Christensen's well-used antenna were on full receive. He went back to his crew and began to speak very quietly: "Cochrane's had a tip-off, stick to his guys like glue." He flicked on his mic: "Joe, d'ya read me?" The producer's voice flickered acknowledgement in his earpiece. Christensen continued: "tell HQ to be ready to flip here for a live link at zero notice, somethin's goin' down, I can feel it." He flipped the mic off: "OK everybody, stay alert, if it's gonna happen, it'll happen real soon."

The TV was on in the Squad Room, but little notice was being taken of it until the linkman said: "... and we're going live to Police HQ in Wichita where there's been a significant development in the Hilary Nicholson case."

Cochrane's face filled the screen: "you can see behind me ..." the camera panned as he spoke "... several patrol cars have just pulled-up and one we believe holds a man who has been arrested in connection with the brutal murder this morning of Hilary Nicholson."

Several burly officers were pushing-back the media corps in an overly theatrical manner to make a space for the rear door of the middle Cruiser to be opened. As it did, a white male, slim, late thirties, wearing jeans, a blood-stained yellow tee-shirt and John Deere cap, emerged in handcuffs before being man-handled up the steps by two of the patrolmen. The camera returned to Cochrane: "we believe the suspect's name is Tommy-Lee Thornton. We don't yet know where he's from or how he came to police notice, but the bloodstains on his shirt are self-evident. I can see to my left Lieutenant Morley, one of the lead investigators; if you stay with me, I'll see if we can get a few words from him."

As the studio reporter précised the development in a well-rehearsed link, Dean's head popped round the door of the Squad Room: "Garcia's here, only this time he's a redneck from El Dorado called Tommy-Lee Thornton."

"And he ain't our killer," replied Kleberson, "because he's covered in blood; but go tell that to Junior Kendrick. Looks like our mornin's gonna be busy doin' nothin' Holdsworth."

Cochrane's voice re-emerged from the TV, along with Morley's face: "Lieutenant Morley, is this the breakthrough you've been looking for?"

"Could be, though we still have a few questions to be answered."

"And how did you find this man so quickly?"

"He was driving erratically along I-Thirty-Nine about four a.m. and was approached by a State Patrol unit. He set-off at breakneck speed, but they eventually forced him off the road near Branson, when he produced a gun and there was a standoff for a while. He kept shouting: 'the bitch was no good, but she didn't have to die. It was all her own fault'. When he was finally overpowered, they noticed the blood all over him and called it in. They took him to Branson Jail and sobered him up a bit, so that we could bring him here for questioning."

"And that, of course, makes everything that's just been reported inadmissible doesn't it Morley, you prat!" Kleberson railed at the TV screen: "even if he was our man, which is totally impossible, that would get him kicked overnight! Hellfire, how I hate these bloody politics."

"And had his gun been fired Lieutenant?" asked Cochrane

"Several times," replied Morley.

"But our victim hadn't been shot," continued Kleberson, "which you would know if you'd bothered to actually collect the M.E's preliminary report instead of looking for opportunities. So what's with all this Morley, whose pocket you really in, huh?"

Dean's head reappeared round the door: "and the Chief wants to see you, says the conference goes ahead as planned."

"OK," replied Kleberson resignedly: "Dean, Holdsworth, find out what Billy-Bob was really doing last night while I torpedo the conference; and do it quickly otherwise the trail will go even colder. That's what you want young Holdsworth, ain't it - the truth? Well, it's time to go find it."

Fourteen

Kleberson walked straight into the Chief's office, where he found Morley and Emil Friedmann in earnest conversation with Stanton, who turned and shouted: "when you gonna learn to fucking knock Kleberson, get the fuck out of here!"

"Didn't realise railroads had doors," said Kleberson "so you won't be needing me for the conference then?"

"Yes I will, and you can fucking wait outside until I call you in to brief you!"

"Sure Chief, nice to meet you too Counsellor." He stared hard at Friedmann: "oh by the way, would really like to talk to your client as soon as possible if that's OK, assuming you know where he is of course."

"I sure do," oozed Friedmann, "and he's way too distressed to see anyone right now. I suggest you concentrate on finding the killer of his fiancé, or haven't we just done that for you?"

"That's why I need to talk to him. Now is he distressed at any particular altitude this time, or distressed as a newt? I do realise there are different timescales involved with these in terms of when he's gonna be compos mentis enough to be interviewed."

"I said fucking out!" screamed Stanton, pointing doorwards.

"Or is it just that he hasn't quite gotten the story off pat yet?"

"OUT!"

Kleberson gently closed the door and kicked his heels in the corridor. A couple of minutes drifted by before Morley and Friedmann emerged in earnest conversation. As they passed him, Kleberson leaned in Friedmann's direction and politely said: "before lunch if you please Counsellor."

"Get your ass in here Kleberson - NOW!" The loud voice came booming from the Chief's office.

"I think the Chief will see you now," said Morley with a vicious grin.

Kleberson marched through the open door to a verbal broadside: "what the f ..." but Stanton couldn't get the words out before Kleberson slammed the door and finished the sentence for him:

"... are you doing Chief? 'Cos you'd better tell me quick or I damned sure am getting that warrant sworn out!"

"I'm trying to find a murderer," Stanton fumed, "of sweet little bride-to-be, whilst you seem intent on going after her soon-to-have-been-relatives, who just happen to be pretty big around here if you hadn't noticed all these years you've been in City Hall."

"So Billy-Bob goes to gaol 'cos he's got no choice or money, or whatever, is that it Chief?"

"Right now, he's a lot closer to our M.O. than the grieving fiancé."

"What, he's got blood on his shirt and he'd fired his gun recently?"

"And he drives a dark-coloured pick-up, wears jeans and a cap, just like someone who arrived at the house around midnight and was spotted by a dear old granny across the street, or hadn't you got that detail yet from your super-dynamo squad?"

"No I hadn't, but I must admit the description pretty-much narrows the field to around seventy percent of the male population of Kansas. Only problem is that less than one percent of that seventy percent ever gets as far south as Derby."

"Unless their cousin lives in Udall!"

"The Udall connection; hellfire why didn't I think of that. Chief you're a genius, I have to admit it."

"Stuff your cynicism up your ass Kleberson and get this, 'cos I'm only gonna say it once. You are coming out with me onto those steps and you're gonna tell the assembled media that Hilary Nicholson was shot dead by a white male intruder whilst visiting a friend's house late last night, that you are currently questioning a prime suspect apprehended in the small hours, and that you fully expect to charge him later today."

"Except that she wasn't and he won't be Chief."

Stanton stared at Kleberson for a moment: "whaddya mean, she wasn't shot. Morley got the report from the M.E. personally."

"If he actually bothered himself to go to the M.E, Chief, then he must've got the wrong report, 'cos Hilary Nicholson wasn't shot, nor did she bleed. Don't know what Billy-Bob had been up to, but he sure as hell ain't our killer. But far be it from me to disobey a direct order from my Chief, if you really want me to issue that statement, then I'll do it."

If the scene had been in a comic book, then right at that moment steam would have been blowing from both of Stanton's ears. Instead he stormed to the door, yanked it open and broadcast at full volume to the empty corridor: "where's that shit Morley - get him in here!"

Fifteen

Morley sat sheepishly in the corner of the Chief's office as Jerry Dean finished the resume of Tommy-Lee Thornton's statement: "... so basically Chief, Tommy-Lee is a well-known trainer of illegal fighting dogs 'round here. He had taken his top bitch to a fight at his cousin's place near Udall, but she got badly mauled by her opponent. He got in the ring to try to save her, but she was too far gone and he ended up shooting her to put her out of her misery. He then got blasted on moonshine and thought the Cruiser was stopping him because he had been at the fight, which as you know carries a bigger potential penalty round here than drink driving. The blood on the shirt was the dog's Chief."

"OK Dean; and we don't need no postscripts from you neither Kleberson!"

"None come immediately to mind," quipped Kleberson.

"Oh, but I have a few questions for Lieutenant Kleberson if you don't mind Chief," Morley sneered from the corner.

"I do mind, Lieutenant Morley, I mind a lot about how we explain to that other pack of hounds camped on our steps out there how, just half an hour ago, we arrested the wrong man for shooting someone who WASN'T SHOT!"

"Not to mention her poor grieving family ..." added Kleberson.

Stanton flicked a withering stare in Kleberson's direction before turning it on Morley, concluding: "... and, of course, to her relatives-to-be."

Morley opened his mouth as if to reply, but the Chief leaned in closer to deliver his coup-de-gras: "the only question right here, right now, Mister Morley, is which of those two explanations you would prefer to deliver. Oh, and here's a clue for you - 'both' would be a good alternative answer to be considering."

"With all due respects Chief, a few pertinent answers from Lieutenant Kleberson here might help us in that decision making process."

"Morley," sighed Stanton, "if you want to examine your own screw-up, you can direct IAD to look into it after this investigation is finished, assuming you will still have an IAD to direct. Because, in case you hadn't noticed, we have a high-profile murder to solve, and you will give Lieutenant Kleberson your undivided attention, support and assistance until it is, is that clear?"

"Crystal clear Chief."

"Good, now we'll both take the press conference, then you can go brief Mr Kendrick Junior because I have a meeting with the Mayor. The rest of you get me something positive to work with, and quick."

As they left Stanton's office, Dean leaned over to Kleberson and said quietly: "that was interesting, the Chief would rather face the Press and the Mayor than Junior."

"Ever the politician," replied Kleberson.

Sixteen

Kleberson left the building by a side door with Holdsworth to avoid the media scrum that was all around the front of City Hall. As they wandered across the grass towards the junction of Central and Main, Kleberson glanced back to see Stanton stepping back from the bank of microphones to make room for a sheepish-looking Morley to step forward. An unmarked Squad Car pulled-up at the kerb and the window dropped down.

It was McKinley: "Dean's finishing-up on Billy-Bob, so I'm on my way to see Ms Rolles - wanna join me?"

"No thanks Chris, but you can take young Holdsworth. I think I'll just stroll down the block and visit the cavalry."

"Already?" queried McKinley, "we haven't given up yet have we?"

"No, I just think a little jurisdiction crisis might be what we need to give us a bit of time without heat from the Chief, don't you?"

"That's your call Paul. See you around lunchtime, then - back here?"

"No, meet me at the Papa John's down on Douglas, then we can compare notes."

McKinley drove off with Holdsworth. Kleberson crossed the junction and walked down Main towards the Epic Center, the tallest building in Wichita. Its strange triangular section was not really visible from this angle - it had originally been conceived as one of a pair, but the second and complimentary triangle had never been built across the other side of Second Street. As he approached, he looked at the Occidental Building on the other side of Main. This was by contrast the oldest commercial building in Wichita, built originally as a Hotel in 1873, its three storeys of colonial architecture quite simply dwarfed by the twenty-eight storeys of the Epic. As he approached the rear entrance that led into a Café area, he looked up at that twenty-eighth floor where the offices of Mulholland, White and Friedmann, lawyers to the Kendrick empire, looked down upon the flat expanse of Kansas.

He was going to visit Emil Friedmann unannounced, but as part of the investigation, which would give him the ideal cover for a private visit with Sam Schneider, head of the local FBI Agency, whose offices filled the twelfth floor of the same building. Kleberson had previously been an FBI Agent for a short while and had worked with Schneider, who was always nudging him to rejoin. Kleberson knew he would get a bit more of that, but also that he could ask Schneider a favour and it would be done, no questions asked. Such was their friendship, both professionally and privately.

He would visit Friedmann first. No doubt Jackson Kendrick III would be there in the office, being prepared for questioning. There was little doubt that Kleberson would not be allowed past reception, Friedmann's receptionist Betty Wagner or, as she was known in legal circles, 'The Rottweiler', would see to that. As he entered the lift that would rocket him to the top of the building, he was still somewhat undecided as to how much of a fuss he would make; he settled on a strategy that would cause enough of a rumpus to get Friedmann out of his office. That way he hoped that he could sneak a look inside that office to see if Friedmann had company. It would also ensure that Friedmann would complain to Stanton and add another blocking move to buy some political wriggle-room.

The door of the lift opened on the twenty-eighth floor and Kleberson stepped-out into a plush foyer leading to the reception area. He turned to his right and at the end of the foyer he could see Betty Wagner sitting at her dominant desk, smiling falsely as she spoke into the tiny telephone microphone on the end of a thin wire looping around the side of her face. As he approached the desk, she disengaged the 'phone conversation, tilted her blonde head slightly to one side and smiled that false, familiarly obnoxious smile before greeting him: "good morning detective," she beamed.

Betty Wagner knew he was a Lieutenant, but this was just the opening volley in the verbal war she always waged with any law officer visiting the offices of Wichita's oldest law firm, or so the words emblazoned across the false wall behind her declared.

"He's in, I assume," replied Kleberson, moving briskly past the desk and towards the executive offices. He had never invaded her turf so deliberately before, they normally swapped jibes for a few minutes before she made him wait an interminable time in one of the soft leather couches bordering the room.

Betty Wagner was completely taken by surprise and shot to her feet, spinning simultaneously on her axis towards what had become a rapidly-disappearing figure. The microphone cord snapped out of its socket and the jack plug flew past her ear as her expression changed to that of the forty-something harridan she really was. After a moment's hesitation caused by her sudden disconnection from the console, she snatched-up the chrome desk microphone for the Tannoy system and bellowed into it: "security to Mr Friedmann's office immediately, intruder on the premises!"

As Kleberson rounded the corner at the end of the corridor that led to the partners' offices, he reached into his pocket and pulled-out his badge and thrust it in the face of the security guard rushing towards him, revolver drawn. "Freeze you bastard", came the command from behind him as another guard crouched in the crook of the corner, also revolver drawn, with it pointing at Kleberson's back. Kleberson stopped, raised his hands towards the ceiling and as he did so rotated his right wrist so that the guard behind him could also see the badge.

At the same moment, an executive office door burst open and Friedmann appeared framed in the doorway. Behind him, Kleberson could just make out a pair of trademark cowboy boots, stretching out of the side of one of the leather sofas. He had confirmed what he wanted.

"I hope you have a warrant Lieutenant!" screamed Friedmann as he slammed his office door shut behind him. "If not, you had better advise your boss that a formal complaint is coming his way. Alright guys, put 'em down, we know Lieutenant Kleberson who is, I'm sure, just about to leave."

Seventeen

Kleberson entered the lift and the security guard leaned in to punch the lobby button. "Have a good day Sir", he remarked with a sinister undertone. The doors closed and the lift started downwards. Kleberson punched the '12' button and the lift glided to a halt. As the doors opened, he exited and turned right walking to the end of the corridor, where he punched the intercom button above which the sign read 'Federal Bureau of Investigation.' The speaker crackled and a friendly female voice asked: "can I help you Lieutenant Kleberson?"

"Is Sam in?"

"Sure is, come on through". The door lock buzzed and Kleberson entered a smart but functional lobby. Behind the reception desk Carla Courtney smiled and, in her thick Georgia accent, said: "mornin' Paul, thought it wouldn't be long afore we saw ya today - ya go on through now."

The two had known each other for years and enjoyed bantering: "wha thank ya Miss Carla", Kleberson smiled in reply using his deliberately overstated mock southern drawl as he breezed past the desk before turning left through the double doors.

Sam Schneider's office was at the end of the corridor; it's occupant was kicked-back with his feet on the desk and the phone at his left ear, the standard pose Kleberson normally found Schneider in. He spotted Kleberson immediately and beckoned him in, then gestured him to shut the door behind him.

"So you don't mind my extending her stay for a while then Pete, if she's willing of course. Any statute of limitations on that?" He stared at Kleberson and pursed his lips in an approving manner, his eyes gleaming with pleasure. "OK, two weeks, that'll be cool. I owe you one Pete", he paused again, "alright, just put it on the tab, huh? Bye." Schneider put the phone down with a flourish, kicked-back again in the chair, put his hands behind his head and smiled his cat-got-the-cream smile.

"What?" queried Kleberson, arms partially outstretched with his palms raised.

Schneider playfully conducted both sides of the conversation: "hey Sam, great to see you. Yeah Paul, great to see you too. How's the wife Sam? She's fine Paul, and your family?"

"OK, OK", said Kleberson, his face relaxing with every syllable, "so the great Bureau man is three steps ahead of me."

"Four," interrupted Schneider.

"Two steps ahead of me as usual," continued Kleberson not even breaking stride, "and is going to extract every second of triumph while I shuffle around on the spot waiting for the results, also as usual."

"You don't have to shuffle on your feet Paul, you can have a chair to shuffle in instead." Schneider gestured to the empty chair on the opposite side of his desk and, as Kleberson manoeuvred into it, Schneider continued: "you know, if you threw-over that blood-pressure job over at City Hall and rejoined us here Paul, leaving that asshole of a Chief to dig himself into oblivion, you'd be at the same place in the investigation that I am, and without having to suffer for your crumbs like y'do now."

"Not that old chestnut Sam, not today buddy please, I told you a hundred times, it ain't gonna happen."

"And I reply now as I've replied a hundred times before, when it does, you know there's a place for you."

"So now the pleasantries are all done, what you looking so all-fired proud of yourself for?"

"Lesley Kryczek."

"Who's he, the latest baseball coach at WSU?"

"She."

"She?"

"She," Schneider nodded approvingly.

"OK, who's she, the latest softball coach at WSU?"

"Top Bureau Profiler out of LA who happens to be on R 'n R after a case went wrong on her and is spending a few days down here visiting relatives."

"And?"

"And, she doesn't have to go back to California for at least two weeks, unless, of course, you want her to?"

"What, you're taking over the case?"

"Hell no Paul, you know I wouldn't pull any crap like that on you, but we have been instructed to give you every co-operation. So …"

"Instructed? By who?"

"DC - come on Paul, you knew it wouldn't be long before Junior was pulling strings."

"Even so, that's pretty-damned sharp!"

"Senator was also at the bash last night," Schneider shrugged pseudo-helplessly.

"Figures," Kleberson responded, "does she know yet?"

"Hell no, I just got off the 'phone with her Lead Agent, Pete Baker."

"And she won't mind."

"Sure she will, but that's my problem - coffee?"

"Yeah, reckon so."

Schneider pressed the intercom.

"Black no sugar, right Paul?" The voice was Carla Courtney's.

"Wha thankya again Miss Carla, that'll be mighty fine."

Sam let go of the intercom button: "why don't you make an honest woman of her Paul?" he quizzed, then immediately threw his hands into the air and said: "whoops, sorry, danger zone!"

"Change the subject Sam."

"So, what you got."

"Zip."

"Thought so, hence the Profiler. From what I hear, scene was a bit strange."

"Sure was, not a lot of clues either, plus the M.E. hasn't given us much to go on yet."

"So Billy-Bob didn't do it?" Schneider quizzed with a wry smile. Kleberson just gave him a stare and they both burst-out laughing.

"Must admit", said Kleberson, "would've loved to hear Morley's explanation, but I needed to find-out if Kendrick was upstairs."

"And he was, right?"

"Yeah. Any idea how long?"

Schneider picked-up the phone: "Bill, yeah it's Sam. Get onto building security and have them send over the CCTV tapes from overnight. Yeah, probably the garage door would be the best to review first." He paused listening to the other end of the phone call, then continued: "Jackson Kendrick the Third, you know him? Right, probably with a few 'supporters'. OK get back to me as soon as you can with a time. Thanks." He put the phone down and lent forward across the desk onto his folded arms: "you've got something though haven't you Paul?"

"Marjoree Rolles."

"Wondered where the media superstar was this morning, where's she figure in all this?"

"Crime scene's her property."

"Whoa, how'd that connection happen?"

"College buddies, now lifelong friends, until last night of course."

"There's something that ain't on the files, that's for sure! She a suspect?"

"No, but the connection gets more convoluted. I've got Chris McKinley taking a full statement as we speak. I'll fax it over when he gets back. You got anything?"

"I know what I ain't got yet, and that's where Kendrick was last night. He is prime suspect, right?"

"After Billy-Bob."

They laughed again and the door opened as Carla brought in the coffees: "wha, you guys're in good spirits this mornin', someone musta died."

All three laughed again and Carla breezed out, flipping her skirt as she went. Schneider made the observation: "like I said Paul, she needs to be an honest woman again."

"Sam!"

"Alright, I'll leave it. Junior was in Topeka, so he could hardly be a suspect, could he?"

"Not out of the frame Sam, but a rank outsider at the moment. Anyway, he wouldn't have done it himself, he'd have had it ordered."

"You're not serious Paul?" Schneider's glib demeanour evaporated.

"Junior's son and son-in-law have been keeping him in the dark on a rather important matter to do with our victim. It's not something we can ignore Sam."

"What matter?" he asked quizzically.

"It will be in Ms Rolles' statement."

"Do I get a preview?"

Before Kleberson could respond he was alerted by the shrill tone of his cellphone. It was Chris McKinley: "I'm over at Marjoree Rolles' place. You'd better get over here Paul."

détente

Eighteen

Paul really enjoyed the holidays that the family spent with Grandpa Walt. There was something more homely about them, a feeling of intactness; that it had ever been so. Which was why the autumn of 1988 was such a sad trip.

Grandpa Walt had finally succumbed to the fatigue of a hard working life, one he had continued to his dying day, at the age of just seventy-two. While the family conducted the wake in the parlour, Paul found himself alone in the workshop, drinking-in the atmosphere for a final time, remembering those hours spent with his Grandpa, just watching him sand and polish while talking endlessly about nothing in particular.

Paul was approaching his eighteenth birthday and had already decided that this would be his last family trip home. The East Coast visits were often fraught affairs and he would rather brave the variable elements back on the fens, where he had acquired true friends. He didn't care for the distracted air of New England so loved by his brother, or the ridiculous opulence of Palm Beach, so desired by his sister; he didn't feel as close to those long-devolved grandparents either. He also knew that his mother and father preferred Arizona to either East Coast option, but Tucson would be very different after Grandpa Walt's passing.

He was in his final A-Level year back in England and could not afford another lost fortnight if he was to get the predicted straight-A's that he needed to move on to Cambridge, which was what Walter hoped for and, for once, something his father desired of him that he wouldn't rebel against as a matter of teenage course. In fact, Paul desired it himself more than anything else in his previous short life, although he was wary that if he let his father know that they actually agreed on something important, then the target may change. So he feigned resistance to bolster his father's resolve.

Three A's were duly accredited the following August, providing the confirmation Paul needed for his passport to freedom. They were in English Literature, Philosophy and, most importantly, History; because that was the undergraduate course he had applied for at Peterhouse, Cambridge's oldest college. On a bright September day, his parents packed the station wagon with everything but the kitchen sink and drove the twenty miles to Cambridge.

As he entered the porters' lodge, he crossed the gate threshold with its reassuringly worn-away step marking the constant passage of academics, famous or otherwise, who had preceded him through the seven-hundred-plus years since the college's foundation by the Bishop of Ely alongside the River Cam. For the next three years, he would be able to sit on benches in the ancient Deer Park, screened from the main road by the overscale Victorian Neo-Classical edifice of the Fitzwilliam Museum, mingling with the spirits of such diverse characters as Hugh Latimer, Thomas Gray, Charles Babbage and Sir Frank Whittle.

He was allocated a room at Five St Peter's Terrace, a small, but elegant, Victorian terrace just two hundred yards back up Trumpington Street. He would be pleased that he had escaped the Corbusier-inspired, but monstrously-gaunt, William Stone Tower, erected directly behind St Peter's Terrace in the 'sixties by the somewhat-misguided college management of the day.

He had a comfortable room on the second-floor, with 'P.W. Kleberson' already emblazoned on the nameplate by the door. He would be sharing the landing with two others whose names, according to their nameplates, were 'A.M. Fleming' and 'R. Prabhakar'. He began the mental detective work regarding who those nameplates may turn-out to be.

Paul and his father made short work of lugging his bags and boxes up the steep stairs. He had already equalled his father's six-feet-three in height, but was yet to fully match the broad shoulders honed through years of physical training in the service. Nevertheless he possessed a wiry strength that would surprise any assailant unwary enough to make the misjudgement potentially encouraged by a heavy mop of blonde hair and the slightly-juvenile lazy stoop.

Meanwhile, his mother put the final finishing touches of cleaning to the already spick-and-span accommodation. He didn't object, he knew that was what his mother did, and that soon he would be free to descend into a level of student decadence of his own choosing. They went through his father's checklist as if preparing for a flight over enemy territory, then it was time for his mother to fight-back the tears of enforced separation from a first-born. In what seemed like seconds, the station-wagon exited the forecourt with a last despairing wave of a mother's arm, and he returned to his room, where suddenly this new world became both silent and inviting.

Paul closed the door and sank deeply into the old leather armchair in the corner by the window, surveying the bags and boxes littering the floor space between him and the door. *'So this is freedom'* he thought, *'I'm now in charge of my own destiny.'* Then it dawned on him that this also meant that those bags and boxes wouldn't unpack themselves. *'However,'* he thought *'when they do get unpacked is down to me.'* He looked out at the clear blue autumn sky, then back at the baggage, then at the sky again. *'Decisions, decisions,'* he thought.

Nineteen

It turned-out to be an easy decision - the sky won. With a selection of coins in his pocket, he strode out to explore the academic heart of Cambridge. He walked on down Trumpington Street, crossing over to Fitzbillies to pick-up one of their renowned and delicious Chelsea Buns that he had discovered on his interview visit several months earlier.

As he finished the last mouthful, he paused to take in the external grandeur of Kings' College Chapel then strolled on as the street narrowed into Kings Parade past the austerity of the Senate House, where he would graduate three-years' later, kneeling before the Proctor for a Latin blessing as his father stood bolt to attention in the crowd, pride exploding from the breast of his dress uniform, alongside his mother in her Sunday best, fighting back more mother's tears.

He carried-on through St Johns' Street to Bridge Street, making a mental note to explore the unusual round Templar Church at the junction, then down to the river and along The Backs, enjoying a swift half in the Granta before heading back to St Peter's Terrace, returning to find his possessions, reassuringly, exactly how he had left them. He was ready to arrange what would be his home for the next ten months.

As he was officially a foreign student, he would not have to tear it apart again at the end of each term, like most Cambridge students are compelled to, in order to make way for the seminar attendees that Cambridge entertains during term breaks. He had unpacked his clothes and was starting on his books, when there was a knock at the door. He opened it to reveal a petite brunette with the most startling green eyes and an engaging smile that lit-up her face. "Hi" said the vision with the clipped shires accent, "welcome to the landing. That's me over there." She pointed to the nameplate that read 'A.M. Fleming': "that's short for Agnetha Morag Fleming." She extended her hand in greeting.

Paul took it into what, by contrast, was his huge right mitt and shook it gently, immediately noticing the perfectly-manicured softness: "Paul Walter Kleberson, pleased to meet you Ma'am. That's me there." He pointed to his own newly-acquired nameplate.

"Hey, you're American!" There was a hint of excitement in her voice.

"Well I try my best not to be all of the time," Paul replied deferentially. "Agnetha?" he queried, "that sounds Nordic."

"Swedish," she replied, "my Mother's Swedish and my Father Scottish, hence the Morag bit." She imitated a Scottish accent more Lothian than Moray: "after me heeland Grannie, but call me Annie - everyone does."

"OK Annie, how long have you been here?"

"Came-up yesterday. Took forever to shoo-off the parents, but I'm settled now. Can I get you a cup of tea, oops I forgot, you Americans prefer coffee don't you?"

"No, no; a cup of tea will be just lovely, thank you." Paul relaxed back into the Californian drawl that he always used at home, but had kept more under control when with his friends in Godmanchester. Here it seemed it would be accepted for what it was, his natural accent.

"OK, leave the door, I'll bring it in." She turned away and he watched with admiration as the pert little backside, fitted perfectly into its tailored designer jeans, skipped off into the kitchen area at the end of the landing, thinking to himself: *'wow, this really is a different world!'*

Over the next few weeks, Paul got to know Annie really well, although not romantically. Somehow, they were always destined to be close friends, never 'an item', although a casual glance in their direction when they were together might yield the latter impression, so relaxed were they in each-other's company. Her father was chairman of a major bank in the City and the family lived in Sussex, in what sounded like a high-end property. But somehow, Annie never evoked the airs and graces that many with her lifestyle would do, like the 'hooray henries' that frequented the bars around Kings and Magdalene.

Even more amazingly to Paul, she was an engineering student, an obvious choice when you knew her highly-practical nature, but definitely not the first guess on meeting her. Neither was she a paid-for student, as were some of her classmates with more money than brain-cells; she had earned her place with straight-A's in the same way that Paul had, and she was proud of it.

Not so the third inhabitant of the landing. Rashid Prabhakar was second-generation Asian money with a capital 'M'. His family had fled Idi Amin's regime in Uganda fifteen years earlier when RP, as he preferred to be called, was just four years old. They had abandoned the largest electrical goods import company in the country, built-up by RP's grandfather through the 'fifties, then taken to another level again by his father in the latter 'sixties.

When they arrived in England in late 1972, they had just the clothes they stood up in. A cousin in Erdington, a suburb of Birmingham, had taken them in and, within weeks, RP's father had set-up a stall in Wilton Market selling kettles and toasters. Three months later he had a shop on Sutton New Road, which developed within two years into a chain of fourteen stores across the West Midlands, supplied from a central warehouse in an industrial estate, next to Spaghetti Junction, where all of the buying for the chain was handled.

Over the next few years, the chain expanded across the Midlands and began to outgrow the indigenous suppliers they had initially been dealing with; RP's father became ideally-placed to emerge as a champion of the newly-elected Margaret Thatcher's enterprise culture. Within eighteen months of her rise to power, the shops had been sold-off, mainly to relatives, and the warehouse re-sited into one of what would become seven regional distribution centres. The headquarters moved to Southampton, near to the port through which own-branded goods were arriving daily in containers from the Far East, where long-term manufacturing contracts had been set-up.

By the time RP, the eldest of four sons and heir-apparent to the family empire, was approaching school-leaving age, the business was the second-largest electrical goods importer in the UK. Unfortunately, though, such business success does not automatically guarantee academic prowess, so RP's rather average A-Level grades had to be bolstered by substantial fees in order to guarantee his place at the Cambridge Business School.

What RP may have lacked in academic talent, he more than made-up for in business acumen. Like his father, he was a consummate salesman. As Annie had succinctly observed: "he could sell ice-makers to Eskimos."

This observation was made after RP secured a terms-worth of free pasties from Ye Olde Bakery Shoppe in return for chaining his bicycle, complete with advertising placard for the shop, to railings occupying the best advertising sites in the town. By the end of their second term, every occupant of number five had a bicycle with a placard mounted in the frame and, although none were ridden around the town very much, just re-located between lectures, in exchange the house-mates were in receipt of free bread, milk, eggs, newspapers, tea, coffee and, most importantly, beer.

Twenty

It came as no surprise that the three landing-mates agreed to rent a house together for their second year, along with Roland Asquith, a gay Art History post-grad that had, rather fittingly, occupied the garret room of number five and filled it with somewhat disturbing comic-book style images of death and destruction, despite being one of the most peaceful characters Paul had ever met.

The house they chose was in Emmanuel Road. It was a small early-Victorian terrace of three single-room storeys and a basement, with a lean-to kitchen/conservatory occupying most of what had been the rear garden. The boys chivalrously allocated Annie the ground-floor room, as it was closest to the bathroom. Roland went for the garret again, while RP took the basement, as he figured that the stone floor was more capable of taking the weight of his ever-burgeoning Hi-Fi set-up and music collection. This left Paul with the first floor, which also had the best view out over Christ's Piece.

They all settled-down to their second years with great expectations. All had excellent grades in year one, except for RP, but his value to the social life of the college made that of less consequence. He would graduate with the minimum that his father's contributions, combined with his own brand of physical input, were destined to provide. The actual numbers on the certificate were of no consequence to his father, the first-ever 'MBA (Cantab)' after the Prabhakar name was his goal. In his view, this was what would guarantee his son the respect needed for RP to take the family business global.

But it was RP's astute nose for an opportunity, coupled with an uncanny knack of befriending people with no preconception of their own ultimately upwardly-mobile destiny, that would bring the later step-change in the company's fortunes. RP was already on the entertainments committee, along with several other college live-wires, who used to visit the basement for regular 'meetings'. Paul soon realised that these were more like musical appreciation sessions due to the vast array of demo tapes that found their way onto RP's sound system. The unusual sounds emanating from the 'meetings' often caused the other housemates to wander down to find-out what new band it was whose tracks were drifting up the stairs, subsequently being tempted into staying longer than intended by the combination of interesting music and free booze.

This became one of the main reasons for Paul to choose to do most of his research writing in the university library, where such temptations were placed beyond his reach. He did, however, meet some interesting folk in that basement, including a member of one of the college bands, a source of some of the promos being reviewed, thanks to his part-time job in one of the High Street record shops. Paul would be surprised a few years later to receive a pre-release CD through the post, via the Peterhouse graduate network, from that self-same visitor, accompanied by a short hand-written note simply saying: "I know you used to enjoy the band's gigs and our chats back at Emmanuel Road, so I thought you might like a copy of our first album which will be released next month." The album eventually broke into the lower reaches of the charts on both sides of the Atlantic.

But the foundation for the increase in the Prabhakar family's fortunes came when RP was introduced by Annie to two fellow engineering students. The two had evolved games that could be played on the new personal computers gaining popularity among the nerdier class of students. RP didn't need a second look; he instantly recognised an opportunity and, within weeks, the games were in production in the Far East, thanks to his father's contacts, following which the new computing division was formed to market them. Funding was never an issue, as Annie's father provided that, in return for a percentage of the equity. The eventual flotation of the division would make all three millionaires several times over, but that would not occur until more than ten years into the future.

At the time, Paul was heavily into the Tudors and the dissolution of the monasteries. He had become fascinated by the way that Oxford and Cambridge, although still primarily monastic institutions in the early sixteenth century, had escaped the worst of Thomas Cromwell's purges. This was to be his main second-year project and he immersed himself in it with gusto. He still made the time to socialise with Annie and RP, Roland rarely joining them on their epic pub crawls unless he had recently finished one of his ever-darker pieces of comic-art, which conversely made him happier than ever. Those carefree nights simply became fewer and further between as the workload grew from their respective courses and cash-earning extra-curricular activities.

Paul would often use the university library late into the evening, poring over evermore obtuse tomes of local history, whilst Annie stayed late in the engineering workshops putting together project pieces, some of which inevitably failed, sending her back to her room to hunch over her drawing board well into the wee hours. She was there when Paul returned from the library late one Tuesday evening in the depths of February; she called to him through her open door and he went into her room.

Annie spoke to him, a look of mild concern on her face: "your father rang, he asked for you to ring back. He said it's important."

Paul looked at his watch: "it's gone eleven now, he'll be in bed. I'll do it in the morning."

"No, he said tonight - he's waiting for your call."

"How did he sound?"

"Serious, but then he always sounds serious to me."

"That's the broomstick they rammed up his arse at pilot training school. They forgot to remove it when he left and he simply refuses to have the operation."

Paul was putting-on his best phlegmatic tone to cover his own concern. His father rarely rang him and never 'awaited a call-back' so Paul realised it must be something serious. He wandered out to the telephone in the hall, picked it up and dialled. As he did so, RP appeared from the basement.

"Problems?" he mouthed to Paul. Paul just shrugged as he waited for the call to connect.

RP wandered into Annie's room and asked: "what's up?"

"Don't know," she replied, "he has to ring his Dad."

"OK, I'll hang around if that's OK? He may need us."

Annie nodded and RP sank into one of her well-worn armchairs. The end of the call overheard through Annie's open door was fraught. Paul had said "No!" firmly on several occasions and finished with an emphatic: "no Dad, it just ain't gonna happen!" before slamming the receiver down causing an audible 'ting' from the unit as the force shook it. By the time he appeared in the doorway again, Paul was looking pale and drawn.

RP looked at Annie: "kitchen meeting," he said matter of factly.

"Tea!" she replied emphatically.

"Hang-on guys ..." Paul meekly tried to interrupt, but was cut-off by RP as he and Annie marched past him through the doorway.

"Come-on you sour-faced Yank," RP told him, "you know the rules, any one of us calls a kitchen meeting, we all have to come immediately, no arguments."

"Not Roland," said Paul.

"Yes - Roland," Annie chipped-in. It was a statement, not a question, and with it she scampered up the stairs.

Five minutes later they were all seated around the table in the cramped kitchen, except for Annie, who was pouring boiling water from the kettle into the large brown teapot Roland had 'rescued' from the dining hall in year one.

"I can't believe him!" Paul was having a bit of a rant about his father's ultimatum, received just ten minutes earlier: "he gets this promotion that takes them all back home and I'm expected to just abandon this course to go back with them! And where am I supposed to continue studying sixteenth century English history? Wichita! I mean, Wichita bloody Kansas! The only place on earth where it's flatter than around here. For God's sake, the place is barely more than a hundred years old itself!"

"Is that where the lineman comes from?" Roland chipped-in, vacantly. Annie picked-up one of the cold teabags she had emptied into the sink from the pot and threw it at him; it exploded on his forehead, breaking the mood and causing them all to fall into fits of giggles.

"She's obviously tea'd off with you," RP observed with a feigned groan.

"Yeah, leaf me alone," whimpered Roland between snorts.

"You should never let a woman treat you with such tea-stain," added Paul.

"Alright, enough you lot," said Annie almost crying with laughter.

RP changed the mood again: "seriously though Paul, just stay here. You're what? nearly twenty now, adult, he can't make you ..."

Paul cut RP off: "he can stop my grant."

The mirth evaporated with a sullen thud. Paul continued: "he pays all my bills, but because we're overseas, he claims it all back from the Air Force. He can't do that if he's not stationed here, so when he goes back I'm beholden to his personal charity."

"So he carries on paying it himself." RP was shrugging at the simple inevitability in his own mind, based upon his own family financial scenario: "what is he now, a Colonel? He must be on a good screw anyway."

"He won't do it guys. If I defy him, he'll cut me off; that's what he rang to tell me. Not that he's got a promotion, oh that's great Dad, congrats and all that. No, he rang to tell me I'm going home - end of."

"Well, your place is safe, Peterhouse won't take that away," Roland observed, then allowed his blacker side to emerge, "unless you decide to kill him and use the insurance money to carry-on."

Annie glared at Roland, then turned to Paul: "plus the Bursar has hardship funds that can be allocated in certain circumstances. Remember Steve Jorgenson last year, his father died and they took him under their wing when his mother found that she couldn't afford to keep him here."

"But that would only cover course costs. I don't think I could afford the accommodation and mess bills on my own, even if I moved back into halls."

"You could get a job," observed RP, ever the entrepreneur, "plenty about in the bars and restaurants."

"Problem is I need the evenings for library time and research. I guess I could get a day-job though."

"And we can split the rent three-ways instead of four," Annie offered.

"Hold-up!" screamed Roland, "that might be OK for you county types, but I can barely cover my book bills. History of Art is the most expensive course here, books and materials-wise, other than Architecture maybe."

"OK then, you carry-on with what you're paying and Annie and I will split the rest two-ways, how's that?" asked RP. Annie nodded her approval.

"I'm not taking charity guys, it's not my way," Paul observed indignantly.

"It's not charity Paul," RP replied slightly miffed at the suggestion, "look on it as an investment in the future. Like those computer games I'm involved in, yes? When they start making me my first millions, I will need to start a Foundation."

"Bollocks you will!" retorted Paul, smiling slightly.

"Problem is Paul," RP continued without breaking stride, "you're so focussed on the past, majoring in history and all that bunk, as one of your country's most successful businessmen once observed I remember, that you don't see the future as we successful entrepreneurs do. Tax-planning my friend, tax-planning." He reclined back in his chair smugly.

Paul looked at him with an expression of vacantness as the notion of tax-planning as a solution to his current dilemma went past him way above his head. RP accentuated Paul's perplexion by waving a flat hand across his forehead, accompanied by a spoken "Voom!"

RP waited in vain for a response before continuing: "you really don't get this finance stuff, do you Paul? When I make my first million, my Father's beloved Maggie and her sleaze-ridden cronies will happily relieve me of four hundred grand of it to squander on rehabilitating druggies so that they can reproduce with the help of the nearest unmarried distant-cousin. But, if I spent the four-hundred grand first, on something fulfilling for society, something for the arts or education, something that the offspring of their expensively-saved junkies can use for their future enlightenment, then they'll let me keep it, so to speak."

"So how does that help me exactly?" Paul enquired.

RP shrugged: "just look on it as Mrs T ensuring that the future academic head of the Prabhakar Foundation for Historical Research gets to finish the Cambridge education he will need to be able to fill the post."

Paul gave him one of his 'you cannot be serious?' looks.

Before he could bat the offer away, Annie added: "and my parents already give me more than double my share in the hope that I will, as Daddy puts it, upgrade from the squalor I have chosen for myself to at least the standard of a slum. So they will never notice. Anyway, I won't need their cash next year when my Trust matures; and I would never be able to finish my course without my trusty backwoodsman to protect me, now would I?"

Paul smiled at the nickname that Annie had coined for him when they had been confronted by a pair of drunks whilst walking home one evening during their first term. Words were exchanged and Paul thought that he had talked the drunks out of any foolish action, when one made a lunge for Annie, to which Paul had floored him with a left uppercut that even he didn't realise he had in his armoury. The other drunk had quickly withdrawn from the fray and was left trying to pick his mate up from the gutter where he had fallen, more humiliated than injured.

"As for the day job," RP continued, "I need someone to research potential stockists for the games. You are brilliant at research Paul and you love libraries, so put the two together and - voila!"

He flourished his arm as if revealing a hidden secret: "the solution - I'll pay you ten pounds for every lead you give me, plus ten percent of their first year's orders. That'll encourage you not to give me any timewasters."

"So that's it," concluded Annie, "I reckon you're staying-on here at Cambridge, don't you?"

Twenty-One

The half-hour bus ride out to Godmanchester had passed quickly and Paul was soon walking up London Road towards the house that the family had occupied those last five years. He had rung his father earlier in the morning to apologise for his outburst the previous night and to arrange the meeting they were just about to have. Having accepted his son's apology as graciously as ever, Walter was seated in his lounge awaiting the subsequent submission to his will, that was the normal and accepted finality to every decision he made within the Kleberson household. He was, therefore, taken by surprise by the reality presented calmly and concisely by his son.

However, Colonel Walter T Kleberson was not a stupid man, even though he could, on occasion, give that impression through bloody-mindedness. Neither was this the defiance of a stubborn teenager that could be subdued by stalwart resistance; it was a well-reasoned alternative scenario, sponsored by the support of third-parties not only beyond Walter's scope of authority, but motivated by true comradeship. This was something he could identify with, the type of unspoken independent backing that he had experienced throughout his service career and that had bolstered his own personal development. It was also in total contrast to the manner in which he had handled his own early departure from the nest nearly thirty years earlier. Walter's pivotal meeting with his own father had not been one of reasoned discussion; it had been a knock-down, drag-out confrontation of two iron wills.

At just turned eighteen, Walter had left Foxborough High and was expected, within the following few weeks, to commence training as a bookkeeper with his father's accountants, Donaldson Terrell and Associates. Instead, he had walked into his father's office in downtown Foxborough to announce that he had just signed-up as a USAF Cadet at the local recruitment office, and would be sent for assessment for pilot-training the following month. His father had gone ballistic and they had both ended-up leaning on their hands, either side of his father's desk, purple faces just inches apart as they shouted-down each-other's viewpoint.

That life-forming event had taken place long before the period of history termed Détente that Walter and his own grown-up son were inhabiting, the perestroika that was about to summon-in the demise of the communist bloc. Back in 1958, the world was deep within the cold war period and although the reds weren't exactly under the beds of US citizens, they were seen as eminently capable of killing them whilst they slept there; the front line of deterrence against any such development was the United States Air Force.

The meeting between Walter and his father had ended with the foyer floor covered in the shattered glass that had showered from the front door of the office suite as it was slammed in the wake of Walter's departure. His father would not physically see him again for several years as, by the time Bill returned home that evening, Walter had packed his belongings and left to catch a Greyhound Bus heading west, leaving his mother, Liz, in tearful shock on the sofa.

There had not been a full reconciliation until nearly ten years later, when Walter had brought home his future wife for the first time. It was Margie's warm personality that had begun the thawing process in the cold relationship between father and son; the presentation of a first grandson barely a year later had finally melted Bill's last vestiges of resistance. Walter also remembered the promise that he had made to Margie on that first trip home after Paul's birth - that he would never allow the stubbornness at the heart of the Kleberson genes to create such a schism between him and his own children.

Margie had been sat across the lounge from Walter during the previous night's telephone conversation. Although he didn't need it, he had been reminded by her of that promise just moments after putting the receiver down. Not by any words, she hadn't needed to say anything; he simply looked across and saw it written in her eyes. But more than all of that, he felt a father's pride in his son's move. He was no longer dealing with a recalcitrant youth. Instead, seated before him was an adult man that had the presence to not only earn the unwavering friendship of his peers, but also commanded the respect of his close family for his new-found independence.

As a result, the kitchen meeting that Paul called immediately on his return to Emmanuel Road was not born of any desperate rearguard action against parental tyranny, but to advise his housemates that their previous evening's generosity would no longer be needed.

"So, he just caved-in then?" enquired RP.

"I wouldn't put it quite that simply," replied Paul, "but he is going to continue with my funding out of his own pocket. The only proviso is that my grades do not fall below my current levels. Any drop and he will stop the support."

"He's just making sure that you don't slack then," observed Annie.

"Sounds more like keeping the screw turned when he's not here to do it himself." RP had a tone to his voice when making the observation, that was not lost on Roland.

"Ever the cynic, huh RP?" Roland quipped.

"Born out of personal experience, my artistic friend," RP observed with a faint sigh.

"I think the one thing we all have in common," Annie commented, "is having a hard-arsed father."

"Born out of the necessity of their professions," Paul added slightly defensively.

"Not all!" Roland interjected somewhat huffily.

"Oh no, I forgot your Dad's in the Civil Service isn't he Roland," RP sniped in a familiar and somewhat unpopular way, "and mandarins just have to sit around waiting for their pensions to mature."

"That's quite enough you two!" Annie intervened. If there was any one of the four that was capable of bringing the group to heel, then it was Annie. So Roland restricted himself to one of his dark sideways glances at RP and the subject was immediately dropped.

"I reckon," Annie continued, "that we all need a night out ..." She paused momentarily: "... to celebrate the maintenance of the status quo."

"Can't stand three-chord blues," Roland muttered.

"Not that Status Quo you grouch!" Annie responded with a smile, and they all laughed. Roland had inadvertently punctured the tension once again.

"I think that's a great idea and the first round's on me," Paul said with some relief. "But just one more thing before we hit the town. RP, I'll take you up on that day-job, if it's still on offer."

"Absolutely!" replied RP with genuine enthusiasm, "just so long as it doesn't put your grades in jeopardy."

"They're exactly why I want to take it. Let's call it my insurance policy, shall we? We history students are not always oblivious to future changes in fortune you know!" A beaming smile burst out across both friends' faces and RP rose to his feet holding his right hand up in the air, palm forwards.

"High-Five my friend!" he said, continuing as Paul's right palm met his with a resounding clap, "or should that be welcome to the Company?"

vitruvio

Twenty-Two

Marjoree Rolles' had a penthouse at the top of the Westview Tower building. As this was only a couple of blocks south of the Epic Center and Kleberson's car was still at City Hall, Sam Schneider drove him there. They pulled into the almost empty garage and parked alongside McKinley's car, before taking the stairs to the lobby where Holdsworth was waiting with the lift doors open.

"What's up?" Kleberson asked.

"We've got another body," Holdsworth replied, "Chris asked me to hold the fort down here until you arrived. There are no stairs to the top floor, you can only ride the lift. Press the top button, he's waiting for you up there."

"OK Holdsworth, stay here and make sure the residents use the stairs until further notice. Get some uniforms over here to take over from you; when they arrive come on up and join us."

"Will do Sir."

They took the lift all the way to the top. The door opened to reveal McKinley waiting for them in the hallway with an older man, who he introduced: "this is Mr Kordowski the janitor, Paul. When I drove over, I didn't get an answer, so I went down to Giuseppe's for a coffee then came back. Still no answer, so I rang all the numbers on her card that you gave me and all I got was voicemail, even on her mobile. It didn't make sense, so I asked Mr Kordowski to open the flat for me. I'm afraid she's dead Paul, worse still, similar M.O. to Hilary Nicholson. However this time no circus, so the scene's untouched. I haven't called anything in yet - wanna look before I do?"

Kleberson was stunned. Not much fazed him these days, but this was totally out of left field.

"You OK Paul?" asked Schneider.

"Sure," Kleberson replied, "better have a look. You want in Sam?"

"Difficult not to, huh?"

"OK Mr Kordowski, is it possible to isolate this floor?"

"Sure is, it's only accessible by a resident's confidential passcode; I have the only override key which is how you guys could get up here. When I get back down I can lock it out the same way. But aren't you going to call an ambulance?"

"All in good time. The lady's dead Sir, nothing we can do for her except find out why and how."

"Mr Kendrick ain't gonna like this y'know, it'll play hell with the rents."

Kleberson felt another wave of shock pass through him. "The Kendricks own this building?" he asked.

"Sure do, bought it four years ago. Not like the old owners, they used to appreciate you, know what I mean? This guy just wants the money without spending any. I told him ..."

Kleberson cut him off: "this guy - what just one of 'em? Which one?"

"Mr Kendrick the younger, Officer, but he don't come here much, just yells down the 'phone normally. He was here last night though."

"Last night, when last night?"

"Oh, he came in just after I came on shift, that would have been around one a.m. 'Good evening Mr Kendrick Sir', I said, but not a murmur, just walked by me as if I wasn't there and got in the lift. Like I said - no appreciation."

"And I don't suppose you saw what floor he went to".

"Would have been this floor."

"Why?"

"Why? Because the other penthouse suite is his of course."

Twenty-Three

Kleberson instructed the janitor that, other than with his own express permission, absolutely nobody was to be allowed up to the top floor, other than the CSI team and Holdsworth when his reliefs arrived. No press, no unauthorised police officers and definitely no residents, regardless of who they were or who they said they knew. Kordowski seemed to revel in this new-found authority, commenting as he entered the lift that this was one day that he hoped the owner decided to turn-up. The doors closed and the fading whine confirmed his progress down to the lobby; the foyer went silent.

Schneider was the first to speak: "when you want a look in the other penthouse, I can get a search warrant through my office. If you try to get one, the politics in play will undoubtedly thwart you."

"Thanks, but not yet Sam, it will just alert the Kendricks; they will know soon enough without us helping them. We'll turn the whole floor into a crime scene which will keep Kendrick out, then who knows, Friedmann might be kind enough to give us permission without the need to go before a judge."

"Altitude getting to you already then Paul? Just try to stay focussed when those pigs come flying by the windows!"

"The only pig nearby here right now will probably be watching us through binoculars from the top of the Epic Center. Tell you what you could do, though, is try to get a look at the CCTV tapes for this building on the quiet."

"I'll get a couple of my guys over to help Mr Kordowski with security down in the foyer, so to speak. What about phone records?"

"Friedmann will make sure we have to crawl over broken glass to get those."

"Only if you tell him you're looking Paul. We're not officially involved yet, are we?"

The two smiled at each other; McKinley sauntered towards the door to the Rolles penthouse, pretending not to be aware of anything that was going on. It was at times like this, however, that he appreciated the advantages that Kleberson's past history brought to the party.

They were all experienced detectives who had worked many scenes. When they entered Marjoree Rolles' penthouse, they walked slowly and deliberately, stopping, observing, moving on. The apartment was conspicuous by its tidiness. Nothing was out of place. It was as if the place had just been valeted throughout. There were no signs of a struggle, no half-empty glasses, no food. The TV was on, but the volume was low. Cochrane's face filled the screen, but they were no longer interested in what he had to say. Nothing seemed strange except that fact in itself.

"This is how you found the other crime scene?" Kleberson asked.

"Other than the cavalry's missing, I'd say yes Paul," McKinley replied.

"Where's the body Chris?"

"Master Bedroom", he pointed to their right.

Kleberson entered the room. It was large and beautifully finished in pale green and grey wallpaper. There was an en-suite off to the left, the open door revealing a sunken bath at the rear, two vanity units to the left with multiple lights over them and a large quadrant-shaped shower cubicle in the front right corner. On the King-size bed was the body of Marjoree Rolles, completely naked and face-down, with her feet against the headboard and her head towards the base of the bed. Her legs were together, the right foot pointing vertically down with the toes pressed into the bedclothes, the left foot at right-angles to it laid across the bed. The arms were outstretched slightly upwards with the tips of the index fingers level with the top of the head; both thumbs were beneath the respective palms.

It was impossible to see the face as, like the toes of the right foot, it was pressed firmly down into the bedclothes. The rest of the head was completely shaven, something it hadn't been hours earlier when she had been seated opposite Kleberson, very much alive, in the booth at Glenda's. Once again, Kleberson thought he detected a slight sheen to the skin, which he noted was beautifully smooth, possibly the most perfect he had ever seen on a naked woman. Her buttocks were also absolutely perfectly curved and in proportion to the hourglass shape of her body. Ms Rolles had clearly been breathtakingly-beautiful, far more so than the expensively-cut designer clothes that she wore had already suggested. He moved to the end of the bed and crouched down so that his eyeline was level with the obscured face, but he could not make-out any expression as it had been pressed quite hard into the duvet.

McKinley broke the silence: "got to be the same perp, don't you think?"

"Hmm, there are too many obvious similarities for it to be a co-incidence, especially with the limited timescale between the two crimes. We are talking about little more than twelve hours at the earliest limit of Mary's estimate for Hilary Nicholson's time of death, even assuming that you walked into the front lobby here as the perp walked out the back. But what on earth is the significance of the way they have both been laid-out; and why is Ms Rolles face down, upside down, while Ms Nicholson was the opposite?"

"Messages?" Schneider offered.

"Seems so Sam, but what message and to who? It's all very meticulous, almost symbolic in a way."

"Has to be for us Paul," McKinley observed, "after all, we aren't going to release any of this at such an early stage, so if it's for a third-party how do they get to see it?"

"Nice to think the perp reckons we are intelligent-enough to suss what they're up to. It sure as hell ain't ringing any bells with me, even with my somewhat-privileged education."

"Photographs!" Schneider suddenly exclaimed. "What if the perp's taken damned photographs of both of 'em and sent them to whoever they're trying to put the frighteners on; bet your boots the recipient understands what it's about."

"So what then - blackmail?" McKinley added, "pay up or you get the same."

Schneider scratched his chin: "or someone else close to you does, and the clock's ticking."

"Or someone who used to be close to you just has," Kleberson said studiously. The other two turned towards where Kleberson was still surveying the top of Ms Rolles head as he expanded his alternate view: "could be an invoice - here's proof that the job has been completed, send the money now."

Schneider was again the first to respond: "stretching it a bit aren't we Paul. We're not even at the point that we could even realistically call this a serial, let alone a hit. How many hitmen have we come across with enough balls and time to have a weird M.O. like this? A pro is in, job done and out again in minutes, the hell with leaving calling-cards, especially ones that take as long as this has to set-up."

"Ah yes, but if it's a serial, what are the odds of them randomly choosing one woman who has become an inconvenience to a local personality and then within hours her close friend, who also happens to know why?"

"Come on Paul," Schneider retorted "systematic, do not rule anything out until it cannot be ruled in. Don't forget the basics you learned and why you were the top scorer at the Academy."

McKinley was surprised at this revelation; he knew Kleberson was good, but not that he had made such a mark in the Bureau. He instantly started thinking: *'so why Wichita? seems Paul could have gone anywhere he wanted.'*

Schneider continued: "even if this were connectable to Kendrick and he's ordered a double-hit, surely even he's not dumb enough to let his employee commit one of the hits right next door to his home!"

Kleberson stood up, still looking intently at the body as he bent over to get closer to the back of the head: "beginning to sound a bit like Friedmann there Sam, not thinking of going over to the enemy are you buddy? No need to answer that and, yes, it's the same perp because Ms Rolles also has that small puncture wound at the base of the neck. OK Chris, call in the bloodhounds, but this time by the numbers."

"Right Paul," McKinley responded going for his radio.

"And reinforce with whoever's guarding the lift that the Chief and Morley don't get in without my say-so; neither does anybody named Kendrick!"

"I'll take care of that Paul," said Schneider.

"Better get that Kryczek of yours over here as well. I want her to see this."

"Kryczek?" McKinley enquired, looking puzzled.

"A little present from our FBI friends, Chris," said Kleberson with a wink. "Then when you've done all that, get over to Judge Frazer and see if we can swear out an arrest warrant for Jackson Kendrick III, plus a search warrant for his apartment."

"Probable cause Paul?"

"It's all in here." He tossed his notebook across to McKinley: "what Ms Rolles would have given you in her statement had she been here to give it. You'll know what to do with it - find him, lock him up, no bail. Better still, go get him from Friedmann's office and arrest anybody else who tries to interfere for obstruction of justice, particularly Friedmann - that way he can't sit in on the interview; and that bitch Wagner as well!"

"Why her?"

"No reason, she just needs taking down a peg that's all."

"Now's not the time to settle old scores Paul," suggested Schneider.

"Anytime's a good time, Sam, and right now is even better!"

Twenty-Four

"So which one of you's Schneider?" The question came from a woman standing in the doorway from the entrance hall into the lounge; and not just any woman, this one was both attractive and beautifully groomed. She wore a simple white tee shirt that hung semi-revealingly over her small, clearly unsupported but perfect breasts; her blue jeans were distressed enough to look old but clearly had only recently left a Madison Avenue store.

"That'll be me," Schneider responded turning slowly then snapping around as his brain registered what his eyes relayed to it nanoseconds earlier.

"Kryczek," she offered her hand. Schneider leapt forward to accept it. As he did so, the visitor fixed him to the spot with a withering look: "so you're the bastard that petrified my Aunt with the message he left?"

"Petrified? I only said we needed you urgently at a murder scene!"

"Not a problem unless dear old, ninety-years-old to be precise, Great Aunt Susie doesn't know her darling niece is a Fed, but instead thinks she's a feature writer on a movie magazine out West. I've never told her because she worries about me. You damned near scared her to death you imbecile."

"Sorry, I didn't know. I'll call round and explain later."

"No you won't! It's done. She thinks Clint Eastwood's directing the Dirty Harry revival here in town and I'm interviewing him this afternoon. Which will only be a problem if one of your clever Field Officers can't forge the Mayor of Carmel's autograph for me on this picture by four p.m." She handed Schneider a twelve by eight black and white studio photograph of a much younger Eastwood.

"No problem," Schneider said somewhat taken aback as he accepted the photo.

"It should say 'to Gladys, my favourite fan.' OK?"

"I thought you said her name was Susie?" Kleberson had joined the discussion.

"It's a long story, and it's on a need-to-know basis. So you are?"

"Lieutenant Paul Kleberson," Schneider completed the introduction, "Head of Homicide here in Wichita, it's his case."

"OK, so you don't need me then. Hick cop here's got it all under control and I'm back on furlough."

She turned to go but Schneider stopped her in her tracks: "failing to answer a specific request from an office to which you have been seconded. That would just about complete the full set of insubordination offences on your personnel record Kryczek, which should put you on permanent furlough this time."

She stopped and turned back: "bastard, you would too wouldn't you Schneider? I heard about your reputation from a friend before coming down here. Straight Arrow Sam huh, that's you ain't it? So what brings you slumming to hick cop's jurisdiction Mister Schneider, charity work?"

"Paul topped his class at Academy, so you have something there in common. Only he listens to advice before he ignores it, whereas you Kryczek just ignore it regardless."

"So why ain't he still in the Bureau with us then?"

"Anal-retentives like you," retorted Kleberson.

"I think that's fifteen-all, so let's just keep the score there shall we," suggested Schneider.

Twenty-Five

"OK Lieutenant Clever Person - that was the name wasn't it?" Kryczek asked cynically, "what's so damned special about this murder that got Schneider here to ruin my holiday?"

"Kleberson, Ms Kryczek. I presume you're a Ms, either because your spiky manner doesn't allow anything with a penis inside the three-mile exclusion zone you've placed around yourself, or because you're one of those damned 'don't you hold a door open for ME you chauvinistic bastard' liberated women who's forgotten why they needed independence."

"Touché Mister Clever Person, I think I'm going to enjoy crossing swords with you for a while."

"You can call me Paul if you keep your tongue in its scabbard."

"And you can call me Kryczek 'cos that's as close as you're gonna get."

"So now that we've got the pleasantries over," interrupted Schneider, "do you think we can get down to business?"

Kleberson began to outline the cases: "two murders Kryczek, approximately twelve to fifteen hours apart, identical M.O.'s on the surface, both women knew each other and were highly influential in the community. The second was due to give us an official statement on the first, but instead we only got another message from the perp."

"Anybody in the frame?"

"Yep, but I don't want you going there yet. I'd like you to look at this scene. It's not been disturbed, whereas the previous one had been. Tell us if it rings any bells with profiling of any other cases you know of."

"You think it's a serial?"

"I don't think anything yet; I want to keep our options open until they are no-longer options."

"Hey, you are a smart cookie, how'd you let this one escape Schneider?"

"Don't go there Kryczek," Schneider responded, "we've wasted enough time on your tangential lines."

"OK, where?"

"Master Bedroom, through there." Kleberson nodded towards the door.

Kryczek sat down and took off her shoes and the thin silk quarter-hose under her jeans. Kleberson stared at her in a questioning manner.

"It's OK, I washed them this morning," she said sarcastically.

"We've got slipovers" said Kleberson.

"Aboriginals thought with their feet. They are our connection to the outside world. That's why modern man has lost touch with the planet - he insulates himself from his surroundings."

"Well you're not walking all over my crime scene leaving your DNA where we don't need it. Here we put slipovers on, either over your shoeless feet if that's your bag, or over your shoes if you wouldn't mind putting them back on."

Kryczek shrugged, dropped her head in a stroppy-teenager manner and held her hand out for the slipovers. Kleberson looked at Schneider as if to ask 'what the hell is this?' but Schneider shrugged and said: "her reputation is somewhat kooky, but she's the best we have, so I'm told."

"That's right, ninety percent clearance rate," she boasted as she pulled-on the transparent covers.

"Tell that to the relatives of the other ten percent, not to me," Kleberson said seriously. He took every failure not only personally, but as a matter of unfinished business. He wasn't interested in scoreboards unless they listed his unsolved cases - four in all. He would solve them one day and then he could retire. Until then they were simply unfinished business.

Kryczek walked into the bedroom and froze in the doorway. The scene before her was both distressing and familiar at the same time; the body of a black woman was spread-eagled on the bed, the head was completely shaved.

"Vitruvio!" she said exhaling quietly, "I knew you weren't dead you bastard!"

"Whaddya mean?" quizzed Kleberson.

"Most of my ten percent are down to this perp. There have been sixteen cases in the last three years, that we know of anyway. This'll be number seventeen."

"Eighteen," said Kleberson, "the other one this morning was pretty-much identical M.O, remember?"

She looked shocked as she turned on Schneider: "how'd you know so quickly?"

"About what?" Schneider responded curtly.

"Why don't I believe you?" she growled. Schneider looked unusually angry. He was about to explode when Kleberson held up both palms in his direction, before turning again towards Kryczek, who had her back to them all, standing perfectly still in the doorway and staring at the form on the bed.

Kleberson asked: "so what you're saying is that this has the hallmarks of a serial killer known to you?"

"Yeah, and if he's on form you have less than twelve hours before there's another body-bag."

"So he has a pattern?"

"The hell with this!" Kryczek turned sharply and barged past Kleberson, grabbed up her shoes and swept out of the apartment. As she went, one of the quarter-hose fluttered to the floor; Kleberson walked after her, gathering-up the discarded hosiery as he passed. When he reached the foyer, Kryczek was by the lift, stood on one leg trying to pull a shoe on to the raised foot while agitatedly punching the button continually.

"It won't come," Kleberson said.

She responded angrily, her face strained with tension: "it damned well will!"

"Not until I say so"

"Then fucking say so, alright!"

"What the hell is the matter with you Kryczek?" shouted Schneider as he marched across the foyer.

Kryczek looked at both of them in turn, then grabbed her head with both hands and slammed back against the wall before slowly sliding down to sit on the floor, by which time she was sobbing uncontrollably. Schneider and Kleberson looked at each other dumbfounded at first. Schneider shrugged and turned as if to launch into Kryczek again, but Kleberson shot him a look and a slight shake of the head. He walked to where Kryczek sat and dropped on his haunches in front of her.

"What's this guy done to you Kryczek?" Kleberson asked.

"He killed someone I knew or, more to the point, he got me to kill them for him."

Kleberson had no idea where to go from that; this whole case was already bizarre-enough without the newly-recruited consultant cracking-up on him. His head raced with options, but nothing made immediate sense. While he was figuring-out how to re-approach her, Schneider interjected: "is that why you're on leave of absence?"

She nodded.

"How long ago?"

"Seven weeks."

"OK Kryczek, we don't need you on this, it's too close; you go back to your Aunt and forget we even existed. Sorry, I truly didn't know there was a connection; if I had, I would never have asked for you. I'll call the lift." Schneider walked away slightly, radio in hand calling his men in the lobby. Kryczek wiped her eyes and began to get to her feet.

Kleberson helped her up: "you OK?" he asked.

"Sure," she replied, "I always knew I would have to face up to it soon, but I didn't expect …" she tailed-off.

"Look," Kleberson said quietly, "I do understand, but if there's anything you can give me that could give us a head-start, I'll be grateful."

"What do you need?"

"The pattern - you said there was a pattern. What is it?"

"He kills in sets of four. There's exactly twelve hours between each of the first three, then forty-eight hours to the last.

"So there could already be another body waiting for us somewhere?"

"How did you hear about the first one?"

"Anonymous tip - we're assuming it was the perp."

"Then no. This guy's into advertising his presence. Your other vic was the first and almost certainly killed twelve hours before this one."

"But he may have done the third in another town."

"No, they're always in the same police jurisdiction. He advertises his presence immediately after the first murder to set the clock ticking, then does it all again after twelve and twenty-four hours to demonstrate to the local police that they will always be behind the game. Of course, they normally are because, unlike you, they have no clue what he's about. Then he stops and they begin to think he may have moved-on. Then the fourth one starts the panic again and while everyone's running round in circles trying to prevent another, he's gone."

"You used the term Vitruvio. Is that what he calls himself?"

"No, he never contacts after the first call. It's what we've christened him because of the M.O. Look-up Vitruvian Man and you'll get it. Were both women left exactly the same way?"

"No, the first was face-up."

"Head on pillow?"

"Yes."

"Then they were an item."

"At some time in the past, apparently. How'd you know that?"

"There's always some connection between the vics and it's usually a dark secret. Vitruvio reveals the link mainly to cause confusion; while you're thinking the symbology is a clue, he's already on the trail of the next vic. If the revelation causes more distress to those close to the vics, then that's a bonus, especially if they've not already been 'outed'; everybody becomes so distracted that it's not possible to get the information you need out of them. It's not rocket science once you've worked it out."

"So what do we do, lock-up all our high-profile females until he's gone?"

"Not just females, he does males too. High-profile is a good place to start though, this guy's not interested in nobodies; and there's always some connection between all the vics, however tenuous. It's as though he gives you three clues, then waits to see if you can work-out who the fourth will be while his clock is ticking. Trouble is, we haven't been able to previously, because we've only recently worked-out the connections. This is the first time any police force has known what it's working on."

Kleberson began to hear alarm bells ringing. "OK", he said "is there anything we need to look for here, or do we just get CSI involved?"

"There won't be anything, there never is; he's too thorough. I understand the first one was Hilary Nicholson, I've read about her somewhere, some high-flyer accountant with a famous boyfriend as I remember. Who was this vic?"

"Marjoree Rolles," he replied.

"From the TV," she replied without any emotion.

"You know her?"

"I watch TV News a lot when I'm visiting my Aunt, she's fascinated with it. So our Marjoree was a dyke, my oh my! Such a beautiful woman."

"This sexuality thing. Our first vic was violated, I suspect this one will have been as well. You said he 'does' males, are you talking just murder, or is there also sexual interaction in those cases?"

"We've had all types. Heterosexual, homosexual, bisexual, all 'violated' as you term it - male or female, makes no difference to Vitruvio."

"But they're all connected sexually somehow."

"Within the foursomes, some were but not all, not that we've discovered to any consistency. We've had so many theories, but never any one-size-fits-all. There will be a link between them all though."

The lift arrived and one of Schneider's Agents stepped-out, followed by Mary Jourdain and three CSI Techs. Schneider took his man off to one side to brief him about Kryczek, handing him the photo. Mary walked over towards Kleberson, who moved away from Kryczek to greet her, then took her through into the apartment.

"What do we have Paul?"

"Looks like a similar scene to this morning, but this time only Chris, Sam and myself have been in the scene. We've touched nothing, so it's all yours - master bedroom through there." He pointed to the open door.

"OK Paul, will you be hanging around for a preliminary?"

"If we can, then yes. We're keeping a lid on it as long as possible, but with the politics in play here, who knows what's coming next, or when. But we do have control of the lift, so you should have minimal distractions."

"Do we know who the vic is?"

"Marjoree Rolles."

"What 'The' Marjoree Rolles?"

"One and the same."

Mary exhaled: "phew, you do have your work cut-out this time Paul."

"All part of life's rich pageant."

She gave him a wry grin, then turned to her assistants: "OK guys, let's go and absolutely by the numbers on this one."

Kleberson returned to Kryczek, who appeared to have recovered her composure, externally at least. He wondered as he approached, however, what was really happening beneath that highly-decorous exterior. "I'm sorry," he began, "but I needed to brief the M.E."

"No need to apologise, I know the drill. Look, give me a few hours to gather my thoughts, then if you have any more questions give me a ring; got a pen?" He pulled a Parker from his inside pocket. She pulled a card from her jeans, turned it over and scribbled a number on it: "here's my cell, I'll do what I can, but don't ask me to come to the next scene, I realise now that I'm not as ready as I thought."

"With any luck, we may not have any more scenes."

"You've got twelve hours until the next one, less whatever has elapsed after time of death on this one. If you work it out before then, you won't just have Schneider wanting to recruit you, you'll have Quantico camped in your front yard."

"How'd you know about Schneider trying to get me back?"

"I'm a Profiler Lieutenant, and a damned good one I'll have you know, yet I've not got close to figuring this perp. But tell you what, if you know in advance when the bastard's striking next, you can come get me. Nothing would please me more than to put a bullet in him - personally!"

Schneider walked over with his companion: "Kryczek, you go with Steinson here, he'll take you out of a side-entrance as we seem to have a bit of a media-scrum building-up out front."

"Oh joy!" Kleberson sighed resignedly. He shook Kryczek's hand gently: "thanks for the help you've been able to give," he continued with a sympathetic tone. She gave his hand a quick squeeze as she managed a weak smile in return, then entered the lift with Steinson. The doors closed behind them and the floor repeater flashed the number changes as the lift dropped away, leaving Schneider and Kleberson considering their next moves. The ringtone of Kleberson's cell broke the short silence; Holdsworth's name on the caller I.D. indicated that there would be little time for such contemplation.

Twenty-Six

The door of the elevator slid open and immediately the sound of a commotion burst into the limited space. There in one corner of the glass-fronted entrance foyer was the slight figure of Kordowski, the janitor, being berated by two tall figures, one in a thousand-dollar suit, the other a scrawny unkempt character in a denim jacket and jeans; the cowboy boots on the latter were unmistakeable.

In the opposite corner, the massive frame of Chief Stanton was shouting at Holdsworth: "... and if you won't take my direct order Detective, Lieutenant Morley here will have your badge!"

"Ding, ding, ding! Laydees and Gentlemen," shouted Kleberson as he exited the elevator, mimicking the ring announcer of an HBO boxing broadcast, "tonight's feature bout is a heavyweight contest of short duration featuring, in the blue corner ... " he waved his left arm in the direction of the Chief but was cut-off by a weaselly voice from the opposite corner.

"Stanton, is this the chicken-shit detective who thinks he's taken over ma buildin'? Ain't ma Pappy told you already to get his ass off this case?"

"I do hope, Mr Friedmann, that your clients are not attempting to interfere with a murder investigation," came the voice of Sam Schneider as he walked from the shadows of the lift cubicle.

The room fell momentarily into silence, which was then broken by the lawyer's voice as he oozed forward towards Kleberson and Schneider, raising his right index finger in their direction: "now listen here ..."

"I should be careful Counsellor," warned Kleberson, nodding past Friedmann and indicating with his eyes something in the background. Friedmann stopped and glanced over his shoulder to see at least half a dozen TV cameras pointing in his direction from outside the building. This was a very public moment.

"May I suggest, gentlemen," continued Kleberson, "if this chicken-shit detective may be so bold as to do so, that Mr Friedmann take our distinguished guest Mr Kendrick quietly back to his office where we can talk about this in some privacy, whilst the Chief here explains to our loving public out there that this little meeting they have been attending is the prelude to a further press conference to be convened later today where details of a second murder that has taken place will be supplied, provided they will get their little backsides out of here as quickly as they possibly can to enable us to carry out our investigations."

"Now you just get this straight detective," came the weaselly voice again, "I ain't goin' nowhere to talk to no-one. This is ma buildin', an' I'm goin' to ma apartment to rest."

"I would think, Counsellor," continued Kleberson, "that it would be much more desirable for your client to leave quickly with you to be driven to your office, than to be handcuffed by me in front of his admirers out there and inserted into a Cruiser to be taken to City Hall. Of course, I could be wrong and if you need to consult dear old pappy first, we can give you a few minutes on your cellphone."

"That won't be necessary Lieutenant," Friedmann replied, lightly holding his client's arm, "let's go Jackson, we'll sort this out later."

The client succumbed to his advisor, fully realising that if he didn't, not only would Kleberson do what he said, but it would open the way for Schneider. He knew the FBI was looking into some of his more dubious business deals and he didn't need to give them any excuse to ask some questions he would prefer not to have to answer. However, he was a Kendrick and they always had the last word - it was tradition: "I'll speak to you later, detective," he said with a threatening voice, then turned to Stanton and glared at him with piercing eyes, "provided you still have a badge that is."

Stanton visibly bristled. He disliked Jackson Kendrick III, but had great respect for his father. If Junior had said that, he would have complied in an instant, but because the 'instruction' came from the son, then it would have to be ignored.

However, Friedmann quickly lowered the stakes: "I'm sure Chief Stanton has the situation under control, Jackson. Mr Kordowski perhaps we could use the phone in your office for a few moments." Disguising his shock, Kordowski led the two men out of the lobby by a side door that led to his cubbyhole in the basement.

"Holdsworth, take the Chief up to the scene so that Chris can brief him. Morley, get a statement from Kordowski when he has finished with our guests, would you please?"

"Get one of your lackeys to do it Kleberson," snapped Morley.

"And what scene is this?" interrupted Stanton.

"I think it's the one that you are briefed on just before you tell Cochrane out there that his boss, and future network meal-ticket, is lying dead upstairs."

The Chief momentarily appeared visibly-shocked by this piece of information, but he quickly recovered, nodding towards Schneider and asking Kleberson: "so does that mean they're looking to take-over this investigation?"

Schneider answered directly: "no Chief, but it does mean that the M.O. has flagged-up on one of our national databases as being potentially connected to a number of unsolved serial murders. That's why, for the time-being, I've advised Lieutenant Kleberson that I can place whatever resources he may need at the disposal of your Department. I will, of course, have to keep my Bureau Chief fully-apprised of developments."

"Jesus!" growled Stanton ,"you best do as you're asked Morley, we're gonna need everything we can get before facing that pack of hounds out there again!"

dinosaurs

Twenty-Seven

Paul graduated in 1991 with a first class degree in History. He had already decided to stay in the UK; after all, if he was to make a career out of history, then where better than to be based in a country where he could visit and touch places that were hundreds, sometimes thousands, of years old. Back home he would struggle beyond two hundred.

In any case, he had become something of an anglophile. He loved the nature of the people, self-deprecating and, to the most part, kind and polite. He had not lived in the 'States for nearly ten years, yet even on family visits it felt alien, even false somehow. Whether this was due to the strange nature of his East Coast grandparents' relationship or, more to the point, lack of it, he was unsure.

He loved his mother and, the older he got, the more he respected his father, as is the case with most sons of successful dedicated men. As for his younger siblings, the less he saw them, the greater the divide between them grew. He viewed his sister as developing into nothing more than a hanger-on within her grandmother's society in Florida. It was an easy option and she would milk it for all it was worth; Paul detested hangers-on. He had hoped that his brother would grow-up more sensibly, but the attachment to his surviving grandfather had become almost desperate. Paul could see the lure of the money in his brother's eyes, something his father had always ignored with almost a passion.

Paul had finally realised why. Money wasn't what life was about, it was about the journey. Sure, money helped to pay the fare, but as soon as it became the destination, then life itself became an unwilling passenger. He had seen for himself how RP's father had made fortunes, then lost them, only to make them again, but as a by-product of his innate passion to succeed. RP had grown-up in a far-wealthier environment than Paul could ever imagine, not even the apparent financial-security and connections of his own paternal grandparents came close. Yet RP was untainted by it and was very much his own man. Annie was old-money, and old-money UK-style is old-money. Again, here was a person who was used to it, wearing it more like a favourite cardigan, never as a badge.

Paul had done reasonably well himself through his part-time work, not just for RP, but also for the Gormaston Foundation who had recruited him in his second year, through his tutor, to help them establish the origins of Hemingford Hall, a large mansion near St Ives that was to be opened to the public in order to finance its survival. The origins of the hall dated back to an eleventh century abbey and Paul had used the extensive libraries in Cambridge to research old documentation, writing a series of papers for the Foundation outlining what he had found. These were used as the basis for their guidebooks.

As a consequence, his two incomes had not only financed him through university, but also allowed him to build-up a reasonable sum in his deposit account. The Foundation had hinted that there could be a full-time post for him as a researcher following his graduation, and he wanted to maintain that as an option, as it would be a good launching point to his chosen career.

Annie, always the steady mind in the house, had advised him to go home for a few months after graduation, before he fully made his mind up. Annie's background meant that she understood the meaning of roots more than any of them. Whereas Paul thought, like many of his countrymen, that three years in one place was akin to permanency, she realised that it took much longer to really establish yourself. A number of her father's favourite little quips at dinner parties often revolved around references to the family's local heritage.

"So how long have you lived in the house?" a guest would ask.

"Oh the family has lived here for nearly three hundred years," would be her father's response, setting up the obvious repartee:

"So you must be one of the oldest families in the area."

This would allow him his favourite put-down: "good grief no," he would respond, "it took the locals around two hundred years before they even realised we were here, but now they occasionally nod to us in the street, so we are on our way towards acceptance."

The lease for the Cambridge house was due to end in July; only Paul had any reason to renew. Annie already had a job lined-up at Rolls Royce in Derby, one of a number of large engineering firms determined to demonstrate the shattering of their glass ceilings by taking-on female engineering graduates, of which Annie was one of the best in her year. RP's software business already employed over a hundred staff in very much a campus environment on the outskirts of Cambridge. Roland was moving to London to suffer for his art.

Although Paul wanted to stay, he knew that he couldn't commit to take the lease alone; the thought of sharing with new, younger housemates appealed even less, but neither did he want to go home with any air of defeat. He knew that his father would seize on that immediately as a lever to make him stay, the least-favourable option of all to Paul.

But Annie's logic prevailed in the end. She convinced Paul that he needed to go home for a few weeks, not as a pretext for staying there, but as the prelude for leaving for good. Paul knew that she was right, but he also recognised the dangers in the process, because of which he would return home with a firm plan.

In early August 1991, Paul flew out of Heathrow bound for Dallas Fort Worth airport, en route to Wichita in Kansas, specifically McConnell Air Force base a few miles to the south. In his suitcase were his summer clothes, a bank statement with enough zero's at the foot to demonstrate to his father that he had acquired substance, a job-offer letter from the Foundation with a five-figure starting salary and the estate agent's details for three flats in Huntingdon, the leases for all of which were well within his budget.

All of his other possessions were in boxes and crates in the loft of one of the many outbuildings at Annie's parents' house, where he had become considered to be a virtually-permanent house guest during non-term times.

Annie's parents adored Paul. His homely demeanour had them half-hoping that a romantic attachment may develop with Annie, given time, which was why Annie's father also encouraged Paul to take a long break back in America.

He knew that absence really did make the heart grow fonder, so why should Paul be immune to the basic rules of nature.

Twenty-Eight

Walter was waiting outside of Mid-Continent airport in his SUV. It may have only been a month since he and Margie had stood in the Cambridge Senate House watching their son graduate, but it had been one of the longest months of his life. Finally, his son, his firstborn, was coming home, for good.

At least he hoped that it was for good this time, which is why the embrace was that little stronger, that little bit longer, than Paul could previously remember experiencing. It was the embrace of a father released momentarily from the straitjacket of his years of military training. It also told Paul that his father was finally offering him his heart, oblivious that it may be subsequently broken by the exposure.

As they drove along I-54 towards the city, Paul could only notice how flat the land was. It had the familiarity of Cambridgeshire, but not the age, or the innate beauty. This was, after-all, one of the fastest-growing cities in the Midwest and among its major employers were four of the largest aerospace companies in the world, drawn there by the weather - two hundred and seventy days per year of guaranteed clear blue skies. They could test aircraft all year round, which was also why McConnell Air Force base was there as well, a refuelling training base where pilots could be processed incessantly, supported by thousands of base staff under the management of their base commander - General Walter T Kleberson.

So this was not the return of some nerdy overseas student, this was the triumphant homecoming of the base commander's eldest son, complete with a First-Class BA Hons (Cantab), one of the highest academic accolades in the world, something that would not be allowed to go unnoticed in this high-achieving metropolis.

The USAF P.R-machine had been in top gear since General Kleberson and his wife had returned from Cambridge and begun preparations for their son's return a month later. They had just omitted to brief Paul who had no idea, as they anonymously took the turnpike to I-235, that he was the subject of a base reception that very evening, followed by a Mayor's reception the following day, an interview by KNKW and a feature in the Wichita Mail.

Twenty-Nine

Paul just about survived the base reception, in spite of the jetlag. It had amazed him that, with their involvement in a business that flew aeroplanes all over the world, so few of the people attending had even bothered to think that he was still on UK-time, the reason that he was struggling to make small-talk as his body-clock chimed five a.m. the following morning.

He also survived the frantic trip the following day to the East Mall to buy a new suit at J C Penney's, for the Mayor's reception. This was due to his logical reasoning when packing back in England, that he wouldn't need anything more than T-Shirts and shorts for his extended holiday in the ninety-plus degrees of the Kansas summer sunshine.

The Mayor's reception was a typical finger-buffet affair where the local great and good press the flesh, swap business cards and generally play the game of appearing to be interested in what the other guests are there for, whilst simultaneously scanning the room for their next business opportunity. It reminded Paul of all he disliked about the East Coast, but again he got through it, despite the obvious job pre-interview nature of casual chats with senior representatives of every blue-chip company in the city.

The Wichita Mail interview the following morning was an entirely different matter. The sensory fall-out from the disinterested hack that turned-up on their doorstep, three hundred and fifty pounds of untrained flab with terminal halitosis and suffering from the combined effects of a twenty-minute drive in both an ill-fitting suit and a fifteen-year-old truck with no air-conditioning, was too much to cope with in the den under the house. So Paul's mother quickly offered iced tea under the awning out back, allowing the gentle plains breeze to carry away the worst of the pollutants emanating from their guest, who she had strategically seated downwind of them. Base commanders don't get to be base commanders without a wife who could glide effortlessly through the entrance exam for the diplomatic corps.

The interview started badly. Hank Raines' opener was meant to be a settler for all concerned: "so you're fresh back from Cambridge then young Paul?"

"That's right Sir," Paul replied, summoning up all of his upbringing in order not to reveal his real feelings.

"So howd'ya like Massachusetts then?"

"Massachusetts?"

"Yeah, Cambridge. It's still in Massachusetts ain't it?"

"No, England Sir"

"New England you say."

"No ... England - Great Britain."

"Gee, what forin' England? They got a Cambridge there as well?"

"Guess so, Sir."

"Damn, I never knew that before. I can see why you done so well young Paul, knowing there are two Cambridges an' that. So did they name it after ours?"

"Hardly!" Paul responded semi-angrily.

In the corner of his eye, Paul caught the look his mother was casting him from the other side of the table. It was a mother's mixture of 'oh you poor boy having to suffer this dimwit' and 'please don't embarrass your Father!'

It caused Paul to pause momentarily, leaving Hank to carry-on in full flow: "so which school did ya go to there, Harvard or Yale?" He caught a glimpse of Paul's scowl in his direction, so clarified the question: "I assume if they named the town after ours, they probably named the schools as well … didn't they?"

"Peterhouse Sir," Paul answered as matter of factly as he could.

"Peter's House … Peter who?"

"No Sir, Peterhouse. That's the name of the college I went to."

"Oh right." Hank scribbled it down on his pad.

"The oldest college in Cambridge," Paul continued, "founded by the Bishop of Ely in twelve eighty four."

"Twelve … Eighty … Four," Raines scribbled again, "that sure is a long time ago ain't it? What was the town called then?"

"Sorry?" Paul asked incredulously.

"If they named their Cambridge after ours, they couldn't have done that back then could they? I mean, in twelve eighty four all we had back here was injuns and buffaloes." He laughed nervously.

"Gosh Mr Raines, your history really is quite comprehensive isn't it?" Paul said sarcastically.

Raines puffed-out his chest: "benefit of a good ole Midwest edyacayshun son!"

"Obviously," Paul continued, "of course they didn't have any buffalo over there you know."

"Didn't they?"

"No, far more dangerous it was. The Bishop and his men had to circle their wagons every night around the camp fire to keep the dinosaurs out."

"Dinosaurs!" Raines scribbled frantically.

"Oh yes, place was infested with them. But they were good God-fearing folk and they knew that if they prayed each day, then they would survive. And when they did, well the Bishop, he was so thankful that he built himself a big church, then added a school to the side for the local children to learn how to pray too. Peter's House he called it, after Saint Peter, the guardian of the gate."

"Fascinating," Raines carried on scribbling, "do they still have dinosaurs there?"

"No, they all died out in the Great Flood." More scribbling. "But they kept the skeleton of one of them and put it in the museum."

"Oh right, yeah, you know I reckon I saw a picture of that in National Geographic somewheres. Huge thing it was, towered over everyone."

"You got it Mr Raines."

"Like that one what ate the guy on the toilet … in the film."

Paul heard a snort from his mother and looked across to see her with her fist against her mouth, tears of laughter beginning to fill the corner of her eyes and desperately trying to stop giggling. Paul couldn't resist. He leaned across and touched her arm, then with a concerned voice he asked: "you OK Mum?"

"Yes dear," she replied recovering her composure marginally, "just a little summer cold coming on I think."

"Oh gosh Ma'am," said Raines, somewhat concerned as well, "I'm sorry to keep you out here like this. I think I have plenty to write about this fine young son of yours here. Just one final question to you Ma'am if I may, you must be really proud of this young fella, what with getting all that fine forin' edyacayshun an' all, so far from home. Did you ever worry, him being so far away an' all?"

She looked across at Paul and with a glint in her eye replied: "oh no, not once I knew there were no dinosaurs any more."

Paul nearly lost it, but held back the guffaw that was trying to explode from his breast. *'How cool are you Mum?'* he thought as Raines bustled his papers into his tatty briefcase.

"Alright then people, I'll make my goodbyes now. No please Ma'am, don't get up, I'll just go out the side gate I can see over there, save tramping back through your lovely house. Thank you for your hospitality, and good luck to you young man, I'm sure there is a huge future ahead of you. He reached forward and shook Paul's hand with his limp podgy mitt, then turned on his heels and waddled across the yard, before opening the gate and waving as he squeezed through it sideways.

As the gate closed, mother and son collapsed into each other's arms roaring with laughter. It took them several minutes to restore some composure. As Margie began to wipe away the tears, she looked at Paul with some pride and said: "you are still a rascal you know - circling the wagons, whatever next?"

"Well you didn't do so bad either Mum, no dinosaurs!" With which they both burst into laughter again.

"They're not all like that here son."

"That's a shame Mum, if they were I think I would take up comedy scriptwriting!"

Thirty

"That was one hell of a wind-up!"

The female voice permeated Paul's consciousness through a channel he had left open whilst dozing shallowly within the shade of the large awning keeping-out the midday sunshine. His mother had gone into the house to make them some lunch, so he had closed his eyes and the jet-lag quickly took over.

"Looks like it fair wore you out - all that mickey-taking."

His mind was still trying to figure-out if this was the prelude to a dream, or if it was real; whatever, it decided that he should best open his eyes and check. When he did, his vision was slightly unfocussed, but aware of a figure close-by, standing with its back to the sun, hands on hips. As his vision focussed, he became aware first of long shapely legs terminating at the hem of beige shorts, above which a bare bronzed midriff with an hour-glass waist came into perspective and above that, a large gingham bow struggled to contain a pair of fairly-impressive breasts within the rest of the undertied blouse.

"This looks interesting' he thought to himself, as his gaze continued upwards to register a large and friendly white-toothed smile beneath high cheekbones and flowing blonde hair, the rest of the features being momentarily shaded by the aura of the sun behind it.

"Oh Leanne, where did you spring from?" Margie had re-emerged through the French doors carrying a tray with some sandwiches and hot tea - English traditions remained strong in the Kleberson household.

"Oh I hope you don't mind Mrs K, I saw your guest was already out here so I thought I would just come in through the side gate and introduce myself. I didn't realise he was asleep."

"Not at all dear, now let me introduce you formally. Paul this is Leanne Henderson, our neighbour's daughter. Leanne, this is my son Paul."

Paul jumped to his feet and offered his hand; Leanne took it gently in hers, which felt immediately warm and soft to his touch. He realised that he was not much taller than this new-found acquaintance, whose features, once fully-emerged from the shade, proved to be even more dazzling than the initial out-of-focus version. "How do you do neighbour," he smilingly offered his greeting. "I have to say, had I known the view from this garden had improved so much, I may have come home more often."

Leanne looked over Paul's shoulder toward his mother: "you were right Mrs K, he is a bit of a sweetie isn't he?" She looked straight at Paul and continued: "you know what they say, there's no place like home." Then that radiant smile lit up her face even more.

"I hope you don't mind Paul," Margie added, "but I asked Leanne round for lunch. I thought you might like a bit of younger company after having to put up with all the so-called grown-ups since you got back."

He didn't look around, but replied: "not at all Mum." His eyes were still transfixed by that smile: "so how come I didn't see you at the reception the other night?"

"Oh I was there, I just didn't think that your brain could register too much, with all that jet-lag n'all. So I kept out of the way of 'the machine'. That's what I call Daddy's little unit here."

"Colonel Henderson is your Father's second in command. He also runs the public relations unit here," Margie explained.

"The roses in our garden get plenty of feed," Leanne continued impishly.

"Now Paul," Margie continued, "let go of Leanne's hand and both of you come sit down and have some lunch."

Paul suddenly realised that he had not released the soft and gentle handshake, letting go quickly and somewhat self-consciously. He was just about to apologise when Leanne simply raised a finger to her lips and whispered, "it's fine - really," before turning and walking, like a model on a catwalk, towards the shaded table under the awning.

Paul watched her, his feet momentarily riveted to the spot. *'My God Mum,'* he thought, *'for once I forgive you your infernal matchmaking!'*

Thirty-One

The next couple of weeks went by quickly, Leanne and Paul rarely being out of each other's company. From their constant conversations Paul learned that the first impressions were mutual, Leanne having had to fight-off her urge to meet him at that first-night reception. She said how glad she was that she held-back, otherwise he might have just put her down as just another girl on the base. He assured her that he had to admit, somewhat ashamedly, that he would probably not have noticed her, as by the time the speeches were over, his overtired brain had long since turned to mush. He was glad that she had accepted his mother's invitation though.

He also learned that she was a couple of years younger than him and in her final year at WSU, where she was majoring in accountancy. Also a forces child, she was born in California, that slight southern twang in her accent coming from her childhood years in Savannah, Georgia, where her father, Colonel Nate Henderson, was head of the Combat Readiness Training Center that shared its home with the nearby Savannah/Hilton Head International Airport. She was sixteen when he was promoted and transferred to McConnell, so her mother decided to set-up home off-base in Savannah until Leanne finished high school.

They then moved to join her father at the base, to the house next door to the Klebersons, a year or so after Paul had decided to stay in England. The reason the two had never met was that, on the very few occasions that Paul had visited Kansas whilst at Cambridge, he was always just joining the family as they started their journey to one or other of the grandparents for a holiday. He was never tempted to stay more than overnight, as England, and its history, were always calling him back. As was still the case.

He had attempted to discuss the offer he had from the Foundation, but his father kept deflecting the subject saying there would be time enough after he had taken the vacation that he deserved following all that effort at Cambridge. Somehow, he knew that his father was scheming quietly in the background.

If General Walter T Kleberson had paid slightly more attention to the infrequent, but highly-detailed, letters that his son sent home to his mother, then he would have been aware that his son's final thesis was on the Italian Renaissance period, in particular the life and works of one Niccolò di Bernardo dei Machiavelli. Paul's natural cynicism had allowed him to understand his chosen specialism to a depth that surprised his tutors. Even at his tender age, he had little left to learn of the basis of high-government, or high-military, political science.

Paul therefore knew that his father had probably already negotiated some cosy position somewhere in the services for his son, he was simply biding his time and quietly observing the lay of the land before casually revealing his hand. Although not in collusion, his mother had quietly injected another factor into the mix by ensuring that Paul met the delightful Leanne as soon as possible. Paul had, therefore, flown into a classic pincer movement manufactured, partly by stealth and partly through good intentions, by his parents, whereby he would settle into a life of public service in his homeland, accompanied by his classic all-American wife and their inevitable resultant two-point-four children. All that would be left to decide was exactly what those children would, in turn, eventually have as their careers.

He also knew that, 'back home' in England, there were other friends and their families awaiting his decision to return and share the rest of his life with them, where he would have the choice of becoming an academic or a company executive. In either case, he would complete his life alongside a steadfast and loyal English Rose of a wife, who most likely at this juncture would also be an aero-engineer that would ultimately inherit a large proportion of a major fortune. Their children, doubtless numerous, would all go to public school, rebel, then either settle into their respective cultural and financial inheritances, or slump into destructive excess.

The choice was the self-control of the new country still wary of the future it was carving for itself, or the irreverence of the older country that had become comfortably over-confident; new world Republican Conservatism with a capital 'C', or the democratic liberalism of the old world conservatives with the lower case 'c'. The wheel was turning, all he had to do was select which shoulder would be applied to it. In the end it would be well-oiled American conformity that won-out over classic English order-from-chaos; but not exactly by the designs already cast.

The first choice was the hardest. Annie Fleming was the person he had become closest to in his entire life; she was his friend, his confidante, his muse and his confessor all rolled into one. She was nothing other than the rock to which his life had become anchored, and all the better it had been for having done so. They could be in each other's company for days on end, or apart for weeks at a time, yet nothing changed. When they made love, which they had occasionally, it was the finest, most tender experience he could ever describe, made even better by the total lack of intimidation that followed in its wake. Although neither felt in any way compelled to be, from the moment they met on that landing in St Peter's Terrace, they were both utterly faithful to the other, neither doubting that unspoken fidelity for a second. It was a relationship of convenient and casual closeness; it felt, in a word, natural, as if predestined at the dawn of time.

Yet he was never sure that it was love, probably because he was still unsure what love actually was; until Leanne had walked through the side gate of his parents' house. That was the day he was hit by the train that would leave him weaving and staggering in its wake between the arrow-straight tracks that carried it beyond the horizon to the station where it awaited his subsequent, and inevitable, arrival.

The feeling had clearly been mutual and the pair were able to steam-up the windows of Leanne's mother's regularly-borrowed pick-up from within days of meeting. However Leanne, being of staunch Baptist upbringing, had made it very clear from the outset that, whoever she married, her husband would marry a virgin. Paul was too much of a gentleman to pressure her into any other viewpoint and, in any case, he would always be a sexual pragmatist. Which is why Leanne also made it clear that she was well aware of, and perfectly happy to provide, such other distractions as would allow him not to be constantly tortured by his animal desires. Hence the steamy windows.

A month after his departure from England, Annie received in Paul's regular letter the first mention of Leanne. Although she too felt closer to Paul than to any other human being, she also privately doubted it would ever evolve into outright, passionate, carnal love. They were, and always would be, soul-mates; but beyond the bounds of marriage. Her reply was instant and unwavering.

She told him how delighted she was at the developments and how she looked-forward to meeting Leanne at the earliest opportunity. She also decided to quietly distance herself whilst simultaneously, but slowly, lowering her parents' expectations in that direction. The announcement of the engagement finally made official what the freighting of the remainder of Paul's possessions to Wichita had predestined.

But that would still be sometime in the future as, although the future of his love-life was already penciled-in by the emotional scribes, the employment status of one Paul Walter Kleberson was still very much up in the air. Which is why the events on the day after the aforementioned letter was posted to Sussex would mark the further evolution of his life-line.

Realising that he was most probably not going to accept the Foundation's offer, Paul began to consider what his options were in the USA. With his Cambridge qualification, he could virtually walk into an academic career in any of the Ivy-League establishments back East, or the more forward-looking Universities of the West Coast. What he was unsure of was whether there would be the demand for the European-bias of his work to date. There sure as hell wouldn't be any such demand should he decide to hang around here in the Midwest.

He had, therefore, begun to submerge himself into some of the more recent associated American history, in particular the other side of the eighteenth century coin that, when flipped, had landed tails-down showing a certain

General Washington's head to the world at large. Part of this had evolved from casual research he had started in England into his family tree, which had proved to have somewhat illustrious roots on his father's side. The Wichita City Library had turned-out to be a surprisingly solid source of books and material on the War of Independence. So on that particular afternoon he was under the awning in the back yard of his parents' house with his nose into a biography of Daniel Morgan, the Revolutionary Rifleman, that had brought Professor Don Higginbotham, a Midwest American with a fine old Yorkshire name, his PhD from Duke University some thirty years earlier.

Paul had put it down and wandered into the kitchen to get a cold beer from the fridge, when he saw the black sedan roll to a halt at the end of the driveway. The passenger looked out of the lowered side window towards the house and turned towards his driver. There was a brief conversation, then the passenger got out of the car and walked up the pathway to ring the front doorbell.

Paul was alone in the house, so went to the door and opened it. Facing him was a man of about his height and build, probably not many years his senior; it was just the severe crew-cut and anonymously-tailored dark suit that made him appear much older. Paul's immediate impression was that the Mormons were about to attempt to recruit him.

"Paul W Kleberson?" the man asked, simultaneously drawing a small wallet from his inside pocket and dropping it open to reveal an identity card. "Sam Schneider, Federal Bureau of Investigation. Can I come in and talk to you for a few minutes?"

'My God,' Paul thought, *'surely to goodness they haven't found out about that party I went to back in Cambridge!'* The previous year, he and RP had baled out of a second floor window and down the fire escape from one of the dorms at Kings just minutes before the police came through the front door; there had been a lot of weed at that one, which was why they had baled out. The raid resulted in a number of successful convictions, and expulsions. Even though they hadn't partaken, like some of the arrested, had they stayed it could still have ended their academic tenure.

Paul must have looked as stunned as he felt, because Sam immediately smiled and said, reassuringly: "I'm sorry, please don't look so shocked, I'm not here to arrest you, I'm here to ask you about your future."

Paul was even more shocked by this approach, but he let Sam into the house and showed him into the parlour. "Please, have a seat; would you like a beer?" Paul asked, "I've just got one for myself."

"Why not," Sam replied, "like I said this isn't an 'official' visit."

As he fished another bottle out of the rack, Paul thought to himself *'OK, so this is the gameplay; this is what Dad has planned. I'm to join the fuzz - and not just any old fuzz, oh no! My Dad's lined me up for the F-B-fucking-I!'* By the time Paul returned with the beers, the adrenaline from the anger welling through him had helped him to recover his composure.

"Listen, Mr ...?"

"Agent Schneider."

"Agent Schneider, sorry. Look, I don't know what my Father may have told you, but I'm a historian, or at least it is my intention to be a historian. In fact, I have already started research on a paper that I intend to circulate to support my application for a place in a history faculty back East. I'm afraid that I am simply not interested in what my Father may have, with all the best intentions, lined-up for me. I appreciate that you may have had to travel some distance to come to see me, indeed I am somewhat flattered that I may be considered as having the potential to join your organisation, but I'm really no action man."

Sam looked at him, still wearing his friendly smile: "that was an impressive speech - have you been rehearsing it for long?"

Paul immediately realised that he had been rumbled by a professional. *'What a plank I am,'* he thought, *'this guy probably arrests international crooks for a pastime and here I am, a naive graduate, trying to convince him that I'm really a man of the world with the entire situation of my future sussed.'* He flopped back into his chair, took a swig of beer then burst out laughing.

"About two weeks - that bad huh?"

"I've seen more transparent assertions, but not recently. However, I also know it was a sincere statement from someone who knows his own mind. So would you like us to start again, with maybe a brief introduction from me about why I'm really here."

Paul lifted his bottle in a toasting action: "Daniel Morgan's not going anywhere these days, so the floor's all yours Agent Schneider."

"Call me Sam."

"OK, fire away Sam."

"The most important thing for any FBI Agent to establish is the trust of whoever he is talking with, whatever the reason for our interest in them. We all have different techniques for that, but mine is simply to tell the truth. And in this case, the truth is, yes, I have spoken with your Father. It was a couple of days after the Mayor's reception, where incidentally I observed how well you handled a clearly-embarrassing situation for you."

"I'm sorry, I didn't realise we had met before, it was all a bit of a whirl that day."

"Don't worry, we didn't meet, I decided that you were probably jet-lagged and that little would register anyway, so I kept out of the way."

"That's spooky."

"What's spooky?"

"You're not the first person to say that to me recently, but never mind. Please carry-on."

"I met your Father in his office, hoping that he would put us together that day. He refused, because he wanted you to have the space to make your own decision."

"Really?"

"Yes really. However, he did add that he expected that you would probably decide to go into a post-graduate programme with the Air Force and that your application was already quite advanced. He said that he could not stop me from speaking with you, but asked that I didn't do so until you had been here a month."

"And the month was up yesterday."

"I got the impression from my meeting with your Father that you may not have been fully-cognisant of the developments lined-up for you. From your little speech, I deduce that you had your suspicions, as yet unproven."

"That's amazing Holmes! But how did you manage to get onto the base to see me this time without my Father knowing?"

"You underestimate me Watson. That was the simplest part of my plan to accomplish."

There was a silence. Paul liked the sound of this stranger, he was quick-witted and possessed a sense of humour, something he had believed would be the first thing to be surgically-removed as soon as someone joined any law-enforcement agency. He leant forward in the chair, as if moving closer for the revelation of a secret. Sam sensed the moment and also shuffled forward on the sofa. He looked left, then right, as if checking whether there was anyone else listening, then craned further forward until he was barely a couple of feet from Paul. In a low whisper, he revealed: "I asked him for a pass."

Both men looked at each other seriously for a split second, then rocked into fits of laughter. They then clinked bottles, took a swig each and burst into laughter again. Sam slumped back into the sofa, still laughing as he blurted-out: "you didn't honestly think that an FBI Agent rocks-up at the gate of an Air Force Base and drives onto it without the Base Commander knowing exactly where he is going, do you?"

"OK, Sam, OK," said Paul, "so that's twice in the space of a couple of minutes that I have proved to you that I am way too naive to ever be an FBI Agent, so why on earth are you not rushing to the door and going back to headquarters to tell them how they made a ridiculous mistake?"

Sam's face turned serious and he drew himself up into a more formal seated position. Then he slowly turned his gaze towards the bottle in his hand, as if focussing his thoughts before making a profound statement. The atmosphere became slightly tense; eventually he spoke:

"Well, for one, the beer's good."

eighteen and counting

Thirty-Two

With the scene under the M.E's control, the Chief outside the building briefing the media and Jackson Kendrick III back in Friedmann's office awaiting interview, Schneider gave Kleberson a lift back to the Epic Center. It was three p.m.

The two had a brief meeting with two of Schneider's Agents, Bill Johnson and Jim Kowalski. The former would provide operational liaison to Kleberson's team, the latter was an intelligence man who would assist with accessing relevant FBI files. It was agreed that they would assemble again at seven p.m. to get a briefing on the files compiled by the staff in the LA Field Office, including Kryczek, that Kowalski was already reviewing. After the two Agents left the office, Kleberson fixed Schneider with a quizzical look. Schneider was the first to speak: "I know that look Paul, what's the problem?"

"That phrase 'for the time being' you used with the Chief back at Westview Tower - was that for his benefit or mine?"

"Both. Stanton needed to be put on notice that the Kendricks have to be kept at arms length in this investigation, for both of your sakes. It was the simplest way I could achieve that."

"And me? What benefit was it to me?"

"Come on Paul, you knew the dangers when you brought all this down the block this morning. Sure, you were just playing local politics at the time. What you didn't know then and, incidentally, neither did I, was that this was a potential serial, or that by coming here you probably have given us an opportunity to catch a major perp that we haven't had previously."

"So is that a 'Royal We'?"

"I guess that's some sort of English thing is it? So would the classics scholar like to enlighten this poor culturally-deprived colonial law graduate?"

"Whenever Queen Victoria was displeased with news, she would tell the messenger that 'we are not amused'. You said I have given 'us' an opportunity to catch the bastard. If that 'us' was spoken with just your FBI hat on, then it has a completely different meaning to you and I, and of course our departments, working together."

Schneider scowled slightly: "I also have to keep my line of command apprised. That's not bullshit Paul, how the hell else do you think I could get you what you're getting at such short notice? Having worked here, you of all people should know that level of resource doesn't come free of political baggage; isn't that one of the reasons you left? Because we couldn't let you play the Lone Ranger like Stanton does over at City Hall."

Kleberson smiled: "guess he doesn't have much choice most of the time."

"Oh he has a choice Paul, he's a lot more shrewd than you give him credit for, and that choice only keeps being made in your favour while you keep him onside with your clear-up rate. Give him a good-enough reason and he'll squash you like a bug. When that happens any support or career choices that you may think are ever-open for you will evaporate as quickly as the morning dew."

A shudder of adrenaline went down Kleberson's spine. The two men had always been frank with each other, but that was in private over a beer. This was the first time that Sam Schneider had given him such a talking-to whilst both were on business, and it had the desired effect. He refocused, quickly moving the discussion on: "so you've got them in the frame as well."

"Who?"

"The Kendricks."

"Everyone's in the frame at this point Paul, I don't need to tell you that."

"No you don't, but you do need to tell me the one piece of information that you're holding back right now."

"Shit, you're good Paul! Problem is that you know it - that's what makes you such a piece of work!"

Both men burst out laughing, as only true friends can to instantly break a tension that occasionally builds between them. Kleberson waited until the guffaws died down and the moment was perfect to push the point: "so what is it Sam? What's the piece of the jigsaw you're keeping in your wallet that you don't want to give me until you think the time's right? Because if we, that means the City of Wichita Police Department with the full support of the FBI, are going to stand any chance of catching this perp before he strikes again - don't forget that he already has the clock-ticking on us - then you know that I am the one to find where it fits."

"Or Kryczek."

"Come on Sam, she's a basket-case, surely you saw that at the apartment."

"That's as maybe, but she's still the one that made the link to a potential pattern of high-profile serials."

Thirty-Three

By the time Paul Kleberson had walked back to City Hall, all of the Squad were back at their desks, except for Morley. At one end of the Squad Room details of the Hilary Nicholson murder were beginning to build–up on one of the whiteboards. On the next whiteboard, just the name of Marjoree Rolles appeared at the top.

"Morley back yet Chris?"

"We think he's with the Chief."

"OK, that will do nicely, close the door Chris."

"Why? We got something secret to discuss?"

The others relaxed momentarily.

"No, it will help Morley to ooze under it when he gets here." There was a loud guffaw from all but Holdsworth, who still found even the thought of Morley intimidating.

"OK, let's review where we are - feel free to add any comments as we go everyone. Hilary Nicholson, fiancé of Jackson Kendrick the Third heir to the Kendrick empire, found dead in what turns out to be her confidential second home in Derby. No signs of a struggle even though she has been murdered, possibly raped or at the very least indulging in some rumpy pumpy. She is found laid-out on her bed in a symbolic manner. She has been shorn completely and it would appear the whole place has been wiped clean of any evidence."

"CSI have finished-up working there," said Moreno, "and they found nothing. They're over at Ms Rolles' place now."

"OK, but we have to assume they will need to take the place apart, and because they didn't find anything at the first scene, at this point all we can hope is that they find something at the second that gives us a break."

Capaldi joined in: "there was no sign of forced entry, so we have to assume she knew the perp. One of the neighbours has a security system that takes stills of the street every two minutes or so. We've been through the tape and there's not much on it; in fact, for the money he says he spent on it, his system's pretty useless. Of the few vehicles it picked-up, all but two were residents, the others were a small car just before eight, looked like a Japanese compact of some sort, then a truck around midnight. But the camera's monochrome and not enough definition on either frame to get a plate. Neighbour thinks he's seen the car before and that it may have been a take-out delivery. But he didn't recognise the truck, so that could be anywhere in a few hundred mile radius by now, or may not have any connection at all."

Dean nodded: "that may help us with confirmation later, but it sure as hell ain't a lead. Do you want me to follow the take-out angle, see if there were any deliveries to the street last night Boss; you never know, may get a break."

"OK Dean, but get uniform to do the canvass, then you follow-up on anything breaking."

"How long would it have taken the perp to clean-up?" asked Holdsworth from the corner. The others all stopped and looked at him.

"Go on," encouraged Kleberson.

"She was found when, one a.m? M.E. estimates time of death between eight p.m. and midnight. Truck on the tape was seen driving-up at midnight. If that was the perp arriving, was there enough time for the deed to be done plus all that cleaning and get clear in less than an hour? Don't think so. So unless that was an accomplice arriving to collect the perp, maybe the truck had nothing to do with that house, just a coincidence."

"Good stuff Holdsworth. Anything else?"

"In the garage you said you thought the Boxster had been used recently. So we have to assume Hilary Nicholson arrived at the house earlier that evening. So did our perp follow her, or was he waiting for her?"

"Marjoree Rolles called the place Hilary Nicholson's safehouse, so presumably hardly anyone knew she went there," added Kleberson.

"So she must have been followed," Holdsworth concluded somewhat triumphantly "so maybe someone saw another car."

"Problem is," said Capaldi, "nobody saw her arrive, even that useless security system didn't pick her car up and as the car was put in the garage, nobody can say what time they first saw it there."

"Hang on," said McKinley, "there's another option."

"What?" asked Kleberson.

"She brought the perp with her. Marjoree Rolles told you in your interview with her that Hilary was in her 'safehouse.' Shall I fill-in the next bit Paul?"

"Sure Chris, you've read the notes."

"The Lieutenant interviewed Marjoree Rolles around five a.m. after he left the house. It was unofficial, but she was going to give us a full statement this morning; of course we won't get that now. The house is or was owned by Ms Rolles. Neither lived there, it was where she and Hilary Nicholson met-up when they were both an item, but this changed once Hilary got engaged to Kendrick. After that, Hilary needed somewhere locally where she could go if she wanted to disappear from view for a day or so, mainly to work undisturbed. She nicknamed it her 'safehouse' because her fiancé had no idea where she was and could not get in her way."

"Doesn't sound like a very close relationship," Moreno chipped in.

"It wasn't," McKinley continued, "it was to be a marriage of convenience. As you will have figured-out, Hilary and Marjoree were both lesbians, but Hilary wanted a child, so she needed a stud. Kendrick qualified because he gave all the financial security and inherited position Ms Nicholson wanted for the child."

"So was she pregnant then?" asked Capaldi.

"No, that wouldn't happen until they were married, neither could Kendrick have his way with her until they were. They had a pre-nuptial agreement setting it all out and Marjoree Rolles was a witness to that pre-nup. But Junior didn't know, neither would he."

"That's it then." Dean stood up purposefully and walked to the water cooler in the corner: "the Kendricks did the deed. Not personally but Junior found out, had both the dykes done by a contractor, then points the whole thing at 'The Turd' who goes to gaol and gets disinherited. Perfect! So how do we prove it?"

"That's where I was until an hour or so ago," said Kleberson.

"So what happened?" quizzed Dean.

"Kryczek happened."

"Who the hell is Kryczek?"

"FBI specialist called in by Sam Schneider."

"Specialist in what?"

"Serials, in particular one known as Vitruvio."

"What, we got a serial now?"

"Looks like it. M.O. is the same as sixteen other known cases, all over the country, all unsolved. They were in batches of four - three killed in a twenty-four hour period, two days space, then one more. All the victims in each batch were connected somehow. I will be having a more detailed briefing over at Sam Schneider's office at seven p.m."

"Does the Chief know?"

"That it's a potential serial, yes. I will give him the rest after we've finished here."

"So do we arrest 'The Turd' or not?" asked Dean.

"At the moment he's voluntarily incarcerated in Friedmann's office waiting for us to question him. Unless someone has tipped-off the Kendricks, neither of them have any idea yet that this may be a serial. If it is Vitruvio, then the connectivity between the vics means that Kendrick could also be on the perp's list, which gives us the option to lock him up for his own safety, an option I rather savour, or to send him out of town with some bodyguards until the time expires. Either way we will have one scared, inconvenienced rich piece of shit out of our hair for a few days."

"But surely he's still a suspect?" asked Holdsworth. "After all, he could have read about Vitruvio and mimicked the M.O. to get rid of his problem."

"He ain't that clever," Dean interjected.

"But he's the only one we have who was close enough to Ms Nicholson for her to let him into the Derby house and he lived on the same floor as Ms Rolles; neither would have suspected he would attack them."

"You haven't met him yet have you?" insisted Dean. "OK, in my opinion he's quite capable of murdering both of 'em in a rage, but all that stagin' shit afterwards? Believe me, he really ain't that clever."

Holdsworth was becoming a little frustrated with the old lag's viewpoint: "so is he simply rich enough to hire the actual Vitruvio?"

Dean nodded his approval with a satisfied smile: "now that I can run with."

"You know, I think I'll take Holdsworth with me to the briefing with the Chief, he really has some interesting input, don't ya think? In the meantime," he turned to McKinley, "Chris, Chief says we can second from other units, so get some more manpower out and about to look for fresh faces around town. Pump all the snitches for anything unusual, see if we can identify any visitors staying in hotels or motels that booked-in yesterday for four nights; concentrate on those that have never stayed there before, or maybe one other time in the last few weeks. Don't ignore anything - if we have to turn the whole city upside down, the Chief will give us the resources to do it. Also try and piece-together Kendrick's movements, known haunts and so on, see if we can put him anywhere in this other than as a potential victim."

"Moreno go sit on the M.E. and get the final report on Hilary Nicholson and any preliminaries on Marjoree Rolles. Then go and talk to Ms Nicholson's associates at her accountancy practice and see if she had any personal employees. She must have had at least a cleaner for that vast pad up at Eastborough. Their Sherriff's department may be able to help you, they've only got about forty houses each to look after up there and they need to know pretty much everything that's going on with domestic staff. Also find out why she needed to use the house down at Derby. Marjoree Rolles called it her 'safehouse', see if anyone knows why she thought she needed one."

"Capaldi, get CSI to go over that Porsche again until they find something - anything that our perp might have left in the car if he was a passenger. Then see if we can put Hilary Nicholson's movements together yesterday. Find out if anyone saw her car with two people in it heading for Derby. Talk to the neighbours again, see if we can make any progress on that truck, or any other vehicles. And check if CSI found any documents at Ms Rolles' apartment; we're particularly interested in a copy of that pre-nup - she must have stashed it somewhere. If it's there, we can blindside Friedmann with it.

"Dean, get in touch with USC and see what you can find-out about our two victims while they were there, who they mixed with, any enemies they made, neighbours, you know the drill."

"Holdsworth, you're with me."

Thirty-Four

Chief Stanton was not a happy bunny. That morning he had had to brief a sceptical media pack about the misunderstanding outside City Hall involving Tommy-Lee Thornton. He had censured them in true political fashion about using tip-offs to preframe stories that turned-out to be way off-beam. That had brought a tirade of aggressive questioning, spearheaded by Tom Cochrane who was clearly targeted as the one who had received the tip-off, not only by Stanton but by his fellow newshounds as well. That in itself was containable as a short term problem. Sure Cochrane would be pissed and be a thorn in their side for a while, but a quick exclusive downstream would soon fix that.

Then just after lunch he had to brief the same media pack outside of Marjoree Rolles' apartment building about the second mysterious death. That wasn't so straightforward, as he had been seen clearly having an altercation with Jackson Kendrick III and his lawyer in the foyer. In the confusion following, he had failed to pre-brief Cochrane that his boss was dead, something he would have done normally and got an agreement not to ask too-pointed questions.

So Cochrane got the news at the same time as the rest of America did via his own live feed. The shock was obvious to all present and it didn't take the producers in their studios more than nanoseconds to get cameras turned on Cochrane. He clearly could not take the first question slot as would be expected of the main local network representative, because the reality of the news was still seeping through the haze that was momentarily his consciousness.

So that honour went to Pete Christensen who took it with all the aplomb of a twenty-year veteran - "Was this also a murder?" "Was there a connection with the earlier one?" "Were the M.O's similar?" All the standard questions that Cochrane should be asking today, of all days, when he had got his break. But he couldn't and yet he had to do something otherwise it wasn't just his boss that was gone.

Christensen moved to the public altercation in the foyer: "wasn't that Jackson Kendrick the Third in the foyer, the fiancé of this morning's victim? What was he doing here?"

Stanton parried all of Christensen's questions, but Cochrane was also recovering his composure. Because he worked closely with Marjoree Rolles, he knew something the others didn't; something he would have been warned-off of using had Stanton briefed him first. But that hadn't happened; Stanton had not covered his back as well as he would usually and he had humiliated Cochrane that morning over the Tommy-Lee fiasco.

Christensen was poised for another question as Stanton finished his latest answer, but he didn't get to ask it. Instead Cochrane's voice interjected: "Chief is this building owned by Jackson Kendrick the Third?"

The pack fell silent, the cameras swung first onto Cochrane then simultaneously back onto Stanton, thrusting forward until they resembled an assembly of expectant children waiting for their parent to give them a sweet.

The shutters whirred. Stanton could only do one thing which he did instinctively - he replied: "I'm afraid we don't have that information right now, but we'll get back to you when we do." As Stanton said it, he realised that Cochrane already knew the answer and that he had just fallen into the bear trap laid by Cochrane's first question.

But Cochrane wasn't going to just bury him with that one point: "is Mr Kendrick a suspect?" The cameras stayed focussed on Chief Stanton.

"At present we are examining several avenues of enquiry."

"And is Mr Kendrick one of those?"

"I couldn't comment on that."

"Has Mr Kendrick been arrested?"

"No."

"Is he being questioned?"

"Mr Kendrick and his family have enough to deal with at this time without our intruding further on their grief."

Stanton could feel the whole nation craning forward in front of their TV's just like the microphones were in front of him. The coup-de-gras was delivered with surgical precision.

"Chief," Cochrane insisted, "Hilary Nicholson fiancé of Jackson Kendrick the Third is found dead this morning in a house owned by my colleague Marjoree Rolles. Ms Rolles is found dead in her apartment hours later, an apartment in a building owned by Jackson Kendrick the Third and, if I'm not mistaken, an apartment on the same floor as one occupied by Jackson Kendrick the Third when he is staying in town. That set of circumstances might be enough to get a man lynched in Mississippi but here, it appears, we have to take grief into account before even questioning anybody. Surely if the people of Wichita are to sleep soundly in their beds tonight, they must expect their appointed officials to do what is right for the people who pay for them, rather than those that bankroll their appointer's election campaign."

As he said it, Cochrane knew he had burnt his bridges here in Wichita, but he also knew that the collective gasp exhaled throughout the country would echo through the National Network studios. Cochrane would not be staying anyway - he had become hot property. As the pre-programmed response of "no more questions" emitted into the microphones, Stanton turned and re-entered the building. He knew that the funding for the upcoming mayoral election campaign had just been jeopardised, so he knew what would be waiting for him back at his office.

And there it was, on his desk right on the top of the pile of messages assembled for his attention - a simple yellow post-it note with the word 'URGENT' printed at the bottom accompanied, in the tidy hand of his secretary, by the command: 'Please call Jackson Kendrick Junior on your return.'

The telephone conversation did not go well; in fact, it was more a monologue than a conversation. So when Kleberson and Holdsworth presented their update on the situation surrounding Jackson Kendrick III, Stanton made a mental note to stop off at St Benedict's on the way home and offer thanks to the Lord for bringing him this almost perfect solution. "So what you're telling me now Kleberson, is that you want to arrest Jackson Kendrick the Third and lock him up, not because you think he committed a crime, but because you want to save his life. And on top of that, you want me to explain why to his father!" He chuckled to himself with amusement, but he was deadly serious. This time he wanted Kleberson to commit to the proposal.

"Well Chief, that's your call. Personally, I'm more than happy to leave him out there as bait, with a detail sitting on him to catch the perp when he tries to strike of course, but if we do that, then he might just run for the hills to save his own arse."

"In which case," Stanton responded, "you wouldn't move heaven and earth to protect him, would you? Don't answer that, I was just thinking out loud."

"What I'm saying is that, in those circumstances, we could not guarantee keeping a detail on him, so it might be safer to have him under lock and key."

Kleberson paused for effect: "plus, if Junior gives the direction to Friedmann personally, his Client will come quietly."

"So get him to surrender himself?"

"If he does that, we won't have to swear a warrant and the family avoids all the accompanying poor P.R."

"Mmm, I think Junior might prefer that, don't you? OK, but I'll have to go over to Junior's place - he won't like hearing this over the phone. How long will his son be at Friedmann's office?"

"After what happened earlier and with the press pack camped on the lawn, I don't think he'll venture out until we've spoken to him."

"OK, I'll go over to Junior's now. You have your FBI briefing at seven, so you go to that and see what else that gives us. We can let Junior do the directing and by the time you get back here, hopefully his son will be here waiting for you. Mr Friedmann can explain the circumstances to the press this time."

As they walked back to the Squad Room, Holdsworth turned to Kleberson and said :"looks like you got what you wanted."

"Yeah," said Kleberson, "but way too easily."

Thirty-Five

"Savannah in late two-thousand-one, Denver and Memphis last year, then Palm Springs two months ago." Kowalski began the briefing by pointing to the highlighted points on a map projected onto the huge whiteboard at one end of the FBI conference room. Around the table were Sam Schneider, Paul Kleberson, Scott Holdsworth and Bill Johnson. Kowalski continued: "and, of course, now Wichita, making it five groups in less than two years. Eighteen victims, and counting."

Kleberson had decided to include Holdsworth as the direct contact from his team with Johnson, the FBI liaison man. Holdsworth had demonstrated a spontaneous analytical approach on the case and Kleberson needed a foil within his own department who could take a contra position when Schneider wasn't around. Schneider was a great help when Kleberson was stuck, but they didn't get much of an opportunity to actually work together. When they did there was a real buzz about them, which was one of the reasons Kleberson was seriously considering Schneider's open offer to rejoin the Bureau, despite his banter to the contrary.

Kowalski continued: "each was obviously seen as a serial grouping locally, but the link between the groups wasn't made until Palm Springs. Kryczek worked on Palm Springs with another Agent, Tom Bonetti, who had transferred from Savannah just before Christmas. When their first two murders happened, Palm Springs PD contacted the local Agency for help, who alerted the LA Field Office where Bonetti spotted the similarities. Much as here, once they realised they possibly had an in-progress grouping, LA put a team together around Bonetti which included Kryczek, who worked the profiling. While cross-checking the various aspects of Savannah with the Palm Springs murders, Denver and Memphis popped-up as well."

"So there could be more?" Schneider enquired.

"No," Kowalski quickly countered that line of investigation, "I've been in the National database which is how you connected these two here, right?" Schneider didn't respond, so Kowalski carried-on: "anyway nothing else came up, so what we have is what we have, essentially the work that Kryczek did."

"So this guy just started working in fours?" asked Holdsworth.

"I don't get you," Kowalski looked a little distracted by Holdsworth's question.

"Like, no singles or doubles with the same M.O. prior to Savannah. It's just that I studied serials at the training academy and they often start tentatively then get bolder as they don't get caught."

"Let's leave the macro analysis until we've got more of an overview shall we," Schneider proposed.

"Sorry, Sir," Holdsworth looked embarrassed.

"No, don't apologise, it's a good line. Just hold the thought and we'll come back to it." Schneider's broad smile reassured Holdsworth who relaxed again. "OK Kowalski, on you go and we'll keep the questions to a minimum until you're done."

"Anyway, the main similarity Kryczek found was the M.O. The pattern was random geographically, the timelines between the groupings were also totally random, there was no consistent victim profile outside of the groupings, all of which meant that once a grouping started, the only way to predict where he would next strike was by profiling the victims within the current group."

"You say 'He', do we have any confirmation of that?" asked Kleberson.

"All the psychological profiling came up male. I can take you through that when you've got a couple of hours."

"No need, just building the picture."

Kowalski changed the slide being projected to one showing a series of bullet points. He began to read them out, adding additional information as he went. "Moving to the individual groupings, all four were consistent in the following:
- The first three murders took place at twelve-hour intervals, then a two-day gap, then the last one.
- The victim was always murdered in their own residence.
- Every scene was completely sterilised - nothing left behind, the perp used what was available at the scene. If he brought basic stuff with him, like gloves and so on, they were taken away for disposal elsewhere.
- There was never any sign of a struggle - this suggests that the perp knew he was not working under any obvious time-constraints.
- There was always a connection between the victims, however tenuous.

- The local PD was alerted to the first scene by an anonymous nine-one-one call reporting a possible intruder on the premises. After that, the connections led to the next one, and so on, at whatever rate the local detectives worked. Nothing else from the perp - no notes, no phone calls, no bragging. He just arrived, did the deeds, then vanished.
- There was always sexual activity either prior to the murder, directly after, or maybe both. But no obvious sexual orientation from the perp, who performed heterosexual, homosexual and deviant acts on the victims, proving that the perp knew he had the time and privacy to do so.
- Where it was possible to confirm that the victims were either gay or ac/dc, the perp showed that he knew this by the way the body was presented for discovery. Those that we have not been able to confirm as such may also have been, but stayed in the closet. Let's put it this way, in some cases the fact that some of the victims actually were not heterosexual came as a huge shock to their nearest and dearest.
- The scene-staging showed any sexual relationships between victims. Again some of those relationships were unknown to relatives and friends of the victims. So the groups of victims were either thoroughly-researched, or the perp studied them over a period of time allowing him to minutely-plan the crimes.
- You won't know this yet, but your first post-mortem will confirm that the ultimate cause of death is a poison injection made at the base of the neck - very precise. So precise in fact that the victim may not even have been aware it had been administered."

Kowalski turned briefly to the screen and studied the bullet points again to check he had covered them all, then concluded: "so in summary so far, the perp never leaves a calling card other than the M.O. Anything he brings to the scene, he takes away otherwise he improvises with local materials. That means there is never anything to trace, no fingerprints, no hair, no DNA, no nothing. He may be a ghost for all we know. Any questions on that or shall I carry-on and give you a rundown on the victims?"

All present were momentarily dumbstruck - information overload primarily. They all studied the bullet points in silence for a few moments, before Kleberson was the first to react: "both of our vics have the puncture wound just as you describe, so I think that confirms what we're dealing with here. This poison that you say is the cause of death, do we know what it is?"

Kowalski flicked through his papers, pulled out an analysis sheet and began to read from it: "I was getting to that. The poison is a composite blend of chemicals, the primary appears to be a derivative of Curare, a poison used by some South American Indian tribes on their hunting arrows. It's taken from vines in the Chondrodendron family and used because it paralyses the muscles, but does not kill immediately. Some animals take hours to die, thus keeping the meat fresh while the natives take it home. At the apparent dosages used, humans will succumb in twenty to thirty minutes. Not easy to trace on analysis, but we have part of the formula here and the testing regime we used, so your lab techs can probably confirm against that if this perp used the same compound; at least that will save them the weeks it apparently took us to break it down as far as we have been able to." He handed the sheets to Johnson.

"So were they poisoned or drugged?" Kleberson asked.

"Possibly both. I said derivative because there are some added ingredients. I won't bore you with the chemical names, suffice it to say they may keep victims alive longer, but are primarily to maintain sexual arousal. Put bluntly, our perp has found a way to paralyse his victims and have sex with them while they die slowly, fully aware of what he is doing. That's why some M.E's have understandably concluded that the sex must have taken place post-mortem, but Kryczek didn't think so as in one of her notes she concluded it would make no sense to use such a sophisticated poison if the perp was simply a necrophiliac. She also queried if the compound could have made the vic initially compliant, but the blend is so unusual that nobody seems to have responded to that one."

Schneider interrupted: "are you saying that there is a task on one of our labs somewhere that hasn't been completed yet?"

"Like I said Sam, I have only had a couple of hours and there's hundreds of pages to go through. There was no response in Kryczek's main file, but it may be in one of the case files."

"Can you quickly lay your hand on the enquiry?"

"Yeah, like I said it's in the main file on my desk."

"OK, find it and give it to Bill. Bill whatever lab the action was on, if they haven't answered make them top-prioritise it straight away." Johnson nodded and scribbled. "I can see where you're going Paul, if this compound works like Kryczek surmised, that would help the perp with moving the body around, because he may not have been dealing with the dead-weight of a corpse."

"It also answers the trust angle," Kleberson added, "if the vic is smurfed-out while this is all happening, then there would be total compliance - what you might call a bad trip coming true." He turned to Kowalski again: "what about recreational usage, were any of the vics into that? If so, did anything show up in the tox-screens?"

"Nothing in the notes I've seen so far, what would be the significance we're looking for there?"

"If the vic was taking recreationals with the perp, then they wouldn't be spooked by the initial effects of the poison compound."

"I'll make sure I check for that in the case files."

"Thanks Jim," Schneider interjected, "can you copy both myself and Bill on your summary of each aspect as you finish. Bill, can you make sure that Paul's team get copies of all of Jim's analysis as he issues it. Timewise we're marching to the perp's drum, so we need all eyes on this in order to find that one mistake that gives us the break we're looking for. Just because this perp's apparently invented the perfect murder doesn't mean that he can't make mistakes; they all make mistakes." Johnson nodded.

Kleberson continued: "Jim, you've used the term residence, why the wide definition? Were they at home or not?"

"Some of the victims were wealthy, so had multiple residences. Some were working away from their main home, some were love-nests."

"So were any killed in their primary residence?"

"Obviously those that only owned the one residence were; from memory some of the vics were single, or not in a relationship at all. So far I've only concentrated on summarising from Kryczek's notes, which are pretty-comprehensive. She did a lot of work after the last grouping, up to when she went on leave. I haven't gone through each case file in detail yet, I'm starting that task after we've finished-up here, but I'll make a point of analysing that as a priority, as well as everything else you guys raise while we're here."

"Also, you said that there is never a sign of a struggle. Do we definitely know that the murder takes place at the scene? Is there any possibility that some vics were murdered elsewhere, then the body brought to the scene? That would cut-down the time needed at the scene and the amount of clean-up needed after."

"From what I have seen so far, I would say transportation was highly-unlikely. Some of the scenes were in high-rises, and at least one of the male vics weighed more than two hundred pounds. Either of those alone raises the probability of observation."

Holdsworth had the next question: "what about those nine-one-one calls, has anyone analysed them to see if they are the same person? Maybe we already know what our perp sounds like."

Kowalski shook his head: "not that I've seen in the analysis. Like I said, I haven't had time yet to look at the case files in any detail."

"OK, let's assume not," Schneider intervened. "Bill prioritise that will you - if we haven't got the tapes, get them."

Johnson continued to scribble as Kleberson added: "we'll get the latest one to you. Nice one Holdsworth, get operations to send that over to Bill then you run with it."

"Sure thing Skip. Can I also ask, Agent Schneider, as it seems that Agent Kryczek is not going to be available to work with us on this, would it be possible to set-up a conference call with Agent Bonetti, seeing as he was heading-up the last investigation?"

"Don't see why not," Schneider responded, "see how quickly you can set that up Bill."

"And requisition a ouija board while you're at it," Kowalski added. The room went silent; even Johnson stopped scribbling as all four men stared at him in shock. Noticing their reaction, Kowalski shrugged and asked: "what?"

Schneider was the first to break the silence: "he's dead? When?"

"He was shot at the end of the last investigation."

Schneider shot Kleberson a glance as they both realised the significance.

Kleberson was the first of the two to speak: "that's what she was talking about at the Rolles apartment. We just didn't make the connection!"

Schneider needed confirmation. He turned to Kowalski and asked: "who shot him?"

"Kryczek," Kowalski responded.

"Why didn't you tell us that earlier?"

"It's all in the next bit on the vics - I was dealing with your questions remember? Bonetti was subsequently identified as Vitruvio, mainly on connections back to Savannah. Must've been that what started Kryczek going off the rails, what with them being an item an' all that. That's why she did all the follow-up work, she was trying to show that he wasn't the perp but the sixteenth victim. Seems she was right."

i may have to shoot you

Thirty-Six

Over the weeks following that first visit to his parents' home at McConnell, Paul had several more meetings with Sam, primarily at his office in the Epic Center on Main Street. That location had been another early embarrassment to Paul; he had no idea that the FBI had local offices, known as Resident Agencies, and even less of an idea that there was one within six miles of his parents' home.

During the meetings, Sam had explained that the FBI was not just about field agents, but that there were at least as many additional backroom professional staff ranging from Chemists to Linguists, who were used for more than just investigative purposes. One of the largest professional branches covered Intelligence Analysis and although this was co-ordinated from FBI Headquarters in Washington DC, most were employed as placements in Field Offices across the country.

Paul's First from Peterhouse, with one of the highest marks achieved there by an overseas history student in many years, made him immediately of interest to a number of Government Agencies. However, it was Paul's abilities as a researcher with the Gormaston Foundation that brought him to the particular notice of the FBI. When he learned this, Paul became immediately concerned about just how this had come about without his knowledge, but Sam quickly explained in matter-of-fact terms what National Security was all about and that it didn't just focus on potential negative influences.

Paul recognised, whatever career he chose, that he would quickly have to shed the conspiracy-theorist nature of the undergraduate mind. Whether he joined the FBI or not, Sam's good-natured approach would be an invaluable fast-track introduction to the elements of reality needed to advance in an unsympathetic world.

His father had accepted the news that Paul would be joining the FBI with the same degree of resignation that he had adopted when his son advised him of his intention to remain in England when the family was posted home over two years earlier. Walter also recognised that this development was going to result in a career for his son much closer to what he had imagined, rather than the potential one brought home from England in a suitcase six weeks earlier.

Walter never told Paul of the groundwork he had put into his eldest son's recruitment into the USAF Intelligence Branch, that he subsequently had to abandon along with the several favours accumulated over many years that had been called-in during the process. Paul never told his father that he knew about it anyway, thanks to Sam's early honesty, the honesty that had swung the deal for the FBI virtually on that first meeting. What had also swung it was the speed at which Paul would find himself at an FBI desk actually working.

The main appeal of pursuing a career in academia, similar to the job offer from the Foundation, was that he would be almost immediately plunged into what he loved most about history - the research. It was the thrill of the chase he enjoyed; that slightly oblique reference in an academic work that hinted at a different aspect of the story to that proffered by the Victorian historians responsible for most of the accepted rite that forms the basis of history teaching today. Once that hint turned into a chink of light emerging from the past through the crumbling mortar between the dogmatic brickwork, sometimes in chinese-walls assembled over hundreds of years by bombastic academics, the whole picture of that particular time in the past changed. When further evidence revealed itself in documents previously dismissed as of no importance, villains became heroes, triumphs became failures, friends became enemies; and of course vice-versa. Sometimes it was as if Paul had found a faded sepia print that, when the light was applied to it, slowly reconstituted itself in glorious technicolor.

Of course, some of his discoveries were neither accepted, nor welcomed, by establishments of learning that pre-existed the original research, particularly where they potentially discredited some of Paul's highly-respected forebears. After a particular roasting from one professor back at Cambridge, for having the temerity to even attempt to revisit the work of that professor's particularly-favourite predecessor, Paul decided that he should keep some of his discoveries to himself, perhaps for self-publication at a later date in his career.

Instead, he resorted to a more opaque style of writing that merely hinted at a suspicion of there being more to a particular story that was still awaiting discovery. This allowed the more rigid of the adjudicating Fellows to believe that he had either not been intelligent-enough to fully realise his suspicions, or had deliberately decided to not embarrass the memory of a previous distinguished career. Either way, they seemed to reward him for this approach.

Attrition was the one aspect of academia, particularly in the UK, that Paul had come to detest, which was why a career with the FBI soon had more appeal. Here was an organisation that not only wanted him to find the cracks in the masonry, but to chip away at them until, if necessary, the wall fell down. There were no egos to be nursed, no sacred cows to protect; nothing mattered unless the clear light of truth shone through. It may not have been his beloved history, well not in the conventional sense, but it was interesting. Should it become less interesting, then he would have honed his intuitive skills and his research techniques. That could only help if he ultimately returned to academia.

Which is how he found himself on the early Monday-morning shuttle from Mid-Continent to O'Hare, then Washington and, after a further half hour taxi drive, to the FBI Training HQ at Quantico. He couldn't help but wonder exactly what he had agreed to as he passed the replica of the Iwo Jima Memorial, gleaming in the mid-afternoon sun outside of the gates of the sprawling US Marines base that the FBI facilities formed just a small part of. Ahead of him, a formal interview process the following day and, if successful, his five-week training course, which would commence the day after that - which it did.

The whole recruitment process would normally have taken six to twelve months, yet there he was, within a month of that first meeting with Sam Schneider, a confirmed employee of the FBI. Paul was being fast-tracked, aided, unbeknown to him, by the completed security screening process that his father had instigated while Paul was still studying for his finals.

There were two things that Paul realised during those first three weeks spent at Quantico before he was able to fly home for the only long-weekend break he would get during the process. The first was that he missed Leanne more than he could ever have imagined. Sure he would call her long-distance every couple of days, but that was no substitute for being with her, whether intertwined half-naked on the bench seat of her mother's truck, or just walking around the East Mall hand-in-hand. He resolved that he would ask Leanne to marry him that very weekend.

As it turned-out, she accepted in a heartbeat, probably because she not only felt exactly the same about the separation, but also because they came within seconds of her losing her virginity on the first night that he was back. Not that Paul knew anything about it; it was Leanne who, realising she was ready to give herself to the man destined as her life-mate, pulled-back from the brink. She had been close previously and knew that was the last time she could stop herself, so the offer of marriage that came just hours later was what she needed to reinforce her self-control - provided there would only be a short engagement.

Paul's second realisation was that he wanted to be an active FBI Agent. Although his training was as an analyst, it included aspects of how that activity keyed into the work of frontline agents. If that wasn't enough to stir his interest, then the visit to Hogan's Alley to observe an ongoing exercise during week two was the clincher. Part of a real town built on the base, Hogan's Alley provided fully-realistic training in staged situations based upon real cases. The exercise that day was a hostage situation and Paul was completely gripped by the psychology involved. Although he realised that he would not be able to apply to become an agent until he had fulfilled three years as an analyst, from that point onwards there was nothing else he would be working towards.

Three months after Paul returned from Quantico, Mr and Mrs Paul Kleberson emerged from the Faith Baptist Church on McConnell Air Force Base into the early winter sunshine. After RP's best man speech had reduced most of the guests to tears of laughter, the reception vanished in a blur of smiling congratulations. The only aspect Paul remembered with any clarity was the wonderful hug he received from Annie, accompanied by her absolutely genuine confirmation that she felt that Leanne was one of the nicest people she had ever met and that his choice was perfect.

Just an hour later, the couple left the base in the hired limousine that took them to the hotel room at Mid-Continent Airport they had taken for the short honeymoon night before their early-morning flight to Honolulu the following day. The presence of Leanne's mother and the bridesmaids all fussing around her, as they changed in her parents' house prior to the trip to the airport, prevented any thoughts the couple had of a quick consummation there; the relatively-short distance from McConnell to Mid-Continent precluded the limo also. In the end, it happened within moments of the over-helpful bellboy being politely persuaded from their hotel room. Both agreed that it was better than either could have dreamed; the additional occasions that day, both before the flight and after reaching their hotel in Hawaii, proved better still.

Within a year, Matthew Nathaniel Walter Kleberson had joined them at their rented apartment on East Harry, all four new Grandparents observing that he was the finest baby they had ever seen in their lives. Even General Walter T Kleberson fought hard to quell tears of joy every time he, somewhat awkwardly, held the little chap in his arms. For he could barely believe the rapid turnaround in his prodigal son's life from the independently-single anglophile living on the other side of the world to the patriotic public servant commencing his personal version of the American dream within a few minutes of the family home.

Unfortunately, dreams rarely last forever.

Thirty-Seven

Paul had submitted his application to be considered for the post of Special Agent within weeks of joining Sam Schneider's team in Wichita in late 1991. In the early spring of 1993, he received an invitation to Sunday lunch from Sam at his home over on Broadmoor. This in itself was not unusual, the two men having become close friends, as had their wives. Sam and his wife Clara were Matt's Godparents and doted on him, having no children of their own. So it was unusual for the invitation to exclude Matt on this occasion, although there was no shortage of volunteers for baby-sitting duties down on the base.

When Paul and Leanne drew-up outside of Sam's house, there was another typically-FBI car standing there, alongside Sam's. Inside the house, Paul and Leanne were introduced to Trent Braxton and Ryan Merrifield, the former from the Kansas City Field Office, the latter from HQ in Washington. Within minutes, Clara had suggested that Leanne help her with final preparations for lunch and the four men adjourned to the deck with their beers.

Merrifield quickly outlined the developing scenario that the FBI was evolving to address. The Gulf War had changed the worldwide security picture, which had been graphically-illustrated by the recent bombing of the World Trade Center in New York. In the wake of that, the FBI was taking on additional responsibilities in the area of homeland intelligence and this remit would extend overseas in certain scenarios.

Trent Braxton took-up the theme: "one of those scenarios may materialise in Wichita this year, as one of the major aerospace companies based here has commenced negotiations to purchase a European rival. If this materialises, then there will be an influx of overseas nationals transferring to the plant here."

Merrifield continued: "the parent of the US Company concerned was a major defence contractor in the Gulf War and therefore is of elevated interest to international terrorist organisations, such as the one that staged the recent attack in New York. There would be no easier way for them to organise an attack on US interests anywhere than by creating a presence within that organisation."

"So who are Raytheon buying?" Paul asked.

"I told you he was sharp," Sam said with a knowing smile.

"Yes you did Sam," Trent responded, "and I can see you were understating as usual." He turned to Paul: "we can't say right here and now, it would be inappropriate at the current stage of negotiations. However, we need to make contingencies of which, hopefully, you will be one, Paul - and before you ask, it's because their target is British. I'm sure you can work the rest out yourself."

"It's my background, obviously - you need someone who understands how it all works over there, that all makes sense. What makes no immediate sense is that, surely, British nationals are the last people in the world that would launch terrorist missions against us."

Merrifield intervened: "generally-speaking, your initial analysis is sound. However, Britain is highly-multi-cultural, and has also recently become a more integral part of the European Union. Since you came back home, they have signed something called the Maastricht Treaty - if you haven't studied that, you will need to read-up on it before refining your analysis. It will change the whole scenario over there, in particular with regard to freedom of movement within employment."

"The upshot of all of this Paul," Trent continued, "and the reason we are here today, is that we need to increase our staffing of Agents here in Kansas. Your application has been brought forward and we want to get you up to Quantico as soon as possible for your training course."

"However, your appointment will not be announced immediately," Merrifield continued, "as it will suit us to have your involvement in any process with Raytheon to be purely as an analyst - as far as they are concerned in any case."

"All sounds very cloak and dagger," Paul smiled.

"It will involve some overseas travel as well - will your wife be up for that?"

"Guess so. She's always wanted to see my old haunts."

As if she had been waiting for the cue, at that exact moment Clara appeared at the patio doors to announce that lunch was ready. Conversation at table was about anything but politics or work and a couple of hours later Sam and Clara waved Leanne and Paul off as they headed back to McConnell to spend the rest of the day with their families.

As they turned south on Rock, Leanne asked the obvious question: "so do I have to guess, or are you going to tell me?"

Paul smiled at her: "if I do, I may have to shoot you."

"I bet Felix Leitner never said that to his wife."

"No he didn't - but only because he was gay."

Leanne cuffed Paul lightly around his ear and with a smile changed tack to speculate whether Matt would have run his grandfather to a standstill again. She had no idea of Paul's ambitions within the Bureau. Somehow the ideal opportunity to even drop hints had never arisen and, to a certain extent, Paul had doubted that his application would be progressed at all, especially as he had continually shown his abilities as an analyst, involving being asked regularly to unravel much more convoluted problems. His mind would occasionally stray in that direction whilst laying awake on a stuffy night, but always evaded the problem by assuring himself that there was no reason to worry Leanne over something that may never come to pass. With the day's unexpected developments, he realised that he would need to summon-up the courage to tell her, and soon, because history was already on the move.

That night, they set another destiny in motion. Matt would soon have a little sister to share the spotlight with.

Thirty-Eight

It was almost a year later, on a typical grey windswept February day, that an American Airlines 747-200 touched down at Heathrow. In Business Class, Paul Kleberson was telling his young son Matt all about the uncertainties of the British weather, while his wife Leanne looked after their little daughter Lucy, who had slept virtually all of the way through her very first flight, taken at the age of just three months. Barely twelve months after being promoted, Agent Paul Kleberson had been assigned to his first overseas posting attached to the US Embassy in Grosvenor Square, London. These were familiar surroundings for Paul; for the rest of the family, this would be their first visit to England.

Paul's original promotion had evolved from the forecast purchase by Raytheon Aircraft Co, of the Corporate Jets Division of British Aerospace, based in Hatfield, barely an hour's drive south of his old family home in Godmanchester. The cause of the overseas posting had been the decision by Raytheon to move the entire British operation to Wichita, together with nearly two hundred of their key British employees. This decision had evolved much faster than had been expected, hence it would be necessary for the Wichita Agency to obtain as much background information on this large band of immigrant workers as quickly as possible.

The first week was spent in the Embassy itself, during which time rented accommodation was secured in Welwyn Garden City, a few miles up the A1 from Hatfield. Having moved his family to Welwyn, Paul took up his cover position as a representative from Raytheon's HR department in Wichita. Leanne, with the help of the wives of several of Raytheon's American staff already living in the area, settled down to being a housewife in a foreign land.

The weekends provided plenty of diversions, either through visits from old friends like Annie and RP, or exploring Paul's old haunts. Just as they were all becoming adapted to their new routine, some worrying news arrived from Wichita. Leanne's father had not been in the best of health for a number of months, but just weeks after their move Leanne was told that he had been admitted to the base hospital for tests. Paul's regular phone calls to his mother revealed that there was a great deal of concern, so arrangements were hastily made for Leanne and the two children to fly back to Wichita, where they would stay at the Henderson home on the base.

Despite the regular transatlantic calls each evening to maintain contact with the three people he loved dearest in the world, and the assurances coming from the Midwest that their visit would only last a couple of weeks until the results of all the tests were available, deep down Paul felt a dread that this was just the tip of an iceberg lurking in the distance, on which his ship of life might founder. Everyone's worst fears were confirmed during those two weeks, when the diagnosis of advanced liver cancer, accompanied by a prognosis amounting to a matter of weeks, was relayed during the latter part of one daily phone conversation.

The first part of each call was spent with Matt who was beginning to talk more coherently and, with Leanne's gentle prompting, conversations were possible lasting several minutes before the butterfly mind of a two-year-old took over and allowed itself to be distracted away from the phone. Leanne's sympathetic assertion that she could not possibly leave Wichita for the foreseeable future was accepted without question by Paul. His offer to fly back was softly deferred until it became 'necessary'. The implications in that word hit home more than anything, possessing a finality in this context for the one situation that would create the inevitable domino-effect. But those things are not discussed at such times; everything is placed on hold awaiting nature's decisive act.

As the weeks passed, the regular phone call took on a major significance in the conduct of the day. Although they actually grew longer over time, the calls felt continually shorter, the silent void that greeted the final click at the other end of the line, followed by the monotone of the dialling tone replacing it, growing darker and deeper. Sometimes Paul would just sit listening to the tone, wondering how long it would remain, before it too gave up on him. He was not aware of the tearful hours Leanne spent in the lonely darkness of her old bedroom every night of her exile from him.

Although he concealed it well, Paul took the longer-term separation hard. Without the proximity of his growing family, he threw himself into his work as a form of distraction. Excursions dissolved to be replaced by piles of files taken home for the weekend, a convenient excuse for declining invitations because he "had a mountain of paperwork", most of which had been cajoled from work colleagues, his own workload being so much up to date that, had his employer been a private company, he could possibly have been considered to have worked his way into redundancy.

It was when he found himself sitting in his lounge late one night, that he realised he simply had to go back to Wichita, even if for just a short visit. The realisation came because he found himself blankly staring at a late-night Open University programme that he had no recollection of selecting, apart from it being the only option available besides going to bed for another sleepless night. What he did recollect was his constant and eternal morbid desire to hear the news of his father-in-law's death. He couldn't believe that he was even entertaining the thought; he knew this man, this was his wife's father for goodness sake!

How could he possibly have such feelings for someone who had not only been so kind to him during their, all-too-brief, family association, but who was also tenaciously clinging to every last second of his existence. It was at that point that he realised that he actually felt guilty that he had not returned to see Nate for a final time. This was a decision that, although the responsibility for making it had been taken from him, he needed to make for himself to recover some degree of humanity. He resolved to file a request the following morning to be allowed compassionate leave. He then went to bed to be instantly overwhelmed by the deepest night's sleep he had experienced in weeks.

The following morning was a fine English spring day. The sun shone, but not enough to remove that early morning nip in the air. The train journey to London went quickly, as did the punctuated tube journey from King's Cross to Bond Street. He had no appointment with his ultimate boss, Lance Wilkins, but knew that he would be seen relatively quickly when he revealed the problem to his line management.

Known to everyone as Lanny, Wilkins had been the head of the London Field Office for seven years. He had led the FBI part of the Lockerbie Bombing enquiry that had resulted in the identification as the culprits, and subsequent indictment, of two Libyan Intelligence Officers. However, their extradition from Libya was proving nigh-impossible, and rumours within the Bureau suggested that Wilkins' expected promotion for the success of the investigation was on hold until they could be brought to trial. Not renowned as a man of great humour, this had done little to improve Wilkins' general demeanour.

It had not been a good morning thus far and the last thing Wilkins needed right at that point was some bleeding-heart story from one of his Agents, accompanying a request for compassionate leave. The Field Office was already undermanned, Wilkins' constant requests for additional resource being just as constantly declined. That morning, just days before it was due to open, intelligence had been received that there was a potential major terrorist threat to attack the first train service through the new Channel Tunnel, on board of which would be a substantial number of American dignitaries and diplomats. As a consequence, the outcome of the meeting was already decided before Paul entered the room.

Wilkins tried, unsuccessfully, to feign sympathy so instead delivered the bad news as humanely as any man might have managed who also had an impending career-ending disaster occupying his mind - he couldn't spare anybody at that point in time, regardless of how up-to-date their workload was, or how pressing the personal circumstances. When Paul emerged once more, totally dejected, into the daylight, the clouds had rolled in and a light drizzle was descending. By the time his walk back to Bond Street was completed, the streets were soaked by steady rain.

The mainline journey back from King's Cross was equally depressing, the raindrops streaking the train window as it thundered through the bleak grey landscape of Hertfordshire on a wet day. During that journey he had made the decision - he was going to resign from the FBI. He had not gone through all of his education, plus all of that training, to end up thousands of miles from his family, combing through security clearance papers looking for reasons to deny visas to foreigners that were more friendly towards his country than some of its own citizens.

When he returned to his temporary home in Welwyn, the light on the answering machine was flashing. His heart dropped a beat; only one person would likely be leaving a message for him, and it was way too early for the daily call. He pressed the play button: "you have one message, Wednesday eleven fourteen a.m." He did a quick mental calculation: that was around five a.m. Wichita time.

He didn't need to hear the message, but the machine broadcast it anyway. His wife's voice filled the room, barely able to contain the emotion breaking through it: "Paul, honey, I know you aren't there right now, but please ring me as soon as you get this. There's some bad news, I'm ..."

There was a silence that lasted maybe twenty seconds after the voice faded away, before the phone hung-up at the other end - a recording of quiet grief. Destiny had once again taken a firm hold of the situation.

Thirty-Nine

The immediate phone call to Human Resources at the Embassy had secured a seat on the last flight out of Heathrow that night. The new circumstances had overridden any decision-making precedent set by the Head of the Field Office. Wilkins would have to live with the consequences of a decision that extended, only for a matter of hours, an Agent's secondment to his Field Office, at the expense of the Bureau losing the abilities of that Agent permanently. Paul had thrown what he could into a carry-on bag, in case the journey across London produced any delay that would jeopardise his being able to make the flight. Everything else would follow, courtesy of the Embassy concierge service, after the Bureau received his resignation letter.

The flight, to New York, was on time, arriving just after ten p.m. local time. He cat-napped the eight-hour lay-over before he could board the first flight in the morning out of JFK to Chicago, where the connection got him into Mid-

Continent just before ten. Walter was waiting for him at the foot of the arrivals ramp; their embrace lasted way longer than his father had anticipated it might, confirming how much his son had missed his family.

The welcome from Paul's own son when, half an hour later, the door of his parents' house opened, was equally emphatic. In fact it would be another half an hour before Matt's arms could be prised from around his father's neck; Paul needed no more demonstrative a sign that his decision the previous day had been the correct one. The disclosure of that news to Leanne would have to wait at least another twelve hours until they were finally alone in her old bedroom, there being all manner of arrangements still to be made for the funeral service.

That night, along with the two children, they had her parents' house to themselves, as Leanne's mother was occupying Paul's old room at his parents' house, having been staying with the Klebersons since her husband had been admitted to the Base Hospital for the final time a couple of weeks earlier. Leanne's mother had not coped with the illness well and could not yet face returning to their marital home without Nate.

Paul and Leanne barely slept that night, they just lay clamped tightly to each other, the relief of their being reunited again overcoming any other emotions or instincts. They finally succumbed to their desires in the early morning light, shortly after Paul had revealed his decision regarding his immediate future. In the resultant quietude both declared their resolve to never subject their family to such pain again.

Colonel Nate Henderson was buried, with full military honours, two days later at Calvary Cemetery. Paul's announcement was made to the extended family that evening, after all the guests had dispersed. His parents also had an announcement to make - that Leanne's mother would be moving-in with them for the foreseeable future. They explained that she would have to give-up the house on the base once she had made the necessary arrangements for her future, which in the long-term may take her back to her native California. In the meantime, with all of her friends there on the base, or in Wichita itself, this seemed the best arrangement to cushion the blow of having to uproot her life so swiftly after losing her husband.

There were no dissentions from the extended family and it was agreed that Paul's family could use her house for a few weeks while they found a new home of their own off-base, at the same time helping Leanne's mother to clear it ready for the handover; effectively, they would end-up doing all of that work for her.

With just a day or two remaining before he was expected to return to England, Paul made the call to Sam Schneider and they arranged to meet for lunch. Sam knew of the reason for Paul's sudden visit, having kept tabs on the situation through Clara, his wife, keeping regular contact with Leanne since her return. He assumed that this would just be an opportunity for the two friends to get together while Paul was home, so was somewhat dumbstruck at being presented with the letter of resignation accompanied by the request to submit it through the internal system so that there was no delay in it being actioned.

Being the professional Agent that he was, Sam did his best to mount some form of rearguard action to prevent Paul taking so irrevocable a step, but he quickly recognised the futility of this. In fact, Sam had some substantial sympathy for the situation such a close friend had encountered, quietly wishing that more agents could be capable of maintaining their family life at the forefront of their responsibilities.

He was more concerned when the answer he received to his enquiry about what Paul intended to do next was that he "had no idea". It was an entirely rational decision to exchange one career for another for the reasons prevailing, but it was an entirely different matter to abandon a well-paid job and embark on the next phase of life with no prospects whatsoever, with no home and accompanied by a wife and two very young children. All Sam could do, in the short term, was to conclude their get-together with an offer of providing any assistance necessary and an insistence that they should "keep in touch."

In reality, Sam needn't have been so concerned, as his friend was a frugal man. Paul had not impinged much on the savings he had assembled at university; in fact, he had added to them by not wasting the substantial overseas allowances he had received even in the short time he had been in England. He had already calculated that the family could live reasonably well, at American standards of living, for around a year if necessary before any financial strictions became imperative. He also had the confidence that he would need nowhere near that amount of time to find something suitable in academia, even though it would likely involve a move East.

It did not take long to secure a short-term lease on a small duplex in North Derby. Leanne wanted to remain as close as possible to the base and, thus, the grandparents, but had not been too happy at their previous apartment in South Wichita. The house in North Derby was just two miles south of the base and in a far better neighbourhood than East Harry had been. They also inherited Nate's two-year-old Ford Windstar; he had changed his previous sedan for a minivan when the first grandchild had arrived, in anticipation of future extended family outings.

Over the next month they cleared Leanne's parents' home so that it could be handed-over to her father's successor. Some of the furniture went into the same store that Paul and Leanne had rented to house their larger possessions while they were in England, possessions that were once again all restored to them in their new home. The remainder, those pieces that Leanne's mother had declared as surplus to her future requirements, filled some of the many gaps in their new, larger home. The arrival of their remaining chattels from England, temporarily-abandoned by Paul in the rented house in Welwyn, completed the re-establishment of the young family in the Midwest. All that remained was for Paul to find a new appointment.

That was the point at which another luncheon invitation was received from the Schneiders.

take-out

Forty

Tom Cochrane's day had not been great. Although his instant and automatic promotion to local network anchor was a boost career-wise, his first report in that position, on the death of his former boss Marjoree Rolles, was not the one he would have wanted to celebrate with. After all, her impending move to the main network would most probably have taken him to that higher level with her. In future, he would have to earn that achievement on his own merits, something about which his mind had its own doubts.

He headed for The Avenue Bar in search of both alcohol and company. The Avenue was the closest thing to a gay bar to be found in a conservative Midwest town like Wichita. Never overtly advertising the fact, these bars existed all across the Midwest and were well known within the gay community as safe havens for visitors and travellers. Conversely to what may be imagined, they tended to exist in the more fashionable parts of towns and cities, away from the innate prejudice of those controlling the seedier areas. The local community knew itself well, but with the rise in international commerce being attracted to Wichita, visitors were frequent and plentiful, so fresh action was generally available, particularly to those with a high profile locally. Tom Cochrane had the added advantage of being able to cover his regular patronage by calling it research into the sexuality of newcomers for a book that he was writing.

Today, however, was not an easy day to be anonymous, with his face filling the various TV screens around the bar, and regular shots of his favourite Jim Beam appearing in front of his stool at the bar, often accompanied by a slap on the back and a "way to go Tommy", plus the occasional whispered adjunct: "maybe see ya later huh?"

But he wasn't after local action, he wanted someone new, a complete escape from the whirlwind of the day. Even so, when the blonde guy in his early-thirties slipped quietly onto the stool beside him, Cochrane barely noticed, distracted by his main broadcast from outside of the building where Marjoree Rolles' lived and died, being replayed for the umpteenth time that day.

"You look younger in the flesh," came the remark from beside him. The voice was soft and friendly. Cochrane turned his glance to see a handsome unblemished face with the most startling blue eyes that were smiling warmly behind rimless rectangular glasses. The hair above them was wispy and fair, short with a Tin-Tin-style quiff. The guy's figure was slight, but strong and the pecs were visible under the white tee-shirt that fitted closely at the shoulders, but loosely at the waist, suggesting a taut, well-toned body.

"The lighting's better in here," replied Cochrane, with the easy glibness of the media professional, unhindered as yet by the half-bottle or so of whiskey already consumed.

"What's your poison?"

"Jim Beam."

"Let me get you one."

"That'll be fine, thank you."

The man attracted the barman's attention: "a double JB for our media star here, and a tonic water, ice and lemon for me please."

"Aren't you joining me?" enquired Cochrane.

"I hope to be, but I don't drink alcohol in bars because it has somewhat calamitous effects on me. I'm what's known as a cheap date back home, one glass of Chardonnay and I'm anyone's."

"And where's home?"

"Little Rock."

"Phew, that must be tough for you."

"Not really. I travel a lot, so it's quite easy not to indulge while I'm home."

"So, is it business that brings you to Wichita?"

"Did I say I travelled on business?"

"I just assumed ... " Cochrane was cut-off in mid-sentence.

"You know what they say about that word, don't you? It's a word that so easily can make an ass out of u and me. Oh dear, there I go again, bringing asses into the conversation already."

Cochrane couldn't believe his luck. This was just what he was looking for and he hadn't even had to move from his favourite stool. Unfortunately, due to his desire to always be in the limelight, that stool was right in full view of the rest of the bar. Leaving with such an obvious stranger would be difficult to achieve without attracting a lot of attention, especially as he wasn't confident that his legs were still fully-operational.

"You staying in town?" he enquired.

"At the Hyatt just across the river."

"You eaten?"

"Not yet, any suggestions?"

"Tell you what, I've got to go back to the studio for a meeting at eight - won't take too long. Why don't I pick you up at nine, then we can check-out one of the places over at Bradley Fair?"

"Do they do take-out? I love Chinese."

"Consider it done, see you at nine in front of the Hyatt."

Cochrane spun off the stool and for a split-second the JB plummeted to his legs. He thought he was going to fall in a spectacular and very public manner, but his brain quickly brought him to his senses, although not before a wag at the other end of the bar had spotted the momentary wobble: "hey Cochrane - take it steady now, we wanna see ya on the nine o'clock news tellin' the story, not bein' one!"

The bar erupted into laughter, all but the blonde guy who pretended, very convincingly, not to notice. Cochrane instinctively raised a digit in the direction of the voice, then walked straight as a die out of the bar.

Forty-One

Just after nine, Tom Cochrane pulled his GMC truck off of South Main onto the road leading along the side of the Library to the front of the Hyatt Regency. The smell of sweet and sour sauce wafted through the cab; the White Zinfandel was already on chill in his apartment near Bradley Fair, less than fifteen minutes away.

He could see his date perched on the wall in front of the hotel, looking across the car park towards the Boathouse, home of the Kansas Sports Hall of Fame, with the Jayhawk, a retired US Americas Cup yacht, perched proudly outside. As he coasted to a stop, he dropped the passenger window and called-out: "excuse me, are you the gentleman that ordered take-out?"

A completely disengaging smile lit-up the face of the man waiting on the wall. As he jumped down and headed across the sidewalk, Cochrane took-in the full vision of his lithe and slender body. The hips were well-defined, the waist narrow, just how he liked his wide-receivers, as he called them, and tonight he was definitely looking for a touchdown. He could feel an erection hardening already and, as the door opened, he was grateful that their destination was not far away.

The blonde swung himself into the passenger seat and pulled the door shut. Cochrane caught a faint whiff of Calvin Klein before the sweet and sour sauce overpowered it again. As they swung-out around the car park, the blonde said: "let me guess - Chow Mein, Sweet and Sour Prawns? Oh I hope so! I just love sucking on prawns, especially king-size ones. And is that Bamboo Shoots and Water Chestnuts as well?"

"You're obviously well-versed in take-out."

"Oh yes, nothing better than take-out!"

The voice was still soft, if slightly effeminate, although not offensively so. More like a pretentious waiter in a California steakhouse, describing the life history of the animal you were about to eat and the 'erbs' that would accompany it to its final destiny.

"I didn't catch your name," said Cochrane.

"I didn't toss it," came the unexpected reply, sharp as a razor.

Cochrane looked at his passenger quizzically, but all he saw was the soft, friendly smile he had encountered earlier in the bar.

"I'm Sean", the blonde offered, extending a small, beautifully manicured hand. Cochrane grasped the hand gently.

"Pleased to meet you Sean, I'm Tom."

"I know", replied Sean, "Tom Cochrane, future anchorman for one of the main networks."

"Hey, steady on Sean, I only got KNKW today, and in somewhat dubious circumstances."

"Oh I don't know Tom. Could be destiny you know. Don't you believe in destiny?"

"Guess I hadn't thought of it that way, but I s'pose I did come lookin' for somethin' tonight, and I seem to have found it."

"There you go then."

"Do you have a second name Sean?"

"I do, but don't you think second names are inappropriate for first dates?"

"Guess I hadn't thought of that either. OK, if that's how you want it."

"That's how I want it Tom, which I guess means that I now have to give you the choice of how you want it as well, doesn't it?"

Cochrane's pants tightened noticeably as the quarterback mentally reviewed the playlist for the game ahead.

Forty-Two

The GMC eased into an empty parking slot near the rear service door to the apartment block. He always used this entrance when entertaining, as it was darker and quieter than the main entrance at the front. They entered the lift and Cochrane pressed the fourth-floor button.

As the door closed, Sean pulled Cochrane round with his left hand behind his neck and planted a full kiss on him, simultaneously groping his groin with his right hand. Sean pulled back and exclaimed: "my, my, Mr Mediaman, we do have our telephoto lens with us tonight, don't we." He then resumed the kiss, plunging his tongue deep into Cochrane's mouth. Cochrane was completely spellbound, so much so that he did not notice the slight prick in the back of his neck.

They tumbled through the front door of the apartment. Both had hands everywhere. Sean broke free and took the take-out bag from Cochrane's hand, placing it on the dining table which was already set for an intimate dinner. He went back to Cochrane, who was beginning to stagger, and helped him back onto the couch; Cochrane was giggling drunkenly.

Sean laid Cochrane's head back onto a cushion, pulled his legs up onto the couch, then sat astride him and began to undo his belt and flies. Cochrane tried to get hold of Sean's belt buckle, but found his arms getting heavy and unwilling to move. He was thinking that he couldn't remember JB ever causing that effect before, as he felt Sean burst inside his boxers and pull-out his dick, which had become, in the words of his favourite author Joseph Wambough, a diamond-cutter.

Cochrane's mind was racing between his dick and his arms, one of which was obviously functioning, while the others were not. Sean put his hand in his pocket and pulled-out a condom then, while holding the diamond-cutter triumphantly in the other hand, put the outer package between his teeth and opened it seductively. He then pinched the teat of the condom between his teeth and lowered his head placing the open end of the condom on Cochrane's dick and deftly unrolled it downwards with his lips, letting go with his hand as he went.

Cochrane was in ecstasy and agony all at once. His arms wouldn't move so he tried his legs, with the same result. Were they anchored by Sean's weight, or were they frozen too? Was he really feeling Sean's mouth, or was his mind telling him what he should be feeling as he watched Sean's head bob and weave in his lap? At that point Sean suddenly sat up and an evil grin burst across his face: "so Mr Cochrane, how you feelin'? Confused I bet!"

He stood-up and began to sexily unbuckle his belt. Once it was undone, he let his trousers drop to the floor - he was commando. And there before Cochrane's eyes stood one of the most magnificent dicks he had ever seen.

"Impressive huh?" said Sean, legs astride and hands on hips, "shall we see how you compare?"

Sean opened Cochrane's legs and knelt down between them, laying his dick neatly alongside Cochrane's. It was not even erect, yet clearly larger in all aspects. "My God!" Cochrane thought, "I'm led here with this Adonis and I can't move. What's the matter with me?"

"I guess you're wondering why you can't take advantage of this glorious situation, huh?" said Sean, his eyes flashing evilly in conjunction with the smile. "It's quite simple, you're drugged. But not with any old drug, oh no - you've been administered with Curare, a little-known poison from the rainforests of Brazil. It has interesting qualities, as you are already discovering. It paralyses most muscles in your body, whilst maintaining you in a conscious state so that your brain automatically sends adrenaline and blood to your vital organs to ensure that they continue to work at full capacity. One of those organs is this little chappie here."

He once again raised Cochrane's dick with his hand so that its owner could see it in its full glory. "As long as I keep stimulating you appropriately, your brain will ensure that you stay erect and I can have some fun with you. Then when I've had enough, I will take this little beauty and nick your dorsal artery."

Sean produced a small Swiss Army knife as if from nowhere, its blade glinting as the apartment lighting caught it. He rested it on the bridge of Cochrane's nose so that he got a good view of the fully-honed blade: "you'll bleed to death very quickly, as your brain is currently sending as much blood as possible down here to assist you in your desires. When it senses the sudden drop in blood pressure, it will then tell your heart to pump faster to maintain your prowess. You'll bleed-out very quickly, thirty seconds tops - very messy I'm afraid."

Cochrane tried to scream out for help, but nothing happened. Sean continued: "yes, and calling-out is also impossible, as you've just discovered, because you are now terrified and your vocal chords have been disabled by your brain in a similar manner to when you have the night fears. You're mine to do with as I wish, until I grow tired of the sport. Then Mr Cochrane, I shall kill you - quickly and mercifully as you will be conscious throughout."

Then slowly and seductively, Sean began to undress Cochrane. As he did so, he would occasionally lower his head and swallow Cochrane's dick, always making sure that Cochrane could see his every move. Cochrane was desperately trying to think what he could do to lower his libido, but his helplessness and the whole sexual experience meant he remained genitally in firm anticipation.

Sean seemed immensely strong. Cochrane weighed two hundred pounds; Sean seemed to be much lighter, yet he lifted Cochrane's body with ease to any position he wanted, all the time giving a running commentary on what he was doing, and about to do, in a low seductive voice. Cochrane's mind was beginning to blow as it processed the cocktail of ecstasy and terror it was being fed.

Then Sean was stood over him again, grinning sadistically as he said: "and now, time for me to have my way with you. That doesn't happen often does it Tom, you preferring to be the dominant partner in any liaison. While you're figuring out how I would know that, prepare yourself for a real treat - you've seen the goods, now enjoy the service."

With these words he lifted Cochrane's limp frame and turned him over. Cochrane could no longer discern what position his body was in, he could feel nothing in his torso or any of his limbs, yet all of his senses seemed alive, except for touch, which only seemed to work in his penis. His eyes told him that he was face down in his sofa cushions, then he began to discern his head moving gently back and forth. He suddenly realised that Sean must be inside him, but he could not feel it. He tried to close his eyes, but he couldn't.

'Dear God!', he thought, 'I have no choice but to stay awake for this,' and as his mind raced trying to imagine what he should be feeling, it was also evaluating how long he would be allowed to live once the inevitable climax was reached.

His eyes relayed to him that his head was moving faster and further on each stroke. The sex must be rough, which was how he liked it when his normal preference of roles were occasionally reversed, but that thought gave him little comfort as there was no enjoyment in this scenario, not even the constant pulsing through his own genitals. All of a sudden, the movement slowed and became irregularly jerky, then stopped completely. Cochrane felt himself ejaculate, again and again, then the only remaining sensation in his body seemed to gradually fade away.

He lay there completely still for what seemed an eternity, until he heard a soft voice in his ear: "hey Tom, you were good you know. Most people in your position just lay back and take it, but we had a real dance there!" Cochrane was aware of his head lifting from the cushions; as it rose he could see, in front of one eye, that Sean was dangling a condom - a very full condom! "Ya know", said Sean, "that was so good, I may keep you for some dessert."

Sean laid Cochrane's head sideways on the couch, so that he could see the dining table. Cochrane could see that Sean was dressed again and was laying-out dinner. Two plates were filled with the take-out, the slight heat haze above them confirming that the food had been quickly microwaved. He also noticed that Sean had donned surgical gloves.

Sean sat down at the table and began to eat. He poured some Zinfandel into a wine glass, then took out a straw and drank through it. "This is delicious you know, shame you can't join me. Hey, would you like some wine?" Sean poured a small drop of Zinfandel into a second wine glass, then carried it over to the couch. He lifted Cochrane's head and placed the glass to his lips, moistening them with the wine and pressing them firmly against the glass. He took Cochrane's right hand and gripped the glass in it, then removed the glass, placing Cochrane's head back on its side on the cushion so he could view the table again.

Sean sat down again and devoured his food. After a few minutes, he looked across at Cochrane again and said: "you know, a roll in the hay sure creates a hearty appetite," at which point he changed his empty plate for the full one and tucked into its contents. When he had eaten enough, he then went through a similar process with Cochrane as he had with the glass, but this time with the other set of cutlery.

He then arranged the table to look like two people had eaten there. Having done that he disappeared from Cochrane's view.

Forty-Three

After what felt like an age to the paralysed Cochrane, once again a soft voice emerged close to his ear: "time for dessert now Tom."

Cochrane was aware of his body being lifted from the sofa, then suddenly he was in a fireman's lift, looking down at Sean's buttocks. He couldn't help notice how perfect those buttocks looked, which only made him imagine what might have been, further adding to his confused feelings. He then realised that Sean must be naked again, but the skin seemed fuzzy, or was it his own sight blurring?

They were moving out of the lounge, then their direction of travel became apparent - he was being carried backwards in the direction of his bedroom. As the facts dawned on him, so the horror of their implications filled his mind. Hilary was found in her bedroom, he knew that from what he had gleaned from that shocked rookie cop at the scene. He had not been so successful at Marjoree's place, but what he had pieced-together indicated a similar scenario. Cochrane had been told he was going to die once enough fun had been had; he dreaded that his visitor had finally become tired of the game.

After passing through the door, however, they swung left into the en suite and he was turned to face his shower cubicle. The door was wide open and from each corner of the aperture makeshift ropes of twisted towelling were fastened. Suddenly he was aware of his body being lifted high as his head flopped backwards and to one side, so that all he could see was the ceiling. Sean must be lifting him, but he wondered how someone weighing no more than two-thirds his weight was doing so with such apparent ease.

Again, after what seemed like minutes, but was probably just a few seconds, his body was lowered until he was facing into the cubicle. His head flopped forwards to be looking down his naked body towards the shower basin, which he seemed to be hovering above. His vision was beginning to distort and the real world seemed to be receding from him.

His head was lifted once more and there in front of him was Sean, who appeared to be naked, but he could have been wearing something. The image seemed to move, almost vibrate, in front of him, but that sadistic smile was unmistakeable. The lips were moving, meaning he was talking, but the voice seemed distant: "still don't remember me do you Tom?" is what Cochrane thought he heard, but he wasn't sure. His head was lowered again onto his chest; he could see a leg outstretched to one side, but no arm. Then that voice again: "ah well, too late now anyways, because it's time for the final cleansing."

The shower was running, he could see the flowing water swirling down the drain. There were gloved hands applying soap and the suds were stubbornly resisting the combined water flow and pull of gravity around the drain. There were black clumps of something falling in the basin and flowing towards the drain. Hair; his hair - he was being shaved! But not just his head, his whole body was being shaved. More and more of it, then less and less until the water was clear again, but still swirling.

His head lifted again; once more there was his guest, naked before him, but distorted. Sean's body seemed to look wrong, bulging in places that it shouldn't; Cochrane's vision had begun to play tricks on him. But that smile was unmistakeable, even through the morphing haze, as was the knife - the one he had seen earlier that Sean was once again holding in front of his nose.

Sean was talking again, but Cochrane's hearing was as distorted as his vision, fading in and out. He thought he heard: "I'll put it in your mouth ..."

'What was he saying?' Cochrane thought, 'what's he going to put - the knife?'

"... think I'll ... cut ... off ... suck on that ..."

'What's that? What's going to be cut off?'

Cochrane's head was slowly lowered, the knife staying in the same position relative to his nose. He was as fully-focussed as his wavering vision would allow, but just on the knife. The hand grasping it moved away from his nose, which was facing straight down his body again. Slowly away, downwards, lightly touching his newly shaven chest. Downwards it went until it slowly circled his groin and then disappeared out of sight, only to reappear crossways, under his dick, supporting it at the body end as it was being held straight-out by the other gloved hand.

Cochrane's mind raced as the adrenaline rush of the realisation of his situation momentarily returned him to a more conscious state. *'Oh my God! He's going to cut it off. That's what's going into my mouth! I'm going to die like some bizarre stuffed pig at a banquet. Oh my ..."*

At that point of realisation, his head suddenly moved up and backwards, as though jerked hard back and he was staring at the ceiling. He saw the bright white of the bathroom light that momentarily blinded him, before fading as he quickly lost consciousness.

His eyes would witness no more of this life.

Forty-Four

Sean spent around twenty minutes washing the shower area, then cleaning and drying all of the surfaces, both on and around his spread-eagled victim. He then released the ties, lifting the body gently before carrying it into the bedroom, where he laid it out in the centre of the double-king bed. He spent another few minutes carefully arranging the body as he wanted it.

Leaving the bedroom, he took caustic soda from the utility cupboard and poured it down the shower drain, then flushed everything through again, drying everything once more using Cochrane's towelling from his linen cupboard. Finally, back to the utility where all the towelling was put into the washing machine, the longest and hottest programme selected and the machine set running.

When he had finished he went back into the bedroom to admire his handiwork for the final time. The muscles of the face on the pillow showed no emotion, having been paralysed long before the coup de gras; somehow the eyes conveyed the final terror somewhat better on a man than a woman - that satisfied Sean.

He then left the bedroom and stood on the open body belt that he had laid-out neatly on the tiled floor of the hallway. Slowly and carefully, he peeled-off the one-piece body stocking he had worn throughout his 'ceremony'. He did so to ensure that any residue adhering to it fell on the body belt, nowhere else. Then the body stocking was carefully folded and pushed into one pocket of the belt together with one of the gloves. The tee-shirt he had been wearing earlier, with the rimless glasses folded inside it, went into the opposite pocket. From the other two pockets in the belt he produced a different tee shirt and a black wig. He put them on, together with the jeans and trainers he had worn on the way in, both of which were nondescript and unbranded, the sort you bought for a few bucks at any local five-and-dime. He then closed-up the body belt and clipped it around his chest, under the tee-shirt.

His appearance was different to what it had been when he came into the building, although equally as anonymous. If there was CCTV in the building, which he was confident there wasn't, then it would have shown that Tom entered the building with a blonde male companion around nine-fifteen, but neither had left. Although various people had entered or left the building throughout the rest of the evening, including this person, he and Tom had passed nobody coming in and doubtless there would be nobody to pass going out either. Even if there was, they would not be able to identify this person as Tom's previous companion.

A quick check of the revised identity in the hall mirror, then he headed for the door, where he listened to check that there was no discernable movement in the corridor outside. His one remaining glove gripped the door handle and, after a quick visual check of the empty corridor, the stranger slipped out of the apartment, down the hall and, via the service stairs, out of the building into the balmy night air.

Nobody had been encountered; once again the triptych had been completed within the self-imposed twenty-four-hour deadline, without raising the slightest alarm. Selection of the final victim could be deliberated over the next two days, while the local police department ran around like headless chickens trying to figure out who it might be.

Forty-Five

Scott Adams was driving along East Central towards City Hall with some trepidation. His original assignment had been to cover a presentation at the Raytheon plant out on Webb, where they were launching a new version of their popular XP series of business jets.

When he got the call from Station Chief Max Huberstein, most of the information he really needed had already been compiled and he was preparing to select the sound bites from the buffet breakfast that he would use to pad-out the three-minute segment he had been allocated in the six o'clock news. The call was short - new station superstar Cochrane had not reported-in, so Adams would be covering Chief Stanton's ten a.m. press conference at City Hall.

The reason that he was apprehensive was that the last time he had been assigned to a major press conference, he had frozen. He had everything prepared, but the questions just wouldn't come out right. He had been swamped by the other stations, but his engineer, the then new-boy Cochrane, had papered-over the cracks by filming the responses to the other hacks' questions, then cleverly editing in some footage he did with Scott after the conference disbanded.

Cochrane had saved his bacon; but it didn't take long before, courtesy of his saviour, everybody who was important enough at the station knew about it, including Marjoree Rolles. Always the one with an eye to the main chance, she took Cochrane on-board and started her rise towards station anchor, then to the brink of going national. Yet here he was, not only heading for another high-profile conference, but also one giving details on Marjoree's murder.

Tom Cochrane should have been there, as he was outside of her apartment building the previous day. He had no-showed before, but normally that was because he was at home, flaked-out on his bed after a bender session, which he could be roused from by a phone call. This time he was nowhere to be found; there was no answer on any of his phones and his truck wasn't parked out front of his apartment. He had literally vanished.

'*Of course*', Scott thought, '*he could just as easily breeze-in to the conference at the last minute and take over.*' He half-hoped that Cochrane would do just that but, if he didn't, Adams was the station's man and, as his was the local station with the most clout, he would get the first question and follow-up. He had only had the twenty-minute drive from the plant to put those together in his mind, a mind distracted by the knowledge that not only were his arch-rivals locally there, but also most of the national networks.

Hilary Nicholson's murder had already made the main network news programmes. Once this had been compounded by the second murder of her close friend, and one of their own, it had become the top story of the day. It was the chance of a lifetime, being seen by every network manager and, if he got it right, who knew where it could lead? But if he screwed-up, he could expect to cover a never-ending round of Women's Institutes and Rotary dinners for the rest of his career. He 'mustn't screw-up' he knew that; his boss's final words to him on the phone not half an hour earlier had been precisely those.

Adams had to park half a block away, as the City Hall car park was a tangle of network satellite trucks and cables. As he rushed into the conference room, it was clear that all of the prime positions had gone, but he quickly found Cochrane's engineer of less than a day, Dave Garton.

"Sorry Dave, only got the call half an hour ago. What's with Cochrane?"

"No-one knows," Garton replied, as bemused himself as to why his new 'boss' wasn't there. "It's too late to do any set-ups Scott, this place is a zoo - we'll do them after, OK?"

"Fine with me Dave."

"Hey Scottie, where's the new superstar then?" It was the voice of Pete Christensen from KNSZ, their main local rivals.

Scott just shrugged, but the rest of the jackals pounced as soon as they knew what was happening: "too much pressure for him yesterday" - "yeah, no stamina!" - "he's still probably with some piece of ass he picked-up last night," all accompanied by lewd gestures and guffaws of laughter.

"Ignore 'em Scott," Garton urged, "get over and tell Lieutenant Morley where we are. Make sure he knows where the first question's coming from - you've only got five minutes to showtime."

Adams pushed through the scrum to the side of the podium where Morley, Stanton's right hand, was deep in conversation with Paul Kleberson. It was not a particularly polite conversation, as Kleberson was doing everything he could to get under Morley's skin. Adams interrupted: "excuse me, Lieutenant Morley."

"What?" snapped Morley, as he turned to see the unfamiliar face before him, "who the hell are you?"

"Scott Adams, KNKW, I'm filling-in for Tom Cochrane."

"What?" Morley snapped again, looking over Adams' head and quickly scanning the room for Cochrane's familiar features. "Where the fuck is he?"

Morley was more antagonised than usual and Kleberson couldn't resist a swift verbal jab to the ribs: "what's the matter Morley, Granma's poodle run off with the neighbour's Jack Russell?"

"Fuck off onto that podium Kleberson and make damned sure you don't upstage the Chief, otherwise I'm bringing you down - you got that!"

"Oooh," Kleberson feigned fear, biting his knuckles mockingly, "what big teeth you have Granma." He turned to the reporter: "nice to meet you Mr Adams." He smiled, shook Adams' hand and waited.

Morley rounded on Adams: "so where is he?"

"Don't know Sir, he didn't show this morning, he's not at his apartment, neither is his truck and he's not answering his cell."

"And Huberstein sends us you instead does he?"

"Yessir."

"And how many national stories have you covered, Mr …?"

"Adams."

"Mr Adams … well?"

"None Sir."

"Oh, that's just great. I hope you have some good questions ready Mr Adams."

"I do Sir."

"Alright, there's no time left to run over them with you - where are you?"

"Over there Sir." Adams pointed to where Garton was set-up.

"OK, I'll give you the nod after the Chief has finished his statement. Get back there now will you."

"Yes Lieutenant Morley," Adams replied and hurried off back through the scrum.

"Yes Lieutenant Morley," mocked Kleberson, "certainly Lieutenant Morley, three-bags-full Lieutenant Morley."

"Podium!" Morley hissed at Kleberson, making a sharp gesture with his finger across his chest with his back to the crowd, so that only Kleberson could see.

"In a moment, I think McKinley may have something for us, better check, eh? Don't want the Chief 'upstaged' do we". Kleberson emphasised Morley's word, smiled then turned and walked over to Chris McKinley who was standing inside the door.

"Anything new?" Kleberson asked.

"Sorry Paul, no."

Kleberson leaned slightly closer to McKinley, then continued in a quiet voice: "OK, listen, Cochrane's no-showed."

"What?"

"Exactly. Superstar status calls and he goes awol. Doesn't fit does it?"

"Damned right!"

"All I've got is that the station can't get ahold of him. He's not answering his phone and his truck's gone from the apartment, so check for any RTA's that may have been reported in the last coupla hours. If that doesn't pull anything up, then get over to his apartment and get the janitor to open it up for you."

"You don't think …" Kleberson interrupted him.

"I don't know what's happening here, but I do know that, if this is Vitruvio, then we've passed the deadline for corpse number three. Cochrane is a definite connection, so if he's caught-up in this somewhere, then we don't need one clever-dick from that rabble out there putting two and two together and getting on the scent before us." He nodded towards the media scrum.

"Gotcha Paul."

"And keep it all quiet. If you find anything, ring me first, OK?"

"What if you're still in the conference?"

"Bollocks to this circus, just ring me, don't use the radio, these bastards have all got their scanners on full earwig."

"OK Paul."

Forty-Six

At ten a.m. precisely, Chief Stanton swept onto the platform, with Morley immediately in his wake; Kleberson joined them both at his own pace. Morley introduced both of them, then did a quick preamble as to order of speaking. The banks of microphones on the desk in front of the three men numbered more than a dozen and included logos from the main national networks . As Morley handed over to Stanton, the flash guns exploded into stroboscopic action and shutter motors whirred incessantly.

Kleberson thought to himself: *'how many photos do they actually need of our ugly mugs to satisfy the public's curiosity?'*

Stanton began the prepared statement: "We reported to you in our previous conference that, at approximately two a.m. yesterday, Friday the ninth of May, a routine patrol found a body in a house in Derby. The body has been identified as being that of Ms Hilary Nicholson, a prominent businesswoman here in Wichita. At approximately midday yesterday, a second body, identified as that of KNKW reporter Ms Marjoree Rolles, was discovered in Ms Rolles' apartment at Westview Tower." Pictures of both women flashed up onto the projection screen behind the podium simultaneously to their names being mentioned.

"We are currently treating both locations as murder scenes and are conducting detailed forensic examinations at both. At this early stage in our enquiries it is not possible for us to establish any positive links between the two scenes, but we are keeping an open mind as to that possibility. The Head of our Homicide Squad, Lieutenant Paul Kleberson, is being given all of the resources he needs to investigate both incidents and when we have more information that we can release, we will of course do so. At this point, I will pass you across to Lieutenant Kleberson, who will give what further information we are able to release at this stage and then we will take some questions, which we would ask you to keep as brief and to the point as possible. Paul ..."

The flashes intensified as the media hounds sensed new blood for their lenses. Kleberson thought again: *'what are you looking for me to be doing? Picking my nose? Scratching my arse? And if I did, what possible relevance would it be to these two deaths?'*

"Thank you Chief," Kleberson began. "Both victims were female, in their early thirties and, of course, well-known to the public both locally and nationally. We can confirm that Ms Nicholson died between eight p.m. and midnight on Thursday, Ms Rolles between eight a.m. and midday yesterday. We know that Ms Nicholson drove to the house in Derby in her silver Porsche sometime on Thursday evening." A picture of a silver Boxster flashed up onto the screen under the photo of Hilary Nicholson.

"We would like to hear from anyone who saw either the car, or Ms Nicholson, or both on either the afternoon or evening of Thursday eighth of May. We know that Ms Rolles was reporting from the scene in Derby at two a.m. yesterday, then she drove home at around six a.m. in her green Chrysler." Another car picture flashed up on the screen under Marjoree Rolles' photo.

"Again, anybody who saw her, or her car at any time yesterday morning, we would like to hear from you. Your press pack contains pictures of both women and their cars and we would ask you all to publish both within your reports of this conference. We are particularly interested to know if either woman was seen in the company of another person during the periods mentioned. Thank you - Lieutenant Morley will now take your questions."

The scrum exploded into animated activity, arms shot skywards and it seemed as though every voice in the crowd shouted either Morley's name, or 'Sir'. Morley fixed Scott Adams in his sights and pointed to him: "Mr Adams."

"Scott Adams KNKW - Chief, can you be a bit more specific on the connections between the two women. Is it true that they were close friends?"

Stanton responded: "I think that's already well known, so there isn't much I can add to what you have said."

"But they were room-mates at college were they not?"

"Yes they were, but it's too early to know if that has any significance."

Adams had used his two bites and had not made the slightest dent in the blank façade being presented by Chief Stanton. Morley began to look for the next questioner when Adams went for a third: "but there is a stronger connection to Jackson Kendrick the Third isn't there Chief? He was Ms Nicholson's fiancé and Ms Rolles' neighbour. Is it true that he has been arrested in connection with these two crimes Chief?"

The look that Morley cast to Adams was withering. Kleberson heard him mutter under his breath: "you little shit! Not only do you take a third question you're not entitled to, but it's also on the 'do not ask' list we gave to your boss!"

The pack momentarily fell silent as every eye in the room focussed on Chief Stanton; Kleberson thought the only thing he could hear was their necks craning. Ever the politician, Stanton replied calmly: "Mr Kendrick is obviously devastated at the loss of his future wife. Despite this, he has voluntarily been helping us to piece together her movements prior to the events that have brought us here today. He and his family are as keen to find out what happened on Thursday night as we are and, therefore, in respect for their loss, I am not prepared to take any further questions along those lines this morning."

Morley immediately pointed at Pete Christensen from KNSZ, but Adams had drawn blood and the hyenas smelt it. He had definitely not screwed-up this time and Garton knew it. As he kept his camera firmly focussed on Chief Stanton, he mouthed to his new colleague: "high-five buddy!"

As questions progressed they became more and more difficult for Stanton. He diverted a few to Kleberson, who simply 'no-commented' most of those in his normal phlegmatic style. As the questions became customarily repetitive, Morley tried to bring matters towards a close, but the pack continued circling; they were not to be denied, particularly as this was going-out live across the nation. It was the Kendrick connection that was creating the interest and Stanton was finding it evermore difficult to balance his official position with his private association.

The latest question was from the Wichita Mail and was regarding the department's ability to deal with such a high-profile case without assistance from outside agencies, such as the FBI. Stanton immediately decided to bat that one across to Kleberson, but before he could get the words out, Kleberson's cellphone rang. Both Stanton and Morley sent dagger-looks at him, but Kleberson calmly took the phone from his pocket, put it to his ear and simultaneously rose from the table, apologising to the crowd for "having to take this."

He headed for the doorway and just inside it said hello to Chris McKinley, leaving Stanton to field the ability question. That he did, but with one eye on Kleberson and the doorway.

"Paul?" McKinley's voice sounded apprehensive.

"Yes Chris."

"We got another one."

"Cochrane?"

"Yup."

"Shit!"

"Same M.O, but much less pretty."

"Can you summon the cavalry without this lot getting wind of it?"

"Already done. I've told everybody to keep to their cellphones, nothing on the radio."

"Good! Keep numbers to a minimum, at least that will allow us some time before Armageddon descends. I'll be there in ten minutes."

Kleberson closed his phone, then headed back to the podium, but he didn't retake his seat. He passed behind Morley and bent to Stanton's ear: "close it down Chief, I need to talk to you." Stanton didn't flinch, his political instinct telling him that he couldn't with national TV in his face. Kleberson continued: "we've got another vic."

Again, without giving any sign of panic, Stanton calmly announced: "ladies and gentlemen, I'm afraid that Lieutenant Kleberson and I are going to have to leave you now, but Lieutenant Morley will stay and round things up for you. Thank you for your patience."

As he rose, Stanton bent to Morley's ear: "keep 'em here as long as you can, we need some time. Tell them there will be another update tomorrow, same time."

Again without flinching, Morley put his best media face on and continued with an explanation of manpower availabilities, as Stanton and Kleberson walked through the door and down the corridor. Once they were out of earshot, Stanton asked: "who is it this time?"

"Cochrane," replied Kleberson.

"Holy Shit!"

"I know Chief, this will bring the world and its brother down around our necks. I sent Chris out there when I heard he had no-showed, but as we found him, we've still got the lid on it at the moment. I'll keep it there as long as I can, everything's on a need-to-know basis until I get out there - I'm going now."

"OK, I'll stay here. If I come with you, we'll have a posse on our tails in seconds."

"That's what I thought as well, Chief."

"Better still, Huberstein's outside. I caught a glimpse of him by their truck, probably making sure their new boy didn't flunk it."

"Or feeding him the lines."

"Hmm. If I go back out there and buttonhole him, it will take them off the scent. Once I've got him in private, I can also put a lid temporarily on his station, 'cos they sure as hell are going to make capital out of this now."

"Thanks Chief."

"Look Paul, I know we don't always see eye-to-eye, but right now we need to put all that to one side, for all of our sakes."

"No problem, just make sure that Morley gets that message, will ya?"

"Just leave Morley to me Paul, you get on with what you do best."

"One more thing, we're going to have to bring Schneider in officially."

"I don't want him taking over."

"He won't, he owes me one."

"And he wants to recruit my Squad Leader." Kleberson looked at Stanton with shock. Stanton continued: "you don't have the monopoly on good detective work, you know Paul - and you'll never make a politician either. Alright, we sure as hell need all the help we can get right now."

"There is one positive for you though Chief."

"And what might that be Paul?"

"Well, it takes some heat off the Kendricks, doesn't it, with the son being in Friedmann's custody and all."

Stanton looked skywards: "thank you Lord for that one small mercy."

Forty-Seven

Kleberson popped his head around the Squad Room door.

"Holdsworth, you're with me."

"Where are we going?" enquired Holdsworth.

"I'll tell you on the way, not another peep out of you until we're in the car. Capaldi, you too."

Capaldi grabbed his coat joining Kleberson and Holdsworth in the corridor. Kleberson briefed him as they walked towards the exit to the car park: "OK Capaldi, when we get out to the car park, there will be media sniffing around. I'm gonna tell you where to go loud enough for them to hear me and you will go smartly off in that direction, lights, siren the lot, got it?"

Capaldi laughed: "decoy duty?"

"Spot-on," replied Kleberson, "when you get about ten minutes out, switch it all off, turn around then come back."

"OK, I'll have 'em out of town like the pied-piper in no time."

The three pushed through the outer door into the car park. Kleberson turned to Capaldi, raising his voice: "you need to get to the airport, quick as you can. He's on the eleven-thirty flight from Denver and I don't want him talking to anyone before you've got him in your car, understood? Bring him straight back here and put him somewhere quiet, I want to be the first to speak to him. We'll see you back here in an hour after we've been to the lab."

There was a sudden stampede as half a dozen secondary reporters sprinted around to the front of the building, where all the TV crews were closing down after the conference. Capaldi jumped in his car, slapped the emergency light on the roof, then shot out of the car park, siren blaring. Within a minute, at least a dozen cars were in hot pursuit as the press pack took the bait.

Kleberson tossed Holdsworth the keys: "you drive," he said.

They calmly got into the unmarked Chevy and sedately pulled away in the same direction. Kleberson checked the mirror as they turned onto First towards the crime lab. He could see a couple of network trucks also heading out of town in pursuit of Capaldi's trail, but nothing was following them. They continued along First until they got to North Minneapolis where the lab was located and Holdsworth began signalling to turn left.

"Not here," Kleberson said, "carry on under the flyover, then turn north onto one-three-five."

"I thought we were going to the lab," Holdsworth said quizzically.

"So did that lot," replied Kleberson, "none of them would follow us here. No stories where they conduct autopsies, just queasy feelings."

"So where we headed?"

"Bradley Fair - Cochrane's flat."

"Why?"

"Because he's victim number three."

"Holy shit." Holdsworth blew out his cheeks as he said it calmly.

"Exactly the words that the Chief used not ten minutes ago. They say great minds think alike - you never know, there may be more of a future here for you than you think young Holdsworth. Now I need to make a couple of calls before we get there."

a fearsome right hook

Forty-Eight

There was a certain déjà vu when the Klebersons arrived at the Schneiders' house that evening in late August 1994. The kids were overnighting with their grandparents and there was another Crown Victoria parked alongside Sam's on the drive. This time, though, it was not black, but a rather non-descript metallic beige.

Inside, the Klebersons were introduced to Sam and Clara's other guests, Frank and Velma Singleton. After five minutes of small talk, the ladies adjourned to the kitchen to prepare some salad, the men to the deck where the barbecue was already on full gas. Sam donned his favourite apron, the black one with the skeleton bones that made him look like a walking X-Ray, and started to load some steaks onto the griddle, making the stones sizzle as the blood dripped onto them.

Paul grabbed three beers from the cooler, flipped off the tops and handed one each to the other men. They chinked the necks together in celebration of their imminent bonding around the large circular table, pre-laid by Clara with all the necessary accoutrements for an open-air dinner party. While Sam prodded the steaks, Frank surveyed the grounds from the deck, like a southern plantation owner from two centuries earlier.

Paul decided to get the potential evening-wrecking subject, from his point of view, out of the way as quickly as possible. He turned to Singleton: "so, how long have you been in the FBI then Frank?"

The other two burst out laughing. Sam held-out his hand towards Frank, who put his beer down and reached into his back pocket for his wallet. He pulled-out a twenty, which he slapped into Sam's hand as he said: "dammit, that must be five on the bounce you've won!"

Paul looked at the other two in turn and smiled: "alright, seeing as I'm the spoof here, you gonna let me in on it or not?"

Frank looked at him with an air of feigned frustration: "see here Paul, not only have you just cost me ten bucks because you asked me that question within five minutes of you getting out here, as predicted by Sam before you arrived, you also doubled-it up by using the exact goddam words he said you would! Every time we come here he does it with one or other of his guests; I reckon it would be cheaper for me to take him and Clara out to the Aberdeen Grill instead."

Paul raised his bottle in acknowledgement to Sam: "nice one Sam, I didn't realise I had become that predictable."

"Oh yes, old friend," Sam countered, "very predictable I'm afraid."

"So I'm not here for an interview this time, that's a relief."

"Ah there, I didn't say that I was any less predictable, now did I?"

Frank took up the baton: "you got the correct M.O, but the wrong I.D." He extended his hand again: "Captain Frank Singleton, Wichita Police Department Special Investigations Division."

Paul stared at Sam, then smiled and took Frank's hand: "Paul Kleberson, wannabe historian whose friend wants him to stay a cop all his life instead, at your service."

"Any joy back East yet?" Frank enquired. "Sam's given me a full verbal CV already."

"Has he, by Jove!"

"Well?"

"No, but I haven't really tried yet - and that isn't just the bravado of someone too proud to admit failure either."

"I wouldn't have presumed it was, not with your abilities."

"Problem with academia is that they want to see contemporary work. I can't really send them any of my research work from the last couple of years as it has this minor drawback of being classified. So I need to produce a couple of papers to show that I can still live up to the billing my qualifications suggest."

"And what are you doing for them?"

"The War of Independence from the English viewpoint. Not too many American authors seem to want to tackle that one - it's not patriotic. Come to think of it, not too many English ones have either, seeing that they lost!"

The men were still laughing as the ladies emerged from the lounge carrying large bowls of salad and vegetables. Leanne placed hers on the table, then came over to Paul and hugged his arm: "you guys seem to be enjoying yourselves, are you going to let us in on the joke?"

"Sure," Paul replied, "Frank here's about to recruit me for the WPD."

Leanne shot Frank a look that mixed 'you cannot be serious' with 'don't even think about it.' Paul continued: "if I were you Frank, I should duck now - she's got a fearsome right hook."

The quip quickly diffused any potential atmosphere developing and, suitably chastised, neither Sam nor Frank attempted to raise the subject again that evening. On the way home, an ominous silence developed in the minivan. As usual, Paul wouldn't let something fester, so he opened the discussion, first sniffing the air theatrically: "do you think there's an elephant in here somewhere?"

"Were you serious back there?"

"About what?"

"About Frank recruiting you. Only he didn't mention it at all for the rest of the night."

"I was spiking their guns, as our forebears used to call it. When a retreating army had to abandoned their cannon, but didn't want the captured guns to be used on them by their enemies, they would ram a spike into the touch hole, that's where the flame is put to fire it by igniting the gunpowder. No flame, no bang."

"So did he say he was there to recruit you?"

"No, because I pre-empted it. Don't be mad with Sam, he's only trying to help."

"But you don't know that was what the evening was about, do you?"

"Of course it was. That wasn't just any old cop, that was Captain Singleton, Head of the Special Investigations Division. Too much of a co-incidence."

"His wife said he was retiring."

"Ah well, another opportunity blown."

"So you don't want to be a cop then?"

"I don't want a career that gets between us." Paul took his right hand off the steering wheel and took hold of Leanne's, squeezing it gently. He looked across at her: "not again."

The car went quiet for a few minutes, then Leanne asked another question: "but will you be happy?"

"Happy with what?"

"Happy with bullying spotty youths into being interested in old stuff every day."

"I'll issue Clearasil at the start of every term."

"I'm being serious."

"So am I - what a great subject! The Zit, it's place in history and the influence of skincare on the Royal Houses of Europe. Maybe I should make that one of my papers."

Leanne thumped his arm.

"Ow!" Paul exclaimed.

"That's for not heeding your own warnings."

"About what?"

"My fearsome right hook!"

Forty-Nine

Regardless of his apparent reticence on the subject in the occasional short discussions they had over the weeks that followed, Leanne remained unsure that her husband was as totally-opposed to continuing a career in law enforcement as it appeared on the surface. He was, however, pursuing several academic openings that would have satisfied his continued desire to be a historian, although most of those would have involved uprooting the family and moving East.

A few weeks after the barbecue, Leanne was again visiting the Schneider house with the children, for tea with Clara. She had left Paul at home putting the finishing touches to a paper he was due to submit at the end of the week. The two ladies had a great afternoon, Matt in particular being at his entertaining best. As Leanne was thinking of preparing to leave, Sam arrived home earlier than expected.

While Clara was in the kitchen making him some coffee, Leanne took the opportunity to ask the question that had been gnawing at her: "Sam, I doubt that Paul wants to discuss this with you either, but do the WPD want to recruit him, or not?"

"Leanne, Paul has one of the finest investigative brains I have ever encountered, but for some reason he doesn't see it. So if you're really asking me if Paul wants to be a policeman any more, all I can say is I don't know - genuinely I don't. If he decides that he does, then Wichita Police Department would hire him in a heartbeat. And to be honest, we would rehire him in the same timescale."

"Thank you Sam, thank you for being a true friend," Leanne replied. She got up and hugged him before starting to pack away all the debris Matt had deposited around the lounge during the afternoon.

Back home a few hours later, having put the children to bed for the night, Leanne and Paul were relaxing in the lounge, listening to some music over a glass of good Californian red. She opened the discussion by asking how the paper on the War of Independence was progressing.

Paul's reply was unusually unguarded: "oh I don't know - it's nearly there, but somehow it lacks a spark. All the papers I did while I was at Cambridge had something, I can't say what it was, but when I read them they excited me as much as the research had. Somehow this one doesn't. Maybe it's the subject matter, maybe it's me - perhaps I've lost it, you know? But every time I read it through, it's wooden, bland, boring even. Dammit, it's ..."

He found it difficult to find the word, so Leanne filled it in for him: "academic?"

He looked at her with that disarming smile of his: "do you think I should have done the one on zits instead?"

"What?"

"You remember, when we were on the way back from Sam and Clara's a few weeks back - when you asked me about educating spotty kids."

She laughed: "oh that - and did you learn anything from how that discussion ended?" He looked at her quizzically. She brought her fist slowly towards his face and gently brushed it against his chin.

He laughed as well and chinked her glass. As the ring from the glasses echoed around them, he lifted his and said: "Round Two?"

"Maybe," she replied, "if you can answer me a straight question?"

"Oh dear, is this confession time?"

"Possibly." She turned more towards him on the sofa: "do you miss being a policeman?" His expression changed to being a little annoyed, mainly by the forthrightness - it was not an easy question to dodge. Leanne realised that he might be withdrawing, so reinforced the lack of danger in her enquiry: "you can tell me, just say it how it is, I'm not looking to start a fight over it, I just want to be sure you're going to be ..."

She also paused through a difficulty of knowing the right word, so this time Paul completed her question: "happy?"

"Yes Paul. Can you ever really be happy writing about stuffy old wars that ended hundreds of years ago? Or how spotty the generals were?"

The lightness of the questioning reassured him: "straight answer?" She nodded. He looked her straight in the eye: "no, I can't, but ..." he raised a palm to stop her from saying anything until he finished, "... I can't be a reason for you, or the kids, or even Mum and Dad, being sat on your own, wondering what on earth is happening to me at work. Those wars - yes they happened hundreds of years ago, which means they can't result in someone thrusting a sword or firing a musket in my direction. If I'm a policeman, I won't just be sitting in an office filling forms all day. I will be out on the street, with little control over what could happen. It may be quiet down here in Derby, but up in the badlands everybody has a knife, or a gun, or both. The worst injury I can suffer researching history is for a book to fall on me from off the library shelf."

She looked at him earnestly: "some books are quite heavy."

They both laughed and, after a few moments of quiet, Leanne continued: "all I want is to live with a husband who is happy with what he is doing, because when this particular husband is happy, he is much more fun to be with. What I'm saying is that only you know what you really want to do and that I will have to live with whatever decision you come to. Just make sure that it is one that means we can still have some fun."

He looked at her with a raised eyebrow, turned and placed his glass on the side table. He snuggled up to her with his arms around her and looked into her eyes: "alright, so exactly what fun do you have in mind right now?"

Fifty

Just over a month after that chat over a glass of wine at home, Detective Paul Kleberson reported for duty with the Wichita Police Department's Drug Squad. All the references received by the city were glowing - academically from his university, vocationally from FBI Headquarters and personally from his close friend and, co-incidentally, new Head of the local FBI Agency. This enabled him to be put in post quickly, without the need for anything more than the necessary local induction training, which had taken two weeks.

Paul's work over the next three years was exceptional. He not only achieved the highest arrest rate but, more importantly, easily the highest conviction ratio in the Squad, a fact that was not overlooked in the higher echelons within the department, including the new Chief of Police who had entered post late in 1996 and promoted Paul to Sergeant shortly afterwards.

A Fearsome Right Hook

Despite the calls on his time caused by the irregular hours, family routine remained fairly unaffected as Paul always strove to be available at important times. With son Matt about to start kindergarten and daughter Lucy at an age where she could be easily left with her grandparents, all three of whom were still sharing the large base commander's house at McConnell, Leanne had been able to take a part-time book-keeping job, two mornings a week, with a small accountancy practice in Derby, a position that could be extended when she was ready to do so.

Life for the Klebersons was, therefore, good, and about to get better. Several senior officers were due for retirement during the second half of 1997 and Chief Stanton was taking the opportunity this presented to reshape his department, from what he had inherited to more how he wanted it going forward. When that reorganisation was announced internally, it included a new person in charge of the Homicide Squad - Sergeant Paul Kleberson. The appointment was to commence on the First of January 1998, at which point his promotion to Lieutenant would also take effect.

The following Sunday, the extended family had all been invited to lunch at his home by General Walter T Kleberson, including Walter's mother and father, his other two children, their families and partners, plus Leanne's mother. Only Walter's mother had been unable to travel, but his father, Bill, was there, completing four generations at the table and looking far younger than his eighty-five years, probably due to the companion he had brought with him, Sonia, who looked suspiciously less than half of that age.

After the main course had been cleared and the gathering were chattering over coffee and cheese, Leanne tapped her wine glass and got to her feet to make a short speech: "as we are all together here today, we have a short announcement to make." She smiled at Paul as she continued: "I know that my husband would probably not say anything until he absolutely had to, but perhaps I could call on the new Head of the Homicide Squad here in Wichita to say a few words. Ladies and Gentlemen, may I present Lieutenant Paul Kleberson."

She sat down still smiling at her husband, who was responding with a wry grin, but was actually inwardly delighted that she had pre-empted the official announcement, due several weeks later. Left to him, it would probably have been the first that his extended family would have known of the promotion. His father was, of course, delighted and the first to walk around the table to congratulate Paul with the warmest of handshakes. So too the rest of the family, who for the next few minutes conducted a question and answer session not dissimilar to some of the press conferences Paul would find himself handling in the future. After this died down, there was another tapping on a glass, this time from the head of the table.

All went quiet as General Kleberson rose to his feet: "thank you Leanne for that unexpected news and may we all say Paul, how delighted we are to hear it." The entire gathering acknowledged their agreement. "But it isn't the reason we have invited you all here today, or the only announcement to be made. I'm not sure if you all know this specifically, but in a few months' time I will have completed forty years of service in the Air Force."

The gathering all indicated their congratulations, by saying so or raising their glasses. When this died down, Walter continued: "that will be twice the number of years that Uncle Sam insists on we servicemen doing before he gives us a pension, and plenty-enough for anyone to have to do to get a decent one!" All around the table laughed as Walter concluded: "so, I have decided to retire on that anniversary date."

More glass-raising was accompanied by several shouts of "well-done." Again Walter politely waited for these to die away before adding: "now, of course, we have had the benefit for a number of years of having this house provided for us, but the Air Force is not known for its overgenerosity in allowing ex-employees to hang around in Government property too long, so having made the decision, Margie and I have had to put some thought into where we intend to live afterwards. I think it's fair to say that for the last thirty years or so, Margie has had little say on where we have lived, she has just had to make do as best she could after receiving the news of where I was going next. So, I think it only fair that, this time, we will be going where she wants to."

There were a few "here-heres" from around the table, but most of the listeners were a little shocked by this unusually deferent attitude from a man who had never really been overly-accommodating when it came to putting the wishes of others within his family before his own. In fact one or two were feeling slightly threatened by where this announcement was going, including Leanne.

Walter continued: "now, I think the kids will probably agree that some of the happiest times we had were when I was stationed at Beale and we lived off-base in Marysville. Probably not Paul, because I know he was happiest over in England - in fact there was a time when I thought he had turned into a damned limey!"

There was a short burst of laughter as most of the family looked briefly at Paul, who was replying quietly - "damned right!"

Walter carried-on undaunted: "certainly Margie was very happy there, so that's where we've decided I will make my final landing - back in Yuba County." Paul was unsurprised, but Leanne felt shocked.

For her personally, there was worse to come from Walter: "now as you are also aware, Olivia here," he indicated towards Leanne's mother, "has been living with us since her husband Nate passed a few years back. What you may not know is that Olivia is a California girl and also wants to get back to her original home turf. So we have decided that she will come as well and continue to live with us out there. She's been great company for Margie, in fact they get on so well they're almost like sisters - plus it will keep Margie out of my hair if I decide to disappear into my den for a nap in the afternoons!"

More laughter filled the room, but there was none from Leanne who was looking at her mother in disbelief, because there had not been the slightest hint that anything like this was coming, and as an only child they had always been close, closer than many sisters. Walter concluded: "it will also be convenient for Paul's family, as they will only have to visit one place for all the grandparents, rather than the three different locations we had to drag the family around back when he was a kid. Anyway, we haven't found a place yet, but when we do we'll let you all know, then sometime next year you can all come and have Sunday lunch with us again, but under a California sun. Thank you."

Walter sat down to a ripple of applause, but Leanne was already nervously scrunching-up her napkin and throwing it on the table. Paul, who had been watching her carefully during the last couple of sentences, leant across to take her hand. Very gently, he said just a couple of words: "easy now."

She looked at him, clearly agitated and whispered: "I can't believe it! Not a word Paul! How could she?"

He whispered back: "look, you're upset, I understand why, but there's not much we can do. She's a big girl, and it's her life."

"But she's said nothing Paul!"

"Well, not about this perhaps, but she hasn't said anything much else since your Father died than her wanting to move back to California."

"I know, but I never expected her to actually do it! And certainly not to take your parents with her as well!"

"I don't think Dad's one to be taken anywhere," Paul replied sarcastically.

"Let's go home Paul."

"We can't Leanne, not right now."

"I can't stay here."

"I'm sorry, you'll have to. See if you can get your Mom to one side and have a chat about it."

"A chat?" she said through clenched teeth.

"OK, don't talk to her then, but don't walk out either. Leave it with me and I'll get us away as soon as it's not obvious that you're pissed-off with the whole thing."

More clenched teeth: "I'm not pissed-off!"

"You could have fooled me."

At that point, Matt ran up and popped his head between their chairs: "Mummy, Daddy! Are we going to Cal - ee - forn - ee - ah too?"

The timing was perfect; Leanne melted as she always did when her kids showed their innocence. She smiled at him: "no - not today dear."

what's that in his mouth?

Fifty-One

When Kleberson and Holdsworth arrived at Cochrane's apartment block, it was quiet. Kleberson could see both McKinley's car and that of Mary Jourdain. Otherwise it was business as usual in this leafy upmarket suburb. They parked and made their way to the apartment.

McKinley let them in. It was a tidy, classily-furnished apartment, much more so than Kleberson had expected - he had always pictured Cochrane as a bit of a slob. He looked into the lounge and saw Mary Jourdain, looking pale and shaken. He caught her eye; she shook her head sadly. McKinley beckoned him down the hallway: "it's a bad one Paul - even Mary's had to take a break." He guided Kleberson to the bedroom.

There laid-out on the bed, in a similar manner to the two previous victims, was a male body, well-built and shorn of all hair. It was Tom Cochrane. He was face-up, with his head on the pillow looking straight-up at the ceiling, eyes wide open and an expression of horror, frozen in death, on his face. There was something in the mouth, but Kleberson couldn't quite make it out from the angle he was looking at. The legs were akimbo in what looked, at first sight, the same formation as those of Hilary Nicholson, but the arms were draped across the torso with the hands together at the crotch, concealing the genitals.

"What's that in his mouth, Chris?"

"It's his dick Paul."

From behind him, Kleberson heard an exclamation: "Oh My God!"

"Tell Holdsworth not to throw-up in the crime scene, will ya Chris."

"I won't do that Sir," Holdsworth responded, "but Christ Almighty, what are we dealing with here?"

"Right now Holdsworth, we can't be distracted by those thoughts. Chris, what's the situation with the janitor?"

"I got him to open the door, then go back to his cubby-hole and not talk to anyone until I get back to him. He thinks we're looking for drugs, seemed surprised we had taken so long to catch up with this particular tenant, which in itself is interesting."

"OK, let's call-in the cavalry and seal it all off, by the numbers. I'll stay here with Mary until her guys arrive. Holdsworth, you run point until the Cruisers get here then set the tape well-back because the nation's media will be here minutes behind them. Then once we've got them under control, get onto locating Cochrane's truck. According to the station they couldn't find it when they sent someone out here earlier trying to rouse him. Shut the door when you go out, let's keep this as anonymous as we can until we've got that tape up."

The two detectives left quietly and Kleberson moved slowly to the foot of the bed; he coopied-down and looked between the fingers covering the groin. He could make-out a gaping, but neat, wound where Cochrane's manhood had previously occupied its proud position, but there was no blood anywhere on the bed or the body. He wandered through into the lounge, where Mary Jourdain stood; as he got closer he could see that she had been crying. He put his arm round her shoulder. They had worked together for over five years, but he couldn't remember her reacting like this before.

He tried to console her: "sorry you have to keep seeing these things Mary."

"Oh I wasn't crying for Cochrane specifically," she replied, "it's all of them. This is one sadistic S-o-B you know and we have to catch him."

"So you think it's a 'he' do you?"

"Doesn't make sense to me any other way Paul. That's a statement in there - figure out exactly what the statement is and you have your gender in that. My kneejerk when I saw it was male."

"Don't forget the Bobbitt woman."

"She didn't kill her man, just cut it off then called nine-one-one so he could have it stitched back on. Alright, that was a statement, but it was world's apart from what this is saying." Mary Jourdain forced a strained smile onto her face: "if you asked me to hypothesise, which I never do, this scene also has similar wronged-lover overtones, but with hints of same-sex interaction and that, coupled with the penetration on the last two vics, makes our perp male."

"Well, I don't know much about Cochrane, except that he was a piece of work. I only encountered him rarely and at a distance, but I sure didn't figure him to be gay. Still, nothing surprises in this job, so we'll explore that avenue and if it turns-up trumps, then we certainly have a strong link to the first two in that alone. Right now though, there isn't much we can do for the poor sod, other than get him justice by catching the bastard who's giving us the run-around, whoever it is."

Mary Jourdain stooped, heavy-shouldered, and picked-up her scene kit, then they walked back though to the bedroom pausing just inside the doorway. She took a deep breath to compose herself: "this is all so calculated," she sighed.

"What I don't get, Mary," Kleberson observed, "is where's all the blood? It must have gone everywhere."

"I had a quick look before you arrived and I reckon it went down the shower drain in there." She pointed to the en-suite: "it's been surgically-cleaned and very recently. That would mean that the killer had to manhandle the body around, because Cochrane sure as hell wasn't alive for long after that was done. Look at him Paul, he's a big guy, gotta weigh one-eighty at least. You can't think it could be a woman doing all this?"

"Fair point Mary, but whoever it is, they're more thorough than a house-proud Jewish mother who's just been given a steam cleaner!"

This seemed to lift Mary Jourdain's spirits. She tried to give Kleberson one of her stern looks, but instead a broad smile swept across her face: "you really are incorrigible. I know I shouldn't be telling you this, but sometimes that black humour of yours does help. Guess we'll never cure you of that, will we?"

"Guess not. So now we've got the professional Mary back, humour me a little longer. Look at this scene, not purely as a Medical Examiner, start as if you have just come in and you're considering whether this is connected to the last two scenes you've been to. What are you seeing?"

"That's not professional Paul!"

"I know, but hey - if this is the same perp, and I don't think we disagree on that, then it's likely to be corpse number three in a series. If it is a series, then there is a time pattern emerging and the intervals are short, so there will be more, the clock is already ticking and this perp is way ahead of us. You're on the punt team Mary and I need better field position."

Mary Jourdain looked long and hard at Paul Kleberson. She felt an air of desperation in his voice, but all she saw in his eyes was steely determination. Although all of her professional training was screaming at her to resist this line of approach, her instincts were overwhelmingly telling her that going by 'The Manual' with this perp was only playing into his hands. If they didn't try something different, her morgue was going to continue to fill with corpses until the perp made a mistake and, from what she had seen so far, that wasn't likely to happen anytime soon.

She turned to face the room and began to recite her thoughts as they came to her: "alright, I haven't given this body even a cursory examination yet, but let's assume I find what I am expecting to, then the M.O. will have been planned to very minute detail each time, but with subtle differences."

"Go on."

"All three locations are domestic and connected to the victim. Let's assume that, like the other two, this body has also been shaved and hosed-down." She raised her eyes and nodded towards the direction of the bathroom: "it will have taken some time, so the murderer was confident that he would not be disturbed while doing so, meaning he was probably here by invitation. The apparent ritual is to cover the fact that each washing was done to remove any of the attacker's hair or DNA fragments because there will have been sexual activity, which would mean that all three could have been sexually assaulted either post-mortem, or immediately pre-mortem, or maybe even both. And let's assume that this one also has the puncture wound in the back of the neck."

"So they have all been drugged."

"Or poisoned, I won't know until we get the toxicology back and I've had to send that to KC. Whatever it is, it's very subtle and we just don't have sophisticated-enough equipment to pick up very low levels of chemicals."

"That's interesting. We'll see if we can get a hurry-up on that, I'll talk to the Chief."

"Fine, but it's what isn't consistent that is most worrying. Hilary Nicholson was the least …" she hesitated, "… damaged. I'm sorry, that's the best word I can come up with to describe it really. It was almost as though she participated, or at least if she didn't, she was treated lovingly. Marjoree Rolles' treatment was more rough, but still not what I would call sadistic, at least not in the context of what we have here."

"What, you think Marjoree resisted?"

"Oh no Paul, I don't think any of them were in a position to resist. No, they were all, at the very least, sedated, maybe paralysed. Which means that the differences in physical treatment were imposed upon them."

"So, with each crime, he is becoming more violent."

"Maybe it is that simple. Yet, I can't help but get a different vibe, as if his disgust for the victim increases. You know, he may even have met all three previously and built-up almost a relative hatred pattern for them."

"So, we are looking for a psycho here?"

"More like a schizo. These are not spur-of-the-moment crimes, like I said the planning is meticulous. He uses local materials for most everything, but he must bring some implements with him. That butchery job in there has an element of surgical precision to it."

"So a medical person, maybe?"

"Certainly that type of training, but that could also indicate a butcher, or a chef. Either could cut meat as precisely and in reality that's all he's done, sliced-off a joint of meat."

Kleberson felt a shudder pass through his body and Mary Jourdain saw his distinctly-masculine discomfort at that thought.

"Sorry Paul, I can't think of any other way of putting it. I've heard stories of scenes like that in there, but nothing prepares you for actually witnessing it first-hand."

"No Mary, it's me that should be sorry - sorry that you have had to."

"Hey, it's all part of the job."

"Anything else you're able to give me before you do the autopsy?"

"Only hunches."

"Doesn't matter, I'll take anything right now. We don't have an awful lot, other than the bodies, and looking at how orderly this place is I doubt we'll get much more here either."

"Yes, that's probably the most worrying aspect. The killer is so fastidious. Even the most prolific serials occasionally exhibit some flaw - the momentary pause at being discovered that drops the guard for a split-second. This one, however, is so confident in his plan, so assured in the execution and clean-up, it is quite chilling. But if I had to guess, I would say that he is gay, or at least bisexual, maybe even a tranny. It's the female side that's motivating the clean-up I think. He's probably a loner, possibly an only child. They can grow up with less fear of discovery through not having any siblings to tell on them, but also they have a greater feeling of exclusion from the world in general. The persona that committed these acts is the alter-ego, the psyche that has confidence in bucket-loads. The normal one doesn't."

"So I'm looking for a shy and retiring cross-dresser."

Mary Jourdain briefly laughed, but uncomfortably: "you do have a way of getting to the point, don't you Paul? Yes, maybe; he's also probably impotent with a big dick - and I mean big!"

"Why impotent?"

"Not impotent in terms of erectile-dysfunction, but in the aspect of not producing semen or carrier fluid. There wasn't any on the first two victims anyway."

"A condom maybe and you did say that the clean-up is thorough."

"Nobody can be that thorough! As for the condom, I've found no sign of the related chemical traces on the first two victims."

"Then a dildo, sex toy maybe?"

"No again Paul. There is a different pattern of 'damage' when an object has been used. No it's definitely him that's been in every orifice."

"OK, just one more thing. Back to the blood - how come, with the surgery this time, that there's no sign of blood in the bathroom either? I mean, surely, you hack the damned thing off, it's gonna go everywhere."

"Not if he was bled-out first, then the surgery performed post-mortem."

"But how long would that take?"

"Oh, he'd be dead in thirty seconds or so - quicker if he was already sedated and the heart-rate was low. Then once the heart stopped, there would be a little gravitational drainage, but not for more than a minute or so. The dorsal artery was probably severed in the shower, with the water running to take the blood away. I'll get one of the guys to take-out the drain and check it, we'll probably get a bit of residue to confirm that. We'll also check the sewer runs to see if anything got hung-up en-route. It's a long shot, but you never know - modern places like this often have sharp bends in the wastes."

"You guys really get the best jobs don't you?"

"We're here to serve, Paul."

There was a knock at the door. Kleberson opened it and Chris McKinley entered with two CSI Techs; Mary Jourdain met them in the hallway to start the briefing on the scene. She turned to Kleberson: "can we take it from here?"

"Sure, he's all yours. Let me have the photos asap can you. I need to put an incident board together covering all three - to see if we can find that little anomaly we need."

"A few hours Paul and they'll all be with you."

"OK, thanks. One thing I hadn't told you is that we're getting some help from Sam Schneider's office. There may be a link with some other cases they have flagged-up, so we will be sharing some of the data in both directions. Can I get their forensic data over to you for comparison?"

"Sure can, I'm not expecting to have any private time while this maniac is running around, so you have all my priorities until it's over."

"Thanks Mary, make sure your guys know this all needs to be kept under wraps. We're going to be running the gauntlet with national media on this one and they won't be as sheepish about doorstepping the morgue as the locals normally are, so if you need any troops out there to shoo them off, let us know."

Fifty-Two

Kleberson and McKinley stepped-out into the dark corridor. Police tape flanked them both sides within a few feet. There was no light other than the overhead fluorescents, one of which was fluttering annoyingly. At the nearer end of the corridor were double fire doors leading to a staircase, the opposite direction led to the lift doors. There were four apartment doors on each side.

"Are we able to do door-to-door yet Chris?" Kleberson asked.

"I've got some more soldiers on the way."

"Anything from the janitor?"

"Nothing useful. This is not the most exclusive of the developments out here, so the staff are to match. Found the truck though, parked round the back; guess whoever came from the station saw the allocated parking slot empty and just assumed Cochrane wasn't home."

"No CCTV I guess." As he spoke, Kleberson looked up and down the corridor again; one of the apartment doors on the left was ajar. As Kleberson spotted it, it quietly clicked shut. Before McKinley could respond, Kleberson was under the tape and walking down the corridor, beckoning McKinley to follow. Kleberson knocked gently on the door; it opened immediately in response, but only as far as the security chain allowed. Part of a small face appeared in the gap, more than a foot below Kleberson's eyeline.

A frail female voice asked a question: "are you from the police?"

"Yes Ma'am," Kleberson responded calmly, pulling his badge from his belt and holding it close to where the aged eye was peeping out.

"Is he alright?"

"Is who alright Ma'am?"

"That faggot along there."

"You know Mr Cochrane?"

"Is that his name?" She cackled quietly: "cocksucker more like."

"Have you been in all night Ma'am?"

"All night and all day, don't get out much me."

"Would it be alright to speak to you inside Ma'am? It's just a little difficult through this gap."

"You'll have to take your shoes off."

Kleberson smiled: "sure thing Ma'am." He bent down to slip both patent-leather brogues off, picking them up to display them. The eye slid away from the gap and the door closed. Kleberson nodded towards McKinley's feet, who followed suit by pulling off his loafers. There was a metallic scratching as a struggle ensued with the chain, then the door reopened. It revealed a diminutive lady, certainly well into her seventies and no more than five feet tall. She was dressed in a long tweed skirt and cashmere top, both of which looked like they had come straight out of their dry-cleaning bags. She had an almost unblemished complexion and not a blue-rinsed hair out of place on her immaculate coiffure.

"Come on through officers," she said as she led the way into the lounge; McKinley closed the door behind him. "Can I get you something to drink," she asked, "maybe an iced tea?"

"We're fine Ma'am, thank you," Kleberson responded as he surveyed the room. It looked how he imagined his grandparents' lounge would have looked back East when it was brand new. The furniture was all high-quality solid wood pre-war style, but with a depth of shine that suggested it had to have been polished several times every day ever since it was first created. None of the soft furnishings had a mark on them, much like their owner.

"I'm Lieutenant Kleberson, this is Detective McKinley," he continued, "and you are?"

"Lillian Maxwell. We don't normally get plain clothes policemen out here, are you from the Drug Squad?"

"Why would you think that Ma'am?" Kleberson deftly avoided having to give any information yet.

"All the comings and goings along there. This was a decent block until the management company was changed, now they let any old riff-raff in here."

"How long have you been here Ma'am?"

"I was one of the first to move in six years ago. My family decided that I couldn't cope with my beautiful old colonial over on North Market, so they made me sell it and move here." Her speech was precise, with a mildly southern lilt to it: "so no more mint-juleps on the lawn with my friends, not that there's too many of them left anyhows. What the family really wanted, of course, was the assets in liquid form in the bank, so that when I pop-off they can get their hands on them more easily. Come out here most Sundays and sit on that couch like vultures wondering why I haven't conveniently died yet. I may be eighty-seven, but my parents both nearly made a hundred, so they'll just have to wait won't they?"

"Sure will Ma'am." Kleberson was smiling at the feisty little old lady who looked more than capable of looking after herself. He glanced over at McKinley, who had moved to the french windows that led out onto the small balcony; McKinley cocked his head slightly indicating that Kleberson might want to take a look.

What's that in his Mouth?

Kleberson moved slowly to join his colleague, asking as he went: "so do you see much of Mr Cochrane Ma'am?"

"Comes and goes at all times that one, can't have a proper job. Then there's all them 'companions' - The Lord calls them all an abomination. Like I said, this was a decent development 'til they let the riff-raff in, with their dens of iniquity. Guess that's why the Drug Squad's here, isn't it?"

Kleberson was looking out of the window. He looked beyond the balcony to the left and could see all the media trucks assembling behind the police tape draped between the pillars guarding the entrance into the main complex car park. To the left he saw a police department recovery truck pulled-up in front of a champagne-coloured GMC truck in one of the marked bays, about to start a recovery operation; he guessed that must be Cochrane's on its way to the lab for a detailed examination. Then as his eyes drew back towards the room, he saw what McKinley was trying to attract his attention to. There on the chair behind the small table on the balcony were a pair of binoculars. He glanced at McKinley, who raised his eyebrows.

Kleberson turned-back to their hostess: "you may want to have a seat for a moment Ma'am. You see, we're not from the Drug Squad."

Mrs Maxwell settled herself into her upright winged chair, her short legs barely touching the floor as she pulled herself into position: "not from the Drug Squad? So what's all the tape for in the corridor?"

"We're Homicide detectives Ma'am."

She looked totally shocked by the revelation, the colour quickly draining from her face: "Homicide ... oh my! Homicide ... in that apartment?"

"'Fraid so Ma'am."

"Oh Goodness!" She grasped both knees and looked at her feet, then went completely silent. Kleberson took a little time to see if she would begin chattering again, but nothing happened.

McKinley asked the next question: "did you see anything yesterday Ma'am ..."

"No!" She cut him off sharply, in mid-sentence, still looking at her feet. McKinley went to continue, but Kleberson raised his hand slightly to stop him; the lady was looking increasingly frail by the minute and he had seen this reaction before. It was either fear or shock, maybe both, but she was not in a condition to answer anything right at that moment.

He tried reassurance: "Ma'am, we get called out to every unexplained death. Most turn out to be not actual homicides, but we have to check them out anyway. This one may be one of those, we just need to check it out, that's all."

There was no reaction, so he continued: "you mentioned your relatives, would you like us to call them and reassure them that you're alright?"

Mrs Maxwell continued to look at her feet, but did speak very quietly: "no, thank you, it's kind of you to ask, but it will only give them an excuse to put me in a home. They just want an excuse to put me away, out of sight out of mind. Please don't give them any excuse."

"We won't Ma'am, please don't worry about that, or what happened along the corridor. We'll get to the bottom of it. But look, here's my card." Kleberson took a business card from his wallet and laid it on the side table by her chair: "if there's anything that's worrying you, please ring me on this number - any time, OK Mrs Maxwell?" She nodded rapidly.

"We'll see ourselves out Ma'am, please don't get up; and remember - any time." The two detectives left the apartment, pulled the door shut and walked back towards the police tape.

"Reckon she must have seen something, Paul"

"Could be, but she's not going to tell us while she's like that and even if she does, how reliable is it going to be? We can come back later and try again. In the meantime, see if you can turn anything else up."

Fifty-Three

Kleberson arrived back at City Hall just after three p.m. His first port of call was Chief Stanton's office. As he entered, he was immediately aware that sitting across the desk from Stanton was KNKW station head, Max Huberstein. Stanton rose from his desk: "ah good, come on in Paul - you've met Max haven't you?"

"Yes I have," Kleberson replied. Huberstein rose to his feet and they shook hands: "I wish the circumstances were better this time Max."

"Thanks for the recognition of our loss Paul; I certainly never expected to be in a position where our station lost three of its top contributors within the space of twenty-four hours."

"Three?" quizzed Kleberson.

"Yes, Hilary did our weekly financial programme. Her national influence meant that we could bring-in almost anyone for a segment."

"Of course, that had completely passed me by. The last twenty-four hours has been somewhat hectic for us as well, plus I'm not much into the business and finance world, unless it involves criminal activity. So that's another connection we need to follow-up on."

"You already have others?" Huberstein adopted the quizzical tone of a seasoned journalist.

Kleberson looked at Stanton with an expression that asked if he was being prompted to reveal evidence. Stanton nodded: "I have Max's agreement that his station will not use anything until we say so, as long as we keep him apprised of our progress. In return, he will give us their full assistance with anything we may need going forward."

'Nice bit of politics going on here' Kleberson thought to himself. 'Still, we need some media help and keeping Huberstein one step ahead of the pack may just pay-off in the long run.'

"I want this bastard nailed as much as you do," Huberstein took-up the point with more than a note of sadness in his voice, although his face betrayed the anger he was holding back. "I'm not going to allow any of my staff to get in your way. Of course, I can't do anything about the networks, they do as they please, but you are already aware of that."

"Understood," Kleberson replied. Stanton gestured for them both to sit and Kleberson took the unoccupied chair opposite Huberstein, and continued: "you may be aware that Hilary and Marjoree were room-mates at USC."

"Yes - with Tom Cochrane," Huberstein replied.

"Sorry, I didn't know that," Kleberson replied, somewhat taken aback.

"Oh yes, it was Marjoree that got Cochrane his interview with us."

"But they didn't work together, not at first?"

"No, that's station policy. It stops little cliques forming, but it was obvious after a few months that, in this case, putting them together would work well, professionally. There was never any possibility that it could be anything other than a professional relationship."

"They didn't get on?"

"No, couldn't stand the sight of each other really, but boy did that make them spark when they worked together. They were both fiercely competitive, always trying to upstage each other. It had to be managed carefully, but the results were superb. We were going to lose them both to the network you know, negotiations were virtually completed."

"So you were already prepared for the loss, professionally-speaking of course?"

"Starting to be. They were going to leave a big hole in our operation. But we weren't going to lose Hilary, she would be a fixture for a long time once she and Kendrick got hitched. The society wedding of the year, station exclusive, network rights presold and Marjoree and Cochrane doing the coverage. But no Paul, we weren't prepared for a loss like this."

"So you see Paul," Stanton interjected, "Max needs us as much as we need him just now."

"Sure do," Kleberson replied. He turned to Huberstein again: "anyone at the station holding any grudges? Sorry Max, but it has to be asked."

"I understand Paul. Let's put it this way, we have over two hundred employees and every one of them had a problem with Cochrane, he was that type of guy. Hell, even I wanted to kill him on more than one occasion - figuratively speaking of course!" Huberstein cast a slightly worried look towards Kleberson. Seeing no adverse reaction, he continued: "but the girls, no. They were both darlings to work with. Marjoree always had time for people off-air, although it would be fair to say that a high-profile persona like hers will always invoke a degree of jealousy in some people - that's just human nature. As for Hilary, everyone loved working with her and not just because of her endless patience, she was also very generous. For example, last year one of our secretaries had a medical problem with her little boy; he needed an operation, but the medical insurance wouldn't cover the cost. Hilary just wrote a cheque and gave it to her. Not a loan, a gift. That's the type of person she was Paul, absolutely genuine."

Kleberson looked at his watch, then turned to Stanton: "well Chief, as you know, I'm holding a briefing down in the Squad Room at three-thirty, so I had better get down there. We've spent the last day collecting bodies and chasing shadows, so I think we need to take stock of what we do have." He turned back to Huberstein as he rose from his chair: "Max, if you'll excuse me. Thanks for the info, I will pass everything we find through the Chief."

"Thanks Paul, I will need to reassure the staff at the station that it's not them that are being targeted. I am right in that assumption?" Huberstein reverted to his journalist persona.

"Right now Max, I couldn't honestly tell you. You will appreciate that we will need to interview all of the staff; when we lift the edge of that carpet who knows what we may find crawling underneath. I'll be in touch later to make arrangements."

"Fine." Huberstein rose himself and turned to Stanton: "what about breaking the Cochrane story?"

Kleberson looked at Stanton and spoke first: "I think we're done with the preliminaries out at the apartment, so I see no reason why we can't release the basic details we have."

Stanton rose and held his hand out to Huberstein: "there you go Max, we will give you a head start. I won't release officially until four p.m."

Huberstein shook Stanton's extended hand: "thanks Chief." Then he turned to Kleberson: "let's just all do our utmost to nail this lunatic as quickly as we can."

"With you there Max, but please don't allow the reportage to get too strident, we've got enough on our plate without encouraging the public into forming a vigilante posse." Huberstein nodded his understanding.

Fifty-Four

It was just after three-thirty p.m. when Kleberson entered the conference room. All of his Squad were already there, plus Morley slumped back in his adopted corner with the ever-present cigarette glow creating a sinister aura around him. Kleberson apologised as he walked to the front of the gathering: "sorry to keep you guys, I've been with the Chief."

"Always the excuse, huh Kleberson," puffed Morley from his lair.

"Button it!" came a booming voice from the doorway. It was Chief Stanton, glowering across into the dark recess from where the cynical comment had emerged: "all departmental politics are hereby suspended until we have solved these murders and put a stop to this motherfucker's activities. And anyone, hear me Lieutenant Morley - that's anyone, who wants to contravene that direct order will find themselves on night duty patrolling the marshalling yards for the rest of their career. Do I make myself clear on that?"

"Yes Chief," came the instant response from all in the room, accompanied by a rustling noise as all took a less relaxed, upright and attentive position in conjunction with their response. All except Morley that was, who just took another long drag on his Marlboro, illuminating his corner with the rosy light from the tip.

Stanton leant against a filing cabinet which visually dimpled on contact: "it's all yours Lieutenant, away you go."

Kleberson walked over to the large whiteboard at the end of the room that had been wiped clean of all other work-in-progress in preparation, a visual indicator to all present that there was, right at that point in time, only one priority for the Squad. He picked-up a marker pen, then placed a picture of the dead face of Hilary Nicholson in the centre-top. As he wrote her name above the picture, he began: "victim number one - Hilary Nicholson, top local businesswoman, fiancé of one Jackson Kendrick the Third". He slapped-up another smaller photo to the right of the first showing the familiar features of the person known to all in the department as 'The Turd'. Kleberson resisted all urges to write this moniker above it, instead just writing 'JKIII', then drew a line connecting the two photos: "she was found in a house she used in Derby, which she called her safehouse. Moreno, did they know anything about this up at Eastborough?"

"Not as far as I could find Boss, I spoke to the cleaner, but as she was only employed to work during the daytime, she rarely saw Ms Nicholson. She did say that it wasn't unusual for her employer to not have used her bed for days at a time, so it looks like she stayed elsewhere a lot. Cleaner didn't think she entertained at Eastborough much either."

Kleberson continued: "we also believe that she drove to Derby earlier in the evening. Did we get anything on the car Capaldi?"

"We had a member of the public respond to our TV appeal with a possible sighting on West Kellogg out near I-two-three-five during the afternoon; hood was down on the car, but just the driver in it. I spoke to him, he was pretty certain it was her - distinctive combination he said. Reckon he had a little fantasy going there." A knowing chuckle rippled across the room.

Kleberson ignored it: "that's near the airport - she could have been picking someone up. Have we checked CCTV at the airport yet?" All the squad members shook their heads. "OK, put a priority on that Capaldi; anything from Mary Jourdain's boys?"

"Still zip Boss."

"Moving on then to the relationship. We know that this was to be a marriage of convenience, because they had signed a pre-nup. We don't have a copy of the document yet, but we do know that it was drawn-up by the family lawyer, Emil Friedmann ..." he slapped a third photo alongside that of JKIII and wrote the name 'Friedmann' over it "... without the knowledge of his father." Another photo was placed the opposite side of JKIII, over which was written the word

'Junior'. "We also know that the arrangement was to be that Jackson Kendrick the Third got to father one child, then that would be the end of his physical involvement. There were conditions, however, which allowed him to carry-on his philandering lifestyle, provided that he did so in such a way that he never brought any scandal upon either his wife or the future child. If he did, then he would lose the family fortune, had he already inherited, or his claim to it if he hadn't, in favour of the child, not Ms Nicholson."

"How could we possibly know all this?" came another cynical enquiry from Morley's dark corner. "Do we have a copy of this agreement?"

Kleberson ignored the interruption and continued as if the question hadn't been needed: "we know this because victim number two, Marjoree Rolles ..." he slapped another large picture, this time of the dead Ms Rolles, in the centre of the space to the left of Hilary Nicholson's and began writing the new name above it, "... witnessed the agreement. She volunteered the outline information to me yesterday morning before she was murdered, when I met her on the way back from murder scene one. She would have given a full disclosure to Chris later that morning, had she not first met with whoever killed her. Capaldi, did we find a copy of the document in Ms Rolles' apartment?"

"Sorry Boss, no," Capaldi responded with a hint of dejection.

"Well she had to have one somewhere, so we need to speak to her lawyer; if that doesn't turn it up, see if she kept a safe deposit box anywhere. So we know that there is a link from our second victim to the son." He drew a line between the two pictures: "in fact there is a second link as well, because murder scene two, Ms Rolle's apartment, is next-door to that of one Jackson Kendrick the Third, in the building he owns." A small picture of the building was placed beneath the picture of Ms Rolles and lines drawn between it and the photos of Ms Rolles and JKIII. "We also have several links to our first victim, because the two ladies were close friends and shared more than just rooms at USC, where they both graduated." He placed a print-out of the USC logo above Hilary Nicholson's picture, then drew lines between it and both victims' photos, then a much bolder line between the two victims.

"Are we saying here that Ms Nicholson swung both ways?" The enquiry came from Stanton: "do we know this, or is it just speculation?"

"No Chief, we know that she was a lesbian and that she wanted a child; not an adoptive child, it had to be her own flesh and blood. What's more, it had to be from a well-connected stud, so that it would be secure for life regardless of what happened to its mother. Marjoree Rolles assured me that if Jackson Kendrick the Third had chickened out of the agreement pre-wedding day, then Ms Nicholson would have just called the whole thing off and carried-on looking for another Mr Right-Connections."

Stanton nodded his satisfaction and Kleberson continued: "Hilary and Marjoree were an item at USC; they were still very close but became more like sisters as their lifestyles had drifted them apart romantically. Ms Rolles said that Ms Nicholson had occasional flings, as she put it, but never let any relationship develop beyond that. I got the impression that neither were much-interested in one-night-stands. So at this stage in proceedings, as of midday yesterday, we had quite a cosy scenario, plus one obvious main suspect." He tapped his pen against the picture marked 'JKIII': "he gains because he is freed from an agreement he never should have made and both other signatories to that agreement are no longer able to tell the tale. At the moment, he has no alibi that we are aware of, but I'm sure that will change as soon as Mr Friedmann here …" he tapped the lawyer's nose on his photo and continued in a more cynical tone "… has arranged it all and condescends to allow his client to speak to us, after he has composed himself from the obvious devastation he is feeling at present, as he showed to us in the lobby of his building yesterday afternoon."

Stanton straightened his pose as if to intervene, but was beaten to the punch by Kleberson continuing: "at which point matters became slightly more complex thanks to the arrival of Kryczek."

"And who the hell is Kryczek?" enquired Morley.

"Ah yes, I forgot, you weren't in our briefing yesterday afternoon were you Lieutenant Morley? FBI Agent Kryczek is a Profiler working on a multiple serial, codenamed Vitruvio, whose M.O. resembles that of both victims."

"Oh I get it Kleberson," Morley responded, "the politics in all of this are already so difficult for you that you pop across to see your close friend Schneider, who finds some obscure excuse for the Feds to muscle-in on the investigation, so they can use it to open-up other lines of enquiry that will end-up with some unconnected high-profile case that gets them all commendations. After which Teflon-cop returns to the Feds unblemished by any of the shit that this department has to clean-up afterwards on his behalf."

Despite his earlier dictat, Stanton chose not to intervene directly in this interchange, instead fixing Morley with a long stare. The recipient was unaware of this, because he kept his focus on the presenter, who in turn found no problem in ignoring his accuser much like a schoolteacher ignores a disruptive child in the classroom, continuing: "Vitruvio is responsible for at least sixteen other murders over the last couple of years, all across the country and in a grouping pattern which, thus far, these cases are following." He turned to Morley, looking him directly in the eye with the same focus that had helped him dismantle many a suspect's story in the interrogation room, and which even Morley found discomforting: "at present the FBI are providing direct liaison to us and are giving us any and all data they have on this killer to help us to establish whether or not we are dealing with a copy-cat or the real thing. Until we have a definite link, because at present our only potential avenue on that will be via forensic evidence, we are all treating these murders as a local matter."

As if to reinforce this line, Stanton chipped-in: "however, because of certain intelligence provided to us by the FBI regarding Vitruvio, in particular the apparent choice of victims, which indicated that Jackson Kendrick the Third, as well as being a suspect, might actually be a potential victim, we decided to make arrangements to take him into protective custody last evening."

"What, we've arrested him and have him here in the building?" McKinley enquired, surprised that he was unaware of such a development.

"No," Stanton responded, "he volunteered to submit himself to our custody and he is currently at a location known only to his legal counsel and the officers who are guarding him. He will be brought here for questioning when we are all ready for that to happen."

'Meaning sometime never,' thought McKinley, but decided not to share that thought with the room, most of whom had already privately come to the same conclusion.

Holdsworth's voice brought the room back into focus: "there is another potential suspect." He pointed to the right of the board: "Junior."

"Nonsense!" Stanton snapped, pulling himself to his full six-four height, "he was in Topeka when the first murder was committed, at a function that I was also attending, along with around two hundred others."

"But he wouldn't have done it himself Chief," Holdsworth responded, determined not to be brow-beaten into being submissive on a vital point, "men like him never do. He would use a hired-hand and from what I've seen of the FBI files so far, they show that these murders are being committed by one cool sonofabitch with a distinct signature, which has not been ruled-out as being that of a hit-man who likes to leave a calling-card."

Stanton decided to back-off a bit. He returned to leaning on the cabinet, which groaned at the prospect, before sending back: "so why would he?"

"Because he found-out about the agreement. So he silences the two ladies and stitches-up his son ... neat!"

Chris McKinley joined in: "but he still has Friedmann to deal with. He also knows about it."

"But if he did the arranging," Holdsworth responded, "then Junior has built-in deniability whilst securing Friedmann's silence through them being partners in crime."

"This is all just speculation!" Stanton responded in an authoritative tone.

"Agreed," Kleberson took control again, "but we can't just rule it out, neither can we make it our prime line of enquiry simply because it's a scenario that conveniently ticks all the boxes."

"Then we mustn't leave-out the box marked son-in-law." All heads swung towards the new voice in the discussion. It was the old-lag Dean, who wasn't renowned for his contributions when open forum was attended by the top brass, although when he did join in, it was always input that had been well-considered and came from the voice of greatest experience in the Squad.

"Come on, it ain't rocket-science is it?" he continued, "everyone's so all-fired concentrated on this pact to produce an heir for 'The Turd' to guarantee the line of succession, you've forgotten that Junior's already got two grandchildren and they've both been fathered by the family's lawyer. Provided the heir remains childless, which bearing in mind his predilection for toxic substances is more than likely how it will pan-out, unless he's already got some unknown piccaninnies from previous dalliances, his line of the dynasty is a cul-de-sac. So who gains most from that line being severed early?"

McKinley pitched-in: "Junior's a hard man. He doesn't strike me as needing to put some convoluted plot together to disinherit his son. He's already done that once when he felt that the family business was under threat from his excesses."

He looked at the Chief as he said this, but it was Dean that continued: "if he doesn't know about the agreement, it's because Friedmann's not told him. And if Friedmann's not told him, it's because the lawyer's holding all the cards. For me, if this is the whole of the picture, Friedmann's the prime suspect. He wins all round if 'The Turd' goes down."

Kleberson, having allowed the debate to run to see where it went, decided to bring it to a halt at that point: "unfortunately, that tidy little histogram became multi-complex today, as we now have a third victim - Tom Cochrane." He slapped a picture of yet another lifeless face into the gap to the right of Hilary Nicholson's and began to write 'Cochrane' beneath, when there was a crash in the corner.

Morley had shot to his feet, knocking his chair over in the process and was staring at the board: "when did that happen?" he shouted, his face turning purple with rage.

The room fell deathly quiet at the unexpected reaction, except for Kleberson, who having completed the name continued without breaking stride, or looking around: "Cochrane failed to show for the press conference this morning and his station was unable to contact him. He was found dead in his apartment when the janitor opened it at around ten-thirty a.m. M.E. estimates time of death at between nine and eleven p.m. last night. Similar M.O. to the first two victims."

"What's that in his mouth?" Morley continued in a louder, almost hysterical voice, still staring at the picture of Cochrane on the board. Kleberson turned to view the scene for the first time, suddenly appreciating that this was not how he had expected to see the normally combative Morley, who was beginning to shake with what everyone assumed was rage.

Before Kleberson could adjust his thoughts, Morley let out a groan and made a bolt for the door, which he threw open before disappearing into the corridor outside. Kleberson looked across at Stanton, who appeared as stunned as everyone else at this totally unexpected outburst. Stanton pulled himself up from his leaning position and there was a slight creak as he did so, almost as if the cabinet was breathing a metallic sigh of relief.

He raised his hand, palm-outwards: "I'll go, you carry-on." He turned to look directly at the rookie Holdsworth: "but keep your speculations in this room, for now at least."

With that, Stanton left the room and pulled the door quietly shut behind him.

the commune

Fifty-Five

Two years had elapsed since that Sunday lunch at the home of the, since retired, General Kleberson. He and his 'two wives', as Paul termed them, had moved to Yuba City over a year previously. They had purchased a large colonial on Second Street overlooking the river, that Paul had christened 'The Commune'. This was due to the bohemian atmosphere surrounding that household, which had been turned into a small bed and breakfast establishment with a twist.

The establishment, run with enthusiasm by the 'two wives', had quickly acquired itself a highly-positive reputation, because they provided an evening meal in the price of the room, but it was the guests' prerogative whether they took it or not. The twist was that all meals were served not in a breakfast room at bijou tables, but in a large dining room around a massive early nineteenth century carved dining table that seated up to twenty, while Walter regaled the guests with forty-years-worth of air force anecdotes. Very few guests declined this regular entertainment, in fact there was a waiting list among the locals who were allowed to fill any spare places at the table each evening at no charge, in return for contributing their own anecdotes to add to the variety.

Family visits by Paul's family had become somewhat restricted by both children being in full-time education. In addition, Leanne's job with the accountancy practice had expanded to five part-days a week, plus some home working and, of course, there were the demands of the Homicide Squad.

Paul himself found the move to Homicide easy. The tasks were all-encompassing and, by and large, self-contained which, as he was a serial completed-finisher, meant there was considerable job-satisfaction. The downside was the sporadic and intense nature of the work. At times of low-activity, other squads could embark on special projects, such as clamping-down on a particularly difficult locality. In Homicide, the jobs came to the squad with no regularity or deference to the detectives' private lives. So there were weeks, sometimes, of perfectly-normal family life - the nine-to-five routine, picking the kids up from school, family dinner together, weekend outings.

These, however, were punctuated by the sudden call at three a.m. followed by twenty-four-seven activity for as long as it took to apprehend a killer, or killers, then building evidence into a case that the District Attorney could take before a Grand Jury, and beyond to a conviction by twelve good men and true.

It was those periods that were the most difficult for both parents to cope with. Paul missed the regular contact with his family as intensely as he had when marooned in England by Leanne's father's illness; in fact moreso as they were within touching distance at all times, not separated by a vast ocean. Leanne resented the sudden demands that threw-over her home life at the ring of a phone, plus the fears of whether her husband would even be coming home during those periods, not through the work-intensity but through being in intensive-care, or worse. These she had to suppress so that the children did not pick-up on any anxiety.

Matt was, by then, old enough to understand cops and robbers programmes on TV and make the connection that his father was on the good-guys' side. This was fine while the good-guys won, but occasionally they didn't, which brought questions, more often than not when combined with Matt not having seen his father at all for several days. These tensions were all to come to a head just weeks before the Millennium.

Fifty-Six

It was the first week after the end of the fall semester and Leanne was balancing work demands with the need to entertain the children, who would be home until early in the new year. Paul had a case coming to an end and expected, within a couple of days, to be able to take-up some of the strain before Christmas. Without the built-in child-support lost when all three grandparents moved West, Leanne relied on friends at times like these, one of whom was Clara, Sam Schneider's wife, who was Godparent to both children.

Sam and Clara had not started a family, for reasons never discussed with the Klebersons. But Clara was a natural with children, so Leanne was more than happy to share her two with someone who treated them almost as her own. Auntie Clara, as the kids knew her, would drive over and collect them early in the morning to take them out on a treat, or to her home, or both. Leanne would then drive across town after work to collect them. Which is what had happened on that crisp, but clear-skied, December day.

Leanne's normal route, one of several that Paul had outlined for her in order to avoid any potential trouble-spots, and updated regularly from his knowledge of what was happening in the city, would be straight back down Rock, taking her all the way to Derby. That day, though, she had agreed to pick-up a neighbour who worked at Wesley Medical Center, because the neighbour's car was in the shop with some serious engine problems. Wesley was on the corner of Central and Hillside, less than a mile from the edge of the badlands.

So Paul had recommended she take Thirteenth from the Schneiders as far as Oliver, then drop across to Central, retracing the last leg having collected the neighbour, then on down Oliver to Kellogg and use that back to Rock.

The first part of the journey was uneventful, apart from having to deal with a standard disagreement in the back seat about who would win a fight between Cat Woman and The Penguin, a debate that had been prompted through them seeing a couple of old episodes of Batman from the 'sixties on TV that afternoon. Leanne used her best diplomatic skills to bring the siblings to the conclusion that it would probably result in a stalemate.

As they approached the junction with Oliver, she became aware that there were several flashing lights which turned-out to be on the roofs of two Police Cruisers blocking-off the turn to the south. All traffic was being waved through the junction by one pissed-off looking patrolman, so she had little choice but to continue. The next crossroads were with Hillside, so she decided to take that road instead, even though it would take her uncomfortably close to the outer reaches of the badlands. The alternative was to retrace her route all the way back to Rock, which could easily add half an hour to the journey.

The lights changed and she swung onto North Hillside. The first stretch of road featured several businesses, mainly fast food outlets. About a hundred yards ahead on her right was a disused gas station, on the forecourt of which were a crowd of youths, some on bikes, some on foot. They seemed at first to be talking but, as she drew nearer, she quickly realised they were arguing; the argument centred on two men on a trail bike. As she watched, the passenger drew a gun and aimed it at one of the standing crowd. There was a sound like a pop, then another, then another. Three of the crowd dropped to the ground, the others scattered. The passenger slapped the driver of the bike on his back, who responded by riding off the forecourt straight at Leanne's minivan.

She realised that they were about to collide head-on, so hit the brakes; as did the bike rider. Then came a moment, as both vehicles slid to a halt, that seemed to freeze in time like a video being paused. In that moment, with the bike broadside across the front of the minivan, the passenger lifted his gun and pointed it towards Leanne. She froze in total fear, only aware of a scream and frantic "Mummieee!" coming from behind her. In the freeze-frame, the passenger, looking directly into her eyes, pretended to shoot her, then to fire two more shots past her - 'pfff, pfff, pfff' he mouthed as he did so. With that, the video restarted and, as quickly as he had done previously, the driver of the bike wound open the throttle and directed the bike across to the correct side of the road before roaring up to the junction. It ran the light and turned left along Thirteenth as several vehicles slewed to a stop to avoid a collision.

It took Leanne several seconds to realise that she had not been shot at. Her first reaction was to slam the car into gear and escape as quickly as she could, but the screams coming from her young daughter in the back demanded her immediate attention. She turned around and did her best to reassure Lucy, recognising quickly that it was the sudden stop that had caused the hysterics. Not so Matt, who was sat quite still and pale - he had seen it all.

Leanne's protective instincts took over immediately. She turned back around in her seat, let off the brake and accelerated away, taking a brief glance to her right where, on the forecourt, three men lay bleeding while some of another half-dozen were already attempting first aid; others stood with cellphones to their ears. Very quickly the buildings in the street evaporated as she drove between the two cemeteries that flanked the next section of Hillside. The screaming from Lucy in the back had stopped, replaced by a regular and repeated tearful 'Mummy' separated by deep sobbing. Matt was still completely silent.

With the lights at Ninth, thankfully, green, the minivan shot across the junction well above the limit. Once over the brow, she could see Wesley to the left and decided to get into one of its car parks. The first opportunity was by turning left onto Murdoch, then left again into a staff car park, where the minivan screeched to a halt in one of the marked slots. Almost before it had come to a halt, her seatbelt was off, she was out of the front and had slid-open the rear door.

She grabbed Lucy out of her child seat and hugged her closely, simultaneously releasing Matt from his harness. He climbed out of the car and stood next to his mother, wrapping his arms around her legs. Leanne put her hand on his back and pulled him closer while she decided what to do next.

As she did so, two WPD Cruisers wailed past the car park heading north up Hillside towards the scene she had fled minutes earlier.

Fifty-Seven

"Here you are Mrs Kleberson;" Jerry Dean handed a mug of steaming black coffee to Leanne. She was sat in her husband's small office alongside the Homicide Squad Room in City Hall. On her lap, the small form of her daughter Lucy, sucking her thumb as she cuddled-into her mother's breast. Leanne would normally have been persuading her daughter to take her thumb from her mouth, but this was not a normal situation.

"How about you young man, would you like a soda?" the kindly senior detective asked the other diminutive figure in the room, who was sat in his father's chair, rotating it from side to side. This was the first time Matt had encountered an office chair at such close-quarters.

"No thank you Sir, I'm fine," the seven-year-old responded politely.

"He's a fine boy Ma'am," Dean said to Leanne, "you must be very proud."

"Yes," Leanne responded, "we are." She smiled at Matt as his motions in the chair became longer, obviously building-up to an eventual full twirl, once he had the confidence to try it.

"The Lieutenant won't be long, he's just briefing the Chief."

"That's fine, thank you." Dean left them alone and Leanne gave Lucy another of the many hugs she had been dispensing for the last hour or so.

When Paul had received her phone call, he was en route to the scene at Hillside with his Deputy, Chris McKinley. With several units already at the scene, they had diverted immediately to meet his family in the Wesley Medical Center car park. McKinley had left him there continuing-on to take charge of the scene. Paul packed the family into their minivan and took them straight back to City Hall.

The minute he saw them, his experience told him that his wife was in shock, his daughter traumatised and his son in withdrawal. Along with the sketchy information he had received from the officers at the scene and the brief description Leanne had given on the phone, he had all he needed to know about what had happened and how close he had come to losing them. However much his professionalism may have tried to persuade him what to do, this was not the time for him to be a policeman. That night in particular, and for whatever time necessary thereafter, he had to be husband and father to his frightened family.

That is exactly what he had told Chief Stanton at the short briefing he had given about the murder of a badlands gang leader and the hospitalisation of two of his soldiers, one of whom was not expected to last the night. Stanton was not happy at the prospect of this particular Lieutenant taking immediate compassionate leave, but recognised that he was being given no choice in the matter. He also knew Kleberson well enough to realise that, if he pushed too hard, he would be looking for a new leader for his Homicide Squad. He took the path to the lesser of those two evils.

Stanton imposed one condition - no, more an instruction. Mrs Kleberson would have to look at some mugshots before she left City Hall. Paul knew he had no choice in that; she was a material witness to a murder and her family connections could not excuse her those aspects of her civil responsibilities.

This was what Paul had been briefing Pete Capaldi about after he had come back to the Squad Room. They already had two names for the pair on the trail bike from the other gang members at the scene, but corroboration of either from a completely independent witness would remove the doubts of any bureaucratic prosecutor from the DA's office, easing the process to a swift arrest. While Capaldi prepared the arrays that would be shown to Leanne, Paul concluded his instructions to the other detectives already on the case, then made a call to Chris McKinley, who was finishing-up at the scene. Having briefed McKinley on what was happening, he handed control of the case to him and walked back across the Squad Room to his office.

"How are we doing?" he asked Leanne.

"We're bearing-up Paul. How much longer do we have to stay here?"

"Not much longer, one more thing to finish-up and that will be me done for a few days."

Leanne looked at him with slight astonishment: "a few days?"

"I've got some time owing, now seemed like a good time to take it."

"But, you …" Paul cut her off by briefly putting his index finger to his lips to stop her saying any more. He turned to his son, still rotating back and forth in his father's chair: "whaddya think Matt, shall we all go Christmas shopping at the mall tomorrow?"

Lucy suddenly perked-up: "can we have an Oreos milkshake at Spangles?"

"Reckon so Lucy."

Lucy looked up at her mother: "that'll be great Mummy, won't it?"

"Scrumptious, just like you." She squeezed her daughter again, delighted at the signs of normality returning.

"Does this go all the way round Dad?" Matt questioned from the chair.

"Why don't you try it and find out?" Paul responded.

With that, his son gave himself an almighty kick-off with his right foot and the chair shot all the way round and carried on to make almost a second circuit. "Wow!" he said as it came to a stop, "you must have so much fun every day!"

"Curses," Paul said with a smile, "now you all know my secret."

Pete Capaldi appeared at the door and nodded almost imperceptibly to let Paul know he was ready. Paul put on his most enthusiastic voice to the kids: "and I've got even more secrets here as well - how about you two let me show you?"

"Oh yes!" Lucy exclaimed, jumping off her mother's lap, "then can I have a go in your chair?" Paul gathered her up in his arms: "oh I reckon we could manage one little spin." He stretched out his free hand towards Matt: "you coming then?" he asked, and his son slid out of the chair to take hold of it.

But before he would leave the room, he asked another question: "is Mummy coming?"

"Not this time, she's going to have a little chat with Detective Capaldi here, then we're all going home." He looked at Leanne with a look that said 'please just go with the flow' and she picked-up on it immediately.

"That's right," she responded, "but you can tell me all about it when you get back, OK?"

Fifty-Eight

That night, while Leanne settled the two children in their rooms, Paul made a call to his father in California. Walter was not too pleased to be summoned from his nightly dinner party, but quickly refocused when the reason behind the urgency of the call became apparent. Father and son quickly agreed on a course of action.

Paul had outlined the situation, but had not included specific detail, such as Leanne picking-out from the arrays Luiz Suarez, notorious head of the Ángeles de la Muerte, one of the most feared gangs in North Wichita. She also identified his second in command, Alberto Peres, as the driver of the bike. This, in professional terms, was good news. Suarez had been running every possible racket from the badlands for years, the tentacles of his organisation rapidly spreading way beyond that limited area over the previous twelve months. Their arrest would slow that down immediately; incarceration on remand would destabilise the hierarchy. Convictions, together with the associated penalty for first-degree murder, would put the organisation out of business once and for all.

The bad news was that Suarez had been arrested many times over the years, several times on solid evidence guaranteeing a conviction. Unfortunately, everybody in the WPD, including Paul, knew that the main reason that Suarez was still at large was the constant stream of witnesses that had either recanted, or disappeared entirely, before any major progress could be made on the case. This time a conviction would hinge around his own wife's evidence.

With the children asleep, the parents curled up on the sofa in each other's arms. Not much was said for ten minutes, then Leanne just opened-up. She needed to unburden it all and, particularly, she felt the need to apologise for being where she had continually been advised not to be. However, Paul was not interested in that minor point, he was just happy that his family was still intact.

Besides, he already knew exactly what had happened from the witness accounts, several of whom had mentioned the Windstar that the bike nearly collided with and how the terrified lady driver had accelerated away from the scene with her kids screaming in the back. The problem was, if he knew about it from those sources, so would Suarez, who was not a man to be put off taking the necessary steps to secure his freedom by the mere fact that this key witness was the wife of a Police Lieutenant - quite the opposite.

Once Leanne had finished relating the events, Paul told her of the agreement he had made with his father that evening - she and the children would fly out as soon as they could to San Francisco, where Walter would collect them and drive them to Yuba City. Walter was fixing-up the flights and Paul was not leaving her side until she went through the departure gate at Mid-Continent.

Leanne looked at him with greater concern than previously: "you know the men I picked-out, don't you?"

Paul didn't lie to his wife, not at anytime. She would never have forgiven him for keeping anything back, even in circumstances such as these: "we do," he replied.

"And they're bad, yes?"

"They're bad."

"How long will we need to be away?"

"It shouldn't take too long to round them up, but just to be safe, we're spending Christmas with the Grandparents this year."

"Will that be all of us?"

"It will, I promise."

"Are you in danger as well?"

"No more than usual."

Leanne let out a deep sigh: "oh Paul, what have I done to us?"

Fifty-Nine

Christmas 1999 was the last that this particular branch of the Kleberson family would spend together as an intact unit. Leanne delivered the news in a tearful walk along the banks of the Yuba river.

The Commune

Paul had arrived at 'The Commune' three days before Christmas. The arrest of Luiz Suarez for what had become a double murder case, had proved remarkably easy. He had been spotted in the passenger seat of a low-rider Honda by the crew of one of Patrol South's unmarked units, who followed it to a building on South Pershing. Having established he was remaining at the building, they called-in the location and twenty minutes later a tactical unit put the front door through to find him, high on crack, with two of his whores. Taking Peres turned out to be just as easy, as he was in one of the rear rooms out of his skull on smack - the Honda had been his.

The pair had been swiftly remanded, without bail, at the El Dorado Correctional Facility, where they were segregated for their own safety. However, the segregation didn't work, because, on the day prior to Paul's flight to California, both were found dead, Peres in the shower block, Suarez in an exercise area. Suarez had over a hundred knife wounds and had clearly paid the summary penalty for a number of previous crimes against other gang warlords, ones that had the reach to even find a way to him in a high-security facility.

The news of the removal of any need for his wife to testify at a trial, Paul expected, would be the best Christmas present he could give the family. Indeed, the celebrations had been some of the happiest they had experienced, with all three grandparents on top form with the children. So Leanne's subsequent announcement that she and the children were staying in Yuba came as a huge shock for Paul.

Even then, he thought it would be for a specific period of time. He had not the slightest inkling that not only would it be permanent, but that his marriage was to end in divorce within months. He had done nothing wrong, Leanne explained, it was her that was at fault. She could no longer live with the fear associated with his job, neither could she be responsible for him having to give up the vocation he was so perfect for. She had seen what leaving the FBI had done to him, but more recently what it meant to have his family exposed to the danger he fought to rid the streets of.

She hadn't met anyone else, neither did she wish to. She would bring their children up so that he could be proud of them, with the help of the owners of 'The Commune'. He could visit whenever he wanted, or have them to visit him, but importantly this would be to his timetable - he must be free to pursue his career unrestricted by them. The divorce was necessary because he also had to be able to have casual relationships free of any guilt regarding her.

This was not some cowardly act by someone who could not take the stress of such a relationship. It was an incredible sacrifice by one who loved another too much.

an assignation

Sixty

Moreno was the first to react to Morley's departure: "what the hell was that about?" he queried.

"Something touched a nerve somewhere," said McKinley.

"Shame we didn't find it years ago," observed Dean, deadpan-faced as ever.

"Enough," said Kleberson, "we'll worry about Mr Morley's sensitivities after we've solved this lot, but with him taking the Chief out of our hair for now, let's move on shall we?" He turned back to the whiteboard and pointed at the deathly face of Tom Cochrane: "Cochrane had links to both previous victims in that he also shared rooms with both of them at USC." He drew a line from the top of Cochrane's photo to the USC logo: "they also all worked at KNKW," with which he slapped a station logo centrally beneath the photos, then drew lines from it to each victim's photo.

McKinley was the first to react: "Hilary Nicholson worked for KNKW?"

Kleberson responded: "she presented the weekly finance show, as all of you will already know, seeing how much spare cash you have to invest all the time." The laughter generated took some of the tension out of the room.

McKinley came back: "this could be anyone at the station with an axe to grind."

"An axe, or a presenter?" quipped Moreno.

The remark attracted a slightly disapproving glance from his boss, who continued: "keep it focussed boys - yes Chris, it certainly could. Also we have very little to link the Kendricks to Cochrane and, unfortunately, 'The Turd' was within our control when this one happened, so he looks out of the frame as far as Cochrane's concerned."

"Unless he was the one that hired the hit man." Holdsworth was developing his theory on the hoof.

McKinley responded: "but why hit Cochrane?"

"Maybe he knew about the agreement. After all, he worked closely with Marjoree Rolles; they could have discussed it, or he may have just picked something up from overhearing a conversation between Rolles and Nicholson. He was in the media after all, wouldn't have taken much for him to sniff-out a situation. What if he decided to blackmail the Kendricks?"

"Or break the story," Dean observed, "that'd spook Friedmann as well."

"Alright," Kleberson was trying to move things forward, "let's have a look at the scenes and see if they give us anything." He slapped up three more photos, one alongside each of the victims, each showing the body in situ at the crime scene: "similar M.O. including the staged presentation of bodies; that all points at Vitruvio, especially when we take the timings into account. The FBI files show that he strikes in groups of four, the first three within a twenty-four-hour period, the fourth forty-eight hours later. We have had three corpses in twenty-four hours, which suggests that we have until nine p.m. tomorrow night to work-out who number four will be and get ourselves into a position to catch this S-o-B in the act. Therefore, we don't have the time or the manpower to follow all potential avenues. So far this perp is ahead of us all of the time and is leaving us false lines of enquiry that he wants us to follow so that he stays there; if we're going to catch-up with him, then we have to start ruling-out some of those. So let's start by ruling-out a local actually committing the crimes, because we've never seen anything remotely like this before, not around these parts. I also don't believe it's a copy-cat because, up until now, no reference to a serial-killer with this M.O, or the name Vitruvio, has made it to the national media."

McKinley responded quickly to that: "I know we have every indication that this could be a serial, but I think we can put that one right at the bottom of the list. After all, what are the chances of a random serial hitting three people with such close connections as these three had. That's a lot of zeros Paul."

"I agree, plus, there is one aspect of these three that does not seem to match the previous patterns and that is the sexual activity. Vitruvio commits sexual assault on all of his victims, either pre- or post-mortem, or maybe even both; this had a consistency that never varied. However, our M.E. has observed that this time the sexual violence seems to be escalating in each case. Cochrane's presentation was particularly violent and matches none of the previous victims. Question is, if this is a hit man with a signature, then why the escalation?"

"We don't know that he always hits in groupings though, do we?" Holdsworth had joined the discussion again.

Kleberson paused to take-in this angle momentarily, then prompted the rookie: "go on."

"That's what came up on the FBI radar because that's what they were looking for - connections from linked murders in Palm Springs. The obvious one was the signature presentation; that's where their codename for him came from after all. But what is that for? If it's a serial, then it would be for publicity - serials get their kicks off of the publicity. That's what makes every murder more of a high because of the apparently futile pursuit by the authorities, which in reality the perp knows is also pulling a tightening noose around their own neck. Then there's the panic each unsolved murder causes in the local population. None of that seems to have happened with the previous groupings, mainly because the perp hasn't stayed around beyond three or four murders in as many days."

"Which brings us back to a hit man," Kleberson responded, "but we've discussed that previously and agreed that professionals don't leave calling cards."

McKinley butted-in: "what did you say at Ms Rolles' flat, Paul? Agent Schneider thought the perp may have taken photos to send to someone. He thought it may have been to put the frighteners on, but you had another idea."

Kleberson was thinking tangentially as he spoke quietly and deliberately: "an invoice, I thought it might be an invoice. I've completed the job, so here, as previously agreed, is the proof the work has been done - send the money."

"What if the perp came for just the one job - Nicholson," McKinley offered, "but then it got messy and he had to hang around. Maybe he's getting pissed about having the extra work put on him. As a professional, he'll know that the longer he hangs around, the more likely we are to find him."

"And the groupings are examples of when this has happened before," Holdsworth added, "Vitruvio went there to do the one job, but then something happened that made him stay around to tidy-up the loose ends. There may well be more single hits all over the place, but they never came-up on the radar because they were exactly that, a single hit that he made, got paid and disappeared into the ether."

"OK," Kleberson continued, "let's follow that for a minute. Will we find the calling card each time?"

Dean had been listening intently and was ready with his thoughts: "not necessarily, most hits are prepaid because most of the clients are criminals. They buy by reputation and the killer got that reputation by not screwing the pooch. The money changes hands, the job gets done, nothing more to be said."

"That's my point, no need for a calling card."

"Absolutely. However, sometimes a client comes along that has the cash, but not the experience. Let's say, hypothetically of course, that you're an heir to a multi-billion fortune with expensive hobbies and habits, some of which might bring you into contact with acquaintances that have criminal connections. You mention, in passing, that you could do with being relieved of a difficult problem, you're made an offer and you decide to take it. But you don't accumulate fortunes trusting everybody with your money, so honour among thieves isn't a concept that has any great resonance with your own philosophy. You're fairly OK with a non-returnable deposit, but you want the goods delivered before releasing the balance."

"There's your invoice Paul," McKinley observed.

"Yes, I see that, but what are the other vics - additional jobs?"

"Maybe," Dean continued, "subject to stage payments. Or …" He paused.

"Or what? Kleberson asked.

"They're penalty clauses." The room went quiet waiting on the old lag for more pearls of wisdom. Dean noticed that all eyes were fixed on him, but he just shrugged: "for any cockroach multi-billionaire the perfect deal has to be when you end-up with the goods and the money, surely?"

Jerry Dean had little time for the upper reaches of Midwest society, having had many run-ins with the Kendricks and their like during his more than twenty years on the local force. Most of those had ended-up with embarrassment avoided or charges dropped through possession of sufficient cash, the right connections, or both. That was something that he knew first-time petty offenders at the opposite end of the social scale did not have access to, which was why the majority invariably found themselves in Winfield. Dean treated all offenders equally and was totally unmoved when confronted by smart-suited lawyers on six-figure retainers, which is why he had never been promoted, despite his clear-up rate being consistently high. His attitude was considered, at the higher echelons, to be anti-privilege, whereas his colleagues knew it was simply straight-talking. It was also why he spent a lot of his spare time working with underprivileged youngsters as part of his personal crusade to stop the state gaols being unnecessarily filled by them.

He continued: "even within the criminal fraternity, history is littered with the bodies of smart-asses who thought they could rip-off a hired-gun. Greed knows no social barriers you know. So what happens in business when a client doesn't pay an invoice, what's the supplier do about it? Send a reminder of course. But we're not talking about thirty-day lines of credit here, are we?"

"Alright, so we could be looking at a multiple hit, or a failure to pay." Kleberson pressed-on: "any other scenarios?"

"Identification," Holdsworth proffered, "somebody knew the perp. Didn't have to be the client or the contacts. It's a small world; you can bump into someone from your past at any time and in the most unlikely circumstances. Sometimes being in the right place at the right time can also be being in the wrong place at the wrong time."

"I agree, and just the same would apply to a serial. So let's concentrate on the strong connections between all three victims, two current ones which are the Kendrick family and the TV Station, plus the historical one of their time at college. The motive could come from any of these. I think we've explored the Kendrick potential as far as we can at this stage and it remains the more likely for me. But these three ..." he pointed at the smaller photos of the two Kendricks and their lawyer "... are going nowhere for the time being and if they have got a contractor on this, he's not going to hang around waiting for us to find him."

Kleberson began a summation of tasks: "so, the TV Station - Moreno, Capaldi, you get out there and interview everybody. Report-in to Max Huberstein when you get there, he's promised us full co-operation; if you need more help, let Chris know. You know what to look for, grudges, politics, noses out-of-joint, rumours. I want every employee covered by midday tomorrow, any no-shows get uniform to track 'em down and pull 'em in here if necessary."

"But there's hundreds of 'em," Moreno whinged.

"Well, you keep asking me for overtime to pay all that alimony, so here it is!"

"I am waiting on a call from the airport to view any footage from the CCTV that looks interesting, assuming there is any," Capaldi advised.

"In that case, if the call comes, break-off at the station and give the airport your priority instead." Kleberson turned to Dean: "have we had anything from USC?"

"I spoke to one of their DPS detectives, who checked-out both ladies and confirmed they did not show up anywhere on their crime record system as either perp or vic. So I contacted campus admin who gave me every assurance that they will do what they can, but it was nearly ten years ago and they have over thirty-thousand students each year, the records are in the archives, blah, blah."

"Well, perhaps they need to know that the longer they take, the more high-profile alumni they are losing. Call the University President's office, tell them that, unless we get what we have asked for by this evening, we shall be making the connection at tomorrow's press conference. In the meantime, they might like to check their TVs, where they will see this story is making headline status on all national news stations, so maybe they need to prepare themselves for some angry Trustee reaction when we point-out how little co-operation we're getting. And if they're not happy about dealing with us directly, then we can always get the local FBI to visit them and give them a hand with their search." He looked at the clock: "it's four-thirty p.m. and they're two hours behind. Call Bill Johnson and see if he can tee-up their LA Field Office in case we need them. Give the campus until eight our time to get at least some preliminary data back to us, but if we haven't had anything by then, I'll ask Sam to send in some Agents."

"That should upset cocktail hour!" Dean observed with some glee. "I'll also get back onto DPS and get them to run Cochrane through their system as well."

"And ask them if they had anything unusual happening during the years the three of 'em were there, what are we looking at early/mid-nineties? We're after anything with a series that they either couldn't solve, or where they caught a perp that was connected to our three somehow, however tenuous. Until we shake the tree we don't know what might fall out. Chris, presumably we haven't come-up with any new faces arriving in the city, otherwise you would have told me."

"A couple, but they both checked-out clean, no potential connection. We've still got our ear to the ground though. More interesting is I'm drawing a blank with 'The Turd', he wasn't in any of his usual haunts, in fact nobody seems to know where he was. So whatever the eventual official alibi transpires to be, it's going to be interesting."

"Right, you continue to concentrate on the Kendrick angle. Find-out each of these victims' lawyers and see if they're holding any documents we need, in particular that pre-nup. We need a copy of that, because I doubt that Friedmann will give one to us. More to the point, he may not even know that we know about its existence, so make sure none of them start blabbing-back to him. If he is behind this, we don't need to spook him until we're ready to."

"Understood Paul."

"Moreno, where are we with M.E. reports?"

"We've got a full autopsy on both Ms Nicholson and Ms Rolles, except for toxicology, which has gone off to KC. Nothing yet on Cochrane."

"Holdsworth you can take those over. What do we have from Sam's office?"

"Bill's sent over the files from Palm Springs and the rest will be here later."

An Assignation

"So you need to get hold of the prelim on Cochrane from Mary Jourdain, plus any toxicology from the first two. If Mary's still getting the run-around from KC on that, tell the Chief straight away - he's already put one hurry-up on them, they won't like another. Once you've got all that back here, go through it and compare it with the autopsies from the earlier files. You're looking for anomalies, anything that shows us this perp's got an Achilles heel. I'm going to grab an early dinner, then I'll be back around seven; you can brief me then on what you've found."

"Sorry Lieutenant, but you are kidding aren't you? That's only a couple of hours to go through nineteen files."

"Out of the twenty eight hours we have remaining before we have file number twenty to add to them. Find a way Holdsworth, find a way."

Sixty-One

Paul Kleberson was suffering from information-overload. He decided that he would get some take-out, kick-back and try to relax. He picked-up some Thai on North St Francis and headed home.

Home had become a rented two-bedroomed apartment in Riverside just west of the river. It was less than ten minutes from City Hall, but being across the river somehow gave that separation that he needed from the job. The apartment was functional, in that it gave him the space he needed on the very few occasions that the kids came to stay, whilst not being too large to keep tidy. After all, he rarely did much other than sleep there, such were the demands of the job. The furniture was light and simple in design, from a great place over on Kellogg that specialised in European imports. Complimenting it were a number of colourful framed modern art prints breaking the monotony of the standard magnolia walls.

He put on the TV while he laid-out the food on a plate, then opened a bottle of Rolling Rock and poured the contents into a long glass. He wouldn't allow his standards to drop like a lot of his colleagues had when divorce inevitably bachelorised them again. The mere action of eating properly, at the dining table using real tableware, underlined to his mind that he was off-duty, not just grabbing a nosebag when the opportunity allowed.

A TV news channel that was full of the day's developments emerged on the screen. He must have been watching it the last time he turned-on the TV, he couldn't quite remember when that was; so he picked up the remote and started channel surfing. He managed to find a channel with a run of old Seinfeld programmes and next up was one of the classic episodes. It was a good accompaniment to an average meal, despite every ad-break including a trailer for the night-time news due to follow later that evening.

When he had finished the meal, he washed-up then turned-off the TV in favour of the Hi-Fi. He put on a CD that reminded him of his times in the basement in Cambridge, conducting impromptu album reviews with his house-mates; it set him wondering what would have happened if he hadn't come home. When the pressure was on at work his down-time thoughts often wandered back to those times. He would begin to doubt whether he had chosen the right career but, quickly realising that those were purely negative thoughts, he would allow them to be lost to the music.

But he couldn't do that today and the music was not creating strong-enough images in his mind to temporarily blank-out the conundrum that he knew he would have to resolve, FBI assistance or not; such were the politics in play. The reality was that there was nobody in Wichita, including the newly-arrived Kryczek, that gave him confidence that they could unravel it for him. In the end, this one would come down to him alone. Inevitably, he began the mental processes that had served him so effectively with the historical research, the process that should have landed him a position back in England - the painstaking examination of each factor in the story, looking for the holes, the missing parts for the jigsaw, the pieces that would not fit. This was why he was head of the murder squad. This was why the FBI wanted him back. This was the curse of the mental abilities that would keep him chained to the Godforsaken job until it chewed him up and spat him out as a bitter and twisted old lag.

'Unless?' he thought. 'Here I go again - unless what exactly? What use is historical research anyway? So you meticulously prove that hundreds, or thousands, of years ago, something did, or didn't, happen in the way some previous researcher had interpreted the same and other, since-eliminated, facts - and the relevance changes what? The perception of the past only. It changes nothing in reality - what's done is done. At least a murder enquiry is in the present; and here and now there's a madman to be caught, to avenge the deaths of people before their due time and, more importantly, to prevent the creation of more grieving friends and family.'

"So OK," he began thinking out loud: "what are we missing? Well, a suspect for a start. It's all very well to think of who would gain the most from these deaths and right at the front of that queue are the Kendrick clan. Yet regardless of which one you choose, are they personally capable of that level of precise planning? Or coldness of action? Politically, yes, but physically, no."

His thoughts took over again: 'so if any one, or combination, of them is responsible, they would have to have used a professional for the actuality - and there is a professional known to the FBI with the same M.O. in previous crimes. But officially, he's been dead for six weeks! So what does that leave? A copycat? An accomplice? It's just too far-fetched. No, ignore the peripherals and concentrate on the facts. What do we have? We have a multiple murderer with deviant sexual appetites and a theatrical method of presentation of his handiwork. So are we dealing with a nutter? Well the first two are such acts, but the third? Is the third a true derivation of Vitruvian Man, or does it show antagonism? If so, then why the change?'

He got up and went into the second bedroom. It doubled as his den when there were no guests staying, which was most of the year. One wall was covered in bookshelves housing his extensive collection of biographies and historical books, everything from Herodotus to Robert Lacey's 'Ford'. He scanned the

An Assignation

shelves until he spotted what he was looking for - a book that he bought at Chateau du Clos-Luce, Leonardo Da Vinci's final home in France, which he had visited on a field trip from Cambridge whilst studying the Renaissance. It was quite a tome, much larger than he remembered, which he found momentarily daunting as he had hoped for a quick scan-read towards revelation.

Nevertheless, he settled back onto his sofa and began summoning known facts from his memory. He knew that the drawing was Leonardo's interpretation of the Roman architect Vitruvius' treatise on human proportion, contained in a ten volume classical architecture masterpiece 'De Architectura', the reference work that inspired Palladio to produce his own four volume 'I Quattro Libri dell'Architettura' in the Sixteenth Century. That later document, in turn, would inspire countless architectural landmarks built during the next three centuries by the likes of Wren, Kent, Wood and Thomas Jefferson.

From his Cambridge studies, Paul was aware that Da Vinci's drawing was a different interpretation of the writing, predating by thirty years another, by Cesare Cesariano, used to illustrate some of the early printed editions of 'De Architectura'. Cesariano only used one figure with triangulation to show proportion, whereas Da Vinci used two overlaid within a square and a circle. The one in Da Vinci's square was almost identical to Cesariano's, except for the layout of the feet and hands. A quick reference to the Da Vinci drawing should confirm whether the perp had used his layout; from their use of the term 'Vitruvio', Paul was already less than confident of the FBI's grasp of classics.

A quick flip through the index brought him to the page where the Leonardo drawing was shown; it quickly confirmed what he expected to see. There were two overlaid frontal views of a naked man, the first standing with arms outstretched to touch the sides of a square; that figure was standing on the base side of the square, and his head touched the top. The other figure was spread-eagled, as if performing a star-jump, and was contained within a circle that touched the feet and the fingertips. The fingertips were level with the top of the head, and they touched the circle at the points where the circle cut the top side of the square.

He scanned the text on the facing page, which referred to Da Vinci's use of both artistic and scientific principles in his work. What caught Paul's eye was the reference to it being Da Vinci, not Vitruvius, who first observed that opening the legs reduced the figure's height by one-fourteenth: *'open the legs to reduce the stature - that's interesting,'* Paul thought.

He read on to discover that it was also Da Vinci who discovered that raising the arms, as he had in the second figure, put the umbilicus at the exact centre of the circle and that the space between the legs when spread to touch the circle created an equilateral triangle. It confirmed that the bodies had definitely followed the Da Vinci layout; so much so, in fact, that even the pattern of the fingers was identical. This temporarily shocked him, as it showed a precision way beyond what he was expecting. *'If is this a code,'* he thought, *'are we supposed to take a more detailed message from these?'*

Reading on, he learned that Leonardo believed the workings of the human body to be an analogy for the workings of the universe, and that the accompanying text on the drawing giving the various proportions of the body was written in mirror writing. This in itself was not unusual, Leonardo used that method of cipher quite often, but he wondered if the relative placements of Hilary Nicholson and Marjoree Rolles were an allusion to the mirror writing.

Cochrane's presentation, however, was a departure from either figure. His thoughts moved from the original observations by Kryczek that the presentations were simply to show sexuality, or relationship between victims: *'we already know they are connected, so it's fair to assume that it might be necessary to illustrate any unknown relationship in some form of revelation; but is this a higher-level statement? For a reduction in stature, should we read bring him down a peg?'*

In the back of his mind Paul remembered seeing something similar at some time back in England during his university years, a visual parody of a Vitruvian Man with his hands on his crotch: *'was it on a poster? Maybe a T-Shirt? If it was a joke, a well-known one, was that another message about Cochrane, or the murderer's view of Cochrane? If it was the latter, then it definitely suggested that this was personal.'*

He glanced at his watch - six-thirty p.m. It was time to think about getting back; the rest of this would have to simmer-away on the back-burner of his brain until something else broke. But first a shower and change.

Sixty-Two

When Kleberson arrived in the Squad Room just after seven, it was deserted. The team had split-up on their appointed tasks. He sat at his desk and mentally surveyed the board that he had created earlier. Nothing had been added to it, yet. Maybe this would be improved with the benefit of Holdsworth's analysis of the FBI files assembled by Schneider's office.

He summarised his thoughts: *'if this is Vitruvio, then we have just over a day to find the S-o-B before he takes his fourth and final vic and disappears into the ether again. So where do we start?'* He leant back in his chair and put his hands behind his head.

"Nice to see you have time to relax," came the voice from the doorway. Kleberson slowly looked to his right to see the bulk of the Chief blocking-out most of the light from the corridor beyond, which was still vainly trying to find a way past him into the windowless blockhouse that was the Homicide Squad Room.

"Chance would be a fine thing Chief," Kleberson replied laconically, "I'm just trying to figure where the FBI connection fits into this. Kryczek reckons it's the serial she killed six weeks ago, which means she got the wrong perp."

"That would make matters a little less complicated," Stanton mused.

"Politically, maybe Chief, but from a case point of view it makes it a hell of a lot more complex."

Stanton sauntered into the room and pulled up a chair. Kleberson gave him an executive overview of the gaps Stanton had missed from the earlier briefing. At the end, Stanton slumped back a bit in his chair and exhaled through pursed lips: "I see what you mean about complexity. We have nothing to give us a clue as to who this guy is, or where he is right now. We don't know where he will strike next, or who the next victim may be. We just know it will happen tomorrow."

"That's about the shape of it Chief. All we can hope is that some unforeseen connection comes out of our canvassing this afternoon, or that we catch a break from the FBI files."

"You can have whatever manpower you need Paul, just make the call."

"If I need it, I'll yell Chief. At this point in time we have to find a new angle. I think it's time to talk to Jackson Kendrick the Third."

"Come on Paul, surely it's obvious now that the Kendricks are just victims here, isn't it?"

"If it's definitely a serial, then yes it would appear that way. But somehow, the killer got into Hilary Nicholson's house without any resistance. Marjoree Rolles told me that Hilary was a black belt. There was no sign of a struggle, so she had to have let him in."

"So she knew him, one way or another?"

"Yep. Same with our other two vics, no obvious struggle at the scene. Could have been social, maybe business. OK, we know that Ms Nicholson's relationship with Kendrick was not, how shall we say, close, but he must know something of what she has been up to recently. After all, she was the family's accountant as well."

"You're right Paul - we have to look under every stone."

"Or in Kendrick the Third's case, every look a stoned one."

"You just keep an open mind here!" Stanton was still nervous of Kleberson's complete disregard for political consequences.

"Maybe you should come with me Chief." Kleberson smiled as Stanton squirmed slightly in his chair. Stanton had felt Junior's displeasure the previous day and Kleberson knew he wouldn't risk that again so soon.

"As much as I would like to Paul, I have to brief the Mayor on progress."

"That won't take long will it?" Kleberson was warming to Stanton's discomfort: "I can grab a coffee while you do that, if you like."

Stanton saw the hint of a wicked grin on Kleberson's face: "if it was going to be that easy, doncha think I would have suggested that already?"

"Well, I can't go alone - even I'm not that politically-naive! Where's your lapdog, he can come; safe pair of hands and all that."

"That won't be possible. Morley's on indefinite leave ... personal situation."

Kleberson was a superbly quick-witted detective and immediately whiffed the scent of something else discomforting for Stanton. His mind delighted at the thought, both at the obvious embarrassment in that short statement and the freedom that Morley's absence would grant the investigation. He continued:

"what's this then Chief? Is it what this afternoon's little 'performance' was about?"

"Damn you Kleberson, can't you let anything just ride on by?"

"Not if it has any bearing on the case Chief - no stone unturned didn't you say?"

Stanton got up and walked towards the door: "let's just leave it that he's on compassionate leave." But instead of going out of the room, he closed the door and returned to his seat. Kleberson suddenly joined all the dots and looked at Stanton in astonishment.

"What are you saying Chief, Cochrane and Morley were an item?"

"I want that kept within this room, it's not relevant."

"Of course it's relevant Chief!" Kleberson was already aboard one of his high horses and spurring it into action: "everything is relevant, including Morley's involvement with our latest victim - highly bloody relevant!"

"He's not involved. I may not be the best of detectives in your eyes, but I do know the difference between a victim and a perp; and Morley is the former."

"Not involved! Victim? What planet are you on Chief?" Kleberson's rage was also fuelling his sharp analytical skills and as the words emerged, several pieces of floating jigsaw suddenly dropped-into place: "let's just think about one or two things here to decide just how 'uninvolved' he is. As one of the main 'victims' of that ridiculous performance yesterday morning with Billy-Bob, did you not wonder for one minute how we were suddenly looking for a shooter in a murder that didn't involve a gun? Shall I join some dots for you? I sent Morley to get the preliminary M.E. report, but he decided not to. Why? Because he already thought he had the cause of death, probably via pillow-talk."

"Oh come on Lieutenant, not everything demands a conspiracy theory, not even when you're a homicide detective."

"At six a.m. yesterday, I had an off-the-record chat with Marjoree Rolles. She knew Hilary Nicholson was our vic, but had no idea how she died, nor was I about to tell her either. Ms Rolles had made-up her mind that she must have been shot, and in her agitated state couldn't imagine any other possibility. So I let her think that to calm her down, with the normal warnings of dire consequences if she used it on her bulletin, which opened her up straight away."

"So you lied to her"

"Oh for God's sake Chief - rule one of interview technique, let the perp think what they want to think." Stanton nodded acquiescence. "We know that after I left her, she must have rung-in to excuse herself from duties that morning, otherwise how did Cochrane get out-front with the crew so early? Answer, she rang him direct, after all they were at USC together. So let's speculate shall we, what words do you think she would have used? 'Tom, Hilary's been shot, I can't do the press conference, so you'll have to take it.' Assuming he was sleeping alone, thus avoiding the image of our erstwhile colleague curled-up alongside him when he received that news, who would be the first person he would contact to set-up any scoop for himself?"

"Morley."

"Exactly, and bearing in mind how economical I was being with relaying facts to your sniffer-dog, he would have gleaned everything he could from Cochrane."

"Morley's a nervous wreck at the moment, take my word for it."

"Oh come off it Chief, he's a material witness. He can give us insight into Cochrane's lifestyle - Goddammit, he was Cochrane's lifestyle! I can accept that it is somewhat unlikely that he is the perp, despite how much I personally would love him to be, but he could be holding the break we need. We must interview him. Where is he Chief?"

"He's gone away."

"GONE AWAY! Chief, you can be the most ridiculous political arsehole at times, but this is way beyond your normal boundaries, however remote they are from reality."

But for once, instead of rising to the bait, Stanton tried to cool the atmosphere: "look, he's not only grieving for the loss of someone close, he's also scared shitless that he's next. You got me to hide Kendrick on that basis, I'm just extending the same courtesy to one of our own."

"Not one of 'our' own here in Homicide, Chief, not in any way, shape or form is Morley anything like one of 'our' own."

"OK, bad choice of phrase, but I'm not revealing where he is until we've locked-up this Vitruvio S-o-B and that's the end of it."

"Dammit Chief, how do I lock-up the S-o-B when you're chaining-up every spare limb I have, one by one?"

"I said no! That's the end of the matter, Lieutenant Kleberson."

But Kleberson was furious: "sorry Chief, you can have all the compassion you want for your little shirt-lifting assistant, but I need - no, this investigation needs - his input. You obviously know how to contact him, so if you're not going to let me interview him, then you tell him to give us a full written statement of everything he knows. Everything Chief!"

"I'll do that for you now."

"Good, at least you haven't completely forgotten you're Chief of Police here!"

"Don't push your luck Kleberson; we all still have to work together after all this has passed."

"I'm not even going there Chief. Get me that statement and I will give it to McKinley to analyse."

"No, only you and I know, nothing beyond this room - remember? You analyse it personally and include whatever is pertinent as unattributed notes."

"Fuck that Chief! You want us to find the perp, Morley goes on that board so that we can see all of the relationships in play here. There is no other way. Morley can cope with his situation any which way he wants, but I'm not going to explain to the next victim's loved ones why we were hamstrung on identifying this killer by your political sensibilities."

"You wouldn't do that, you're just blustering."

Kleberson shot him a cynical glance: "no, you're right Chief, I wouldn't. I would let them see it on the national news channels when I'm interviewed about why I resigned my post."

Kleberson looked hard into Stanton's eyes and he saw defeat. Stanton looked back and saw iron resolve. Stanton had no choice. He had tried, but deep-down he knew he couldn't win: "I'll get you the statement, just try to stay focussed on the real goal here."

"I always am Chief; sometimes I wish there were more like me around here."

Sixty-Three

Paul Kleberson was walking down Main Street again, towards the Epic Center. Stanton had rung Friedmann a couple of hours earlier and arranged for Kleberson to meet him with his client at ten p.m, in Friedmann's office on the top floor. The other members of the team had received large amounts of data from their various lines of enquiry, but not until late-on in the evening; they were all sifting-through what they had on their desks in preparation for a full review at seven a.m.

Kleberson's workaholic instincts would have liked them all to work through the night, but even with the implied deadline set by Vitruvio's previous M.O, he recognised that after them all having very little sleep over the last forty-eight hours, without some meaningful rest that night none of them would be in any condition to work at the pace the following day would ultimately demand.

He had arranged to meet Sam Schneider in the coffee shop in the rear of the foyer, which was dark and lifeless as he entered, but for the glow from the panels of the vending machines that ran twenty-four-seven to service the security staff and any late-night workers. Chief Stanton had agreed to Schneider being in on the interview; it would avoid Kleberson having to take one of his own detectives off of their assignment, as well as adding some weight to the occasion on the enforcement side.

Friedmann was clever. You didn't get to be lawyer to the Kendrick empire if you weren't, and you definitely didn't marry into the family by just being a top lawyer. Jackson Kendrick III, on the other hand, was nothing short of a redneck playboy with a powerful father and more money than sense. The interview was clearly not going to be with Kendrick, it was going to be with Friedmann.

Kleberson had floated taking Kryczek as well, but Stanton refused point blank. Not only would it appear that the FBI were taking over the investigation, which he definitely didn't want, but also he felt that Kryczek would be a distraction. He hadn't met her yet, but from the comments he had picked-up in the Squad Room, a philanderer of Jackson Kendrick III's reputation would not be put-off by there being a badge pinned to a neat little waist. Kleberson knew that he had a point there.

An Assignation

There was time for Kleberson and Schneider to grab a coffee and a savoury snack from the machines before the meeting. So in the corner of the otherwise-deserted coffee shop overlooking the manicured lawns backlit from the searchlights illuminating the building, Kleberson briefed Schneider on the new development.

Schneider was genuinely shocked by the news about Morley, but also concurred with Stanton's views about keeping him stashed away from everything, although he quietly thought that he should try to persuade Stanton to let him put covert surveillance on Morley. This killer had been clever enough to amass three victims within twenty-four hours whilst apparently not leaving any trace. There was, therefore, no reason at present to believe that he couldn't find his next victim at will and if the target was Morley, then at least it would provide an opportunity to catch the perp.

He observed to Kleberson: "Morley's an obvious target Paul, as is Kendrick. We know that Stanton and Friedmann will keep Kendrick safe, which means that we also will know where to look for leaks if he turns out to be victim number four. Ditto Morley, eh?"

Kleberson hadn't thought of it that way. If he was brutally honest, he wouldn't be against using either as bait to catch this monster, as long as it was apparent that they were potential targets; at least he wouldn't be as worried as to their welfare as he was regarding most anyone else in the city. Having said that, logically if they could identify the specific link between the victims, then it followed that there wouldn't be too many people who were potentially victim number four. Having two less to directly supervise when the time came would only ease his logistical problems. But that was for later.

It was five before ten as they entered the lift from the foyer and punched the button for the top floor.

Sixty-Four

As the doors slid open, Kleberson and Schneider were faced by the two security heavies who had 'escorted' Kleberson from the floor the previous day. They were stood, legs astride with their hands cupped in front of their manhoods. *'Probably not much for such huge mitts to cover,'* Kleberson thought to himself. They were stood far enough back to allow Kleberson and Schneider to step from the lift, but close enough to prevent them from passing, if that became necessary. What happened next even took Kleberson by surprise.

Schneider pulled his badge from his belt with his left hand and thrust it in the face of the larger of the two, catching him totally off-guard: "Agent Schneider, FBI; face down on the floor please, both of you, arms to the side where I can see them." The smaller hulk began to reach inside his jacket, but before he could get the ends of his fingers inside the lapel, he felt the end of the barrel of Schneider's department-issue Luger against his temple. Schneider had drawn it with his right hand and cocked it literally in a microsecond: "sorry," Schneider continued looking them both in the eye in turn before continuing in a calm voice, "which part of 'on the floor' was it that you didn't understand?"

Both goons raised their hands slowly, turned and knelt down, before prostrating themselves on the floor of the foyer. As they did so, the alarm sounded. Betty Wagner, called-in specifically for the meeting, had pressed the button under her desk and was looking-on horrified as the Company's security was neutralised.

"Take their weapons Paul; we'll let them have them back after we've checked that this establishment is correctly licensed for armed security." Kleberson bent over to frisk the first goon as Friedmann appeared behind the reception counter, having run from his office.

Without removing his gaze from the two goons, Schneider addressed Betty Wagner: "Mrs Wagner, would you please advise Mr Friedmann that Lieutenant Kleberson of the Wichita City Police and Agent Schneider of the FBI are here for their ten o'clock appointment as arranged."

Kleberson had pulled the Glock from the shoulder holster of each goon, plus a P32 from each ankle holster; he was holding them in both hands.

"Gentlemen!" Friedmann said with a beaming smile, trying to diffuse the situation, "so nice of you to visit us this evening." He walked around the counter extending his right hand towards Schneider in greeting. Schneider holstered his gun and returned his badge to his belt hook.

He turned to Friedmann, then with a matching smile he shook Friedmann firmly by the hand: "nice to see you again Mr Friedmann. I hope you don't mind, but your security men here looked so tired when we got here, that I suggested they might like to have a little lie-down. I'm sure if you were to let them take a rest while we're here, then they will be a lot more alert for you afterwards."

"Very kind of you to suggest it, I'm sure they will be most comfortable down there, won't you boys?"

"Yessir Mr Friedmann," both responded begrudgingly.

"And Lieutenant Kleberson, nice to see you again." Friedmann extended his hand, but Kleberson held both of his forward showing the guns.

"Sorry, I seem to have my hands a bit full at the moment." Kleberson replied with a grin.

"Maybe Ms Wagner can take those for you." Friedmann turned to the counter: "Betty could you help Lieutenant Kleberson with his baggage here?" Turning back to Schneider and Kleberson, he continued: "now gentlemen, if you could follow me, we'll go through to the office. Betty, some coffee for everyone please." Friedmann turned and walked briskly through the reception area towards his office in the corridor behind.

Kleberson and Schneider hung back slightly, then followed. The guards stayed flat on their faces. As Kleberson passed the counter, he handed the four weapons to Betty Wagner: "there you go Betty, I should find somewhere safe for these, we wouldn't want them falling into the wrong hands, would we?" She didn't reply, just sent a snarling look back in his direction.

As Kleberson moved alongside Schneider, he leant towards his ear: "nice one."

"Yeah - d'ya think we've got his attention now?" Schneider whispered back.

Sixty-Five

Friedmann ushered the two into his palatial penthouse office. The views out over the lights of the western part of Wichita went on forever and beyond, into the blackness of the flat plains of Kansas. The large mahogany desk was noticeably clear of clutter and the bookcases that lined the internal walls contained volume upon volume of law books, none of which showed any evidence that they had ever left their shelves.

The large Chesterton-style sofas, upholstered in dark burgundy leather, surrounded a low glazed mahogany coffee table that had nothing on it other than the familiar cowboy boots worn by Jackson Kendrick III, who was kicked-back horizontally into the corner of one of the larger sofas, wearing somewhat grubby Levi's, a lumberjack shirt and a contemptuous countenance.

He was a complete contrast to his lawyer in every way. Friedmann's thousand-dollar suit bore no indication that he had been wearing it for the entire day, his black patent shoes reflecting the view of the room in whichever direction they pointed. Nobody really liked the person that was 'The Turd'. Not his lawyer, not his staff; not even his close friends. But he cared not a jot, because he knew that his implied power held them all in his orbit. He was typical third-generation redneck new money; his lawyer was anything but.

"Please be seated gentlemen, I believe you both have already had the pleasure of meeting Mr Kendrick on previous occasions." He paused to allow for them to exchange greetings and handshakes, but Kendrick didn't move and the visitors had no intention of putting their interviewee at any ease. Friedmann continued: "I'm sure that we can get this over with quite quickly. My client is ready and willing to co-operate in every way, isn't that right Jackson?"

"Waste ma time all ya like, officers," he scowled, "I ain't got nuttin' ta do 'til ya catch the Goddamned maniac what killed ma betrothed, an' apparently wants ma ass too."

"It must feel real good to be wanted by someone for a change," Kleberson sniped as he sat in the sofa opposite Kendrick, fixing him with a steely glare.

"That'll do Lieutenant," Friedmann intervened, "right now, we're happy to assist you - just remember that! We can just as easily decide not to."

"Either way's fine by me." Kleberson responded, "just remember that the alternative is handcuffed through the front door of City Hall past the nation's gathered media."

The Mantis Pact

"Lieutenant Kleberson," Friedmann's voice hardened, "there is no need for aggression here. You forget my client is currently in protective custody, at your suggestion, being a potential target of this killer who has already made him the grieving victim of a vicious crime. Have some respect!" He immediately turned to Schneider, who had seated himself alongside Kleberson so that both were confronting Kendrick. "And whilst we are on the subject of aggression, Mr Schneider, I did not appreciate the manner of your entrance to my offices this evening, which will be the subject of a formal complaint to your HQ. I do have good friends in that establishment, you know."

"Who you will doubtless meet on business should we find-out that those fifth-rate goons you laughingly call 'security' are not licensed to be performing the duties you have employed them for. Now, if you don't mind, we have a number of questions for you and your client who, whether he likes it or not, remains a suspect in this case until such time as he persuades Lieutenant Kleberson here otherwise. Perhaps you can start showing some respect for the public offices that Lieutenant Kleberson and I hold, in-line with your sworn oath as an officer of the State Courts of Kansas, whose jurisdiction we all operate under."

Friedmann looked about to explode as the outer door opened and Betty Wagner entered with the tray of coffee. The room virtually crackled with the silence that fell, only interrupted by the light tinkling of the bone china cups and saucers as she crossed the room and set the tray down on the coffee-table.

Kendrick broke the silence: "wha thankya kindly Ms Wagner, at least someone here has some feelins fer ma tragic circumstances." He beamed at her as she visibly blushed at his attentions; having set the tray down, she looked towards Friedmann somewhat sheepishly.

"That's fine Betty, we'll manage from here," he responded, "and send Laura in would you." Betty nodded and quickly scurried from the room.

'Hellfire' Kleberson thought, 'I never thought of using flattery as a way of lowering The Rottweiler's defences.' He looked across at Kendrick, who was obviously enjoying watching the somewhat middle-aged rear end wiggle through the door. Kleberson's thoughts wandered further to the thought of 'The Turd' and 'The Rottweiler' as an item, then felt a slight shudder pass down his spine as he imagined the fictional offspring. *'That's enough of that'* he thought, although the exchange had confirmed what a lot of people believed, that nothing in a skirt was safe when Kendrick was around.

"She is one mighty-fine person," Kendrick mused, "you're a lucky fella Emil."

"As is her husband Jackson," Friedmann retorted, somewhat pointedly as he re-arranged the crockery in front of his guests. "I have arranged for one of our stenographers to join us, if you have no objections. Obviously, we will furnish you with copies of the transcripts of the conversations we will be having."

Both nodded compliance, at which there was a quiet knock at the door which opened to reveal a dumpy lady in her mid-fifties carrying a stenotype machine.

"Come on in Laura and have a seat." Friedmann directed her to an upright chair by his desk, directly behind the sofa Kendrick was occupying, who looked-up hopefully, only for his face to register momentary disappointment before he shot Laura his falsest of smiles.

"OK gentlemen," Friedmann began, "let's forget all that has passed these last few minutes and get this over with, shall we?" He poured himself a black coffee and sat down in the third sofa, neutrally between the two factions and ready to referee proceedings. He had noticeably failed to pour coffee for anyone else, which Kleberson took on board as an indication that he may just be a little jaded with nursing his client. Schneider went for the coffee-pot; Kleberson went for the jugular.

"Well, firstly Mr Friedmann, we would like a copy of the pre-nuptial agreement between Mr Kendrick here and Ms Nicholson."

Friedmann dropped his cup quickly onto its saucer and glared across the table: "if you wish to examine any documentation pertaining to my client, you'll need a warrant gentlemen. Of course, you will need to specify exactly what documents you require and we will be pleased to assist as soon as practicable, provided of course that the documents do actually exist and are not the subject of conjecture, or the fruits of any over-productive imagination."

"Being arranged as we speak, but seeing as we are all a little bit pushed for time here, how about some quick bullet points?"

"Not going to happen Lieutenant, don't even think about going there. The document has no relevance to these discussions."

Kleberson seized on the underhit backhand and slammed it back across the net for a winner: "ah, so there is a pre-nup then."

Friedmann instantly felt his stomach churn. He had fallen for the easiest trick in the book and he knew it. He was furious with himself, but not as furious as Kendrick, who slammed his cup and saucer on the table glaring at his lawyer. Kleberson realised they had their adversaries on the back foot; clearly Schneider's dramatic entrance had rattled the cage more than could have been hoped.

Friedmann tried to recover: "I didn't say there was a document Lieutenant, you just assumed that."

Kleberson continued: "then let me tell you what else I'm 'assuming' about the possible document that doesn't exist, then you can give us a quick yes or no on each point."

Kendrick shot-up in his sofa and pointed at Friedmann: "it's that bitch Rolles, she's spilled the lot. Ah told ya she were trouble, but you said we had a signed non-whatever agreement, which would shut her goddam mouth. So, that didn't work, did it?"

"Is that why you killed her as well?" Kleberson asked calmly, again fixing Kendrick with an unrelenting stare and thinking *'set-point already and we've only been playing a few minutes.'*

Kendrick was bristling. He was clearly not the sharpest nail in the toolbox, but he had the basic instincts to know when he was in trouble. So did his lawyer, who quickly moved to diffuse the situation.

"That's out of order Lieutenant and you know it. Alright, let's get the pre-nup on the table." He got up, walked to his desk and pressed the intercom button. Within a second, Betty Wagner's voice responded.

"Yes Mr Friedmann."

"Can you arrange a photocopy of the Pre-Nuptial Agreement from the Kendrick/Nicholson marriage file for Lieutenant Kleberson please Betty and stamp it Private and Confidential please before you give it to him. Also prepare a non-disclosure to go with it."

"Yes Sir." The machine clicked-off.

Friedmann returned to his sofa. He looked across at Kleberson: "you heard what I said Lieutenant, the document is Private and Confidential. We are loaning you a copy purely so that you can eliminate any misconceptions you may have formed regarding the relationship between my Client and his fiancé. When you have satisfied yourselves in that matter, we require you to return it to us and not to keep any copies."

"Unless of course it becomes material evidence," Kleberson responded.

"In which case you will need to subpoena it Lieutenant," Friedmann replied.

"We can leave such legal niceties to the D.A. and yourself to sort-out, Counsellor, should that become necessary." He turned back to Kendrick: "why did your fiancé need a safehouse?"

"How the hell should ah know?" came the instant response.

"Have you ever visited her there?"

"You don't need to answer that one Jackson;" Friedmann had started to lay-down the boundaries of the conversation.

Kendrick looked across at Friedmann without any change in demeanour or posture: "look Emil, I know you're coverin' ma ass as ever, that's what ah pays ya fer, but the more ya follow convention, tha more this pair a'dipshits are gonna think they've got us by tha balls, when in fact we got nuttun' ta hide here. I'm tellin' 'em what they need ta know so that they can leave ma ass alone after they've covered it while they're catchin' this mo-fucker that's runnin' aroun' making human copies of old masters."

Friedmann raised his right hand in surrender, before continuing the motion to grip his temples between thumb and forefinger as if shielding his eyes from the light. His voice expressed total exasperation: "whatever Jackson, just remember there's a lady present. Whatever you may feel about senior law enforcement officers, at least show her a little respect in what she's having to transcribe."

"Oh Lord!" he responded pivoting in his seat to look, Chad-like, over the back of the sofa, continuing in a somewhat pathetically-false tone: "I'm real sorry Ma'am, but these gentlemen are putting me under some strain at this time of ma' grievous loss, please ignore anythin' that you may find in any way embarrassing." Laura ignored him, professionally keeping her eyes on the stenotype keyboard as she continued to record every syllable.

Kendrick pivoted back and continued: "officer, ah am not gonna try n'hide tha truth from ya, as ya already know ma fiancé and I were not the closest of couples - yet - but that wuz becuz we wuz both very busy with our own biznissis which meant that we had ta be happy ta see each other whenever we both were in town at the same time, which weren't often enough. That don't mean that we didn't have any affection fer each other, or that our relationship would not have blossomed after we got hitched. Cuz whatever ya may think, ah luved ma fiancé, an' ah believe that she loved me too. As fer her 'safehouse' as ya like to call it, ah have no idea wha she needed another property, ah knew nothin' about it or where it was, an' ah've never been there either with her or without her. But if she wanted ten properties, then she could have 'em;" he waived his hand dismissively in the direction of the sofa opposite, "as many as she wanted. We can afford whatever we wants and no green-eyed, divorced, sonofabitch with a badge can find any law o'this land that says otherwise!" At which he pivoted again to look across the back of his sofa continuing: "an' ma apologies again Ma'am for any disrespect to your sensibilities in that statement."

He slowly rotated back catching Friedmann's black stare in his direction as he did so. Kleberson and Schneider had been quietly absorbing the tirade, picking-out the plums within it as it went. Kleberson had registered that Kendrick knew about the method of presentation of the bodies, which could either mean that he had seen them, or pictures of them, or that the information had been relayed to him after being leaked; that would be easy to tease out. But he also registered an undertone that, regardless of the content, suggested an ease with the situation: *'there's blind contempt and there's guilty defiance',* Kleberson thought, *'and that felt like the former.'*

Schneider had picked-up the references to Kleberson's personal situation, clearly showing that this information had been discussed within the Kendrick circle. He had also been watching Friedmann throughout for any tell-tales in the body language and had seen the momentary anxious glance in his direction straight after the personal references, Friedmann almost as quickly looking back down at his navel when he saw that he was already under surveillance. Friedmann knew that he and his Client were in a roller-coaster that was out of control, and that he would have to wait for a suitable opportunity to arise before there would be any chance of getting back in the driver's seat.

Kleberson had no problem with blind contempt, the feeling was mutual, so he continued without showing any reaction: "can you tell us where you were on Tuesday night?"

"Tulsa."

"Where in Tulsa?"

"Friend's house."

"Name and address please."

Friedmann intervened: "we would rather not at this stage."

Kleberson stayed focussed on Kendrick: "you were doing so well, don't give us reason to believe that you are trying to obstruct our investigation."

Kendrick stayed silent, staring back as Friedmann replied: "it's delicate."

Kleberson had maintained focus on Kendrick, creating a staring contest. He responded to the lawyer without diverting his gaze: "so's your client's situation, Counsellor."

"Can we go off the record at this point please?" Friedmann looked somewhat anxious. Kleberson looked at Schneider, who nodded. Friedmann looked across at the stenographer: "stop for a moment please Laura." Her fingers came to an instant halt.

Kendrick smiled triumphantly: "Penny Clarke."

Schneider looked across at him: "Penny Clarke?"

Kendrick nodded slowly, still smiling like the cat who had got the cream. Schneider continued: "as in Oklahoma Senator Clarke's wife?"

"One and the same!"

"So what are we saying here, that you had dinner with the Senator and his wife?"

"Woulda been a bit difficult that, what with there being an important vote on in Washin'ton Frida' night. Ya can check that out with DC if ya want."

"So you had dinner with Mrs Clarke?"

"Sure did."

"At what restaurant in Tulsa?"

"Guess it's called the Senator's Dining Room."

"So no witnesses then."

"Other than Mrs Clarke, I guess not."

"And what time did you leave?"

"About ten."

"Late dinner?"

"More like early breakfast."

Friedmann finally intervened: "that's all you need, Agent Schneider. I hope that the FBI will be treating this information confidentially."

"We will need to confirm it with Mrs Clarke," Schneider insisted and noticing Friedmann begin to move forward in his chair he held out his hand to halt him, "but we will be happy to do so discretely." He turned and glared at Kendrick before firmly continuing: "for Mrs Clarke's sake." He turned back to Friedmann: "if you are happy to act as the conduit, I will ask our Field Office down there to contact you tomorrow with the details of who we need her to speak to, then they will arrange a convenient appointment."

Friedmann nodded and his body language eased: "thank you for that, will there be any more tonight?"

"Oh I think so Counsellor," Kleberson took up the conversation again, still focussed on Kendrick: "where did you go after ten p.m?"

"Ah came back home."
"And which of your many homes might that have been?"
"Westview Tower."
"What time did you arrive there?"
"Around one, but then ya already knows that doncha?"
"So you drove?"
"Plane's in dock."
"What do you drive these days?"
"That night it was ma truck, ah love ma truck, nice n'nonymous a truck."
"Make?"
"Ford - Harley Special crewcab."
"Very anonymous!"
"We Kendricks has standards to keep up y'knows."
"And you were home all night?"
"Nah, just 'nuff time fer a shit n'shave - ah had plenty of rest earlier, so t'speak." He winked at Schneider; Schneider bit back on his reaction.
"Where did you go then?" Kleberson continued.
"Marlena's."
"And after they closed."
"They were closed, it was a private party - invitation only."
"For anyone we know?"
"Nah, just a few businessmen from out a'town who decided to hire it out for the night - some people can afford privacy."
"And you got an invite."
"Ah get all sorts of invites, some are more attractive than others."
"So you were there all night?"
"Till about five, then we all moved-on."
"Where?"
"Friend's house up off Webb. I was there until I got the call from Emil."
Kleberson turned to Friedmann: "OK Counsellor, we need names and contact details for any of Mr Kendrick's acquaintances that may have been compos mentis enough to provide corroboration of this."
"I anticipated your request Lieutenant," he got up and walked to his desk, picked-up a typed sheet and handed it to Kleberson: "now, will that be all gentlemen?"
"Not quite Counsellor, I have a question for your stenographer." Laura looked up in some astonishment, seeking out her boss for a visual assurance. "Just a clarification of the transcript please; can you read out to me the last sentence of Mr Kendrick's direction to his lawyer early in our conversation."
Laura looked again at Friedmann, who nodded his approval. She picked-up the loop of paper and began to check through until she found the passage, then began to read: "I'm telling them what they need to know so that they can leave me

alone after they've protected me while they're catching this person that's running around making human copies of old masters."

"That's fine," Kleberson smiled in her direction, "and thank you for translating some of the more colourful wording that was used. Please add to the record my request for you to ensure that particular passage does not mysteriously disappear from the transcript before it arrives at City Hall."

"And Laura," Friedmann's strained voice continued, "please also record my personal protest at the mere suggestion that it would!"

Sixty-Six

Schneider and Kleberson re-emerged into the plush foyer. As they reached the reception desk Betty Wagner handed Kleberson a sealed envelope: "can you please sign here that you have received it, as requested by Mr Friedmann."

Kleberson opened the envelope, pulled-out the four pages of photocopied agreement, gave them a cursory glance-through, then pushed them back into the envelope. He accepted the pen that she was offering with her hand hovering over another piece of paper laying on her otherwise clear desk. He leant over the desk and perused the document, ran a line through the entire second paragraph, then signed the dotted line above his name at the foot of it. He lifted himself back up, handed the pen back with a flourish and started to walk away.

Betty Wagner shot a look behind her, where Emil Friedmann was standing observing the exchange. He shook his head to tell her to leave everything as it was, at which her head swept back towards the direction that the visitors were leaving, with a look in her eyes that would have bored two neat holes in the back of Kleberson's head, had she the power to do so.

The two approached the lift, which was being held open by one of the goons that were disarmed by Schneider earlier, while the other sat motionless on the sofa opposite the lift entrance.

"Thank you gentlemen," Schneider said, "I'm pleased to see that you have benefitted from your little rest." In a virtual repeat of the previous day, the standing goon punched the lobby button and stood back to allow the doors to close and the lift, obeying his command, started downwards.

Schneider punched the '12' button immediately. He breathed-out as if destressing, then murmured: "every time I have to meet that Kendrick, I leave feeling I need a shower."

Kleberson responded: "first time I've had the dubious pleasure of being in his company for any length of time - what a piece of work! Was he really suggesting that he was screwing a Senator's wife while his betrothed was being raped and murdered?"

The lift pulled to a halt at the twelfth floor and the doors slid open again. As he walked from it, Schneider observed: "oh that was no suggestion Paul, not from that arrogant shit! Coffee?"

Kleberson followed Schneider out of the lift and along the corridor, hanging back as Schneider punched-in the security code for the FBI office suite. The door lock clicked and they walked through into the suite, which seemed to be humming with unusual activity for nearly eleven at night. Schneider continued: "I've cancelled our weekend as well Paul, as you can see."

Just before they reached Schneider's office, he turned left into the small kitchen area where full flasks of coffee were warming on the two hotplates. He picked-up one of them and poured coffee into two mugs standing on the work surface. He handed one to Kleberson: "help yourself to cream and sugar," he said, nodding at the various jugs and bowls laying haphazardly on the same surface, before picking-up his mug and carrying it undiluted to his office. Kleberson followed a few seconds later with his coffee customised to requirements.

"Close the door Paul, I don't like to the staff to hear my expletives." Kleberson dutifully obeyed, then accepted Schneider's gestured direction to sit in the chair opposite his desk; Schneider remained standing, with his back to Kleberson and looking out of the window at the lights of East Wichita."

Kleberson broke the silence: "you know the Clarkes don't you?"

Schneider breathed deeply again before responding: "I know Bob Clarke," he began, "one of the best lawmakers we have in the Senate, despite being a Democrat." Schneider, not unusually for an FBI Agent, never made any secret of his strong Republican views. The high compliment conveyed in those few words was not lost on Kleberson. Schneider continued: "I've not met the new Mrs Clarke, but I did know the previous lady that held that title. Deborah Clarke was an old friend of my mother's. I met her occasionally while I was growing up, when the Clarkes came for dinner. She was a wonderful lady, always had time for us kids, genuinely interested in how we were doing. And a very attractive woman as well, always looked at least twenty years younger than she actually was; she must have been a real stunner when Bob married her."

"You said 'was' Sam?"

"She committed suicide three years ago; took a massive overdose. Bob was in Washington as usual, working on yet another welfare bill. The cleaner found her the following day. Bob was devastated."

"I must confess, I didn't pick-up on that one; did it not make the networks?"

"No, we covered it up for him. Standard story, succumbed to a long illness they had kept quiet; wasn't difficult for the media to swallow, that's the type of people they are - were - so masses of sympathy for Bob and an unblemished memory of the wife he was devoted to."

"You say 'we', you mean the Bureau?"

"I mean me and his son; Chandler's an Agent down in Mississippi - we were at The Academy together. The cleaner rang Chandler first, which was the best thing to do in the circumstances. Chandler called the family doctor, who managed to keep a lid on it until Chandler got there. I was an hour ahead of him, because I got his next call after the one to the doctor. I found the note."

"Should you be telling me all this Sam?"

"About time I told somebody;" he paused while he took a long sip of his coffee. "She felt she had betrayed her husband; she had become involved with another man, who she had originally met at a reception in Washington. This man looked her up when he was in Oklahoma a few months later and they had a short fling before she called it off. Nobody's a saint in that world, however much we like to think they are; truth is it happens all the time because of the enforced separations caused by the political position. It only becomes an embarrassment if someone wants to make it one and that normally only results from multiple situations; there was no indication that she ever strayed more than the once."

"So why did she have to kill herself? Did the media get ahold of it somehow?"

"No, it just evaporated into the ether as is normally the case, until her ex-lover contacted her nearly a year later. This guy was younger than her and she felt flattered by the renewed interest, but she kept him at arms length that time, avoiding meeting him other than at public functions. He then started to ask her for help in persuading the Senator to assist with a particular business problem that he had; she kept telling him that her husband took little notice of her views, which politically was true. Eventually, this man managed to get her alone; that was when he delivered the coup de grace."

"He tried to blackmail her."

"No, he didn't try, he just showed her the evidence he had of their previous liaison and told her straight that if she didn't help him, then he would use it whatever way he felt necessary to bring her husband down, so it was up to her how she told Bob, but the clock was ticking. The evidence even included photos; she had been set-up all along. That was when she realised how it would end Bob's career - not the scandal because Bob would not have allowed it to get that far. He's an honourable man, not something that can be said of everyone in Washington. She knew something that her blackmailer could never have imagined - that Bob would have resigned to protect her, and if that happened she could never have lived with being responsible for ending his career. That's what the note said."

"I know the type of lady. Did she name the blackmailer?"

"She did better than that, she included one of the photos with the note. It showed her with her lover - Jackson Kendrick the Third."

Kleberson was dumbstruck by this revelation. He couldn't believe that this case could become any more convoluted than it already was, yet it just kept doing so. He waited for his friend to continue, but Schneider just stood there staring out of the window. He decided to prompt Schneider gently: "did Senator Clarke see the photograph?"

"No, neither did Chandler. I made the decision that the note was enough for both of them to take in the circumstances; as it didn't contain any hint at the identity of the lover, I pocketed the photo. I had intended to reveal it at a later point, when they might both be in an emotional condition below the threshold where either of them might decide to act as judge, jury and executioner. That scenario never materialised."

"You mean they both would still kill the S-o-B if they knew?"

"Totally the opposite. You don't know Bob, he's a very rare individual. He was devastated, as I said, but he was able to accept what he perceived as his wife's decision not to reveal the identity; he saw it as her way of saying to him that he should not pursue revenge in any way."

"And because of that he went along with the cover-up?"

"Not exactly; he wasn't keen on that initially, but he quickly realised that Chandler couldn't take seeing his parents' reputations being raked through the media, so he did a deal with his son. He would go along with what his son wanted to do, if Chandler agreed to not hunt-down and identify the lover."

"So neither of them know."

"No. And, as far as I was aware, only I knew that it was Kendrick, until ..." Schneider tailed off into silence again, still focussed on the view from the window whilst taking another long sip of his coffee.

Kleberson waited a respectful few seconds before prompting again: "until?"

Schneider turned to face him. His face was drained and pale and his eyes were sad and moistening: "until he winked at me upstairs." He looked for a reaction from Kleberson, but when he didn't get one he continued: "so you didn't see it then, right after he made that glib remark about getting rest earlier."

Kleberson tried to review that part of the meeting quickly in his mind, but drew a blank: "I remember the remark, but didn't catch anything else - sorry Sam."

"Goddam it! If it wasn't bad enough that this piece of shit Kendrick brought so much sadness to good people, he's now saying he's gone back to the same well for more!"

"Hang on Sam, that's one hell of a leap from the simple wink of an arrogant toerag that thinks he's the real-life incarnation of Glenn Quagmire, to it being an indication of him having an agenda in specifically winking at you, at that point in the discussions."

"He knows Paul, every instinct in my body sensed it; I'm compromised." Schneider held out both of his arms in resignation, then flopped into his chair: "don't you see that?"

"What I see, Sam, is a friend in turmoil who's not thinking straight. What I want, no, need to be seeing is the Agent that persuaded me to join the FBI instead of being a history professor. The career policeman that told me there was no investigation that was a dead end, no situation that could not be stripped-down, analysed and then reassembled to reveal the whole truth standing like a beacon shining it's light on the debris of the bullshit strewn useless at it's feet."

"I said that?"

"You did."

As Schneider's face relaxed, the smile returned to his lips: "then maybe I should have been a philosophy professor."

"OK, you be Plato to my Herodotus and let's see if we can make any sense of what we just heard up there. Who's Penny Clarke?"

"You would know her as Penny Ostergaard."

"The Hollywood starlet?"

"That's the one."

"She's gorgeous."

"And, by all accounts, very happy, as is Bob - it's given him a whole new lease of life."

"Forgive me Sam, but marrying someone like that would give me a whole new lease of life - and I'm apparently younger than Senator Clarke's son."

"Bringing you back to the flatlands of Kansas from your imaginary Elysian idyll, so is that piece of crap from Hades upstairs!"

"OK, so if she's a distraction, then let's leave her out of this for now."

"How can we do that Paul? This is anything but a distraction, this is an alibi we're talking about."

"Is it? We only have his word for that. So what did he really tell us up there? That he was having an assignation with a Senator's wife until 'about ten'. Time of death for Hilary Nicholson was between eight and midnight. At that time of night you could drive from Tulsa to Derby in around two hours. Say that he left nearer nine than ten, he still didn't get to his flat until around one. That's gives him two hours between Derby and downtown Wichita with no alibi at all; meaning he's still in the frame for Ms Nicholson."

"But he's got a posse lined-up to place him on the other side of town when Ms Rolles was murdered."

Kleberson paused while he momentarily analysed that one, continuing: "but again, we've got a provisional time of death range from eight a.m. to midday. He's at Marlena's until five, then they all adjourn to some sprawling pad over East. Doesn't take Einstein to figure that there were more of them that left Marlena's than arrived there, for 'private party' read 'selection process' and if these 'out of town businessmen' were from Kendrick's usual social circle, then there would be plenty of stimulants involved once they got to their destination. So when we interview this list, which if you hadn't noticed has a dozen names on it, all male, we're going to find that they think he left Marlena's with them, and that he also arrived at the house with them. Then he must have disappeared into one of the rooms because he was well away with one of the girls and, 'well you know Jackson' and she must've been one hell of a lay because they didn't see him again until late morning. Circumstantial the lot of it."

"So he flashes a load of cash at one of the girls at Marlena's, takes her on to the house out East, makes sure she is publically all over him for a while then takes her to a room, where he makes some excuse, doubles her fee to keep her quiet, sneaks her out the back way and drives her home, leaving him free from maybe seven a.m. to whenever he sneaked back into the house for his reappearance."

"So he has an alibi for Ms Rolles that cannot be proved or disproved."

Schneider leant forward on the desk and rested his chin on his clasped hands: "because those supporting it have either been blackmailed, duped or paid-off. It will take us ages to get a break out of that combination that would allow us to get any actual evidence that we could use in a court."

"Then, of course, he was in protective custody when Cochrane was murdered."

"Meanwhile we have less than twenty-four hours before we're expecting another corpse."

"Which is why we shouldn't pursue any of it - not right now anyway."

Schneider shook his head at that suggestion: "forget Cochrane for a moment. If Kendrick is our man for either of the first two murders, that means he gets a head-start on us."

"Oh he's our man for all three Sam, I was convinced of that right from that first tirade upstairs. That wasn't the blustering defiance of a perp covering his tracks, that was downright contempt for two law officers that he knows he has completely wrong-footed. He knows that he didn't do any of the deeds, because he's hired the professional to do that for him. Plus he thinks he has an alibi that will, however obtained, stand up for long enough to be a blind scent to take us off the trail of that professional."

"Which shows a high degree of planning," Schneider observed, "which is when it all starts breaking down doesn't it? This is 'The Turd' we're talking about."

"We could simply be underestimating him. This is the same man that set-up Deborah Clarke. That took time and patience, not qualities that would normally occupy the same sentence as the name Jackson Kendrick the Third. It went wrong for him, but he didn't give it up. He waited until he could get another line on the Senator. Whatever he wants the Senator to do for him, I don't think it's connected to this. But it provided an opportunity which he took advantage of - that shows ruthlessness as well."

Schneider's face dropped again: "this will kill Bob Clarke you know."

"Which is one good reason why we shouldn't follow this through."

"One reason, so there are others?"

"Just one - Kendrick's expecting phone calls from this list, to tell him the police have been sniffing around." Kleberson held-up the piece of paper in his hand: "but most of all from Mrs Clarke. If he gets them all, he'll know we've taken the bait."

Schneider's face lifted again: "but if he doesn't he'll want to know why."

Kleberson nodded: "and when he asks that question, we will know what we need to know."

flush it again

Sixty-Seven

The alarm scythed through the memories of a Cambridge night-out with Annie that were preventing Paul's mind from dragging his sub-conscious back to the images that had accompanied the early fitful stages of sleep that night - images of an aged balding Da Vinci with his long grey beard and tousled shoulder-length hair sculpting corpses in perfect proportion. The green digits read 05:30 as he smashed his fist down on the top of the baby-blue plastic shell of the bedside clock with the inadvertent hope that it would find its target - the ridiculously-small off switch.

He had eventually left Schneider's office after midnight, finally getting his head down around one-thirty after reading the pre-nup agreement for the third time. He had concluded that it said exactly what Marjoree Rolles' summary had given him two days before - either party could have walked away at any time prior to the wedding, no penalties, no disclosures necessary. The final clause even used the phrase 'tear-up this document'.

His final self-question before he put himself at the disposal of the sandman was: *'are we trying to pin this on Kendrick simply because that would solve so many other problems as well?'* Other than it being almost definitely unknown to his father, the document held no terrors for Jackson Kendrick III. In fact, it demonstrated that he had no motive whatsoever for committing either of the first two murders, either directly or indirectly.

Kleberson's first realisation after dragging himself back to consciousness four hours later was that, with little over fifteen hours to go to the expected murder of an, as yet unknown, fourth victim, his department were no closer to preventing it than they had been for the last few days. It was a depressing way to start what could be nothing less than a manic day.

He prepared his usual breakfast of oatmeal and tea. The cereal was the closest he could get to the porridge he had grown to love whilst in the UK, but it was accompanied by genuine English Breakfast Tea, imported by a little shop off South Webb, that had been set-up to cater for the influx of Brit appetites following the relocation of ex-British Aerospace staff during the 1990s, the very project that had taken his young family back to England at that time. The oatmeal wasn't exactly the same, however, the American product being somewhat coarser than the original British recipe that, for some obscure reason buried deep in the copious US Food Import Regulations, could not be brought into the country. But it still was far more preferable to sacrificing a waistline on the altar of the heavy fry-ups, pancakes and syrup, or biscuits and gravy, served-up in every breakfast joint across the Midwest.

Kleberson walked into the Squad Room just after six-thirty. Chris McKinley was already at his desk, as was Scott Holdsworth; both acknowledged his arrival. He looked at McKinley and cocked his head towards his office before walking in and draping his jacket over the chair.

McKinley walked through the door a few seconds afterwards and closed it behind him: "morning Paul," he said, "get any sleep?"

"Couple of hours I suppose - you?"

"About the same."

"I know we're gathering at seven, but do you have any bullet-points for me beforehand?"

"Some good, some not so good, but we might have caught a break out at the airport. Capaldi's been out there most of the night going through the CCTV with security and he's on his way back now."

"Is this from the Hilary Nicholson sighting?"

"Sure is, looks like she was on the way to the airport and we may have some video of who she met there."

"Well that sure is a break, anything else?"

"Dean's picked-up on another girl who may have had some association with Hilary Nicholson at USC; it came up when DPS widened their search parameters to include contacts of perps and victims of crimes on the campus. On the surface it doesn't seem more than a tenuous connection, but Dean's got them working with the admin people going back through the student records to see if she ties-in anywhere with our three vics. We're waiting for more details."

"Are we expecting that info before the briefing, or are they all still asleep in California?"

"DPS have been working through the night and I don't think they've given the University Admin any choice but to do so as well. It seems that it was a combination of a third connected victim and the national media involvement that woke them all up."

"Typical West Coast, ignore anything except bad publicity," Kleberson observed with a weary disdain.

McKinley ignored him. Very little sleep in the last forty-eight hours was beginning to erode the edges of his concentration and when that happened his professionalism automatically fail-safed to just focussing on the specifics, otherwise he would be less than effective over the important hours in front of them. He moved-on: "Mary's also coming over for the briefing, seems like they may have a few things for us from the last scene."

That last piece of information acted like an adrenaline-shot for Kleberson, bringing him into full-focus for the day. His eyes widened as he sat upright looking straight at McKinley: "so our man's started to make mistakes?"

McKinley felt the new focus from his boss and that served to re-energise him as well: "seems so, let's just hope we can string them together quickly."

At that point Kleberson's phone rang. It was Sam Schneider: "morning Paul, what time's your briefing?"

"Seven."

"OK if I sit in?"

"No problem."

"See you in fifteen."

Kleberson replaced the receiver: "Sam's coming over for the briefing," he advised McKinley.

"How'd you both get on with 'The Turd' last night?"

"If bullshit were brains, he'd be president."

"Wouldn't be the first time," McKinley sneered. He did not hold a high opinion of politicians.

"Yeah, but they still did as they were told, unlike Kendrick." Kleberson smiled as he recalled part of the previous evening: "Friedmann was not at all happy with his client when we left."

"So is he still in the frame?"

"He's got alibis for the first two, nowhere near watertight but difficult to disprove, and we had him under guard for the third. So no as the perp, but if it turns out to be a multiple hit, then definitely as the one who ordered them. Plus we got a copy of the pre-nup."

He handed the envelope containing the document to McKinley, who responded with some surprise: "wow, that was easy!"

"Not really, I've read it several times and it's just as Marjoree Rolles outlined; there's no motive in there."

"Not for Kendrick maybe ..." McKinley mused as he pulled the document out of the envelope.

Kleberson immediately finished the sentence for him: "... but certainly for other interested parties. I assume that's what you were about to say Chris."

"So we're not letting the family off the hook then."

"Not while we can keep 'em squirming Chris!"

Sixty-Eight

There was a positive atmosphere in the crowded conference room as Kleberson entered just after seven, along with Schneider. They left the door open as individuals repositioned themselves to make space for their guest. The entire Squad was there, plus the Medical Examiner Mary Jourdain and Schneider's liaison man Bill Johnson.

As Kleberson walked to the end of the table where the whiteboard filled one wall, Holdsworth rose to close the door, stopping abruptly as he realised the massive frame of Chief Stanton was stepping through it as well. Other members of the Squad quickly picked-up on this additional presence and began to reshuffle again in an attempt to create enough space in the already cramped accommodation. Stanton quickly stopped them by holding up his hand and saying: "as you were everyone, I'll be fine here." He took control of the door handle from Holdsworth, closed the door behind him, then leaned back against it, causing the hinges to visibly protest at the extra stress they were not designed to accept.

Kleberson began the briefing by bringing everybody up to speed with his interview of Jackson Kendrick III, including cursory details of his movements and the contents of the pre-nup. He left the details of the lady being a Senator's wife out of this summary, which brought an immediate, and surprising, challenge from Stanton: "so who is this, so-called, lady - and when do we intend to interview her?"

Kleberson looked slightly shocked by the intervention, but Schneider quickly picked-up the question: "as it's across State lines Chief, I've passed the details to our local Agency down in Tulsa for them to check-out."

"And these so-called out-of-town businessmen?" Stanton continued.

Schneider also fielded the follow-up: "we've got that covered as well."

Kleberson tried to close-off the angle, as he didn't want to reveal the tactics that he and Schneider had agreed upon the previous evening: "as you're about to hear Chief, we've got several other avenues of enquiry opening-up and with time running tight, I want to keep this Squad focussed on those in the short-term."

But Stanton was on another tack altogether: "so are you telling us, Lieutenant, that Jackson Kendrick the Third is no longer a suspect in this investigation?"

Kleberson picked-up on the trajectory immediately: "no Chief, I'm not telling you that at all, not until Agent Schneider's men have confirmed the details are correct." He paused momentarily and looked Stanton directly in his eyes before delivering his final riposte: "or otherwise."

The atmosphere in the room was becoming uncomfortable, causing several of those present to shift uneasily in their chairs. But Stanton was also not finished: "just as long, Lieutenant, as you're not looking for non-existent pretexts to rule either him, or any other members of his family, in." Stanton also paused for effect while he surveyed the room making eye contact with as many present as he could before finishing: "I should not need to keep reminding you that the Kendrick family has suffered a severe bereavement themselves, do I make myself clear?"

There were nods from those that could not countenance the thought of missing a single paycheque; those that wished to stay neutral focussed on their shoes. Holdsworth stood perfectly still, Dean gave Chief Stanton a steely look which he held, Schneider looked directly at Kleberson almost imperceptibly shaking his head. He recognised that Stanton must have received a very serious phone call from either Junior or Friedmann, or both, between their leaving Friedmann's office and this briefing. He also realised that they were causing discomfort where it wasn't wanted, but if Kleberson chose not to back down this time, then Stanton would have no hesitation in removing him from the investigation and if that happened then he would be replaced by one of the Chief's more ambitious lackeys from another squad.

He needn't have worried, because Kleberson was almost telepathically on the same track, the intervention having buoyed him even more in his purpose. The cracks were showing and Kleberson wasn't about to let them be papered-over, having never been afraid of living with a little short-term public humility in the name of justice: "fully noted Chief," he responded, without removing his gaze from Stanton's eyes. Stanton nodded his approval and his body language altered slightly; several chairs sighed in silent relief as the atmosphere relaxed.

"So let's go back over each case in order and see what we are able to add to this picture up here. Capaldi you have something from the sighting of Ms Nicholson in the afternoon?"

Capaldi got to his feet and picked-up a VHS tape from the table, before jostling his way to the TV unit in the corner of the room. He pushed the tape into the player on the shelf beneath and picked up the remote, stepping back marginally as he began playing with the buttons whilst beginning to summarise the information he had. "After the briefing yesterday afternoon, I faxed the best photos we had of Ms Nicholson and her car to Jerry Bruckner over at Mid-Continent and he got his guys to go through their footage for two days ago. They came-up with this."

The screen fuzzed, then a series of jagged black and white lines appeared across it before it cleared to show a monochrome picture of the main corridor leading down from the boarding gates. Every ten seconds the camera angle changed, first to the main lobby area, then the check-in area, then the carousel area where a Big Dog motorcycle, one of Wichita's more iconic products, stood permanently on display.

"This is the composite footage of the groundside part of the terminal building," Capaldi continued. He pushed the pause button as the camera switched to a view of the entrance opposite the main corridor. There, frozen in time pushing her way through the revolving door towards the camera, was Hilary Nicholson, dressed in a smart plain white blouse and straight knee-length skirt, as if arriving for a business meeting. She carried no briefcase or laptop bag, just a small plain shoulder bag. The timer in the bottom right corner showed 17:34.

Capaldi pressed the play button again and the assembled company watched as the different cameras recorded her movements to look at the arrivals board, then ambling along to the carousel hall, which was empty, apart from one battered suitcase that was rotating constantly, forgotten and unloved. She returned to the junction with the main corridor and stood looking up the ramp towards the security checkpoint, un-needed prior to nine-eleven, but latterly becoming a fixture along with its humourless attendants. The timer read 17:37.

Capaldi put the tape into fast forward; the timer raced, but Hilary Nicholson appeared frozen in the strobing of the frames. The timer reached 17:48 and Capaldi returned the video to normal play. The view up the corridor, previously only sporadically-populated, showed a steady stream of people appearing through the checkpoint, mainly businessmen in slightly-dishevelled suits or smart polos and chinos, towing their one carry-on in their wake. Every few seconds, as the tape flicked-through the camera covering where Hilary Nicholson was standing, it recorded her non-movement along with a look of rising anticipation on her face.

The steady stream had become a throng. A mother and father with two children, aged probably eight and ten, emerged through the stream, at which point the younger girl broke ranks and ran down the slope, her pigtails trailing in her wake and the camera angle changed just in time to see her fly into the arms of an older lady who was bending down to receive her in a matriarchal hug, much to the satisfaction of the silver-haired gentleman in a smart blazer stood at her side. In the background Hilary Nicholson moved through shot towards the ramp. The timer read 17:52.

They all waited while the camera sequence cycled through to the view looking up towards the security gate. There walking towards each other were Hilary Nicholson with her back to the camera and a man probably of similar age, short hair, slightly taller maybe and looking very trim in what looked like a lightweight linen jacket, light t-shirt and jeans; he was carrying an airline-style shoulder-bag. They met and hugged; Hilary gave him a peck on the cheek, then took both of his hands before stepping back one pace as if she was saying 'let's just look at you'. At that point the camera view changed to the next cycle and everybody seemed to sigh impatiently in unison.

The tension in the room was palpable, but nobody dared say yet what they were thinking: *'was this Ms Nicholson meeting her murderer?'* They all waited with bated breath for the cameras to cycle again until the one on the corridor came back onto the screen. There, walking towards it, chattering intently and as close as they could be to the lens without walking out of shot, were Hilary Nicholson and her companion. At that precise moment, the man looked-up straight into the camera lens. Capaldi hit the pause button - the timer read 17:54.

Sixty-Nine

Kleberson was the first to break the silence, although still staring at the face on the screen that was looking straight back at him, almost defiantly: "what flight is arriving?"

"United commuter from Chicago," Capaldi immediately responded, "but he wasn't on it." Everybody exchanged puzzled glances.

Chief Stanton drew himself up to full standing height and interrupted: "whaddya mean he wasn't on the flight? He's just come through the damned checkpoint! How the hell did he get airside without a ticket?"

"He didn't do that either Chief," Capaldi responded and put the player into fast forward again as he continued: "we checked the gate and concourse footage and he didn't come off the plane, so we checked elsewhere." He put the player back

The Mantis Pact

in play and this time a single fixed camera played constantly, its view on a buffet area. The timer read 16:42 as Capaldi continued: "this is earlier footage from the food concession next to the security gate."

As they watched, the same man they had seen with Hilary Nicholson, still carrying the airline bag, wandered between the chrome bars demarcating the queuing area for the counter, took a tray, placed it on the slider in front of the counter and moved to the cold food display. He lifted the clear plastic door and selected a packet, placed it on the tray, then moved to the beverage servery. The assistant served him with a container, presumably of coffee, then moved to the till as he slid the tray in front of her again. He handed her a note, she smiled as if he had said something to amuse her, she gave him his receipt and some change, then returned to her station behind the beverage counter ready to serve the next customer. He moved to the condiment area, picked up some sugar and a spoon, then carried his tray to a table in the corner, away from the corridor. The timer read 16:45.

Capaldi put the tape in fast forward again, the bars jagging across the screen, but still allowing the viewers to see the man sat at the same table, eating his sub and drinking his coffee, then getting a book from his bag to read, then getting another coffee before returning to read his book again. Capaldi pressed the play button and the tape returned to normal speed. The timer read 17:51.

The concession had become more crowded, with additional people seated at tables looking periodically out of the area. Capaldi began talking again: "those people gazing out of shot are watching the security gate, which is over here." He pointed to the left lower part of the screen. As he did so, the man looked across in the same direction, then got up, packed his book in his bag, put the bag on his shoulder and walked towards the camera across the shot then out of screen bottom left. The timer read 17:52.

The footage changed again to the long camera shot looking up the corridor towards the gate; the timer again read 17:51. As in the previous footage, there were a steady stream of people coming through the gate. The timer changed to 17:52 and the family group appeared again in shot as Capaldi paused the tape: "when I start the tape again, don't be distracted by the little girl running away from her family down the ramp, but watch the background in this corner here."

He pointed to the top left corner of the screen, stood back and pressed play again. As the footage progressed to the point that the girl broke ranks, the man with the airline bag momentarily appeared in shot for just a split second exiting the concession and walking across shot into the crowd. He was invisible for about ten seconds before he emerged towards the front of the crowd, walking down the ramp towards Hilary Nicholson, who moments later appeared in shot walking towards him. They met in the familiar footage from the earlier montage and Capaldi paused the player again.

Kleberson once again broke the silence: "so Hilary Nicholson was meeting this person that, we have to assume from what we have seen, she knew and who she believed was flying-in on the Chicago shuttle. But he wasn't, he was already at the airport. So did he come in on an earlier flight from somewhere else?"

"No Boss," Capaldi responded, "Jerry's guys checked all the gate footage for the day and he did not get off any aeroplane." He put the player in fast forward again: "then they checked the composite footage again, going backwards from when he arrived in the concession area." He stopped the tape as the camera angle pointed across the carousel area; the timer read 16:29. In the background, the man appeared through the revolving door nearest the car rental counters and walked across to the empty Hertz Rental counter. He waited for a few seconds, then a female assistant appeared and spoke to him. He then handed her a set of keys, at which point Capaldi froze the shot again.

"Bingo!" Kleberson exclaimed.

"The bastard drove-in," Schneider continued.

"Yes, but he drove-in in a hire car," Kleberson added, turning to Capaldi: "do Hertz have the details?"

"That was why I was out at the airport for so long. We couldn't raise the kiosk manager on his contact number, so I had to wait for them to open-up at six. They're onto it now, so I'll head back out there if that's OK Boss."

"Sure Pete, get right on it. Can you put his face back on screen."

"I can do better than that Boss," at which Capaldi handed Kleberson half a dozen ten by eight prints of the frame: "we should have smaller ones printed by eight for circulation to all officers, I set that up before I came in here."

"Fantastic," Kleberson smiled as he slapped one of the large prints onto the board dead centre, "thanks Pete - odds are this is our perp, ladies and gentlemen!"

As Capaldi left the room, everybody momentarily focussed on the photo. The image was somewhat in soft focus, as happens with stills taken from VHS footage, but it was clear enough to see that this man was in his late twenties/early thirties, with short fair hair, the front of which was slightly longer and formed into a small Tintin-style quiff. Other than that, there didn't appear to be any distinguishing features on the face, in fact it looked like the face of someone who had not had to worry too much in those thirty years, certainly of someone from an affluent background, upper-middle class at the very least. The highish cheekbones added to the overall handsomeness of the face, only the eyes appeared to depart from this comfortable overall persona - eyes that seemed to pierce the camera lens to look out from the whiteboard and invade the intimacy of the conference room.

"Those eyes," Kleberson mused.

"They're cold as ice," Mary Jourdain observed, "I've seen too many like them in the past, some on the slab but mainly on courtroom defendants."

"Maybe that's what I'm getting from them," Kleberson continued, "for a moment there I thought I had seen them before. But it must have been the generic familiarity - you're right Mary, they're a perp's eyes, no doubt of that."

"Looks like a faggot to me," Dean observed with his customary brusque manner.

"Actually, that's an interesting angle." Kleberson was moving to pick-up the remote control that Capaldi had left on the table. He pointed it at the player and rewound the tape to the point where the man emerged from the throng to walk down the ramp towards the camera. He pressed play and the man walked towards them. The gait was neither masculine nor effeminate, but it was unusual, maybe slightly flat-footed. He paused the tape again to study the full body form.

He was about to make some observations when Dean beat him to the punch with a succinct summation: "yeah, he's a fag!"

"Didn't know you were such an expert Jerry," Moreno chirped-up and the room relaxed into quiet mirth.

Dean glared at Moreno, but Kleberson cut-off the tangential trend: "it makes sense. All three of our vics were gay, so they wouldn't feel threatened by one of their own. In fact, maybe they all knew him." He put the footage into play again to watch Hilary Nicholson greet the visitor, then paused it again: "that's somebody she knew, maybe not recently, but from somewhere in her past - USC! Dean, you've got something from them haven't you?"

"Only a tenuous link Boss, nothing concrete yet. It came from when I faxed over the photos of the vics; one of the longer-serving DPS cops recognised Hilary Nicholson's. She thinks it was back in the early 'nineties, Ms Nicholson went to the aid of a fellow student who had been attacked on campus. It would appear that the girl was not going to report the incident, but Ms Nicholson persuaded her to go along to DPS, where they interviewed her. They got a description of the attacker out of her, but when they tried to have the doctor examine her, she just flipped-out. Not unusual, as we know, so Ms Nicholson agreed to take the girl home to see if she could calm her down then bring her back later. But they never came back. The officer did the usual initial follow-ups in terms of looking for other witnesses, etcetera, but nothing came of it because the description the girl gave of her attacker was pretty-inconclusive. DPS logged it all, then moved-on."

"Does this girl have a name?"

"Not yet; in fact the DPS Officer couldn't really remember the girl, other than she had dark hair and was very shy. She remembered Ms Nicholson because of her kindness towards someone she had never met until earlier that same evening. They see this sort of thing regularly of course, normally turns-out to be a date that went further than expected and any stranger that gets pulled-into the situation is often more keen on getting back out of it as quickly as they can once that becomes obvious. But Ms Nicholson's attitude was different, certainly different-enough for the memory to last with that officer for around ten years. So I'm waiting on the University for full details. But all they've had to start from were rough dates, so it's not easy for them."

"Well, sounds a bit peripheral to me, but stay with it because even if this doesn't connect they may come up with something else that gives us another break. At the moment, USC is looking like the common link."

Schneider interjected: "you asked yesterday, Paul, if our LA Field Office could be involved, and they have confirmed they are keen to help in this if you want. They've got unfinished business with this perp remember."

"Sounds like the University Police could do with some help up there, you OK with that Chief?" Stanton nodded.

Schneider turned to his liaison man: "Bill, give LA the green light and feed everything they find back to Dean." Johnson scribbled on his pad as Schneider continued: "also check if there's any USC link to the Palm Springs grouping."

"Sorry Agent Schneider, I think that's a blind alley." It was Holdsworth piping-up from the back of the room: "I've been going through all the files that your office passed over to us and although they're definitely by the same perp, the groupings don't seem to have any links between them aside from the M.O. Within the groups, absolutely there are connections. Palm Springs had three vics from the movie industry, Memphis included a love triangle, Denver three IT specialists and Savannah three people from the same company."

"But these were groups of four," Kleberson responded, "you've mentioned threes?"

"That was what Kryczek was working on; the fourth victim each time had some link to one or more of the other three, but it was more tenuous. Except for Bonetti of course, he had no link other than being an investigating officer on previous murders elsewhere."

"So were the three with the definite links always the first three?"

"No; they were in Savannah and Palm Springs, but not in the others."

"So with our three having a strong connection, does that mean we're looking for the odd-one-out this time?"

"I don't know Skip, I haven't had enough time to fully-analyse it all yet. We have a link between all three at USC, so that would make the next target needing a tenuous link to USC. But then, we have two with a definite link as full-time employees of the TV station, but Ms Nicholson as the tenuous link, being a minor presenter; so the target could be another full-time employee at the station. Then we have Rolles and Nicholson as lesbian lovers, with Cochrane a tenuous link as a gay friend; so the target could be somebody in a love triangle with the two ladies. None of which helps us narrow anything down from what we have at present."

"Except," Stanton intervened again with a look of some satisfaction, "none of those involve the Kendrick family."

"Actually," Holdsworth paused staring momentarily at the board. The room focussed on him as he turned to Chief Stanton: "you've just added another scenario I had missed Chief - thanks for that." He turned back to Kleberson: "Ms Nicholson, Ms Rolles and Mr Kendrick all signed the pre-nup didn't they?"

Kleberson nodded and Holdsworth continued: "just the three of them?" Kleberson nodded again. "In that case, Mr Kendrick could be the target for victim number four making Cochrane the tenuous link. Maybe he knew more about it than was safe for him and that meant he needed silencing, particularly if this turns out to be a series of contract hits."

Chief Stanton was glaring at the young detective, his extraction plan for the family already in tatters just seconds after it had been quickly-conceived. Kleberson couldn't resist tweaking the silence against his boss: "looks like we may have some bait after all."

Stanton once again sprung to his full standing height, this time focussed on his Lieutenant: "not a snowball's chance in hell and that is the final word on the idea, get that implanted firmly up here Lieutenant." He prodded the side of his temple several times with the end of his index finger to reinforce the order.

Before Kleberson could respond, Holdsworth continued: "actually Skip, the Chief's right. That's precisely what got Bonetti killed."

Seventy

The entire room was focussed on its youngest occupant; even Johnson had stopped his incessant scribbling on the reporter's pad he used to keep his notes.

Holdsworth didn't appear fazed in any way by this, continuing: "by triangulating the first three vics, much as I have been doing overnight, Bonetti and Kryczek had identified two prime candidates for the fourth - a young up-and-coming actress and a make-up artist, both from Hollywood and both working on a location in La Quinta. The production company was already spooked by the previous murders, so agreed to the stake-outs. Bonetti split his team into two to nursemaid both, just in case. The actress was staying in a rented villa and requested close guarding, whereas the make-up girl was in a motel about a block over, but she wouldn't allow anyone in her room with her. Bonetti decided to head the group covering the make-up girl from outside the motel wing, with Kryczek taking the actress with all her group inside the property.

About two a.m, Bonetti's crew picked-up on a figure in the shadows at the back of the motel block, who appeared to be working around to the emergency exit. While they moved into position to take the intruder, he became spooked and ran off. Bonetti and one of his Agents went in foot pursuit, the other remained to check that the make-up girl was OK. He found the room still locked and in darkness, with no sign of forced entry, so assumed the girl was asleep undisturbed and radioed Bonetti for instructions; Bonetti told him to stay-put outside the room. They lost the runner about half a block from the motel, so Bonetti radioed Kryczek to check that all was OK, but did not get a response. He tried the other Agents in her group and got no response from them either.

Realising that they had been running in the direction of the other stake-out, they both made a beeline for the villa, which was in darkness when they got there. Bonetti then caught a glimpse of a figure shinning over the wall to the rear of the property. Assuming this was the same figure they had spooked from the motel, he decided to follow and send his companion round the opposite side to pincer their quarry. Bonetti went over the wall and dropped into some bushes. He may have tried to radio again, we don't know, but we do know that, when the other Agent was at the opposite side of the building, he tried to radio Bonetti but also got nothing. Bonetti moved to the rear of the villa and found a window open; assuming the intruder had gone in, he decided to enter the building through that window. Kryczek was on the other side waiting for him.

She had picked-up on the shadowy form going over the rear wall and had tried to radio Bonetti, but got nothing; she had also tried to radio the others in Bonetti's group and also got nothing. She assumed the worst and made her way to the den at the rear of the villa, where she saw that the window was open. She knew it had been checked as secure earlier and just as she was about to check closer, a figure climbed through silhouetted against the moonlight, that she could see was carrying a gun. She shot twice. When she turned the light on, she saw it was Bonetti - he was pronounced at the scene.

The other Agent from Bonetti's group had not seen anyone come out of the villa garden, their quarry had just vanished. They had to use the landline to summon the cavalry; when they arrived they all found their radios were not working. A local jammer was later found under the eaves of the villa. Bonetti's sidekick rushed back to the motel, but when he got there everything was calm. They roused the make-up girl and she was unharmed in her room - she had slept through unaware of anything."

Schneider intervened: "it was put down to a total screw-up by Bonetti and Kryczek was exonerated. However, she didn't see it that way, she thought it was a set-up, that the shadowy figure was Vitruvio and that Bonetti had been pulled into a trap. She wanted to continue to investigate, but was told to drop it. Afterwards, she rang her office and said that she realised that she was suffering from PTSD and asked for time off. Her boss was already considering putting her on garden leave, so was relieved that she had come to her senses and gave her indefinite leave of absence."

"Are you saying then, Agent Schneider, that the expert you foisted on us is a head-case? Stanton was back on his political high horse and riding furiously: "in which case I would be dumb to carry-on accepting your department's so-called assistance."

"No Chief, I'm not. What I am saying ..."

Stanton cut him off: "and are you telling me Holdsworth, that if I approve the use of Mr Kendrick as bait, the result might be that my Head of Homicide here could become a potential victim instead?"

"Not necessarily the Lieutenant, Chief, but I think that ..."

Holdsworth was also cut off in mid-stream: "pity," Stanton looked wickedly at Kleberson as he continued, "I was beginning to think there might be a silver-lining in all of this after all!"

Seventy-One

The United Regional Jet taxied slowly up to the terminal building. It was half-empty, not unusually for the first flight of the day from Dallas Fort Worth. It left too early to catch any international arrivals, so it carried mainly domestic businessmen and retired people visiting relatives in Wichita, who knew that it was easy to book in advance for substantial discounts. Today, it also carried one relative who had had to book suddenly and unexpectedly.

Madeleine Nicholson had a formidable presence. Not only did her appearance reek of comfortable affluence, but her demeanour shouted loudly that it had not been recently acquired, silently reassuring anybody around her that she was well-used to carrying the burden that old money bequeathed on its guardians. The even tan she wore had not been acquired in a downtown strip mall studio, but on the island of St Lucia, where her home had been since the death of her father, from whom she inherited it. It was in that home that she received the terrible telephone call from her lawyer in Dallas, news of another death, this time her much younger step-sister. It was that telephone call that had begun the tortuous journey to Kansas via three separate flights, the time in-between punctuated by stays in unfamiliar hotels.

Madeleine Nicholson hated flying. There was only one thing that she detested more - a forced stay in an unfamiliar hotel. Her body language, therefore, gave clear signals that today was certainly not a day to be getting in her way - she was on a mission and the target of that mission would soon be screaming "incoming!" at the top of their voice.

Unusually, she was waiting at the door as the hostess slid it open. Not for her, today at least, the slow and deliberate gathering of possessions whilst the plebs rushed-off to their working breakfasts. Today's trip would be brief but of significant influence, before she departed on the same plane on its second rotation later that afternoon. Neither would her designer luggage be allowed to make its normal high-profile laps of the carousel, because she did not have any.

The limo was awaiting her as she stepped through the arrivals lobby doors. It had been booked by her Dallas law firm; they arranged every part of her itinerary when she was forced to make an unwelcome visit to the mainland. The driver had been instructed to not stand in the lobby with a hastily scribbled name on a piece of unevenly cut white card. Madeleine had become irritated by the consistent inability of ethnic drivers to spell her surname correctly, so the instructions were to wait by the car and wear a red carnation, her favourite flower. Additional directions to the limo company were always the same: 'your client will find you, she is a middle-aged lady who does not enjoy travelling, so treat her with care.'

There were just four stops on today's schedule. First was the City Morgue where the driver was to await the client while she viewed the body of her newly-deceased sister, after which she was to be taken to an address in Eastborough, where a representative of a local law firm would meet her with the keys. Again, the driver was to wait, before taking both the client and the representative to Cafe Bel Ami for lunch. Following lunch, the client only was to be taken to City Hall for a short meeting with the Police Chief scheduled for one p.m, after which she was to be taken directly to Mid-Continent airport for her return flight at three p.m. There would be no baggage to be handled.

Madeleine Nicholson's only payload was secreted in her memories, but for its intended target, it carried the potential destructive power of a cruise missile

Seventy-Two

The briefing broke up just after eight. In the final twenty minutes, Mary Jourdain was able to confirm that the drug cocktail used on the first two victims matched the profile provided by the FBI and, having conducted initial tests before sending it off, that she expected the same result to come back from the Kansas lab on Cochrane's blood sample as well. More depressingly, the CSI Techs had not turned anything up that was remotely useable, despite going over the first two scenes twice. She confirmed that they had also taken a second look at Cochrane's site and had turned-up one or two possibilities, but she would rather wait for test results before raising any hopes. Johnson was detailed to provide her with copies of all M.E. reports on the previous groupings so that she could see if anything might open-up any other avenues forensically.

Similarly, Moreno had found nothing of any major significance at KNKW, but had more interviews scheduled that morning. He summarised the victims individually: "Hilary Nicholson was extremely popular among the people she worked with, nobody having a bad word to say about her. Marjoree Rolles was a consummate professional, hard working to the point of being a workaholic, but also highly-respected by everybody who worked with her, although some were quick to say that she did not socialise much with any of the staff and what private life she had remained very private."

He paused, momentarily, before continuing: "Cochrane, on the other hand, was almost universally loathed. Nobody liked working with him and many could not understand why Marjoree Rolles tolerated him like she did, because he was brusque, bad-mannered, short-tempered, rude and confrontational. Some of the technicians commented, nevertheless, that it was those traits that made him such a perfect news cameraman. He was not openly gay, but most of the staff either knew, or suspected, that he was. The majority also referred to well-known bouts of heavy substance-abuse, everything from alcohol to cocaine and even heroin at some time in his recent past, an episode that saw him taking extended leave to attend a residential rehab facility in Utah. There were many theories on how this was funded, but it was almost unanimously agreed that he could not have afforded to pay for it himself, as his habits ensured that he did not accumulate much wealth."

There was little more new information. The last ten minutes of the briefing descended into a blazing argument between Chief Stanton on one side, with Kleberson and Schneider on the other. This arose initially over why Morley had not yet formally provided his statement, as promised, which resulted in McKinley being detailed-off by Kleberson to conduct a formal interview after the briefing. The animosity then developed into whether the picture from the airport should be issued to all media at the ten o'clock conference. The Chief wanted to plaster it across every TV screen in the country, the detectives wanted to hold their fire a little longer while they tried to put more of a profile together and also so as not to spook the suspect if he was still around.

In the end, Schneider had asked Stanton to step outside, both returning a couple of minutes later with a compromise. The picture would be circulated to all FBI Field Offices with an urgent request for response if it was a known face. In addition all City and State Police would be issued with a copy of the photo with orders to alert the Homicide Squad immediately if spotted, but not to apprehend unless unavoidable. Stanton would postpone his press conference to two p.m, at which point he would issue all of the information they had, whether anybody else liked it or not. He then left the gathering with the customary thunder cloud brewing over his head.

As everybody returned to their desks and tasks, Schneider and Kleberson grabbed a coffee each and headed for the Squad-Leader's office. Kleberson slumped-down in his chair, throwing the airport photo on the desk in front of him. Schneider cosied-up to the filing cabinet in the corner next to the desk.

Kleberson was the first to speak: "so what do we really have? A photo, a possible connection to a hire car, but that's about it. This guy comes out of nowhere, then disappears back into nowhere; he's a ghost Sam, so that has to make him a pro. If we're right on that, then we have twelve hours, tops, to find out where nowhere is, otherwise we get another stiff and he gets clean away again."

"It's a bit more than we've had previously, so let's take a positive out of that."

"Yes, but we still have no real idea of where he might strike next. He's hit three people connected by the TV Station, so we could stake that out. But then two of them worked mainly outside news broadcasts, so does that mean we have to stake-out the press conferences? Then all three have a connection to USC, but if that's the connection then it's more your jurisdiction than mine. Two of 'em are connected to Kendrick and we've got him under guard; but what if it's the family? Could it be Junior next, or his daughter? Or will it be just someone random, like Bonetti? Which, while we're on the subject, brings another question - did you know about all that? You seemed to be able to close-off young Holdsworth's dissertation quite succinctly; so what did you know and when? Are you holding-out on me with something Sam? 'Cos if you are, buddy, you'd damned-sure better tell me now!"

"You're losing focus Paul."

"Brrr - wrong answer! That's one of your strikes gone, so do you want to try again, or pass to the next contestant?"

"Your problem, as always Paul, is that when facts won't fit into the neat row of boxes you've pre-created for them, then you start flailing-out at anything in range because you think there's a fact that's being deliberately hidden from you. Alright, carry-on, shake the damned tree - all you'll get is the usual crop of rotten apples falling on your head."

"Brrr- oh! Another wrong answer, that's two in a row. One more and you won't make it through to the last round where you get the chance to win tonight's star prize."

"OK, stop that bullshit right now Paul and read my lips." Schneider was still relaxed against the filing cabinet, but had put the coffee cup down on the top of it and was pointing at his mouth, his gaze fixed sternly on Kleberson's eyes: "I am not holding anything back from you - why would I? As you like to remind me, constantly, you're the one with the analytical brain and I'm the one with the gun."

"And the political nous."

"Don't change the subject - you asked for this, so you're going to get it. Hilary Nicholson's death came onto our radar because of the political nature of her connections, i.e. the Kendricks, and in particular one specific Kendrick who is under investigation on several aspects of both his business and personal lifestyle. I was hooked out of my bed at five a.m. by a call from Connolly ..."

"What, Alan Connolly?"

"One and the same." Kleberson whistled quietly and leant back into his chair. "Exactly," Schneider continued, "the Deputy Director must've been on the case well beforehand to be getting down to my level by five a.m! And that was all way before we knew anything about Vitruvio and all that additional shit. He wanted me to bowl straight in, kick Stanton into touch and take the whole thing over there and then - doesn't rate your Chief much by all accounts."

"Amazed he even knows who Stanton is."

"Oh, don't you worry your little head in that direction, he knows all about this wonderful department of yours and he's got none of it from me, but you can ponder on that after we've got the cuffs on this perp, not now. So I put my sorry ass on the line by saying how there's actually an ex-one-of-our-own in the department, who's likely to get a handle on this more quickly than I would."

"And did he know who I was as well?"

"He gave me another bollocking, as you call them, for letting you go - does that answer your question?"

"Another ...?"

"You can go there later as well. So he accepted my recommendation, which is why you're it and I'm quietly covering your ass with every resource I require. But beware Paul Kleberson, that's my valued and trusted OLD friend Paul

Kleberson, you give me the slightest hint that you're losing the plot and your ass will follow Stanton's into the prairie grass so quickly you won't be able to even form a huddle, let alone call the play."

"OK mother, I'll be a good boy and eat-up all my greens."

"Glad to hear it, now like I said … FOC-US!"

Kleberson adopted his finest mock Yorkshire accent: "what, both of us?"

Schneider looked about to explode, but confined himself to slamming his fist down onto the top of the filing cabinet. Everything on the same surface seemed to simultaneously jump upwards, to varying heights based upon relative weight. Kleberson visibly started at the sudden violence exhibited by his old friend, immediately jumping to his feet and backwards against his chair as he realised that Schneider's coffee cup had failed to land squarely and had launched itself off the top of the cabinet to hit the office floor, expelling its hot contents towards Kleberson's legs. He just avoided the main flow as his chair cannoned back from the wall to provide another obstacle that nearly caused him to lose his footing. He shot out a hand to help him balance, grabbing the arm of the chair which, because it had no other weight on it, immediately tried to rotate on its spindle.

Kleberson only managed, barely, to avoid falling into the puddle of muddy liquid created by the spill by jamming himself between chair and wall like an inebriated tramp in the boondocks. The sight of his friend's predicament brought a huge guffaw from Schneider's throat, a reaction not dissimilar to that of a companion tramp in similar circumstances, the previously-strained atmosphere evaporating as the two men dissolved into laughter at their joint recognition of the total ludicrousness of the scene.

Seventy-Three

"You OK in here?"

The enquiry came from a surprised-looking McKinley who had just opened the door of the office as the hysterics died-down, with Kleberson regaining his balance and a modicum of composure.

"Sure Chris, Sam here didn't like the blend of instant we're using; hang around a few minutes and you'll see him doing his famous impression of Mrs Mopp."

"I'm off to see Morley. He's at his home waiting, sounded a bit weird on the 'phone, nothing like his usual arrogant self. Do you want to come along?"

"No thanks Chris, I want to see if there's anything in the analysis that Holdsworth has been doing on the previous cases. Don't waste too much time on Morley, he's a bit of a sideshow really. Just see if you can get anything about Cochrane that would give us a break - what was his lifestyle, where did he hang-out, that sort of stuff. If anything sounds interesting, follow it up straight away. If you get a break, ring me."

McKinley acknowledged the instructions and left the office. Schneider looked at Kleberson and shrugged: "guess I'd better get a bucket."

"Don't be daft Sam, we've got janitors to clear this up. What are we going to do about this press conference?" He picked-up the photo: "two p.m. - doesn't give us much time before the Chief spooks this guy."

"No, but neither can we sit on the info until it's too late to save victim number four. I would rather scare him off than have that on my conscience."

Kleberson nodded and shrugged: "still, let's see if we can at least put a name to this face."

"The hire company is your best bet on that. Ring me on my cell when Capaldi gets something out of them."

"Where are you going?"

"I'm driving down to Tulsa to see Penny Clarke. Friedmann left a message on my cell that he has made the arrangements, but he thinks I'm sending someone from the local Agency. I've got to handle that one myself, Paul." He pointed at the photo: "I know that this bastard is our priority, but I can't just stand by and see old friends put through the wringer just because Kendrick wants to play games. I've got to find a way of keeping a lid on that, for the Senator's sake and his son's. I can't let some Field Agent who doesn't know the background just barge in there and destroy their lives again. Who knows, I might just get some dirt on Kendrick."

"So, will you be back for the press conference?"

"Pushing it, Paul, but I'll do my best. You don't need me though, you can run rings round Stanton. Make it happen how you want it to happen and if we get a break, then follow it and leave him to what he does best."

Seventy-Four

When Kleberson re-entered the Squad Room, it was very quiet. Capaldi was at the airport, Moreno had gone back out to KNKW and Dean was over at the Epic Center with Johnson having a conference call with the LA Field Office. Only Holdsworth remained, hunched over his desk, diligently combing the FBI files of the previous cases looking for something that didn't fit.

Kleberson started the conversation: "that was an interesting summary you gave us earlier, do you have anything more that you weren't letting everybody in on? Something that your instinct tells you doesn't fit?"

Holdsworth lifted his upper body from the relaxed stoop that characterised his studious phases. He was a tall man, long in the body, so the small desks in the Squad Room, combined with the inadequate seating, seemed to accentuate his apparent physical discomfort when working in there.

"This is a bit of a fool's errand, you know Skip?" he observed.

"In what way?" Kleberson replied.

"I'm trying to find consistency, as if we're looking for a serial. But this isn't a serial, this is a professional hit man - the Palm Springs grouping tells us that."

"How?"

"Bonetti. He doesn't fit anywhere with the other three vics in Palm Springs; the only way he links-in is that he investigated the first grouping in Savannah. So he must have spotted something that gave him a chance of catching Vitruvio who, as a result, led him into an ambush - completely different M.O."

"Some serials have been known to change their M.O."

"Yes, rarely, but then they stick with the new one for subsequent victims. Vitruvio has gone back to the original M.O, which makes no sense."

"But if he thought Bonetti was close, then he adapted."

"But a serial wouldn't do that, especially a serial who moves locations. That is very rare, because a serial wants to cause fear; he needs to see the results of his work through that fear spreading across a community. Serials that have nearly been caught go to ground, leave a time gap, then come back when they are least expected. Up until Palm Springs, Vitruvio had the drop on everybody, because he arrived, did the first three murders, then waited two days, did the last and disappeared, in most cases before the local police even realised they had what they thought was a serial. Why? He can't have been fearful of capture. It makes no sense, nobody got near him, until Bonetti that is."

"OK, we need to make something break, so tell me how you see it."

"If we change our primary approach from serial to hit man, then we can apply different criteria. The motive changes from a psycho satiating some weird fetish that results in similar murders, to simple business. And if this is business, then money has changed hands. So we follow the money."

"But how do you propose doing that? We don't know who this character is, so we can't do a trawl on bank accounts when we don't know whose accounts we need to trawl."

"But we know who the victims were, and to be a victim of a hit you have to be associated, in some way, with the person ordering it."

"But you said yourself that there is no consistent connection between all four vics in a grouping, no common-denominator that gained from their deaths."

"True. But what if one or more of the victims is a red herring - a random killing performed using the same M.O. to muddy the waters of the investigation? Or, taking your own thoughts, what if the method of presentation of the corpse is a form of invoice? And what if the customer fails to pay? Is the indiscriminate killing a way of re-inforcing the demand for payment - if you don't pay-up I will commit more murders until you do. Worse still, I will kill someone you know and if you still don't pay-up, then I will come for you. You have forty-eight hours to decide."

Kleberson went quiet, studying the face of this young rookie as he tried to assimilate what Holdsworth was suggesting. It was a radical theory, but one that fitted the facts too closely to ignore. Then a thought scythed across his mind like

Flush it Again

a lightning bolt. He reconsidered the thought out loud: "and the defaulter becomes the fourth victim!"

"Yes they do, but not necessarily each time. They may pay-up. In which case, for the threat to be valid and to reinforce the deterrent for future customers to not take the risk, he kills a fourth victim anyway; randomly, maybe, or not, as he feels relevant. It's his game, he directs it as he goes. There are no hard and fast rules, as there would be with a serial - just the pattern."

"But if that's the case, then the first vic must be the prime target."

"And payment is due on delivery. No payment within twelve hours, someone else dies, then someone else twelve hours later, then finally the defaulting customer two days after."

"And if payment is received as requested?"

"Then the perp is long gone, leaving just one victim - a casual murder with no clues, so any investigation will soon become a cold case."

Kleberson nodded involuntarily. Bizarre as it sounded, it all fitted too neatly for it not to have some relevance. Then another thought seared across his brain which, again, he pondered out loud: "there would be no need to attract any attention to the hit if the payment is received would there?"

Holdsworth thought momentarily about this new angle, then replied: "none at all. Best hits are the ones that we don't recognise as such. That way perp and customer walk away squeaky-clean."

"So, if it's a standard hit, payment up front, the perp walks in, does the deed, walks away and the customer learns of the success accordingly. M.O. doesn't matter, so other victims could have been shot, strangled, whatever. But if the customer is a distrusting soul, or is maybe careful with their money, then they will want some confirmation before releasing the cash. So is that where the poison comes in?"

Holdsworth looked at his boss, somewhat puzzled by this tangential leap: "where are we going now Skip?" he asked.

"Try this." Kleberson stopped momentarily to assemble the disorganised thoughts, put his finger to his chin, then continued: "customer places order, supplier asks for payment up front as usual, but gets a rider - you get your cash when I get the proof. Supplier is immediately suspicious, so changes M.O. to the poison injection. This disables the vic, but doesn't kill them immediately, although they will die within a set time. Having done that, the request for payment is made - could be a coded text message, could even use a camera phone, there's enough of 'em on the market now, especially among the level of society that orders hits. The vic would be disabled, so a photo of them laying there would look like they're dead to all intents and purposes. The perp's not going to hang around waiting for cash, so terms and conditions would be instant payment on proof into a nominated account, that he would be monitoring. If the payment arrives, then he finishes the vic off, or just leaves them to die. If not, then he's into the afters; that's when he changes from Joe Schmo the hit man to

Vitruvio the perverted serial-killer. The ultimatum is the presentation of a second proof - this is what's going to happen to your friends, and to you, if you don't keep your end of the bargain."

Holdsworth took a deep breath, then continued: "and after that, Vitruvio has a reputation to maintain."

"Yes, and you know what makes that sick scenario even more valid in our cases?" Holdsworth shook his head slowly, knowing the revelation would be quickly forthcoming. Kleberson looked him straight in the eye: "there can be few families in this State who are more protective of their money, or calculating in their business dealings, than the Kendricks."

Seventy-Five

Kleberson was more convinced than ever that the Kendrick family was behind the murder of Hilary Nicholson. He didn't particularly care which one it was, that person was the paymaster - the murderer in thought, not the murderer in deed. If the motive was surrounding the pre-nup, whether the existence or concealment of it, then that could explain the second murder of Marjoree Rolles and the elaborate interpositioning of the bodies; a failure to pay made Cochrane the randomly-connected victim.

He smiled to himself at the thought that, if they still hadn't paid-up, then the Police Department may not have to prove which one was the Client, Vitruvio would establish that for them within twelve hours. His amusement quickly evaporated as he realised that the alternate scenario, that payment had been made, meant that there was an innocent victim out there awaiting Vitruvio's deadly embrace within the same timescale. They had to pursue both potential scenarios - one perp, two completely different potential victim profiles.

"OK Holdsworth, let's follow the money. Get over to Sam Schneider's office and have Kowalski help you trawl through financials. Look at the fourth victims first. Did any of them, or maybe their companies, have financial problems; did they hold large insurance policies on any of the related victims? Maybe they were trying to cash-in on credit, as it were, get the deed done then pay the perp out of the proceeds. Also look for any largish payments made by them in the weeks preceding the first murder, that could be a deposit, balance on delivery. See if any of that builds-up to a motive for having the first vic killed."

"Hopefully the Feds have already done some of that."

"I doubt it; they have not been looking for perpetrator-turned-victim, remember. These are completely new lines of enquiry and we haven't got time to analyse any more, so run with the results wherever they take you, just keep me apprised of anything that turns-up."

After Holdsworth left the Squad Room, it seemed eerily quiet. Kleberson looked at the clock; 09:42 - less than twelve hours to make something break. He wandered through to the conference room again and started surveying the board. His eyes kept returning to the airport photo. Those eyes seemed so familiar, but where from? The shrill ringtone on his cellphone broke his concentration.

It was Chris McKinley: "hi Paul. As expected, not much out of Morley, he's pretty shook-up though, seems to have convinced himself that this is some homophobic maniac and he's next on the list. Tried to persuade him that there's no real logic in that but he can't, no won't, see it. Seems his conspiracy-theory tendencies have flipped him over the edge on this one. One thing's for certain, he ain't coming out of his hidey-hole until we've caught this bastard."

Kleberson smiled again as he responded: "if I get any more good reasons like that, I might decide to leave Vitruvio out there."

"I don't get you Paul, are you OK?"

"Ignore me Chris, private joke, tell you later - maybe."

"Anyway, I did get a bit of background. Seems he and Cochrane were an irregular item; if both of them were at a loose end and needed 'company' then they would get together. I got the impression that Morley would have liked it to develop further, but it never did, probably because Cochrane just used him. Know a few guys who've strung a broad along that way, never thought of gays doing it though - quite sad really."

"Yes, quite, I'm bawling my eyes out here Chris. What else?"

"They also socialised occasionally with the two ladies; seems that all three vics were still close friends. Morley said they invariably had a fun evening, mainly because the three were always reminiscing about college times and so on. Even so he didn't feel left out at all, they were all very relaxed in each other's company. But all three liked a one-night-stand with a complete stranger, then they would exchange those experiences as well, quite graphically at times. That's how I got to The Avenue."

"The bar down south of Kellogg?"

"That's the one. Seems that Cochrane used it when he was on the pull, it's a well-known pick-up point if you're an out-of-towner looking for action. Showed the airport photo to one of the owners and he recognised him from the other night."

"What, he picked Cochrane up?"

"No, that's the weird thing. He saw them talking at the bar, in fact our man bought Cochrane a drink. Then Cochrane left alone, a bit worse for wear apparently. Our man stayed around for half an hour or so chatting-up anything in trousers, then suddenly he wasn't there. Owner didn't see him leave, but thought he must have pulled and gone off with someone."

"Is there anything on the CCTV?"

"Nothing, but then that's not surprising as there's no CCTV installed."

"You're kidding me!"

"Owner doesn't believe in it, says it's one of the main reasons they've been in business so long."

"What, not even on the exterior?"

"Sorry Paul."

"So another dead-end."

"Looks like it, but there's another thing Morley said. More often than not, they would end-up at Cochrane's for the night, often arriving late. You remember Mrs Maxwell?"

"The old southern lady along the corridor from Cochrane's."

"It seems that whatever time of the night they arrived, her door would be cracked-open and they would hear it close when they were at Cochrane's door."

"Godammit, so she must have seen Cochrane arrive with his killer."

"That's why I'm on my way over there now."

"OK, I'll meet you there."

Seventy-Six

Kleberson pulled-up outside Cochrane's apartment block, alongside McKinley's car; both men climbed-out of their cars simultaneously. Kleberson looked-up at the fourth floor as he closed his car door. He saw a net curtain snap back into place as he did so.

They climbed the stairs to the corridor where Cochrane's apartment was sealed-off. They walked past the police tape criss-crossing the door and continued to the door of Lillian Maxwell's apartment; this time it was shut firm. McKinley pressed the bell push and the shrill ringer sounded in the distance. There was a long pause before they heard a shuffling from behind the door, which opened to the extent that the security chain would allow. Kleberson pushed his badge gently into the gap: "it's Lieutenant Kleberson Ma'am. You remember we came to see you the other day."

The door closed temporarily followed by a prolonged rattling of chain behind it, then it opened fully to reveal the same tiny form they had met previously, as immaculately dressed and coiffured as before, but somehow looking years older. Kleberson bent to remove his shoes, nodding to McKinley to do the same.

Lillian Maxwell smiled warmly at the gesture and some of those extra years fell from her face: "that's good of you to remember gentlemen, please come on through." She turned and led them down the short lobby: "now will you let me get you a drink this time, I have just made-up a nice jug of iced tea."

"That would be very nice Ma'am, thank you," Kleberson replied.

"Sit yourselves down in there," she pointed at the door to the lounge, "and I'll bring it through."

Kleberson and McKinley settled into a sofa and chair respectively. Within a few moments a tinkling sound drew closer from the kitchen area as Lillian arrived carrying a silver tray with three glasses and a large pitcher of iced tea, with several slices of lemon floating in the neck around the silver serving spoon that was the source of the sound. She placed it on the coffee table in front of the sofa: "please help yourselves gentlemen, I have a little difficulty lifting that pitcher these days."

"Will you have some as well Ma'am?" Kleberson asked as he poured-out the first glass.

Lillian nodded as she climbed into her wing chair by the window and settled herself with her back as upright as she could make it. Kleberson carried the glass over to the chair and placed it on the side table, noticing his card still on the same surface.

"Thank you," Lillian said, seeing Kleberson's glance at the card: "actually, I was just about to ring you gentlemen. I have remembered something about the other day. I don't know if it's of any use to you."

"That's OK Ma'am," Kleberson replied as he poured another glass and handed it to McKinley, "just tell us what you remember and we'll take some notes." He poured the final glass and sat down again on the sofa: "now take your time."

"I suppose it would have been around nine-thirty p.m. It was a warm evening, so I was sitting out on my balcony, reading as usual. My neighbour, Mr Polanski, he must read a book a day, so he lets me have my pick of whatever he has been reading recently. I normally take the thrillers, I like a good yarn, especially if it's a bit racy, you know what I mean?" She giggled softly at the thought, like a naughty schoolgirl: "I'm currently reading 'The Five People You Meet in Heaven'. It's a lovely story about a janitor who dies, then gets to meet some folks that he knew who went on before him. I suppose it won't be too long before I get to see if it's fact or fiction myself." She giggled again.

"I'm sure you have plenty of time with us yet Ma'am," Kleberson reassured her.

"Not as much as you two though, eh?" She smiled a little as she let out a quiet sigh: "anyway, it's not at all as morbid as you might think from the title, so we mustn't be any different, must we? Now, where was I?"

"You were reading on the balcony Ma'am."

"That's right, I was. That's when he pulled up in his truck, you know, him - the faggot; actually both of them."

"Mr Cochrane, from along the hall?"

"That's what you said his name was, so I guess so. They were all over each other, it's not right you know. I mean, you can't stop people doing what they do in their own homes, but they should keep the drapes shut when they're a-doing it. I don't want to know what they're up to, do I? But in broad daylight, it ain't right."

"So they were, what, arm in arm?"

"Lord no, Lieutenant, they was all over each other like I said, touching each other and kissing n'canoodling all across to the building. I tell you, ain't right if it's a man and a woman; but two men - what are we coming to? I mean, God gave you a pecker to do one of two things - to pee with or use it to get us ladies pregnant. That's it! It ain't meant to go anywheres else, is it?"

McKinley smiled broadly, straining to keep back the loud guffaw that he wanted to emit; he was taking to Lillian quite well.

Kleberson couldn't look at him, because he knew they would probably both lose it if he did. Instead he replied: "well, it's no longer against the law Ma'am, but we do try to discourage it in public."

"If you say so. But they just don't care, any of 'em."

"This other man with Mr Cochrane, did you get a look at him at all?"

"The one with the neat little butt, oh yes I got a good look at that as he flaunted it along in those ludicrously tight jeans of his. Looked more like a woman's ass, but that's probably because that's what he wanted to be wasn't it. He obviously knew what he was doing with it as well but they can't be completely right in the head can they? I mean parading himself like that for another fella."

"You're sure it was a man Ma'am?"

"Oh you couldn't miss that either. When I said those jeans was tight, I mean they was tight and he wasn't a small fella in that department, I can tell you. Time was when a man went to his tailor to hide a bulge like that, not accentuate it."

"And you saw all of this from your balcony Ma'am?"

Lillian blushed slightly. She looked at Kleberson a little sheepishly, then continued: "I'm a lonely old lady who used to be able to sit on her verandah watching the world go by. Down on North Market the world used to go by all the time and most of it said 'good morning Mrs Maxwell' or 'good afternoon Mrs Maxwell' or 'what a lovely evening it is Mrs Maxwell' and sometimes they would join me for a few minutes for some iced tea, just like you are today. And we would talk about life and what was happening in the world - normally that it was all going to hell in a handcart! But it's not only difficult for me to see all down there, nobody sees me all up here. So I can't talk to them much, but I can at least still watch them go by."

"So is that why you have the field glasses?" She nodded guiltily. "And why you open your front door when someone's in the hallway?"

"Folks see me sometimes and if they do they stop for a chat. People are still very nice, you know, generally."

"And this man, the one with Mr Cochrane, did you see him in the hallway?" She nodded, this time more frantically. "So could you describe him, other than his ass of course, we've already got that." Kleberson smiled at her and the self-imposed weight seemed to lift again from her small frame.

"He was a lot younger, in his twenties I would say, whereas that Cochrane, he must've been forty I s'pose." Kleberson assumed this was because of the receding hairline, because he knew that Cochrane was only thirty-two. "He was quite slim, had fair hair, short cut except for that weird quiff at the front. He looked like he was smiling most of the time, but it was false."

"Why do you say that?"

"The eyes, they were cold. Seen eyes like that before, never on nice people though."

"Did you get any idea of how tall he was?"

"Sorta; he was taller than me, but shorter than you two. How tall are you?

"About six-three Ma'am."

"Same as my husband, he was six-three. At least he was when he was your age, he shrunk later on. Said it was a good job he did, 'cos his hearing was going and it got him closer to me so he could still hear what I was saying. When he wanted to that was - amazing how the older you get, the deafness gets better or worse dependant on the question you're being asked, isn't it?"

Kleberson smiled again, remembering Grandpa Walt in his workshop: "I suppose it is Ma'am. So are we saying, what five-eight, five-nine?"

"Guess so."

"So would you recognise this man if you saw him again."

"Sure would. They wasn't eyes you forget in a hurry."

Kleberson pulled the airport photo from his pocket: "is this him Ma'am?"

Lillian took her spectacles from where they were lying on the side table, put them on the bridge of her nose and bent forward. As she focussed on the picture, she let out a gasp and sat back suddenly."

"Don't worry Ma'am, please, we don't think he's around here any more."

"Is that the one?"

"Which one?"

"The one they keep talking about on the TV - killed those two other ladies?"

"We're not sure yet Ma'am, it's early days. We don't even know his name yet."

"Oh I can tell you that! It's Shaun. At least that's what your Mr Cochrane called him as they walked past m'door."

Seventy-Seven

When McKinley and Kleberson returned to their cars in the parking lot, Kleberson leant against the boot of his Chevy with his arms folded looking-up at Lillie Maxwell's apartment. The lace curtains were hanging normally, but he was sure that her small face was just behind them looking down in their direction. McKinley noticed the direction of his gaze and observed with a smile: "she's a lively old bird that one."

"Sure is," Kleberson replied, pulling the airport photo from the pocket of his jacket, "and thanks to her we now not only have this fellow placed with two of the victims, but a possible first name on him. This is our perp Chris, no doubt about it." He looked at the photo: "so, Shaun whoever, where might we find you today? Not too far away from here I'll wager."

"You don't think he's bolted then?"

"Not a chance Chris. This is a professional and I somehow think he's got a number of reasons to hang around here at the moment. He has a job to complete and be paid for. We know when he's going to do that, we also know that he's going to do it within our jurisdiction, we just don't know exactly where. But we do know what he looks like now, so our task is just to stop him."

"Sounds simple."

"It's a lot more simple than it was last night."

At that point Kleberson's cell rang, it was Mary Jourdain: "hi Paul."

"Yes Mary, for once I'm hoping this is not a social call."

"We've got something - it's not much, but it might be a small piece of the puzzle. On our second search of Cochrane's apartment, we took up the bathroom floor and went through the drainage pipes, looking for anything that might have not been flushed away, but might give us some DNA; any hairs or whatever that were not Cochrane's."

"Remind me not to put-in for a transfer to the crime lab when the Chief finally loses patience with me." Kleberson could sense Mary Jourdain smiling at the other end of the phone.

"We found a condom - a rather full condom. It had somehow snagged itself on one of the bend joints; it happens sometimes, but will eventually loosen or tear and be flushed away, so it couldn't have been there too long. Obviously, there was no chance of getting anything off the outside because of the environment it had been in, but we were able to test the semen inside. When we found it was Cochrane's, we first assumed it must have been used on a recent previous liaison. But something bothered me about it, you know, those little nagging thoughts about something not being quite right. So I sent one of my guys out there again first thing this morning while I was at the briefing."

"What was he looking for?"

"Anything with a potential sexual usage, stimulants, creams, magazines, toys, used or otherwise. There was plenty of it, dotted all over the place, Cochrane was into all sorts. But there was one thing missing - the condom we found."

"Forgive me Mary, but surely it would be missing, he had used it."

"No, not the actual condom - the make and model. Cochrane had an array of condoms in all different shapes, colours and flavours, but no plain ordinary ones like the one in the pipe. So I analysed the latex; it's a different compound from any of the ones he used and it's from a maker's range that he didn't even have in the apartment. There was no matching empty packaging in the trash either."

"I still don't get the significance Mary, sorry."

"Until this, Paul, we have been following an evidence trail that shows our murderer performing various sexual acts on the victim, some possibly post-mortem. We assumed that he uses whatever he finds locally for the crime and the clean-up, but this confirms that he brings items with him as well. A condom makes sense, so as not to leave any of his DNA on the victim and there would be no guarantee that there would be any lying around in the victim's home. But surely that would be for his use on the victim. So how did Cochrane's semen, and plenty of it, get on the inside of the murderer's condom?"

"Cochrane had voluntary sex with him before he was murdered."

"In which case, wouldn't he have used one of his own condoms? He had them strategically placed everywhere in the apartment. Sexually, Cochrane was as much a predator as his murderer, but he was careful, like most gay men. This was his ground, so he made sure at any point that he would be able to lay his hand on a condom - one that he knew he could rely on and that would give him the sensations he wanted."

"So the condom was brought by the murderer and he played games on Cochrane with it. He's a careful pervert, hey, I think we already worked that one out didn't we? But there's no DNA on it, so how does it help?"

"It's the make of condom. They're not on general sale, because they are made primarily for the medical market by a manufacturer that includes, among other products in their range, full-cover body stockings. The total lack of DNA deposit by the murderer would make more sense if he was wearing such a stocking, if only during clean-up."

"Mary, you're a genius!"

"Oh it gets better Paul. The manufacturer only supplies those body stockings direct. I have them compiling a list of customers as we speak, which they have promised to fax over in the next half hour."

"That's quick."

"It's not a long list apparently."

"Chris is here with me Mary, we're outside Cochrane's apartment block; I'll get him to collect it on his way back to base. I owe you Mary."

"I'll put it on the tab Paul. Bye."

McKinley had been quietly listening to one half of the conversation, becoming increasingly intrigued. As Kleberson clicked the end call button on his cell, he observed: "that sounded interesting."

"Mary's found another angle. She's waiting for a list to be faxed through to her that might just include our perp. Can you pick it up on your way back to City Hall? I'll let Mary explain it to you in full when you see her. When you're back at City Hall, give the Chief a quick brief, then get on the phone and see if you can narrow the list down to one name ..." he pulled the photo out again and continued: "... this name. And get some troops out here to do another door-to-door with this photo. We need to find out if anyone else saw Shaun out here. Do the same in Derby and Westview Tower."

"I'm running tight on resources Paul."

"Then the Chief will find you some more. If necessary pull Moreno out of KNKW; after what we've found out this morning, I don't think he will find anything there."

"What are you going to do?"

"When you have a turd stubbornly floating around in the pan, what do you do with it?"

"Flush it again."

"Well that's exactly what I'm going to do - some more flushing."

apeiron

Seventy-Eight

Ten minutes after leaving Cochrane's flat, Kleberson was turning off of North Webb towards Greenwich. Two blocks across he swung a right onto a spacious loose-gravel entranceway, pulling-up in front of a pair of massive iron gates. A large figure in a dark suit emerged from the gatehouse to his right and walked slowly, but purposefully, across the bows of his stationary car, observing the driver closely as the electric window lifter wound down to its full extent. The figure came to a halt about two yards from the driver's door, legs astride with his hands joined across his crotch, peering down from his full height of about six-six. He said nothing, just stared at the car window. Kleberson initiated the conversation: "I've come to see Mr Kendrick Junior."

The goon responded in a low, sub-woofer voice: "is Mr Kendrick expecting you Sir?"

"I doubt it," Kleberson responded, slowly raising his badgecase before allowing it to unfold, revealing the badge. "Lieutenant Paul Kleberson, Wichita Police Department."

"Wait here Sir," came the booming response. The massive frame slowly walked towards the rear of the car, around it, then back to the gatehouse, watching the car and its occupant all of the way before disappearing through the door.

Two minutes later he re-emerged, walking to the driver's window in an almost identical manner to previously: "open the trunk please Lieutenant," he rumbled, to which Kleberson popped the remote release and the spring-loaded lid moved to the fully-open position, completely obscuring Kleberson's rearward view in the internal mirror. He watched the goon in the door mirror instead, as he crunched to the rear, looked inside and then slammed the lid back shut, to which the car reacted by twitching noticeably on it's springs. The goon looked across at the gatehouse and nodded; following his signal the large gates began to swing open.

Kleberson acknowledged the goon as he started the car forward through the opening and along the gravel drive towards a copse of trees about two hundred yards ahead. He glanced in the rear-view mirror to see the gates closing towards the solitary figure, who had readopted his legs-askance pose as he watched Kleberson's car disappear into the trees.

Kleberson suddenly realised that he was in - just like that. He had been granted access to the Kendrick Estate, a vast area of land to the North-East of Wichita that had been acquired during the immediate post-war years and on which

Jackson Kendrick Senior had erected a southern-style country mansion deep into the centre, surrounded by landscaped gardens incorporating thousands of imported mature trees to conceal it from external curiosity. Even after more than fifty years of eastward expansion of the urban sprawl of Wichita, most of which was built on Kendrick land, the ten-foot stone walls that circled the entire estate border still stood over a mile from the outer reaches of the city.

As the driveway meandered through a densely-wooded area, Kleberson began to wonder why it had been so simple. His visit had been intended just to cause a fluttering in the dovecotes, a phrase from Shakespeare's Coriolanus that his old English teacher would use to describe an unexpected development. He had anticipated being turned away, politely of course, following which he would await the identity of the first enquirer who might ask what exactly he had intended to achieve by his visit. He therefore had no preset agenda for any discussion that might ensue. Nevertheless, the opportunity was not to be wasted, even though he would have to wing it from here on in.

The trees suddenly evaporated to reveal a long, winding driveway, curving slowly to the right and down over a rolling landscape to end in a slight rise onto a large forecourt in front of a white-painted house. The whole scene looked as if it had come straight out of 'Gone With the Wind'. As he drove up that final incline, he realised that this house was far larger than it had first appeared from the tree line, showing how clever the landscaping design had been.

He pulled up in front of a flight of wide steps that led-up to the front door; at the top of the steps stood a manservant in full livery awaiting him. Kleberson got out of the car and ascended the steps, allowing himself to survey the scenery as he did so. To the left of the house, partly obscured by a tall grassy knoll that was also not apparent until the viewer was close-up to it, was what appeared to be a large stable block, complete with clock tower over the entrance gates. To the right an enormous artificial lake that disappeared into the distance, complete with islands and a large boathouse on the shoreline. In its fifty short years, this pastiche-property may not have amassed the history of the grand English mansions of his schooldays, but it possessed all of the grandeur - and some.

At the top of the steps the manservant greeted him. He was dressed in full white tie and tails, the epaulettes on his jacket appeared to be edged in gold braid and he wore spotless white gloves: "good afternoon Sir, I am afraid that Mr Kendrick is away on business today, but Miss Gloria will be happy to receive you. She is on the terrace - if you would like to follow me please."

He indicated that he was going to move off along the colonnaded terrace at the front of the building in the direction of the lake end; he proceeded with a metered step with Kleberson following him. As they walked along with the Doric pillars soaring above their heads to support the canopy two full-stories above them, Kleberson noted that there was not a blemish on any of the whitewashed stonework; it was as if the whole building had been painted just that morning. Beneath his feet, the flagstones were perfectly level and the pointing between them totally regular and undamaged. He began to think that this was more like a film set than a family home.

They rounded the corner of the house and the vista opened up even further. If anything, the side of the house was longer than the front, stretching off into the middle distance; the colonnade continued for a short distance, then ended as the terrace spread out before them. It was vast and on at least five levels leading down to the lake's edge. Each level comprised formal garden areas, all perfectly manicured with box hedges, statues and fountains, the lower levels curving around away from the house to end in open steps that also led down to the lake level, almost simulating a form of ancient amphitheatre.

Far along at the opposite end of the top level of the terrace, the colonnade began again to maintain the symmetry of the house; between the colonnades a orangery-style glazed extension rose to the full height of the house. There appeared to be no support for the glass, nor any obvious joins in it, but as he moved closer Kleberson realised that this was a trick of the light, as there was a thin stainless steel framework that ran between each of the, still enormous, glazing units.

On the terrace in front of the orangery were a series of round tables, all uncovered except for the most central one, which had a crisp linen table cloth spread across it with a large silver tray placed exactly central, on which were an elaborate silver teaset and two white bone china cups and saucers, both with gold edging. The table was shaded by a huge round white canvas parasol, suspended from a looping cantilevered support that disappeared into a concealed housing in the terrace flagstones. Nothing in this property was, in the remotest manner, unplanned or temporary.

The servant stopped at the end of the colonnade and extended his left arm towards the terrace: "if you would like to take a seat at the table Sir, Miss Gloria will join you shortly." He then walked back the way they had come, leaving the visitor alone on the terrace.

Kleberson began to move towards the prepared table. At the precise moment that he passed the outer wall of the orangery, as if choreographed, the figure of a lady emerged from the central door, heading in the same direction. Kleberson stood still; she also stopped and turned towards him, surveyed him momentarily, then smiled and extended her right hand towards him.

"Lieutenant Kleberson," she began in a distinctive East Coast accent, "welcome to our home."

Although Gloria Friedmann was in her mid-thirties, she looked to be easily ten years younger. She was slim and tall, probably five-nine; her skin was perfectly tanned and toned and her impeccably-groomed black hair formed into a 'sixties bob-style that flicked forward at the shoulder level. Kleberson remembered the early black and white photo he had seen of her mother wearing an almost identical hairstyle. The simple black dress that further accentuated her hourglass figure may, to the uninformed eye, have looked like any number of such designs on the rails in the fashion department at Macy's, but was in fact a unique

Caroline Herrera creation purchased straight from the catwalk at New York fashion week. First impressions were that she was not only one of the more beautiful women that Kleberson had ever met, but she possessed the natural class that had, no doubt, been inherited from her mother's side of the family.

Kleberson stepped forward and shook her hand. She extended her left hand towards the table: "let's sit," she said. Kleberson moved first to pull one of the chairs out for her, which she gratefully accepted and sat down: "thank you Lieutenant," she continued, "I can see you learned more in England than just history. We have tea, I asked for Assam, I hope that's acceptable."

Kleberson did not quite know whether he was impressed or disturbed by these two quick-fire revelations of such intimate knowledge of his private life, but he was not going to be destabilised by them: "perfectly," he replied with a smile, "shall I be mother?"

A full smile burst across Gloria Friedmann's face, lighting it up as if the sun had just emerged from behind a cloud: "I haven't heard that expression for years," she laughed as she spoke. "Mom sent me to England for a year when I was eighteen, basically to get Emil out of my system. I found that I loved it, much to my Mother's delight. I also found that I loved Emil - Mom was not so delighted with that, but she's learned to live with it."

She gestured towards the teapot: "please ..."

Kleberson began the tea ceremony: "how do you prefer it?"

"Milk, no sugar please. Assam is your preference I hope."

"It is - I'm assuming that wasn't a guess."

She smiled again: "very perceptive of you Lieutenant, I can see why you're able to get under my husband's skin so readily."

"So, does your family have a file on everybody in Kansas, or just those that may be of occasional use, or nuisance?" He looked straight at her as he asked the question; her relaxed smile remained, there was not the slightest perceptible flicker of change in emotional state. He made a quick mental note not to be drawn into a game of poker with this lady.

"A family like ours, Lieutenant, operates on two levels. The men deal with the business side, the ladies with the social. The general perception is that the two do not mix, but they are, in reality, inextricably interwoven. A successful husband and wife are a team, each knowing the necessary steps to achieve a mutual goal and as they grow in each other's success, they develop an almost clairvoyant ability to do so. Take my Mother and Father, for instance. You would know that my Father is one of the richest people in the country, maybe even in the world, but you are probably unaware that my Mother's various foundations are worth, in total, a similar amount of money. That isn't happenstance, Lieutenant, the two are indistinguishably linked and not just by the sources of the money."

Kleberson had continued to pour the tea as she spoke; he handed one cup to his hostess, who nodded gently as she took it. She lifted the cup to her lips and took a small sip, before returning the cup to the saucer: "mmm, exactly how I like it. So you see Lieutenant, a man and a woman working together to a common goal. I supplied the exact tea that you prefer and you mixed it with the milk to the exact proportions and temperature that I like to drink it. Yet we had never met until five minutes ago, so how did that happen? Should we be worried about it? Or should we just accept it? After all, because of it we have got off to a good start, have we not?"

Kleberson lifted his cup and saucer from the table and sat back in his chair. He smiled a broad smile as well: "we have."

"Good!" She also sat back into her chair: "there are two types of social guest we receive here, Lieutenant, those that wish to learn more about us as people and those that wish to experience the surroundings. I am happy to assist with either, or both, so which would you prefer to commence with?"

"You said social guest, what if I was a business guest?"

"Then you would be waiting in the foyer of our headquarters building while one of my Father's pretty secretaries fussed around you so that you did not realise how long he was keeping you waiting. You see, that is where my Father's world centres, this estate is the hub of my Mother's. If you wish to understand one, you also need to understand the other."

"Well, I would not wish to be the wrong kind of social guest, not for such a gracious hostess. So as I am experiencing the surroundings for the first time, why don't we start there."

"An encouraging choice, Lieutenant. Are you aware of the name of the estate?"

"Apeiron - the principle of all things."

"Ah, so you did some research before you came."

"No, it is emblazoned across your gates."

"Yes it is isn't it? - in Greek." She lent forward to deposit her empty cup and saucer on the table: "I apologise for momentarily forgetting that I am in the company of a classics scholar of some distinction. But we prefer the definition that it is the mysterious glue that holds the elements together, that supports opposites such as hot and cold, wet and dry and directs the movement of things, by which the host of shapes and differences in the world are grown."

"Ah, Nietzsche, yes. I prefer Anaximander's view that it is the primordial chaos to which everything ultimately returns."

"Nietzsche thought Anaximander a pessimist."

"Was that before or after he entered the mental asylum?"

Gloria Friedmann burst into a roar of laughter, throwing herself back into the chair clapping her hands once like a child experiencing the glee of discovery: "how wonderful Paul! Oh sorry, Lieutenant Kleberson, may I call you Paul? I am already having the nicest morning I have had for some time, it would be so much more fun if we could dispense with some formality."

"Well, you did say that I am not here on business, so as you have essentially taken me off-duty, why not?"

"In that case you must call me Gloria. Now, Paul, you may know the name that my Grandmother christened the place, but I bet you don't know what my Grandfather called it." He shook his head. Gloria shot forward to sit on the front edge of the chair to get closer to him, as if she was about to whisper a deadly secret: "Boom-Dee-Ay."

"Boom-Dee-Ay?"

"As in Ta-Ra-Ra-Boom-Dee-Ay." She giggled like a young child: "isn't that wonderful?"

He looked at her somewhat puzzled.

"Oh come on Paul! You can't have missed the similarity of the main part of the house to Tara, you know the mansion from Gone With the Wind. You see, when my Grandfather asked my Grandmother what sort of house she wanted, that's what she asked for. So he gave it to her, although as the work continued she kept adding and adding to it. When it was finally completed, they held a grand ball - yes we have a ballroom in there as well - during which one of the guests asked them whose idea it had all been. My Grandmother said they had done it together and my Grandfather added: "yes, she came up with Tara and I just added the Boom-Dee-Ay!"

Seventy-Nine

Gloria Friedmann continued to describe to Paul Kleberson how the Apeiron Estate had developed over the years. She explained how the main house and landscaping had been created by her grandparents, including the digging of the lake, the spoil from which had been used to create the rolling landscape around the house on which the trees had been planted, a necessity in the flat prairie lands of Kansas. The many illusions that this landscape introduced had been created by subtle use of space and enclosures, Paul expressing some surprise when he learned that the house itself was not only on the same level as the gatehouse, but much closer to it than visitors realised, due to the entrance driveway incorporating subtle bends and gradients upwards whilst winding its way through the woodland.

The stable block, terracing and lakeside views had been mainly developed by her mother. Her father took far less interest in the development of the estate than his father had, although he had been instrumental in the addition of several of the islands in the lake, which although they appeared uninhabited, actually contained facilities that even included a small power station and satellite communication systems: "if a state of emergency arose," she declared, "we could survive here for months on our own resources." To which he found himself wondering if even the government itself was as well prepared.

As the facts became less surprising and more macro, Paul decided that it was time to move on to the other subject that social guests were allowed to enquire about: "is this the main home of the entire extended family?"

"Yes it is," Gloria replied, still very relaxed in her overall manner, "although the house is divided into individual self-contained units so that we can all live separate lives when we wish to. My apartments are at the back overlooking the swimming pool, makes it easier for the boys to use it when they're home."

"So they're away at school?"

"Yes, they're both at Bement and from there they will go on to Deerfield; my Mother's family have long associations with both."

"Is that the same education that you had?"

"Yes and my little brother. I had the task of looking after Johnson from a very early age."

"Johnson?"

"Oh! sorry," she giggled mildly, "the problem with having this damned family tradition of calling every firstborn in the male line by the same first name is that when that gets called-out at home, they all come a-running. So we gave him a family nickname. Quite easy to understand really, Jack and John are often alternates used within families, take JFK for example. We were just going to call him John, but he had grander ideas and declared that if his father was called Jackson, but nobody ever called him Jack, then we should at least do him the honour of adding the 'son' to his name as well. Not bad for a toddler, Pops was almost impressed, although a five-year-old is too young to realise that Johnson is a nickname for something else; he found that out later, of course, at school. Didn't faze him at all though, because people often have far worse nicknames for him - but then you already know that don't you? Still, I expect the Squad Room will find it amusing that he chose to be called a prick as early as the age of five."

Paul was momentarily stunned into silence by this graphic flow of information, so Gloria just continued on the original subject: "then we all have our own properties as well. Mom has places in Boston and The Hamptons, Pops has a house in Washington, I have a lodge in Aspen for the ski-ing, plus a small house in Deerfield so that we can spend weekends with the boys during term time. Emil has his beach house in Malibu. Insists it's for entertaining his showbiz clients, but he's just an old beach-bum really - he's even still got his old VW camper in the garage there."

"Is that how you met him?"

"Yes, I went to stay with a school friend in Santa Monica for the summer recess. She was the daughter of a family friend, so Mom was glad to be able to ship me off somewhere safe and not to have to worry about entertaining me for an entire summer. Emil's family were part of that circle of West Coast society, so we met at a party, then spent most of the summer on the beach; problem was I didn't want to come back to school afterwards. Big fuss, I was dragged back to Deerfield screaming, Emil came to find me, Pops had to run him off back to California. Result was I was grounded for the entire year, then sent off to England. Thing was, though, Emil never lost touch - must've cost him a fortune in transatlantic phone calls. We got it all planned during that year, so when I came back home we told both sets of parents that we would see our education through, then get married. If they didn't like it, then that was their problem."

"Bet your Father didn't like that."

"Sort of. You see, he likes people that demonstrate independence. But he also loves Mom, and she wasn't happy because she had plans for the deb balls and so on. So Pops brokered the compromise, I did all the society stuff, Emil went to law school, graduated top of his class and we all lived happily ever after."

"What school?"

"Stanford"

"Wow!"

"Oh yes, clever boy my Emil, as Pops soon figured out."

"And your brother? You haven't mentioned him much - does he live here, or in town at Westview Tower?"

"Westview Tower? Oh Lord no! That just belongs to one of the real estate companies. They have properties all over the country and at least one of the better apartments in each is maintained for company use; for entertaining or accommodating the more important clients that they don't want to put in a hotel. We all use them from time to time if we're travelling and want some privacy. Johnson's probably been the main one to use that resource over the past few years, because he runs most of those companies and he's always zipping-about between them doing deals and so on. No, his main home is still here, although since he's lost Hilary, I fear he might go nomad again."

"Go nomad?"

"There's no point in hiding the facts from you is there? His colourful history must be well documented in police files all over the country, and it's all my fault."

The conversation had been candid enough already, but Paul still started slightly at this latest revelation: "your fault?"

"He's three years younger than me and I am supposed to look after him. So while Mom and Pops were sorting out my teenage rebellion, nobody noticed that he was having one as well. By the time I came back onto the rails, he was already way off them. Got in with a very bad crowd and no matter how much Pops tried to clean up the mess they left in their wake, they were always a few steps ahead of him. After many years of that, he just snapped one day and threw Johnson out. Strange, that seemed to bring Johnson to his senses; it was like having my little brother back again."

"What, you acted as an intermediary?"

"Oh good Lord, no!" She looked slightly anguished for the first time in the entire conversation. "Pops has a mantra - never let anyone crap on you twice. It's stood him in good stead throughout his life, so when he's severed the cord, that's it. No point in anybody acting as an intermediary once Pops has taken such a decision, unless they want to be on the business end of a similar one."

"So how come ...?" Gloria interrupted the obvious question.

"How come he's back in the fold? That's a good question you know. I wish I could answer it for you, but the truth is I don't know. Look, Johnson's every bit his father's son, whilst he's full of sobriety, that is. In that state, he can make genius judgements and decisions, charm the birds from the trees and be the life and soul of any party. You, and most of your colleagues, have probably only met him while he's acting-up to his nickname. That's his alter-ego and it's not pleasant. Problem with Johnson is that, under the influence of any form of stimulant, his mind does not perceive the change. He thinks he's behaving normally, but everyone else knows that he isn't. Polite society won't tolerate it, but the hangers-on will, because they know what's at the end of the rainbow. I guess that Pops realised that taking-away the pot of gold was the best way to remove the influences - and it worked."

"But that must have taken some time."

"Oh yes, it took about a year for all his personal money to run-out, then another few months for all the friends and business acquaintances he hit on to realise that Pops wasn't underwriting the loans they were making any more. That was when he finally got himself into rehab and out again clean and dry."

"But if he had no money, how did he get the rehab?"

"I paid for it. Like I said, it was my fault so I had to put it right."

"So is that when he met Hilary Nicholson?"

"Oh … dear Hilary." As Gloria paused, her face grew very sad. Then she looked away from Paul and off into the distance, clenching her right fist and bringing it against her lips. After her incessant chatter, the silence was almost overwhelming. Although it was just a matter of seconds, it felt like it was going on for much longer, broken only by the occasional cuk-cuk of a coot echoing across the lake.

Paul felt that he needed to bring her back, because he had accidentally slipped across her invisible divide between social and business: "I'm sorry, I should have …"

Gloria cut him off again, still looking away: "no - no! It is I who must apologise. I suppose I have been bottling it all up since we heard the news. Oh that poor dear girl!"

She turned back towards him. Her eyes were wet and red and her left cheek glistened where a small tear had attempted escape. Paul instantly whipped a handkerchief from his trouser pocket, quickly checking that it was fresh before handing it to her. She accepted it graciously and gently dabbed it against the offending moisture in a manner more akin to the heroines from the black and white afternoon matinee films that he had been forced to endure as a child when staying with Grandma Liz. Gloria thanked him, but her manner had become more agitated: "I can't think how Johnson must be feeling, he must be beside himself with grief."

Paul decided not to go there. He was already developing a warm respect for his hostess and he had no intention of popping any of her many balloons, not unless this all turned out to be an Oscar-winning performance, which he doubted: "so you haven't seen him since it happened?"

"No, but I know that Emil has. He has reassured me but, well, what do you men know about emotions? I keep leaving messages on Johnson's cell, but he hasn't replied yet." She seemed to recover her composure almost instantaneously, the professional hostess returning to the surface, masking the big sister's concern for a sibling: "are her family coming to Wichita do you know? It's the funeral arrangements; they will need help if it is going to take place here. Otherwise, we will need to organise the travel details if they're taking her back to Dallas."

Then, the persona changed again, the anguished face of a frightened woman returning: "tell me Paul, professionally of course, what sort of monster does something like that? I mean, walks in off the street and murders a complete stranger? Because that's the only explanation I can see - Hilary wasn't the sort of person that made an enemy of anyone."

"I know this will sound like a cop-out, Gloria, but if I could explain that I would not only be able to solve all of the open files in our current caseload, I could also stop most of the future ones from opening. In this instance, we appear to be dealing with a serial, because there are two more victims as well."

"Two?" Gloria appeared even more agitated: "I heard about the TV presenter, Marjoree Rolles wasn't it? I did meet her once, briefly, when I went to a Chamber of Commerce event. She was on the same table as Hilary - she seemed very nice. You think that was connected?"

"We believe so. Hilary and Marjoree were at USC together."

"Really? I thought they were just thrown together on that table, I didn't realise … gosh … you know what those junkets are like. Networking I think they call it - ghastly term. And the third?"

"Ms Rolles' cameraman, Tom Cochrane."

"No, doesn't ring a bell." She shook her head; that was all the concern a mere cameraman was going to get from this location.

Eighty

Paul and Gloria were both so deep in conversation that they hadn't noticed the manservant approaching again across the terrace. He came to a halt a discrete distance from the table, but within the arc of Gloria Friedmann's vision. She started with surprise momentarily, then acknowledged him: "ah, Woodhouse, I'm sorry I didn't see you there."

The servant bridged the final distance to the table: "excuse me Miss Gloria, but we were just wondering whether your guest will be joining you for lunch."

Paul glanced at his watch, amazed to note that it was already past midday.

Gloria responded immediately: "oh, how rude of me - will you join us Lieutenant?"

"I'm sorry Mrs Friedmann, but I have a press conference at two, so I will need to get away."

"Of course, I understand. Maybe another time, once this ghastly business is behind us?"

He smiled: "I would be honoured."

"In that case Woodhouse, it will just be me. I think I will have lunch out here, it's such a lovely day."

"Certainly Miss Gloria." The servant gave a courtly bow, then turned and walked back across the terrace in his metered fashion. As the figure faded out of earshot, Paul took on board the fact that they were alone at the house, an obvious reason why he was allowed entry, which would doubtless have been denied had any other family member been at home.

He turned again to his hostess. He couldn't resist the next question: "is that really his name?"

Gloria's wonderful smile returned to her face as she absorbed the query: "oh yes, absolutely! Mom has always wanted a butler called Jeeves or Wooster, or something similar; she has a wicked sense of humour you know, loves to see her guests slightly discomforted by it. Anyway, when the applications arrived the last time we advertised, there it was - a CV with the name Woodhouse on it. He had the job before we even saw him, Mom wouldn't have cared if he couldn't buttle for tuppence, in fact she may even have preferred that!" Gloria giggled again at the thought: "anyway, he turned out to be the best we've ever had. Makes you wonder why anybody bothers with all that human resources nonsense, doesn't it? The world might just be a better place if we just picked a name out of the hat and hoped for the best, don't you think?"

Paul nodded agreeably, recognising that he was in the company of someone else that lived up to her name - the ones given to her by her parents in any case. He decided this would be a good note to leave on: "anyhow, I really must be getting back to City Hall," he said apologetically, slowly rising to his feet. He offered his right hand as Gloria also rose from her chair: "it really has been a pleasure meeting you and thank you so much for telling me all about this wonderful home of yours."

She moved towards him and took his hand as if to shake it, but instead pulled herself towards him and, raising herself on tiptoe, brushed her right cheek against his before depositing the gentlest of kisses next to his ear. She immediately withdrew to the requisite distance: "no Paul, the pleasure has been entirely mine. It is always enjoyable to entertain a true gentleman and you have fulfilled the expectations that I had been given. Let me walk you to your car."

Paul was, once again, momentarily distracted by the apparent reference to some personal knowledge of him: "I hadn't realised that I was the subject of

The Mantis Pact

conversation in such elevated places, except perhaps negatively I suppose, if my boss was involved."

Gloria burst out laughing again: "what that crushing bore Stanton?" She laughed aloud again: "oh my Lord, I give him a wide berth when he's out here cosying-up to Pops; even he can only take Stanton in small doses!"

"I'm sorry, I assumed ..."

"You assumed Stanton was in Pops' pocket; of course you would, but only because he climbs in there of his own volition. Pops would have him replaced in a heartbeat if he had the inclination to - someone more independently-minded would suit him." She stopped and turned towards Paul, who also stopped in his tracks: "someone like you, Paul - someone who isn't a voluntary lapdog."

He just stood still, his mouth slightly open.

"You'll catch flies in that this time of year," Gloria pointed at his mouth, which he shut quickly. "You really don't get it, do you? Families like ours don't run empires like we have by buying influence. We no longer have to because we ARE influence - we permeate everything we touch, to such an extent that we ultimately have no need to touch any of it."

Gloria looked straight into Paul's eyes and could see they were full of many more questions: "the next thing you're going to ask is why, then, do we use someone like Stanton? Simply because he's there, ready and willing to be used. But one thing you can be absolutely sure of - absolutely sure - is that Pops would never tell Stanton what decision to make. If Stanton wants to mentally ponder how his decisions might be received by Pops and perceive compliance or otherwise, then act accordingly, that's entirely up to him. Life in the stratosphere of society is far more subtle than anyone up to their ankles in the mud of existence could ever understand."

She began to walk on and he followed, almost spellbound by this new flow of information. Gloria continued as they entered the colonnade: "I was told you're a flyer, a free-spirit. Now I've met you, I can see that more than you can. Free spirits get things done - make things happen. Oh, they may not be the things we might like to happen, but life moves on and we quickly adapt to the new circumstances, taking the positives from them. There will always be positives while life is moving forward; negatives come when it stagnates, thanks to stick-in-the-muds like Stanton. 'If you do what you've always done, you'll get what you've always gotten' - Tony Robbins - if you haven't read any of his stuff, you really should. 'Awaken the Giant Within' would be a good place to start."

They had reached the top of the steps and Gloria stopped again: "alright Paul, I'm sure that's more than enough information for one day." She smiled at him again. He stood and looked at her, as if hesitating to leave. He had one burning question that he needed to ask before he left and was pondering the best way to ask it. Once again, Gloria beat him to the punch: "come on, spit it out man, the question you want to ask me, 'cos I sure as hell ain't gonna ask that one for you."

"I cannot think," he stumbled unusually, "who on earth I know who could possibly have such opinions of me."

"Ah, but you see Lieutenant, that's the policeman thinking, not the historian. Try a little harder, using the analytical researcher's part of your brain."

She smiled teasingly, but when no response was forthcoming, she pushed a little harder: "we have a mutual friend, Paul. Now who on earth could that be, you wonder? Someone who is just as comfortable circulating among the aristocracy as they are with the hoi polloi."

"Annie!" he exclaimed, "you know Annie - but how?"

"Simple really - Pops borrows money, Sir Nigel lends it. One deal, back when I was about ten I think, Sir Nigel brings Lady Liz over with him for a holiday, she meets Mom, they get on like a house on fire and we all become family friends, actually they are some of Mom and Pops' closest friends. So where do you think might be a really pleasant place in England to send a somewhat unruly young colonial in need of some stability and protection? She sends her love, by the way, and says not to be a stranger."

Paul's rapidly returning memories quickly intermixed with pangs of guilt. It must have been over a year since he last wrote to Annie; their regular direct correspondence had long since faded once he married and Leanne had taken over the writing duties. It resumed, sporadically, following the divorce. Sporadically because, as always, Annie would reply within a week with at least four times as many pages as Paul could ever manage. He would eventually find the time for a one-page guilt response, always starting with the phrase: 'I'm really sorry it has been so long ...'

"She said that the coach house hadn't been used for a few years," he mused quietly out loud, "but that as my predecessor was one of my own countrymen, she knew I would love it like they had". He looked, somewhat sheepishly, at Gloria: "that was you?"

"Wonderful family the Flemings. They just give you all the space you want, yet somehow when you have it, you no longer need it, so you spend all your time with them, don't you? They were such a perfect contrast to the restrictions of this country. We might be the home of the brave, but since that time over there, I always felt England was the real land of the free; shame most of its indigenous people never realise it."

Paul nodded, once again drifting through the memories that were flooding back of those university summers spent in rural Sussex: "forgive me for saying so," he began, "but you must be a few years older than Annie."

"No need to be embarrassed by it Paul, it's only length of life experience. Yes, about three years, in physical age that is; when I arrived I quickly realised that, in terms of maturity, I was light-years younger. I sure caught-up quickly. Even so, having met you, I don't think I would have been able to accept the rejection as readily as Annie did, let alone manufacture it in the first place. You're so obviously soul-mates."

He had only met this lady for the first time less than an hour earlier, but he already felt so comfortable in her company that he no longer found this analysis disturbing: "I understand why you would see it that way, we were always very close right from the time we met, but somehow it never went to that final level."

"For you Paul, maybe not, but I don't think that was mutual you know, not at the time anyway. I was forcibly separated from Emil and that was probably where we both derived some of the strength we needed to make it happen. But if someone had suggested to me that I send him back to where he came from and ask friends to make it as easy as possible for him to stay there, I can tell you they would have got a two-word answer, the second word being 'off'. People tell me I have class but, even if they're right, I'll never have that level of it."

"Make it easy for me to stay?" He was once again wrong-footed.

"Oh come on Paul, you can get away with feigned naiveté some of the time, but don't overdo it. You surely don't think that all those offers from Ivy League institutions were caused by that one little article that excuse for a society columnist wrote about you in the Wichita Mail, do you?"

"That was you?"

"No, it was Mom. Good friends like the Flemings don't ask many favours, which is why they get the A-Team when they do."

"But I rejected all of them," he responded somewhat horrified.

"Yes and became a cop instead - which is why you will always have the respect of both families!"

Eighty-One

The drive back to City Hall was made on autopilot, that mode of consciousness where the instincts deal with the mechanics of the task in hand while the mind races trying to make sense of other, more pressing, matters.

The first part, between Greenwich and the junction of Webb and Central, was spent attempting to come to terms with the revelations about Annie's true feelings for him, and the way that the relationship between the Flemings and the Kendricks could have sent his life into an entirely different orbit. The lights at the junction alerted him to the need to focus back on the case, the entire length of Central being spent on analysing exactly what new information Gloria had revealed about the potential connection between the murders and the Kendricks.

He had got under the skin of Emil Friedmann, at least to the extent that it had come to the notice of Friedmann's wife, which meant that there was something he had to be concerned about Kleberson digging-out. Potentially, this could mean one of two things - Friedmann was simply nervous about his involvement in the pre-nup being exposed to Junior, or he was up to his neck in any conspiracy involving the murders.

There was the overall aspect of the family double-act between business and social, husband and wife working seamlessly together but in different spheres of influence and, of course, totally-legally. Was tea with Gloria just an elaborate charade, one where she wove an image of a family watching from the sidelines as life went on, biding their time to take advantage of an emerging game plan? On the flip-side of that, she had no idea that he was going to pay an unannounced visit to the estate that morning, until the call had come through from the gatehouse. She was highly-intelligent, no doubt of that, but could she have conceived such an elaborate deception during his short drive from the gatehouse to the mansion? She would have had no time to have a telephone conversation with either parent, neither of whom were at home because she would be lunching alone. Or maybe they were there, watching from a distance, sending the servant out to create the impression that their daughter was home-alone, that this little tete-a-tete was an accident of opportunity.

How could he tell? He didn't know Junior and his wife, had never met them and so could not perceive them in any way other than through third-parties - third-parties with agendas. But he did know the Flemings; he had virtually lived with them for over two years. Were they people who could be close friends with a Machiavellian dynasty? The short answer was no - not a hope. Sir Nigel and Lady Liz were lovely people, kind, gentle and accommodating; they were also no pushovers. Sir Nigel was particularly astute and Paul could imagine him negotiating a business deal in his quiet calm manner, whilst politely not giving an inch beyond his pre-chosen boundaries. And their 'little place in Sussex', as Lady Liz called it, would no doubt have impressed the Kendricks on their first visit as much as Apeiron would have amused the Flemings on theirs. Even John Le Carre would have struggled to weave an old-money family like the Flemings into any new world political intrigue.

Then there was the servant named Woodhouse: *How many Americans actually read P G Wodehouse these days, for goodness' sake?* Paul thought to himself. *How many would recognise the irony in the fact that the author spent more of his life in America than he did in Britain, hence the immense popularity of his books here in the 'thirties, books that, despite their Englishness, were actually written primarily for the American market. Not enough to give that private joke much impact at dinner parties - but tea on the terrace with an anglophile cop?*

And what of her apparent perception of her brother as an emotional wreck following the tragic loss of his fiancé of convenience? This was diametrically-opposed to the reality Kleberson and Schneider had witnessed in her husband's office. If she genuinely perceived her, recently-reformed, brother in such a light, then he was still very-much capable of creating separate existences, one in full-view of the family, at Apeiron and in wider society, the other in the shadows of the many grace-and-favour apartments at his disposal around the country. Plus, of course, the homes of his acolytes.

The fact that Gloria appeared to have no recognition of how close the friendship had been between Hilary Nicholson and Marjoree Rolles, suggested that she may not have been as familiar with her future sister-in-law as the impression she had tried to convey. Although she would have worked closely with Junior within the Corporation, just how much had Hilary Nicholson actually been absorbed into the family? Gloria's lack of detailed knowledge of someone ostensibly so close to her, made little sense in the context of how much she clearly knew about individuals barely-peripheral to their social circle; people like Paul Kleberson himself.

Then, finally, there was Stanton. If Kleberson took the Kendricks at Gloria's version of face value, then Stanton was more dangerous than he could ever have realised. He could cope with his Chief being in the pocket of a multi-billionaire, that was a simple dynamic to understand. But a Chief of Police following some kind of self-delusional or auto-suggestive breadcrumb trail towards - well, who knows? Kleberson was apolitical at the best of times, but even he recognised how volatile that situation could be.

He came to two conclusions. That he had gleaned very little substantively from the visit, except for one or two new snippets that might just make sense when they slotted-in with other, yet to be learned, facts.

And that, when this was all over, he was taking a long holiday with his real friends back in England.

Eighty-Two

Kleberson's first recognition of the journey was slamming the door of his Chevy in the City Hall parking lot. He looked at his watch; it said one-fifteen p.m. Still time for a review of what had transpired that morning with the investigation team prior to the press conference. He considered calling-in to the Chief's office on the way to the Squad Room, but then thought better of it; he would have enough opportunity to fill Stanton in at the conference and after.

The room was empty, so he grabbed a coffee and wandered into the conference room, which was heaving. Capaldi was writing on the whiteboard, Dean and McKinley were poring over several documents and Holdsworth was scribbling frenetically on some pieces of scrap paper.

"So there you all are!" he said.

McKinley looked-up, with a somewhat annoyed look on his face: "where have you been Paul?"

"Flushing, like I told you."

"And what about your cell?"

"Got it here." He pulled it from his jacket and held it up.

"Have you checked your messages recently?"

Kleberson's mood tightened. He looked at the cell - it was dead. He pressed the 'on' button and the keyboard lights flashed momentarily, then extinguished again: "sorry Chris, looks like the battery's flat."

"No matter - we've got a name." McKinley pointed at the whiteboard.

Capaldi stepped away from the board to reveal a name in red capital letters beneath the airport photo: 'SEAN SHEPHERD'.

Capaldi added some detail: "that was the name on the booking for the hire car deposited at the airport by our man on Friday afternoon before he met Hilary Nicholson. It was rented on Wednesday from Tulsa International Airport."

"Was there any home address given?" Kleberson asked.

"It was rented on a company account; seems our Mr Shepherd is one of their club gold members. We got a printout of the rentals over the last two years and, among many others, we found two hires in the Palm Springs area, three in Memphis, two in Denver and two in Savannah, all the dates co-inciding with the periods that Vitruvio was active in those cities. All hires were pre-booked through the account; some were collected from airports, the rest from hire offices in towns. Some of the hires overlapped."

Holdsworth cut-in: "I've taken a look at the overlapping hires, in particular the first one here. He hired a second car from the East Wichita branch office which he collected at around two p.m. Friday afternoon. That would have given him sufficient time to drive the car down to Derby and park it up, then still get out to the airport."

Kleberson was momentarily dumbstruck by the flow of data: "whoa there boys! Let me get my head around that a minute. What you're telling me is that this Shepherd drove from Tulsa to East Wichita in one hire car, collected another, drove that down to Derby and parked it, went back to the first car, then drove that over to Mid-Continent airport half an hour before Hilary Nicholson arrived there, dropped it off, had a cup of coffee, pretended to come off the plane from Chicago, got a lift back to her place, murdered her, then drove off in the second hire car he had parked in Derby earlier?"

Capaldi responded: "that's about it, Boss."

"But that's pretty complex. There are any number of elements that could go awry there. It's not the actions of a serial, or a hit man."

Holdsworth joined in: "why not? It's all pretty-much under his control throughout."

"So how did he get back to collect the first hire car - does he have an accomplice?"

"We've guessed taxi," McKinley joined the discussion, "I've currently got enquiries into every taxi company - did they pick-up this man Friday afternoon in Derby and drop him in East Wichita, or vice versa? We tried the company he works for, Berger & Pastore Enterprises Inc based out in California, but just got voicemail. Incidentally, that company was also on the list you asked me to collect from Mary Jourdain this morning."

"What the list of customers for the special condoms?"

"Exactly that and, among other things, full-overbody stockings; so I've asked Johnson to see if they can track down either owner of the company. Seems a bit unusual to find a German and an Italian in business together, although the listing says they provide services to the film industry, so I guess it's anything goes in that area."

"French and Italian, Chris." Kleberson was smiling as he corrected McKinley, "and tell Johnson not to waste his time, he won't find them."

McKinley looked at Kleberson with an expression that mixed puzzlement and anger. Puzzlement at the correction, but also anger at the more recent uncontactable absence of his senior officer just as they were beginning to hit pay dirt. Kleberson quickly put McKinley out of his misery: "Berger and Pastore are the French and Italian words for Shepherd - this sonofabitch is playing games with us."

McKinley threw his pen at the table in front of him. It bounced back up, hit the wall and rebounded narrowly missing Dean's bald pate as he ducked in anticipation of it hitting him: "Jeez!" McKinley exclaimed, "just as you think you are getting a handle on this bastard, it gets turned into another dead end!" He rounded on Kleberson: "what the hell are we really dealing with here Paul?"

"A very professional hit man," Holdsworth interjected again, scrabbling through a sheaf of papers on the table in front of him as he did so: "here it is." He handed a copy of a bank statement to Kleberson. It was from the First Tennessee Bank in Memphis, for an account in the name of Jordan Michael Harrison, dated September 2002.

"What am I looking at here?" Kleberson enquired.

"This entry here." Holdsworth pointed at a line two thirds of the way down.

Kleberson read it out: "twenty-third October two-thousand-two, wire transfer to Cayman National Bank, George Town, Grand Cayman to the account of B&P Enterprises for fifty thousand dollars."

"Mr Harrison was a lawyer, who was widely predicted to be a future Governor of Tennessee; on eighth November o-two, he became Vitruvio's fourth victim in Memphis. Three days earlier, the first victim had been Harrison's wife, a member of one of the oldest-money families in the State; in March o-two he had taken out a three million dollar life insurance on her. The previous year there was a botched kidnap attempt on their eleven-year-old daughter."

"Looking at this statement, the fifty-grand near cleaned-out the account."

"Turns out, he had made some large investments in Tunica casinos."

"Tunica. Isn't that the area they're developing into the Las Vegas of the South?"

"That's the one; if he had invested in the developments, he would have been fine - problem was, he preferred the tables."

"So this was the down payment on his get-out-of-jail scheme."

"Looks like it, which makes the group pretty-much fit the pattern we were discussing earlier, because victim two was Jose Ramos, the Harrison's gardener and rumoured to be Mrs Harrison's lover. Number three was Kathy Parker, a cocktail waitress in a bar on Beale Street often frequented by Jordan."

"His mistress?"

"Lots of smoke, not enough fire. Local police found indications of the odd liaison, but couldn't put them together regularly."

"OK, let's examine this a minute. Jordan Harrison pays the deposit to an offshore account belonging to this supposed entertainment company in California, but is actually our hit man Shepherd here." He pointed at the whiteboard. "Two weeks later Jordan's wife is murdered and the balance is due, let's say another fifty grand. But he doesn't have the cash, only the insurance payout to come. So Shepherd murders the lover next; that's two in twelve hours, closely connected and both pointing straight at Jordan. He still can't raise the cash, so his current squeeze gets it. This makes it a serial, but there's not enough for the locals to connect Harrison to that one, so the heat's off him for the time being - except that he's got the message, via the waitress' body, that he has forty-eight hours to live, unless he pays-up. He doesn't, or more likely he can't, so Shepherd forecloses on him."

McKinley had been listening intently: "fits like a glove, Paul - and we have similarities here, don't we?" McKinley moved to the whiteboard: "if Hilary Nicholson is the ordered hit, then a deposit will have been paid by whoever, although I think we have a good idea who whoever is, someone that has a reason to be rid of her re the pre-nup. But the balance isn't paid on time, so Marjoree Rolles becomes victim two; because she's not only a witness, she's the next-door neighbour of the defaulter, which points us right at you-know-who." He pointed at the photo of Jackson Kendrick III. "Still no money forthcoming, so Cochrane gets it next. If we hadn't known what we did, we would have gone straight for a serial and we would have been diverted from our prime suspect, who if he is our prime suspect, is the next victim in ..." he looked at his watch "... just over seven hours time. Fits like a glove again, except ..."

McKinley tailed off, so Kleberson prompted him: "except what Chris?"

"Except Kendrick doesn't have any money problems. If the price is the same, what's fifty grand to him? It's pocket change, so why would he play games with this guy that's sending him messages that he's a dead man unless he pays up?"

The room went momentarily quiet, then Holdsworth broke the silence: "because he's not the one getting those messages. He's being set-up!"

Eighty-Three

"You know, that's some excellent detective work there gentlemen."

The words came from the doorway behind Kleberson, who swung round to see it almost completely blocked by the massive frame of Chief Stanton: "it just amazes me that you've taken the last couple of days running round in circles just to arrive back at the same place you started from - although I must say that I am pleased that you have finally come to the conclusion that Jackson Kendrick the Third did not murder his fiancé. So, who was it that was telling you that back in the early hours of Friday morning? Let me think a minute." Stanton stroked his chin between thumb and forefinger, looking up at the ceiling for effect: "oh yes, that would have been me wouldn't it."

"Now hold on Chief …" Kleberson tried to interrupt, but Stanton had waited three days to take the high ground and he wasn't going to lose it - not this time.

"But of course you, Lieutenant Kleberson, do not want to listen to anything your superior has to say on the matter, do you? What on earth could some hick ex-football player like me know about detective work, all I'm useful for is playing politics, cosying-up to people with influence, because that's the only way someone like me could possibly advance a career in anything. Then, of course, if I say that a certain aspect of an investigation, or a family maybe, or even a place, is off-limits, I'm only saying that because I know they're as guilty as sin and I want to pervert justice to their ends which, by such definition, must be my ends as well. But then, if that's true, those ends must also be applicable to the Mayor of this fine city, who I have just had the pleasure of sharing lunch with, as he updated me on certain developments this morning. And of the Governor, who had passed that information down to him just prior to our meeting for lunch. Who knows, Lieutenant Kleberson, how many more layers of government may become embroiled in this simple murder investigation, a Congressman or two, maybe even a Senator? Or do the tendrils stretch all the way to the White House itself? What are the limits of your ambition, Lieutenant?"

He held up his hands in a defensive, but theatrical pose: "no Mr Kleberson, don't bother to respond to my rhetorical questions. You see I already know the answers to all of them and there was a slight clue in that previous sentence." He held out his right hand towards Kleberson. "Lieutenant Kleberson, you will deposit in this hand your shield and your gun. You are hereby suspended not only from this investigation, but also forthwith from the Wichita City Police Department, for gross insubordination and deliberately ignoring the direct orders of a superior officer. The suspension will remain in place until such time as an internal enquiry can be assembled to examine the evidence that will be presented to it and from that decide upon the punishment that you will receive. Is that understood?"

McKinley leapt forward, his face dark with anger: "for pities sake Chief!" he exclaimed.

Stanton stopped him dead in his tracks: "unless you want to join him, Detective McKinley, something I don't believe that you can afford to contemplate with your current financially commitments, you are instructed to accompany ex-Lieutenant Kleberson to his office, where you will ensure that he recovers all of his personal effects. You will then escort him directly from the building."

"Are you out of …" McKinley began the obvious question to Stanton, but Kleberson grabbed his arm.

"Do as you're ordered Detective," Kleberson said, turning towards the door, where Stanton moved aside as Kleberson removed his shield from his pocket and his gun from its shoulder holster, depositing them in the Chief's hand as he passed him, eyes straight ahead and offering no acknowledgement as he did so. McKinley glared at Stanton as he followed.

Stanton launched a parting volley in Kleberson's wake as he made his way down the corridor towards what would become his old office: "and that suspension includes an embargo on any correspondence that you may wish to make to the Federal Bureau of Investigation, whose local Lead Agent is currently on his way back to his office, from Tulsa I believe, having received a similar instruction from his State Bureau Chief."

Stanton turned back and entered the conference room to address the remaining detectives: "you, gentlemen, will continue with this investigation under the command of Detective McKinley, but there will be no further assistance from the Bureau, you will have to make do with the evidence that you have assembled. It looks to me as if you now have a good idea who our murderer is, so I suggest you make every effort to arrest this man before he causes any more grief to our citizens. Because you are so close, I have cancelled today's press conference, as I believe that releasing any information at this time might jeopardise your chances of apprehending him. I will be briefing Detective McKinley as soon as I can on an operation we are setting up this evening which, I believe, may help conclude this unfortunate episode and I firmly expect to be able to call a fresh press conference tomorrow morning where we can announce a successful outcome. Thank you gentlemen."

At which, Stanton turned and marched out of the conference room and down the corridor towards the stairs to his office. He made no attempt to change the straight-ahead direction of his gaze as he passed the open door to the Squad Room, where Kleberson was just about to emerge, carrying a small briefcase into which he had packed his childrens' photos from his desk; he had no room for anything else, physically or mentally. He and McKinley had exchanged few words since the Chief's bombshell had exploded in the conference room, but as they moved down the corridor towards the door into the car park, McKinley took his cellphone from his pocket and pushed it into Kleberson's jacket pocket.

"Don't be daft Chris, you can't take any risks for me." Kleberson went to take it back out again, but McKinley grabbed his arm to stop him.

"I need to be able to get hold of you Paul; I'll recharge yours and use that. The Chief won't know, how could he, operating at the altitudes he does?"

As they reached the double doors, they opened to reveal Emil Friedmann entering the building. He held the door for Kleberson to pass through, making his farewells in the process: "goodbye Mister Kleberson, I doubt we shall meet again, so you'll forgive me if I don't say it has been a pleasure."

Eighty-Four

"What on earth happened there?" The question came from Holdsworth, holding his arms out in disbelief, as McKinley re-entered the conference room.

McKinley shrugged with an air of exasperation, realising that his immediate priority would be to focus the troops back on the task in hand: "listen guys, we all know the politics in play here, we have known them right from the get-go. We also know that Stanton is an asshole - and if any of you want the job I have just had thrust on me, then feel free to go tell him what I just said so that he can take my badge as well."

McKinley gestured to the open door; there were no takers. So he moved to the door and quietly closed it, returning to the table in the centre before resuming in a calm, but quiet, voice: "our Boss has been sailing very close to the wind throughout this investigation - not because he was trying to cause problems for his superiors, but because that was the only way to get at the truth. As police detectives, gentlemen, we have one goal - to get to the truth. That's the real truth, not some convenient truth that fits a billionaire's preferences, or some ass-crawling politician's ambitions; we need to get to the truth that brings justice for a victim and their family. Therefore, we will continue with this investigation without our Boss, just as we would have with him. We owe that not only to the victims, but also to the finest policeman it has ever been my privilege to work with. That is what professionals do, gentlemen, and what professionals expect of their colleagues. Any questions?"

All in the room silently shook their heads in a resigned manner.

"Good. We have just a few hours to locate Sean Shepherd before he kills again, so let's concentrate on that and leave the other baggage until tomorrow. It would appear that the Chief intends to go ahead with the press conference, so I had better get out there, see what other rocks he intends to throw in our path."

"He's cancelled it," Dean said gruffly.

McKinley turned to him with a quizzical look on his face: "he's what?"

"He's cancelled it, told us after you escorted the Lieutenant from the room."

"Did he tell you anything else?"

"That you're in charge and that he's planning some operation this evening, which he will brief you on later, although he didn't say whether we were involved or not. Oh, and we can't talk to Schneider no more."

McKinley stood silently in some disbelief for a few seconds then, recovering his thoughts, he continued sarcastically: "so, I guess it was good of him to let the new officer-in-charge in on all those decisions up front. Right! Let's just sit down a minute, go through what we have and what we can and can't use, then we can see what strategy we have left. First, does anyone have a phone charger?"

"I have Chris." Moreno started digging in his briefcase, pulling-out a large black unit from its depths with leads trailing behind it.

"Good. Put this on charge will ya." McKinley slid Kleberson's phone across the table to him and Moreno connected everything up before plugging the unit into the nearest wall outlet.

"Let's start with the hire cars. Capaldi, what do we have?"

"He's on his third car now, a red Dodge Intrepid hired from the branch on Douglas yesterday afternoon, license number S-G-four-seven-five-two. He returned the Stratus he had previously to East Wichita sometime last night."

"OK, let's get an ATL out on that license State-wide and to Oklahoma as well; he came in from there and we're only an hour's drive from the State line. He may be hopping across the line when he goes off our radar. Do we know what time he returned the Stratus?"

"No, the branch was closed so he just parked it up and posted the keys in the box. He's a corporate account holder, so doesn't need to check-in."

"So we have another overlap and presumably more use of taxis to achieve it. Who's covering the taxi companies?"

Moreno responded: "just uniform at the moment Chris, but I can take that if you want."

"Yes, do that. Shepherd does seem to be a creature with some habits, so let's hope that he used the same company both times."

"Maybe three times Chris." Moreno started flicking through his notebook as he spoke: "yes, here it is - a Mr Danielli out at Cochrane's apartment building. I spoke to him earlier on the door to door and although he couldn't identify the photo, he thought he saw someone of a similar physical description getting into a taxi on Saturday afternoon. The guy wasn't familiar, so he was pretty sure it wasn't a resident."

"What time?"

"Around six p.m."

"How long would it take a taxi to get from there to Washington and Lincoln?"

"Twenty minutes tops, even at that time on a Saturday."

"That fits then. Shepherd was seen talking to Cochrane in The Avenue Bar between six-thirty and seven; he must have parked-up the hire car outside of Cochrane's, then called a cab to take him to the bar. The bar owner saw Cochrane leave alone, around seven, but didn't see Shepherd leave. Maybe Cochrane was waiting outside for him."

"No, Cochrane went back to the station that evening." Moreno was flicking through his notebook again: "here it is, he did some voiceover work on the afternoon footage, ready for the morning news."

"How long was he there?"

Moreno checked his notes again: "about half an hour, left soon after eight."

"That's it then, he had arranged to meet Shepherd later, because they arrived together at Bradley Fair in Cochrane's truck around nine-thirty. Shepherd had parked the hire car there earlier, so after he killed Cochrane he was able to walk out of the apartment block and drive off into the night. But without the car, he had to get from The Avenue to wherever they met. How many taxi companies over on the East side?"

"Four or five."

"Then start with them. All of the taxi rides we know of start or finish on the east side and if he did use the same company, then you never know, on one of those journeys they may have taken him to or from somewhere we haven't got on the list yet, maybe even where he is staying."

"If we could find that out," Holdsworth observed, "we could possibly save the Chief the embarrassment of what he's planning for tonight."

McKinley turned to Holdsworth with a wry smile: "I didn't know that we had someone on the squad that was privy to the Chief's inner thoughts."

"Come on, he's not likely to be planning anything radical, is he?"

"And nothing we can do much about, so let's not waste any more time on that. What about the Bureau stuff? As we are apparently cut-off from that channel from here on in, is there anything in what we already have that helps us?"

Dean was the first to respond: "we seem to have hit a dead-end at USC. Problem is, it was nearly ten years ago, so all that we have is what is in the University records, plus odd tidbits from staff who knew them and are still there. So we know that all three vics were close socially, they even shared a house at one time, but nobody else seems to figure in the mix as far as all three are concerned. The only other thing we got was the Schaeffer girl, the one that Hilary Nicholson helped-out when she was attacked."

"Schaeffer?" Holdsworth suddenly sat-up.

"Yeah, Norma Schaeffer. But nothing came of it, she didn't even return to make a statement; that's why the file was closed. We don't even know if Hilary Nicholson ever saw her again afterwards."

"I've seen that name somewhere," Holdsworth pondered, "in the Bureau files. Where was it?"

McKinley continued: "while you're thinking," he turned to Dean, "did we get anything else on her from the Bureau?"

"No, I let it go once the trail went cold."

"Got it!" Holdsworth exclaimed, "the make-up girl!"

"What make-up girl?"

"The one that Bonetti was nursemaiding in Palm Springs - her name was Schaeffer!"

"Co-incidence?"

"Maybe," Holdsworth responded, "but how many genuine co-incidences have there been in this so far?"

"None," Moreno observed, "and I doubt this is either. Schaeffer is German for Shepherd." All eyes instantly focussed on the member of the team least-renowned for insight, in some disbelief at this detailed knowledge of a foreign language. He shrugged: "my Grandmother, she bred German Shepherds, or Schäferhunden as she would put on the pedigree certificates."

At that point there was a knock on the conference room door. It opened, and Stanton's secretary poked her head into the gap: "Detective McKinley?" she asked looking from one face to another.

"That's me," McKinley responded.

"Chief wants you in his office in five minutes, please Detective, for a briefing." The door closed as pre-emptively as it had been opened.

"Looks like you're going to find out the Chief's plans Chris."

"As if I need to right now," McKinley sanguinely observed.

Holdsworth continued: "my money's on setting up Kendrick somewhere, leaking it through the TV News so that Shepherd knows where to find him, then surround the place with SWAT guys expecting him to walk straight into the trap, like the idiot the Chief seems to think Shepherd is, but we know he's nothing like."

"He's not going to take a risk like that."

"Course not, because Kendrick will be somewhere else safe and sound, somewhere only the Chief and Kendrick's close circle know - and, of course, Shepherd."

"Sorry, you've lost me there."

"Where had we got to when the Chief decided to break us up half an hour ago?"

"Shit!"

"Exactly, that Kendrick has been set-up - and to be set-up like that, it would have to be someone close."

McKinley exhaled as he realised the significance of developments: "that's why Friedmann's here."

"Friedmann's here?" Holdsworth queried.

"He came in as Paul was leaving, very full of himself - cat-got-the-cream type full of himself."

"What odds will you give us he's in on the Chief's meeting?"

"I don't take bets on certainties. Dean, do you have the right contacts at USC to get addresses on the Schaeffer girl?"

"Reckon so."

"Then get what you can as quick as you can. Holdsworth, do you have any way of checking-out the make-up artist without involving Schneider's office."

"If there's anything in the file, I'll use it."

"Good, then you all get on with what we've just discussed, while I waste my time in this damned briefing."

Eighty-Five

McKinley ascended the stairs and walked along the corridor towards the Chief's office. Stanton's secretary was at her station outside of the closed door, but she indicated that he could go straight in. He knocked on the glazed portion of the door, opened it as the "come in" instruction issued from within, and entered, closing the door behind him.

Stanton was seated purposefully behind his desk, looking every bit in full control of his empire - this specific part of it at least. On the sofa to the right of the desk were Deputy Chief Dick Harper, commander of the Support Services Division, and Captain Carlos Delgado, head of Special Investigations. In the chair to the left of the desk was Emil Friedmann.

McKinley immediately understood why Harper was there, as the SWAT Team came under his command, but was a little puzzled by Delgado's presence, which he assumed was because he was the longest-standing senior officer on the force. Homicide was part of the Personal Crime Bureau, itself part of the Investigations Division, but as the heads of both had been missing for several months, one on long-term sickness, the other under internal investigation for staff harassment, there were two gaping holes in the org-chart that Stanton seemed very reluctant to plug, even temporarily. This meant that Homicide had fallen directly under the Chief's control, along with the other parts of the Personal Crime Bureau.

Thanks to Stanton's most recent outburst, McKinley found himself with three empty boxes on that chart between his level and the Chief of Police, something anyone of his rank would find themselves uncomfortable with, so if Delgado had acquired some extra responsibility, even in the short-term, that would suit McKinley fine. Delgado was a bit conservative, but that meant he would also be a steady hand, something the Squad needed in order to dissipate some of the worst excesses of Stanton's direct management style.

McKinley's hopes were quickly shattered as Stanton indentified the two senior officers to him and outlined why they were in the briefing. Delgado was there because Jackson Kendrick III was being nursemaided by two of his best undercover officers. Stanton concluded: "… and of course you met Counsellor Friedmann the other day at Westview Tower, so you know that he is Mr Kendrick's lawyer." Friedmann smiled falsely as he acknowledged McKinley.

Stanton continued: "do sit down Detective McKinley." He indicated to a small chair positioned centrally in front of the desk, almost interrogation-style: "I think it would be most helpful to all of us if you could bring us up to date, as succinctly as possible, with where your investigation has got to."

McKinley looked at Friedmann, then back at the Chief: "with all due respect Sir …" he paused, looking again at Friedmann.

"I have asked Mr Friedmann to sit-in on this session because he has brought us his Client's personal permission for us to involve him in the next part of this operation." Stanton continued, with some gusto: "I would remind you as to exactly what the content was of the discussion we had recently downstairs and ask you once again to bring us all up to date, as quickly as possible."

McKinley had done all he could; it had become impossible to keep the facts away from an individual who had so recently evolved, at the very least, into a potential accessory to three murders. Even if he refused, Stanton would just dispense with him and turn the heat onto the next in-line, none of whom would be capable of resisting the pressure either. So he gave a fairly brisk executive summary of the previous three days, concluding with brief details of how they had identified their suspect, Shepherd, along with the leads they were following in their attempts to locate him. McKinley also took the opportunity to say how beneficial the Bureau assistance had been in getting to where they were, but fell short of complaining about losing that assistance; he ducked the opportunity to expound the theory of Jackson Kendrick III being set-up. As he finished, there was a heavy feeling in the pit of his stomach as he recognised that he had not been as brave as his ex-Boss would have been if he were occupying that chair.

Stanton took-up the baton: "yes Detective, but I also observe that the main breakthroughs that have been made these last couple of days have come from your department, in fact from your desk and that of Detective Holdsworth in particular; which is why I have made the changes I have today. This is a Wichita Police Department problem, Detective, and therefore needs a Wichita Police Department solution." Harper and Delgado nodded obediently in unison; Friedmann's cheshire-cat grin widened and McKinley's stomach knotted further. He realised that he was completely intimidated by the scenario. Worse still, he recognised that both Stanton and Friedmann knew it. He reluctantly nodded as well.

Stanton, content at finally being in complete command, passed the baton on: "so, gentlemen, Deputy Chief Harper will give us details of the operation he has set-up for tonight to catch this, so-called, Vitruvio." The accent on the nickname was particularly dismissive. He looked directly at McKinley as he completed the introduction: "dead or alive, we don't much care which."

Harper used the whiteboard behind Friedmann to lay-out the details; they were exactly as Holdsworth had predicted. They would use a house owned by one of Kendrick's friends where he was staying secretly, or at least that's what would be leaked to the local media with enough detail to allow them to speculate where the location might be. Two of Delgado's people would be installed there, looking exactly like Kendrick and a lady companion. The perp, an obviously resourceful individual, maybe even part of the media if they followed the connections between the victims, would have little trouble in identifying where they wanted him to go and he would walk straight into the waiting ambush; meanwhile, the real Jackson Kendrick III would be ensconced safely, miles away.

During the five-minute presentation, Friedmann never looked at the board once, instead watching McKinley's face intently. As Harper concluded, Stanton took over: "so, any questions gentlemen?"

McKinley thought of his friend Paul Kleberson and realised that, regardless of what was going to happen, he no longer wished to be part of a Police Department that was under the control of someone either this stupid, or that controlled by external influences. As his stomach began to unknot itself, aided by the sudden recognition that freedom from the fear of consequence allowed his bravery to return, he started his personal fight back: "do you not feel that we are underestimating this perp? After all, he has not only eluded capture for nearly two years, the last time a team thought they had him cold, he killed one of them."

"Come now Detective," Stanton leaned forward, elbows on his desk heightening the intimidation on the outnumbered McKinley, "you've read the reports of that operation, it was a total screw-up and you know it. Just because the Bureau runs an operation, doesn't mean that they are infallible, although they sure might want us to believe that."

"But any operation can go wrong Chief."

Stanton's face began to darken. He appeared to lean even closer, not removing his gaze from McKinley as he asked Harper a question: "Dick, would you like to apprise the Detective of your success rate with your SWAT team?"

"One hundred percent since I took it over four years ago Chief."

"Them's pretty impressive numbers there, Detective, don't you think?"

But the more Stanton tried to intimidate, the more strength McKinley gained from it, because he realised that Stanton was moving further and further out on a limb - a limb that would eventually snap bringing him down, along with his cohorts, in a blaze of publicity. From a human standpoint, his instincts were to protect. Politically, however, the best place to be at that juncture was as far away from the Chief as it was possible to be.

Nevertheless, he feigned deference: "absolutely Chief," and turning to Harper, "that comment was not meant in any way to show any lack of confidence in Deputy Chief Harper's team." Then turning back to Stanton with a look of determination, he continued: "but having analysed this perp's previous actions, he does always seem to have a Plan B. Do we have a Plan B?"

Stanton seemed a little startled by this challenge to his, previously undisputed, authority within the briefing. But he quickly recovered due to his overlying assumption that he had the drop on this detective, if only through his power to suspend him without pay, something he was sure McKinley would never countenance.

"Do we have a ... Plan B, Dick?" Again the emphasis was disdaining.

"Don't see we need one Chief. This guy either shows up, or thinks better of it and hightails it out of here. Either way, we're rid of him."

Stanton had not taken his eyes off McKinley. He continued: "maybe the Detective has a ... Plan B?"

"What about Mr Kendrick?"

"What about him?"

"I'm assuming the majority of our resources are going to be concentrated at the target location. Will we have extra protection on Mr Kendrick as well?

"Mr Kendrick has the advantage of being at a secret location, Detective; one only known to those who need to know. Only two people in this room know it Detective, are you one of them?"

"No Sir."

"Do you know it Dick?"

"No Chief"

"And, it may surprise you Detective, neither do I. So are you ... concerned ... Detective, that we might have a mole? In Captain Delgado's unit perhaps?"

McKinley was about to respond, but Delgado beat him to it: "I have my very best officers on that duty, Chief," then he looked directly at McKinley, "unless Detective McKinley thinks I may be in personal touch with this elusive felon."

'That's it' McKinley thought, 'all the bridges are burning now, there's nothing for it but to call Scotty on the Enterprise.'

Emil Friedmann came to his rescue - with a lit torch: "which of course leaves me," he smarmed. Then with eyes as cold as ice he delivered the coup de grace: "surely the Wichita Police Department doesn't believe that a lawyer would be setting-up his own client?"

betsy

Eighty-Six

Sam Schneider reached forward to press the receive button on his hands-free kit. The phone had started ringing just after he crossed the State line into Kansas. The caller I.D. read 'Paul Kleberson'; the time was just after three p.m.

"Where the hell have you been Paul, I've been ringing you since noon?"

The response came: "it's not Paul, it's Chris McKinley Sam."

Schneider slowed the car. He was approaching the turn to Wellington, which he took so that he could stop the car and concentrate on the conversation: "sorry Chris, but the I.D. came up as Paul."

"That's because I have his phone. I saw all the messages."

"What's happened Chris?"

"You mean you don't know?"

"Don't know what? Look we're running out of time here Chris, what game is Paul playing now?"

"No game Sam, Chief took his badge just over an hour ago."

"WHAT?"

"And we've been told that we will receive no further assistance from your office."

"On who's fucking authority?"

"I have no idea. Look Sam, it all happened out of the blue. Stanton barged in on a case review and suspended Paul for insubordination; made me escort him from the building. Stanton has told us no more Bureau involvement. He seemed to know where you were, gave the impression you had been instructed to back off as well."

"I haven't been Chris, I think I would know if I had. What else has that idiot Stanton done?"

"He cancelled the press conference this afternoon and he has just briefed us on an operation he's set-up for this evening that I can't tell you about, but he thinks he's going to catch Vitruvio red-handed and it involves the Kendricks. And I also didn't tell you that the man's now completely up his own ..."

"OK Chris, I realise you are taking a risk even talking to me, so you had better stop right there, 'cos we can't afford to lose you off the case as well. I'm about an hour out, so I will talk to my office as I drive in. Has Paul gone home?"

"I don't know Sam, he was pretty quiet when he left, so you know that means he was fuming, so who knows where he went? He was off the radar this morning for about two hours before the Chief showed-up, so I have no idea what he was doing. When I left him this morning, he was talking about flushing something-out, but you know Paul, he didn't elaborate."

"Where were you when he left you this morning?"

"Outside Cochrane's apartment block."

"And you say Stanton knew where I was?"

"He said you were on your way back from Tulsa. I just assumed …"

"Have you seen Friedmann today?"

"He was coming into the building as Paul left. He was in on the briefing as well."

"Alright Chris, I'm getting the picture. I'll try Paul's apartment."

"He has my cell Sam, I gave it to him as he left the building; that's why I now have his."

"Good move Chris. We haven't had this conversation, you carry-on as you are and I'll see what options I still have from this end."

Eighty-Seven

Paul had chosen to walk home. He knew that it would take him over half an hour, but as it was a normal Kansas blue-sky day and the route included Riverside Park, it would give him time and the right environment to make some decisions.

The first had been made within minutes, as he crossed at the junction with Waco. He was not going to wait for any disciplinary hearing, he would submit his written resignation the following day. The second had been made earlier, after he had spoken to Gloria Friedmann. It just needed ratification, which came as he walked along West Central towards the Nims Street Bridge. He would be returning to England for a long holiday; after that, his life would evolve as it was destined to.

He began to wonder about that destiny. Would he return to academia? Maybe become a widely-published professor of history who would later be encouraged by his publisher to produce an autobiography. A smile rinsed across his face as the thought that this potentially-pivotal point in his life might form a key chapter in that work. By the time he slammed the door of his apartment behind him just before three p.m, he had calmed-down sufficiently to ensure that the force of the slam would not take it off its hinges. He went straight to the CD rack and selected a disc that had always been cathartic at times of previous crisis.

Paul had always been a bit of a closet-rebel, so when this album filtered through the underground scene into the halls of residence in Cambridge during his final year, like many others of his generation he identified with it well before the mainstream had realised the significance of the howling basslines and anarchic lyrics. He could also remember his pride on discovering that the band were American.

He had come to accept that the British were the race most-capable of spontaneously-disinterested rebellion and therefore it followed, on first-listen, that this band must be British. So the combination of an awakening in the dark recesses of the American sub-consciousness being discovered six thousand miles away and pulled triumphantly into the daylight through the English student scene chimed with his own persona. As a consequence this album was to become, for Paul, a statement and the second track an anthem.

He looked at the cover insert and his thoughts wandered again to that imagined autobiography: *'ten or twenty years from now, what might they all make of an Ivy-League professor, especially one who was also an ex-cop, salving his frustration with music like this?'*

The truth was, more than twelve years on from originally hearing it, he had no idea what had happened to the band. Back at uni he could have recalled all manner of rock trivia at the drop of a hat, but he had lost touch with the scene - his music collection had frozen from the mid-nineties, and any random listening was confined to mainstream radio. If the band had since issued a string of successful albums, he was hardly likely to have heard them there - FM Rock stations were rarely into polemic lyrics. Maybe they had just made the one album, then broken-up and gone their separate ways, some to other underground bands, others to beachside condos - irreconcilable musical differences, that's the phrase they always used on the press release. He thought again of his current situation and mused on that phrase: *'irreconcilable differences.'*

He smiled an ironic smile and took the disk from its case. He put it into the player and cranked the amplifier volume up to eight, then went into the bedroom. The abrasive strains of the opening track began to filter through the quiet building while he discarded all of his detective clothes until he stood there just in his boxers. As that first track morphed into the second, he strolled through to the lounge, stood behind the sofa and gripped the upholstery at the top of the back tightly in his fists. The compulsive rhythms began to seep through his veins, as he rocked back and forth, allowing the lyrics to wash through his mind, quietly at first, then building.

Mrs Warnock next door started to bang on the wafer-thin party wall; Paul looked at the wall with disdain as the chanting grew louder. Then the phone began to ring. He turned his gaze towards the handset, glaring at it's insolence, but the attempted psycho-kinesis couldn't stop it ringing, or hurl it against the wall. So he let go of the sofa, marched to the amplifier and cranked it all the way to the stop. As the track wound on to it's crescendo, he focussed on the phone and joined-in with the culminating line, screaming the expletive at the top of his voice that nobody else could possibly hear above the booming speakers.

As the album progressed into track three, Paul marched back through the bedroom. He removed his boxers as he went, throwing them against the wall. He walked on into the en-suite, where he turned the shower fully-on cold, stepped in facing the nozzle and let the freezing-cold water flood down over his head and body. He must have stayed in there for easily twenty minutes, because when he strode back into the lounge, stark naked and dripping wet, but much calmer, track seven was just finishing.

He turned the volume down to four and was immediately aware that someone was apparently trying to beat his front door in, plus the phone was still ringing. He punched the amplifier power button off. He had made the point for his own benefit; there was no further need to punish anybody else. The pounding on the door stopped, but the phone continued to ring.

He picked up the receiver, held it for a couple of seconds aware of a distant-sounding voice saying something like: "Paul, where have you been? Paul? You there?" He calmly replaced the receiver for a couple of seconds, then removed it and placed it on the table, with just the low buzz of the dial tone emitting from the earpiece.

The pounding started on the door again, then just as suddenly stopped. A voice strained through the firedoor thickness: "fuck you Kleberson, disturbing our afternoon, now keep that damned thing turned off!" It was old man Sampson from the floor above, the three-hundred pound couch-potato grouch for the whole block.

Paul smiled, thinking: *'probably ruined that repeat of Jeopardy he was watching.'*

Then he turned to the door: "but you might have figured that nobody tells me what to do anymore," he said out loud. He turned the amplifier back on, flipped his index finger at the back of the door, then returned to the bedroom.

He towelled himself down, pulled a fresh pair of boxers from the drawer and a clean pair of Levis from the closet, yanking both on with a purpose, followed by clean socks and a pair of black leather boots. Back to the closet, he flicked through the tee-shirts hanging on the lower rail until he found the white classic-pose Springsteen he got at the Kemper Arena back in 2000, the only time he had seen The Boss perform live. What a night that had been, accompanied by fellow-aficionado Carla Courtney, who had sneaked-off to a concession stand to buy it for him following their fists-in-the-air duet during the finale.

"Here you go," she had said on her return, "from one true fan to another."

He stood looking at the shirt dangling on its hanger for a few seconds, Sam's words echoing through his mind: *'when you gonna make an honest woman of her ...?'*

"Maybe sooner than you think, Sam," he said - again out loud.

With the shirt flipped over his head and hanging almost as well on his upper torso as it had on the hanger, he lifted his black leather biker jacket from the top rail, put it on and slipped the pair of mirror Ray-Bans from the top pocket, sliding them up his nose to nestle on his ears. He pulled the drawer of the bedside cabinet open and grabbed the bunch of keys it housed. As he did so, the cellphone in his suit jacket pocket started chirping. He retrieved it, glanced at the caller I.D. which said: 'Agent Schneider'. He hesitated, countering his instinct to hit the green button, then held-down the on/off button until the closedown sequence started, threw the dying unit on the bed, swept some change and his wallet off the bedspread, then headed towards the door.

The Mantis Pact

As he emerged into the hallway, it was again empty and quiet. He took the back stairs down to the rear forecourt, which he strolled across until he arrived at the garage door in the corner. The padlock resisted momentarily, having not been troubled for more than a year, but this was soon overcome and one door was opened to reveal a familiar outline at the back covered with a sheet. Paul spoke to the shape: "hi again Betsy, sorry it's been so long old girl. I hope you're not going to be obstinate today, not today there's a good girl."

Paul strolled through the open door and took hold of the sheet covering the shape, pulling it gently away to reveal Betsy's classic black and chrome curves. She was older than her owner, having celebrated her fortieth birthday the previous year, alone in her current home. Paul apologised to his oldest companion: "still looking good old girl, bet you would like a run wouldn't you?"

Betsy was a 1962 BSA Rocket Gold Star, frame number GA10 114, one of the earliest survivors of the less than 1600 produced in just over a year to mark the final, and ultimate, development of the classic model that had first started in production twenty-five years earlier prior to the second world war. Paul had found her, rusting and unloved, but in one piece, under a tarpaulin in a school friend's back yard two years after the family arrived in England. The friend's father did not need much persuading to part with the machine, a long-intended restoration project that never happened. Paul parted with the majority of his savings, twenty pounds, to acquire the sad-looking relic. Another friend's father was enlisted to transport her from Huntingdon to Godmanchester in his van.

When the van arrived, it was the first that any member of the family knew of Paul's purchase. Margie was apoplectic; not only was this pile of scrap metal not going to be allowed anywhere within the confines of her dwelling, Paul did not know the first thing about mechanics, he was too young to ride it, even if it did ever work, which seemed highly doubtful, and the roads of England were way too dangerous, narrow and congested in any case. Betsy, as she had already been christened, was wheeled sadly into the narrow alleyway at the side of the house, covered with the tarpaulin that had accompanied her from Huntingdon and Paul dispatched to his room to contemplate his fate "when your Father gets home."

He was summoned to the hastily-assembled tribunal in the lounge just after seven that evening; to his utter amazement he found himself acquitted on all charges. He was also to be allowed space in the garage to carry out the work - the family's new car they were taking delivery of a few weeks later was too big to go in there in any case. Walter had persuaded Margie that a project like this was just what their teenage son needed to focus his spare time - time that, to Walter, appeared constantly wasted at friends' houses on TV and what his son's generation claimed to be music. What Paul never heard, or knew, was his father's reassurance to his mother: "don't worry Margie, he's not got a snowball's chance in hell of ever falling off it, as it will probably never make it to the road in the first place, so stop fretting."

What Walter had not factored-in were his son's perseverance and the involvement in the project of two men - Grandpa Walt back in Tucson and

Master Sergeant Abe Lebwinski, NCO in charge of the Engine Bay at the base. Abe was a motor-cycle nut and had spent most of his spare time after arriving in England tracking down classic British bikes and shipping them back home to fellow enthusiasts courtesy of the USAF Transport Service. This activity not only earned him a substantial income on the side, it also meant that he had built-up a wide range of contacts among British bike enthusiasts, who he could use to track-down difficult-to-locate spare parts.

When he first heard of his commanding-officer's son's new project, he soon found the excuse to make contact, primarily because he had gained the impression that the boy would not stick with the project too long, and a Rocket-Goldie was a prize in whatever condition it could be found. He soon realised, on meeting Paul, that here was a chip off the old block, someone who was unlikely to deviate from a chosen path once selected. In Abe's eyes, here also was a younger version of himself, an apprentice biker to be encouraged and assisted. It was Abe who pointed-out that Betsy was equipped with all the performance extras, including siamese exhausts and close-ratio gearbox, all of which cemented Paul's confidence in his decision to buy her in the first place.

Over the next two years, Betsy was systematically dismantled and reassembled by Paul in the family garage at Godmanchester. Back in Tucson, Grandpa Walt became a consultant for the project. Letters went back and forth continually, questions from Godmanchester, detailed answers with diagrams from Tucson. Sometimes the letters were within a package, sent by USAF-Mail, accompanied by a small part that was too intricate for the teenager to restore.

Grandpa Walt used his vast experience and patience to painstakingly overhaul those parts, returning them to his Grandson complete with detailed logs and photographic records of the process for Paul to retain should he ever need to do the work again. Abe had control of all of the right machinery in the engine shop at the base, from shot-blasting equipment to plating tanks. He dealt with refurbishing all the larger parts, including the plating and/or painting of them.

But both mentors made sure that they never took any process away from Paul that he was capable of doing himself, because of which Paul became familiar with every bone and sinew of his mount. When she finally burst into life in the garage, three weeks before Paul's seventeenth birthday, the entire family was there to witness it, plus Abe; Grandpa Walt was also there, at the other end of a very expensive transatlantic telephone call. Her mother later told Margie that Grandpa Walt had burst into tears as, six thousand miles away, he heard the throaty roar of the six-fifty twin accompanied by his grandson's whoops of joy.

Walter also found himself bursting with pride when his son, who had become a very competent rider having obtained his restricted US License with the help of the MT Section at the base, insisted that Abe should have the first ride on Betsy, having done so much to help restore her. Abe said afterwards that he never remembered such a rush as the old girl gave him when he momentarily opened her up for a few hundred yards on the nearby A-14 that afternoon.

Betsy sailed through her M.O.T. test the following week, where Paul, having accompanied Abe as pillion to the test centre, had to politely decline a substantial cash offer from the garage owner for the machine, one that would have seen him net a profit in the thousands of percent.

But that was never what Betsy was about. On his seventeenth birthday, Paul passed his British motorcycle driving test on a borrowed Yamaha trail bike from Abe's collection; after that, he and Betsy were virtually inseparable until Paul went up to Cambridge. Even then the separation only lasted a few weeks, until he had located suitable garaging for her during term time. Weekends that were not spent on the road to one historic site or another, were allocated to maintenance and cleaning. When Paul returned home to Kansas, Betsy had stayed behind in the coach house at the Flemings' estate, but followed him across the Atlantic, once again courtesy of USAF, with the rest of his belongings a few months later, after he had decided to stay. As ever, she had started instantaneously minutes after emerging from her crate.

That unblemished record would not be tainted today. Once Paul had painstakingly gone through the normal unmothballing processes detailed to him by Abe and Grandpa Walt all those years earlier, he wheeled her out of the dark recesses of the garage and propped her on her stand while he locked the garage again. The bright afternoon sunshine glinted off of the chrome tank, the rays momentarily turning the gold star in the centre of the resplendent red BSA badge into a starburst. He sat astride her, tucking away the stand, then gently primed the cylinders a couple of times with the kick-start lever, flicked-on the ignition switch and then, with a familiar single sharp tap of his right boot, the engine once again roared instantly into life. With first gear engaged, a quick flick on the throttle took him up the ramp towards freedom.

Eighty-Eight

Schneider drove straight to City Hall. There was little point in going to his office as the first call he had made after talking to McKinley, to Carla, had revealed that there was a message for him to ring Special Agent Normanson in Kansas City. Schneider detested Normanson, his immediate superior, a desk-jockey politician who ran the Bureau's State Field Office in any way that would bring him a peaceful life and rapidly advance his career.

It was typical of Normanson not to call Schneider on his cell, in fact he was probably relieved when Carla Courtney told him that Schneider was out on a case and would not be back until the afternoon. Like all of the best PA's she had asked whether it was an urgent matter and when Normanson indicated that it would be fine for Schneider to respond when he returned, she picked nothing up in the tone of voice that gave her any indication otherwise. She knew that Schneider did all he could to avoid contact with Normanson, so the Post-It just lay on his desk blotter awaiting his return and his decision as to its priority.

Schneider had considered ignoring the message, after all if he found a reason not to return to the office he might just not get it until it was too late. But McKinley's news meant that he would need some substantial clout to override Stanton, so he would need to do everything by the numbers.

The call to Normanson was short and sweet. There was little point in starting an argument with his superior, who had clearly been 'got at' politically, if not by Stanton then by the Kendricks. The message was loud and clear - the Wichita Police Department no longer needed the Bureau's assistance, they had an operation in progress that Bureau involvement might compromise, there was enough of a caseload to deal with in the Wichita Agency without going looking for more. A brick wall would have had greater flexibility and Schneider did not have the time, or the patience, to start pushing against it; he needed a demolition squad instead.

The next call was to Pete Baker at the LA Field Office. When Schneider dropped the bombshell, the phone went quiet for a split second, followed by several bangs and crashes; Baker had cleared his desk - literally. They quickly hatched a plan that would circumvent Stanton without taking the current cases out of WPD's hands. After all, if Stanton was hell-bent on courting disaster and Normanson was determined to help him, why should they be given any potential scapegoats for after it all went pear-shaped.

Schneider then code-three'd the last forty miles in order to gain some time. All the way back he continually called Paul's home number and McKinley's cell, leaving multiple messages on both. Eight miles out the call came back from Baker confirming the authority he needed.

He tried one more call to Paul's apartment. This time someone picked-up, but did not speak; after about ten seconds they hung-up. Schneider redialled, but the number was engaged.

Eighty-Nine

McKinley was at his desk in the Squad Room, poring over his notes about the evening operation, for which he was expected to field his entire staff. He was looking for ways in which he could phase-in their assignments to keep them on the current investigation as long as possible, in the hope that they might get a break that would change the whole scenario. It was looking to be a vain hope.

Holdsworth and Dean were working the phones. Holdsworth had tracked-down the film production company involved with Palm Springs and was through to their HR department. Dean was being shunted from desk to desk within USC Administration, becoming increasingly frustrated with every call. He caught McKinley's eye as he looked-up from the operation notes, putting his hand over the telephone mouthpiece: "you won't believe how many administrators this danged University has, this is my third hold on this call alone!"

"Maybe they could lend us a few," McKinley responded dejectedly.

"Gotcha!" Holdsworth exclaimed as he put his receiver back on the hook. Both detectives swivelled their chairs in his direction.

"Norma Schaeffer, make-up artist. Film company took her on a short-term contract for the film in Palm Springs and guess who invoiced them for her services." He waited momentarily for them to respond, but couldn't maintain the suspense: "B&P Enterprises Inc!"

McKinley stared at him, unable to respond immediately as he tried to assimilate this latest twist. Dean spoke first: "an accomplice?"

"Sure looks like it. Makes sense when you think there's two names on the company owners list, Berger and Pastore."

"Shepherd and Shepherd."

"Exactly! One on the inside, the make-up girl, one on the outside; Shepherd himself. It makes sense of how he stays ahead of the game so easily. It also explains how they set Bonetti up."

"But that would mean they were targeting Bonetti."

"With an insider, they would know if he was getting close, plus maybe they would have recognised him from the Savannah cases."

McKinley joined in: "but surely he would have recognised her as well?"

"Maybe he did and it spooked them."

"So why would he have thought she was a target?"

"To play them along."

"In which case he wouldn't have fallen for the attempt at the motel, he was too good an Agent."

"Good point Chris." Holdsworth's enthusiasm drained from him and he slumped back in the chair.

"Unless …" McKinley pondered for a moment, then he continued: "maybe he couldn't have recognised the insider on the Savannah jobs because they had swapped roles for Palm Springs."

Dean looked exasperatedly at the other two: "so what are we looking at now, Bonnie and fucking Clyde?"

"Why not?" Holdsworth responded, "husband and wife, starstruck lovers, what does it matter? Pairs have a different momentum to a solo; they drive each other on in a sort of contest to best each other's achievements. Criminal history is littered with 'em and they were all very powerful combinations."

"There's another option," McKinley stopped the discussion with another thoughtful intervention, "siblings."

"Brother and sister?" Holdsworth queried.

"Would explain why they're so fixated on the Shepherd name."

At that point Dean heard a voice in his phone handset. He swivelled back around grabbing his pen: "yes, I'm here … OK … yes I do, fire away."

McKinley looked back to Holdsworth: "don't suppose they had a home address for her?"

"No Chris, sorry, they don't bother for short-term staff provided by agencies, they leave that to the supplier."

As he spoke, McKinley noticed a familiar shape walk past the glazed area between the Squad Room and the corridor. Holdsworth picked-up his gaze, turning around just in time to catch the back view disappearing past the open Squad Room door and down the corridor.

"Was that Sam Schneider?" he asked.

"Sure was and it looks like he's heading for the Chief's office."

"With some purpose, by the look of him."

"Yes," McKinley smiled for the first time in a few hours, "maybe I should go and brief the Chief on our latest discovery."

Ninety

Schneider climbed the stairs and turned in the direction of the Chief's office. He arrived with a purposeful walk, striding straight past Stanton's secretary, who reacted slightly too late, rising to her feet as he passed her desk: "excuse me Agent Schneider, Chief Stanton's in a conference, you can't go ..."

It was too late, Schneider had the handle of the door in his hand, which he turned and, having opened the door, walked straight through. Stanton was stood with Harper and Delgado, their backs to the door, poring over a map spread across his desk. Stanton turned slowly, initially thinking he was addressing his secretary: "I thought I said no ... what the ..."

Schneider cut him off: "we need to speak Stanton. Thank you gentlemen, you can leave us now."

Stanton's secretary appeared in the doorway: "I'm sorry Chief, he just ..."

Stanton held up his hand: "that's OK Debbie, it's not your fault. Agent Schneider obviously has the wrong building." The secretary withdrew rapidly; having worked for the Chief for two years, she knew the signs of when to take cover.

Schneider closed the door behind her and turned back to the group facing him: "right building, right office, wrong company." He stared at the two uniformed officers.

"I guess it was about time for a break. Dick, Carlos, why don't you go grab yourselves a coffee, I'll join you in a few moments." The two men departed with as much aggressive body language as they could direct at the intruder. When the door closed behind them, Stanton glared at Schneider, his face turning purple. He grabbed-up the telephone handset from his desk.

His secretary responded instantly: "yes Chief?"

"Get Special Agent Normanson in Kansas City please."

"Yes Chief."

Stanton thrust the handset towards Schneider: "you can take this."

Schneider took two paces towards Stanton, took the phone from him, then continued past him to place it back on it's cradle. He turned back to Stanton. They were standing less than two feet apart: "I've spoken to Normanson. He told me that you no longer need our help with your current cases."

"Therefore, Agent Schneider, we have nothing to discuss." Stanton pointed to the door: "close it as you leave would you."

"However, what Normanson failed to tell you Chief," Schneider continued, "was that my Agency is currently working in conjunction with four other Field Offices on a national enquiry, co-ordinated from the Director's Office in Washington. As the senior Agent on the ground locally in that investigation, I have, with your approval, been receiving assistance from your Homicide Squad and in return have ensured that the Bureau has provided whatever assistance we could with their current cases."

"Which you have been advised, via the correct channels, is no longer required, thank you." Stanton again pointed at the closed door.

"OK Stanton, you wanna play hard ball politics? Then try these apples! My case is a Federal case because it involves the murder of a Federal Agent. If I decide your case is directly connected, I make one phone call to Washington and that also becomes a Federal case - my Federal case - and your department is off of it, after which I can investigate it as far as I want to, in whatever direction I want to. And if that investigation reveals any other illegal activity of a Federal nature, whatever that may be, I can take those aspects as far as I want to as well, regardless of what inconvenience that may cause to anybody, whether they be felon, victim, law enforcement officer, businessman or politician. Are you with me thus far Chief Stanton?"

Stanton said nothing, he just glowered at Schneider. However, he immediately understood the implications of what was being said. Schneider continued: "I will take that as a 'yes' shall I Stanton?" There was still no reaction.

"In which case it may surprise you to hear that I have no intention of making that call - not yet awhile anyway. You see Stanton, man to man within these four walls, I really don't care if you want to make an ass of yourself with some half-baked PR-related stunt this evening, one that, whatever it is, has as much chance of catching this perp as I have of becoming Director of the Bureau. But, even if I'm wrong about my ultimate career path, I still prefer to be a million miles away when it all goes belly-up on you. Instead, in return for such a favour which, incidentally, you do not in the remotest sense deserve, you will continue to provide me with all of the liaison facilities with your department that I need on my case. You never know, if you are very lucky, we may just have time to resuscitate the investigation sufficiently to save your career."

"And what if I refuse."

"If you had been paying attention Stanton, you would have heard that I wasn't making a request."

"I'm not re-instating Kleberson."

Schneider moved closer, close enough for the Chief to detect the hint of chipotle from a rapidly-consumed sub the FBI man had picked-up en route from Wellington. He spoke softly, but deliberately, almost in a whisper.

"I said ... I have no intention of taking over your investigation. What you do, or have done, with that investigation is your business and for you to answer for when the time comes. Comprende?"

Stanton continued the staring contest, but Schneider had already detected that the fire behind those eyes had been replaced by hollow doubt. No further words were necessary, so Schneider turned, calmly opened the door and walked out of the office, quietly closing the door behind him with a distinct 'click'.

Stood alongside the secretary's desk, was McKinley. He looked concerned, having been stopped from entering the Chief's office by Stanton's secretary.

"Sam," McKinley said, a little surprised at Schneider's stern countenance, "we've caught a break. I'm waiting to brief the Chief, do you want to join us?"

"Go ahead Chris," Schneider responded as he walked past, "I think he could do with some good news. I'll wait for you in the Squad Room."

Ninety-One

Paul had been riding for about forty minutes. He had gunned Betsy along River Boulevard, then dog-legged via Thirteenth to McLean, after which Amidon and Womer took him all the way to the I-235 interchange, from where he took the short link to his favourite road going west - the State Fair Freeway.

A little while after getting on the freeway, he had slowed from his initial illegal speeds, brought on by the need to relieve those final strands of frustration, to a steady sixty-five in respect of Betsy's age and her lack of recent use; she made no complaint either way. Although it carried the name and had long stretches of four-lanes, K-96 was not a freeway along its entire route. What it did have were long, flat, straight sections where you could ride and think at the same time, or just contemplate the almost-distinguishable curvature of the earth way ahead on the constant horizon.

It was a typical Kansas early-summer day, not a cloud in the big blue sky above and a balmy warmth to the air rushing past Paul's face. *'What a contrast to Cambridgeshire,'* he thought. Not to the infinite flatness of the fenland, or the similar arrow-straightness of the A-14 through Huntingdon. But to the stinging coldness of the late spring showers that would, no doubt, be drenching him through, were he on that stretch of road instead of this, once again fulfilling the role of windbreak for his pinion companion with her arms around his waist and her crash helmet nestled between his shoulder-blades.

During those university years, Annie had accompanied him on many of his weekend field trips to historic sites around England. On the ones featuring stopovers, they had always shared a bed, Annie never forgetting to wear the gold wedding band she had acquired for a couple of pounds from the local fleamarket, just to quietly save any potential embarrassment for the oft-conservative bed and breakfast owners.

Paul allowed his thoughts to stray to the implications of his earlier chat with Gloria Friedmann. Did he really make a wrong decision all those years ago? If he did, then he would not have had those wonderful years with Leanne, plus two super kids to show for it, even if they were a thousand miles away these days. Like most policemen, it was the job that would cause him to neglect his relationships, all of them, for far too long. He and Leanne were still good friends and although any chances of that ever becoming romantic again were probably well past, it was not too late to resume the role of a proper father, even on a part-time basis.

It was also time to link-up with those real friends that he had similarly neglected. In reality, beyond Sam Schneider and his own family, everyone else he knew in the 'States was no more than an acquaintance. He had never made the close connections in his homeland that he managed to do regularly in his adoptive country. As an ex-cop, which was what he had become, whatever he decided to do would have to be able to fulfil two basic criteria - give him real amounts of time with his kids and allow him to make extended trips to England.

The miles had quickly passed under Betsy's wheels, but he had still not decided where exactly he was heading. Focussing again on the scenery, it took him a few moments to realise that he was further out than he thought. When he saw the signs warning of the possible proximity of horse-drawn carriages, he realised that he was approaching Yoder. What better way than to decide on his destination than over a cup of coffee at the Carriage Crossing, along with a home-made cinnamon bun from their bakery. He pulled onto the ramp and dropped his speed until he was doing just twenty miles per hour as he completed the few hundred yards to the crossroads at which his destination stood, where the old State highway crossed the road leading into the village.

As the oldest part of the main Amish settlement in Kansas, Yoder's traffic flow was dominated by their familiar single-horsedrawn carriages, hence the need to drive at moderate speeds there. Named after its founder, Eli Yoder, the village was little changed from the time that he founded it in the late nineteenth century. Paul loved the contrast created by a community that maintained the ways of life of a bygone time, whilst the twenty-first century charged past just yards from its centre. Even so, little pockets of modern life were breaking into the area, with some of the more progressive farmers using tractors for field work instead of the more familiar teams of plough-horses.

With the normal tempo of his life suddenly diffused, Paul was able to sip his coffee and consume the cinnamon roll at the reduced pace that he had rarely experienced over the last few years. He glanced at his watch; it was approaching five p.m. All of his main decisions for his future had been made in just a couple of short hours and he could only wonder why it had taken him so many years to realise again what he had been told by Grandpa Walt when he was just ten years old - that you are in control of your own destiny, and that changes only when you allow others to make the decisions for you.

Even so, unfinished business kept trying to hijack his thoughts. One of Paul's main strengths was in his being a completed finisher. Despite being forcibly denied the facilities to resolve what would be his last three cases as a policeman, the historian in him felt the need to find the truth, even if just for his own peace of mind. There was something they had all been missing, something that was probably hiding within plain sight. Maybe his being relieved of all responsibility might just give him the cutting edge he needed to actually find it.

Four hours to go. However much his head tried to persuade him that the best course of action was to keep on riding into the sunset, his heart told him that while there was time to find the answer, then he must at least try to do so. He quietly cursed the impetuousness that had meant he had come all the way out here without McKinley's cellphone. But Betsy would have him home within an hour, still leaving him time to make the one phone call that could provide that missing link.

Ninety-Two

In the ten minutes that it took McKinley to brief Chief Stanton on the latest developments, Holdsworth had also brought Schneider up to speed in the Squad Room one floor below.

As McKinley re-entered the room, he hurled his notepad at his desk in frustration: "that man is on such a distant planet, even the Starship Enterprise wouldn't be able to find him!" He continued in sheer exasperation: "not only does he not want to even consider the possibility of there being two perps, he looked me straight in the eye and told me that as this Squad was no longer capable of coming-up with a tangible line of enquiry, it was of no further use to him on these cases! He doesn't want us involved tonight, in fact he thinks that we would be more of a hindrance to the operation due to our negative attitude towards it. He finished off by saying that once this is all over, it may be best if he disbanded us and found a better way of organising the division."

"Don't worry Chris," Schneider responded, "you guys will still be on this Police Force long after Stanton has left it."

"I won't." The voice came from Dean, who was at his desk facing away from the discussion, scribbling notes on his pad. He stopped and turned to the others: "I've got enough years for a reasonable pension, as soon as we're finished here, I'm putting my papers in."

"Hold on ..." McKinley tried to intervene.

"No point in trying to persuade me otherwise Chris, I was already ninety percent there before this latest circus even started, but seeing a klutz like Stanton suspend one of the best officers I've ever served with on the grounds of, well what? That was the final straw."

"We've still got work to do though, isn't that right Sam?"

"So he did tell you," Schneider replied with an air of surprise.

"Oh yes. Throwaway line as I was leaving his office - you can assist Agent Schneider with his other caseload if you wish, but you will release no information to the FBI on the three murders here in Wichita. If you do, you will be on garden leave as well."

"Fair enough, I'm up for either of those assignments," Dean smiled, "so would you like to hear what I found out from USC? I've decided it fits within those guidelines."

Ninety-Three

Dean ran through the information he had pieced-together from the various bits of data he had gleaned from different areas of USC: "I had to speak to at least six different administration departments to get all of this, but basically Norma Schaeffer was attacked during the spring semester of her first year. She had switched courses at the start of that semester, because during the winter break of nineteen-ninety, she had married a US Army pilot whose unit was being posted to Saudi in support of operations in Iraq. She transferred-in to the School of Cinema-Television, but as yet they have not been able to trace what course she was on before, or what her maiden name was. They're still working on it."

"Anything on the husband?" Schneider enquired.

"First Aviation Battalion based out of Fort Riley. I've contacted the base and they're checking the records for me; I'm expecting a call back any time now. I did get a contact address from USC, though - a Mrs Ferguson, South Monroe, Hillsboro."

"What, Hillsboro here in Kansas?"

"Yeah, looks like they're all fairly local."

"But the husband wasn't listed as primary contact?"

"No, but he was in the army."

"Fair point, guess I'm grasping at straws a bit. So could the husband be our man here?" Schneider lifted the photo from McKinley's desk and looked at it: "there does seem to be some hint of military precision about all of this."

"Schaeffer to Shepherd, maybe it's that way round," McKinley mused.

"Sorry Chris," Schneider looked at McKinley somewhat puzzled, "is there something I'm missing here?"

"My fault Chris," Holdsworth interrupted, "when I briefed Agent Schneider on the twin perp angle, I mentioned the Berger and Pastore link, I forgot to add that Schaeffer is also German for Shepherd." He turned to Schneider: "sorry Sir."

Schneider held up his hand in a conciliatory gesture: "that's it, this is our man! Military training, wife on the inside, damn it fits! Dean, when Fort Riley get back to you, find out when he got out of the Army - and see if he had any connection to Special Forces."

Dean nodded and scribbled on his pad. Schneider continued: "what was that contact address again?"

"Three-two-one South Monroe, Hillsboro."

"Hillsboro's about forty miles out - whaddya think Chris?"

McKinley shrugged: "we've not picked-up on him in any hotels locally. Hillsboro's a quiet town, he's using hire cars, so if he's visiting a relation with his wife, then nobody would find that unusual. He could be into Wichita and back in a couple of hours. We've got nothing else that fits."

"It's five-fifteen, so we can be there by around six. It still gives us time."

"I'm with you Sam."

"And me," Holdsworth added as he went to grab his coat.

"No," Schneider stopped him, "we could be on a fool's errand - we can't arrive like the cavalry. In any case, we need some eyes back here on what's going on. Dean's got to sit on that 'phone at least until he gets the rest of the info from Fort Riley and in any case Stanton won't trust Dean if he goes sniffing around what's happening, he'll smell a rat straight away." He turned to where Dean was sitting smiling to himself: "no disrespect Dean."

"No offence taken, Agent Schneider, the Chief has every reason not to trust me; if I can do anything to bring him down in my final days in the department, I will."

Schneider continued: "but you Holdsworth, you're a rookie. You have a career ahead of you that you won't wish to jeopardise by being associated with what we're doing. So you need to build some bridges."

"So what? I go to the Chief and volunteer for tonight?"

McKinley reassured him: "if nothing else, it keeps your options open for the future. This Squad has simply become dispensable in the Chief's mind, so he's going to love the thought of one of us deserting to his side."

"And you don't want me to keep you informed as to what's happening."

"I can't order you to do anything," Schneider resumed, "but we may need someone to contact if we find ourselves on the trail of a perp heading for somewhere in Wichita in a couple of hours' time. What you do with that information will be entirely up to you."

Ninety-Four

It was coming up for a quarter before six when Paul re-entered his apartment. Betsy had been put back in her garage, but not polished-down and covered-up as usual: "I'll give you some real cosseting tomorrow old girl," Paul had promised as he paused in the half-open garage doorway, "but right now I have some unfinished business and very little time to complete it."

All the way back from Yoder, he had been turning-over in his head some of the more obscure facts from the last couple of days. He wandered over to the telephone, where the voicemail light was flashing relentlessly; he flicked the play button and headed for the bedroom.

"You have fourteen new messages ..." the soulless recorded female voice announced with an air of accusation, as if he had been ignoring her deliberately - which of course, he had. "Message one, Monday, three-o-three p.m."

'Oh joy,' he thought as he visualised how many people had been trying to contact him over the last few hours, 'and there's McKinley's cell to come as well!' The voice was familiar - Sam Schneider was asking him to pick-up. He waited a few seconds, then rang off.

"Message two, Monday, three-o-five p.m." Same voice, same message, same result. As was message three, and the next six after that, except for the one from old man Sampson screaming down the phone what he would do to Kleberson if he didn't turn the music down. Paul was hanging-up his leather jacket in the closet, having checked the pockets to make sure he hadn't left anything in them.

"Message ten, Monday, three-twenty-seven pm."

"Hi Paul." The familiar female voice made him stop in his tracks. He dropped the jacket and ran into the lounge to pick-up the phone, momentarily forgetting that he was listening to a message recorded after he had left the apartment over two hours earlier: "it's Leanne, I'm sorry I haven't rung you for a few days, but I see from the TV that you are up to your eyes in a case at the moment. Saw you at the news conference yesterday; you looked tired Paul. I can see from the people involved that you have to put the hours in right now, but don't neglect yourself. You'll be of no use to anyone if you're exhausted, and that pompous idiot Stanton isn't going to solve anything without you."

Paul stood frozen to the spot; he began to wonder what was happening here. He hadn't had space for any thoughts of his family for the last few days, yet the minute he was released from his tasks sufficiently for his mind to allow them through, here was his ex-wife leaving a message for him. In fact she must have been leaving it at virtually the same time that he was riding Betsy up K-96 deciding to visit them.

The message continued: "look, the case will be over sooner or later and you will be due some time when it is. So why don't you come out and visit for a few days; take a break with your family. You haven't seen your Mom for over six months, you know, and she misses you. So do the kids, although they are riding the wave of having their Dad in charge of a high-profile celebrity homicide case. They're following every minute when I let them. Matt's already solved it - three times yesterday, twice the day before! Looks like he's a real chip off the old block. In case it's any help, he was convinced at first that it was the boyfriend, but then he got a bit sidetracked, even decided it was Chief Stanton at one point; he's gone back to the theory on the boyfriend now."

"That's my boy," Paul mouthed quietly and a broad smile burst across his face at the thought, almost as rapidly evaporating as the flash of his eleven-year-old son having constant fights with the likes of Stanton invaded his mind.

"Anyway, all I wanted to say was that we're here and you're there and I know that you will be for a little while yet. But there's no reason we can't all be here afterwards, even if only for a little while. Ring me when you can. Bye darling."

He wanted to snatch-up the phone right there and then and make the arrangements, but somehow he was rooted to the spot, as much by the farewell as his need to finish-up, properly, here in Wichita. *'Bye darling?'* he thought: *'Leanne hasn't called me that since those damned divorce lawyers on both sides conspired to up their fees by leading their clients into unwanted battles three years ago.'*

"Message eleven, Monday, three forty seven pm."

"Paul, it's Sam again. I'm on my way to see Stanton right now. If you're there, for goodness sake pick-up buddy ..." There was a long pause: "... OK, if you're not there, then ring me as soon as you return, because we have some developments that mean that we still have work to do here, and you can help. I know how you will be feeling, but fuck Stanton, he's not relevant any more. Just don't start thinking about going all vigilante on me, I don't need to be worrying about stuff like that as well. RING ME!"

"Message twelve, Monday, four fourteen pm." This and the last two were all from McKinley, typically efficient, just asking for his call to be returned at almost spot-on half-hour intervals; the last one had been left just before Paul had returned to the apartment. Paul looked at his watch - coming up for six. He turned back towards the bedroom, grabbing-up McKinley's cell and switching it back on as he went.

It took what seemed an interminable time to wake-up and produce sufficient signal bars to show that it was ready for him to use. It started bleeping and the notice appeared on the screen: 'You have 18 new messages - Press OK to see list.' He pressed the 'back' button and the notice evaporated. The phone bleeped again. This time the notice appeared: 'You have voicemail messages - Press OK to hear them.' Once again he hit the back button. Finally the notice appeared: 'You have 16 missed calls - Press OK to see list.'

This time he pressed OK; the list only held two numbers in almost equal proportions, his old cell and Sam's. There was no point in listening to the voicemail, as they would be the same as he had already received. He pressed 'back' to leave the list, then displayed the list of text messages. They were also all from Schneider and McKinley, bar for the last one which was from the Chief. The time was just minutes previously.

He pressed read and the message appeared: 'McKinley. It seems that not all of your staff are as loyal as you think. As I need all the men I can find, I am taking those that still want to work in this Department for the operation tonight. As you have your cell switched off, I can only assume that you no longer wish to. I expect to have a call from you within the next thirty minutes to confirm one way or the other.'

Paul just shook his head sadly: *'the man's just completely lost it,'* he thought, but instantly realised that McKinley couldn't respond, as Paul had his cell. He quickly dialled his old number; it went straight to voicemail. He waited for the recorded announcement, then left a short message: "Chris, sorry I've had the phone switched off. I've just got all your messages. I've got one more thing I want to do; if that comes up trumps, I will ring you again. If not, there's no point. There's also a text from Stanton on this phone. I will forward it to you. You need to ring him urgently. Don't ring me, I'm turning the cell off again." He hung up, then found Stanton's message and forwarded it to his old cell.

He then rang Sam - same result, so he left a voice message: "It's Paul, sorry I've been out. I've got all your messages. I'm not going to get in your way Sam. I hope you can get a break, if not, then heaven help the next target, whoever it is. I do have some unanswered questions and there's only one person who can help me with them. If it brings any results, I will text you. After that I'm leaving town and at present I don't know when, or if, I'll come back. Thanks for everything. I'm sorry."

He hit the end button, then turned off the cell, tossing it back into the middle of the bed. He then went back into the lounge and walked over to the TV. On the table to the right hand side was a pile of business cards. He picked the top one off the pile and looked at it for a few seconds. Then he walked over to the phone, picked up the receiver and started to dial.

Ninety-Five

It was six p.m. as Chief Stanton swept into the crowded conference room, closely followed by Deputy Chief Harper and Captain Delgado. It seemed that half of the Wichita Police Department was crammed in there, including Holdsworth, who had stationed himself as close to the whiteboard as he could, in case the Chief wanted him to provide any insight into the investigation so far; he wasn't holding his breath at the prospect though.

Alongside him were Moreno and Capaldi; discretion had proved the better part of valour as far as they were concerned. As Stanton had already alluded, with three sets of alimony between them to finance, they were not in any position to challenge the inevitability of the impending reorganisation. Both had made semi-panic phone calls to McKinley late in the afternoon and received his blessing for 'deserting the sinking ship', as he had so eloquently termed it. Dean had also apparently relented, as he was leaning against the wall just inside the door with his arms folded to match the smouldering body-language and grim expression on his face. McKinley was nowhere to be seen.

To maximise the effect of his entrance, the Chief walked through the crowd and positioned himself at the furthest end of the room from the door, flanked by his two uniformed cronies. "Good evening gentlemen," he said gravely. The room mumbled a response.

"As you are aware, commencing three days ago there have been a series of murders in this city with high-profile victims. It is believed that these have all been committed by one perpetrator, a serial-killer who is known by the nickname of Vitruvio. This person is responsible for at least twenty killings across the country during the last two years and thanks to assistance received from the Federal Bureau of Investigation, we have more insight into this killer's modus operandi than previously available to the Police Departments in the other cities where he has operated. Earlier today, we received intelligence that this killer is still in the city and that he intends to strike again this evening. We also have reason to believe that he has a particular victim and location in mind for this crime. It has therefore been decided, at a very high level, that this one-man crimewave should come to a halt here, in Wichita, tonight. This Police Department has therefore been given a massive responsibility, despite the missed opportunities of apprehending this felon over the last two days due to one of the senior officers previously in charge of the investigation being focussed in entirely the wrong direction. I therefore welcome the decisions of most of that officer's squad members to join us to assist this evening …"

At that point there was a massive crash at the opposite end of the room. Dean had prised himself from the wall, opened the door and exited, slamming the long-suffering entrance back in its place as hard as he could manage, leaving the glass portion vibrating close to its shatter-point. As he would advise his exit-interview panel weeks later, he had "… finally had enough of this ridiculous man's bullshit."

Stanton barely broke stride: "… showing their willingness to take upon their shoulders, as well as the rest of us, this opportunity to restore the tarnished reputation that the Wichita Police Department has unfairly received as a consequence. I will now hand over to Deputy Chief Harper, who will give you the details of the operation and your individual assignments. Good Luck Men!"

Moreno and Capaldi both lowered their heads in order not to be able to catch the Chief's gaze. Both felt the shame of their situations welling through their bodies. Moreno was aware of his own shallow personality and knew he would recover as quickly as the events of this day became yesterday's news. Capaldi had more scruple than his colleague and would transfer out to Topeka within weeks.

Holdsworth's fists, already clenched to dissipate his rising temper at this unwarranted and, in his view, unnecessary politicising of the investigation, tightened further, his nails pushing to the point of breaking through the skin on his palms, despite their being hardened by years of manual work during his youth helping his parents out on their farm.

He quietly resolved to break Stanton's jaw at the earliest opportunity.

gardenia

Ninety-Six

The phone call had gone straight to voicemail, so he left a message: "It's Paul Kleberson. Look, I don't know if you're going to get this message, but if you do I really would like to meet-up - over dinner tonight if possible. I'll be out of town after tomorrow, so that sort-of restricts things. It's six-fifteen and I've got a table booked for seven at Gardenia on Douglas in Old Town. I'll be there a couple of hours, so if you can join me, don't worry if it's after then. Thanks. Bye."

Gardenia was Paul's favourite restaurant in town and he was a regular there, so he knew it would be highly-unusual if he couldn't get a table, especially on a Monday night. The next call, to the owner Angelo, confirmed his anticipation and the booking was made. Finally a call for a taxi, then a quick shower and change and he was out of the apartment just after six-forty, down the stairs and through the front doors of the building just as the taxi rolled to a halt in front of them.

Unfortunately, the driver recognised him from the press conferences and started up a conversation about the case, offering his theories, as well as his views on whether police officers should really be gallivanting around to restaurants when there was a killer at large out there: "I'm on nights this week, and my wife can't sleep soundly in her bed knowing there's no-one to protect her if this guy should pick our house as his next target."

Paul wanted to say what he was thinking: *'not my problem any more buddy and unless you have really upset your boss in the last day or so, I don't think he will be ordering a very-expensive hit on your wife to teach you a lesson.'* But knowing that the first bit of news had not filtered out into the general community, plus the driver would never understand the second bit, he decided to use his law-enforcement experience one last time to bunt the never-ending torrent of questions and assertions.

"Please assure Mrs ..." Paul looked at the licence on the dashboard, "... Mrs Sanchez, that we are doing all we can and that we have no reason to believe that the killer is operating in the north-west district."

"Hey, how did you know I live in the north-west district?"

'Hellfire,' Paul thought, *'what do you want me to do, give you a Holmes-style rundown - the company you work for is based in the north-west, a quarter of the population there is Hispanic, you Mr Sanchez, unless I'm very much mistaken, are Hispanic, so it's elementary my dear Sir!'*

Annoyed as he was with the situation, Paul could not resist the urge to play a little game with the driver, however. *'It's not politically-correct for me to make such observations nowadays,'* he thought, *'so how about this instead'* - "we receive a lot of training that the public are unaware of, so that we can observe certain behaviours that normal people can't. For example, you are left-handed, you have a mild hiatus hernia and your dinner this evening was a Fiery Hawaiian with extra Jalapenos."

The driver almost ran the lights as they changed at Broadway, slewing to a halt just in time. He turned to Paul: "that's amazing! And you got that just by talking to me?"

'Talking TO you?' Paul thought, *'maybe if I could get a word in edgeways I could talk TO you.'* Instead he just acknowledged: "uh huh."

"OK, you gotta tell me how," Sanchez gabbled excitedly as he turned to look over his shoulder at the ex-detective, "no, that would be giving away State secrets wouldn't it? Come on, just a clue, my wife and me, we watch all the cop dramas and the repeats. We nearly always get it right."

'Well I should hope you do on the repeats at least!' Paul thought. After a moment's consideration, he was beginning to think better of the idea: *'I dunno Mr Sanchez, do you really want to know that you involuntarily scratch your balls with your left hand while you're driving; that every time you belch, which is about twice a minute, you grab the centre of your breastbone because it's burning; and that the Dominos box on the passenger seat has your order scribbled on the top in felt-tip?'*

"No sorry," Paul responded, "you were right, State secret. Lights."

"Lights? What's that some kind of codeword for the secret."

"No, they're green."

"What are?"

At that, the redneck in the Dodge Ram behind lent on his horn as he pulled-out from behind the taxi and gunned his truck across the junction, offering some pertinent advice and flipping the finger at the taxi driver as he went. Sanchez quickly took his foot off the brake and the taxi shot across in pursuit. He stopped talking for about half a block, then resumed where he left off: "anyway, I should have realised you would know where he was, from what they said on the radio while I was driving over to your place."

"Oh, and what were they saying on the radio?"

"You mean you don't know?"

"We tend not to get all of our information just from KSQT."

"They was saying that you were concerned that he was more after rich folks, you know those Kendricks and the like. Then one of the reporters managed to grab ahold of the Mayor and he said that you were making a lot of progress and he wouldn't be surprised if you made an arrest as early as tonight.

'Dear God!' Paul thought, *'what the hell game are you playing now Stanton?'* He looked-up and realised that they were about to drive past Gardenia: "we're here."

"What? Oh! Sorry." Once again the beaten-up Impala shuddered to a halt, then Sanchez completed a rapid U-turn and pulled-up in front of the restaurant; the meter read $9.70.

Paul climbed out of the back then leant through the passenger side front window. He pushed a twenty towards the driver: "you can keep the change if you promise me you will not tell anyone where you have taken me. I am still on duty Mr Sanchez and this is a very important investigation, as you have been reminding me all along the road."

Sanchez coloured-up as he sheepishly took the note, then hung his head slightly realising that he had been running his mouth off at the wrong guy.

"And tell your boss to get those brakes fixed if he doesn't want one of our traffic officers paying him a call next week to inspect his entire fleet."

Paul pulled his head out of the window and watched with amusement as Sanchez fumbled around with the cash and the various levers before flooring the throttle and disappearing back down Douglas in a haze of blue smoke.

Ninety-Seven

The restaurant was fairly quiet. There was a middle-aged couple in one of the window tables who talked occasionally as they ate, filling the long intervals with bouts of watching the world go by outside. A table of six at the back were having a working dinner while they thrashed-out some deal or other and a young couple had grabbed a dark table for two in the nook, where they gleefully discussed the night's prospects in hushed tones. Paul took a table about halfway back, seating himself facing the door so that he would not be taken by surprise when his guest arrived. He advised Angelo that he would await the arrival, then ordered a beer. When it was deposited on the table in front of him, he allowed himself to slip back into detective mode as he weighed-up the day's events, taking involuntary sips of his beer as he did so.

What he couldn't figure was how quickly his own situation had altered once he had spoken to Gloria Friedmann. He still did not see her as the type who would play him along though; she was sharp, sure, but she had no idea that he would turn up at the gatehouse that morning. He hadn't gone there to see her, she wasn't even on the shortlist of who he had hoped to spook that morning. Yet even so, within hours of his arrival he was being frogmarched out of the Wichita Police Department. So assuming Gloria was genuine, which he was happy to do, who activated Stanton? And how?

'Well the how is quite easy to figure,' he thought to himself. '*The goon on the gate rang somebody. Resulting from that phone call, the jungle drums beat until someone within the higher reaches of the Kendrick organisation rang the Governor, who rang the Mayor, who had lunch with Stanton, where he got the order to remove his senior investigating officer from the case. Or did he? What was it that Gloria said? 'If Stanton wants to perceive compliance or otherwise and act accordingly, well that's entirely up to* him.' So whoever started the dominos falling knew that Stanton would probably over-react, and when he did that would clear the way for them to finish their process without my interference. So who do we have within the Kendrick organisation who could mobilise the Governor?'

He paused for a few seconds while he drew-up a mental shortlist, then continued: *'Junior, of course, but again if Gloria was telling the truth and Junior genuinely wanted a more independently-minded police organisation, why would he want to intervene? Only if he was as guilty as sin, which somehow seems unlikely in the light of the close family friendship with the Flemings. Sir Nigel is no fool, he is also a superb judge of character and would never have allowed a dark, criminal version of Junior past the front door of his bank on a second occasion, let alone into his family circle. No, Junior must be on the outside of all of this. Consequently so are his wife and Gloria as well.'*

Before Paul realised it, the beer was gone. He looked at his watch; just seven-twenty. He decided to wait another quarter of an hour before calling for the menu, so another beer was summoned. The analysis continued with the aid of the second bottle: *'which brings us around, once again, to 'The Turd'. He has all of the motives and opportunities. What he doesn't have is the Governor's ear.'* Paul had overheard some Democrat wag, at a State function the previous year, proffer that the Governor was only holding-back on repealing the death penalty in Kansas in the hope that he might get 'The Turd' onto death row beforehand. So much was the Governor disgusted by the younger Kendrick's recent life history, even the family reconciliation had not thawed that relationship.

Paul surveyed the label on the front of the bottle: *'which leaves just one person - Emil Friedmann. He could certainly pull any of the strings that Junior could, even do so in Junior's name and nobody would question it. As legal counsel, he has access to everything in the business, even parts where 'The Turd' would still be marginalised. But more importantly, at the very point that we were homing-in on 'The Turd' being set-up, the squad is blown-apart by the family lap-dog, Stanton. Some juries would find that co-incidence somewhat more than circumstantial. Gloria had summed it up in four words - 'clever boy my Emil.' He had even made sure he arrived at City Hall in time to ensure that the instruction was being carried-out.'*

Paul paused his thoughts and took a long sip of beer, then wrote the conclusion on the imaginary whiteboard in his mind: *'ergo, 'The Turd' is a dead man ...'* he glanced at his watch again: it said seven-thirty, *'... and within the next couple of hours, which we are powerless to prevent, because the missile is in flight and Stanton is on the ground lighting-up the target.'*

At that moment in time, Paul found himself equidistant between the two aspects of his persona. The argument was going with the dark-side, something that he fought with regularly. It was happy to stand back and let life, or in this case death, take its course. To his dark persona, there was no downside to this proposal. The world would not mourn the passing of a parasite like Jackson Kendrick III; even the family would get over it in time. Stanton would go down with him - ingloriously, publically, incompetently, spectacularly! Paul would be exonerated and his squad, with Sam's help, would mop-up the fall-out by nailing the perp, then Friedmann from the evidence gleaned. This wasn't a win; it wasn't even a win-win. This was a win-win-win-win, even though there would be no glory for him, other than to be in the position to decline the plaudits and ride off into the sunset, High Plains Drifter-style - symbolically, victoriously, enigmatically, deliciously!

As usual, the light-side had just the one argument: *'if you allow someone to suffer a preventable death, you will never be able to live with yourself.'*

As usual, that was the irresistible argument.

Ninety-Eight

"Hello Clever Person."

The voice came out of the blue from behind Paul. In his surprise he jumped to his feet, turning as he did so to see Kryczek standing there smiling, looking every inch Madison Avenue in close fitting designer jeans and a loose fitting light pink satin top that draped itself delicately over those same small breasts that still appeared to have no visible means of support. The look was finished-off with a pair of colour-co-ordinated gradated Oakleys.

"Oh hi," he managed, somewhat unbalanced by this sudden and unexpected appearance. He continued, wondering how she had slipped past his view of the front door: "please ..." he indicated to the seat opposite him. She glided into it and he resumed his seat facing her.

"Given up on me had you?" she enquired.

"To be honest, I was just about to."

"And now you're wondering how I got behind you."

Still somewhat unbalanced, he tried to respond: "well ... I ..."

"I saw you as I came up the street; you seemed lost in your thoughts and I noticed there was another entrance through the patio area. Second week at Quantico wasn't it?" She smiled again; he hadn't noticed on their previous meeting what an engaging smile it was.

He nodded: "I guess you forget some of those early basics after so many years away."

"Yes Clever Person, but they're forgotten at your peril."

Paul caught Angelo's eye, who brought over the menus. "What are you drinking?" Paul asked his guest.

"Just a soda please, ice and lemon."

"And another beer for me."

Angelo nodded and departed the scene. Paul opened his menu: "I can recommend the Sole Bonne Femme, it's really quite exquisite."

"And unusual for the Midwest! Sounds fine to me." Kryczek's menu lay unopened to the left of her placing.

"And to start?"

"Not for me thanks." She raised her left hand in a slight gesture, "but don't let me stop you."

Angelo returned with the drinks and they ordered. As Angelo departed again, Paul picked-up his beer and gestured the glass toward Kryczek: "cheers," he said, "I'm glad you could make it."

She raised her glass marginally in her left hand: "bottoms up," she replied, "I think that's what they say in England isn't it Lieutenant Clever Person?"

"Paul. The name's Paul Kleberson."

She smiled and offered her right hand across the table: "sorry, we were never formally introduced were we? Lesley ... Lesley Kryczek."

He took her hand and shook it gently: "you've obviously done some homework, Lesley," he responded.

She withdrew her hand, picked-up the fan-folded napkin and draped it across her lap: "I had a quick briefing from Agent Schneider before we met the other day, plus there is still a hint underneath that hotchpotch of an accent of yours. I can only say your phone call was somewhat of a surprise. There's obviously a reason for this unexpected invitation, so what is it Lieutenant, sorry, Paul? Are we about to embark on some interesting philosophical adventure, or is it just my body you're after?" She leant back in her chair, her arms dropping to her side in a presentational gesture.

Still a little destabilised by this continued frankness, but aware of the time-constraints he was working under, he decided to come straight to the point: "please don't take this the wrong way Lesley, but it's your mind I'm after."

She leant back further and laughed aloud for a few seconds, causing the middle-aged couple in the window to look over, semi-disapprovingly. Moving closer to the table she leant forward with a beckoning gesture, to bring him closer as well; he leant forward towards her as requested. She spoke very quietly, so as not to cause any embarrassment: "you know, the last man who said that to me wasn't being totally honest - turned-out, all he wanted was to fuck my brains out." She moved back slowly, observing his reaction as the impact of the words took hold.

No longer phased by this quasi-aggressive attitude, he just focussed his gaze on her as best he could, being unable to fully-see the eyes behind those rose-red gradations: "Bonetti?" he queried, straight-faced.

She blew-out her cheeks. This was looking like being a fairly evenly-matched contest: "Schneider told me you took few prisoners - he was right!"

Knowing the circumstances, Paul would normally have backed-off at this stage, but he no longer felt that he had time: "look, I'm sorry if I'm hitting raw nerves, but there is little time left if I am going to finally understand what we're all up against here. I need to talk to you about that fateful night, because I think we're about to experience a similar one here in Wichita tonight."

She looked at him slightly quizzically: "I thought you were off the case."

His recovered equilibrium was once again disturbed by this totally-unexpected remark: "you know about that?"

"Schneider told me."

He looked at her even more quizzically. She continued: "I rang him after I got your voicemail." He glared at her and she sighed in response. Then with a first sign of irritation in her voice, she continued: "I'm an Agent out of territory, OK? In fact I'm not even supposed to be working anywhere, remember?"

He relaxed again: "I'm sorry, kneejerk reaction. I guess I'm a little raw myself at the moment."

"Schneider also asked me, if I did actually find you, to give you a message."

"Shit, I've been ignoring his calls all afternoon. What does he want me to do?"

"Nothing."

"Nothing?"

"Nothing - Schneider said he's got everything covered and he doesn't need you coming out of left field at the wrong time."

"I can't just sit here!"

"You seem to be managing it quite well just now."

"But that can't be right."

"Then ring him."

There was a prolonged pause: "I don't have my cell."

She dug in her pocket and pulled out her cellphone: "use mine."

He waved his hand at it: "no, you're right ... I mean he's right. The last thing Sam needs is another loose cannon out here. And in any case, I have nothing to add, which is one of the reasons we're here."

"One of the reasons," she exclaimed, "now this is getting interesting."

The waitress arrived with the food, then conducted the customary offerings of garnish and condiments before wishing them both bon appétit and departing again. Paul grabbed his napkin from the table top. While adjusting it he restarted the conversation: "look, if you don't want to talk about Palm Springs, then I'll just drop it. But if you can, then I would really like to hear what happened from somebody on the spot. I've read the report, but we both know that is never the whole story."

"Actually, it may be time that I talked about it to someone outside of the Bureau. I've just been bottling it up since it happened - what the hell, if it helps you, it may help me as well."

"I understand you and Bonetti were an item."

"Tom Bonetti and I had an interesting relationship. Very physical - my God no! Totally physical!" She paused as she took the next morsel of food from her fork, as if savouring more than just the flavour of the food. Paul felt something stir within him as he surveyed his guest, an unusual feeling that he had no recollection of experiencing previously and that he was unsure was either appropriate or desirable. He chose to just observe where this all went.

She continued: "we just clicked the moment we met in the office. Tom told me some time later that even with a dozen or so other people around he just wanted to rip my clothes off and have me right there and then on the desk! I have to say, the feeling was mutual. Instead, he waited until end of shift and invited me out for dinner; I still don't know how we managed to stay at that table as long as we did. Good job he had taken me to the restaurant at his hotel, with just a lift shaft separating us from his bed."

Paul felt somewhat embarrassed at these revelations. He had never been one for indulging in the review of sexual conquests with either friends or workmates; even if he felt it necessary for the purpose of bonding, he would always make some excuse to leave before there was ever any danger of revealing his own. He had sometimes wondered whether he was a bit repressed, but ultimately decided that he was simply more of a private person than many.

She concluded: "that night just confirmed that we were right for each other - sexually that is. So after his wife and family moved over from Savannah, we snatched what moments we could, normally during the day."

"Bonetti was married?"

"Oh yes and very happily too. He had no intention of breaking-up the home and I sure as hell did not want any type of permanent relationship. I just needed my libido servicing." She noticed his expression was becoming very accusative: "and before you think about moralising at me, I don't just jump in and out of married mens' beds. Bonetti was the first married man that I had ever allowed to make me his mistress. I have long-term relationships with men that I can relate to, but who don't want total commitment, and when I'm in such a relationship, I don't cheat on them."

"I'm not a moraliser," Paul responded, "and I don't make judgements on other peoples' private relationships."

'How could I,' Paul thought to himself, recognising the similarities with the way he conducted his relationships over the years. Other than those occasional encounters behind the bikesheds in his teens, he had only really ever been with three women - Annie, Leanne and Carla. He enjoyed constancy, which was why he had never cheated on any of them, even though he had had no legal commitment not to do so, other than with Leanne.

"I'm sorry," she responded, "that wasn't particularly nice of me was it? What I was trying to get over was that I miss him, I miss him like hell - and not just because I miss the sex. That may have been what brought us together, but the relationship had developed way beyond that without me realising it, even though it would never, ever, have evolved into marriage."

"Forget it," he replied, "I guess you're a bit of a loner really, like me. If we allowed ourselves to admit it, that's why we're drawn to this job. It probably explains why divorce rates are so high in the law enforcement community; in fact, your philosophy probably keeps you saner than most."

"I hadn't looked at it that way, but yes, I suppose I am a loner. I've been on my own most of my life. Anyway, we're not here to review our life histories, are we?"

He was beginning to wonder what he was actually doing there. He was a man of reasonable private means who had just left a job that he never really wanted, with no pressing commitments to anybody, other than himself and his ex-wife and children, who he could provide for, financially, more than adequately. Yet there he was, sat opposite a very attractive woman who gave no indications that she did not want to be in his company and had openly declared that she was not seeking commitment. Why was it, he wondered, that he was distracted from a scenario that most men could only dream about, by the need to solve a series of crimes that nobody, not even his best friend, wanted him to be involved with?

He looked at her closely as she consumed another morsel of sole and he felt another sensation, this time in his loins. Not a rip-her-clothes-off-here-and-now sensation, but still an involuntarily recognition of the potential in the evening. She looked-up and caught him watching her.

"What?" she asked.

"Sorry," he diverted his gaze to his plate and busily filled his fork, "now it's me being rude."

She put her knife and fork down on her plate, placed her elbows on the table then rested her chin on her interlinked fingers: "look, we have been thrown together by circumstance, we've tried our best to alienate each other, but we haven't done so. To me, that seems to indicate that we won't end up throwing these plates at each other, so maybe we can turn this into a nice evening together instead. I have no idea where it will ultimately lead to, maybe a roll in the hay, maybe just a friendly handshake. Frankly, I don't mind which it is, but we won't be able to find out unless we can get the elephant out of the room. And the only one of us who can do that, Paul, is the one who brought it with them."

He also parked his cutlery and leaned back in his chair as if trying to take a wider-angle view of the situation. *'Have I really just been propositioned?'* he thought to himself. *'More to the point, do I want to be propositioned? Or do I want to join the posse instead?'*

He concluded that there was only one way to find out.

Ninety-Nine

Schneider had, thankfully, found the traffic quite light along Kellogg and once onto I-135 going north he was able to put the lights on and make quick progress to clear the city boundaries. They pulled off I-135 north-east of Newton and took Fifty for about five miles before turning north again for the last part of the journey to Hillsboro along the aptly-named Thirteen Mile Road, which became South Ash as they passed the City Limit signs west of Alfred Schroeder Field.

En route they had received a call from Dean. Fort Riley had no record of any Schaeffer serving in the First Aviation Battalion; he was awaiting their wider search for any Schaeffer or Shepherd connected with the base. He also had a confirmation from USC that the address they were heading to in Hillsboro was

Gardenia

the same address that Mrs Schaeffer had given when she arrived as a single woman at USC, when her maiden name was Shepherd. Mrs Ferguson was listed as her aunt.

This caused some discussion in the car as to what would be the best way to approach Mrs Ferguson. It was beginning to dawn on them that they could be dealing with two perps who were related, somehow. They had a handle on the female one, quickly concluding that, being the aunt of the female, Mrs Ferguson would have to know the male as well. If he wasn't the husband, then he could be a sibling, in which case she was his aunt as well.

It was just before six when they turned east onto the old Highway 56 that cut the town in two, passing Tabor College on their left before turning north again onto Monroe. They were in a fairly-typical well-established residential road, a mixture of small plots carrying small 1960s bungalows, some a bit run-down, fronting the road behind an area of open-plan lawn, and more mature plots with larger houses hiding within wooded areas back from the road; 321 South Monroe was one of the bungalows. They drove past slowly before pulling-up slightly beyond, under some trees.

McKinley looked back towards the house, making some observations: "looks very quiet, no vehicles on the drive."

"Could be in the garage," Schneider responded.

"Not by the look of that door - it hasn't been opened for a few years I would say."

"Mmm, let's take a closer look."

They got out of the car and wandered slowly over to the bungalow. It was not set back as far as some of its neighbours, with just a narrow strip of lawn between the sidewalk and the front porch, bridged by a short dirt pathway. The front porch was the width of the small building and accessed up a small flight of steps; the front door was set back under the porch roof. Several large ash trees shaded the porch, making the whole area quite shadowy. They both walked onto the porch and Schneider knocked the door. There was no answer. Another, louder, knock produced the same result.

"I'll take a look round the back," McKinley offered, walking off the porch to the right side and disappearing down the dirt driveway towards the garage. There was a gap between the garage and the house, leading into the back yard, which was just a large patchy lawn area, sheltered by more ash trees. McKinley went through the gap to take a look.

Schneider tried one more knock, then a female voice came from his left: "can I help you?" He looked out from the porch to see a large, jolly-looking lady in a light blue dress protected by a red gingham kitchen apron, standing across in the next-door driveway.

"I'm looking for Mrs Ferguson," Schneider replied.

"Oh, you've missed her I'm afraid, she's at the church - it's their weekly communal meal."

"Oh that's a shame," he replied.

"Forgive me, you're not from Hillsboro are you? Have you come far?"

"Not really, just from Wichita."

"Oh, are you there with Sean?"

Schneider felt an icy shudder run down his spine. They had hit paydirt; this lady obviously knew the family well. He had to react quickly, but also correctly, otherwise the opportunity would be lost: "yes," he adlibbed, "we got-in today. Sean left a message to meet him out here."

"Oh what a shame, he went to the church with his Aunt. She doesn't get around so well, what with her eyesight going, so she was really excited at being chauffeured by her favourite nephew, especially as he doesn't get home so much these days."

"Oh I didn't realise he was from these parts."

"You wouldn't with all that California suntan would you? Yes, born and bred in Marion County, quite a local celebrity what with all his Hollywood connections."

"So, he's staying with his family?"

"All that's left of it, yes."

"Oh I'm sorry, I didn't ..."

"No, no, you wouldn't know, it was a long time ago. His mother died when he was just a child, so Mrs Ferguson took him in. His mother was her niece."

"So he grew up right here."

"That's it, right here in Monroe Street. Who knows, maybe the local historical society will put a plaque on the house one day."

"So you've known him since he was a child."

"Oh no dear, no - we've only lived here for about six years. He had left home long before that. He gets back when he can, but only for a few days at a time; he's such a busy boy with all the films he works on. But you would know that wouldn't you? In the same business."

"Oh yes, never a dull moment."

"And this one sounds so exciting. Who would have thought it, Clint Eastwood coming to Wichita!"

Another shudder went down Schneider's spine. His mind was racing with where this was taking them. Once again, his response had to be right. If he could have, he would have been crossing all of his fingers and toes, not just for the right response, but also that McKinley wasn't going to suddenly appear from the other side of the porch. He summoned up all of his experience and training: "it's not fully-settled yet."

"Oh I'm sorry, yes I know, Sean said it's still all hush-hush. I've not told anybody else, I promise. But I'm such a fan, I've seen all his films." She joined her hands, narrowed her eyes, then slowly brought her arms up until they were pointing at Schneider, still clasped together, with her right index finger pointing out towards him. "Make my day punk!" she said earnestly, then dropped her hands and began laughing, continuing: "oh, I'm sorry, I just can't resist it thinking he might be saying those words downtown somewhere soon. I just can't wait to show everybody that signed photo Sean got me."

Schneider wasn't sure how well he was concealing how much his brain was racing, but he instinctively knew he had to get away as quickly as possible: "maybe I can find them both at the church?" he asked.

"Oh no, sorry, Sean said he had some business back in Wichita this evening, so he was dropping his Aunt off, then carrying on. I'm going to fetch Susan for him later."

"In that case, it looks like I'm headed back there as well then. It's been very nice to meet you …" Schneider tailed off to try to prompt a name.

"Gladys," she blurted out quite happily, "Gladys Breitner."

"Alright, thank you Gladys, maybe we'll meet up again after the decision is announced."

"Oh!" she responded a little flustered at this apparent confirmation of her hero's future visit to the area, "oh yes, that would be wonderful!"

Schneider waved, then turned and walked off the porch down onto the sidewalk, turning away from Gladys towards his car. As he walked past the far wall of the bungalow, he was aware of McKinley waiting behind it.

"Has she gone?" the whispered voice came.

Schneider looked back over his shoulder just in time to catch a small area of red gingham disappearing through the rapidly closing door of the next-door house: "yes Chris."

As the two men headed for Schneider's car, he asked the question: "did you get any of that Chris?"

"Enough," McKinley responded.

Schneider tossed the keys to McKinley: "then you drive back, I need to make some calls."

One-Hundred

The briefing broke up around six-thirty with a final rousing battle cry from Chief Stanton. The troops filtered out of the conference room to collect equipment and vehicles and get themselves into their assigned positions by seven p.m, some with more enthusiasm than others.

Deputy Chief Harper had outlined the overall parameters of the operation, essentially an inner protection detail with outlying surveillance units, all backed up by the cavalry of his SWAT units laying in reserve half a block away. What was colloquially known within the service as a spider and fly operation and not entirely dissimilar to the one mounted by the FBI in Palm Springs a couple of months earlier, other than this time just one location had the deployed net.

Captain Delgado then took over to reveal some of the covert information that had led them to this opportunity to finally bring Vitruvio to justice. The implication was that the information had been gleaned through his undercover unit. Nobody in the room, besides the three senior officers and the three remaining members of the Homicide Squad, was aware of any reason not to believe the line being spun. What the three detectives were not privy to, although Holdsworth had already deduced, was that the member of the public who was Vitruvio's anticipated prime target had already been salted-away somewhere safe to be replaced by one of Delgado's men.

Moreno and Capaldi had exchanged surprised glances when Delgado announced that there would be a second member of the public to be protected at the address to be surveilled, a female companion of Vitruvio's prime target. They knew from the investigation thus far that Vitruvio had never risked hitting an accompanied target, every murder had been a solitary act. Both had also shot an enquiring look in Holdsworth's direction at that point, only to receive a barely-perceptible head-shake in return. Even though he was by far the most junior Squad member present, his performance thus far on the case had been authoritative; Moreno and Capaldi obeyed the gesture without question and kept their own counsel.

Delgado also gave a warning to all present about the need to avoid any contact with media personnel and crews that were on the lookout for any WPD operation, hence the need for them all to follow their individual deployment schedule details to the letter and that if any of them felt they were about to be compromised, they should advise their chain of command immediately. He gave the impression that the media were just hosepiping around looking for something to latch onto, whereas his division had been part of a carefully-orchestrated earlier leak involving the payment of two trusted informants to spark the story. Within minutes of them all leaving the conference room, the Mayor himself would be adding sufficient fuel to have the local media roasting this little chestnut nicely by the time they were all in position.

Every instinctive cell in his body wanted Holdsworth to scream-out what a load of bullshit this entire operation was, but he knew that they had to play the game so that he could at least tell Schneider the one location in the city where there was absolutely no chance Vitruvio would be that evening. He was also hoping to get the chance to tease-out from somebody where 'The Turd' might be, to give Schneider and McKinley a chance of homing-in on the more potential scene of crime instead.

All possibilities of the latter had evaporated after Delgado had handed back to Harper to announce the individual details for the night. All three Homicide detectives would be on the outermost remote observation points. They had been as marginalised as they could be, not only from the heart of the operation, but from each other, as the operation was to be conducted on secure radio frequencies only via defined chain of command, outside of which there was a strict communication blackout. This included the instruction that all cellphones, departmental or personal, were to be handed-in as they left the room. Holdsworth gave a silent prayer of thanks for Schneider's foresight in giving him an FBI cell earlier, that he had secreted in the glovebox of his car; at least he would be able to make one call on his way to the operation.

The stationing of the three officers most familiar with Vitruvio was justified by their familiarity with him, in other words they were the most likely to recognise him if they saw him. Holdsworth allowed himself a silent chuckle at that line, which everyone else swallowed without the slightest question. Copies of the airport photo were then distributed to everyone in the room, including the SWAT team members. Holdsworth smiled at the fleeting image in his mind of them pointing their guns at a cornered, and armed, Vitruvio whilst quickly checking the photo to make sure they had the right guy.

At a quarter before seven, Holdsworth climbed into his department-issue Falcon and drove out of the City Hall car park. He was alone in the car and turned east on Central as instructed before taking Broadway North to Twenty-First, then doubling back west via Arkansas and Twenty-Fifth to the location in Burlington Hills.

The house belonged to a business associate of Jackson Kendrick III and had been well-selected. It was not too large a property, but was set in reasonable sized open grounds with not too many trees and bushes near the house to provide cover. The rear to the west and part of the side of the property to the north backed-onto I-235, so there was little opportunity for approach from those directions. The frontage was on a dog-leg road with just two access points, to the south and the east. There was a school across the street whose upper floors provided a good viewpoint, and a church at the south junction where a car could be stationed in the car park among several others attending an evening prayer meeting there, so as not to attract attention to itself. That was Holdsworth's observation point, where he arrived at two minutes to seven.

He radioed-in to his chain of command confirming he was in place and that he had a good view of the junction with the road to the surveilled house, plus east and west along Twenty-Fifth. He was given instructions to report all vehicle and pedestrian movements in and out of the subject road, the frequency to change to at seven p.m, plus a codeword to use if he spotted Shepherd himself. The codeword was 'volcano'; he shook his head at the superficial nature of American general education.

He had called Schneider en route to give the basic details of the location and timings. The Bureau cellphone was resting in the cupholder to his right, in silent text mode as instructed by Schneider, a recent technique the Bureau had developed for one-way communication in just this type of surveillance scenario. If Schneider needed to contact him, he would send a text and Holdsworth would be alerted by the backlight on the phone screen illuminating; he could then read the message without compromising his operational situation. Having completed all of his preparations, Holdsworth settled back for a long and tedious evening.

One-o-One

Paul pushed his plate away slightly, then pulled himself forward, folding his arms to rest them on the table where the plate had been. He looked directly at Kryczek as he spoke: "what led you and Bonetti to believe that Vitruvio had two potential targets?"

"Process of elimination really. We had the advantage of Tom's previous experience in Savannah, then from that, together with the analysis we had done, he was certain it was going to be a female. Out of the connections to the first three victims, the only two that fitted the bill were the actress and the make-up girl."

"So it was Bonetti that made the connection between Savannah and Palm Springs."

"Yes," she replied.

There was a pause after the answer and he waited for additional information. When it wasn't forthcoming, he pushed gently: "and what?"

"Sorry, I don't get you."

"Well, when was the connection made?"

"Oh, straight after the second victim was found. Palm Springs Police only have a small personal crime unit, so they were pressed to deal with two separate scenes and called-in our local office for help."

"How was it made?"

"Tom spotted the M.O. when it came in from Palm Springs."

"And when did Denver and Memphis come into it?"

"They just showed-up on the National Computer when I started my analysis."

He was becoming a little uncomfortable with the reticence of the answers. He could understand that Kryczek would find dealing with the night of Bonetti's death difficult, he remembered the situation at Marjoree Rolles' scene. That was why he had started from a more oblique angle, to spare her feelings and test how far and how quickly he could push to what he really wanted to know.

"So was it your analysis that helped Bonetti to his conclusion about the two potential targets."

"I guess so, we were sharing all sorts of information between us, you know what it's like."

"Sure. So when did it start to solidify?"

She looked at him a bit puzzled. If he hadn't known she was such a highly-qualified Agent, he would have started to doubt her experience; she almost seemed out of her depth. *'The scars of that night must really go deep,'* he thought as he continued: "I mean before or after the third homicide."

"Oh after. Everything was moving so quickly at the start."

He identified with that scenario and the response reassured him.

"So back to the two ladies, where did they fit in the pattern?"

"The most obvious was the actress, she had slept with everybody on the crew at one time or another, so it was easy to make that connection to all of the first three victims."

"Yes, I saw that part of the analysis. She was ac/dc and with the other victims being one female and two straight men who both had connections to the dead female, the conclusion was that the final victim had to be female. But why not another male?"

"Another male?"

"Yes. If you're looking at connections and going with the sex angle, the dead female could have been the link. Why not another male who was also sleeping with her?"

"Because there weren't any."

"Fair enough, then why the make-up artist?"

"Tom interviewed her, several times. He wasn't sure about her, thought she was holding something back."

"Did he say what?"

"No, he just couldn't put his finger on it."

"But he must have thought she was the more likely target, otherwise why would he take her motel that night and put you in the actress' house."

"That's just the way it fell."

"So it wasn't that he thought the make-up girl the most likely."

"Why would that make a difference?"

"It would for me."

She shrugged. Paul was not getting what he had expected, so he decided to stop skating around the issue and ask the questions he needed answers for: "what actually happened at the actress' house?"

"I shot Bonetti. It's all in the files."

"What's in the files is what I expect to see in the files. It doesn't tell me what was going on."

"What, in my head you mean?"

"Seeing as you mention it, yes."

"One of my men told me we had an intruder on the property, he came through the window, I shot him."

"First shoot-out?"

"No!"

"First kill then?"

"What has that to do with anything?"

"You had no idea it was Bonetti."

"How could I? The radios were out. Look don't you think I've been over and over this for the last two months?"

"But you weren't happy about something to do with that night, other than the shooting that is. What was it?"

"I don't know what you mean." She was getting a little tetchy.

"Well, there were no more murders after that night, not in Palm Springs anyway. As a result, the Bureau seems to decide that Bonetti had been the perp all along and closes the files. Were you happy with that?"

"Of course not!"

"Which is why you took leave of absence."

"The world seemed to have fallen-in on me. I just needed away."

"Oh come on Kryczek, give me credit for some intelligence here will you. You took leave of absence, but you didn't drop the case did you? You've been working on it privately. What other reason could there be for you being here in Kansas the next time Vitruvio strikes. You know who it is don't you?"

Her shoulders slumped and he could see that she was doing all she could to keep it together. He backed-off: "look, I'm sorry, you're not a suspect here, I shouldn't have come on that strong."

She took a deep breath and seemed to recover her composure: "it's OK - and the answer is no, I don't know who Vitruvio is, he is way too professional. But I do know who his paymaster is."

He looked at her initially with some shock, then continued: "are you saying what I think you're saying?"

She looked at him without responding. He waited until it was obvious she wouldn't reply, so he answered his own question: "they're all linked aren't they? Every single murder has a link to the others."

She still didn't respond, so he carried-on himself: "this isn't the work of a contract professional, this is an employee."

"Which is why you have nothing to prevent tonight. Unless the paymaster has decided to commit suicide."

"They're all connected to the Kendricks?"

"No, they're all connected to one Kendrick."

"Bonetti was connected to the Kendricks?"

"No."

"But the pattern. He completed the pattern, meaning there has to be a victim tonight if the pattern is consistent."

"Which is exactly the trap we all fell into. Tom; me, initially anyway; the Bureau; now you. Why does there have to be a pattern? This isn't a serial, these are hits. I have found more that fit the pattern, in other locations and various numerical combinations."

"But it doesn't explain Bonetti."

"Bonetti was a loose end. Vitruvio would have done the three and left town, except he must have recognised Tom from Savannah somehow and needed to remove the danger that may have posed to his business. So he set him up, Tom took the bait and walked into his own trap. Any of this ringing any bells yet?"

Paul felt a shudder run through his body. He didn't need to say anything, his face said it all.

"Penny's dropped has it?" she continued: "now answer one question for me." He nodded. "Why did you call me this afternoon, despite being off the case?"

"Are we ever off a case that's current?"

"Exactly. You know there are aspects that don't fit, which is why you're a loose-end that needs tying up, just like Bonetti. The difference this time is that you won't be taking the bait."

"I won't"

"You won't"

"And why not?"

"Because I'm here to stop you."

"So Sam appointed you to be my minder then?"

"Schneider doesn't know I'm here."

"But you rang him."

"Only to find out why you rang me. He told me you were off the case, so I said I wouldn't return your call."

"So Sam knows nothing of what you've just told me."

She went silent again. He was getting the pattern of the conversation; or was it a test? She would give him a morsel, he would chew on it until he got the flavour, then when he had correctly identified the flavour, he could have another morsel. If he spat it out, he failed the test. He considered this latest set of facts, then responded: "you don't trust Sam's office."

"I don't trust the Bureau."

"There's an alternative to Vitruvio identifying Bonetti, isn't there?" The question caused her to smile for the first time since the discussion began. He took the cue and continued: "which is why you're operating on the outside."

"As are you, now."

"Whoa, hold on right there; you're thinking we might team-up and covertly bring these bastards down?" She smiled again as he continued: "you're forgetting one or two small details - you're still an Agent on extended leave, I'm a suspended cop. Worse still, I'm a loose end, according to your theory anyway. They might miss me tonight thanks to your timely intervention, but they're not going to give up."

"Unless they think you've given up. It wouldn't take much in the way of deductive skills to figure-out that you're pretty-pissed with what's happened. So I'm guessing you're not going to wait for the disciplinary."

He didn't respond: *'two can play this game,'* he thought.

So she continued this time: "in which case, you have already decided to resign, so why wait? Hand it in tomorrow and leave town; their concerns leave with you."

"And where do you suggest I go?"

"California - my place; I've got all the evidence there that I've gathered so far. Two heads are better than one, especially when one has more inside knowledge of who is behind all this."

"I've got a better option," he responded, "we go back to my place, and you tell me what you have on the Kendricks. I fill whatever gaps I can, then we decide where we go after that."

"Is that a proposition, Paul?" She smiled a more knowing smile; there was no response. "Good," she continued, "I was beginning to think you were never going to ask!"

One-o-Two

McKinley was driving at way above the limit along Route 56 in full code three; even at those speeds it would be close to eight p.m. before they could reach Wichita. They were heading towards McPherson, where they would pick up I-135 South. It was the long way around but, being a US Highway, it had good cellphone coverage. They had lost signal several times for long stretches on the minor roads between Newton and Hillsboro on the way up; they could not afford interruptions on the way back.

Schneider had picked-up Holdsworth's message after they had set-off from Hillsboro, which meant that Holdsworth was on station and could only receive text messages. So first, he rang his own office and asked them to patch him through to Pete Baker in LA; it seemed to take an age for the return call to come in, but eventually he was through.

"Hey Sam, how are things with you. Did we get you back in the game this afternoon?"

"Sort of Pete; I've let Stanton dig his way into his own pile of shit. He wasn't likely to give-up on what he sees as a publicity-coup operation, so he may as well run with it; it will keep him out of our hair for now, maybe even permanently. In return for that he had to let me have Chris McKinley on liaison, he's with me now. We've also got one of Chris' Squad on-line in the operation just in case."

"So you think Stanton might get a show?"

"With this perp anything's possible, but realistically? No. Something else is in play here, which we are trying to get our heads around, but we may not have much time. Look, I let Kryczek go because of her state of mind the other day, but she might be able to help us with something. Is she still down here?"

"Far as I know, yes Sam; do you want me to get ahold of her?"

"No, that's OK, my office will put a call into her cell. In the meantime, maybe you can help me get a handle on the relationship with Bonetti. He was married wasn't he?"

"Yes, and very happily - lovely wife, super kids. That was why we kept trying to allocate the two of them to separate cases in the office."

"I can sure see why he would have been tempted."

"You can? You'll have to explain that one to me when we next get together! Damned if I could work out what he saw in her. I mean, I suppose she's not unattractive in her way, but I never liked tiny women, especially ones with an attitude like Kryczek. I have a real problem when I have to work with her, a bit like having a gremlin on the team."

"So nobody else in her life other than Bonetti?"

"I very much doubt it. Moody, unreliable, probably the worst dress sense I've ever come across, but I suppose that didn't matter much to Bonetti, as far as I could make out, when they were together he had her clothes off most of the time!"

"So you're better off if I keep her down here a little longer then?"

"Decor wise, hell yeah. But don't you get any ideas, just because nothing can clash with those multiple shades of brown in that shabby office of yours, she's still the best Profiler I've ever worked with and I'll have her back here as soon as she's fit again."

"I hope you're not disappointed on that last count. Still, let's get tonight out of the way, can you manage a conference call in the morning?"

"Sure thing Sam, how about ten a.m. Central?"

"Fine for me."

"OK, you set it up from your end. Speak to you in the morning."

Schneider hung up and slumped back into his seat staring out of the side window across the flatlands towards the sun that was beginning to settle towards the horizon. They had turned south on I-135 and McKinley was driving very rapidly down the outer lane. He waited a little for Schneider to say something, but when the silence wasn't broken, he prompted: "I got half of that, am I right in assuming the other half confirmed what we heard back there in Hillsboro?"

The silence continued for another mile or so. When he finally spoke, Schneider's voice was strained by a mixture of rage and exasperation: "how could we have missed something as obvious as that?"

"Krycek's involved, right?"

"Kryczek's a midget with no dress sense! Did a midget with no fucking dress sense visit the Rolles crime scene? How the fuck could we have missed that? Jesus Christ, this bastard's accomplice walks straight into his fucking crime scene right under our noses impersonating an FBI Agent!" He punched the trim on the passenger door, leaving a distinct dent.

McKinley was trying to get his head around what he had just heard; the car began to slow noticeably. Schneider looked ahead to see what the obstruction was, but only saw a wide-open road.

"Why are you slowing down Chris?"

"Sorry," McKinley responded, snapping back into driving mode; he floored the throttle and the Crown Victoria quickly picked-up speed again. He asked the only question he could frame at that moment: "so where's Kryczek?"

"Holy shit!" Schneider responded, suddenly recognising an aspect he hadn't even considered to that point. He felt a deep hollow forming in the pit of his stomach, before the professionalism began to kick back in again: "no idea, but we don't have time to go off on tangents Chris, the only way we can answer all of these questions is to catch this, no these two bastards. Shepherd's not in Hillsboro, he's gone back into Wichita. We have no idea where the false Kryczek is. Shit! We're virtually back to square one again! They're so far ahead of us in the game, but what is the game? Is there even a fucking game? Are we missing something, or do we have all the pieces but no diagram of how they go together? Think! We have to think!"

McKinley considered for a second, then offered an idea: "maybe we've got too many pieces."

Schneider stared at McKinley, his mind turning-over this fresh approach trying to find a flaw in it. When no obvious one appeared, he went with it: "that's a good angle you know. All of these cases are over-elaborated - multiple-murders, accurate timings, clean-ups, posed bodies, apparent connections all over the place, now two perps not one. It all adds up to information overload, and we're left thinking they're playing games with us, like a serial, but it's all done to muddy the waters so we chase shadows and don't see the real connections."

"That's because there are no loose ends. That's what the false Kryczek was doing, tying up a loose end. We had to think Kryczek was still alive."

"Because if she wasn't, that would be a second FBI Agent dead in connection with these cases and the Bureau would take everything over. WPD wouldn't have got a look in, because we would already have been all over it down here from the minute Hilary Nicholson was found with that known M.O!" He paused and McKinley was about to speak when Schneider suddenly shouted: "shit - she found them!"

McKinley's mind was battling with driving at nearly a hundred miles an hour and trying to keep up with Schneider as he started to piece it together. He decided to keep them both alive and let Schneider's thought-processes run their course. Schneider turned towards McKinley as the veils began to drop away from the facts: "Kryczek and Bonetti must have got close, which is why Kryczek took furlough. She's a highly-rated Profiler; she must have made the right connections. She wasn't ill, she needed to follow her hunch without the Bureau knowing - or at least, someone within the Bureau knowing. What she found meant she didn't trust somebody. So she went native to build the picture. That's when they killed her."

"We don't know she's dead Sam." McKinley's sympathetic side wanted that to be true.

"With all due respect Chris, that's why you're a Police Officer not an Agent, and also why you should stay that way. By and large, Police Officers retain their humanity. Unfortunately, Agents are picked because we can think the unthinkable without it affecting us."

"Is that why Paul left the Bureau?"

"That's a whole different discussion for another time Chris; keep your focus on the here and now. But yes, she's dead. You said it yourself - these are professionals, they do not leave loose ends. They've also had her cellphone since they killed her, and probably her access codes to the Bureau Computer System amongst other things, so they could keep the lie running as long as they needed to."

"But to walk in to the middle of the investigation posing as her, that not only takes balls, the risk-factor is off the scale!"

"Yes, but it was a calculated risk - cold, hard and calculated. She was running interference for Shepherd and it worked. I'll wager that if we had sussed her, that would have been sufficient of a diversion in itself to tie-up your investigation until Shepherd killed Cochrane. Then where would you have been with a suspect in custody when a third related murder was committed? No Chris, we're dealing with killers here of the most sinister kind that simply don't fear capture, probably not even their own deaths. In fact, this could be some form of symbiotic relationship."

"Like the Sumners a few years ago?"

"In that they were husband and wife, I guess so. But they were a dysfunctional couple, these two are nowhere near that. Kryczek must have picked-up on something like this that took her to them. It's going to be in those files somewhere."

"We don't have the time to go through them again. In any case, our expert on them is watching traffic for the Chief as we speak."

"Shit! Holdsworth - I forgot about him!" Schneider flipped-open his Motorola and started pressing buttons rapidly.

One-o-Three

Holdsworth had been on station for more than half an hour; nothing had happened. In fact, despite the constant flow of traffic he was quite surprised at the small amount that turned-off, or joined, at the junction he was watching: *'no wonder the plots up there are all so large,'* he thought to himself, *'it must be a real quiet area to live, if you can cope with the noise from the Interstate, that is.'*

That was the source, or destination, of most of the traffic on Twenty-Fifth and the reason why he had positioned himself so he could see into every vehicle approaching from the intersection, because that was considered by his chain of command as the most likely direction for their target to arrive in a vehicle. Just in case, though, he had also made sure that he could see easily into the driver's side of vehicles approaching and turning from the city side. He knew from the files that they were dealing with a much higher-level of criminal intelligence than Harper had indicated at the briefing.

To the rank and file, Deputy Chief Harper was a career administrator, with an ability to efficiently organise schedules and compile reports that exonerated anybody in the department that his bosses at the time needed to remain employed. Thus, he had acquired a Teflon reputation that attracted ambitious toadies into his division who, in return for rapid promotions, absorbed all the dirty jobs whilst protecting him from any political harm; people like Morley, whose IAD section was part of Harper's Division. This gave Harper an outlook that saw the entire WPD through the rose-tinted specs that came free with every copy of every report he issued. In the eyes of the executive, he could do no wrong; proper policemen distrusted him and everything he stood for.

The operation in progress was typical Harper. Analysed by the book and organised to the nth degree, it could not possibly fail - provided that the target to be arrested had been briefed by the same personnel, or was completely stupid. In the event that they were neither, then the SWAT team, headed by Harper's toadie-in-chief Lieutenant Rusty Lomax, a barely-literate redneck thug in uniform, would take no prisoners. Nobody on Harper's team would have batted an eyelid if the words 'Target to be taken Dead or Alive' had been writ large across the bottom of the briefing document. With a sidekick like Lomax around, such words were unnecessary.

Holdsworth had probably not been on the force long enough to fully-appreciate that being marginalised on this operation, in the wake of the Chief's dismissal of Paul Kleberson, was actually a blessing in disguise. Instead, he felt frustrated by his situation, a frustration that was ratcheted-up every five minutes by the pedantic check-in calls on the radio from the next up his chain of command, Sergeant Walewski, who was ensconced in the mobile control van concealed in the equipment storehouse at the back of the school. Spot on cue at seven-forty, the radio crackled: "Delta Three, anything to report?"

Holdsworth flicked the tx button on his radio: "Control this is Delta Three - nothing to report."

"Thank you Delta Three, stay alert."

The radio crackled off. That last phrase, used on every contact thus far, rankled with Holdsworth. Why would he not 'stay alert'? That was why he was where he was, why he had been chosen to be an early-warning, even though he didn't expect there to be anything to report at all that night. In Holdsworth's view, this operation was just a complete waste of everybody's time.

A few seconds later, his attention was distracted by the backlight on the FBI cellphone screen lighting up. It read: 'You have a Message.' He waited until sufficient gaps appeared in the traffic, then grabbed-up the phone and hit the 'Read' button.

A short message appeared on the screen: 'All my Agents, including Kryczek, advised to stay clear of your op. If any show - report to your chain of command, then text name to me.'

Holdsworth resumed his concentration on the road junction until another gap occurred, then he read the text again. It didn't differ from the first reading.

He put the phone down, returning his gaze to the junction. At every gap in traffic, he mentally analysed it, but only one question emerged consistently - why mention Kryczek specifically?

That brought him to reconsider what he could recall from the Palm Springs files. He had likened the current operation to the previous one where Bonetti was killed, but other than for the spider and fly methodology and the possibility of it also going badly wrong, there were no significant similarities; until that text message when Kryczek had become a feature in both. But this time was she a suspect or someone on a vigilante mission?

Only Schneider knew the answer and, either way, Holdsworth wasn't in a position to ask the question. That heightened his frustration as the radio crackled again: "Delta Three, anything to report?"

He sighed deeply as his finger moved to the tx button.

don't vex me now

One-o-Four

Deputy Davy Fitzhugh was coming towards the end of his shift. He was completing his final sweep through Riverside that would take him back to the County Sherriff's Office on West Elm. It had been a quiet shift, one speeding ticket and a failure to yield. The first driver, a businessman late for a meeting, had accepted culpability and with nothing showing on his record the matter was dealt with in minutes.

The second, a brother with an attitude and a 'seventies Sedan de Ville, had been more trouble. He knew that the offence was down to his word against Fitzhugh's and that some Deputies would let it go if enough fuss was made, rather than have to suffer the court paperwork and non-payment follow-ups. When he realised Fitzhugh wasn't one of those, and that he was about to call for back-up, the driver had backed-off and taken the ticket; that was the point at which Deputy Fitzhugh knew the County had little chance of it being paid. Still, minimal paperwork at the office meant that he could catch Gravy's second set at The River's Edge on the way home, plus a couple of beers of course.

Fitzhugh had looped around The Botanica then back along Murdock before turning up Aldridge. He had done this sweep several times during the day, but this was the first time he had chosen Aldridge for the cut-through. Just after crossing Van Buren he caught a glimpse of a red Dodge Intrepid parked in the Bethlehem Baptist Church car park, catching a partial on the plate at the last minute. He turned right onto River Boulevard, then right again into Fitzgerald, that would bring him back around the block. As he was doing this, he called in:

"Forty-Nine to Dispatch."

"Go ahead Forty-Nine."

"WPD put an alert out on a red Dodge yesterday, is it still current?"

"Let me check ... Roger that alert Forty-Nine, red Dodge Intrepid, licence sierra golf four seven fiver two. Location to be reported, observe only, do not approach driver unless cleared to do so."

"I may have the vehicle, dispatch. It is parked and unattended. Will do another pass to confirm."

"Roger that Forty-Nine, call back when confirmed."

"Roger dispatch, Forty-Nine out."

Fitzhugh turned right onto Van Buren, then right again back onto Aldridge. He took a slower pass to confirm the plate and that there was nobody inside. This time when he reached the end of the street, he turned left onto River Boulevard, standard procedure in case a subject was watching the location. He accelerated away up River Boulevard. As he did so he called-in again: "Forty-Nine to Dispatch."

"Go ahead Forty-Nine."

"Affirmative on the red Dodge Intrepid. It is in the Bethlehem Church car park, no occupants. Have vacated immediate area, heading north on River Boulevard approaching the Eleventh Street Bridge."

"Roger that Forty-Nine, hold in vicinity for further instructions."

"Roger Dispatch, will hold on West Eleventh, Forty-Nine out."

Fitzhugh, turned left on Eleventh, then fifty yards down did a U-turn, returning to park just short of the junction, looking across River Boulevard to the bridge. This was a regular observation point for catching speeding drivers on the junction with River Boulevard and unlikely to alert anybody local to any other interests he had. He looked at his watch; it said seven-fifty. The alert wording suggested this was not something as normal as a stolen vehicle, meaning he would probably be on station for a while: *'so much for getting off shift on time'*, he thought to himself, as he settled back to await his next instructions.

One-o-Five

The Taxi had arrived quite quickly, for a change, and the conversation in the back bore no relation to the earlier discussion at the table.

Both had been mildly embarrassed by the discovery that their assumption the other would have transport on hand had been wrong. After Paul had ordered the cab Kryczek apologised for being insensible to the side-effects of his recent change in circumstances. Paul waved this away, in turn apologising for assuming she had driven-in from where she was staying. "You weren't to know I had decided to go back home," she reassured him, "and I can't abide a long drive before an early-morning flight, so I prefer to dump the rental the previous evening and get a room at the airport, then just curl-up with a good book. My Aunt doesn't sleep well at nights in any case, but she wouldn't sleep at all knowing I had to be away at some crazy early hour. Like all old folks, she takes the responsibility for making sure others meet their commitments."

Both had submitted the potted verbal CV of their life so far, such that in the ten minute journey they had enough background to feel like established friends. He had found her upbringing somewhat disarming, her mother dying in childbirth, then her father committing suicide when she was eleven, leaving her and her elder brother to fend for themselves. However much he looked-back on those aspects of his youth that he disliked, there was no doubt that he had experienced a far more stable family life. Yet despite a back-story that he was more familiar with hearing in a courtroom, here was someone who had ended-up graduating from Quantico in just the same way that he had.

His fascination with social history was pushing him to probe more deeply into her early years, but he was unable to find an opportunity amid the constant flow of questions about England. Despite her obvious advance in lifestyle, she had apparently never travelled outside of America, so her questions were ostensibly those of a one-dimensional tourist, someone who had seen the pictures, but never sampled the sensual atmosphere that could only be transmitted by those who had. Even so, between the answers his detective instincts kept bothering him. Something didn't add-up here; he just couldn't put his finger on quite what it was.

Almost before they realised, the cab pulled-up at the kerb outside of his apartment block. She got out of the car while Paul paid the driver, then he followed her, releasing the cab to depart for its next job. She was looking-up at the building when he joined her: "nice place Paul, although forgive me for observing that it seems a bit above the pay-grade."

He smiled: "I don't have the penthouse, just one of the broom cupboards on the third floor."

"Even so, I'm impressed."

"I made some good friends when I was in England and one of them knows an awful lot more about business than I ever will. He helped me with some investments and I guess I got lucky. Meaning, I have the advantage of some independence that others on my pay grade may not."

She looked at the building again: "you must give me his number."

Paul smiled in response to the suggestion: "so I guess this is the point at which I offer you coffee." He gestured towards the front door; she nodded approval and moved-off towards it.

One-o-Six

Much to his relief, it was only a few minutes before Deputy Fitzhugh's radio crackled back into life: "Forty-Nine this is Dispatch, do you copy?"

"Dispatch, this is Forty-Nine - go ahead."

"WPD want the vehicle kept under surveillance until they can get one of their units to the location. Do you have visual?"

"Negative on the vehicle at present."

"Can you attain visual without revealing your position?"

"Only on foot."

"Roger that Forty-Nine, hold please."

The radio went quiet; Fitzhugh realised that dispatch must be in conversation with another unit, from where they were receiving instructions. The radio crackled again: "Forty-Nine this is Dispatch, proceed on foot to attain visual and advise status when you have."

"Roger Dispatch, Forty-Nine out."

Fitzhugh moved off and turned right to head back down River Boulevard. As he passed the Palace Inn, he realised that the car park next to Saint Agnes's was almost full: *'must be something on tonight'* he thought as he pulled-into their car park. This would be an ideal location to leave his patrol car, as it would not stand-out as much as it would if it was parked on one of the quiet side streets or in a half-empty car park.

He drove around behind the church building and picked one of the empty spaces shielded from Hodge Street by some trees. The L-shaped car park had two entrances and the one on Hodge was across from Stover. From his local knowledge of this beat, he knew that there was an entrance off Stover into the alleyway that ran behind Bethlehem Church and, with the sun setting, there would be enough cover in the shadows for him to take-up a good observation point from there.

He entered the alley and walked to the end. To his left, the alley ended in a low wall behind which there was a ten foot drop to the yard behind the five-storey apartment block that completely screened any view of River Boulevard. To his right, the alley ran all the way along the back of the church car park. For the first twenty yards the hedge and trees screened the car park from his present viewpoint, but after that the hedge became sporadic, petering-out halfway down the alley to give a full view of the church building itself. He could see the Dodge Intrepid and that it was still unoccupied.

He pressed the button on his radio: "Forty-Nine to Dispatch."

"Go ahead Forty-Nine"

"In position in the alley behind Bethlehem Church car park. I have visual on subject car, it is in the same position and still unoccupied."

"Roger that Forty-Nine, maintain observation and report any change. Dispatch out."

Fitzhugh surveyed the situation; he had good cover and the Intrepid was in full view. However, because of the trees, the apartment block and the church buildings, this only afforded him a very narrow angle of view on a short stretch of Aldridge. He realised that this would give him very little reaction time if anyone approached the car from there - the most likely scenario.

He moved across the alleyway until he was behind the hedge, then inched along the hedge until he came to a narrow gap that led into a thicker area of vegetation under the trees. He slipped through the gap and found himself in a small cleared area beneath the trees and surrounded by hedging. From the remnants of a couple of small campfires and the positioning of pieces of wood and canvas, this was obviously a den made by some local children.

It could be a bit risky using this area, but being a school night, it was a calculated gamble to assume that the kids would not be using it in the next few hours. He moved around a bit until he found an ideal location which aligned with several gaps in the hedging. Through those, he not only had a good view of the entire car park, but also of the entrance. In between the trees on the opposite side of the car park he had fairly-unobstructed views of stretches of the sidewalk on his side of Aldridge, plus parts of the junction with River Boulevard.

The church was in darkness, but the car park was not empty. There were a dozen or more other cars sprinkled around, probably belonging to local residents or visitors. Aldridge Avenue was also very quiet, with no movement other than a taxi moving away from the apartment building behind him. Deputy Fitzhugh settled down for what might be a long evening.

One-o-Seven

Schneider and McKinley were just approaching Park City. Schneider was driving, the two having swapped seats at the truck stop at Newton, allowing them both to use their phones, Schneider's car being equipped with handsfree for his Motorola, but not for McKinley's Nokia. The first call came through to Schneider from Bill Johnson: "Sam it's Bill."

"Hey Bill, what've you got?"

"Nothing on Stanton's op, just a constant stream of check-ins. But I've picked-up something on the Sherriff's frequencies. They may have something on the hire car."

"Do they have a location?"

"Don't know yet, a Deputy just radioed in for confirmation on the alert."

"OK, keep me informed."

Johnson rang off. McKinley looked at Schneider, who was totally focussed on the road. They were getting closer to Wichita so the traffic was increasing and at these speeds things happened fast.

"You're monitoring Stanton - I thought our radios were encrypted?"

"They are, but who developed the encryption?"

"Jeez, he'd have apoplexy if he knew."

"Just as well he doesn't then."

McKinley's phone rang next. He answered: "McKinley."

"Lieutenant Kleberson, this is Central Dispatch. We have a call patched-across from the Sherriff's Office; they have a positive I.D. on the red Dodge Intrepid that you put the alert out on yesterday. We have an operation on tonight and there are no free units we can dispatch. Do you want to take it?"

"This is Detective McKinley, the Lieutenant is busy right now. Do we have a location?"

"Yes Detective - Aldridge Avenue"

"Which one? North or South of the river?"

"Please hold while I get confirmation."

McKinley turned to Schneider: "positive on the hire car."

"Where?"

"Just getting specifics."

At that point Schneider's phone rang: "Sam, Bill again. Positive I.D. on the car. It's parked, no occupants."

"Where?"

Johnson's reply: "car park of Bethlehem Church," was simultaneous with McKinley's dispatcher: "South, in the Bethlehem Church car park with no occupants. Sherriff has offered surveillance until we can get a unit there."

Schneider shot a glance at McKinley, who continued his conversation with the dispatcher: "OK Dispatch, ask Sherriff's Officer to observe, but keep their car out of sight and report immediately the occupants return. I will take it, e-t-a…" he looked at Schneider, "… ten to twelve minutes?" Schneider nodded.

"Roger that, Detective McKinley, Central out."

Schneider resumed his conversation with Johnson: "you may have heard that Bill, McKinley has it. We're on our way there now."

"Shall I keep monitoring?"

"Yes Bill, we will get an update quicker from you than we will via the Sherriff and WPD dispatches."

"OK Sam." Johnson rang off.

"Where's Bethlehem Church?" Schneider asked.

"Behind Paul's place … JEEZ!"

Both men shot a shocked look at each other that they held for a spilt-second before Schneider forced himself to look back at the road, immediately hitting the brakes, throwing both of them forward against their seatbelts. An eighteen-wheeler had chosen the precise moment that Schneider took his eyes off the road to pull-out to overtake a similar rig.

Schneider had forgotten that activating the handsfree also muted the siren which, as a consequence, he needed to restart; when he did so, it immediately caused the truck driver to slow and pull back in so they could pass. Schneider floored the throttle and the Interceptor leapt forward like a horse given full spur.

"Shit that was a close one! What's the quickest route, stick on One-Three-Five to Thirteenth, or Twenty-First then Mclean?"

McKinley looked at his watch - it read five past eight: "Thirteenth. This time of night traffic is lighter and there are less lights to shoot, plus we can cut over on Bitting. You don't think …?"

"I don't want to think anything Chris, other than how to get there. Try his, sorry, your cell." McKinley hit the speed-dial and waited for the dial tone; instead he got a voice message.

He told Schneider with a frustrated tone: "gone straight to voicemail again."

"He's not carrying it, forget that. What was it he said in that message he left me earlier? Find it will ya."

McKinley leant across and pressed the buttons on Schneider's phone, leaving it in the cradle so that they would both be able to hear it. When he found the message, he pressed play and Paul's voice came out of the car speakers: "It's

Paul, sorry I've been out. I've got all your messages. I'm not going to get in your way Sam. I hope you can get a break, if not, then heaven help the next target, whoever it is. I do have some unanswered questions and there's only one person who can help me with them. If it brings any results, I will text you. After that I'm leaving town, and at present I don't know when, or if, I'll come back. Thanks for everything. I'm sorry."

It was the first time McKinley had heard the message; to him Paul sounded somewhat defeated. Schneider detected more sadness in this hearing than previously when he wasn't as fully-concentrated as he should have been.

Schneider was the first to speak: "we know who that one person is, we've just got to get there. How long do you think?"

McKinley surveyed the landscape. They were coming-up on the I-235 Interchange: "still ten minutes, minimum. Have you got any troops you can mobilise?"

"Only Johnson, but I would have to take him off monitoring; even if I did, he wouldn't get there before us. You?"

"Chief's got 'em all and half the department as well; dispatch said they have no spare units anywhere. Paul has, would have had, the authority to yank one of those off whatever they're doing, but I can't without the Chief's blessing, and he ain't likely …"

"Holdsworth, he's closer! He's only up on Twenty-Fifth."

"He would have to desert his position …"

"Ask Him!"

"He's a rookie Sam, he won't …"

"Got another option? ASK HIM!"

"What about the Sherriff, we've got that Deputy on the car, I could patch through …"

"So he goes in all guns blazing and it turns-out another Palm Springs, we need someone with some savvy. Holdsworth!"

"SAM!"

"Fuck you Chris, this is my friend!" Schneider leant forward and punched autodial eight.

One-o-Eight

Holdsworth looked at his watch. He couldn't believe how slowly the evening was passing and it was coming-up on ten past eight - time for yet another tedious check-in.

The screen on the cell flashed alight. He looked at it expecting to see it reading 'You have a Message'; instead it said 'Schneider Calling'. He picked it up to make sure his eyes weren't deceiving him, but that's what it said alright. He couldn't believe it; Schneider had promised him he wouldn't do this! The message was flashing, as if compelling him to answer. He knew that he couldn't. Right then, the radio crackled again: "Delta Three, anything to report?"

Holdsworth diverted his attention from the cellphone, flicked the tx button on his radio: "Control this is Delta Three - nothing to report."

"Thank you Delta Three, stay alert."

The radio crackled off again. Holdsworth threw the handset at the dashboard and mumbled to himself in a childish voice: "yes Sergeant, I'll stay freakin' alert Sergeant." He looked down at the cellphone. The message had changed: 'Missed Call, Schneider. Press redial to call back'. The backlight dimmed.

'Shit,' he thought, 'something must be going down.' He considered for a few moments whether he should ring back, then the backlight came on again: 'You have a Message from Schneider - Press Read to see it.'

He pressed the read button. The message was short: 'PICK UP!'

The only thought he had was that it was in caps with an exclamation mark; the caps showed it was typed in a hurry, but the exclamation mark - that took time on a cell keyboard, meaning this was not normal. The cellphone screen flashed. Once again it said: 'Schneider Calling.'

At the same time the radio crackled: "Delta Three, respond."

This was not a routine check-in. Holdsworth once again had to divert his attention from the cellphone as he scrabbled in the footwell to locate the radio handset. When his hand located it, he picked it up and flicked the tx button: "Control this is Delta Three."

"Delta Three, I am patching Chief Stanton through to you."

"Roger that Control."

There was a short pause before the radio crackled again: "Holdsworth?"

"Holdsworth receiving Chief."

"Your Squad filed an alert yesterday on a red Dodge - was it on this case?"

"Yes Chief, licence was for Shepherd's current rental car."

"Roger that, out." The radio crackled off again. He looked down at the cellphone, beginning to dread what it might say; something was definitely going down - but what?

The screen read: '2 Missed Calls'. As he watched it changed to: 'You have a Message from Schneider - Press Read to see it.'

He pressed read again. The message was slightly longer: 'PICK UP DAMN YOU!'

For the first time in a long while, he felt uneasy. Something was definitely happening and it involved Shepherd's hire car; plus the Chief, the senior officer running his operation, was all over it. He had an unauthorised cellphone, an FBI phone, in a WPD car, on the other end of which was Agent Schneider trying to tell him something clearly very important. The jeopardy question was simple - answer the call, or lose the phone?

The various permutations for 'answer the call' ranged from receiving crucial information from the FBI that would lead to apprehension of the perp, to being compromised when Shepherd's car arrived at the junction, so being unable to call it in. The only thing he was on station to watch-out for was Shepherd arriving at this location; if he missed his assignment for any reason, everything that happened subsequently, good or bad, was definitely on him.

He picked-up the phone, turned it over and pulled off the battery cover. Having pulled out the battery, he threw both into the door pocket and resumed his study of the junction.

One-o-Nine

Paul put the key in the lock and pushed the door, which opened directly into the lounge of his small apartment. He removed the key, then stepped across the threshold rotating to have his back against the wall as he chivalrously ushered his guest into the flat. He was immediately taken by surprise as that guest threw her arms around his neck planting a passionate kiss full on his lips. The door crashed shut behind them, kicked there by the visitor's right foot.

All evening as they had talked, there had been signals that she may have had thoughts in this direction, but his mind could not determine whether, if she did, he would want something to happen or not. In the interludes between trying to figure-out what it was about Palm Springs that bothered him, the hormonal side of his brain was saying 'yes please!' to the thought of being entangled by a pair of beautiful legs. The instinctive side was strangely revolted by the thought.

It was the hint of revulsion that he could not come to terms with. Was it something in this woman herself that repelled him, or was it simple distrust? He had a continued doubt about the final fateful moments of that operation in Palm Springs, because something just didn't fit. Her apparent reticence in answering his questions, almost as though she hadn't been there at all, didn't help. Could it be her way of concealing a vital piece of information, particularly concerning the radio communications - or the lack of them?

Or was it simply the amount of time since he had been presented with the opportunity of a no-strings one-night-stand like the one that was confronting him? Paul was somewhat old-fashioned by the standards of the day; he was one for the long-haul and preferred to court his ladies before committing his body to them. He was simply not the one-night-stand type, hence the few women in his life romantically since the fumbling experimentations of adolescence.

The love of his life, his wife, had left him three years earlier, due to the familiar mixture of fear and frustration that blights so many police marriages. Frustration that, although everything about the husband permeated the wife's life twenty-four-seven, the physical presence was fleeting and often emotionally distant; fear that, one day, even that sporadic presence would be suddenly and permanently snatched from her to be replaced by a framed triangular memento.

Since then, Paul had confined his romantic interest to the occasional evening with Carla Courtney. Those liaisons had started innocently enough, but had developed into amorous oases in life's dispassionate desert. They happened irregularly, but were an instant battery-charge for both parties. Both yearned secretly to make them more regular; more permanent. Both equally feared that doing so would remove the essence of the thrill they imparted. It had been ten weeks since their last event - ten long weeks.

But here he was with another woman clamped to his face forcing her strong tongue past his own as she pressed him against the wall. Not only had she taken him by surprise, but this was the most aggressive first kiss he could remember experiencing. At that point, he had no choice; she had control and it felt decidedly uncomfortable. He liked his women soft and gentle, to take time building to the main event; even in adolescence he had never enjoyed 'wham bam, thank you ma'am'.

He lifted both arms in an attempt to cool things a bit. His right hand was the first to make contact with her body, nestling against a beautiful soft round breast, unfettered and unsupported, nestling sensually beneath her diaphanous blouse. She mistook this for a positive signal, quite the opposite of the intention in Paul's mind. She unlocked momentarily, pulled her face slightly away, smiled broadly, then spun them both further into the room until they collided at an oblique angle with the back of a sofa. They bounced off of the sofa still twirling until Paul's back hit the wall of the hallway leading to the other rooms.

She giggled, then clamped on another intense kiss. As she did so, both of her hands went to Paul's trousers. In what seemed like a split second, his belt was undone, his zip was down and her right hand was thrusting inside the waistband of his boxers like a hungry snout trawling a trough for a tasty morsel.

Paul really felt out of control, but unsure whether he cared or not. The probing hand found his penis; it was already half-erect and rising rapidly. That part was an ecstatic feeling. The kiss, however, had become almost brutal. It produced a contrasting sensation that confused him; but it was all happening so fast, his mind was unsure whether his senses were trying to warn him, or he was just experiencing complete naiveté of being on the receiving end of this type of full-on sexual advance.

She unclamped again, pulled back slightly and smiled seductively as her right hand gave his penis a little squeeze: "my goodness Paul, you are pleased to meet me aren't you?"

She grabbed his right hand that was still on her breast and pulled it down to her belt. The signal was obvious, so he began to fumble with the buckle. He moved his left hand behind her waist, then down to her buttock to balance his moves. The buttock felt firm and muscular, with little trace of flab: *'she obviously works-out regularly'* he thought, almost as if he was trying to distract himself from the sensations already welling in his groin. The buckle freed and he popped the waist button on her jeans, then found the zip toggle which he pulled down as far as it would easily go. At the same time he slipped his other hand inside the loose back of her jeans and grasped a handful of bare buttock. She was either wearing a g-string, or had come commando.

The jeans dropped away slightly and slipped over her hips. As she felt this happen, she wrapped her left arm around Paul's neck, pulling him closer, then around so that her back was against the wall, simultaneously lifting her right leg over Paul's hip. She relaxed her other arm so that Paul could pull back slightly to gain easier access to her groin with his right hand.

Her jeans dropped away further revealing a tightly-fitting red g-string. As Paul began to slowly explore downwards with his fingertips, she clamped the kiss harder, urging him on towards their joint goal. As he edged his fingers gently south, he encountered the top of the g-string, which was initially reluctant to allow an intrusion to the sanctuary it was protecting. A little gentle manipulation, however, soon persuaded it to yield and he began to slip his fingers inside.

As he gently massaged his fingers across her lower pelvis, he realised that he was not encountering any pubic hair. He had never previously been with a sexual partner who completely shaved that area. He had observed it on the occasional prostitute laid-out on a morgue slab, of course, but not up close and personal like this. It felt strange; this was all very different for him and it made him hesitate momentarily.

She sensed the change, unclamping the kiss and moving her head to the side, pulling Paul's neck closer as she brought her lips close to his left ear: "don't stop Paul, please … not now," she pleaded with a low whisper in his ear.

He continued to edge downwards, seeking the soft edges of her labia. She felt hard and slightly misshapen, but the few women he had previously known had never been this instantly compliant. His experience had always involved slow, painstaking foreplay, so he had nothing to compare the physical signals with - no yardstick to judge his senses against.

She tightened her grip on his penis and began to rub her thumb along the dorsal artery. His animal instincts took over in an instant and as she sensed this, her right leg moved outwards allowing him full access with his hand. As she did this his hand moved swiftly down between her legs to cup her and he extended his index finger towards the opening he expected to unveil itself.

Instead he found himself running his finger toward the end of something detached and unusual. At the same time, what was cupped in his hand began to move and detach.

'What the …?' he thought, 'it can't be!'

'Oh my God!!'

'Tubesteak!!!'

One-Ten

Paul opened his eyes as he jerked his head back in revulsion, only to realise that the expression on his companion's face had changed to something entirely evil. This was no longer the attractive female FBI Agent he had dinner with earlier; the resemblance was there, but this was something altogether different..

He tried to let go, but the visitor had moved like lightning to bring their right leg back down, clamping Paul's right hand between a pair of strong thighs. He had no choice but to hold on to what he realised was a semi-erect penis, somewhat larger than his own. He tried to break free, but not only was his right hand anchored, the stranger's left arm had his neck in a full lock. Their other hand clamped harder around Paul's penis, which began to ache and convulse: *'Oh no!'* he thought, *'I can't cum now, not like this!'*

His guest had also noticed the involuntary spasm and let go quickly: "oh no Paul, not yet," came a slightly lower, more sinister-sounding voice. "You have far more pleasures to endure tonight before your little Vesuvius erupts."

With that the clamping thighs were released and Paul's right hand immediately let go of the already fully-grown organ. *'My arm's free,'* Paul thought, and in an instant he moved to use it to land a punch on the imposter's jaw.

At least, his brain commanded his right arm to do so, but there was no response. He tried to pull away further, but he couldn't break the armlock around his neck; in fact he couldn't move at all. He realised that all that was stopping him from crumpling to the floor was the stranger's tight grip on his neck. His thoughts raced, repeating the same question over and over: *'what on earth is happening?'*

The unfamiliar face slipped away sufficiently to look straight at him with an evil, piercing grin. Paul tried to speak, but couldn't. Then as he stared at what still looked something like Kryczek, the imposter's right hand slowly ran through their luxuriant brunette hair, then yanked it swiftly downwards ripping away a wig to reveal a completely hairless head. The right hand returned to remove the gradated glasses, then the stranger deliberately licked their right thumb and slowly moved it across each eyebrow, removing the make-up that had masked the lack of any hair there.

Paul was contemplating an entirely different face, hairless, slightly effeminate thanks to high cheekbones, but no longer a female face. Leering back at him were a pair of familiar eyes - piercing, sinister and cold. He was no longer looking at the face of a stranger, it was one he had seen before in a photograph - the airport CCTV photograph. He was looking straight at Sean Shepherd.

"Yes Paul," the pretender said triumphantly, "not the beautiful woman you thought you had brought home tonight, but something else entirely. And so that you understand what is happening, while you were distracted by one big prick, you didn't notice the other, much smaller, one in the back of your neck that rendered you mine, to do with as I wish. But don't worry, you don't have a lot of time left to you this evening, so in that precious time, let me entertain you with ecstasies that you would scarcely have imagined. Although your body will not be able to fully register them, your mind will - I can assure you of that."

In that instant, Paul realised that the hunter had fallen prey to the monster he was pursuing. He had brought her, no ... him, to this apartment; with them both locked within his own safe haven, there was nothing to save him from suffering the same fate as Hilary Nicholson, Marjorie Rolles and Tom Cochrane.

He was going to die tonight, slowly, humiliatingly and, ultimately, publicly, and he was powerless to stop it.

One-Eleven

With the help of the sirens, Schneider's Crown Victoria had devoured the distance between I-235 and Thirteenth Street. It had brought several cars screeching to a halt as the car emerged from the bottom of the ramp around the edge of the School baseball field, Schneider barely lifting the throttle as it did so.

McKinley was on his cell and had managed to get a patch through to the Sherriff's Office, where the dispatcher was relaying his instructions to Deputy Fitzhugh, who had already been told to abandon his observation of the Intrepid: "he's to obtain access to the building, but wait in the foyer to let us in when we arrive, then assist us from there."

"Roger that Detective McKinley, please hold."

There was a silence on the phone as the dispatcher flicked over to talk to Fitzhugh. The volume of the siren momentarily crescendoed into the car interior as it echoed through the concrete tunnel when they flashed under the railway bridge at Santa Fe.

The dispatcher came back on the phone: "Forty-Nine will expedite access asap Detective. Will confirm when he has secured it."

"Our e-t-a is four minutes; are the paramedics on their way?"

"Roger - paramedics have e-t-a six minutes. Support units also en route, e-t-a eight minutes."

"Tell support units to hold back until our arrival and please keep this line open until we do."

"Roger that Detective, you have our highest priority."

The lights at Broadway were green allowing Schneider to blast straight through. *'Let's hope the same happens at Waco,'* Schneider thought, *'then we're almost clear from there.'*

McKinley lowered the phone momentarily from his ear and said quietly to Schneider: "that's everyone we can call-in, I think."

"There's one more, Chris. You can put your hands together and send a prayer for us all - mine are a bit full right now."

One-Twelve

Paul didn't know whether it was his senses slowing, or the speed that Shepherd was moving around, but suddenly there was nobody in his field of view. He realised that his body was falling backwards, to be stopped just before it hit the floor. He then became aware that he was moving, no being dragged, backwards out of his lounge and down the narrow corridor towards the bedrooms.

As the ceiling moved past him, he imagined himself being laid-out on his bed in a similar manner to the previous victims he was investigating. He expected to be taken first into the shower to be shaved and prepared, but as they entered the master bedroom, he was turned to the left into the room itself, not to the right into the en-suite. Before he could register anything else, he was on his back on his own bed, looking up at the ceiling.

'*I really need to paint that ceiling,*' he thought, bizarrely in the circumstances, as if trying to hang-on to something mundane and ordinary in the highly-abnormal situation he found himself in. He lay there for what seemed like minutes before he was drawn backwards again and his back rose against the headboard. He had been moved to a semi-seated position, looking straight down his body. The next thing that he realised was that he was entirely naked; he also still had an erection.

He could see everything in front of him within his arc of vision. He tried to move his head, but nothing happened. So he tried to move his eyes, but again nothing happened. He suddenly realised that his earlier intuition, that whatever was about to transpire he had little power to stop, had been entirely optimistic. He was totally powerless. '*When the time comes, I'll close my eyes,*' he thought, attempting to practice the action; his eyelids disobeyed the instruction from his brain as resolutely as most of the rest of his body. He then felt intense despair, something that Paul Kleberson had never experienced before in his entire life.

'*Is this really it?*' he thought. '*It must be, because the poison is in my system and we know that it kills eventually, even if this monster doesn't have a reason for hastening the inevitable, as happened with Cochrane. There is nobody to help me - hell, nobody even knows I was meeting Kryczek, let alone coming back here with her ... him. And what if they did? Last time I spoke to Mary, her lab still didn't know what the full make-up of the poison was, so they sure as hell won't know how to make any antidote. So this really is it. I can't fight, I can't even plead, not that this ...*' his thoughts paused momentarily '*... whatever he's really called, would grant any pardon. He hasn't done before - he's not going to now.*'

'Lord!' He rummaged his thoughts for a silent prayer, then realised he hadn't even been to a church service since his wedding; he began to lose his temper with a Deity he rarely even acknowledged. Not in his usual controlled manner, but irrationally, something he had not allowed himself to do since he was at school: '*surely you can't let me go just like this - this simply; this terribly. My kids!*

What will happen to my kids with no father in their lives! No Lord! Not now, not yet, please!'

Paul realised it was more of a demand than a plea, but that was how he felt: 'right here, right now, this is the real me. I haven't lived quietly, why should I die quietly?' At that same point, he sensed hot breath near his left ear.

"So Paul, are you ready?" The voice was still familiar, but more sinister than before: "it's so much better with the drug, you'll understand that as we go. It maintains the vital functions, deadens the unnecessary parts of the body, unnecessary for this purpose anyway, just accentuates the pleasure nodes. The eyes can see, the ears can hear, the skin can feel. It's just the muscles that don't obey ... except for those in the pleasure zones, that is."

The voice faded away, resuming after what seemed like minutes: "damned clever those Amazonian tribes. With none of the external distractions of the outside world to enhance their experiences, they developed ways to artificially enhance their erogenous zones by disabling the neural pathways to some parts of the body and rechanneling the power saved to the ones they wanted to enhance. A bit like an I.T. guy turning-off unnecessary programmes on a computer to make the other ones run faster. Being a female-dominated society, they concentrated on ways to enhance the male's experience and hence his fertility. Any mate prepared to make the ultimate sacrifice would be granted pleasure beyond belief; in return they would guarantee a fertilised ovary. The male would offer himself for the continuance of his tribe in a final act not dissimilar to that of the Praying Mantis. But what a way to go, as you will soon experience."

Once again, the voice faded for a few seconds before resuming: "of course, genetics began to play nasty tricks on them and by making the male sperm so powerful, it created more female offspring than males. So they eventually realised that they needed to develop the means to reverse it all after the event, to save their studs for encores. But don't get your hopes up, darling Paul; I wasn't interested in those reversal drugs. I have no need for saving my studs, after all there are plenty enough men in our society to last someone like me a million lifetimes. So now, let me show you something truly unique, a sight that few have seen in this life, and even fewer have survived."

The hot breath receded and the room seemed silent again. Paul tried once more to move; any part of his body would do, but still nothing seemed to want to co-operate. All he could do was stare down his body towards the wall opposite his bed, in front of which stood the chest of drawers with his family pictures on it. Looking back at him were his mother and father, his ex-wife and his two children. He felt overwhelmingly ashamed that they were apparently to witness his final degradation.

Again, the silence seemed endless: 'what am I about to see? What has this fiend planned for me that I haven't already seen the results of? I know the M.O, that's no real surprise. So, do I get the full sexual treatment or the slow lingering end? Well come on damn you, let's get it over with!'

At that thought, right on cue, his assailant appeared at the foot of the bed. If the drugs allowed Paul's eyes to widen, then they did: *'is this really Shepherd? Maybe it's an accomplice,'* he thought. *'No, there can't be more than one of these. This has to be a hallucination brought on by the drugs. This cannot exist, not for real.'*

At the foot of the bed stood a totally naked form. It was completely hairless from head to toe, no head hair, no pubic hair, just bare flesh. The facial expression was pure evil, like a mad clown with no make-up; eyes wide and staring - mouth wide and sneering. The chest area was female, with two perfectly formed and pert breasts; not huge, but genuine, of that there could be no doubt. Beneath them, a trim waist - very trim. In fact as the bodyline moved down to the hips it formed almost the perfect hourglass. The skin was flawlessly toned, the belly flat with a hint of a six-pack, as though at that point this body was morphing to a different form.

Because there, below the belly-button, was an enormous erect penis rising from the groin and pointing directly towards Paul. As penises went, this was a thing of beauty; a sight to behold. As perfectly male as the breasts were perfectly female. And, as if to accentuate it all, this person, no this thing, was stood legs akimbo, hands on hips in the classic 'look at me' pose. Not that he was any expert in such areas, but Paul knew that any teenager approaching puberty, if offered such an endowment, would willingly do anything to achieve it. Beneath this member unveiled before him there appeared to be no gonads, no scrotum.

The legs were muscular and again perfectly toned. There wasn't an ounce of unwanted flesh on this body, neither were there any signs of surgical scars. Whatever it was, this was no assembled Frankenstein monster.

"So whaddya think Paul?" The voice was arrogant and assured: "I told you to expect something unexpected didn't I? Oh, but hey, you don't get the full effect head-on, so take a look from this angle."

At that, the figure turned to its left until it was at right-angles to the bed. The penis was revealed in its full glory, arcing gently upwards from the groin to almost a foot in length and almost two inches in girth. It extended incongruously beyond the breast line, clearly also unsupported and looking textbook shape in profile. The back arched inwardly from the shoulder blades into the waist, from where the buttocks flowed outwards in a perfect flat curve around to the undersides, which appeared almost rock-hard - no sag, no cellulite to be seen.

However, from this angle the body looked almost like a composite of two distinct halves - female down to the hips, male below. It somehow reminded Paul of Egypt, of the peculiarly androgynous nature of the Pharaoh Akhenaton, whose images had been virtually wiped from history by his successors. That and the statues of Min, the God of fertility, that he had encountered during his study trip in his second year at Cambridge - the ones that had caused such amusement to the teenage Californian girls that had joined their tour party at Thebes.

"I know what you're thinking Paul," came the sinister voice again, "you're thinking, this can't be Shepherd, this must be an accomplice. Of course, you're right ... and you're wrong. It is not the Kryczek that so nearly unravelled the mystery that you see before you, but it is definitely the Kryczek that you first met a couple of days ago; the one that has recently occupied the space on this mortal coil vacated by that very clever young lady. Then you're thinking, this is just a monster, like the Minotaur or Centaurs of ancient legend; half human, half beast, or in this case, half male, half female. So am I a true hermaphrodite, the progeny of Hermes and Aphrodite? Would you like to see?"

It removed its hands from its hips, then motioned across its body as it spoke: "the top half is clearly female." The hands moved slowly across the breasts, cupping and caressing them before moving downwards: "the bottom half apparently male." The right hand dropped below the penis and gripped it, completing a loose fist around the base, as the girth was too big for thumb and forefinger to touch above it. The loose fist moved seductively along the shaft towards the tip, producing an involuntary stiffening twitch as it did.

Paul felt his own erection also stiffening, which immediately sent a chill of revulsion through his mind: *'God Almighty, don't let me leave this world thinking I'm gay!'* he thought, angrily.

"I can see that interested you Paul. I was wondering whether you might enjoy our little couplings later - some do, some don't. It matters little to me in the circumstances, but it seems that you may, more than you might have thought." The smile grew more evil at the thought.

Paul felt total revulsion: *'if I could move, I would kill you with my bare hands,'* he thought, *'you ... freak!'*

"Yes I know Paul; you want to kill me don't you? If you don't, yet, believe me you will as we go further in our little dalliances together. But don't fear, the more you hate me, the greater the sensations you will experience - the drugs will see to that."

He leaned forward as if to accentuate the next part: "so what exactly am I? Actually Paul, my birth certificate says that I'm male, Sean Shepherd at your service." He bowed extravagantly: "so I guess you will just have to accept that you have been flirting and frolicking with another man this evening. Legally Paul, and we know how much the law means to you, you're going to die gay." Shepherd laughed as he said it: "but first, we have that unanswered question, and as I would not want you to go to your maker with any doubts in your mind, let me show you something that I don't show many people. You may feel very privileged at this."

Shepherd turned with his back to the bed. Once again the almost perfection of the lines and toning of the body produced an unusual feeling within Paul, as if his brain could no longer process the merged male and female forms against its memory banks.

Shepherd spread his legs, then leaned slowly forward as if to touch his toes. The muscle control was of the quality of a gymnast in slowing his movements.

As he bent forward, he thrust his buttocks up and back until the groin area was fully visible. There between the neat circle of his anus and the long shaft of his penis was a perfectly formed vagina - small, but complete.

The voice began again: "can you see Paul, the lower half is not entirely male. Behold, a true hermaphrodite! So you were not seeking in vain with your fingertips earlier on; had you not allowed your revulsion to rule your actions, you would have found it. But you couldn't have used it I'm afraid, it is not physically possible, unfortunately. Only two have ever tried and they both died gruesomely, I can assure you! Who knows, I may even have let you touch it, that's how much I like you; not many have and only one has survived to tell the tale, not that he would. Not even dearest Hilary - oh but you didn't know did you? We were old friends, in fact she was probably the only true friend I ever had, other than Aunt Suze. Only two ladies in the whole wide world aware of all there is to know about me, yet they never told anyone."

Shepherd pulled himself back to the standing position, then part turned to look over his shoulder at the paralysed form on the bed: "Hilary always had the curiosity, she even talked about it - what would it be like to be loved by someone who was half what she desired, half what she loathed. That's what made her death so easy to arrange, because all I had to do was offer what she was intrigued by and the rest was routine. I didn't have to overpower her, or shock her, so the end was peaceful, almost beautiful."

"But why? That's what you are asking in that fevered mind of yours; oh, I can tell even though your face can't reveal it. It's in the eyes Paul, I can always see it in the eyes - the terror, the anguish, the anger, even the love. It's not love I see in yours, not even anger. No, with you it's hate - total unrelenting bestial hate. If you were able, you would tear me apart with your bare hands, wouldn't you? Oh I'm sorry, of course you can't answer can you, not even give a gesture; not a nod of the head or a flip of the finger. I understand how frustrated that must make you feel. But I digress and we, sorry, you in particular, do not have the time for digression I'm afraid. So back to the question - why did the wonderful Hilary have to die? Because nobody survives their death warrant when it is signed by my masters and handed to me. Not their enemies, not friends of their enemies, not enemies of their friends; not even enemies of theirs who were friends of mine."

Shepherd turned fully towards the bed: "none can survive and neither will you - not now anyway. But you could have, you know - you are, in fact, Plan B for tonight. Ah the eyes show puzzlement at the conundrum, but yes you were given the chance to live, but you chose not to. You were supposed to run off into the sunset, never to return; not of your own free will that is. And you nearly made it, you so nearly escaped your fate. But you were curious, as usual; you cannot abide loose ends, so you had to tie them up. Not for your paymasters, the citizens of Wichita, not for your colleagues, not even for your friends; but for you alone, the great Paul Kleberson. Oh, and you are great, no doubt one of the best I've come up against, not that that is too difficult, most homicide detectives couldn't locate their own noses without a mug shot. But Kryczek wasn't one of those, and neither were you, which is why I pay homage to her and may also to you in time."

One-Thirteen

Paul was still trying to deal with all of this. The suspension was pre-planned? Surely not? But he did run; so if he was meant to, who was tonight's appointment really with - who was Plan A? Shepherd was not about to allow him to work it out.

Having allowed just enough time for the thought processes to reach this level, he resumed the monologue: "ah yes Paul, you have two questions - who was Plan A? and what triggered the change of plan? Let's deal with the latter first - it was the phone call, the one to Kryczek. That was always left open for you since the morning at Marjoree's apartment, of course. It was my checkstop for you - as long as you didn't make it, you would not be as good as I thought you might be and therefore no danger. But you did and, by doing so, you sealed your fate - and reprieved someone else in this building."

'In this building!' Paul's mind reacted quickly: *'Plan A was in this building? Who on earth ...?'*

Shepherd interrupted the flow again, right on cue: "ah, now that has confused you, so let me put your mind at rest. You see, I never really made my mind up on that one. You would be surprised how many people in this building had an opinion of you, even though you barely communicated with any of them. Mostly negative opinions as well, it has to be said; you didn't know, but why would you when they were discussed regularly behind your back.

I had a shortlist; the janitor - he's not the best is he? Not particularly efficient, as you would tell him most-every time you did speak to him. Then there was Mrs Warnock next door - thought your lovemaking with Carla was a bit too noisy for her comfort. And old man Sampson - you upset him just this afternoon didn't you? And not for the first time, was it? So, one of them would have chosen the wrong time to tell you their thoughts, and in the mental state you were in - it was obviously just too much and you snapped. Of course, that would not have been discovered until after you flew out tomorrow; you would have had to run away, nothing else you could do in the circumstances. But you came back instead, so now you're 'The Plan.' And I have to say, by far the best choice for what we are about to do - from my point of view that is."

Paul was trying to digest that the alternative to this reality would have been a living hell in exchange for someone innocent having to suffer a similarly degrading death. There would have been no escape from 'The Plan', whichever one had been selected, and events were moving faster than his rapidly-addling mind could process them. Then Shepherd knelt onto the foot of the bed, with his legs either side of Paul's.

"So Paul, shall we begin our first dance. What will it be? What would you prefer? We have a number of choices, oral, anal, dextrous. But first, let's make sure we have taken our precautions shall we? Can't be too careful these days." As if from nowhere, Shepherd produced a condom, holding the teat gently between thumb and forefinger: "as you are unable to put this on, perhaps you will allow me." Shepherd put the teat of the condom gently between his teeth: "now, where shall we put this, hmm?"

He edged forward, putting his forearms either side of Paul's hips. *'No!'* Paul thought, losing all his will in an instant, *'don't put anything in that mouth - please Lord, take me now, before that can be done.'*

Paul's groin pulsed and ached with pleasure, while his mind screamed with repulsion. The two contra-feelings mixed into some form of combined ecstasy and he felt every unsedated nerve-ending in his body tingle with dread. If his eyes could close, he would have shut them tight; instead his fate was to involuntarily watch whatever his tormentor chose to do. Shepherd focussed his gaze into Paul's eyes, grinning fiendishly, as if he was looking directly into his soul: "just a little sampler, I think, we can't have you climaxing too soon, as I doubt you have enough time left in this world to manage a second time."

If thoughts could be transmitted into effects, then what Paul was thinking would have killed Shepherd stone dead on the spot. He had never felt such hate for anybody; in fact he realised that he had never felt real hate before. He finally understood the true meaning of the word, forced to lay there, powerless to resist the sensual torture he was undergoing. Paul felt his heart pounding within his chest and the stress was both unbearable and exciting all at the same time.

Shepherd hesitated, then took the condom from his mouth: "I can see the fear in your eyes Paul, so you're not quite ready for oral are you? We can't let you accelerate your fate, so we'll just have to try something a bit more relaxing for you." With that, Paul's limited vision registered that he was rolling over on his side, away from the door. The window came into view as the movement stopped momentarily, then it continued until he was face down. He stared at the pillow for a few seconds, then his head was on the move again, back towards the window.

"There, that's a bit better." That awful, condescending voice rasped through his ears again: "you can look at the outside world while I take my pleasure with you. Don't worry if the window begins to move, back and forth, back and forth; that's all part of the pleasure - for me that is."

'Dear God', Paul thought, *'can this get any worse?'* He couldn't feel his body moving, but the angle of his head changed slightly, as if his legs were being lifted off the bed. He then felt a pulse in his own penis again: *'why can I not feel anything of my body, but I can feel that?'* Paul thought.

"Ooh!", Shepherd exclaimed, "judging by that, you're anticipating me at play aren't you Paul? My latest developments to the drug must work better with you than they did with Cochrane, because he didn't react like that. Then again, he had been a bum-bandit for years, not like you my little anal-virgin."

Paul tried to blank-out the pictures his mind was creating from the input information that his brain was being permitted to receive, but it was of little use. He was about to be sodomised and by some being that had no right to exist, not by all the normal rules of creation. Then he heard a large crash from behind him, from beyond the bedroom door. Suddenly, his body dropped onto the bed; whatever had been supporting him was gone.

'What the...?' he thought, trying to piece together what could possibly be happening. Then there was something that seemed like shouting; yes it was someone shouting - a commotion and it was getting closer. Suddenly a shape appeared in his line of sight, silhouetted against the window; it was naked. It was holding something - a knife!

"In here!" he heard a shout; it was a male voice. Then there was a loud explosion, then another. No, not explosions, gunshots. The shape by the window lurched upwards, then collapsed backwards towards him. It hit the side of the bed, then rolled over. The head landed right in front of his eyes. It was bald, its eyes were staring straight at him and blood was oozing from a hole in the temple.

It was Shepherd - and it was dead.

One-Fourteen

"Oh my God! Paul!"

This was another male voice, behind him and it sounded familiar: "is he alive? Set him over on his back." The voice sounded panicked: "Medic! Where's that fucking MEDIC?"

Paul was aware again that his head was moving, upwards ... away from those evil, staring, dead eyes. Then he was looking at the ceiling. A familiar face appeared between it and him: it was Sam Schneider.

"Paul!" he shouted, "can you hear me?"

'YES!' Paul's thoughts screamed, but no sound would come from his mouth. His head was moved slightly away from Sam.

"There's a pulse." It was a different voice, one he did not recognise.

"Can he see me?" Sam asked, clearly anguished.

"Don't know," came the other voice, "he seems paralysed and the pulse is weaker than I would expect."

"So, fucking do something about it then!" Sam shouted.

Paul could hear clasps snapping, plus crunching and rustling. Another face appeared on the other side of the bed. It was Chris McKinley and he looked shocked: "throw a sheet or something over him, for Christ's sake!" he said angrily.

Then Paul felt his head lifting up. It lifted and lifted, moving past the figures around the bed towards the ceiling. He felt like he was floating: *'they must be moving me'* he thought, but as he neared the ceiling he rolled over until he was looking straight down at the bed. He was able to see the whole room. There were two paramedics to the left of the bed, working feverishly with syringes and lines, plus some electrical equipment. Sam was standing at the foot of the bed, Chris to the right. Next to Chris was a crumpled corpse that had been bleeding onto the carpet. A large pool of blood had spread out from its head.

There was a shocked-looking uniformed policeman in the doorway, staring wide-eyed and ashen-faced at the scene. Paul recognised the uniform as that of a Sherriff's Deputy: *'I hope he's not a rookie, I don't want him throwing up on my carpet,'* he thought.

There was a man on the bed spread-eagled, being worked-on by the medics. His eyes stared up at Paul; it was like looking in the mirror. *'Just a minute,'* he thought *'that looks like ... me down there.'* But instead of panicking, he felt calm.

The whole picture began to fade; the colours began to tone away towards monochrome and the edges of the picture lightened to white. It was like looking at one of those old sepia vignette photos from Grandpa Walt's albums.

"We're losing him!" one of the medics said, sounding anguished by the thought. The other medic grabbed some pads with wires coming out of them, the other ends of which were attached to a box on the bed.

"Charging," he called. There was a whistling noise, then he placed the pads on the man's chest: "CLEAR!"

There was a dull thud and Paul felt himself jolt back against the ceiling. Immediately all of the colour returned to the room, like a TV screen powering-up: "OK, we have a trace again," said the first medic.

"Come on Paul, hang in there old pal," Sam pleaded from the foot of the bed.

Paul saw the Deputy turn from the doorway into the hall, putting his hand over his mouth as he left the room: *'he is going to throw-up on my carpet,'* Paul thought. The picture began to fade again and he was aware of a light coming from his right; it was growing brighter. He turned to look at it and became aware of a woman's voice faintly calling him from beyond it. He looked back into the room. Most of the edges of the picture were clear white. Just the bed, the figure on it, the two medics and Sam were visible - the rest had gone.

The voice to his right grew more defined, the soft tones audibly recognisable. It was his grandmother calling him for tea. He was back in Tucson, in Grandpa Walt's workshop: "come on you boys, it's getting cold," the voice called.

Below him, he faintly heard another voice: "charging," it said. He looked down, but all that was visible was the head and torso of the figure on the bed: "CLEAR!"

Another dull thud. The picture enlarged again, but only to just beyond the bounds of the bed; it remained monochrome. He became aware that Sam was on his knees at the foot of the bed, his head resting on his hands. He looked like he might be praying, but then Paul realised that he was sobbing gently. The light to his right brightened and the voice came again, this time much louder: "come on boys, don't vex me now."

"Coming Grandma," he called, then turned to the light and began moving away from the room. The room faded to white behind him and he was enveloped by a warm comfortable feeling. There was no pain, no commotion, no monsters; just the smell of beeswax and a room full of old tools.

The first medic turned to Sam Schneider: "we've lost him," he said in a matter of fact way, as if it happened every day, which of course it did in his job. He had never met the body on the bed previously, so he had no idea what connections and emotions were in play. He realised just in time that something was headed his way, something heavy. He ducked as a medical bag rushed past his head before hitting the wall behind him, its contents exploding from the opening to scatter all over the floor on that side of the room.

It had come from Chris McKinley's side of the room. Chris just stood there silently, glowering at the lifeless body on the bed. It was the only way he could express himself in that brief instant. The medic looked at him, then nodded and bent down to pick up the various packs and boxes, putting them back into the fallen bag.

a pilgrim returned

One-Fifteen

Paul found himself standing in the doorway to the kitchen of his grandparents' house in Tucson. His grandma had laid-out three places on the table for lunch, but she was the only other figure in the kitchen. He looked behind him, towards where the door led from the workshop, expecting to see Grandpa Walt walking through it just behind him, as usual, but all he saw was a white corridor with a faint image of a room at the far end. He looked back at the kitchen, where his Grandma was taking her apron off as she stood by the table looking at him. She looked younger than he remembered, her face was smooth and more relaxed; she looked beautiful like his mother when she was younger.

"So?" she asked quizzically, "are we eating today?"

"I'm not sure I'm hungry, Grandma," Paul replied slightly unsure of himself. He felt confused and, if truth were known, a little scared.

"Well you've sure been doing enough to work up an appetite," she replied, matter-of-fact as ever.

"Yes Grandma, I have, but the job's not finished."

She looked at him momentarily with a reassuring expression, then smiled that kind, sweet smile he could never forget: "would you prefer to go finish it before you have your lunch?"

He thought for a few seconds before replying: "yes ... if that's OK with you Grandma."

"Of course it is Paul, you know I can never argue with my favourite grandson. Go on then, away with you, finish the job then I'll make you a sandwich."

He wanted to rush forward and hug her close, but somehow he knew he couldn't. The door was open, but there was something stopping him from passing through. He smiled and gave a weak wave with his left hand; his Grandma's expression remained unchanged.

He turned away and looked down the corridor; it was growing shorter and the room at the far end was rushing towards him. Suddenly, he felt himself fall and there was a huge jolt through his body as he landed heavily on his back on top of his bed. He was back in his bedroom looking up at the ceiling. He felt puzzled: "have I just fallen from up there?" he thought.

"I've got a pulse!" Another voice he didn't recognise was speaking with some excitement.

Paul tried to regather his thoughts of what he had seen in his bedroom before his visit to Tucson. He remembered that Sam was there, with two paramedics: 'The voice must be one of those,' he thought.

"Thank God!" That was Sam's voice.

"The adrenaline must have done the trick," the unknown voice continued.

Then another unknown voice joined-in, the first one he had heard when he was previously in the room: "the trace is still very weak though. We can get him to St Damian's in five minutes, but we need to go now, we can't afford to have him arrest again."

'Arrest?' Paul thought, *'what does he mean by arrest?'* He was getting his thoughts back together. He tried to move his head to see where the voice was coming from, but nothing happened; he was still looking straight up at the ceiling.

Then a face appeared in front of his eyes - it was Sam. He looked long and hard into Paul's eyes as though he wasn't sure that Paul was there: "can you can hear me buddy?" Sam asked slowly.

'Yes I can!' Paul's thoughts screamed back, but he quickly realised no sound can have been coming from his mouth.

Sam continued: "don't worry buddy, we've got the medics here, they've got it all under control."

'Got what under control?' Paul tried to answer: *'hellfire, what's the matter with me?'*

"The trace is unstable," the first voice was talking again, "best let him relax."

"OK," Sam nodded in acknowledgement, then looked hard at his friend again: "don't worry Paul, we're putting you on a gurney then we will get you to the ambulance. Just hang in there buddy."

'I'm hanging, for Christ's sake, I'm hanging!'

Sam's head disappeared from view to be replaced by Chris McKinley's.

'What's this a police convention in my bedroom? Paul thought. *No, it must be a party, because you look like shit Chris; too much Liffey Water huh?'*

McKinley spoke: "don't worry Paul, we got the bastard."

'What?' Paul thought, *'got which bastard? There's so many of 'em.'*

McKinley's head disappeared and Paul felt himself lifting once more: *'oh no, not the ceiling again,'* he thought. But this time he only rose a foot or so, then moved sideways before lowering gently onto another flat surface just below the level of the bed.

The ceiling began to transit above him as he moved head first out of the bedroom and through the lounge towards the front door. As he emerged into the corridor, he saw the young Deputy looking at him, still ashen faced.

'I hope you threw-up out here,' Paul thought.

One-Sixteen

The trip in the ambulance had taken minutes. Once into E.R, Paul was quickly assessed then whisked through into intensive care; within hours his condition had been reported as stable but critical. The following day, the satellite trucks that had decamped from City Hall to occupy half of the car parking space at St

Damian's Hospital were relaying that Lieutenant Paul Kleberson was lying in a coma there, having been the intended fourth victim of the serial killer known as Vitruvio, but this time it had been the killer who had died in the attempt.

The media were not to be denied. They had lost some of their own to a monster in the line of duty, so how else could they salute the avenger of those acts, the brave public servant who had put himself in harm's way to save the innocent from a fiend, but had come so tragically close to losing his own life in the process - and might yet do so. That was the storyline they had latched onto and no facts were going to get in the way of it. Paul was their current national hero, and his life story was about to be sieved remorselessly for tidbits to satiate the 24-hour news networks. Yet so little did they know of the man himself, that they could never have realised that he would likely wish to arrest the lot of them for making him such a public property.

They had already picked-up on the lineage that Paul had discovered whilst studying at Cambridge fifteen years earlier. Through his grandmother Liz, he had a direct ancestry line back to the Howland family from the village of Fenstanton, just a few miles from Cambridge. One of the Harlands had sailed on the Mayflower as a servant to the first governor of the Plymouth colony, John Carver. This meant that it was quite possible that his ancestor had been sponsored by the Cromwell family, whose country home of the time had become Paul's old school.

It also meant that he was distantly related to a number of US Presidents, including Roosevelt, Nixon and Ford, as well as one of Britain's national heroes, Winston Churchill. At the time that he made the discovery, another distant relative, George Bush Senior, had recently been elected as US President. Even as a cynical student, he could not help but be excited by the whole scenario.

He rang his grandmother in Florida, at huge expense, to ask her if she knew: "oh yes," she replied, "I seem to remember my Grandmother mentioning something about it. Now tell me dear, what would you like me to get you for Christmas?"

As a Democrat, Paul's father Walter had been quite excited by the tie to Roosevelt, but mention of the shamed Republican Nixon brought a particularly curt end to that conversation. Later, after George W Bush was elected courtesy of some Floridian hanging chads, Paul himself would regret ever having mentioned his illustrious connections. Colleagues often teased him with the question: "hey Paul, you're related to the President, so you'll know what the Dubya stands for won't ya?"

"I don't know," Paul would reply, "I don't care, and I don't want to hear what you think it might be either!" He was not a fan.

Pictures had also been broadcast of his family arriving from California to be at his bedside. One plucky junior reporter attempted to ambush General Kleberson on his way in, thrusting an intrusive microphone under Walter's nose as he and Margie walked-up to the hospital door. The reporter was greeted with a steely stare that silently said: 'if I had my gun, I would shoot you right where you stand, in front of the world; and the world would probably give me a medal for it.' Nobody came within yards of Paul's parents when they left hours later.

After that visit, Walter drove straight out to McConnell to meet his successor, General Pete Vrabel, his old squadron adjutant from years back. General Vrabel was a career officer who had never married, so found himself in this, his first posting in charge of a station, rattling around in the base commander's house that had been the Klebersons' home for many years. Immediately he became aware of the situation with Paul, his first action was to contact Walter and make the house available to him and the rest of the family. To give them privacy he moved himself into guest quarters at the officer's mess, a location he much preferred in any case.

Vrabel's next move was to make arrangements for the very best Air Force medical specialists to travel to McConnell and set-up their equipment in a reserved section of the base hospital. Although the neurologists at St Damian's had a superb reputation, their immediate prognosis was that Paul would probably never be able to come out of the coma. If he did then he would probably have suffered serious brain damage.

That was not the sort of prediction that military men care to hear. While there was hope, General Kleberson had no intention of giving up on his boy, and if General Kleberson was not about to surrender, then neither were his comrades in arms. As soon as the medics at St Damian's were satisfied that Paul could be safely moved, then he would be heading for the base.

Some three and a half days after Paul was rushed into St Damian's, the Mayor and Chief Stanton called their first major press conference on the case since Shepherd's death. It was arranged at City Hall and, as expected, it pulled all of the star anchors and most of the satellite trucks out of the hospital car park, like hyenas stalking a pack of lions for the leftovers of the hunt. The junior reporters left behind on coma-watch completely swallowed the hospital administrator's explanation for the need to clear the intensive care area to provide the quiet conditions needed to allow Lieutenant Kleberson to be moved to a room better equipped for his long-term care.

Realising that this probably meant that there was little hope of a miracle recovery, they all agreed to go for coffee and work-out a shift-pattern between them for what appeared to be turning into a long assignment. They were entirely unaware of the specially-prepared USAF Truck that had pulled into one of the loading bays at the back of the hospital.

With the efficiency only a military operation can command, within minutes Paul Kleberson had been disconnected from the fixed apparatus in his private room and reconnected to the mobile apparatus that would ensure he made the eight-mile journey equally-well monitored. His bed was then wheeled to a service elevator which took him down to the loading dock. Before the reporters had been able to sprinkle the chocolate on their cappuccinos, the truck was already heading, undetected, south on I-135.

As the Mayor walked-on to the dais at City Hall with the Chief, the truck was passing through one of the rear gates at the base. Paul would not only have the best care that a military budget could provide, he would be receiving it half a mile beyond a fence that would also protect his family from the prying lenses of the media. More importantly, the gates in that fence were manned by armed guards. If the Wichita Police Department and the FBI were unable to absolutely guarantee to protect his son from attack by another hired hand, then General Walter T Kleberson, USAF (Retired), sure as hell could.

But that wasn't the only favour Walter had been able to call-in. Within hours of his hearing of the reason for his son's paralysed state, a representative of the US Army's Medical Research Center at Fort Detrick in Maryland was receiving a sample of the latest version of Vitruvio's poison compound, taken from the syringe recovered from Paul's flat by Sam Schneider; this time, not only had Shepherd not got away, neither had his equipment. A team of scientists in Maryland began working around the clock to analyse and remanufacture the compound. Once they were able to do so, there was an even chance they could produce some form of serum from it. Whether it would be effective was another matter, of course, but if there was even the slightest chance of producing it, then Walter was not going to allow that chance to go begging.

It wasn't only Paul's story that was attracting interest. Shepherd's death had allowed the Chief to conveniently draw a line under the case; there was not going to be a trial, hence there was no major urgency in releasing information. Because of this, and the sensational nature of the small number of facts that had inevitably leaked to such a voracious band of top-ranking hacks, the press conference was being beamed live around the world. This had become a political event, and Mayor Ramsey was not about to miss the opportunity to bolster his ratings ahead of the forthcoming election, or the future possibility of standing for higher office. This was the time to get his face on every front page and TV screen that he could.

Stanton was also the ace politician, so when the baton was passed to him to talk about his officer, he delivered what could almost have been a eulogy, had its subject not still been alive. Nevertheless, what he said was not only to the tone of the moment, but respectfully accurate to what Paul would have appreciated. There was not a mention of their professional enmity and at the end, had Lieutenant Kleberson been seated alongside Chief Stanton, he would probably have shaken his hand and invited him for a beer.

Such was the clever usage of this aspect of the subject matter, by two men considered relative amateurs by their battle-honed interrogators, that the first segment effectively limited the amount of time available to discuss specifics about Shepherd. This helped the city officials to comply with Schneider's insistence that only the minimum was released while there was still an ongoing Federal investigation in progress. Therefore, the officially-released information centred around the facts that had already been sniffed-out by the media pack, turning the Q&A afterwards into almost a series of "yes" and "no" replies. This also suited Stanton's situation, because it deflected, for the short term at least, the press-pack's deeper analysis of the details surrounding his suspension of Kleberson during the afternoon preceding the events in the apartment, and the operation the Chief mounted that had pulled most of his department into another part of the city.

Also on the podium was the head of the Neurology Department at St Damian's, Doctor Alvin Sperring, who provided a similar analysis of Paul Kleberson's future as he had supplied to the family two days earlier, an event that had reduced Leanne to a sobbing heap in the corner of the small conference room where he had taken her and Walter to break the news. Walter had tried to comfort her, but soon surrendered to the obvious need to exchange roles with Margie, who had been keeping the two grandchildrens' spirits up in the private waiting area beyond.

Doctor Sperring made no reference whatsoever to the removal operation that he knew would be in progress while he was speaking. In the medical analysis, the assembled media had all it needed for the straplines in Friday night's news bulletins. The nature of Shepherd's physiology and modus-operandi were strangely of secondary importance for the time-being. This was a slow-burner and, in the absence of anything even moderately-sensational in a more attractive area of the country, the anchors knew they were going to be able to milk their expense accounts out here in one of the more modern and refined Midwest cities, possibly for the next week at the very least.

By the time the more investigative of the journalists were beginning to ask penetrative questions, the producers from the main networks were already fidgety about the amount of time that had elapsed since the last ad-break. So it became quite easy for Mayor Ramsey to call a halt, knowing that the weekend would create even more space for him to strategise the next such event, scheduled for the following Monday. Once the halt had been called, the three men quickly left the dais, aware that it would not be long before cellphones were transmitting the news from St Damian's.

Within minutes, that news was filtering through and it didn't take long for the main anchors to recognise that they had been duped; some were abandoning their intended copy almost as quickly as they had composed it. Huddles quickly formed to plan the weekend's coverage, which ostensibly would be from a road verge alongside miles of barbed-wire-topped fencing, whilst attempting to focus long-lenses across half a mile of draughty airfield. This was most definitely not the original shared plan - of satellite trucks ensconced back in the hospital car park, just a couple of blocks from their hotels in Old Town, from which the star anchors could be ferried within minutes to do a five-minute link, tops, then back to the cocktail bar.

The mood became noticeably more ugly and it was obvious that the local officials were going to be given anything but a comfortable ride on the following Monday.

A Pilgrim Returned

One-Seventeen

Sam Schneider's first call, as the ambulance left Paul's apartment building, had been to Pete Baker in LA. As usual, Baker was still at his desk and, for the very first time he could remember, Sam had not been in a position to curse the two-hour time difference that normally worked against him. Sam had then telephoned Leanne Kleberson in Yuba City, just as the ambulance had arrived at St Damian's; much to Sam's relief, Walter had picked-up the phone. The family were preparing for the communal evening dinner with their guests, so Leanne and Margie were busy in the kitchen. Sam had limited the content of the call to the absolute minimum necessary to convey the seriousness of Paul's condition and the fact that transportation was already being arranged to take the family to Wichita that evening.

Within an hour, Walter's logistical skills had placed his paying guests in local restaurants for dinner, and rebilleted them with neighbours for their overnight stays. By the time the FBI Suburban from the Sacramento Agency pulled-up outside of 'The Commune', Walter, Margie, Leanne and the two children were waiting packed and ready on the verandah. A call to an old friend at Beale had secured clearance for the NetJets Lear, arranged by Pete Baker, to land there to collect them for the three-hour flight to McConnell, where two WPD Cruisers were waiting to escort another FBI Suburban at high speed across town to the hospital. Four and a half hours after Paul Kleberson was admitted into intensive care, his family were at his bedside.

Paul was completely unaware of any of this, because within half an hour of his being hooked-up to the monitoring equipment, Doctor Sperring had directed that he be put into an induced comatose state - not an unusual decision in the case of a patient having suffered two cardiac arrests, as Paul had experienced at the apartment. By mid-morning Tuesday, the doctors were able to confirm that this action had brought-about complete stability in his condition and that Paul was out of immediate danger. The medical team would wait before making any further changes, until they were in a position to decide that the time had arrived to bring Paul out of the induced state and gauge what damage may have been caused. However, they were not going to consider that for at least a week, during which time they would conduct a myriad of tests and observations on the patient, whilst they also awaited proper analysis of the, as yet not fully-known, chemical cocktail that had been used on him. Because of this, the situation at the hospital turned essentially into a round-the-clock vigil that would last until at least the weekend.

General Vrabel's kind provision of accommodation at the base gave the family the opportunity to arrange a rota so that there was always at least one of them at the bedside, whilst the others were able to take periods of downtime and sleep in relatively-familiar surroundings. Added to the family names on the rota were

Sam Schneider and Chris McKinley, who took short periods away from the casework whenever they could to support whichever family member was on duty. The investigation was not concluded by the death of the real Vitruvio; there were still too many loose ends to tie-up before the full story could be known of why their friend and colleague was on a hospital bed in a state of suspended animation.

During his stints alone in the room, while the other participants were taking a necessary comfort or refreshment break, Sam took to talking about the case to Paul's motionless frame; he found this not only cathartic, but by talking out loud about the facts, they sometimes made a little more sense. Because he was acutely aware that the family themselves were not yet asking for any specifics, meaning they were still in a form of shock and denial, he made sure that he stopped any analysis before any of them walked back into the room.

On Wednesday evening, the number of participants increased by two when Annie and RP arrived at St Damian's. The news had arrived with Annie via a telephone call from her father on the Tuesday evening; he had received the information from Gloria Kendrick. Annie contacted RP, who immediately dropped everything to be at her side when they caught the first available flight out of Heathrow on Wednesday morning, which got them into Chicago in time for an internal flight that landed at Mid-Continent at five-thirty p.m. that evening.

As well as being one of Paul's oldest and closest friends, RP also had another, more grim, reason for needing to be in Wichita; if the worst were to happen, he was the primary executor for Paul's estate. As he and Annie boarded the plane that morning, all they knew was that Paul was on a life-support system, they did not even know if they would get to his bedside in time. It was a nervous flight, neither feeling able to hold any length of conversation, probably for the first time since they had met all those years earlier on that shared Cambridge landing.

Paul had made the appointment in his will, the one he had prepared four years earlier when he had learned that he had become a reasonably wealthy man, courtesy of a shareholding in RP's computer games company that he didn't even know that he possessed. Paul had been extremely successful in identifying potential retailers for RP whilst at Cambridge and had earned a reasonable amount of money from the task that he had used to ease his time there after his family had returned home. What he didn't know was exactly how his work had built the bedrock from which RP rapidly developed the company into a major player in this new niche industry.

Maybe it was his father's Democrat genes, maybe the socialist reaction to Mrs Thatcher by all university students in the UK at the time, or maybe it was just the extreme practicality of Grandpa Walt, but Paul was extremely anti-anything related to acquiring wealth that wasn't earned by sheer hard work and toil. This made him very cynical around the subject of high-finance, so whenever RP had offered Paul the opportunity to have a small stake in the company, Paul politely, but firmly, turned him down.

So RP had decided that he would use the money that Paul declined to accept in the form of bonuses, to purchase shares for him that were registered in Paul's name, but administered by RP himself. Dividends and scrip issues were all taken in shares, so when the company was floated, this little nest egg had a dollar value well into seven-figures. The rules of the flotation dictated that shareholders of the old private company had to elect whether to exchange their existing shares for the equivalent in the new plc, or to sell them. RP's position on the board of the new plc meant that he could not take that decision on Paul's behalf, so he dropped-off into Wichita whilst on one of his whistle-stop round-the-world trips, to confess his 'sin' to Paul over dinner at his hotel.

Paul had been speechless, one of the very few occasions that RP could remember the phenomena. But he had not been rendered thus by anger, rather with the embarrassment as to how generous his friend had been, despite the stridently left-wing views he had expressed to RP, quite forcibly on many occasions. At that time, with over five years as a cop behind him, he had long-since realised that the world at large was not the benevolent society that Cambridge had heralded, but a dog-eat-dog place where you rarely got second chances. This was a second-chance, financially, one he had not felt he had earned, but would take graciously. Homicide cops could never expect to retire on the sort of numbers RP was placing before him.

He decided that he would take RP's advice and sell the shares, but by the end of dinner his democratic tendencies had got the better of him, coupled with the stark realisation that a comfortable cop is a careless cop. Paul hadn't told RP at the time, but essentially he had to make up his mind there and then whether he wanted to stay in his job, or leave it for something less demanding on his wits. Paul's marriage was already in trouble, mainly because of the job, and his first thoughts were that, maybe, this could rescue it. Instead, he recognised quite quickly that he was still a cop at heart and that, instead of retiring to a comfortable self-financed academic lifestyle, he would use a little of the cash to take the family on a long-overdue holiday, pay-off the mortgage and use much of the rest to provide a trust fund for his children, primarily to provide them with the educational opportunities that he had lucked-into by dint of his father's profession.

He had asked RP to help him do this and his friend was not only able, because the money would have no further connection with his company, but more than willing to do so. Over the next few years, RP had administered the trust extremely well, making very shrewd investments to the effect that, when it matured for them, Paul's children would be substantially rich themselves as the main beneficiaries.

The will was very specific and as both RP and Annie were named as executors, all of Paul's requests would be followed to the letter. If the worst were to happen, these would include an eventual interment in the Cambridgeshire countryside, the place that Paul knew, despite having stumbled into it by chance, to be his true home. It was also where he had already made provision to retire should his life be allowed to run its natural course. The headstone was to have a simple inscription: 'Paul W Kleberson - A Pilgrim Returned.'

As a realist, however, Paul recognised that a policeman, particularly one in his line, was statistically less-likely to even reach retirement age, so it was necessary that provisions were made for all eventualities. Hence the stipulation that there were to be two services should he die in the line of duty, one in Wichita that would allow for his wider family, friends and colleagues to pay their respects locally, followed by a second smaller ceremony for nearer family and close friends that were prepared to make the transatlantic journey for the interment. He could never have anticipated, however, that should his demise occur within the next few days, it would be widely-reported in the national media due to what would be, in that case, his final investigation, the final act of which had been played-out in his small apartment.

It was probably best that he, and his family, would never know that contingency plans were already being drawn-up for that public service to be a full-blown city and department ceremony, with dignitaries from State, City and County being put on alert to be ready to join the Mayor in receiving the coffin with full honour guard at New Spring Church, the only church in the city able to take the intended size of attendance. However, such were the aspirations of the political opportunists at City Hall that none had yet made any direct or personal enquiry as to their employee's precise condition, relying instead upon the constant news ticker running beneath the latest update from KNKW. To them, at that precise time, celebrating a life had a higher priority than saving it.

Annie and RP ensconced themselves at the Hyatt Regency, just a few minutes' drive from the hospital. Walter had immediately offered them guest rooms at the base, but they both felt it would be better for them to be physically closer to Paul. They also wanted answers when the time was right for their questions to be asked, and they were more likely to get those if they were somewhat more detached from the family environment.

On Thursday afternoon, they were sharing a shift that would conclude at five p.m, when they were to be relieved by Carla Courtney. Paul was, by then, apparently out of any immediate danger of deterioration, but still in a condition where there was no obvious indication of whether ultimate recovery was even a possibility, let alone what form that recovery might take. Walter had called a summit meeting at the base commander's house for six p.m. that evening for the family and close friends to discuss the options; RP and Annie were invited, along with Sam Schneider.

Sam had initially declined, preferring to take a shift with Paul to enable the others to all meet. When this had been mentioned at his office, Carla immediately insisted that she be allowed to take his place, having only been able to view Paul through the small window in the door when she had visited the hospital two days earlier. She had not wanted to impose on the family at the time, but they all gratefully accepted her offer, thus releasing Sam to be at McConnell that evening.

Around a quarter-to-five, RP slipped out of Paul's room to make a business call, leaving Annie to await Carla's arrival. He was sitting in the foyer making that call when he noticed a smartly-dressed figure who entered the reception area and walked over to the desk. Despite the unfamiliar tidiness of his appearance, he recognised Roland's slight features immediately. RP ended the call, then strode over to stand behind the figure, who was waiting patiently for the receptionist to conclude a telephone call she was handling.

"May I be of assistance Sir?" RP asked gently.

The figure turned slowly before the face displayed the immediate pleasure of encountering an old friend. Ten years as a civil servant had changed Roland radically, but the warm and easy smile had survived the experience unscathed. The two men embraced for several seconds. When they separated, RP kept his hands on Roland's shoulders and asked: "look at you! Where on earth have you been old friend?"

Before Roland could answer, there was a shout from behind them: "Roland!"

As RP let go and turned to see where the voice was coming from, Annie flashed past him and threw her arms around Roland, almost knocking him over in the process. Roland's expression was one of total shock, as Annie gripped him tightly with both arms around his neck; she apparently didn't want to let go. As Roland began to recover some stability, Annie released her grip slightly, but only enough to allow her to plant a long kiss on his left cheek. Roland looked at RP almost appealing for help, but RP just smiled back reassuringly.

"Er ... hi Annie," Roland started to speak almost apologetically, as he placed his hands either side of Annie's waist as a first tentative move to release himself from his apparent embarrassment.

After a few more moments, Annie finally let go and lent back, grabbing Roland's upper arms as if forcing him to maintain his hold on her waist: "Roland, oh my goodness, where on earth have you been all these years?"

"I was just asking the same question," RP added, "although somewhat less dramatically, it has to be said."

The three all laughed, almost in joint relief, a momentary lifting of the weight that had been placed on them by their other old friend's predicament. Annie continued: "and how did you get to be here? Oh sorry, that sounds awful - of course you should be here."

Roland very gently pushed Annie away slightly and let go of her waist. She received the signal and let go of his shoulders, then stepped back slightly to look at him, but this view just made her lunge forward again and give him one extra short hug: "oh, it's so good to see you!" she added, then let go and stepped back positively.

"So?" RP asked again, gesturing with both hands as if awaiting an answer.

"I was in New York on business," Roland began. "It was all over the networks, I just couldn't believe it. Sat there all alone in my hotel room, it just hit me like an Exocet. When they said about him being stable in intensive care, I just dropped everything and flew over. I couldn't not come."

Tears tried to break from the corner of Annie's eyes as she responded melancholically: "of course not - but why did it have to take something like this to get us back together?"

Roland stepped forward, only this time it was he that put both hands on Annie's shoulders: "that's enough of that. I haven't flown over here to make anybody more unhappy than they are already." He turned to RP: "can I see him?"

"He won't know you are there," RP responded, "you do understand?"

"Absolutely, but I still want to be with him, if I can."

"Of course. There is someone with him, Carla, a close friend."

"Oh! In that case, I can come back …"

"NO!" both Annie and RP responded simultaneously. RP continued: "no, it's not a problem, she will love to meet you I'm sure. We've all been taking shifts to be with him, his Mum and Dad, Leanne and the kids …"

"Leanne and the kids?"

"Oh, of course, sorry, you wouldn't know. Leanne is Paul's wife; they have two children, Matt and Lucy."

"I thought you mentioned a Carla?"

"Paul and Leanne divorced a few years back. We obviously need to bring you up to speed, but I'm sorry, we have to go; Walter, Paul's Dad, you remember?" Roland nodded. "Well, he's called a summit for six p.m."

"Sounds like some things don't change," Roland observed.

"Quite. Look, why don't you come with us, the family won't mind I'm sure."

"No … No," Roland held his hands up showing his immediate reluctance, "please, just let me see Paul, then I'll get out of your hair."

"You will not!" Annie exclaimed: "oh, sorry - get out of our hair I mean. That is absolutely NOT going to happen, not now we've found you again Roland."

"Where are you staying?" RP asked.

"I'm booked into the Broadview, it was the closest I could find to the hospital."

"We're at the Hyatt Regency, it's not that far away either." RP attracted the attention of the receptionist and asked if she could place the two hotels for them; from her response they established they were less than a block apart.

"Why don't we have dinner tonight," RP suggested, "do you have a car?"

"No, I've just used a taxi to get here from the airport."

"Then why don't we pick you up from your hotel between eight and eight-thirty, then we can find somewhere quiet to eat and chat."

"Sounds fine to me, I'll wait in the foyer for you."

"Good," Annie responded, "now, let me take you through and introduce you to Carla."

One-Eighteen

RP and Annie were the last to arrive at the base commander's house; Sam Schneider had arrived just minutes before. Walter began the introductions, forgetting that all three had met years earlier at Paul and Leanne's wedding. He also introduced Doctor Sperring to them, who they had not met previously. Finally, the newly-arrived Doctor Jerry Manderling from the 59th Medical Wing's Department of Neurology based at Wilford Hall in Texas was presented to everybody. The formalities over, Walter advised that the children were being shown around the base by Pete Vrabel, so there would be about three quarters of an hour in which to discuss specific details before their return was expected.

Walter commenced by outlining the plans for moving Paul to the base hospital the following day, to which Sam added that he had persuaded the Mayor to use their press conference as a diversionary tactic. Of those present, only Walter, Sam and the two doctors knew anything about this change. All three ladies were immediately concerned about the dangers of moving Paul, but were quickly reassured by the two medical men, Doctor Sperring explaining specifically how this would be achieved with regard to Paul's medical care during the transfer, concluding by advising the limitations he felt with regard to the ability of his department at St Damian's Hospital to give Paul the type of highly-specialist care he would need to give him the best chance not only of surviving the poisons he had been attacked with, but also with making any form of full recovery.

Doctor Manderling then explained that he was in close contact with the scientists at Fort Detrick, and that they were dealing with compounds they had little, or no, experience of in the past. He continued: "however, from what they have been able to deduce thus far, the compound used on Lieutenant Kleberson was similar, but not identical, to the one previously analysed by the FBI from earlier victims at other locations. Because of that, it would be unsafe to assume that any of the originally-identified components were still valid. So, although a derivative of Curare had been identified as the main component, and elements of that plant would provide the same symptoms as those displayed by some of the victims, it is not just a case of simply treating the effects of that plant. It may not be Curare, it may be something similar that they have not previously encountered; without that information they are unable to ascertain exactly how the compound has been working within Paul's body, so they are not confidant that they can produce an effective serum to reverse the effects. Remember, in all previous cases the medical examiner was simply attempting to identify a cause of death; the nuances of that were of little importance to the victim. In this case, those nuances are imperative in keeping the victim alive."

Everybody in the room felt a shudder pass through them as they recognised, once more, the fragility of Paul's circumstances. The doctor continued: "therefore, because of the unique nature of this compound, in parallel to the Fort

Detrick analysis, we have called-in assistance from tropical medicine research specialists, who have been scrutinising the effects of the elements of the compound, as opposed to their identities. From that they are developing predictions based upon known plants and chemicals that cause similar results. From their initial projections, they believe that there is a distinct possibility that, having survived the first couple of hours after the poison was administered, Paul's body has effectively warded off the worst physical effects."

At that point, RP interrupted: "then are you saying, Doctor, that you believe Paul will live?"

"What I'm saying is that the way we think that the compound is intended to work is on two levels. Firstly, the body's muscles are physically paralysed, but only for a relatively short-term, after which the body's natural functions diminish the effects - putting it simply, the paralysis wears-off. The problem there is that the heart is also a muscle, and if there are any inherent weaknesses in that organ, then the physical paralysis element will shut it down. It would appear that, firstly, Lieutenant Kleberson is a very fit man with a strong heart and, secondly, the timing of the administration of adrenaline directly to the heart by the paramedics may have given it that extra assistance that it needed to resist the temporary paralysis."

"The other victims did not have the benefit of that," Sam added, "so they were on their own."

"Yes," Doctor Manderling continued, "but some of those could also have survived as well, but for the other elements of the compound that provide the secondary effects that spelt their death warrants. Those include chemicals that may affect the neural pathways to the muscles and organs, opening or closing those pathways selectively, regulating what is allowed to work and what is not. There are also traces of components that may possess hallucinogenic properties. It's too early for us to know exactly how all this interacts with the body, but the first investigations are based on an action where, once the effect of the initial paralysing agent wears off, the neural signals then take over. What this could mean is that, effectively, the muscles are no longer physically paralysed, but the brain thinks they are. That is the area where Lieutenant Kleberson appears unique - something inherent to him corrected the neural channel to his heart."

Leanne jumped to her feet: "he didn't want to die!" she called out, as much in relief as recognition, then tears began to roll down her cheeks. Annie was seated on the same sofa, nearest to her. She also jumped-up and enveloped Leanne in her arms; as she looked across Leanne's shoulder towards RP, he could see that Annie was also crying.

"I'm sorry," Doctor Manderling interrupted his flow, "perhaps I should stop. I appreciate this is very distressing for you all."

"No, please," Leanne insisted, recovering her composure, "that's the first really positive thing I've heard since Monday night. Does that mean that you have a plan? Can we have Paul back?"

"It would be wrong of me, at this time Mrs Kleberson, to raise any hopes - we need to take this one step at a time. We are at the edges of our understanding with these types of compounds and this theory could be wrong. As we have no intention of experimenting when we have a life at stake, perhaps I should, instead, outline what we would like to do, with the permission of all in this room of course."

"That's why we're here Doc," Walter interrupted, then turned to Leanne. She was drying her eyes with a tissue passed to her by her mother-in-law, who was also bravely fighting back tears of her own: "are you OK to carry-on?"

"I am, thank you." Annie helped Leanne back to the sofa so that, once again, the doctor had the floor.

"We need to complete the transfer from St Damian's tomorrow, then we will just observe for twenty-four hours. If we see no obvious deterioration, we then intend to carefully bring him out of the induced comatose state to check that he will be able to support himself. Once we are satisfied that he can, we can commence a process of cleaning the Lieutenant's bloodstream by exchange transfusion, in order to remove any remnants of the compound from his body. All of the time we are doing this, we will be monitoring his neurological patterns; once the first phase is completed, we shall have sufficient data to assess the best way forward from there."

"I assume that you want our yes or no on that," Walter asked, "is that correct Doc?"

"It is Sir."

"Then I'm sorry ladies, but I have to ask a couple of potentially-distressing questions before I can make my decision, is that alright?" All three nodded. Walter continued: "what happens if Paul appears to be failing to support himself?"

"Then we put him straight back on life-support and wait a while longer."

"So this isn't a once-and-only chance?"

"Not at all, sometimes the body is ready, sometimes it isn't; we wouldn't try again, however, without consulting you as we are now."

"OK, then let's hope that isn't necessary. Assuming it isn't and he can survive unaided, how soon will you know the extent of any damage he has sustained?"

"Fairly quickly; we know what we are looking for. We will keep you apprised at all stages."

"In that case, I think we should go ahead, but I am not the final arbiter here; what are the views of the rest of you?"

Leanne responded immediately: "we have to do this. I don't want to just sit there looking at what may or may not still be my husband, it's too cruel to everybody, Paul especially. If he doesn't want to leave us, then we must give him the opportunity to come back."

Nobody in the room missed the Freudian slip in Leanne's plea and by that the decision was made. Walter observed the unanimous nodding of heads and concluded the meeting: "OK Doc, I think that means you have our blessing. Now, I don't know about the rest of you, but I sure need a drink!"

Both doctors declined the offer, excusing themselves by the need to complete the arrangements for the following day. They received the thanks of everybody individually and left. Leanne and Margie also declined the offer, but announced they would be making coffee, and tea of course for their transatlantic visitors if they preferred, which they did. Sam also went for coffee, he was still officially on duty; Walter went for the fridge.

One-Nineteen

For a few moments, RP, Annie and Sam were left alone in the lounge. Annie took this, her first, opportunity to tackle Sam; she quickly précised the facts that she had gleaned since her arrival in Wichita, sparse facts to which she wanted greater detail added. But before Sam could respond, the door to the lounge burst open and two very excited children tumbled through it, followed by a uniformed officer; almost simultaneously Walter reappeared at the door to the kitchen.

"Granpa, Granpa!" Lucy exclaimed as she ran across the lounge towards him, "we've been flying an aeroplane!"

"Have you?" he replied, Wow! You had better tell me all about it, but not until we've thanked General Vrabel for putting the entire metropolis of Wichita in danger by letting you!"

Matt turned to the General and very politely shook his hand: "thank you Sir, that was so cool!"

"You're welcome young man. I remember doing the same for your Father when he was about your age."

"Thank you Gen-er-al," Lucy chimed in, "do you think I can fly planes again when I grow-up?"

"I don't see why not Lucy, we have lots of women pilots in the Air Force nowadays."

She turned back to Walter: "oh Granpa, won't that be fun!"

"It will Lucy." He looked across at his host: "thanks Pete - now, would you like one of your beers?"

"Don't mind if I do," Vrabel responded.

"Now then kids, let's get those coats off and see if Granma has got something for you to drink." With that, the mini-tornado completed its passage through the lounge and out into the kitchen. General Vrabel acknowledged Sam, having also been in on the arrangements for moving Paul; Sam introduced him to Annie and RP, then Vrabel also exited the room towards the fridge.

"It doesn't look like we will get much opportunity to talk here tonight," Sam observed, "how about dinner?"

A Pilgrim Returned

"That's a great idea, actually Sam," RP replied, "we've just met another visitor who would also be interested to hear what you have to say."

"Really," Sam responded, "and who might that be?"

"Roland Asquith - he's the fourth member of our house at Cambridge. He arrived at the hospital just as we were leaving, so we invited him for dinner tonight. Is that OK with you?"

"Of course, Paul mentioned him a lot - he's an artist right?"

"He was. Truth is we had lost touch for a few years, so we need to do some catching-up as well."

"In that case, I can leave dinner until another night if you prefer."

"No Sam," Annie replied very firmly, "we all need to know and we have no idea how long Roland is staying. Tonight is fine."

Margie returned to the room with a large tray of tea and coffee, which she set-down on the low central table. She was followed by the others, who all settled into the various chairs and sofas; Matt and Lucy cosied-up to their mother as they sipped the home-made lemonade provided by Margie.

"Now," said Margie addressing the visitors, "Leanne and I have started preparing dinner, so we do hope you will all stay and join us - we have plenty. I'm sure the Hyatt must have a great chef, but I bet he doesn't do real home-cookin'."

"We would love to," Annie responded, "but just before we left the hospital, another friend of ours arrived to visit Paul - Roland Asquith - and we have already made arrangements to meet him for dinner in town."

"Roland's here?" Leanne asked, "Paul always used to talk about him; he said they had lost touch. I know Paul tried to find him when we were over there, but couldn't."

"Who's Roland Mummy?" Lucy was looking at her mother, quizzically.

"He's an old friend of Daddy's when they were at school, like Auntie Annie."

Lucy looked across at Annie: "Auntie Annie, Mummy says you were at school with Daddy, is that right?"

Annie and the others felt almost relieved at the intrusion: "yes Lucy," she replied, "but not school, university."

"In England?" Lucy asked as she jumped from the sofa and ran across to where Annie was sitting.

"That's right, at Cambridge - RP was there as well."

"What was he like at u-ni-ver-si-ty?" Lucy asked, struggling slightly with the unfamiliar long word, "was he a rascal like me?"

They all laughed as Annie replied: "a little bit, but not as much as RP here."

Lucy turned to RP: "are you still a rascal, Mister RP?" she asked.

RP felt amused for what he thought must be the first time in days: "not as much as I would like to be any more." He beamed at the child, seeing Paul's glinting eyes looking back at him, with that same quizzical look that his friend often showed when he hadn't quite grasped the meaning of a phrase.

"Why not? Daddy says its good being a rascal sometimes."

"I'm sure he does," RP replied, feeling a strange pull on his emotions, for here in front of him was one of the people whose financial future Paul had personally entrusted to him.

"Tell me about Daddy being a rascal," Lucy insisted.

RP glanced across at the rest of the family and realised that they were all looking at him. Leanne's face again showed an expression of such sadness that it was almost appealing for some outlet from these awful few days. Matt, Paul's eldest, just seemed lost, the elation of the brief interlude in the hangar having quickly evaporated at the mention of his father again. At eleven, he was old enough to feel the pain, but too young to understand what it was, or why he felt it. He was also in need of some solace; after all, he had only seen his father two or three times a year since the separation and RP knew they were still very close.

Piled on top of all of that were RP's own feelings, subsumed in the maelstrom of the past few days. He needed a lift as well: "now let me think," he said, putting his hands on the child's shoulders, then pulling her up onto his knee, "ah yes, there was this time when we all went on a stag night in Cambridge. Do you know what a stag night is?"

Lucy shook her head, so RP continued: "it's when we men all go out together to celebrate when one of us is about to be married."

"Oooh, a party!" Lucy said excitedly.

"That's right, a party. But this party does not have a home, it's a travelling party that goes from one house to another."

"That sounds like fun! Do they have lots of balloons and ice cream and cakes at each one?"

"Not exactly," he replied grimacing slightly at the family without Lucy seeing, as if to acknowledge that he might need some help at some point should Lucy's innocence place him in a corner: "but we do have some drinks at each one."

"What, lemonade and cola?"

"Well, something and cola, yes." A smile emerged across each face, as if to reassure him that he was doing fine and to carry-on with the welcome interlude.

"Do you go to lots of houses, Mister RP?"

"Oh yes, in fact the night I'm talking about we were trying to go to every public house in Cambridge as I remember."

"So you had lots of something and cola?"

"We did, Lucy, but that's what a stag night's all about really."

"Mummy doesn't let me have lots of cola, because when I have lots and lots and lots of cola, I'm sick. Does lots of something and cola make Daddy sick?"

"Sometimes Lucy, yes it does."

"But why doesn't his Mummy stop him from having lots and lots of something and cola?"

"Because, Lucy, Mummies aren't allowed on stag nights."

"That's right Lucy," Margie joined-in, "only men can go on stag nights."

"Oh." Lucy stopped as if deeply in thought, then continued: "my Mummy let's me go to my friends' parties on my own sometimes, but she always tells me to be careful not to drink lots of cola."

"And do you do as Mummy tells you, Lucy?"

"Oh yes! Only naughty rascals don't do as their Mummies tell them. So does Daddy's Mummy tell him not to drink lots of something and cola?"

RP smiled across at Margie: "probably Lucy, yes."

Lucy looked across at her Grandma, who smiled and nodded in confirmation. Then Lucy turned back to RP: "but he is still sick?"

"Not every time, but sometimes, yes he is."

"Then Daddy is a naughty rascal isn't he?"

The entire room erupted into laughter. RP nodded knowingly and gave Lucy a big hug. The laughter was like a relief valve, which began a round of further recollections, each taking it in turn to relate an amusing anecdote from Paul's life that generally raised the whole spirit of the gathering.

They all suddenly realised how time had rapidly passed by. RP and Annie got up and apologised for having to rush away. Sam also announced that he had to return to the office and, while the others were momentarily taking their leave, he took Leanne to one side and spoke to her: "Leanne, I will be going over some aspects of Paul's case with his friends. They are full of unanswered questions, like the rest of us, so I really can't let them go back with those half-answered. I am having dinner with them tonight, question is - do you feel up to joining us?"

"In all honesty Sam," she replied, "I don't think I'm ready for that level of detail yet and I certainly don't want to leave the kids alone. They are being very brave little souls and, although they won't say so, at the moment they really need me around all of the time. It's been another long day, so if it's alright with you, I'll have dinner here with the family."

"I thought that might be what you would prefer, but I had to ask."

"Sure thing Sam, you're a good friend and I know you will help me make some sense of it when I'm good and ready, sometime in the future when you have some resolution to your own unanswered questions. There must be so many of those."

"There sure are Leanne." He took her in his arms and hugged her.

She gave him a peck on the cheek, then released herself before she broke down. She turned to the kids with a forced smile and asked: "so guys, who's for dinner?" Smiles lit their faces and they leapt across the room to her side. She concluded: "now say goodnight to Auntie Annie and tell her we'll see her tomorrow."

"Bye Auntie Annie," they chorused. "Bye Mister RP," added Lucy, "thank you for telling me about stag nights?"

RP smiled "You're welcome Lucy."

One-Twenty

Sam led the way back to Wichita and to the Broadview, where Roland had been waiting in the foyer for a few minutes; Annie dashed-in to collect Roland, apologising for their lateness, before whisking him out to the car to complete the journey. Sam had already continued on to the Hyatt, where they had decided to eat, mainly because it did not seem to be accommodating any media staff. This had been due to it hosting two large back-to-back conventions when the original story broke, which meant that it had been fully-booked when the media circus hit town, commandeering virtually the entire accommodation around Old Town instead. The newsmen were not unhappy, as it meant that some of the liveliest bars in the city were within a drunken stagger of their rooms.

It was a fairly lengthy walk through the Hyatt itself from the car park to the bar. When the three arrived there, Sam was awaiting them and, after introductions, he advised that he had booked a table in a booth at the back of the restaurant which would be ready in about half an hour, and that dinner would be on him. There were a few businessmen on the stools at the bar and one or two couples at tables, but as it was Thursday night, the bar was otherwise quiet. They ordered drinks and moved to a table overlooking the river terrace; shortly afterwards the waiter arrived with a tray carrying beers for Sam and RP, a Martini for Annie and a mineral water for Roland.

They had barely settled when Annie began the questions: "so this, I don't know, monster, was what - a hit-man? God! I suppose that we can't even use gender can we? What then - a he, a she or an it?"

"He was registered at birth as male and christened Sean Norman Shepherd," Sam began. "Biologically, he was all three. Shepherd was a true hermaphrodite, or intersex as some scientists prefer to call them. He possessed the reproductive organs of both sexes. However, the chemical and hormonal imbalances in the body, along with certain physical difficulties, essentially made him incapable of being wholly either. For example, the autopsy confirmed that the vagina was too small to allow him to copulate with a normal male, although had he been able to, he possessed a fully functioning womb and fallopian tubes that could have allowed him to become pregnant. As a consequence, he did menstruate occasionally. On the other side, his penis was fully-functioning in terms of his attaining and maintaining an erection, at least sufficient to allow him to penetrate another person. But he could not ejaculate, as he did not possess functioning gonads, hence could not create either sperm of carrier fluid. So he could copulate as a man, but not impregnate a woman. Having spoken to several scientists, I personally believe this was nature's way of preventing him from impregnating himself."

"So technically, he was a she?" Annie asked, still somewhat perplexed.

"In reproductive terms, I suppose yes. He ... she also had full breasts that could lactate in the case of pregnancy, so yes I guess we should call him a her."

"And she died as a woman," RP interrupted, "Kryczek wasn't it?"

"An FBI Agent!" Annie added, "how on earth did it ... I'm sorry I just can't view it any other way, how did it manage to conceal all that additional equipment for all those years. Good grief, don't you people have regular medicals or something?"

"Yes Annie, we do, but Shepherd was only masquerading as Kryczek for a short time, during which the real Kryczek was officially on extended leave from the Bureau. Nevertheless, this has sent shockwaves through the organisation and there are internal enquiries going on as we speak to establish how all of this occurred, the details of which I'm afraid I'm not allowed to discuss with you."

"Oh come now Mister Schneider," Roland intervened, "I accept your public candour whilst the enquiries are being conducted, but once complete they will be accessible by means of freedom of information legislation and I doubt the media will be slow in finding them and publishing the gory details. Even if you do manage to suppress it as far as the general public is concerned, I certainly will be able to access them via my position in MI6. So come along, we are not the tabloid press, we are not digging for a Pulitzer Prize, we are Paul's closest friends and we are not looking to do anything other than understand what happened to our friend.

"OK," said Sam, "but only on the understanding that none of this goes beyond the three of you - agreed?"

"Agreed," they all acknowledged.

Schneider began in fairly hushed tones. He did not want the details carrying too far beyond their table, least of all to any other table where there may have been other ears ready to hear them: "from what we have pieced together so far, Shepherd was always a loner. That probably developed from his being abandoned by his mother when he was six. Nobody knew who his father was, not even his mother, apparently - the mother was a user. She was a pretty-hopeless case, so when it was apparent that Shepherd was a true hermaphrodite and that it would involve expensive medical bills, she just disappeared."

"Disappeared?" queried Annie, "how does a mother just disappear?"

"They were attending a clinic where the decision was to be made about an operation to fix whichever sex the child was to become and she just walked-out of the building, leaving the child behind. The local police knew her well, but all their searches just came up negative. She simply vanished off the face of the earth. That's where Susan Ferguson came in, or Aunt Suze as she is known. She took the child in after the police contacted her, even though she was much older. She was Great Aunt Suze really, the child's grandmother's sister. She was already losing her sight, but she is a devout Mennonite Anabaptist, so she saw it as her Christian duty to look after an abandoned child of her own blood."

"So did she know what she was taking on?" asked RP.

"Oh yes. The doctors explained what they wanted to do, but she would have none of it. She decided that the physical defects were God's will and, much as her own disabilities, were to be lived with. As far as deciding the sex of the child, that was straightforward - he had a penis, therefore he was male. She would raise him as a boy and, with God's help, that is what he would become."

"Misguided faith," sighed Roland.

"Not really, more like exceptional faith that nature overtook. You see, everything was fine until puberty. Shepherd was a late developer, female-wise, so even he thought that he was just a normal boy during early teenage years. But he was a shy individual, although he was devoted to his guardian. When the breasts began to develop in the ninth grade, he became very insular, withdrawing from all social activity. The family doctor was aware of the situation and had a meeting with both Shepherd and Aunt Suze where he explained it to the boy, apparently advising both of them, once again, on a sex-change operation. But Aunt Suze was still adamant and Shepherd was never going to go against her. This was the period of his life which concluded with him winning a place at USC. Aunt Suze was so proud, as nobody in the family had ever gone to university. What she didn't know was that Shepherd had decided to use the distance from home to live a double life. He had made the application as a female, not a male. His doctor had provided a reference because he saw it as the first independent move towards the sex-change that he felt would provide the necessary grounding for Shepherd to live as normal a life as was possible. Aunt Suze would never have known, as she was by then virtually blind, so could not read the address labels on the envelopes. So Sean Norman Shepherd became Sian Norma Shepherd, preferring to use her second name, Norma, at university, but coming home as Sean. He had already learned to hide his female aspects with tailored undergarments and a clever choice of clothes, so when he came home the neighbours just saw Sean as the slightly-effeminate adult version of what they had known from a child. In fact, some have indicated that they knew the boy would turn out to be gay - it was 'in the eyes' one of them said."

"Perception becoming fact," RP observed.

Sam nodded and continued: "Norma would never have been able to hold-down any close relationship whilst at university, any physical interaction with a man would have blown her cover completely. So, she tended towards the lesbian and gay community, which is how Norma originally came into the periphery of the group containing Hilary Nicholson, Marjoree Rolles and Tom Cochrane. We know that Norma and Hilary eventually became friends, but with Hilary and Marjoree already in a strong relationship, there was no chance of any love triangle forming. Cochrane was gay anyway and had no interest in that direction, so Norma just became part of their little clique, all of which was perfect for Norma. 'She' could survive university with friends, but without relationship complications; 'he' could come home to Aunt Suze with no risk of being troubled in that environment either."

"So what went wrong?" Annie asked, puzzled: "it almost sounds like a perfect normality for someone with a dual identity to hide."

"From what we have pieced-together so far, it fell apart when Norma was attacked on campus in nineteen-ninety. Dressed as a woman she was physically attractive and that had consequences, particularly when one individual who obviously really fancied her was continually rejected. In order to put this individual off, Shepherd even faked a marriage to a US Army Pilot, arriving back at USC after winter break as Norma Schaeffer. She even changed her course to avoid any contact, but it didn't work; in fact it appears that her being married encouraged that individual to press his attentions even more. She was walking home late one evening when the individual approached her again. When she turned him down, he became violent, pulling her into bushes and attempting to rape her. Norma fought him off and it would appear that as she ran off she encountered Hilary who was walking home to her apartment nearby. Although at that time, they only knew each other by sight, it was Hilary who took her to the campus police and reported the incident, but charges were never pressed."

"Presumably because a physical examination would also have exposed him/her/whatever," observed Annie with a hint of resignation.

"Possibly, we don't know. We have to remember here that these were campus police, not the area of law enforcement in our country renowned as seeking out a heavy workload. What we do know is that her suspected attacker, who the campus authorities could not take action against because no charges were laid, suffered a fatal accident a few weeks later."

"Victim number one?" queried RP

"An accident according to the coroner, but now, of course, that verdict is called into question and the case may need to be re-opened, along with a few more 'accidents' that occurred over the following two years."

"What more victims?" asked Roland.

"Not all, but some - maybe. The rate of accidental deaths on campus dropped after they all left, but that could just be a statistical anomaly."

"So what then," asked Annie again, "did they all move on together?"

"Hilary and Marjoree did and, as we know, Cochrane followed a little later. Shepherd, as Schaeffer, went into the movie business, which meant that he could travel around as either persona, but come home to Aunt Suze always as a male. What we are beginning to piece-together is the distinct possibility that this dual-persona, plus the dual covers of Aunt Suze and Berger & Pastore Enterprises, allowed Shepherd to develop into a serial killer or hit man, most likely the latter. We don't know as yet what happened to initiate this activity, or when it started. Until we establish that we can only assume that there are victims out there that we know nothing about. He certainly had plenty of money, much more than the apparent career in assessing movie locations would bring-in; a lot of it came in large denominations from offshore accounts. We are still working on whether those offshore accounts were his, or those of his clients."

"But when did Shepherd the movie locator become Kryczek the FBI Agent?" asked Annie.

"Very recently, a few weeks at the most. The last positive contact from the real Kryczek was a telephone call to her family home in Minneapolis on March twenty-fourth, in which she told her mother she would be travelling around for a few weeks on a case, but hoped to get back to see her after it was done. They normally talked at least once a week, but she told her mother not to worry if she didn't call because the case was very complicated. Her mother was familiar with these occasional periods of silence, so was not alarmed in any way by there being no phone calls recently."

"So do you know where the real Kryczek is?" RP enquired.

"We don't. She almost certainly was murdered by Shepherd, but of course we can't ask him. She certainly wasn't killed in his usual way and displayed for us to find. Truth is, we may never find her."

"That poor woman!" Annie said in an anguished voice: "her mother - what must her mother be going through? Not only did she have no idea her daughter was missing, she doesn't know whether she's alive or dead; if she is dead she may never have a body to bury. In the meantime, her family name is all over the media tangled-up in this business." Tears were welling in Annie's eyes as she spoke; it was as if there were just too many tragedies to absorb at once.

"The Bureau will do everything we can for her Annie," Sam replied, "I can assure you of that."

Annie looked straight at Sam: "is there any way I can talk to her?"

"I'm not sure that would help either of you Annie."

"Maybe not," Annie's shoulders slumped. Noticing this RP put a comforting arm around her shoulder as she continued: "but even if, heaven forbid, we are to lose our dearest friend, there will be a reason, whatever adjective we may individually wish to apply to it - unnecessary, senseless, unwarranted, needless, I could give you dozens dependant on the mood I find myself in at any particular moment - but we will know the how and the why, however unfathomable they may be."

She looked again directly into Sam's eyes: "but Mrs Kryczek has none of that, Sam. She just has an empty space full of question marks. The FBI cannot guarantee to mend that, can they? And deep down you know that they are not going to keep trying forever, it's not practical in the grand scheme of things. So what happens to Mrs Kryczek when that decision is made? I'll tell you - she is just forgotten, another of life's unrecorded tragedies."

Annie straightened her back pulling herself out of the slump to demonstrate her resolve: "I'm not going to allow that Sam. I won't forget how her daughter's image was raped by this maniac, then misused to deceive my wonderful friend and lure him to what was to be his end. I intend for her to know how I feel and that there is someone out here connected to her by this tragedy who feels the same pain, who will be there for her whenever she needs them."

She fixed her eyes on Sam's so that he could not avoid her gaze: "I know you are a good man Sam, I know that, because you are Paul's dearest friend on this side of the pond. And I know that you are going to help me contact Mrs Kryczek - not today, maybe not next week, but sometime soon."

Sam said nothing; he didn't have to, because he knew that silent assent was the answer that Annie demanded - the answer that he was happy to give. At that point his cellphone rang. He looked at the screen and got up from the table: "sorry, I have to take this, I'll be back in a few minutes." He wandered outside onto the terrace with the phone pressed to his ear and disappeared from sight.

"Actually," Annie said, "I wouldn't mind just nipping up to my room to freshen-up, I've been in these clothes all day."

"Me too," RP added, "would you mind if we left you on your own again for a few minutes Roland."

"Of course not, you carry on. I promise not to grill Agent Schneider any further before you get back."

"You'd better not," RP replied as he got up, "MI6 eh? Well, well."

Roland drained his glass of the rest of the mineral water. He waited a few minutes, but when Schneider did not reappear, he pulled-out his pen and began to sketch on a napkin. It was a dark sketch, the type that he hadn't produced for years. Nothing much happened in the civil service to give him the dark thoughts of the nature he was thinking at that juncture.

The waiter came over to the table to clear the debris and asked Roland if there was anything else he could bring him; Roland declined explaining they were about to go in for dinner. The waiter glanced at the sketch and looked somewhat shocked. Roland noticed the reaction: "I'm an artist," he said with a smile, "and I'm visiting a friend who is in hospital - it's possibly terminal."

"I'm sorry to have intruded Sir," the waiter said, bowing his head slightly to avert his gaze from the sketch.

"Better out than in, eh?" Roland replied, with that disarming smile that he still possessed. The waiter forced an uncomfortable grin and withdrew.

Roland looked at the sketch. Even for him, it was rather shocking. He had never been able to quite figure-out where these images came from within his psyche, especially as they were so diametrically-opposed to the sunny personality that he displayed to the world so comfortably and consistently. Strangely, they never worried or scared him, like they had so many of his acquaintances over the years. He had tried to make a go of selling them when he left Cambridge, with some small degree of success in the first couple of years. The only problem was the type of clientele that they attracted - some of those people were really scary!

So he decided to let that career go and answered an advertisement for a curator at the Tate Gallery, a rather loose job title that covered all manner of tasks that would fall on the successful candidate's desk. His First in Art History, and his intense knowledge of modern artists, meant that he was at the top of the short list of names for interview; his sunny disposition at the board made it a futile journey for the rest of the applicants.

He had taken-up residence in an office on the second floor of the gallery building, overlooking the Thames on the opposite side of the river from the MI6 building, or 'Legoland' as his colleagues disparagingly termed it. That was the closest he had ever been to that shadowy organisation, as he knew Schneider would discover, should he ever bother to check-up. Roland's outburst earlier was just public-schoolboy bravado; nevertheless, it had had the desired effect.

Somewhat perversely, compared to his recollections of the past, Annie was the first to rejoin him: "you beat the boys to get ready as usual then?" he quipped sarcastically.

"You know me Roland," she replied, "never one for the endless performance in front of a mirror."

"You never needed it," he observed.

"Good job I know you're gay," she smiled, "otherwise I might think you were making a pass at me." They both laughed at the thought - it was just like stepping back in time to those halcyon days at St Peter's Terrace.

"Still the artist then?" Annie pointed at the sketch.

"Yes" Roland replied, "don't know where that came from. Haven't done anything like it for years."

"Better out than in," she observed. Roland smiled and nodded, folding the napkin and tucking it away in his inside pocket, together with the pen.

"So what's your story then Annie? What have you been up to all these years?"

She held out her left hand. On the ring finger was a sizeable solitaire diamond set in a platinum ring, in front of that a simple platinum band.

"Married then," he said, "who's the lucky guy?"

"I suppose you should address me as Mrs RP." She watched for his reaction.

"You're kidding me? he responded. "Really? I always had you and Paul down as the potential item. Somehow RP was just going to be married to the money."

"Very perceptive, as usual," she nodded. "You're right, Paul was always the one for me, right from the day that he opened his door to me at St Peter's Terrace, but somehow it never happened. Then when he invited us both over for his wedding to Leanne, RP and I, well, we suddenly clicked. Whether it was just that we were both alone in a foreign land, or whether it was the removal of the barrier of the Paul option, I don't know. What I do know is that within six months the roles were reversed with Paul stood alongside RP as his best man."

"Any Kids?"

"Yes two, the heir and the spare so to speak. Tom is four and Jerry is two. Both wonderfully grounded unless their grandparents are about, which is probably too often; then they imitate spoilt brats. Never have millionaires as both sets of grandparents, it just turns every Christmas into a one-upmanship contest!"

"Tom and Jerry? You are pulling my chain aren't you?"

"Sort of. Tamonash is our eldest boy, it means Destroyer of Ignorance; Jayashri, Goddess of Victory, is our daughter. I just prefer the shorthand versions. Rather apt really, they are always chasing each other around the house, as you can imagine."

At that point, RP slid into the chair beside her and squeezed her hand.

"So, congratulations you old fox," Roland said.

"We would have invited you if we had known where you were. But you just disappeared. Even the college didn't have an address."

Roland sighed: "the least said about those few years after uni, the better. Let's just say it was better to have no ties to the past and leave it there."

"So what are you doing in New York, meeting an opposite number from SMERSH - or shouldn't we ask?" RP smiled knowingly.

"You figured-out that was bullshit then. Nothing gets past you does it?"

"Let's just say that you never struck me as double-o-Roland." They all laughed again at the incongruous image.

"Don't tell Schneider, I may never get a visa again!" Roland grimaced.

"Don't tell Schneider what?" came a familiar accent to the side of the table. They all looked around at Sam, then collapsed again into fits of laughter.

"I have a confession," Roland said, still laughing.

"That you're not an MI6 Agent I presume," Sam replied with a smile.

Roland turned back to the other two sheepishly: "oops, he sussed me."

"I'd be a pretty poor FBI Agent if I didn't, wouldn't I?" Sam slapped Roland on the back: "come on Bond, I'll buy you dinner."

"Why, thank ya Felix," Roland imitated the accent, "that'll be mighty fine."

One-Two-One

They walked around to the restaurant and the Maitre'D showed them to their table at the back where they settled down to order. They needn't have worried about privacy, as they were the only customers; being the Midwest, the main service was normally finished by eight. Once the waiter had finished with the preliminaries and delivered their wine, the conversation returned to the earlier subject matter.

Annie once again launched the conversation: "you were telling us how Shepherd, the hit man, became Kryczek."

"That's the sketchy bit at the moment. You see Agent Kryczek shot and killed the serial killer Vitruvio, the persona given to the perp responsible for various similar murders across the country, or so it was believed."

"She killed the hit man?" RP looked shocked: "when?"

"A couple of months ago in Palm Springs. There had been a similar pattern of killings to those we have just had in Wichita. Kryczek worked out of the LA Field Office, primarily as a Profiler. About three months before the killings started, an Agent called Tom Bonetti was transferred there from Savannah. The two of them became an item fairly quickly. When the Palm Springs Police were faced with dealing with a second murder within so short a timescale, they called for help and Bonetti was assigned. By chance, he had covered a similar set of murders in Savannah while he was there, so he pulled Kryczek in on the cases to see what she could glean. It was she who found two additional sets in Memphis and Denver in between, all with similar M.O's. The third murder occurred before they could get any handle on things, but somehow the two of them managed to work-out where the potential fourth murder might occur. They narrowed that potential victim down to two possibilities and staked-out both locations. Somehow, a sighting at his location led Bonetti to think that the hit was going to go-down at the other, but there was a comms-failure so he trailed what he thought was the perp to the other location and tried to apprehend him, but in the resulting confusion, he was shot and killed."

"What, by this Vitruvio?" RP asked.

"No, by Kryczek."

The three friends once again found themselves staring in disbelief at each other. Roland was the first to speak again: "hold on, hold on - now I'm really confused. Bonetti and the real Kryczek were tracking this Vitruvio, who I assume is also Shepherd and the false Kryczek."

"Yes and Norma Schaeffer," Sam responded.

"Well … yes, back at university he was her. But how did Bonetti and the real Kryczek end up shooting at each other?"

"Because the possible victim that Bonetti was guarding was Norma Schaeffer."

"Oh this is bloody crazy!" Roland said, totally exasperated, "you're telling us that the FBI was guarding victims that are also killers, then end up killing themselves! No wonder Paul ended up in a hospital bed, what's the matter with you people?"

"Calm down Roland." RP was trying to take the heat out of the situation, even though he felt just as angry inside: "don't forget that this is just as hard for Sam as it is for us - he is Paul's friend as well you know."

"Alright," Roland responded quietly with his palms slightly raised from the table, "I'm sorry Sam."

"Not a problem Roland, like I said earlier, it's still all very sketchy. Why don't you let me continue and give you the full Palm Springs story, then it may become a bit clearer."

At that point their starters arrived and while the waitress served them, they all busied themselves with napkins and condiments. Once the waitress had withdrawn, Sam continued as he tucked into his seafood pate: "the main piece of the jigsaw that you are missing at this point is that the Palm Springs murders involved victims that were all part of a Hollywood movie team shooting on location there. Norma Schaeffer had got herself onto the team as a make-up artist working on contract. We have since realised that this was Shepherd's

A Pilgrim Returned

cover to perform those murders, thanks to what Paul's Squad were piecing together just before he was attacked. Neither Bonetti nor the real Kryczek would have had any reason to suspect that name. And we can't ask either of them why they thought that Schaeffer was a possible victim, although Pete Baker in LA has his team combing through every piece of information on the cases and their individual notebooks to see if there are any hints. The only theory we have, and it's just based on the presence of a radio jammer at the location where Bonetti was killed, is that Shepherd set-up the whole situation deliberately."

"I don't see why you would think that," RP pondered, "if this is a professional assassin, surely that's way too complex, almost a gamble."

"Except it worked, because afterwards the Bureau decided that Bonetti must have been Vitruvio, because of his links with Savannah - case closed."

"That's a bit sloppy isn't it Sam?"

"In hindsight, of course it is. But I wasn't there, they didn't know what we know now, so it all fitted the scenario they had at that time."

Annie had been listening intently: "Kryczek couldn't have taken that well. She's killed her lover, who then suddenly turns-out to be a serial killer. But then, you said that she had been analysing all of the cases, so was it she that found the links that brought that conclusion?"

"No, and that's where I think it all started to unravel. You see Kryczek had never been involved in any form of shooting outside of the academy, where they are realistically-staged, but still staged. That, and the death of Bonetti, just devastated her, so for obvious reasons she was put on garden leave. She was interviewed by the internal enquiry team, who concluded it was a righteous shoot, but that took a couple of weeks and she had no contact with the Field Office during that period. By the time she returned to duty, the conclusion that Bonetti was Vitruvio had already been made and approved."

"Smells of a cover-up to me," Roland observed somewhat bitterly.

"Yes," Annie sighed, "but would I be right in assuming that she didn't accept that version of events?"

"Absolutely right Annie," Sam resumed, "in fact she was suspended for a couple of days for damaging Bureau equipment."

Annie smiled: "she threw something at her boss, right?"

"Several things actually, including a bronze bust of J Edgar Hoover that had been presented to the LA Field Office by the current Director. It only narrowly missed Pete Baker's head before demolishing a plate large glass screen between his office and the reception area."

"Right on Sister!" Annie punched the air symbolically, "sometimes you men do leave a lot to be desired, you know." At that point, their waitress arrived to clear the starter debris, looking slightly concerned at the outburst.

"Steady-on Annie," RP intervened, turning to the waitress with a reassuring smile: "don't worry, there's at least one 'New-Man' at this table." The waitress forced a smile, but still cleared everything away rather more quickly than usual.

After she had moved away, arms full, Sam continued again as RP topped-up the wine glasses: "when Kryczek returned to duty, she had calmed down considerably, apparently-so anyway. She did, however, persuade her boss that, as Vitruvio was a particularly unusual, if not unique, persona, to let her look over all the files and produce a full profile for the database of serial killers that we keep. Profiling was her primary function in the organisation and Pete thought it might also be cathartic for her in the circumstances."

"So was it?" Annie enquired.

"It appeared so. Baker had no reason to believe there were any problems; she worked steadily on the profile whilst holding down all her other tasks. Then, a week or so later, she turned-up one morning and announced that she couldn't handle it any more. She produced a letter from her doctor, who diagnosed that she was suffering from acute stress caused by the recent events, recommending that she take leave of absence for as long as necessary, during which time she should receive counselling. Pete handed it all over to HR, who interviewed her and rubber-stamped the diagnosis and recommendations. That was a week or so prior to her last phone call to her mother."

The waitress and Maitre'D returned with the main courses, offered and dispensed all of the appropriate condiments and garnishes. The friends ordered another bottle of wine which came back by return, after which, once again they were left in peace with a polite: "please enjoy your meal."

Roland had barely contained himself during this forced interlude: "she found something, didn't she?"

"Almost definitely", Sam replied, "and as a result had decided to take-on the investigation personally."

"She didn't trust her bosses to believe it," Annie observed.

"Be fair Annie," RP added, "what we've heard so far is all quite unbelievable, and we're being briefed by someone that we trust, who is not unhinged-enough to throw a bust of his organisation's founder at his current boss!" He turned to Sam to conclude: "at least I hope I'm right in making that statement."

Sam smiled broadly: "not so far anyway - if you'd ever had the dubious pleasure of meeting Clyde Normanson, you might admire my restraint!"

They all laughed briefly, but Sam brought the conversation back to the serious aspects: "thing is, Annie, they do believe her now."

"Yes Sam," she responded curtly, "but too late for her and a few others."

"I know that Annie, but I can tell you that I am now heading-up a national enquiry, with two other offices assisting mine, plus additional priority resource wherever I need it."

"Aren't you just bolting stable doors, though?" Roland enquired.

"No Roland. Although we are talking here about a disturbed and calculating individual who we believe carried-out all of the killings, we don't know, yet, who his paymasters were. If, as it appears from what Paul was piecing together, Shepherd was paid to carry-out these murders, then the money-men are as guilty

A Pilgrim Returned

of the crimes as he was - and that's Federal crimes we're talking about. But they are walking-around out there somewhere, free as a bird. More importantly, if we are dealing with just one paymaster, which we haven't ruled out, then there is nothing to stop him finding a replacement for Shepherd. For all we know, they may already be scouting-out their next victim."

"Victims surely," Roland intervened.

"Ah yes, let's explore that tangent for a moment shall we? You see, the killer we named Vitruvio killed in sets, but we don't know if this was always his modus-operandi, or one he reserved just for his 'spectaculars' as one of our more literary contributors noted in the files. We don't even know, yet, if the connected people who died were just a sideline to satiate his dark appetites, or part of the contract."

"But why?" asked RP, "surely a hit man needs anonymity. Turn-up unannounced, kill the target, disappear without trace. Why would he announce what he was doing, then hang around to do more?"

"For the answer to that question, RP, I think we can go to one of Paul's theories, which was that the hit man, he didn't know it was Shepherd at the time, offered a disguised service for his more expensive clients. One of the reasons why we are often able to nail the buyer of such services, if not the hit man themselves, is that a motive becomes obvious. It could be as simple as cashing-in on an insurance policy, or gaining control of a company, even avoiding a divorce settlement. One victim creates a motive."

"But if there are multiple victims, there can also be multiple motives," Annie observed.

"Exactly," Sam continued but was stopped almost immediately.

"Just one thing if I may," Annie interrupted the flow, turning to her husband: "when you tire of me darling, a simple divorce will suffice. As much as I sometimes dislike your Mother's busybodying around the children, I would never want to see her as collateral damage." She touched his arm gently, smiled, then returned to her risotto. Roland nearly choked on a piece of crab.

Sam, looking slightly bewildered, continued: "it's the old question about where is the best place to hide an oak tree, to which the answer of course is in a forest of oak trees. If people who, initially anyway, appear unconnected, die in a similar manner in close proximity, then it is likely that the manner prompts the motive; in that scenario, the investigation team is immediately looking for a serial. To try to get one step ahead, they analyse the pattern of the killings, look for a wild-card perpetrator and also for potential victims of the pattern that may attract him. But if the pattern is a ruse to hide the real target, who has already been selected and scouted, without any clues from the killer it is much more difficult to ascertain if one particular, ostensibly-random, victim was a specific target."

"And if the victims are related in some other way, then their selection may point the finger in an entirely different direction, away from the client," RP added.

"Exactly. My goodness, are you sure you're not all detectives already!" Sam exclaimed.

Annie, however, didn't hear that comment. Her thought-patterns were running riot. She rested her chin on her hands and stared out into space past Sam, who was sat opposite her. After a few seconds she said, slowly and pensively: "or - the finger could be pointed at somebody that the client wants framed."

Sam's flow stopped suddenly. He looked at her with an expression of realisation: "go on," he said.

"Well, you get an added bonus. You remove a certain problem permanently and, as a by-product, another by discreditation. A golden-bullet."

"My God, thank you Annie!" Sam exclaimed and leapt up from the table. He threw his napkin in front of him, leant across to Annie and, cupping her head in his large hands, planted a gentle kiss on her forehead. He stood back up and left his seat: "excuse me everyone, but I need to make another phone call. Please carry-on with your meal."

He shook them all by the hand in turn and parted saying: "don't worry, I'll be in touch over the weekend. I have a lot to do and not a lot of time to do it in." At that, he attempted to dart from the restaurant in the direction of the car park, but Annie ran after him. Catching up with him in the foyer, she tugged his sleeve causing him to turn round to face her.

"Just one more thing Sam. I know I don't have to ask you this, because you are also one of Paul's closest friends, but will you promise me that you will never give up on finding who is behind all of this. Even if you can't bring them to justice, at least identify them, confront them and tell them about who they tried to kill and who his friends are. Then come and tell me all about it."

Sam felt the repressed emotions of the past week welling within him as he looked at the determination on Annie's face. He grabbed her in his arms and hugged her close, as if he was bear-hugging his old friend after a night-out together. Then he kissed her gently on the ear, as he whispered to her: "I will Annie. I will pursue them until I nail them, until I draw my last breath. I promise you; his friends; his family; my family - all of you!" With that he turned and left without letting Annie see the tears in his eyes.

She returned slowly to the table, wondering quite what she had unleashed on Paul's enemies, when she was brought back to reality by a familiar voice: "well done Watson!" Roland aimed his congratulations at Annie, "now we may never know how Kryczek got switched."

"I'm no longer sure that I want to know," Annie replied. With that, she raised her glass and said: "cheers Sam and thanks for the meal."

"Not so fast with the thank-you's," RP replied holding-up the bill: "he shot off so quickly that he obviously forgot it was his treat!"

At which the group erupted into laughter once more.

what a caring boy

One-Two-Two

Schneider was still at his desk approaching midnight, making a few final scribbled notes for the meeting that he had pre-arranged for eleven-thirty a.m. in his conference room. He had been making phone calls from the moment he got back from the Hyatt and had managed to get all of the attendees confirmed.

He then went across to the hospital to relieve Carla a little after midnight, as pre-arranged. He had decided to take the complete night-shift so that he would be already in the room when the transfer was made, and therefore his arrival couldn't awake any curiosity in one of the more alert junior reporters prowling the corridors. It also meant that the family could stay on the base and await Paul's arrival. Finally, Sam alone would provide the civil security escort for the transfer, again avoiding the need for marked police vehicles to be involved, thus avoiding alerting the media in any way.

At eleven a.m, Schneider's unmarked Crown Victoria pulled-up outside a rear gate to McConnell, and he watched as the truck completed the security checks and slowly moved through the gates onto Airforce land. As the gates closed behind it, Pete Vrabel leaned out of the passenger side cab window and gave the A-OK sign. Sam acknowledged with a wave, then gunned the throttle for a swift drive back to his office. He pushed through the door of the conference room just before eleven-thirty; waiting for him were McKinley and Holdsworth, plus four FBI Agents. Schneider slumped into the chair at the head of the table.

"Jeez Sam," McKinley exclaimed, "you look like shit!"

"I took the red-eye shift at the hospital."

"Any change?"

"Not in condition." Schneider's attention seemed to drift away for a few moments: "he looks so peaceful led there with all those pipes coming out of everywhere. I still don't know if that's a good thing or not." He refocused: "but there is a change in status Chris. As of half an hour ago, Lieutenant Paul Kleberson has been transferred to the base hospital at McConnell, where his care has been taken-over by the USAF fifty-ninth medical wing's specialist neurology unit. This has been with the full co-operation of the medical staff at St Damian's, who believe that they do not possess the specialist knowledge necessary to deal with the unusual causes of Paul's condition."

"Does that mean we can't visit any more?"

"No Chris, the rota stays in place and arrangements have been made with the base for special visitor clearance for close friends who are to continue as before. You are one of the names already on their list."

"Thanks Sam, I appreciate that. Is this off-the-record?"

"No. The media don't know yet, but they will find out fairly soon, probably after the Press Conference."

"The Chief knows?"

"And Ramsey; they agreed to stage the conference this morning to get the media trucks out of the hospital car park."

"You could have told me."

"It was an Airforce operation Chris - their call on need-to-know I'm afraid. Now, did you get what I asked for?"

"Sure did, here they are." McKinley slid two books across the table to Schneider: "green one's the official log, red's our internal one."

"Two logs?" Schneider looked askance at McKinley.

"The Chief put Morley on us right from the get-go. You know that Paul doesn't trust him, so he asked me to keep one with what we were happy for Morley to know and the other for us with everything in."

"So, do I ignore the green one?"

"Don't think so Sam, in the circumstances it shows you what Paul was happy for them to know. That in itself may prove significant."

"Point taken. Does Stanton know they're here?"

"No Sam, nor that we are either. Chief thinks the case is closed."

"Good, let's keep it that way, for the time being anyway."

Holdsworth leant forward on his arms and looked at McKinley: "can I just clarify something here Chris, we're not here officially?"

"Not exactly," McKinley replied.

"It would have been nice to know that in advance you know."

"Sorry kid, couldn't risk it. Any roads, weren't you the one that said to me after we cleared-up at the Lieutenant's apartment that something still didn't fit?"

"Yep. Is that what this is about?"

"Sure is," said Schneider, "Paul Kleberson is one of my oldest friends. He was put in intensive care helping us apprehend a multiple killer, who we all believe may have been hired to be in Wichita. That killer took a secret to the grave with him - who it was that hired him to be here in the first place. Which means that there may be individuals out there walking around enjoying the fresh air that Paul cannot at this juncture, people who were ultimately responsible for Paul's injuries, as well as numerous deaths. We could just accept that, or we can make the bastards pay for their involvement. I intend to do the latter, but if you're not comfortable with helping, Detective Holdsworth, feel free to leave now."

"I'm more than comfortable with that, Agent Schneider."

"Good, because that saves me having to shackle you and stash you somewhere only I would know where. From here on in, nothing that we discover or discuss goes beyond these four walls; that applies to everybody in this room, understood?" He looked in turn at the four Agents, who each nodded affirmation as he did so. McKinley and Holdsworth followed suit.

"Right, you have probably already introduced yourselves, but just in case," he pointed to each in turn, "Bill Johnson and Jim Kowalski from my office here, you have already met our visitors from out of State. Chris McKinley and Scott Holdsworth from Wichita Police Department's Homicide Squad, you already know Bill and Jim."

Schneider than indicated towards the first of the two new Agents joining the team. He was in his early forties, tall with fair hair, a genuine West Coast tan and not an unwanted ounce of weight: "Pete Baker is my equivalent in the LA Field Office who, as you know, handled the previous set of murders in Palm Springs. He's flown down this morning to be with us."

Baker rose and shook hands with McKinley and Holdsworth, saying as he did: "so, I'm looking for answers and not only as to who is responsible for me losing two of my best Agents."

Schneider continued, indicating the final person at the table - early-thirties, five-ten, impeccably-groomed dark hair and clothes that hinted at his being of comfortable means and some class: "Chandler Clarke is from our Field Office in Jackson, Mississippi and is currently conducting an investigation into political corruption where he has found connections to the Memphis murders." What Schneider didn't add was that, in his phone call the previous evening, he had revealed to Chandler Clarke the substance of Jackson Kendrick III's alibi for the first murder; it hadn't taken many questions from Clarke before he had joined the dots to the events leading to the death of his mother. This was the main reason for Clarke's instant agreement to join the investigation. Schneider concluded the introduction: "incidentally, Chandler's office doesn't have Pete's budget, so thank you Chandler for driving up here overnight to be with us."

This comment brought some levity around the table as Clarke repeated the handshaking ritual without saying much other than: "hi guys, nice to know ya." He then sat down again before continuing: "I will apologise in advance for not being able, necessarily, to share everything I have at the moment, some of which is subject to National Security restrictions. But I want you to know that I will not hold anything back that is pertinent to your investigation here; you'll just have to trust me sometimes as to how I came by it. Is that OK with you guys?"

McKinley and Holdsworth both nodded their acceptance, Holdsworth somewhat sheepishly, as this all seemed to be reaching an altitude well above his pay grade. But he quickly reassured himself that he must have something to offer, otherwise he would never have been invited. Thus he privately resolved to go with it for as long as it took.

Schneider then outlined their joint purpose: "let's start by laying the basic guidelines so that we all know why we are here. Five days ago, my best friend was hospitalised by a murderer by the name of Sean Norman Shepherd, a-k-a Sian Norma Shepherd, a-k-a Norma Schaeffer and given the codename of Vitruvio by this Bureau. None of us in this room believe that he was working on his own initiative, or that he was just a serial killer, per se. If we did, we would not be here."

They all nodded as he continued: "so this investigation starts and continues from the premise that Sean Norman Shepherd was a hit man - a prolific and successful hit man. We are no longer interested in how the murders were set-up or committed, or how Shepherd became what he was; we know enough of that already and have been distracted by it for way too long. What we are interested in, gentlemen, is the why? There was a reason for each murder and we need to find it. When we do, we will find who benefitted from it and how. When we have that, it will lead us to who it was that ordered the hit."

Schneider paused and took a sip of water: "I shouldn't have to tell you how important that last part is, because that is the key to putting these people in the defendant's chair and, if we get it absolutely right, onto death row. Because all of the States that these murders were committed in, including this one, still retain capital punishment, which is the minimum sentence we will be going for. So our evidence assembly must be painstaking and meticulous with no corner-cutting; just good, solid, old-fashioned police work. Wherever possible, we must acquire multiple evidence strands or independent corroboration to close-off every loophole or rat-run that a defending lawyer may try and wriggle through. If our instincts are proved right, there will be some very high-powered and expensive lawyers lined-up against us, because we suspect that Shepherd's client for at least some of the murders here in Wichita may have an important status in this community, high-enough to hire that standard of defence counsel and to have, shall we say, conduits within the corridors of power, right down to City Hall. But not here in this room. So Chris, Scott, no discussions in that building about any of this and no phone calls using city property - Bill ..."

Agent Bill Johnson stood, walked to the side table and picked-up two cellphones. He returned to the main table and slid one of them across to each of the two city policemen. They both picked up the phones and looked at them; Holdsworth recognised the model immediately.

"If you need to contact us," Schneider continued, "use these, but do not use them within any city asset; that includes your cars. All our numbers are programmed-in, as are each one of these."

"So, if I want to talk to Chris, I use this one?" asked Holdsworth.

"Only on this case," replied Schneider, "on your normal cases, work normally."

"Check," Holdsworth replied.

Schneider turned to another of his Agents: "now Kowalski, tell us what you have put together from the case files."

One-Two-Three

Jim Kowalski was the oldest Agent on Schneider's staff in Wichita. He should have been retired after suffering a heart-attack three years earlier, but such was his record of detection as a Field Agent, that he was retained on desk duties. Regardless of the illness, he had lost none of his mental abilities and was used by

What a Caring Boy

the team to look over cold case notes for anomalies that may justify the case being re-opened. So good was he at this, that of the fifteen cases he had revisited in the past year, all had been re-opened, of which twelve had resulted in a positive arrest; the other three were still active. Vitruvio was the first current case that he had been allowed to work on since his return and he was relishing every minute.

He placed a copy of the airport photo near to the top left corner of the whiteboard and began his analysis: "Sean Norman Shepherd - born in Marion, Kansas in nineteen-seventy-three and lived there with his mother until she deserted him at the age of six, after which he was raised in nearby Hillsboro by his great aunt, Susan Ferguson. According to IRS records, Shepherd's permanent address has been three-two-one South Monroe, Hillsboro since he left high school. He files his tax returns every year, which show that he currently earns less than eighteen thousand dollars, below the level of household income that would lose his aunt her State benefits."

"What a caring boy!" McKinley observed.

"Since nineteen-ninety-eight," Kowalski continued, "he has been employed by Berger & Pastore Enterprises Inc of Palo Alto California, as their Midwest location agent, an occupation he lists as casual. The only qualifications we could find listed against his name are his high-school diploma, which showed him in the top quartile of his class, but no further education is listed."

"That's pretty watertight," Clarke observed, "there's nothing there to raise any eyebrows at the IRS. His aunt is on benefits, low income, disability, etcetera, so she could live without his income; she's a Mennonite, so she will live pretty frugally anyway. But he injects just enough into the household to make her life comfortable, probably paying for some sort of home help when he's away, but not enough to make her think he is up to something he shouldn't be. With the general level of earnings in a place like Hillsboro being in the lower medians, it all fits - he was an intelligent child from a poor background in a small Midwest town. That essentially precluded him from affording a place at any university without some form of scholarship, so he basically becomes just another redneck boy getting work best he can. You know, that's not just clever, that's damned clever. If it's an indication of what we are going to find when we get to the real income, then we had better be prepared for a long haul on this one."

There was a general degree of thoughtful nodding around the table at this observation. Kowalski moved on: "we know that he managed to get a place at USC. We don't yet know how it was financed, but we have enquiries out to find that, because it could provide some clues as to an early connection with somebody with money."

"With a payback clause maybe," Schneider observed, "good angle Jim."

"So he moved to LA in nineteen-ninety where he became Norma Schaeffer." Another photo was placed to the right of the first; it was obviously a blow-up of a photo taken in a passport booth and showed a woman's face, attractive with high cheekbones, probably late twenties and with long brunette hair.

"That's Kryczek!" McKinley exclaimed, almost immediately correcting his obvious mistake: "sorry, of course, what we thought was Kryczek."

Kowalski continued: "Norma Schaeffer has lived in San Diego California since nineteen-ninety-five, from ninety-eight in an apartment block on Front Street, right in the centre of the local gay community, a community that has a strong attraction for transgenders, so she would have fit right in without causing any question. The apartment block is owned by Berger & Pastore Enterprises."

"What the entire block? Schneider enquired, "how many apartments?"

"Sixteen," Baker added, "mainly studio and of reasonable quality. Not condos, but certainly not a dive. Probably netts ten grand a month."

"And the company acquired it when?"

"Nineteen ninety seven."

"Mortgage?"

"None."

"So between leaving USC and ninety-seven, he's come by enough money to buy a small apartment block in central San Diego. What's that a cool million?"

"And change probably."

"So by then he's already into something highly lucrative. I suppose we have to acknowledge that it was likely illegal, at least including some contract killings." Schneider readdressed his questions to Kowalski: "so this Norma Schaeffer, presumably there's no IRS record for that name?"

"On the contrary," Kowalski responded, "she has been filing her tax returns since graduating in ninety-four. On her more recent ones she listed her occupation as a Key Make Up Artist - that's the person who actually designs the look for each actor and runs the whole make-up area on a set, assigning individual tasks to artists working for her. Last year, she declared earnings of fifty grand from her employer, Berger & Pastore Enterprises."

"But how could she hold down a job like that?" Holdsworth enquired, she would need qualifications, experience, references."

"She had all of those," Kowalski resumed, "that was the major at USC she switched to after she apparently married. She worked on several B-Movies after leaving USC and features in the credits for them. But we have found nothing on the movie database after nineteen-ninety-five and certainly none as the Key."

"Of course that doesn't mean she wasn't working on movies," Baker observed, "just not mainstream movies. Whatever, that was still enough for her to land the job on the Palm Springs location and hold it down sufficiently for the crew not to suss her."

"And it explains how she was able to pass herself off as both male and female at will," McKinley added.

"It doesn't explain the Social Security number, Clarke interjected: "Shepherd retained his, so where did hers come from?"

"Norma Wosziecki," Kowalski replied, "died July eighteen, nineteen-seventy-three in Salina, aged one day. That was the name she used for her marriage in

What a Caring Boy

ninety-one to George Schaeffer, who died December twenty-three, nineteen-seventy-one, also aged one day."

Schneider was beginning to disbelieve his ears: "so even all that way back, aged what? - eighteen/nineteen, Shepherd is able to create not one identity, but two, and marry them to each other? Where?"

"Vegas," Kowalski answered.

Schneider looked at Clarke and Baker: "I don't know about you guys, but to me this is already feeling like we have an organised crime element involved."

"Don't see any other way that a penniless teenage redneck tranny pulls-off that sort of complex deception," Clarke added.

"Has Berger and Pastore turned-up on any databases?" Schneider enquired.

"Nowhere," Kowalski responded with a hint of despair, "totally off our radar."

"So what do we know about them?"

"Berger & Pastore Enterprises - you guys from City Hall already noted the fact that all three surnames, including Schaeffer, are foreign translations of the word Shepherd." Kowalski added a photo to the board of a fairly nondescript office building frontage, which could have been in any business district of any town in the country: "registered office is this five thousand square foot detached unit on El Camino Real in Palo Alto, close to the Stanford Campus. It has been owned by the company since nineteen-ninety-nine. CEO is Jean Berger, age thirty-nine, French national, moved to the USA in nineteen-eighty-nine to work in the movie industry, obtained his green card four years later."

Another enlarged passport photo went onto the board to the right of Norma Schaeffer. It showed an older face, with a droopy moustache and long dark brown hair, receding slightly at the sides and apparently drawn back into some form of pigtail. "This is the photo from his latest French passport which Interpol obtained for us. They also sent us the previous one, from nineteen-eighty-eight." He added another blow-up underneath the first photo, this time a black and white shot of a younger man also with long hair, in more of a mullet style, but no moustache; to more than a cursory look, these were pictures of the same person a number of years apart.

Holdsworth got up from his seat, walked over to the board and looked closely at the two photos, then at the one of Norma Schaeffer. He turned to the table and pointed at the later photo of Berger: "this is Schaeffer," he pointed at the eyes on her photo, "the eyes are the same." He pointed at the earlier black and white photo of Berger: "this isn't."

All the others at the table got up and moved to the board to scrutinise the photos, except Johnson who continued scribbling his notes. "My God," Schneider said quietly, then turning to Kowalski: "have you got any of Pastore?" Kowalski nodded and moved to place two more passport photos on the board. The others stood back slightly to give him space to work.

The one he placed next to the later one of Berger was of a lady, again very attractive with relatively short blonde hair, styled into a generic flyaway look that could place her age anywhere from early thirties to mid-forties. The one below, again black and white, showed an equally-attractive woman in her mid to late twenties with long flowing blonde hair framing her face and falling well below her shoulders. Once again, these were ostensibly the same person, but closer examination showed that the eyes didn't match, although those in the upper photo matched all three photos to its left. The room went very quiet as all but Kowalski returned slowly to their seats.

"I'll finish-off this part for you if you like," Kowalski resumed; Schneider nodded agreement. "Berger stayed around the LA area until ninety-six, when he moved to Palo Alto, where he founded the company. His home is a restored colonial in the University District, also owned by the company and the address that the company operated from until they moved to the registered office."

Schneider's next question sounded somewhat exhausted, maybe due to his lack of sleep: "and I guess, Pete, we're not talking low real estate values here either?"

Baker responded: "the offices a couple of mil, the house probably upwards of three."

Schneider shook his head, staring at the board. Kowalski concluded with the details on the final photo: "Sofia Pastore, age forty-one, dual Italian/US Nationality. Born Sofia Carlotti in Turin, came to Hollywood in nineteen-eighty -one having been discovered," he intimated inverted commas with his fingers as he said the last word, "on Italian TV by one Bruno Paoletti, a wise guy from Brooklyn who became her agent. He couldn't break her into any movies before her visa expired, so she married him and became naturalised in nineteen-eighty-five. Shortly afterwards they were divorced, claiming an irreconcilable breakdown of the marriage. Once he was out of the picture she picked-up a few minor roles in insubstantial movies over the next few years. In the late eighties, she became an agent for Italian actresses looking for a break in Hollywood. During one of her scouting trips, to Rome in ninety-six, she married her second husband, Fernando Pastore, who was apparently involved in the Italian soft-porn industry. On returning to California, she moved to La Crescenta-Montrose in the San Fernando Valley, where she continued her agency work, using her new husband's contacts to primarily source actresses for porn movies. She has lived there ever since and became a partner in Berger's company in ninety-eight, when her second husband died."

"How and where did he die?" Schneider enquired.

"We have no idea. In fact, he probably never existed, Interpol have found no trace of him anywhere so it looks like a repeat of the Schaeffer story."

"I guess if it worked once …" McKinley began to observe, but Schneider interrupted, his thoughts apparently elsewhere.

"Yes Chris. Jim, thank you for all of that, but I think we had better stop there and digest what we've heard, do you agree gentlemen?" All around the table nodded, except Johnson who was still scribbling. Schneider continued: "OK, let's take a break, get some lunch, check our messages and so on, then reconvene at …" he looked at his watch, "… shall we say - two-thirty?"

One-Two-Four

When Chandler Clarke walked back into the conference room at just gone two-twenty, Sam Schneider was already there, stood in front of the whiteboard pondering the photos.

"Just you so far Sam?" he enquired.

"Yes, oh sorry Chandler, Carla couldn't find you. We're not reconvening until three-thirty now. Chris and Scott had to go back over to City Hall, some meeting with Stanton regarding the reorganisation of their Squad."

"Stanton's re-organising his Homicide Squad? Why would he need to do that? From what I've seen of McKinley so far, he's a shoe-in for promotion in place of the guy in intensive care ..."

Schneider rounded on Clarke with a fierce look on his face: "Paul Kleberson, his name is Paul Kleberson."

"Oh sorry Sam, that was a really dumb way of putting it."

Schneider relaxed and refocused on the board: "no, not your fault, just a mixture of insufficient sleep, a very raw nerve and this lot." He pointed at the board.

"Yeah, the guy certainly had some balls ... figuratively, if not physically."

Schneider allowed himself a light burst of laughter, uncomfortable though it felt. Pete Baker was the next through the door; he walked over to join them. Schneider welcomed him: "ah Pete, sorry we're not reconvening until three-thirty, although actually ..." Schneider broke off and walked to the door, closing it, then turned and beckoned the other two to sit around the table again.

Baker continued: "yes, I saw McKinley on his way out. Good man, in fact both of them are, especially for a local PD. Why on earth would their Chief be reorganising at a time like this, and on a Friday afternoon?"

"Oh that's typical Stanton; don't worry about him, he's got enough problems of his own - man's an asshole!"

"Is that on top of his problems, or part of them?"

"Both." Schneider shook his head as though to push the conversation to one side; he was trying desperately to focus on something. "Look, whichever way we come at this, it's just a rat's nest of facts that will take us months, maybe years to unravel. By which time, there will be yet more layers added on top by whoever is behind it all."

"OK, so what are you suggesting?" Baker asked.

"We've got to be the first to shake the tree - see what's hanging loose and might fall off. If we don't it will all be pruned before we get the chance."

"You want to come out all guns blazing?" Clarke asked, "like Butch Cassidy?"

"They both got slaughtered you know," Baker observed, "the movie may have gone to freeze frame, but in real life they both died."

Schneider sighed: "I know what you guys are saying, but look at this." He gestured back to the board, "this guy's got four separate valid identities, he's probably killed two of them to take them over, he's into all sorts of things, murder to order, porn, money laundering, impersonating a Federal Agent - and that's what we've turned-up in just a few days. But he's been operating for at least ten years and during that time he has been moving around as different sexes, different nationalities and there's nothing to say that his reach is just confined to California and a few random other States. He could have been operating all over the world for all we know. But one thing is clear - he couldn't have done all of this without help."

"What you thinking Sam?" Baker enquired, "the mob? The Italian connection makes that a distinct possibility."

"Yes of course, but then why is none of this turning-up on any databases? Not the company, not the individual names - and not just here, at Interpol as well."

Clarke looked at him with a slightly shocked realisation: "you're not thinking CIA are you?"

Baker quickly batted that one away: "no, can't be, we would have been getting all sorts of missives from above to step back. I don't know about you guys, but I certainly haven't had any, not even in coded form. In fact, quite the opposite."

Clarke shook his head, then pondered: "unless we're supposed to be tidying-up after them." The other two looked at him puzzled. He continued: "say that this operative has gone way off-piste recently, they could just take him out, but that wouldn't be the end of it if his main handlers were also out of control."

Baker was not convinced: "no guys, if that were the case then we would be getting all sorts of anonymous guidance - you know, tips, leaks, plants, anything to point us where we need to go. I got caught-up in something like that a few years ago and it was made so simple for us, a child of two could have sussed it."

Schneider took up the point: "then if it's not them, or the mob, whoever it is has money - and influence. Regardless of how clever Shepherd was, that money didn't come from a State Lottery win."

"You're still thinking of the Kendricks aren't you?" Baker concluded.

"There's nothing we've seen yet that excludes them."

"No there isn't. But I've met Junior and his wife, only briefly and at a huge UNICEF benefit back home a few years ago; they just didn't come across as that type and I know you've met plenty of the type I mean as well."

"That's not enough Pete and you know it, certainly not to exclude the son."

"Now there's a piece of work!" Clarke interjected.

Baker looked at them both thoughtfully: "alright, then let's go with the son shall we? What has he to gain from having his own private assassination service? How would that fit in with his business, his lifestyle? We would need a pretty long list of possibilities before we could get enough probable cause to even get him in an interview room, let alone get a judge to issue us with any warrants to search and seize."

Clarke glared at him: "how long you got?"

"Alright Chandler," Schneider intervened, "look guys, this is all getting a bit pointless. Even in death, this bastard Shepherd has got us chasing our tails. We've got to cut through the crap, not keep piling it up. I don't know about you, but it's been a long week, I'm exhausted and rapidly losing focus. What do you say we call time for today and sleep on it?"

"Suits me," Baker agreed. Clarke shrugged and nodded as well.

At that point Kowalski opened the door and put his head around it: "just had a call from McKinley - they can't make three-thirty."

"That's OK Jim, we've decided to call it a day anyway. Get Carla to reschedule for the morning, anytime after nine for me." He looked at the other two; they both nodded. Kowalski also acknowledged and was just about to leave when Schneider had a thought: "Jim, how far have you got with putting the company finances together and so on - enough to brief us in the morning?"

Kowalski thought for a moment before replying: "Agent Baker's staff are still going through the documents they seized from the home addresses, not that there was a lot." He looked at Pete Baker: "have your I.T. guys got anything from the servers at the office?"

"I don't know Jim, is the short answer, but I'll ring them for an update and get them to send you anything new."

"In that case," Kowalski addressed Schneider again, "I can give you an overview, but little more unless there's anything new overnight. I'll get in early and go through what's waiting for me and add it in if it's relevant."

"OK, thanks Jim," Schneider replied, "see you in the morning then."

One-Two-Five

The Homicide Squad meeting had been short and sweet, there being only three active personnel left - McKinley, Holdsworth and Moreno.

Dean had handed-in his papers for retirement, as he was allowed to by his length of service. As a result, he was placed immediately on what the old lags called rehab, a programme of lectures and meetings designed to ease the subject back into civilian life. He had left a message telling his colleagues that he would give them details of his retirement bash when he had made the arrangements; from similar events he had organised for others, they knew it would be a long and liquid affair.

Capaldi had applied for a transfer to the State Capital, which was immediately accepted. He was ordered to take his remaining leave awaiting confirmation of his start date in Topeka, so that he could begin organising the move of his family.

Chief Stanton had very little to say. He outlined the new structure that would be introduced at the end of May. It was typical Harper; there would be no Homicide Squad any more, instead a department entitled 'Crimes Against the

Person' would be created. This would be headed-up by Sergeant van Allen, currently in charge of Narcotics, who would be promoted to Lieutenant to do so. It would also absorb Sex Crimes, Assault and Domestic Violence, all currently smaller units; Holdsworth would be re-assigned to what had already been internally nicknamed the Cr-A-P Squad.

Moreno was to be transferred to Burglary, a section that guaranteed plenty of overtime, but also more social hours than Homicide. That would go down well not only with Moreno, but also his third wife, who regularly suspected that the night call-outs he received were not always on police business.

Chris McKinley was to be transferred to the Narcotics Squad, where he would be promoted to Sergeant to take-over from van Allen. Although he knew this was nothing more than he deserved, having taken the exams years earlier, but subsequently being overlooked several times despite Kleberson's constant recommendations - or perhaps because of them.

Stanton finished the briefing with instructions on how the caseload would be handled in the interim. No new cases to be taken on by the three detectives, as many open ones as possible to be closed to minimise the amount of paperwork to be transferred to the new unit, and so on. He concluded with the usual platitudes, the reassurances of how this had been in planning for some time, had nothing to do with recent events and would make for more-efficient crime solving. All three knew it was just another load of corporate bullshit; even the Chief appeared to be aware of the unfortunate smell surrounding his words.

As Stanton moved to leave the Squad Room, McKinley gently took his sleeve and quietly asked if he could have a few words. Stanton seemed somewhat surprised by the approach, although his ego quickly suggested that this may be a prelude to a thank-you, a degree of capitulation in the light that McKinley's erstwhile protector was not likely to be around for some time, if at all - a recognition of his new dependence. Stanton suggested that they go into Kleberson's old office; McKinley followed him in and quietly closed the door.

Stanton parked his ample rump on the corner of the desk, which creaked in futile protest: "so - Sergeant," he began, "and not before time may I add. I'm sure you have many questions about your new role and I just want you to know that my door is always open. If you need anything, just come along and ask."

McKinley cringed internally at the patronising nature of those words. He heard Kleberson's voice scream in his mind: *'just twat him one!'* a British phrase that he understood the meaning of, but whose context he had never fully understood - until then.

Nevertheless, he restrained his instincts: "Chief, I think it's a bit early to use that title. I have not, as yet, accepted either the transfer, or the offer of promotion that goes with it. This will be a major move for me, one that will change my working patterns and I think it only fair that I talk it over with my wife and family before I do so."

"Of course," Stanton replied, "we would not expect anything else."

"I do have one immediate question though," McKinley continued.

Stanton looked at him, but with some apprehension: "carry on," he replied.
"Man to man Chief, no ranks."
"If you wish;" the apprehension was more apparent in that reply.
"Why did you suspend Lieutenant Kleberson? The real reason."
"I don't have to answer that." The response came with a degree of bluster.
"No Chief, you don't, but I would rather hear it from you than have to drag it out of other people."
"Whatever. You're not going to."
"Alright. So let me rephrase my question - can you assure me that the action taken was entirely your own decision and not influenced in any way by anyone outside of your chain of command?"

Having looked McKinley constantly in the eye prior to that question, Stanton momentarily looked down at his feet, then back at McKinley again: "I don't believe I need to answer that question either."

"You just have - thank you Chief."

One-Two-Six

"Good morning Carla!"
Sam Schneider seemed more his usual sunny self as he entered the Bureau office suite, smiling at Carla Courtney who had already been behind her desk for more than an hour. The clock on the wall above her read 09:09.
"Wha good mornin' Sam, you look like you had a good sleep last night."
"Yes Carla, I must have gone off as soon as my head hit the pillow just after eight last night and the next I knew it was almost twelve hours later. Long hours have some drawbacks, but they sure do knock you out for a good long sleep sometimes. What's the situation?"
"Briefing is scheduled for ten a.m, so you have some time to catch up first. Agent Baker is working with Jim; it seems they had some success out in LA overnight and they are looking through the results together."
"Sounds good - in that case I will leave them alone."
"Agent Clarke is using the conference room at the moment, he has a conference call in progress with Interpol. Detective McKinley is with him, he's been here since seven-thirty. He needs to speak to you before the briefing - seems urgent."
"That was early, he must have come straight here. It's probably to do with the re-organisation over at City Hall."
"Jungle drums say he's been promoted."
"That's not before time - good for him!"
"Yes Sam, but he doesn't seem too happy."

"OK thanks for the heads-up; give me five minutes while I grab some coffee, then let him know I'm in."

"Sure thing Sam."

Schneider filled his mug in the kitchen, then went through to his office. There were a few messages for him, but none that needed any urgent action, bar for the one asking him to ring Normanson in KC. He pressed the intercom.

"Yes Sam," came Carla's voice.

"This message to ring Normanson?"

"Oh that came through yesterday after you left; it was his secretary, not him. Usual non-committal - nothing urgent, ring back when he can, you know the form." Schneider nodded involuntarily, he had experienced five years of similar messages; Normanson seemed to revel in the deployment of uncertainty. Carla continued: "I told her you would not be in this morning, she didn't seem bothered by that, so you can leave that one until Monday. In fact you can leave all of them if you want to Sam, I've been using the same cover for everybody."

"Don't know what I would do without you Carla, thank you again."

"Oh I'm sure you would manage, but if you really want to thank me, just nail whoever was responsible for putting Paul in that hospital bed. In the meantime, I'll keep all the timewasters away."

The intercom clicked off. Schneider was slightly taken aback by what was Carla's first reference to Paul Kleberson's attackers since he was hospitalised. The consummate professional, she had not displayed any emotion whilst at work, although he had made the point of privately letting her know that he was available whenever she wanted to talk. She had just replied with a quiet 'thank you', with no further reference during the ensuing time - until now.

As he was considering the implications, there was a knock at the door; it was McKinley. Schneider beckoned him in. As McKinley closed the door, he began apologising: "sorry about yesterday, the Chief kept us hanging around for ages."

"Not a problem, we were all tuckered-out anyway, myself more so. How'd it all go?" He indicated for McKinley to sit.

"Oh, the usual bullshit." McKinley took the seat in front of Schneider's desk: "he's transferred me to Narco and given me promotion."

"So, congratulations!" Schneider enthused, rising and offering his hand.

McKinley leaned forward and shook it unenthusiastically, continuing: "thanks Sam, but it's a bit premature because I haven't decided yet whether I'm accepting it."

"I see," Schneider responded slightly deflatedly; he sat down again and waited for McKinley to expand on the bald comment.

"To be frank, Sam, I don't know how much more I can take of that man. Oh, I know about the Chief of Police having to be a politician first, but he also must be a policeman as a close second. Stanton has forgotten what his title means and he's in so many pockets I'm not sure even he knows who his real paymaster is.

That might be liveable-with, just, as long as those pockets belong to politicians who have a say in the budget. But he's not even answering to them any more."

Schneider was puzzled at this unusual frankness from a man he knew well, because of which he also knew that Chris McKinley was not one for going behind peoples' backs with mere tittle-tattle. Schneider suspected that overnight he had found something out.

McKinley continued: "after the meeting, I asked for a private audience - no ranks. Stanton agreed, but I don't think he realised what I was going to ask, which was why had he suspended Paul; he wouldn't answer. That didn't surprise me, so I focussed the question - I asked for his assurance that the decision had not been influenced from outside the chain of command. Again, he wouldn't answer, but he couldn't look me in the eye to say so."

McKinley looked down towards his hands, which Schneider noticed were clasped in his lap. Knowing that McKinley hadn't finished, Schneider held back from any comment, allowing a silence to develop in the room. After about ten seconds, McKinley looked-up, straight at Schneider; his eyes were moist. "Sam, that bastard is as dirty as a cop can be. He not only sent Paul to what may have been his fate, he did so on the orders of someone. That someone can only have been a Kendrick. Sam, your instincts are right; you must follow them and nail those sons of bitches!"

That was the second time Schneider had been implored to do so within a few minutes, again by someone close to Paul Kleberson. But he knew he couldn't do it alone and he was unsure whether this latest discussion meant that he would be losing a strong ally, so he asked: "what about you Chris? You've pieced as much of this together as we have."

"Oh, don't worry about me Sam, I'm in for the long haul; I'll do whatever it takes, but the Vitruvio cases over at City Hall have all been closed by order of Stanton, except for the IAD enquiry into the final shooting in Paul's apartment."

"IAD? That was a righteous shoot! There's no need for any IAD involvement other than a rubber stamp!"

"Got the summons on my desk this morning; it was issued at eight p.m. last night."

"After your little tete-a-tete with Stanton."

"I'm to be interviewed Tuesday by the investigating officer - Captain Morley."

"Captain?"

"Another recently-decided promotion."

"I thought he was on garden leave."

"No longer, apparently - resumed his duties this morning."

"Chris, you're not to worry about this. I have a vacancy here, if anything goes wrong I will cover you."

"I appreciate that Sam, but it's not necessary, not for me anyway. I'm going to see this through with you, then I'm getting another career; hopefully one mundane enough for the Stantons and Morleys of this world to have no interest,

The Mantis Pact

one way or the other. Stanton's helped actually, because he's stopped any new cases from coming to us; for the next month or so we can only tidy-up what we already have on the books. Far as I'm concerned, there's still work to do on the attack on Paul. If the Chief don't like it, he'll get my resignation sooner than I prefer to give it."

"Chris, I can see that this isn't the time to try and persuade you against this course you've set out on, so let's concentrate on what you, I and Carla all want. Then we can talk about it again."

"Carla, Jeez! I had completely forgotten about how she must be feeling."

"Don't worry, I'll look out for Carla; she is OK, no need for you to worry."

"Sure thing Sam, but I do have a specific request."

"Anything Chris, shoot."

"Holdsworth. He's at the beginning of his career and he's damned good; could be as good as Paul if he has the room to develop."

"That's a hell of a statement Chris, but I can't disagree."

"Moreno's in with Morley on Monday morning, then it's Holdsworth in the afternoon. Moreno's going to say anything that Morley wants, he can't afford not to. But Scott's not that type, he's going to take Morley on."

"He told you this?"

"No, but he didn't need to. He's been seething under the surface since he ignored your text messages to the stake-out the night Paul was attacked. He feels responsible, that he could have got there if he hadn't put his career first. That's why he was here yesterday."

"But we both know that's garbage. He might have got there a few minutes before us, but that would still have been too late to stop the injection being administered, after which there was nothing any of us could have done."

"Of course and I've already told him that several times, but it makes no difference. He marches to the beat of his own drum, and we know that's what the very best do. So that vacancy - I want you to give it to Scott Holdsworth."

"If he wants it, we'll be sure to take him. In the meantime, let's keep him out of this building and away from you outside of City Hall. If he's going to take Morley on, then likely Morley's going to put surveillance on him, in the hope that he will make revenge easy by doing something outside of the rulebook."

"I would prefer we take him out of the frame altogether."

"No Chris, we need someone on the inside and that isn't you any more. You are already being marginalised, soon nobody will be talking to you about anything that could affect their career. If they think Holdsworth is distancing himself as well, then Morley may ignore him. If not, he's toast already."

"You want me to talk to him?"

Schneider looked at his watch; it was still a quarter of an hour until their briefing. "Yes Chris, and use our phone - don't tell him to back-off of Morley, that will be a good diversion. Just make sure he knows not to give any indication of having any involvement with us any more. He should also tell Morley that I approached him to keep me apprised of the stake-out operation, but that he refused. He needs to keep them guessing whether he may still be on their side."

"What if he decides not to help any more?"

"Then he isn't what both of us think he is. And if that's how it plays-out, then make sure he ditches my phone - none of us need Morley being given any free hits at this stage."

One-Two-Seven

Everybody had assembled in the conference room just before ten, except for Chris McKinley who was making the call to Holdsworth from Schneider's office. He arrived shortly after Pete Baker had begun giving the details of what had been found overnight in LA. Schneider welcomed him, asking: "any news?"

"No change Sam," McKinley replied, "we'll get another update this evening."

Satisfied with this confirmation of Holdsworth's continued involvement, Schneider asked Baker to start again for McKinley's benefit. He commenced by explaining that very little had been gleaned from the searches of the residential properties in San Diego, Palo Alto and La Crescenta-Montrose. The following half an hour provided a lot of financial data that had been obtained from the servers recovered from the offices of Berger & Pastore in Palo Alto.

He explained that the network had been set-up with servers that worked using RAID hard drives, allowing those drives to be removed and taken to other locations. From the system records, they had deduced that there were at least three drives missing and were fairly sure that these were at separate sites, two of which would have been back-ups - most likely held in safe deposit boxes, locations to be determined. The third was almost certainly in Shepherd's possession. As nothing had been recovered thus far, that one was most likely still somewhere in the Wichita area and would contain the very latest data.

The recovered drives showed many files from which a more detailed picture of the financial structure of the company and its assets was beginning to emerge. There were numerous bank accounts in more than ten countries; the main ones were in California, Paris and Rome, plus offshore accounts in The Cayman Islands and Liechtenstein. There were also previously unknown subsidiaries in Rome and Grand Cayman, each with their own buildings, plus residential properties in Grand Cayman, Strasbourg and Naples. A quick estimate of cash and property assets alone added-up to more than seventy million dollars, exceeding the declared assets on the company's latest filed accounts by a factor of at least twenty.

Pete Baker explained that some of that discrepancy was due to a lot of the property being actually vested in trust and pension funds. Regardless, the mere fact that the named beneficiaries of those were all aliases of the same person, as indeed were all of the employees of the companies and their listed directors, this was sufficient to make everything subject to seizure by the IRS under tax-evasion legislation. In order to do that, there would no longer be a need to prove whether the source of the wealth had been the result of criminal activity. This was a major fillip to their own investigation, as the IRS had agreed to share everything they found with the Bureau. As a further result, similar investigations had been commenced by Interpol and the Cayman Islands authorities which would result in further searches and seizures at the other locations.

The main breakthrough, however, had come not from any of this but from one file found on one of the drives applicable to the pension fund. The simple spreadsheet listed additional investment holdings in the form of shares in hundreds of corporations, stretching right back to 1993; two of those companies aligned with references in the Vitruvio case files for Memphis and Savannah. Three-quarters of the holdings had been sold, but the file also gave the date and value of each transaction. As a result, Kowalski was collating all of the share information with the filed accounts for the companies plus lists of directors and shareholders. Initial research had shown that there were several holding companies and shell corporations showing-up, so where the shareholders were other corporations, they could follow the trail to wherever it led.

Pete Baker's conclusion was highly-satisfying: "I believe that at least some of the hits have been paid for not in cash, but in the form of stock certificates. If that is the case, it will give us a paper-trail that should lead us back to the client. This is most-definitely not the way that the mob works, certainly not in any case I have been involved with over the last twenty years. As well as being an ideal laundering methodology, the advantages for the contractor are that they can realise their assets into cash at whatever time and pace that they wish to, whilst receiving dividends in the meantime. In some of the private corporations, the shares have been bought-back by the issuer over a period of time; this may have been a way of concealing a stage-payment contract. Of course, if the company's fortunes improve while the holdings exist, then so does the price to the contractor as their shareholding increases in value as well. But perhaps more importantly, the contractor has some degree of insurance in that they would have an extended hold over their client."

"What, a type of protection racket?" Schneider enquired.

"Maybe, or a way of ensuring future assistance with another project. These companies have all sorts of assets, office facilities, cars, planes, hotels, who knows what leverage could have been applied by Shepherd."

"Or his paymasters."

"Yes, and although we mustn't rule out organised crime in some form, such criminals don't usually display this degree of subtlety. For me it suggests a highly-creative and high-flying business mind behind this, which of course could well be Shepherd himself. Nevertheless, at this early stage, I firmly believe that we are going to find something that links this to a corporation of some standing with multiple subsidiaries, one not unlike The Kendrick Corporation."

"So how long before we find something we can act on?" Schneider asked.

What a Caring Boy

Kowalski responded: "five hours, five days, five months, who knows? There's no way of short-circuiting this Sam, it's just going to be an old-fashioned slog through thousands of documents."

"Even if we find something," Baker added, "it doesn't make it admissible in a murder trial. Tax-Evasion, Corporate Fraud, Money Laundering, yes, but procuring a murder, that needs much more, because it requires the payment to be tied to the deed. You know how it works Sam, it's easy when someone pays their best friend to bump off their wife for the insurance money. But this is probably hundreds of hits for multiple clients. Sorry to pour some rain on the parade, but we have to be patient."

"No Pete, you're right," Schneider responded, "but I can't help thinking that the longer it takes, the easier it will be for these bastards to be able to distance themselves from it."

"Which is why I think I'm going to be of more practical use if I go back to LA and get as many Agents onto this as I can round-up. Because Berger & Pastore is registered in California, the IRS investigation team are based in offices just two blocks from ours. So we can liaise directly and include them in conference calls at our end. I'll obviously keep Jim fully in the loop on everything we find."

"Makes sense Pete, but there is one thing I would like you to do before you leave. We'll talk afterwards." Baker gave a curious look, but acquiesced.

Chandler Clarke then gave an overview of the conference call with Interpol. Basically, it was giving the Europeans an update on what had been found thus far on the computer drives - names, addresses and so on. Arrangements had been made to have daily update calls to interchange information and, in return, assurances received that sufficient resources would be allocated.

Chris McKinley provided a quick update on developments at City Hall, which brought unanimous disapproval from the senior Bureau men opposite him, expressed through shaking heads. They agreed, reluctantly, with releasing Scott Holdsworth, Schneider deciding not to take any risks at all by concealing, in the short term at least, his continued undercover role. McKinley concluded: "while I appreciate that all of this financial data is of great use to the investigation overall, I don't see where it gets us in terms of convicting an individual for ordering the hit on Paul Kleberson." He turned to Schneider: "that was our declared primary intention as stated yesterday afternoon, was it not? OK, they didn't succeed, but it's still attempted-murder and that carries enough of a tariff here in Kansas for them never to see the outside world again."

"You're right, it was Chris," Schneider responded, "and still is."

"Good! In which case, gentlemen," he addressed himself this time to Clarke and Baker, "you are all obviously well in your comfort zone when it comes to data files, spreadsheets and corporate records; that stuff just goes right over my head." He passed his flattened right palm above his head with a smile. All of the others also smiled, so he continued: "I'm from the old school, scribbling in notebooks and 'just give me the facts ma'am'. So the best assistance I can give is as the good old-fashioned gumshoe, talking to people, searching premises, stake-outs. So why don't you guys give me all of that stuff, then you can build the evidence that will nail them in court."

"Sounds good to me," Baker responded, and the others all nodded in agreement. Baker continued: "in which case we need that missing hard drive. Nothing was found at his aunt's house in Hillsboro, she doesn't even have broadband, which makes sense when you consider how much trouble he took to keep her away from what he was doing. So he must have had somewhere else fairly close by where he could work. We're not talking a laptop computer here, this would need to be a server installation, so we're looking for a tower computer at the very least."

"OK, I'll get right on it. I know Charlie Watson out at Hillsboro, we were on Patrol North together years ago before he went in search of an easier life."

"You don't rate him?"

"No - I mean yes. He's a good cop, he's just out of practice. Nothing much happens up there and that suits Charlie down to the ground. He does everything you ask of him, efficiently, thoroughly and by the book. Just don't expect him to think outside of that box of his own volition."

"What about all this IAD stuff?" Schneider enquired.

"Oh, don't worry about that! Paul taught me how to run rings around them. Morley's no bloodhound - he's so far up the Chief's ass, he has no sense of smell anymore. I can cover Hillsboro with my current duty which is to tidy-up and close cases, so Stanton and his lackeys won't know what I'm really doing. They will just think I'm being a good boy, especially after I tell the Chief I'll take his offer."

"You will?" Schneider queried.

"Tell him? Yes of course I will if it makes him feel snug and secure, why not? Doesn't mean it has to happen though. After all, it's nearly six weeks until the reorganisation goes live - a lot can happen in six weeks." He surveyed the three senior Agents: "I'm relying on you guys to make sure that it does."

One-Two-Eight

Pete Baker stayed in his seat in the conference room as the briefing broke-up and Schneider indicated to Chandler Clarke to remain for a few minutes as well. Once the three were alone, Schneider walked over and closed the door.

"So what's with the cloak and dagger Sam?" Baker enquired.

"Not really cloak and dagger, I just want to share a few of my own thoughts, then hear your candid views on where we really are with this. Because, you see, I am completely with Chris McKinley. My words yesterday were not a rallying cry to the troops, I know that the Kendricks are behind all this. Oh sure, I have no evidence, no proof, not even any probable cause. But I was with Paul Kleberson for most of those three days before he was attacked, so was Chris.

And I can tell you, just like Chris is telling us in his own way, Paul knew this was the Kendricks. He sensed it - the more he probed, the less they liked it and the more he knew he had the right scent. Even if my own instincts were not shrieking the same message at me, Paul's senses would be enough for me to go with him. So maybe all this," he once again swept his hand in the direction of the ever-filling whiteboard, "will eventually give us the answer, but eventually just won't cut it for me. I want the bastards and I want them now!"

"Phew Sam, I don't know." Baker blew out his cheeks as he spoke: "look, you've always been the instinctive one, I just grind my cases into submission. What you see there," he nodded towards the board, "is our best shot at getting people in court. Far as I see it, that's all we can do; that and providing lorry loads of evidence to help get a conviction. And I can tell you, buddy, from just the tip of the iceberg that I've already seen, there will be a lot of people, many with high-profiles even public figures, who will soon be hiring expensive defence lawyers, regardless of which we will get a shedload of convictions, maybe even a Kendrick or two. We're talking household names here - this is a big one. So I don't really care what they are convicted of, that's for the Federal Prosecutor to decide, just so long as they all go to jail for as long as possible. To me, that's justice; sure, it's not perfect, it takes forever and it's often disappointing, but it's still better than simple vengeance. That's what you're talking Sam, not justice - vengeance."

"To a certain extent," Clarke added, "I'm with Pete on this. Lord knows I've got reason to see one Kendrick in particular facing the Grand Jury, but it doesn't matter to me what the charges are, as long as they stick and he spends the rest of his days in Leavenworth as a bitch for some iron-pumping, faggot lifer."

Pete Baker looked visibly shaken by this: "damn Chandler! It doesn't take much to guess the one you mean and you do conjure up a highly-tempting image for his future. So is there something, maybe, I should know here?"

"Not right now Pete, maybe one day when this is all over. What I'm saying, I guess, is I know where you're both coming from. But Sam, however much I want to see one particular Kendrick discomforted, in doing that we could also just spook them enough to lose what we could get by foregoing that pleasure."

Baker looked at Schneider: "nevertheless, this is still your case - so what did you have in mind?"

"I want to shake the tree. That's what Paul Kleberson did the morning of the attack. Problem is we don't know what tree he shook, but I'm sure it was the one that nearly got him killed."

"But City Hall must know who he saw that day," Clarke responded, "surely it's in his notes?"

"That's the problem, Stanton suspended him before he had a chance to write them up for that morning. All we know is that he was at Cochrane's apartment block with McKinley until after eleven, then he just went off the radar for a couple of hours until he walked back in the Squad Room around one-thirty. His Squad were briefing him when Stanton walked in around two and had McKinley escort him from the building. Chris and I both tried calling him on his home phone and his cell all afternoon, but the only contact we had was a message from him around six. We know he was at his apartment between three and four, because the neighbours were banging on his door to get him to turn the music down, and that he met Shepherd posing as Kryczek at Gardenia on Douglas just after seven, so there's another few hours we can't account for either."

"Did he not discuss anything with McKinley?"

"Chris asked him where he was going before they left Cochrane's, that was his job - to know where everyone was on the investigation. Paul just mumbled something about flushing a turd down the pan; doesn't take much to figure out what he meant by that. When he got back to City Hall, Chris asked him where he'd been. All he said was he'd been flushing like he said he would. He didn't say a word on his way out of the building, probably because he was fuming."

"Did the Squad not try and contact him?"

"Battery in his cell was dead. Not unusual for Paul, he's renowned for it."

"So we can't get a trace off any towers, dammit!" Clarke thumped the table: "where's Cochrane's apartment?"

"Bradley Fair, out on the East side."

"And Kleberson's?"

"Riverside, 'bout a mile west of here."

"Doesn't help then, in all those hours I guess he could have criss-crossed the city several times."

"Depends who he saw and for how long, but essentially, yes."

Baker had been listening quietly. He added his thoughts: "it's the morning two hours that are significant. I've never met Kleberson, Sam, but would you say that he is an intense character?"

"He doesn't suffer fools gladly, Pete."

"So he has a temper?"

"Oh yes, but he is good at controlling it most of the time."

"But not after being suspended - that's why the music was on loud. Discount the afternoon, he was cooling-off. He wasn't interested in any of this for those few hours, that's why he didn't answer your calls. Cochrane's apartment's out East you say?"

"Yes, Bradley Fair's at North Rock and Twenty-First basically."

"Kendrick's estate is out East isn't it?"

"Greenwich, yes."

"How far from Cochrane's?"

"Fifteen minutes tops."

"I'm not a gambling man, but I would wager that's where he went. Does he have the balls to walk in on them unannounced?"

"Undoubtedly. Only one problem though - Jackson Kendrick the Third wasn't there, he was under police guard somewhere else. Paul thought he was a potential target."

"Did Paul know where he was?"

"No, just his lawyer, Friedmann, and Delgado, one of Stanton's deputies."

"Better still ..." Baker pondered for a few seconds, then continued: "... he saw someone else, talked to them - if not, he would have been back at City Hall much earlier. He must have said something to that person that touched a nerve, or maybe just having the front to walk right into the lions' den spooked them. Presumably Stanton had put the family off-limits?"

"Constantly."

"But Kleberson ignored him."

"Also constantly."

"Then he found the connection he was looking for. Only he hadn't bargained for being suspended, just for getting a good chewing-out for it. That's why he was so angry - angry with himself for underestimating Stanton's response."

"Thanks Pete, because that's put the logic behind my instinct and brings me to what I was going to ask you to do, based only on that instinct. You see, I am convinced that Stanton was a part of Paul being set-up as the victim for that night. There was not the remotest piece of genuine evidence that warranted launching that flytrap operation, but what it did was move half the city's police force away from normal duties and give them all a cast-iron reason for not being able to respond quickly to any emergency elsewhere in the city."

"You want me to shake Stanton's tree for you."

"As long as there's no reason it would jeopardise anything else. If I do it, he will just stonewall and tell his paymasters that he saw us off again. But if he's got an unfamiliar Agent from what is, now, a Federal investigation asking awkward questions, he will still stonewall, but it will have an entirely different effect. Behind all his bluster, he knows he's the one most exposed. If I'm right, and they think he is becoming a weak link, they'll just hang him out to dry."

"I don't see any downside, how about you Chandler?"

"None at all"

"Then I'll be delighted to continue to take your excellent Midwest hospitality for a little longer, Sam, in order to give me the opportunity to make Stanton's acquaintance. I'll get my office to set up the meeting to reinforce the thought that this is outside of your remit."

"Do you want me to go with him Sam?" Clarke enquired.

"No Chandler, I want to keep your involvement under wraps for the moment as far as the Kendricks are concerned. I think your appearance will cause one of them some considerable anguish and I want to be there when they find out."

"Mmm. It's obvious that both of you have a shared secret," Baker added, once again slightly surprised by the revelation, "I'm somewhat disappointed that I won't be there as well!"

that's my name!

One-Two-Nine

The privacy afforded by the base hospital was ideal for the family to conduct their bedside vigils. They were able to take their turns at much more frequent intervals and, thereby, shorten the length of the individual visits. Doctor Manderling was satisfied that the transfer had gone smoothly, with no immediate matters that should cause any concern.

Because the hospital was much smaller and personal than St Damian's, it provided the ability for the allocation to Paul's room of a dedicated nurse on twenty-four hour rotation. With the base commander's house just a couple of minutes' drive away, the doctor had also been able to persuade the family that it would not be necessary for them to be at the bedside throughout the night as, should anything happen, they could be summoned immediately.

Annie and RP were unaware of this when they arrived at the base hospital on Friday afternoon for their expected shift at the bedside for that evening and into the early hours of the morning. They were immediately aware of how relatively peaceful the atmosphere was. Other than the noise of the medical equipment, intermittently accompanied by muffled aircraft noise from the distant runways, Paul's room was almost eerily silent. The contrast revealed just how much the constant bustle of a large urban hospital infiltrates even the areas housing the most desperately ill.

They found they were taking over from Leanne. This was opportune, because they had brought Roland with them, so he was able to meet Paul's ex-wife for the first time. Leanne found him charming and was immediately aware of why the four had become such close friends through their being thrown together by the apparently random nature of accommodation allocation at Cambridge. This would be Roland's first and last opportunity to visit the base at this time, as he was booked on a morning flight the following day out of Mid-Continent to Minneapolis, where his connection would have him back in the Big Apple in time for a late dinner at his hotel. He needed to be there to prepare for an important meeting at the Museum of Modern Art on Monday morning, where he was assisting with arranging the loan of a number of items from the Tate's reserve collection that were to be included in an exhibition to be staged during the summer. He was also booked on a transatlantic flight back to London on Tuesday evening, but he had promised to return to Kansas within the month.

Because of his restricted schedule, Leanne persuaded him to accompany her back to the base commander's house so that he could meet the rest of the family. As usually happened, he had enchanted them all within half an hour.

Immediately the children discovered that he was an artist, he was presented with their drawing books to inspect and approve. Having done that to their satisfaction, Lucy demanded that he draw something in hers. The resultant cartoon had none of his usual dark elements, instead it showed Roland leaning out of the pilot's window of a Jumbo Jet about to take-off, waving goodbye to the family and friends on the ground. The sign by the side of them announced they were at McConnell and the direction sign showed that the plane was headed for England. Most importantly, sat up in his pyjamas in a bed alongside the family, also waving, was Paul Kleberson.

The positivity and fun in the image was uplifting for all that saw it. When RP and Annie joined them around eight o'clock, having been gently-encouraged by the nurse to leave things to him for the night, Lucy rushed across to show her latest possession: "look Auntie Annie, Uncle Roland drew me a picture!"

She thrust the book into Annie's hands who, knowing the normal images Roland produced, momentarily dreaded what she was about to see. When she saw it, all she could do was stem back the tears that were rushing to her eyes and hand it to RP, who stared at it also in disbelief. He turned to Roland: "goodness Roland, I never knew you had it in you."

"Neither did I," Roland replied. RP noticed that there seemed to be genuine disbelief in the reply.

"Looks like you may have a new career open to you."

"One swallow doesn't make a spring."

"But it does make those who see it hope that it will." RP kept his gaze on Roland, who was looking at Lucy bouncing around the room from one adult to another. After a few moments, Roland became aware that he was being watched; he turned to RP, from whom he received a broad approving smile.

This time Margie was able to persuade the visitors to stay for supper and, once the children were packed-off to bed, Walter outlined the latest report from the doctors, which essentially confirmed that Paul had not suffered any reversal from the transfer and that, provided there was no reaction through the night, they would commence the process of removing the life support in the morning.

"When will we know whether Paul can support himself?" Annie enquired.

"Doctor Manderling says that he will know if he can't within a couple of hours and, if that is the case, then Paul will be immediately put back into this stasis state. However, if all goes well, then he feels that they should be able to start some basic neurological tests by early afternoon."

"So what are the rota arrangements for tomorrow?" RP asked.

"Basically, they don't want us there in the morning at all. Because of that, Leanne and I are going back over tonight to spend an hour or so with Paul, then we will leave it to the medics. Doctor Manderling has promised to come over at Midday to give us an update."

"So when should we be out here?" Annie asked.

"Doctor Manderling wants to have a conference with us all at three p.m. Are you in contact with Sam and Chris?"

"Not regularly, but we have Sam's number."

"Could you let them know as well then?"

"Of course."

"Can you ring me afterwards?" Roland enquired, "I should have landed in New York by then."

Annie nodded: "sounds like tomorrow is going to be a big day."

One-Thirty

Sam Schneider's conference had broken up around midday on Saturday. He had received Annie's message among the other's left on his desk by Carla and arranged to meet Chris McKinley at around two so they could both drive out to McConnell together. There being no messages from anybody left during the morning, either in his office or on his cell, he assumed everything was going well at the hospital up to that point.

Kowalski intended to work the weekend on the analysis and Baker had arranged for his staff in LA to do likewise and liaise with Kowalski throughout, in the hope that something might break ready for his meeting on Monday with Chief Stanton. That had been arranged for after lunch due to the next press conference being scheduled for ten a.m.

That left Baker and Clarke at a bit of a loose end, but it transpired that, like them, Johnson was a keen fisherman. So Sunday had been quickly arranged for a day at Kingman Lake, about forty miles east of Wichita where Johnson had a licence to fish from his boat. The day would be finished off with dinner back at Johnson's place, hopefully of Channel Catfish or Largemouth Bass.

With no new caseload arriving, leaving just the prospect of endless paperwork, Holdsworth had decided not to work overtime that weekend. Instead he would drive over to his parents' farm near Webb City, just across the border in Missouri. He knew exactly what he intended to do at his interview with Morley, so there was no need for endless preparation and review. Instead he would chill-out in familiar surroundings.

Annie and RP had taken Roland to the airport for his mid-morning flight. As they parted at the gate, they felt they were saying farewell to a different person to the one that had arrived at the hospital two days earlier. Somehow his whole being was lighter, as if the weight of whatever had happened in those intervening years whilst he was lost to his friends had lifted from him. He still wouldn't talk of it, despite the several opportunities that arose at dinner Thursday night, and in the car back from McConnell on Friday evening, but both Annie and RP knew there would be plenty of time in the future for him to do so, should he feel the need. Because there was going to be no escape for Roland in the future - every possible phone number had been exchanged, as well as e-mail, home and business addresses. He was back in the fold, whether he liked it or not; all indications were that he relished the prospect.

The friends had stopped at the hospital before they left the base on Friday to allow Roland half an hour alone with Paul, his having been whisked-away by Leanne before he had the opportunity earlier. Strangely, for Roland at least, he felt that he could talk to Paul's motionless frame about his own feelings on the situation. With nobody else in the room, the nurse having discretely retired to the monitoring station in the next room, he opened-up more than he had to anyone for many years. This seemed to progress the feelings that had awakened in him when he drew the cartoon for Lucy, and he left promising to return within weeks. This time he meant it and he fervently hoped that, should Paul have heard any of what he had to say, then he would at least be able to latch onto that last promise as even the slightest encouragement for the future.

On the way back from the base, the conversation quickly moved to that cartoon. Even Roland had no idea where it had come from, in much the same way that he did not know the source of all those dark images that had emerged from his brushes and pencils before he became deskbound. He could only explain it like most creative types do: "it just happens." His friends were happy to accept that, just expressing their pleasure in his apparent new-found ability, whilst privately hoping-above-hope that it could continue unabated.

When Annie had arrived back at the Hyatt, there was a message waiting for her from Gloria Friedmann, inviting them both to dinner at Apeiron on Sunday evening. RP was happy to attend, but somehow Annie felt uneasy about it; not about meeting Gloria, they had been good friends for years and had maintained a constant correspondence - it was the venue.

She had visited Apeiron several times over the years and each time had found it uncomfortable. It wasn't the grandeur of the place; after all, having grown-up in a minor stately home with substantial acreage that had been in the same family for centuries, a pastiche imitation was hardly likely to intimidate. It wasn't even that 'created' tradition of apparent longevity. There was something else there; something unseen, intangible, that impinged on the atmosphere.

Her parents just dismissed her feelings, with a smile, as juvenile snobbery. They found the whole place amusing from the traditional aspect, but they were also very fond of the Kendricks themselves. Annie found Gloria's parents less endearing, probably due to their attitude towards the younger generation, which was less loving than that of her own parents. Annie's mother had explained this away as the difference in cultures between the transatlantic nations, but it still did not satisfy Annie's sensibilities. She did not savour the thought, at any time, of having dinner with the entire family. She therefore decided to decline the invitation, on the basis of their having a previous engagement. However, to reduce any potential misunderstanding, she extended an invitation to Gloria herself to have lunch with them at the Hyatt instead on Sunday. That reciprocal invitation had been accepted by return.

One-Three-One

As promised, Doctor Manderling arrived at the base commander's house just after midday on Saturday. The interim news was good, in that Paul was responding well to the process and there was no reason to believe that he should not continue to make progress. The doctor confirmed to Walter that his staff had already commenced the neurological monitoring and that the family conference scheduled for three p.m. would go ahead as arranged.

Walter was the first of the attendees to arrive at the hospital, just after two-thirty. He wanted to make sure that arrangements were all in place and to be able to welcome everybody and settle them down ready for three o'clock. Paul's progress was still providing encouragement and this lifted Walter's mood considerably. However, he was not allowed to visit the bedside, as he had hoped, because of the tests that were in progress.

Sam Schneider and Chris McKinley arrived shortly afterwards and Walter took them to the small meeting room that was to be used, where coffee and cookies were available on the side table. This gave Walter the opportunity to extract a quick situation report from Sam on the FBI investigation, which Sam managed to initially summarise within a few sentences before anyone else came into the room. Walter still possessed a high-enough security clearance for Sam to have no qualms about talking about any details with him, and Walter expressed his satisfaction that they were beginning to build a picture of Shepherd and his background.

He also checked with Sam that his office was receiving copies of all of the research results coming out of Fort Detrick, to which he not only received an affirmative response, but also Sam's assurance that the detail of the compound components that they were managing to retrieve were being cross-checked against purchase invoices and manifests that were emerging from the Berger & Pastore records being combed-through by the LA Field Office. As well as identifying Shepherd's clients, Sam's office also had a priority on flagging-up any potential supplier or manufacturer for the contents of the syringe used on Paul.

Next to arrive were Leanne and Margie, who had detoured via a house on base where a birthday party was in progress; the children had been deposited there for the afternoon. Just behind them were RP and Annie. Annie also took the opportunity to have a quiet update from Sam who, in doing so, invited her, RP and Chris over to his house for dinner that evening. Chris declined, as he had already arranged to take the family out for a rare Saturday treat, but in doing so assured that there was nothing he felt he could add to what Sam could tell them; Annie and RP gratefully accepted.

Just after three p.m, Doctor Manderling arrived. Having encouraged everyone to take a seat, he began his report: "I am very pleased to tell you all that we began to remove the artificial support to Lieutenant Kleberson at nine a.m. this

That's my Name!

morning, and that by midday we had established a sufficiently stable status to enable that support to be downgraded to a secondary level. That situation has persisted for a further three hours, unaltered, so I believe that we will be in a position by six p.m. this evening to completely remove that artificial support."

There was an immediate rush of elation around the room as several of the attendees hugged each other in relief. Doctor Manderling resumed: "I can obviously see how welcome that news is to all of you, but it would be wrong of me not to council caution - these are very early days."

Walter responded: "rest assured Doc that we are not getting ahead of ourselves, but this is the first bit of really positive news we have had for nearly a week, so forgive us for allowing our feelings to show for a short while." It was the nearest Walter's emotional straitjacket, imposed by his training, would allow him to get to actually punching the air. He continued: "on behalf of everybody here, I want to thank you for doing all that you are to help our son, our relative, our friend, to have every opportunity to recover."

The rest all acknowledged their support and there was even a brief ripple of spontaneous applause; it may have been inappropriate, but nobody cared. The doctor quickly brought them back to the matter in hand: "thank you for those words, General, but it is just my job. I have a little more news for you, also positive news I believe, which is that although your son is still unconscious at this point, we are already seeing evidence that his brain patterns may be beginning to restore." Leanne let out a gasp of joy, immediately clamping her hand over her mouth to curtail it; Margie put an arm around her.

Manderling carried-on: "we will continue to monitor this, but if everything remains as it is, then we shall commence the cleansing process this evening. Consequently, I can let you all have a few minutes in turn with Lieutenant Kleberson after we finish in here, but I must then ask you to not return until tomorrow. We will, of course, keep the General apprised of what is happening, and I'm sure he will pass those details on to you."

"What time tomorrow?" Sam asked.

"We should be in a position to let you visit after, say, two p.m. But I need to give you a few guidelines while I have you all here, if I may?" They all nodded their agreement. "He may have achieved some degree of sensory awareness by then, in which case you will need to avoid anything of a sudden nature. He is still very seriously ill and anything may cause him to relapse. What I mean by sensory awareness is that his hearing, maybe even his sight, should begin to return to him, but his brain may not be able to process the information being relayed to it. This could translate into a form of reaction, but we are not expecting any immediate return of muscular control. You will see no movement for a considerable time yet, the only indication of a reflex reaction will show on the monitoring, meaning our staff will have to be in the next room watching the screens while you are with him. So no loud noises, no sudden movements, nothing that could accidentally alarm him. If we start picking-up signals we do not like the look of, we will have to cut your visit short until we can restabilise."

"How will we know if he can tell we are there?" Margie asked.

"You won't, not for a few days at the very least and probably not for weeks I'm afraid. Ostensibly he will not appear any different from how he does now, except that there should be a lot less tubes and equipment around him. All we can do is sit, watch and wait. If he's coming back to us, he will do so in his own time."

"Is there anything we can do to help him?" Annie asked.

"As soon as we are sure that he is starting to function again, we will open his eyes. Then we will put some special goggles and headphones on him. They will allow us to regulate the levels of light and sound that he receives, which we will raise systematically as we are assured that his brain is able to process again. When we have completed that part, we will just use them when we want him to sleep, as we will need to reintroduce his body to sleep patterns and routines. This is going to be a long process, I'm sorry."

"But will he hear or see us?" Leanne asked in somewhat anguished tones.

"What I would like you to do, regardless of what he is wearing when you are with him, is to speak to him. You can speak to him about anything you like, but do so quietly and calmly in an even timbre; also touch him, hold his hand, but again very gently - no surprises. Finally, when you arrive and before you leave, let him see your face. Hold a position in front of his eyes for a few minutes so that, if he is able, he can focus and then re-associate your face with your voice. If any of that produces a physical reaction of any kind, tell us straight away."

As there were no more questions, Doctor Manderling took his leave and, after accepting everyone's handshakes and thanks, plus an impromptu hug from Leanne, he went out into the corridor. He was followed there by Walter, who stopped him: "Doc, I just wondered if I can be here when you switch that infernal machine off. It's just that I was there when he was born," he paused as the emotion took a hold momentarily, "and I guess this will be a sort of rebirth, so I want to witness it as well."

The doctor smiled: "of course General, but just you, OK?"

"Sure Doc, you have my word." Both men nodded.

Walter returned to the meeting room and to commanding-officer mode: "alright everyone, we have a little time available to see Paul so I suggest that we do so in pairs and, unless there are any objections, Leanne and Margie should go in first so that they are free to fetch the children afterwards. Do you want to bring them over Leanne?"

"I don't think so, not after ice cream and soda, but I will bring them over tomorrow, assuming everything is going to plan."

"In that case I will take the final slot this afternoon to let these fine folks get away." With that, Leanne and Margie left the room.

Walter turned to RP: "I understand that we have a bit of a media presence out by the main gate."

"Yes," RP replied, "but I don't think they are doing much except sitting there - nobody approached us when we came in."

"They will," Walter replied, "we had an incident a few years back and they descended on us in their droves; just watched at first until they were able to work out who to ambush. If you get any trouble, tell the guards on the gate and they'll let Pete Vrabel know. He'll get the base liaison officer to sort it out."

Walter encouraged Annie and RP to see Paul next. He intended to glean extra information from Sam and Chris, but there was little more they could tell him. They perceived Walter's need-to-know as a way of his coming to terms with the circumstances that had brought his eldest child to death's door, and a small way back. In some manner, this was similar to the needs of Paul's close friends, but not to the depth that Annie, in particular, wanted to understand the killer.

Sam summarised it to Paul as he completed his short visit accompanied by Chris McKinley: "I think your Dad's conducting a form of private military enquiry, a way of understanding what went wrong so as not to let it happen again. He's looking to work-out where to put the cotton-wool to protect you when he has you back. Annie, on the other hand, wants to get inside heads; she wants to know why on earth you put yourself in harm's way like that."

He concluded with a smile: "I warn you my friend, the first thing she's going to do when you prove you're fit and well again, is kick your ass good and hard!"

One-Three-Two

Dinner at the Schneiders was a happy event; most of the chat was about England and the times the friends had spent there with Paul. Sam was not aware of some of the scrapes they got into, and certainly had no previous knowledge of the showdown at Godmanchester over Paul's continued study at Cambridge after the rest of the family moved back to the 'States. It finally put some background behind that first meeting with Paul all those years back at the base commander's house, something that neither Annie nor RP had any real knowledge of either.

It was during these exchanges that the link between Annie's family and the Kendricks emerged. Although he didn't show it, Sam was taken-aback by the revelation, but quickly established, by a few discrete questions, that there was no direct link between Paul and the Kendricks, other than being the next occupant of the coach house at the Flemings' country home after Gloria had returned to the USA. Having also discovered that Annie and her husband were to have lunch with Gloria the following day, he decided to not pursue the subject any further at that point, but also to be somewhat more selective with the information he passed on to Annie.

The opportunity of a one-to-one was afforded by RP's gallant offer to assist Clara with clearing away. It was obvious that RP had received the same briefing from his wife as Clara had from her husband because when, in the kitchen afterwards, Clara offered to show him around the garden, he accepted without a moment's thought; RP hated gardening.

Sam underwent a cross-examination by Annie as good as any he had been subjected to by a reasonable defence lawyer. Because of that experience, he was able to duck the more dangerous questions and filter the answers to others without Annie having any indication that she was getting anything other than a full and frank disclosure of what it was possible for Sam to tell her. What he couldn't reveal, she recognised as being either pertinent to his investigation, or simply part of the many unknowns at that point. Sam concluded by assuring Annie that he would be more than happy to update her going forward, but in return she must not disclose anything he had told her to anyone, including RP.

Although that request had surprised her, Annie gratefully acceded to it; what she hadn't told Sam was that RP wasn't seeking that level of detail, not yet-awhile in any case. Sam was also content that her acceptance meant, if Gloria Friedmann's luncheon appointment the following day was not intended to be just the simple meeting of two old friends, that at least the 'enemy' would not have a conduit into his investigation. Just to be sure, he had fed-in a couple of red herrings that should cause a reaction in that camp, should they be disclosed. Sam had not risen to his current position by being anything other than the consummate Agent.

One-Three-Three

The following day at midday, Pete Baker was hauling-in an eight-pound Walleye that would provide that evening's dinner, Holdsworth was assisting his father deliver an Angus calf, Chris McKinley was buying funnel cake for his kids at McDonald Stadium before settling them down for a crucial Butler Grizzlies game against Hutchinson, and Schneider was contemplating another beer on the deck at the back of his house as his wife pruned some roses. At the base commander's house, Doctor Manderling was delivering another promising report to the Kleberson family.

At the Hyatt, a glamorous and sophisticatedly-dressed woman approached the front desk. The reception manager had recognised Gloria Friedmann even before she pushed through the revolving door that led from the front terrace; the Kendrick Corporation was one of the hotel's most important corporate customers.

He greeted her as she completed the traverse of the foyer: "good afternoon Mrs Friedmann."

"Good afternoon George, it's unusual to see you on duty on a Sunday."

"I'm glad I am, Ma'am - how can I assist you?"

"I'm having lunch with Mr and Mrs Prabhakar; they are guests of yours here."

"They are indeed. I didn't realise they were visiting the Corporation."

"They're not George, Mrs Prabhakar is an old friend of mine." If Annie and RP's guest status had not been high-enough through their occupation of one of the best suites in the hotel, it had just gone stratospheric.

"I believe they are in their room," George replied, "shall I call them and tell them you're here?"

Gloria was looking across the foyer towards the lifts. One of the doors opened and Annie stepped-out, followed by RP: "I don't think that will be necessary, thank you George," Gloria concluded. She walked towards the couple as they crossed the marble floor towards her. The two women met in a warm embrace. George picked-up the phone and dialled the restaurant to alert the Maitre'D.

Annie kissed Gloria warmly on the cheek; she was British, none of that Hollywood kissing-air nonsense for her. Gloria stood back slightly grabbing Annie's hands and making the usual opening noises: "let me look at you darling. Goodness, how long has it been?"

"Five years?" Annie replied, looking at RP quizzically; he nodded.

"Since the wedding I suppose," RP added holding-out his hand, which Gloria took gingerly.

"My goodness, you've put on some weight." She gestured with her head towards Annie: "she must be a much better cook these days than I remember."

RP laughed: "God no! But she knows how to employ one."

Annie boxed his arm and gave him an indignant look: "then, if you've really put on that much weight, I'm going to sack her as soon as we get back!"

"I haven't," he appealed, pulling his abs in theatrically; all three laughed. "We've got a table here," he continued, "if that's OK with you Gloria."

"Perfect!" she responded, "actually their luncheon menu is much better than the dinner one as I recall. Now tell me, am I still to call you by your initials, or have you finally succumbed to the needs of society?"

"You're our guest, so you can call me Rashid if you prefer. But I warn you, I may not realise you're talking to me."

"What he's saying Gloria," Annie observed, "is that as well as getting fat, he's going deaf as well. Won't be long before I'm pushing the old buffer around in a bath chair!"

"A fate that is best avoided by regular feeding," RP responded with a laugh. He indicated with his hand in the direction of the restaurant: "shall we?"

The Maitre'D welcomed the group at the entrance and showed them to a discrete table in an alcove where they could talk happily, whilst still having a good view across the river towards the Lawrence-Dumant Stadium. He fussed around their table constantly, much to Gloria's delight and Annie's quiet annoyance. The three exchanged recent family histories over the intervening five years, swapped anecdotes on children whilst nibbling at their starters, issued medical bulletins on parents whilst devouring their mains, then bemoaned the social mores of siblings over dessert. It wasn't until they were on coffee that the reason for the Prabhakars' visit came into the conversation. Annie was welcoming the fact they had finally got together again, to which Gloria observed: "which makes it such a shame that you were brought here by such awful circumstances."

"Yes," Annie mused, "poor Paul."

"I understand they've moved him. Have you seen him since that happened?"

"Oh yes, we saw him briefly yesterday."

"And how is he?"

"Outwardly, unchanged, wouldn't you say." She looked at her husband.

"In that he's flat on his back with a load of pipes coming out of him," RP responded, "absolutely. But the prognosis is better."

"In what way?" Gloria enquired, "I thought he was in a coma."

"He was, still is I suppose," Annie responded, "but the doctors think they might be able to bring him out of it - eventually."

"Really? That is good news, we thought there was little hope for him."

"You did?" Annie felt surprise at this response, "how did you get that impression?"

"From the media. Television's been full of the story, although I guess you have been too busy to see much of that."

Annie felt a little guilty at her reaction: "oh, of course, television. How silly of me - no, we haven't seen much since we've been here."

"Of course you haven't, in the circumstances. To be honest, as you are so close, probably best you haven't. Usual mixture of half-truths and rampant speculation, you would find it upsetting - best to stay away from it. Have they been bothering you?"

"Who?"

"The media."

"Good Lord, no! I don't think they even realise who we are."

"Keep it that way darling, you don't need that bunch of wolves on your trail."

"What are they saying?"

"Oh, mainly historical stuff, putting two and two together to make twenty-two. All they really know is Paul Kleberson the cop, so they're basing it all on that persona - which of course is nothing like the real thing."

"No it's not. If you had been able to meet him before," Annie hesitated, "before ... this ... well, you would know what he is really like."

"But I have met him."

"You have?"

"Yes darling, twice. At your wedding, of course, and then last Monday, not hours before he was attacked."

"What?" Annie and RP responded simultaneously.

"Where?" RP asked.

"How?" Annie added.

"He came out to Apeiron."

That's my Name!

Annie and RP looked at each other in shock. It was RP who tried to get a handle on the situation: "what - not on business, surely?"

"Oh, I expect so; he said he wanted to talk to Pops, but he was away."

"He wanted to talk to your Father? On the case he was on?"

"Probably - don't forget the first victim of that animal was my brother's fiancé."

"Oh my God!" Annie's jaw dropped open. She didn't know whether to speak, hug her friend, or just burst into tears for being so self-centred. All that came out was: "oh Gloria?" Then she clamped her hand over her mouth in anguish.

RP tried to take a hold of the situation: "I'm so sorry Gloria, we ..."

"Oh goodness," Gloria said with some surprise, "look, it's not ... I'm not ... oh, whatever way I put it, it's going to sound awkward." She took a deep breath then continued very matter of fact: "Hilary was a lovely person, we got on well, she would have been a wonderful addition to the Kendrick fold, but we weren't - close. What happened to her was utterly horrible, but it doesn't have the emotional baggage attached to it for me that your situation with Paul Kleberson has for you guys."

"But what about Johnson?" Annie was trying to piece these revelations together, "how must he be feeling?"

"Johnson's Johnson," Gloria responded with a slight degree of exasperation: "who the hell knows? I've barely seen him this last year, let alone since this all started happening. Emil sees him more than I do, business, you know? He says he's bearing up," she looked at RP, "whatever that means in male-speak."

"It means he's hurting like hell," RP observed sympathetically.

"Exactly, which for Johnson means that he's tearing-up the town looking for solace at the bottom of a bottle ... or worse."

"Can we help?" RP's humanitarian instincts kicked-in automatically.

Gloria laughed out loud, which just made the whole atmosphere even more uncomfortable for the other two at the table: "help? Johnson? Oh you darling man, you really are too kind to be involved in things like this!" She turned to Annie: "you are such a lucky girl to not only know two such men as Rashid here and Lieutenant Paul Kleberson, but to have them as soul-mates as well."

"But ..." Annie tried to say something, anything, to puncture the bubble that was enveloping them all.

"Annie," Gloria said peremptorily: "stop - stop now! What you know of Johnson is what you have pieced together from the very few encounters you had with him when he was a kid, like we all were at the time. The grown-up Johnson - no, that gives the impression that he ever did grow-up - the evolved version of Johnson, yes that's better, is not what you might have thought that apparently shy little brat turned-into. The tragedy in Hilary being murdered, from Johnson's viewpoint, is that it's probably destroyed what was left of his ticket back into the corral that his father threw him out of around the time that you two married. It's a very long story and one that I have no reason to bore you with, other than to say that my husband has invested a huge amount of his time into making it happen, probably all wasted." She laughed quietly to herself, finishing with a throwaway aside: "just like Johnson probably is as we speak."

"I'm so sorry ..." Annie's old-fashioned Englishness tried again to mitigate.

But Gloria wasn't having it: "no, Annie, I'm sorry. I'm sorry that wonderful friend of yours that I met just those few days ago is now fighting for his life in a hospital bed. Do you want to know what we spoke about?" Annie nodded. "We chatted for over an hour on the terrace, yet not once in that time did he ask me a single question about his case. Oh, he wanted to, he wanted to like hell, but he didn't; he was the perfect guest. So instead we talked about Nietzsche, Gone with the Wind, private education, surfing in California ..." She broke off and looked directly at Annie: "you."

"Me?"

"He had no idea we were old friends. I thought about that afterwards - he couldn't even remember meeting me at your wedding, you know? I don't feel insignificant very often, it isn't something I've had to deal with much, so I didn't know whether to be offended or flattered. A hack reporter wouldn't understand that, but you two must."

RP nodded: "yes, I understand. So what did you decide?"

"I was," she paused again, "I still am ... flattered. He wasn't talking to a reputation, he was talking to a person - me. I realised that I could count on that ..." she held up her left hand and spread the fingers "... the number of people who have done that to me in my life, and one of the others is here." She looked directly at Annie, who began to feel very uncomfortable. Gloria continued: "I can see why you were in love with him; hell, I could see why I would have fallen in love with him if I had met him before Emil."

"She still is," RP observed. Annie shot him a withering stare, so he gently modified the bald statement: "not like that, Annie, but there's no point in avoiding it. Gloria mentioned it just now - you are soul-mates. He will always be your closest friend, that's just how it is. I recognise it, it's nothing to be ashamed of because I feel the same way. It's not a ménage a'trois - Paul is special to both of us."

"To all of us." Gloria lifted her glass; the others copied her, silently.

One-Three-Four

Paul Kleberson became aware of some noises; they were muffled and distant, but they were noises. He tried to concentrate on seeing what they might be, but everything was black; there was no light at all. He wondered if his eyes were closed, so he tried to open them; nothing appeared to happen. He tried to figure-out what position he was in, but with nothing to use as a datum, it was impossible.

That's my Name!

He began to feel a momentary panic, but then, almost co-incident with that, his instincts told him to analyse instead: *'OK'*, he thought, *'my eyes could be closed, or they could be open and I'm in total darkness.'*

Next he tried to move his arms; he felt nothing. Then his legs - nothing again; his torso - ditto. He decided that he must be led on his back, because if nothing moved, that was the only position he could be in. Could he move his head to see if there was anything around him? Apparently not. He suddenly felt exhausted, as if he was drifting off to sleep ...

He became aware again of the muffled noises; he started to focus once more on his situation. He began to remember the process he had just gone through, or had he? Just gone through it, that is, or had he been asleep? If he had, how long had he been asleep? He quickly recapped his previous actions and confirmed his status. He couldn't move, he couldn't see, but he could hear something.

He decided to concentrate on the noise. It was muffled, as though permeating through from somewhere else to where he was. It was rhythmic, almost like a heartbeat: *'is that what it is, a heartbeat? Is it my heartbeat?*

He listened more intently. It was more mechanical, so not his heartbeat: *'do I have a heartbeat? If I don't, am I dead? Is this what happens after you die? Just endless nothingness - a transition maybe?*

Paul was not a religious man, but religion said there was life after death, so if there was life after death, it was supposed to be heaven or hell - an eternity in light or in darkness: *'well, this is darkness alright. Then again, if I can't feel anything, I wouldn't feel my heart beating, so I could be alive - no, I must be alive.'*

He suddenly saw an image, he was on his back, moving head first, he saw a ceiling, there were lights moving past him. He went through a door. Somebody looked down at him, somebody wearing a uniform - they didn't look well. The image receded and it was all black again; the muffled sound continued rhythmically. He felt exhausted again as sleep reclaimed him ...

Once again the muffled noises returned and the thought processes were repeated, this time a little easier. A type of Q&A began - there was another presence in the same space, but out of sight. An interrogator.

Paul heard a question: "so are you in something?"

'Maybe; something where light cannot penetrate, but sound can - just.'

"A box?"

'A box big enough for me?'

"A coffin."

'So, have I died? Then they would put me in a coffin?'

"But if your heart is beating that would mean you are in a coffin, but alive."

'They've buried me alive?'

Paul felt a sudden feeling rush over him - despair. No fear; maybe both. He was so tired ...

The noises again - less muffled this time, but still not discernible. The previous image reappeared momentarily.

The interrogator began again: "you're on a trolley."
'Yes'
"But the uniform is a police uniform."
'What should it be?'
"A paramedic?"
'Yes, a paramedic; but not looking at me, that's a police uniform.'
"Is the paramedic pulling the trolley?"
'Must be.'
"So how did the trolley become a box?"
'Not a box, a coffin! No, not a coffin, can't be a coffin. If it was a coffin, that would mean I died.'
"But you can't be dead, because your heart is beating."
'That's right - and they can't have buried me alive.'
"Why not?"
'Because if I had died they would have done a post mortem - then I WOULD be dead!'
"Why WOULD you be dead?"
'Come on, I'm a policeman, I know what happens at a post-mortem.'
"You're a policeman?"
'I don't know.'
"But why would you think you're a policeman - do you have a uniform?"
'No I don't.'
"So you're a detective?"
'Yes! I am - I'm a detective.'
"So what's your name Detective?"
'I don't know.'
"What do you mean, you don't know? You said you're a detective, so surely a detective would know enough to know their own name."
'I can't remember.'
"Well maybe I can help you Detective - is it Sherlock?"
'No.'
"You sure?"
'No - why would it be Sherlock?'
"Sherlock's a good name for a detective, don't you think?"
'How should I know?'
"Because you're a detective, Detective, or so you say."
'Yes I am.'
"So what's your name?"
'I don't know.'
The invisible interrogator became more aggressive: "come on - you don't really expect me to believe that, do you? Well Sherlock?"
'My name's not Sherlock.'

That's my Name!

"Then what is it?"

'I can't remember. Why can't I remember?'

"Because you're holding-out on me."

'I'm not!'

"Then think! Can you see anything else?"

Paul was feeling tired again, but a determination passed through him that he was not going to succumb this time, not until he remembered his name at least. It was quiet, but for the muffled noise. The interrogator was silent, waiting in the shadows for an answer.

Another image began to emerge - he was in a room, looking up at the ceiling. The ceiling needed painting. A face appeared - it was a familiar face. He didn't know who it was, but he knew he should know.

It was an important face and it began to speak: "can you can hear me buddy?"

'Yes I can.'

"Don't worry buddy, we've got the medics here; it's all under control."

'Buddy? Is that my name - Buddy?'

There was no response from the interrogator.

The face was talking to someone else, someone else out of sight, but it was garbled. All that could be heard was the last word: "OK"

The face nodded to the someone, then looked at him again: "don't worry Paul, we're putting you on a gurney ..."

'That's my name'

'Paul - that's my name'

'I know who I am'

'I'm Paul!'

you know what you have to do

One-Three-Five

"My goodness, Chris McKinley! What're you doin' all the way out here in the sticks?" Sergeant Charlie Watson had leapt up from behind the desk in his office at the back of the Civic Center as soon as he saw the familiar face approaching down the corridor. Watson was the same age as McKinley, but the slower pace of life in Hillsboro weighed more heavily on his midriff, demonstrated by the pile of papers cascading to the floor from the front edge of the desk where the bulging pocket of his 44R service issue trousers had made brief contact. McKinley extended his hand as his old friend appeared in the doorframe.

"Oh, you know me Charlie, I've always liked the travel opportunities afforded me by the good citizens of Wichita."

"Must be five years."

"More like seven - Joe Morton's wake as I remember."

"Lord ... good ol' Joe - has he been gone that long?"

"Time waits for none of us Charlie."

"Damned right! Come on in, have a seat." Watson indicated to the uncomfortable-looking upright wood-framed chair facing his desk: "can I get you a coffee?"

"No thanks, I'm fine."

"Good choice, the machine's on the blink again." He gathered-up the fallen papers and replaced them on the corner of the desk, ready for their next excursion: "they should just relabel all the buttons 'tepid nondescript brown liquid', that'd solve the problem for good."

"Machine coffee! How does a connoisseur like you cope with that?"

"Basically, I don't. Too busy, what with all those emergencies to deal with every day over at the Little Pleasures Coffee Shop on Main." Watson winked as he sat down.

"Good do'nuts as well by the look of it," McKinley eyed the portly figure descending into the ample swivel chair on the opposite side of the desk.

Once ensconced in the soft leather, Watson swivelled round to face McKinley: "by the look of your sorry skinny ass, there's enough stress in your job for the both of us!" They both laughed out loud. After a few seconds Watson continued: "but you haven't come all out here to advise me on my new fitness regime, have you? More to do with Sean Shepherd I guess."

"As much as I would like it not to be, 'fraid so Charlie."

Watson's demeanour darkened: "bad business all around. Everybody round here's still in shock, just unbelievable. Poor Susan Ferguson's had to go into hiding, all them press hyenas camped-out in front of her porch twenty-four-seven. They're still trying to find her, which is why her church are looking after her - good people."

"Mennonites aren't they?"

"Yeah. They just accept it all as God's will; even so, I can't see how she'll ever get over it. She raised that boy single-handed from a whipper-snapper, got him into university, proud as punch she was. Whatever's she to think? She's blind you know. Still, at least she can't see all those newspaper headlines. Doesn't have a TV either, guess that's a blessing as well."

"He moves in mysterious ways."

"Amen to that. She was damned scared the other day though, when they moved her. Her people were so dignified you know, asking politely for the press to stand back and give them room to get her to the car. Did they listen? Not a hope! Kept pushin' 'n shovin', rammin' microphones an' cameras in her face. She couldn't see them of course, so couldn't understand what it was all about; thought they were tryin' to kill her! Me an' the boys had had enough after about thirty seconds; went over, asked politely as well, they took no notice, so we broke a coupla' heads - they listened then. Got her in the car and away, but then the press just chased the car over to the church and laid siege to it. We moved 'em on every half hour or so, but they just came back after we left; like tryin' to mop-up mercury."

"So, is she still in the church?"

"Nah, we managed to clear it long enough for them to get her clear sometime after midnight."

"Broke a few more heads, huh?"

"No need. Just started lockin' 'em up, litterin' the sidewalk's a capital offence out here y'know," he smiled, "that put a few of the more ansy ones off; y'know, thems that's all mouth 'n trousers. So they went off back to the city to whinge at their bosses - police brutality, press freedom, all that shit. Once we had filled the jail here, we started shipping them over to Marion. That got the Sherriff's department interested, so they came on over and spotted all sorts of minor defects with their 'spensive vehicles with all them dish things on top. Started talkin' 'bout impounding 'em, but before the tow trucks could get here, they'd all high-tailed it back up the fifty-six as well."

McKinley was smiling, thinking how much easier city justice might be with the application of such flexibility: "so how long did you keep them locked-up?"

"Oh, they was here longer than we intended. Judge Jacobs set very reasonable bail, least we thought so, but they all refused to pay a penny; said their lawyers would be over in the mornin', so we just left 'em where they were till that happened. Then suddenly, they was all bangin' an' shoutin', pushing cash at us, or askin' if we'd take credit cards for the bail. Was 'bout three in the mornin' right after one of my boys brought 'ol Leroy Baxter in; found him nursin' the results of a bender on the school field. We always bring him in, let him sleep it

The Mantis Pact

off in the cells, cold on that school field, can't let him get hyperthermia. Poor ol' Leroy, not what he was - terrible flatulence these days."

McKinley couldn't contain his amusement. This was bringing back memories of the fun he had working the beat with Watson all those years back: "so I guess you're in a bit of trouble with the networks."

"Oh they sent a few suits in to the Judge makin' a fuss, so he gave them the option of payin' a fine or arguin' their side at the next vacant time in the calendar. There were so many of 'em to hear that the first date he could deal with 'em all at one sitting would be 'bout three years' time, or he could fit 'em in one at a time in between. Seems they took the option to pay the fines. Day after, the Mayor got a letter threatening all sorts of legal action, civil rights, health 'n safety, that sort o' thang. Far as I heard, he filed it in the shredder."

"So they're all gone?"

"Hell no, hard core's still camped out over on Monroe out front of the house. Wastin' their time, Susan ain't comin' back any time soon. She's at one o' the church members' houses, no idea which one. They wanted to tell me, you know, just in case, but I told 'em - what nobody knows, nobody else can."

"That's a pity."

Watson's expression hardened: "you're not interviewin' her Chris. Even if I knew where she was, I wouldn't let ya'. Take my word, she knows nothin', God's Honest Truth." Watson placed his hand across his heart to reinforce the statement.

"No Charlie, that wasn't what I was going to ask."

Watson relaxed and sat back into his chair: "OK, shoot."

"Did your department conduct the search of the house?"

"Yep, day after Shepherd died; I was there with your Captain Delgado."

"Delgado came out to supervise the search?"

"Your Chief rang me first thing, said it was high-profile, man down, how we had to give him every co-operation and so on. Did you know the guy what nearly got killed, Kleberson wasn't it?"

"My Boss."

"Jeezus! Chris!"

"He's one of the good guys Charlie, likes a good laugh, you would have got on with him real well."

"Why the past tense? Somethin' happened?"

"He's in a coma Charlie; we don't know if, or how, he's coming out."

"Shit, don't know what's worse, that or dyin'. Obviously you're friends - when did you find out?"

"I was there."

"What, when it happened?"

McKinley didn't say anything, he just looked expressionless at Watson. Watson sat there, his mouth partially open in shock. Eventually he forced a response: "Chris, I'm so sorry … I don't …"

"Then don't Charlie. I'm dealing with it, best I can. This is helping, OK? I need to know a few things … we all need to know a few things, so let's get back to it."

"Sure thing Chris."

"Delgado, did he meet you at the house?"

"Yeah. Soon as I heard about the circumstances, I went over to break it all to Susan. Her neighbour had called-in here to report Sean missing the previous night, but there'd been no road accidents or the like, not with injuries anyhow. Duty officer just told her that he had probably stayed in Wichita; hell, he's in his thirties, we're not going to launch a full-scale missing persons in those circumstances. Glad I did that, don't think she would have got it quite so sympathetically from Delgado, cold fish that one."

"So you were at the house first?"

"Yeah, but we didn't start nothin' till Delgado arrived."

"Thorough search?"

"Hell yeah, he's a stickler that Delgado."

"Find anything?"

"Some spare clothes in Sean's room, otherwise just an old lady's life story."

"No suitcase, travel bag?"

"Nothing Chris, I thought it was weird too, but then I didn't know the whole story then. After I heard that, it sorta seemed ordinary."

"And you searched everywhere - garage, outhouse?

"Everywhere Chris. Like I said, that Delgado don't leave no stone unturned. Probably had a post mortem done on that dead rat we found under the porch."

"Did you talk to Mrs Ferguson at all?"

"Susan? You don't talk to Susan, you try to interrupt when she draws breath."

"So did she have anything to say about the previous night?"

"She had little to say about anything else. She'd just lost her boy, Chris."

"Anything of interest?"

"Just kept going over when Sean dropped her off at the church, that he couldn't pick her up after but that her neighbour, Gladys Breitner, was going to do that for him. He promised her that he would be back by ten and she was to wait up for him because he wanted to make her bedtime cocoa. Seems it was a bit of a ritual they went through the night before he flew home."

"So he was leaving; when, in the morning?"

"Didn't ask Chris, sorry."

"But he was coming back here that night?"

"Seems so."

"So where's his travel bag?"

"In his car I guess."

"No, there was nothing in the car, I was there when CSI searched it. So you found nothing? No keys, travel documents, nothing like that?"

"Other than the closet with the clothes in, his bedroom could have been a hotel room waiting for the next visitor."

"And no computers?"

"Not a chance. Susan Ferguson only had a phone installed a few years ago. She did that under protest and only because Sean wanted to be able to contact her. So she never used it to call anyone - these are simple people Chris. I have to say, there are times I envy them that ideal; just look at us - desk phone, e-mail, radio, cellphone. We're the ones in prison, but the only bars it has to hold us are the ones that show the signal strength and when there ain't any of those, we still don't try to escape - we go hell for leather to get 'em back!"

"Are you aware of anywhere else he could have used when he was in town? Did he have an office anywhere, or anything like that?"

"Not that I'm aware Chris. He wasn't a high-profile individual, in fact I never met him. Thinking about it, why would I? He never did anything wrong!"

"Would Mrs Ferguson know?"

"Susan, no she wouldn't know, but if anybody does, it would be Gladys Breitner. She's very close to them, helps Susan out a lot and she keeps her eyes open; sweeps her porch a lot, you know what I mean? Apparently she's known in the street as 'Neighborhood Watch'."

"OK, then I need to talk to Gladys. Am I likely to cause an attraction if I go down there on my own?"

"Car they haven't seen before, carrying a plain clothes officer? Sure will, press are like limpets, especially when nothin's been happening for a while. Tell you what, how d'ya fancy being on the beat together again?"

One-Three-Six

Scott Holdsworth had positioned himself outside of the office of Acting Captain Morley at five minutes to two. He was young and inexperienced in these matters, as this was his first summons to be interviewed by an IAD enquiry. Nevertheless, he knew what was expected by those interviewing him, and had no intention of providing IAD with any ammunition with which they could alter his current status and thus prevent him from fulfilling his role in the FBI investigation that only he and Chris McKinley, within the Wichita Police Department, had any detailed knowledge of. He also believed, although nobody had intimated this to him, that the intended conclusion of the enquiry was that his colleague, Chris McKinley, was in some way palpable in the hospitalisation of McKinley's close friend and their squad leader, Lieutenant Paul Kleberson.

Scott Holdsworth was not going to have anything to do with any such moves even if this meant that he would find himself in hot water as a consequence. He had let himself down by not assisting on that deadly night, even though to have done so would have put him in-line for an insubordination charge. He also could not dismiss from his mind his failure to recognise the threat in the Chief's apparent joke at the briefing that fateful morning, regarding Kleberson being a potential victim for Shepherd. In the short time that he had worked homicide, he had sufficient memories of the example Kleberson set his staff in not allowing politics to determine the direction of an investigation. If he was ever to aspire to such a rank and role himself, then he had to be just as fearless of the pressures that could be applied. He had resolved that those events would be the last time in his career that he would allow internal politics to override true justice.

The office door opened at precisely two p.m. and Holdsworth was ushered inside by Sergeant Mike O'Malley, his Union rep. O'Malley should have met Holdsworth outside of the office but, following the events of the morning session when Moreno was interviewed, had insisted on initially meeting the two presiding officers on his own. He had been sickened by the way that Morley had framed the morning's questions, pre-empting replies with barely-veiled threats of the consequences of his not receiving the answer he needed, essentially prompting Moreno to answer to the potential detriment of his fellow officers.

O'Malley, like many of his colleagues, had nothing but contempt for Morley, but at least his position as the Union rep gave him immunity from any repercussions of his expression of such views given in his official capacity. He took advantage of that by providing both officers with a severe reminder of their responsibility for the correct conduct of the sessions, something he made perfectly clear had not happened that morning. He also reminded them of the relative inexperience of their next interviewee, warning them that the first indication of any repeat of the morning's proceedings would result in the immediate withdrawal of his Union's co-operation, in place of which legal representation would be mandatorily provided for his members at all future sessions. That despite all of the members concerned having voluntarily waived that right in order to be done with this process as quickly as possible.

The first thing that Holdsworth noticed as he entered the office was the ambient temperature coupled with the slight hint of staleness in the air, due to the failure of the air conditioning in the room. This was not an unusual occurrence, the general view being that it was a preferred tactic in Morley's enquiries, which ensured an uncomfortable environment conducive to instigating perspiration in those susceptible, resulting in his being able to imply that such a reaction was caused by the questioning.

The conference table grew out of the front of Morley's desk. On the door side were two uncomfortable tubular-framed blue plastic chairs, probably borrowed from the canteen, one of which Holdsworth took when indicated to do so; O'Malley sat in the other alongside. The other side of the table, in rather more comfortable upholstered meeting chairs, sat Morley and to his right Lieutenant Joe Mackenzie from Patrol North, sitting as the independent officer.

Mackenzie was popular among his divisional staff and known as a very fair manager. Although he couldn't voice criticism during the morning session, to do so would have undermined the proceedings, he too had been highly-embarrassed by its conduct. He had informed Morley of his views within seconds of O'Malley leaving the office with Moreno. He had also suggested a change of venue because of the uncomfortable conditions in the room. Both aspects had been brushed aside by his, now, senior-ranking officer.

It wasn't the manner in which this was done that ultimately infuriated him. It was the arrogant dressing-down that he received for having the temerity to make such comments to a senior officer, that had been delivered by an officer with less than half of his years on the force, and little more than a day at that senior level. In doing so, Morley had made yet another enemy within the department. Unexpectedly, on Morley's part anyway, Mackenzie immediately told him so, following-up with a withering dissection of the morning's evidence and why not a shred of it would be usable because of the manner of its being obtained.

"And who will determine that?" Morley had asked, haughtily.

"I will," Mackenzie had responded with a look of steel resolve on his face. That was the point at which they had parted for lunch.

Morley was not concerned in the slightest. He had no intention of using anything he had extorted from Moreno within the report. It would be far more valuable as a way of extracting facts from the more loyal soldiers, Holdsworth, Capaldi and Dean, which he would then use to nail McKinley himself. He knew that Dean would never give him anything other than grief, so he needed something to hold over him in addition to the potential loss of pension rights. Even so, he knew that Dean was still most likely to answer 'fuck you!' when taken down the more obvious avenues of enquiry and there would be little, in reality, that Morley could do if he did. Capaldi would also be able to stonewall because there was little that Morley could do to derail his transfer, but there was still the potential of hinting at future career damage by name-dropping senior Topeka officers that he knew, or at least could suggest that he did. But Holdsworth was a different matter, a young and promising detective at the start of his career did not need to make any enemies. But he was loyal, no doubt of that, so that loyalty needed to be discredited before he would spill the beans. But spill he would; they all did once their careers were threatened.

It was the unexpected bonus from Moreno that reinforced Morley's confidence - the revelation of the two case logs, kept by McKinley at Kleberson's instruction. That would be the clincher if all else failed to come together. O'Malley and Mackenzie could make as much noise as they liked, Morley's task was to dismantle the Homicide Squad root and branch, leave nothing remaining that could attach itself to his Chief. Dean and Capaldi were already gone, Moreno neutralised, not that he was ever likely to be any threat to the plan in the first place, and McKinley was well in the frame. Which just left this rookie sitting across the table from him, already looking intimidated by it all. Would he stay in the light, loyal to the last, in which case the frame would just be grown to accommodate him. Or would he capitulate and move across to the dark side to join all of the malleable cops that had made the transition before him? In IAD logic, either way he was fucked.

Morley began the session by turning-on the tape machine placed at the head of the table. He announced the time, the purpose of the session and those present, never removing his gaze from the young detective, who in turn looked directly into Morley's eyes, unfazed: "Detective Holdsworth, I believe that you have already been apprised of your legal rights by your Union rep," he stared at O'Malley knowing full well that this was unlikely due to the outburst just prior to the session, "and that we expect you to provide us with truthful answers to every question put to you. Are you happy to acknowledge this so that we can move on quickly."

O'Malley tried to interject, but Holdsworth simply answered: "I am."

O'Malley interrupted again: "just a minute …"

He was cut-off by the unexpected response: "in which case, having been apprised of your inexperience in such matters, I will hand over to Lieutenant Mackenzie who has some questions for you." Morley sank back in his chair, but maintained his intense gaze on Holdsworth.

O'Malley and Mackenzie shot each other a look of surprise; they both knew that they could do nothing but go along with this, more to save the department embarrassment than anything else. Mackenzie was saved from his potential initial struggle by Holdsworth, who changed his gaze from Morley to Mackenzie and asked: "I have no idea what is supposed to happen here Sir, but would it be possible for me to first make a short statement."

O'Malley leant across and took Holdsworth's elbow in his hand, then moving his mouth close to Holdsworth's ear he whispered: "not a good idea, as your Union rep I certainly advise you against it."

Holdsworth turned and whispered in reply: "and I accept your good intentions, but I do want to do this."

O'Malley moved away again, shrugging as he did so and thinking: *'OK, it's your funeral.'* Mackenzie asked Holdsworth the next question: "is this a prepared statement?"

"No Sir."

"Is it relevant? After all, we have not yet given you any indication of what it is we wish you to assist us with." He looked at Morley as if wanting some guidance from him. Morley stayed perfectly still, continuing to stare intently at Holdsworth, who was ignoring him.

"I believe so Sir."

"Then there being no obvious objection from the chair of this enquiry," he glared at Morley, to no effect, "then I do not believe that I can stop you."

"Lieutenant, I have been with the Homicide Squad here in Wichita for nearly a year, during which time I have been under the command of Lieutenant Kleberson. Although I have little experience from which I can draw to compare, I would first like to state that I do not expect to serve with any better commander during the rest of my career, no disrespect intended to anyone else present Sir."

"None taken Detective," Mackenzie responded with a kindly voice.

"Probably be a short career anyway," Morley mumbled, maintaining the stare; Mackenzie shot him a withering look. Holdsworth did not change his body position, appearing not to have heard the remark or, if he had, choosing to ignore it. *'Mmm,'* Morley thought at this apparent coolness of spirit.

"I believe that this enquiry will be looking into certain aspects of the cases involving the killer known as Vitruvio, whose final intended victim was Lieutenant Kleberson. I was very closely involved with the interpretation of the evidence available to the Squad and I am aware of certain aspects that were, shall I say, overlooked during those three days - aspects that may have altered the whole direction of the enquiry had they been followed-through."

Morley strained forward placing his elbows on the table, while still maintaining the constant gaze: "go on," he whispered in anticipation, almost to himself.

Holdsworth continued to address Mackenzie: "exploration of these avenues of enquiry were restricted by two specific factors within the Squad at the time."

O'Malley gripped Holdsworth's elbow again, whispering: "careful!"

Holdsworth ignored him: "those factors were the diversion of the Detectives in the Squad, by a senior officer, away from the important lines of enquiry onto other areas that proved irrelevant and the absence of that same senior officer at a time of intense workload, which placed considerable strain on the available manning at a time when there were multiple lines of enquiry in progress."

Morley could barely contain his glee at this apparent ease of capitulation to the dark side. *'Come to daddy,'* he thought, but instead asked out loud: "and for the record Detective Holdsworth, this senior officer - would that be the Head of the Homicide Squad, Lieutenant Kleberson?"

Holdsworth turned to face Morley, looking him directly in the eye: "no Sir, it was you Sir." Turning to speak directly into the tape machine he continued: "for the record, I am addressing Acting Captain, at that time Lieutenant, Morley." He then returned his gaze to Morley, awaiting the reaction.

One-Three-Seven

By coincidence, Pete Baker's meeting with Chief Stanton had also been arranged for two p.m. This was due to the scheduled morning press conference, which was likely to be a turbulent affair, in the circumstance that the entire media pack had stored-up two days of frustration from receiving typically monosyllabic medical bulletins from the military, coupled with some almost unprecedented levels of inter-station co-operation on framing the order of questions, to unload on what they expected to be an unsuspecting set of local officials. However, Mayor Ramsey had anticipated this. He pulled Stanton into a meeting in his office as soon as he had arrived at eight a.m. that morning, to meet two PR consultants that Ramsey had engaged over the weekend to advise on the best way to take personal advantage of the situation, although the official purchase order from City Hall said something completely different, along the lines of protecting the City of Wichita from unwarranted media criticism.

By the time the two had walked onto the dais just before eleven a.m, they had received three hours of intense personal coaching, not only in how to handle themselves, but in the type and level of questioning they were about to be bombarded with. In the end, they escaped an hour later relatively unscathed but, particularly in Chief Stanton's case, mentally exhausted. In Footballing parlance, the underdogs were holding their more experienced opponents to just a field goal apiece at the end of the first quarter.

Baker, as he often preferred to do when meeting someone for the first time and on their own turf, arrived just a couple of minutes late. This was still within an acceptable timescale to arrive, as well as being blameable upon unanticipated external factors, such as traffic or tardy receptionists; it was rarely taken as rude, which a few minutes more would have been. More importantly, it invariably meant that the other party would be at their desk or residence when he arrived, removing any possibility of the subject taking stock of their visitor in advance.

Stanton rose from behind his desk as his secretary showed Baker into the office, stepping around the desk to welcome his visitor. He indicated that they should sit in the sofas surrounding a long coffee table, where coffee and cookies awaited on a polished tray. Pete Baker settled on the smaller of the two plush-leather sofas. Stanton took the further corner of the larger one, which sighed in resignation, positioning himself at right angles to his guest whilst cutting-off the exit route from the room. Baker recognised this, wondering if Stanton had taken the same FBI course, in the power-arrangement of meeting rooms, that had been part of Baker's training before taking-up his first management post.

Stanton started the pleasantries, another recommendation of the course: "so, it isn't often that we have the pleasure of meeting an FBI Agent from another State. How long have you been here in Wichita?"

"A few days. I like the Midwest, it doesn't have the urgency of LA."

"I have to admit I haven't been to California more than a coupla times - I didn't enjoy it much."

"Was that on business?"

"Once, for a Seminar in Sacramento about three years ago, the other time was way back for a College game."

"Ah yes, I heard you were a star linebacker for the Wildcats."

"I was working behind a great D-Line; nobody liked playing us back then."

"How far did you get?"

"Not far enough. When I said nobody liked playing us, I shoulda said offences; opposition defences just loved us! We got something going offensively in my second year, even made the Independence Bowl - lost of course. But yeah, good times."

"Wasn't there a possibility of you going to the NFL?"

"Oh sure, I was all lined-up for the draft. Chiefs were all over coach Dickey, but they were up against a few others. Bears were favourites, even met Mike Ditka for ten minutes, seemed a good guy. Imagine that, might even have been a member of the Shufflin' Crew lined-up alongside Singletary, Phillips, Dent and The Fridge." He held out his right hand: "who knows, you could have been lookin' at a Superbowl Ring right there."

"So what happened?"

"A-C-L, last game but one of the season; only one we won that year but I didn't get to see it, I was in the ambulance on my way to Truman. I had surgery, hell I had a lot of surgery, but it was never really right again. Don't even think a Heisman Trophy winner would get into the Draft on crutches."

"Tough break."

"Shit happens. But you ain't come all the way 'cross the Rockies to talk Football. Kryczek was one of your Agents, right?"

"She'll be past tense only when we find her body and not before."

Stanton shuffled in his seat. He had made a simple and silly mistake and instantly knew that he had been placed on the back foot: "I didn't mean …"

Baker interrupted him. He wasn't going to surrender any advantage, particularly one provided on a silver platter: "of course you didn't Chief, but we can discuss the real Kryczek a little later, as it is only one of the matters involving the Wichita Police Department that is causing me concern."

'One of?' Stanton thought. His body language was already demonstrating signs of mild panic, all of which was registering on Baker's sharp antennae. Stanton slipped easily into bluster mode, his default defence that was so effective in deflecting subordinates: "I fail to see where the FBI could have any concerns about this department, or the assistance it has provided on these cases."

Unfortunately for Stanton, Baker was neither subordinate, nor easily deflected: "that will become clear as we progress. Firstly, as you have not yet asked me what it is that I want to speak with you about, let me just outline why I am here in Wichita. My Field Office has lost two Agents, two outstanding Agents, in recent weeks, both because of the activities of Sean Shepherd - one killed, the other missing. In addition to them, we also have three open murder cases currently attributed to Shepherd. Because of all that, I have been included in the national enquiry team which has been assembled to piece together his activities, and that includes the recent murders committed by him here in Wichita."

Stanton sensed a chink of opportunity to re-establish some status in the discussion: "we have closed those cases, for what I think should be obvious reasons in the circumstances. I fail to see why you need to reopen them."

"Who said anything about reopening them Chief?" Baker paused momentarily for effect, allowing Stanton to start to digest what he had said. A few seconds of silence elapsed, sufficient to allow Stanton to think that maybe he had read that previous statement wrong. Just as his mind began to relax, Baker continued: "the FBI hasn't closed the Federal cases Chief - why should we?"

Stanton's mind was racing. Although there was, occasionally, political wrangling over high-profile cases as to whether a felon should be tried by the State or Federal Authorities, only one investigation led-up to that point, during which the felon was identified, arrested and charged. The perception given by the statement he had just heard from Pete Baker suggested that there was a separate investigation in process, even before the recent events in Wichita. So did that mean the involvement of the Bureau in Wichita had not been initiated by Kleberson, as Stanton had previously believed? Just at the point that he thought he had finally got a handle on everything, here was something new coming at him out of left field.

He could only do what he did best: "because it is painfully obvious who committed the murders and that person is dead. Ergo nobody to prosecute, case closed, we move on to other cases where the taxpayer wants us to devote our already-stretched resources."

"Ah yes Chief, the taxpayer, a-k-a the voters. Might there be a mayoral election coming up sometime soon?" Stanton's mouth opened in preparation to answer, but Baker kept talking: "no need to worry, the Bureau being apolitical, our spending only influences presidential elections."

Stanton was beginning to shift uneasily in the sofa, which occasionally issued a complaining groan in response. *'I can deal with Schneider,'* he thought, *'why didn't Shepherd impersonate one of his Agents instead of bringing this guy into our lives?'* He was beginning to realise that he may not be a match intellectually for Baker, neither did he have any strings to pull jurisdiction-wise. His political instincts were persuading him that because his only obvious superiority at this point was physical, which was not a viable option in the circumstances, he had best go along with Baker until an opportunity presented itself to reverse the balance of power in the room. If that didn't happen, then he needed to get out of this meeting by acquiring as much information as he could whilst absorbing minimal damage. So he ignored the jibe and created another silence.

Baker sensed the change in vibe almost instantly; over the previous fifteen years he had fried much larger, and astute, fish than Stanton. He quickly moved the game to the next level: "there is one thing that puzzles me about the events on that fateful day a week ago ..." He paused for a response, but it obviously wasn't coming: "... where did the intelligence come from? What was the information that persuaded you to run that surveillance operation?"

Stanton felt his anal sphincter tighten involuntarily - this was not a question he had anticipated. He knew he needed to answer quickly - hesitation could be fatal: "like all police departments, we have a network of informants ..."

Baker cut him off again: "sure Chief, I understand that would have been the source, after all there was no other channel for it to arrive here was there?" Again, the pause, a little longer this time to watch for a tell. He detected at least two - the rhetorical question had hit the mark: "sorry for being a bit oblique there. What I meant was, what part of the information was it that persuaded you that you should set-up a flytrap operation? You see, there's nothing I could find in any of the notes of our Agents who were assisting you. What I was looking for were similarities with the information that prompted Tom Bonetti back a couple of months ago. I was quite surprised to find absolutely nothing."

Stanton could feel his temperature rising, again involuntarily. It was becoming very uncomfortable - he needed to diffuse this: "you'll have to forgive me for not being able to answer that off the top of my head. I wasn't involved in the analysis, that was done by our undercover team. They brought the scenario to me and from what they were telling me, we not only had a situation developing, but we had, for the first time in three days, some advantage in the timing. As for there being no notes, that could well be because we decided to keep everything on a need to know basis."

"And in your judgement at the time, the Bureau didn't need to know - is that what you're saying?"

"There wasn't time, not for setting-up a multi-agency operation. We could handle it, so we did. I kept Schneider in the loop."

"Not quite how I heard it, unless you interpret a noose as a loop."

"Now just hold on ..." The bluster was back.

Baker sidestepped it deftly: "I'm not interested in your local bureaucratic squabbles Chief, that's for you and Schneider to sort out between you. But why did you suspend your lead investigator just before you launched the operation?"

"That's the subject of a current Internal Affairs enquiry, so I'm not going to discuss that until it is concluded."

Baker shot Stanton a puzzled look: "you've called an enquiry into yourself?"

"What? ... No! Why would you think that?"

"Because it was your decision I guess."

"The suspension, yes. The enquiry is trying to get to the bottom of what was going on in the Homicide Squad during those three days - they were out of control."

"But they were getting close. From what our local liaison, Bill Johnson, told me they had more of a handle on what was going on than any of our Field Offices had managed previously."

"They were hosepiping around, not concentrating on the obvious lines of enquiry."

"So you were aware of how close they were getting."

"To what?"

"To whatever they were getting close to ..." Baker paused again, watching for a reaction. Stanton's instincts stopped him from responding; was he being tricked? Best not risk finding out.

Receiving no reaction Baker continued: "... which was presumably what the information from your informant network was confirming?" Another pause, again no reaction: "so why remove your lead investigator just as you're hitting paydirt. Surely you needed him to bring all the strands together?"

"He was gone before the information came in. The two were not connected, unless you want to look at it from the viewpoint that with Kleberson out of the way, suddenly we get an important break." Stanton's mind applauded him on not only spotting the political opportunity, but utilising it. Baker's brain just recorded three words: *'he's winging it.'*

"So you suspected Lieutenant Kleberson of blocking the investigation?"

"It became obvious somebody was."

"Yes, I can see where that thought came from." Another pause.

'Damn!' Stanton thought, *'that's not good!'*

Baker continued: "but why Kleberson? Oh and let's keep it away from personal animosities, I know how those operate in a small city department, but you don't get to be Chief of Police anywhere by settling personal scores in the middle of a high-profile murder enquiry." Yet another pause.

Now Stanton was even more confused: *'that was a compliment, right?'* he thought, *'Lord, this guy is really fucking with my brain. This needs to stop - and soon!'*

But Baker was already back in flow: "wasn't there anyone else who could be running interference? What about the lawyer, Friedmann?"

"He's not a member of this department."

"No, but he's here often enough to be …"

Another pause with no reaction: "… he was here that afternoon wasn't he?"

"He was here to discuss his Client's protection."

"But he arrived as Lieutenant Kleberson was leaving …"

Baker paused again and Stanton's spirits lifted: *'at last! You've given me something!'* he thought, *'McKinley. This is all coming from McKinley - and we have him where we need him. This can go away!'*

Baker sensed the change in Stanton as he continued again, but couldn't pinpoint the cause: "… if the information was not received until after Lieutenant Kleberson was taken off the case, how could Counsellor Friedmann be arriving to discuss your operation that resulted from it being received?"

"I said he was here to discuss his Client's protection. We had already had his Client under guard for a coupla days, at Lieutenant Kleberson's suggestion I might add. The Counsellor wanted to know how much longer this might continue."

"Couldn't he have phoned you to find that out?"

"He was across at the courthouse, it was just as easy for him to pop-in. Just as well he did, seeing as he was here when the break came made it easy to get a decision to use his Client as bait." Stanton's confidence was returning as his own mind once again congratulated him on his ingenuity. The lies came easier once they fitted the facts; his patience was paying off.

Baker's brain registered just two words this time: *'keep digging.'*

Baker continued: "was that an easy decision? What I mean is, this was a really high-profile piece of bait. Why didn't you use someone else? Wasn't there one of your officers who thought he might be a target?"

"Lieutenant Morley? He was in no condition at that time to take part in an operation like that. In any case, his fears were irrational."

"That's interesting."

"What is?"

"That you are happy that irrationality is an acceptable personality trait for a Head of Internal Affairs."

"The irrationality was temporary, brought on by transient personal circumstances."

"Nice phraseology Chief, I can see why the media don't look forward to your Press Conferences. But getting back to Mr Kendrick, you had seen the results of how Palm Springs had gone awry; did that not worry you?"

"We weren't using him physically, he would be in no danger at all."

"Unless your resources were being diverted away in order to expose him."

"Only one person in the department knew where he was and before you make any assumptions, that person wasn't me. It was Captain Delgado, my head of Undercover Operations."

"The very head of section that brought you the information on Shepherd's intention to hit Mr Kendrick that evening."

"I have known Carlos for years, I would trust him with my life!"

"I don't doubt it Chief and there is no reason for you not to. But tell me - do you trust all of his undercover officers? All those characters who live dual lives for months on end, years sometimes, cosying up to seriously criminal minds on a regular basis? Just stop for a minute and think how many of them you know ..."

Baker paused again, but this time just for effect: "... I mean really know - and not just as a name on an assignment sheet. How many can you put a face to when you read that name? How many of their wives' names do you know, or their kids, or even if they have a wife and kids? How many support The Chiefs, play golf, go on hunting trips with their pals? How many have to moonlight because they can't pay the mortgage on their salary, or drink or gamble too much, or both? How many are susceptible to blurring the lines between work and reality? How many of them would you trust with your life?"

Stanton neither responded nor displayed any emotion; he just sat there waiting.

'Gotcha!' Baker thought, then raised the game one more notch continuing in a more aggravated manner, startling Stanton: "did you not think for one minute Chief that your department was being set-up? Set-up by someone with another agenda? Someone who needed the department's attention and resources diverted at a particular time in order to achieve their goal?"

The heightened tension returned Stanton to bluster-mode. He screamed back at Baker: "even if that was the case, it didn't work did it?"

Pete Baker cranked himself forward onto the edge of the sofa and in a contrasting very soft voice, delivered the coup-de-gras: "didn't it?"

Stanton just sat there dazed and drained, trying to get a grip on what just happened.

Baker stood up and offered his hand: "anyway, it's been an interesting discussion Chief, thank you for your hospitality." Stanton shook his hand, almost on autopilot. Baker released finishing: "please don't get up, I'll find my own way out." With that, he left the room.

After a few minutes sat in silence, Stanton got up and shuffled across to his desk. He pressed the intercom: "no interruptions for the rest of the afternoon please Debbie, I need to make some calls."

One-Three-Eight

It was just after two p.m. when Charlie Watson turned south onto Monroe. Alongside him the figure of Officer Nyman, a-k-a Chris McKinley, peered down the street he had first seen just a week earlier. As then, today it was quite deserted, but for a small group of ragtag-looking individuals gathered in front of a small bungalow on the right, talking. The bungalow itself was as deserted as it had been on his previous visit, but this time that was because it was surrounded by police tape, put there by Sergeant Watson as a deterrent against any daring media type that might attempt some form of photo-scoop.

"I can't believe they're still here," McKinley said.

"It's just the dregs," Watson responded, "all the high-flyers are long gone. These are the failures and wannabes that the networks use as lookouts, just in case something breaks. This lot think they will get the exclusive, putting them en route to a Pulitzer. Reality is that their first phone call will bring all the trucks and star links back in a heartbeat - sad really."

The appearance of the Cruiser injected some animation into the group on the sidewalk, especially as it pulled to a halt in front of the bungalow's overgrown drive that led to the garage set back behind the rear building line to one side. Watson climbed out first and wandered around the back of the Cruiser to meet the first wannabe, a young man, barely out of college, who greeted him with an earnest question, as if he were a network link thrusting his microphone forward in a desperate photo-finish to win the Olympic Gold medal: "Sergeant Watson, can you give us an update on the latest developments in the case?" Watson just smiled at him sadly.

McKinley extricated himself from the passenger side of the Cruiser and stood up to survey the scene. There were half a dozen media types, the older ones hanging back near the porch, their experience telling them that this was not a visit likely to bring them the career break they had almost become resigned to never receiving. He was immediately approached by a second wannabe, this time a young girl with straggly blonde hair and wearing a worn parka that hadn't seen the inside of a surplus store for a few years. If it wasn't for the reporter's notebook, opened hopefully at a blank page, and the pen hovering in anticipation above it, ready to record every minute detail of the response, he would have expected her first words to be a request for a few coins to buy a coffee.

Instead they were: "good morning Officer ..." she strained to read the name badge on McKinley's crisply laundered uniform, leant to him by one of Watson's patrolmen who was about his size, "... Nyman. Are you here to prepare the building for the return of Mrs Ferguson?"

McKinley looked at her from behind the mirror shades, recovered by Charlie Watson from the unclaimed property room and given to him, together with a jaunty smile, back at the Civic Center to 'complete the look' as Watson put it. McKinley was just deciding whether to pretend that he was chewing as he replied, commencing with the customary "well, ma'am ..." when Watson shattered the moment.

He had moved to stand alongside McKinley in the classic US Cop pose, legs apart, hands on hips, thumbs tucked in his belt: "let's get this clear young lady, as I repeatedly tell you people when I come down here, Mrs Ferguson ain't coming back, so you're wastin' your time. Now why don't you go and find a real story you can devote your undoubted talents to and give these folks down this street a bit of peace?"

McKinley shuffled to adopt a similar pose, with his left hand on his nightstick just to add some authority, but suddenly realised that there was little point, as the stick was still in the Cruiser. It was so long since he had been on patrol, he had forgotten to pick it up: *'good job this ain't a riot,'* he thought.

The young man took up the questioning, with the earnestness of someone who believed they had just found some profound meaning in the scenario: "but if there is no chance of her returning, Sergeant, then why are you here today?"

Watson began to chew as he stared at the boy. *'You bastard'*, McKinley thought, *'that was going to be my effect.'*

Watson leant forward so that his face was within inches of the young reporter's, then said in a low and metered tone: "because, 'Sir', we are here to placate the locals who have asked us to clear this street of the garbage that has been littering it this past week or so. To attempt, one last time, to assure them that you, as members of the fourth estate, have every right to be doin' what you're doin', however annoying and offensive having such a constant blemish on their fine landscape has become. So now, with your kind permission, Officer Nyman and I are going into that property there," Watson pointed at Gladys Breitner's bungalow next door, "to meet with their representatives who are advocating that we should use a little more 'persuasion' in your direction. If you will take my advice, it might be a good idea if none of you fine folks was here when we come back out, just in case their argument has been successful in encouraging us to make more substantial use of our nightsticks in support of their case."

Watson stood back upright, observing the two young journalists. What colour they had was rapidly draining from their faces; the boy noticeably swallowed hard. They turned without a word and walked back to the place where their compatriots were gathered. Watson turned and began to walk towards Gladys Breitner's bungalow; McKinley followed him. When they were out of earshot,

Watson turned to observe the two youngsters, who were once again talking earnestly with their companions. He looked at McKinley with a wry smile: "of course, that may have had a little more impact if both of us actually had achieved the complete image by remembering to have their nightsticks swinging from their belts!" McKinley stifled a juvenile laugh in response.

They climbed the short flight of steps to the side door, which Watson was about to knock when it opened to reveal Gladys Breitner, wearing her customary red gingham apron, but this time over a dark blue plain dress: "good afternoon Sergeant," she greeted them enthusiastically, "I see that you have been successful again in shooing-off the vermin for us." She looked past Watson's shoulder, where the group of reporters were wandering disconsolately up the street towards their parked vehicles.

"Let's hope they finally take the hint this time," he replied, "may we come in Gladys?"

"Of course Charlie," she looked at McKinley, "and who is this you have with you, I don't believe we have had the pleasure." She extended her podgy hand towards McKinley.

"McKinley Ma'am, Chris McKinley." He shook her hand gently.

Gladys pointed at the badge: "but it says …"

Watson cut her off: "we'll explain inside Gladys."

She looked at him slightly quizzically, then turned to lead them inside. McKinley shut the door behind him. Gladys led them through into a neat parlour, decorated with frilly doilies and numerous floral ornaments, in between which smiling faces looked out of dozens of inconsistent photograph frames.

"My my, another mystery!" she exclaimed as she indicated for both of them to sit in the massive corner unit surrounding a glazed square coffee table: "can I get you boys a drink? I've just made a batch of lemonade."

"That'll be wonderful Gladys," Watson responded and turning to McKinley: "Gladys makes her own lemonade Chris, won numerous prizes with it, finest in the county!"

"In that case, I'll have the same please Ma'am."

"Good," Gladys responded, scuttling out into the kitchen, from where she returned almost instantaneously with a silver tray carrying the largest pitcher of lemonade McKinley had ever seen, its neck choked with lemon slices and ice cubes, accompanied by three empty glasses. She deposited the tray on the coffee table and started to pour.

Watson began to explain: "Detective McKinley here is with Wichita Police Department's Homicide Squad and needs to ask you a few questions. We were a bit worried about him just rolling-up in plain-clothes at your door, so we sorta disguised him so that we didn't raise your profile with them outside."

Gladys smiled: "thankya for that Charlie, I really appreciate your thoughtfulness. I'll bake a batch of those blueberry muffins you and your boys love and drop them round to your office tomorrow."

Watson looked at McKinley, who smiled back, then looked down at Watson's ample midriff. Watson was scowling at him when he looked back up, so McKinley decided to start work: "Mrs Breitner ..."

She interrupted him immediately: "Gladys dear, please call me Gladys."

"OK Gladys," he smiled, "we are trying to get some sort of a handle on Sean Shepherd, tie-up some loose ends so that we can be sure we know all there is to know about him, if you understand what I mean."

"I do dear. What an awful business this all is - and poor Susan." She cast an anguished look at Watson: "she's aged years you know, just in these few days. Pastor Reimer is very worried about her, says she just sits there looking out into space. Of course she can't see anything, but she's not talking he says, and you know how Susan loves talking." Watson nodded.

McKinley continued: "so would you have seen Sean when he came home? How often was he here?"

"He didn't get back as often as he used to, probably only three or four times in the last year. But he did stay longer when he came and yes I saw him each time. This time was quite unusual I suppose, because he was only back a few weeks before, but that was only for a day or so. I was a bit concerned when he came again so quick; thought something must be wrong with Susan. So I was quite relieved when he told me about the film - I suppose that was all a load of hooey as well?"

"'Fraid so Ma'am."

"It's just so difficult to take it all in, you know." The look on her face was almost that of a lost soul pleading for guidance: "is it really how they are telling it on the TV? Did he really kill all those people?"

"Possibly more Ma'am. Like I said, we're still trying to get a full picture."

"Oh my!" She pulled a handkerchief from the pocket of her apron and dabbed her eyes with it, then returned both hands to her lap, wringing the handkerchief between them like a child with a comforter.

"Did he ever bring anyone with him?" McKinley asked.

"No, never. Always on his own. Seemed uncomfortable when girls his age were around, could see that at the church; much happier mixing with us older generations. The young girls used to say he was gay, whatever that really means. To be honest, I don't think he was interested in any way, if you get my drift."

"What about visitors?"

"Up to that previous visit, not that I saw and if there were any Susan would have commented, I'm sure."

"You're talking about the visit before this one, the short one a few weeks back?"

"Yes. There was this young woman, little thing she was, reckon she must have been colour blind or something, no dress sense at all you know. I don't like women wearing trousers anyway, but that woman, I mean, honestly - pink jeans with a sunshine yellow top and a purple jacket. And they wasn't tidy clothes either, nor was she - hair all over the place. Still, that's what these kids do with their hair these days isn't it, all straighteners rather than curlers, no perms. No wonder poor Mary has so much of a struggle making her salon pay over on Main."

"So you saw this woman where, at the house?"

"On the second time she came, yes."

"She came twice?"

"Yes, first time was a coupla days before he came home. Susan told me this woman turned up enquiring about Sean. Said she was a friend from college staying down here for a week, so thought she would get back in touch. Susan told her she would mention it to Sean next time he rang and to come back later in the week so she could pass any message on. When Sean heard, Susan said he was so pleased, he flew home special to meet her when she came back."

"And that's when you saw her."

"Yes. She didn't stay long, in fact I'm not sure she went into the house that time." Gladys stopped as if running the data through her mind: "no, she didn't, they both got in her car and drove off."

"Can you remember the date, or anything else?"

"Let me see, it was a Thursday morning, because I was washing my windows; so probably around eleven. And it would have been about a month ago. Do you want me to look on the calendar?"

"Not right now Ma'am, thanks anyway. Did they come back?"

"Oh, I don't know dear. Thursday afternoons I have my hair done over at Mary's, so I wouldn't have been here. He was back by the time I got home, because I saw him take some coffee out to his Aunt in the garden shortly afterwards."

"And what time would that have been?"

"Around four-thirty."

"Did Mrs Ferguson mention anything else?"

"Only that they had lunch somewhere and a nice chat catching up on old times."

"Did you get a name?"

"No dear, I didn't. Susan would know though, she had quite a long chat with her first time she was here, although knowing Susan, I doubt she was listening for too long. You know what I mean Charlie?" Watson nodded again.

"So you haven't seen her since?" McKinley continued.

"No dear, she said she was only in the area for a week."

"Of course. What about friends? Did he have any friends locally that you were aware of?"

"I didn't know him back when he was at school, you understand, but Susan told me he was quite a solitary child. She suspected he was bullied a bit and you know some of them low-lifes in his generation Charlie, so I guess that would be quite a reasonable assumption."

"All too well Gladys." Watson again nodded in agreement.

"But he used to see that Thackeray boy most times when he was home."

"What Mort's boy?" Watson asked.

"Yeah. Now he's a bit of a strange one, probably to do with being around dead bodies all day."

McKinley shot Watson a quizzical glance. Watson responded: "Mort Thackeray is our local funeral director Chris, as was his father before him and his father as well. Jake, the son, went into the family business straight from school, he does most of the heavy work - you know, all the embalming and so on. Mort's got real bad arthritis in his fingers, so he does all the up front stuff with the families. He's real good at that, put's everyone at their rest." Watson turned to Gladys: "I guess they'll be doing all the business with Sean when the M.E. is able to release the body."

"Oh I don't know dear," she replied, "I don't think the pastor's even got round to talking to Susan about that yet. Bit of a blessing, the delay I mean, I don't know that anybody would have known what to do about it a week ago if the body had been released straight away."

McKinley turned to Watson: "so have they been friends since school?"

"Guess they must have been," Watson replied, "like I said, Sean never came on my radar, Jake neither. We can check that out over at the school though, later on if you want, or ask Jake himself."

"Yes, that might be a good next port of call." McKinley turned to Gladys again: "so, when they met up, Jake and Sean that is, what did they do? Did they go for a beer, go fishing, play golf?"

She laughed: "play golf? Jake? Oh Lord, that would be a sight wouldn't it Charlie?"

Watson laughed as well: "I guess it would Gladys." He turned to McKinley again: "shall we say that Jake's not the most co-ordinated of individuals, would probably increase business for the family if he played golf!" Gladys laughed along with Watson at that thought: "yet Mort says he is amazingly skilled with his work. One of them strange things, I guess, doing a job that works perfect for him. Fifth generation, so it must be in the genes now - doubtful he could do anything else."

"Except play those video games of his," Gladys added, "Mort says he does little else but that and work."

"He's not married then?" McKinley asked.

"Lord no dear! It would be a brave girl that took that one on. Like I said before, strange, and ..." she lowered her voice noticeably, as if someone might be eavesdropping on them, "... a bit of a personal hygiene problem as well."

"Did Sean play video games with him?"

She paused, as if her brain was processing again: "you know, they did, come to think of it. I seem to remember Susan complaining occasionally about the number of times Sean went round to Jake's when he was home. Sean would have to go there to play. Susan doesn't even have a TV."

"So you didn't see Jake here much?"

"Only when he picked-up Sean. Susan hated it if he came round in that van of theirs."

"Van?"

"The Black Van, the one they collect the bodies in. Susan always wondered if he had one in the back when he pulled-up, you know collecting Sean on the way back from a job."

"Did he always drive the van?"

"No, mostly he came in that beat-up truck of his."

"This last visit, did Jake come round when Sean was here?"

"Come to think of it, no; not that I saw anyway."

"And the one before?"

Gladys processed once again: "yes, I did see him then. Would have been in the evening, same day that young woman came."

"Did he arrive in the truck or the van?"

"It was the van."

One-Three-Nine

"This session is suspended at two-fifteen p.m!"

Morley had leapt to his feet and was leaning on the table with his face thrust towards Holdsworth on the opposite side. Holdsworth had not flinched, but continued to hold his gaze directly into Morley's eyes. He had learnt what was likely to happen from the similar previous scene he had witnessed in the Squad Room on that very first morning of this nightmare case. Morley reached for the button on the recorder but found his wrist grabbed, preventing him from taking the final action.

"The hell it is!" came the normally calm voice of Lieutenant Joe Mackenzie, the owner of the hand preventing the recorder being turned-off: "the questioning of this Detective Officer has been put in my hands and it will not be interrupted until I give my permission, is that clear gentlemen?" He waited for a reaction, but when none was forthcoming, he continued: "for the record, I have prevented Captain Morley from switching-off the tape machine. Now, Acting Captain Morley, please resume your seat and refrain from any further such unprofessional conduct!"

Mackenzie began to release his strong grip, but as soon as it had relaxed sufficiently, he found the captive's wrist wrenched theatrically from his hand. It's owner, equally theatrically, intensified his stare in the direction of Holdsworth before dumping himself back in his chair with the body language of a pubescent teenager that had just been grounded. Mackenzie took a deep breath, cast one more disapproving look at Morley, gave a glance back towards O'Malley signifying mild exasperation with his errant colleague, then resumed his seat, composing himself ready for the next round of questions: "does that conclude your voluntary statement, Detective Holdsworth?"

Holdsworth turned back to Mackenzie, leaving Morley's eyes burning a metaphorical hole in his skull: "yes Sir, I think it would be politic for me to refrain from adding anything further at this juncture. I would, however, request the facility of adding any other pertinent facts at the end that do not emerge from any questions posed to me by either yourself or Acting-Captain Morley."

Both Mackenzie and O'Malley were slightly shocked by this apparent show of confidence by the young Detective - that, despite the outburst from the other side of the table, he was prepared to answer direct questions from his obvious adversary.

O'Malley realised that there was little point in counselling caution to this young colleague, apparently so hell-bent on self-destruction, but he had a duty to ensure that no precedent was set that would allow any of his members to be disadvantaged in the future. So he took-up the discussion: "for the record, I would like to state that the course of action taken by Detective Holdsworth is against any advice that he has been given by his Union and is not to be used as a precedent for any similar enquiries in the future. I intend to observe very closely how the rest of this interview is conducted and repeat my previous warning to the panel, given privately, that we reserve the right to suspend the sessions at any time in order to have legal representation present."

Mackenzie, privately admiring Holdsworth's bravery, reassured O'Malley, also for the record: "I am happy to concur with all that Sergeant O'Malley has just stated and give my personal assurance that I have no intention of using Detective Holdsworth's ..." he looked directly at Holdsworth as he continued, "... unusual conduct in these circumstances, which I have to say I find somewhat refreshing, to any advantage and particularly if to do so will prevent us from getting to the truth of this unfortunate case."

O'Malley nodded his approval and Mackenzie recorded: "for the record, Sergeant O'Malley has acknowledged his acceptance of that statement. Of course, I am unable to speak for my colleague who will have to make his own comments." He turned to Morley, as if to prompt him to say something, but Morley remained motionless, staring intently at Holdsworth. Mackenzie continued: "also for the record, Acting Captain Morley has made no physical indication, whether positive or negative."

Mackenzie resumed his relaxed posture in his chair in order to continue the examination: "Detective Holdsworth, you stated that members of the Homicide Squad were diverted onto irrelevant lines of enquiry. Could you give us any specific instance?"

"Yes Sir. On the first morning, after the discovery of Ms Nicholson's body, we were attempting to analyse the evidence we had in order to assess the best lines of enquiry. From the initial information received verbally from the M.E, there was no obvious cause of death, certainly no violent M.O. was indicated. We were awaiting the M.E's preliminary report, from which Lieutenant Kleberson would be able to formulate our initial information release to the media at a press conference that he had been instructed to prepare for at ten a.m."

"Just for clarification, Detective," Mackenzie interrupted, "what time of day are we talking here?"

"Around nine-thirty a.m. Sir."

"So only half an hour prior to the conference."

"Yes Sir." Mackenzie nodded and gestured for Holdsworth to continue: "the TV was on in the Squad Room tuned to one of the local channels, just in case the media were breaking anything that we were unaware of."

"Is that normal Detective?"

"No Sir, but Lieutenant Kleberson had previous experience of dealing with a high-profile case that the media took a particular interest in, and had advised us that, because of the competition between the networks, in the early stages they will often exaggerate minor pieces of information in order to be the first to break pertinent facts. As these were almost always irrelevant, he needed to be aware of them so that he could have an answer for them at the press conference. Of course, if something came up that might be relevant, it gave us a heads-up as well."

"So it's fair to say you were keeping all your options open."

"We had no choice Sir; frankly at that point we had virtually nothing to go on other than associates of the victim. One of those was a reporter for one of the local stations, one with major network influence, so we couldn't take the chance of her revealing more information via her station than she had thus far to us."

"This is the second victim you are referring to - Ms Rolles."

"Yes Sir. Lieutenant Kleberson had briefly interviewed her earlier to obtain as much background as quickly as he could; he had arranged to meet her later in the morning to get a formal statement. She had given her word not to say anything prior to making that statement, but the media do not always keep their word."

"Quite. So the television was tuned to her channel."

"Yes Sir, but she had not made an appearance to that point, her assistant Mr Cochrane was handling the links instead."

"The third victim. So a pattern was already there."

"With all due respect Sir, both were still alive at that point."

"Of course, carry-on."

"Just after nine-thirty a.m, we became aware of a commotion being shown on the screen from the outside broadcast in front of City Hall. As we watched, we saw an individual covered in bloodstains being taken in through the front door by some of our patrolmen. Cochrane was talking into the camera and it was clear that he already knew the name of the individual."

"So had someone from the Homicide Squad spoken to him?"

"No Sir, we had no idea of who this person was, or what connection he had with our case."

"Just for clarification, Detective, the Homicide Squad had not arranged the arrest of this person."

"No Sir, he had apparently been picked-up by a State Highway Patrol unit earlier in the morning."

"Did the State Police apprise you of this?"

"Not the Homicide Squad Sir. I have no idea when the information was received at City Hall, or how it was processed."

There was a loud bang, causing a startled reaction from everybody at the table bar one. It was caused by Morley's chair, which had rocketed back on its castors and collided with the credenza behind it as Morley stood up and shouted: "we're getting nowhere!" May I remind you that we are conducting an enquiry into the shooting at Lieutenant Kleberson's apartment three days after these events. This has no relevance to the enquiry and I do not intend to waste any more time on it. Therefore, if you're finished, I wish to question this officer on the later events."

Mackenzie reacted remarkably calmly in the circumstances. He remained seated and turned to look at Morley: "on the contrary, I believe that all of the events during those three days have relevance and I intend to pursue them so that this enquiry has all of the information it needs to determine what circumstances brought about an attack that nearly resulted in the death of one of our colleagues. I recognise, Acting Captain Morley, that you called this enquiry in your capacity as the Head of IAD, but this officer has introduced potential information that, should it prove relevant, may compromise your future participation in it. I am keeping an open mind at the moment as to whether this officer is in a position to substantiate his earlier assertions, but if you feel that you wish to remove yourself while I continue my examination and nominate another of your officers to act in your stead, then I will fully-understand the reasons for that action. However, if you wish to stay, then I am also happy to continue with you doing so, provided there are no further disruptions to proceedings. Because if there are, and they are initiated by you, I will have no alternative but to have you replaced by an officer of my nomination and to recommend to Chief Stanton that you are suspended immediately from your duties. So are we clear, Acting Captain Morley, on exactly how proceedings are moving forward from this point, or are you requesting an adjournment to consider your position?"

Morley did not noticeably move. Maybe there was a barely-perceptible alteration in his body posture, but to all of the other three in the room, he suddenly looked defeated. He grabbed the back of his chair and pulled it forward towards the table, resuming it as he did so: "continue," he said, with as much authority as he could muster, adding with false bravado, "for now." He folded his arms in a display of intransigence, but the stare was gone and he was no longer focussed on any other individual, instead appearing to be deep in thought.

Holdsworth had sat motionless throughout this most recent outburst, not wishing to display any emotion externally, despite his inner feelings racing with the excitement only a detective can experience at the point that a suspect is unmasked by his own actions. Mackenzie once again addressed Holdsworth directly: "now, Detective, I believe you were advising us of Mr Cochrane's live reportage that morning. Other than mentioning the arrested person's name, was he in possession of any other information?"

"Not until he conducted an interview with one of our officers."

"And that officer was who?"

"Lieutenant Morley Sir."

Mackenzie shot a look at Morley; there was no reaction.

"And what did Lieutenant Morley disclose?"

"The basic facts of how the suspect was apprehended by the State Patrol, the events that had brought him to their notice and that the gun found in his possession had been fired recently."

"But you said earlier that no violent M.O. was apparent, so are you saying that Ms Nicholson had not been shot?"

"Correct Sir, she had not been shot."

"And presumably, the M.E's preliminary report showed that fact."

"It did Sir, but we did not have it in our possession at that stage."

"When did it come into your possession?"

"Around eleven a.m. Sir."

"So Lieutenant Morley would not have known the correct M.O. at the point that he spoke to the reporter."

"He would have done, had the report been collected when it was ready."

"And what time was it ready for collection?"

"Eight a.m. Sir."

Mackenzie's expression changed to show some annoyance and the cadence of his voice confirmed this: "so why did it take the Homicide Squad three hours to collect it, Detective?"

"Because the officer detailed to do so did not collect it Sir."

"And who was that officer?"

"Lieutenant Morley Sir."

Mackenzie again shot a look at Morley, this time holding it for a few seconds as if considering his next action before, seeing no reaction, he returned to address Holdsworth: "did Lieutenant Morley volunteer to take the task?"

"No Sir, Lieutenant Kleberson requested him to."

"Wasn't it a somewhat mundane task to request of an officer of his rank?"

"In my experience in the Homicide Squad, there has never been any application of rank. We are normally working within time-constraints, which is why we all work together as a team and do what we have to do to advance the investigation."

"Does that statement include Lieutenant Kleberson?"

"Probably more than any other member of the Squad Sir; he never flinched from any task."

Mackenzie deliberately looked directly at Morley while he asked the next question: "so he would expect others of his rank to follow his example." Again, there was no apparent reaction from Morley.

"Of all ranks Sir, and he wasn't afraid to tell them so either."

"Had any other tasks emerged, or been assigned by Lieutenant Kleberson to Lieutenant Morley that may have distracted him from obtaining the report from the M.E?"

"Not that I am aware of Sir."

"So Lieutenant Kleberson could have done so without your knowledge."

"I don't believe so Sir, because Lieutenant Kleberson was working with us in the Squad Room throughout that part of the morning. We would all have been aware of any other conversations, that's how we work."

"And you were in the Squad Room all of that time?"

"Yes Sir."

"What time did Lieutenant Morley leave to collect the report?"

"Around seven a.m. Sir."

"And what time did he return?"

"He didn't return Sir."

Mackenzie again turned to face Morley as he asked the next question: "so between seven a.m. and nine-thirty a.m, what task was Lieutenant Morley performing on the investigation?"

"I don't know Sir, you will have to ask Lieutenant Morley that question."

Mackenzie had maintained his gaze on Morley during the reply, so continued in the same pose: "oh I will Detective - rest assured I will."

There still being not a hint of reaction and having taken another few seconds apparently considering the situation, Mackenzie again returned his pose to face Holdsworth: "so, as a result of the arrest of this suspect and the subsequent media interview, what was the reaction in the Squad Room?"

"Lieutenant Kleberson sent Detective Dean and myself to conduct an interview with the suspect and Lieutenant Kleberson went to see Chief Stanton regarding the developments."

"What was your total manning in the Squad on that shift?"

"We were at full strength Sir, five Detectives and the Lieutenant, plus Lieutenant Morley who had been temporarily re-assigned to us."

"Did Lieutenant Morley return to the Squad Room after the interview?"

"No Sir, he was instructed by the Chief to assist at the press conference."

"So during the period immediately after the suspect was brought into City Hall and the press Conference, Squad strength was down to five actually working on the evidence, is that correct?"

"No Sir, in my opinion it was down to three, because Detective Dean and myself were interviewing a suspect that could not possibly have had any relevance. But we had to officially eliminate him in order to have complete case notes, which took us some time because of his condition - he was inebriated Sir."

Mackenzie sighed and considered the notes he had made on his pad, before concluding: "is there anything else you wish to add Detective?"

"Only that - and this is only my opinion Sir - having looked through Lieutenant Kleberson's notes a number of times since the attack on him, this matter delayed the interview of Ms Rolles. Lieutenant Kleberson had arranged that she provide a statement at her home and had we not been diverted onto these other matters, I believe that two of us would have been dispatched to do that while Lieutenant Kleberson was in the press conference. Instead, we did not arrive at Ms Rolles' until after eleven a.m. The M.E's report places time of death in a window that included that hour of delay."

"Are you saying, Detective, that without the delay, you believe that you may have been able to save Ms Rolles life?"

"There is no way of knowing that for certain Sir, but personally I cannot eliminate it from consideration either."

Mackenzie let out another deep sigh and consulted his notes one more time. He looked again at Morley, silently imploring some reaction. Instead Morley remained motionless, as if his mind was far from what was developing in the room. Mackenzie returned to his notes, then spoke without looking up: "one last question, Detective Holdsworth. From what you know, was there any indication, anywhere in the evidence you had at that early stage, that may have brought anyone to believe that Ms Nicholson could have been shot?"

Holdsworth was momentarily distracted from an immediate answer by a barely-audible, low, almost bestial groan, emitted by Morley at the end of the question, but only momentarily: "there is one possibility Sir. In Lieutenant Kleberson's notes, he said that during his first brief interview with Ms Rolles in the early morning, she indicated that she thought Ms Nicholson had been shot. As a very close friend of Ms Nicholson, who knew her abilities and lifestyle, that was the only way that she could perceive it happening. Lieutenant Kleberson allowed her to believe that in order not to reveal any details - she was, after all, a reporter."

"Did he tell you this in the Squad Room?"

"No Sir, it was only in his notes, which at that time he had not introduced into the files."

"So how did that information come to be in the possession of a member of the Squad?"

"I can only conceive one possibility. Again, it is just a theory, but Ms Rolles, having decided not to take the press conference at City Hall, must have given some form of handover to her assistant, Cochrane, during which she may have mentioned that her friend had been shot."

"But how could that information then have passed from Cochrane to Lieutenant Morley?

"Because they had a relationship Sir."

Mackenzie was startled by this. He looked first long and hard at Holdsworth, but saw no obvious body language to indicate that the Detective was unsure of what he had just said. He then looked yet again at Morley, but getting absolutely no reaction to what he at first believed was an outrageous statement, he returned to Holdsworth. With an air of quiet despair and an innate instinct to protect a colleague, however obnoxious, from such an unacceptable slur, he launched an attack that would either dismantle or confirm his statement once and for all: "Detective, I have been very patient with you up to now, so you had better have something to give me that will substantiate that last statement. Have you?"

"It is in the case notes Sir. Lieutenant Morley was noticeably upset when the news broke of Mr Cochrane's murder. Chief Stanton granted him immediate leave of absence and prevented us from interviewing the Lieutenant for almost a day. When Detective McKinley finally was able to do so, the Lieutenant confirmed the relationship in his statement."

Mackenzie was completely floored by this, but summoning up all of his professionalism, he brought everything to a conclusion: "gentlemen, I am suspending this session at two-fifty-five p.m. Before I do - Detective, this will not be the conclusion of your interview, so you will maintain yourself available to continue it when we are ready to summon you again. You will discuss none of what we have spoken of here with any of your colleagues, or indeed anybody outside of this room, regardless of their rank - is that understood?"

"Yes Sir."

"In that case, Sergeant O'Malley will you please accompany this officer from the room. I will apprise you immediately I know when we are ready to meet you again."

O'Malley rose and left the room with Holdsworth. As the door closed, Mackenzie stood and turned-off the tape recorder. He faced Morley, who finally looked up at him. All Mackenzie could do was shake his head sadly.

Having waited again for some words from his erstwhile colleague, he decided to hand him the metaphorical service revolver: "you, of all people, should know what you have to do." He extracted the tapes from the machine and placed them in his folder: "I will go and get these transcripts typed-up, which will take around an hour. I will then take them to the Chief. It is up to you whether you wait here for his inevitable visit or, in the meantime, save him the walk. Either way, my advice would be that you find yourself some good legal counsel."

With that Mackenzie walked from the room, closing the door behind him, leaving the soon-to-be-former head of IAD staring blankly at the back of it.

find us some felons

One-Forty

The Hillsboro Funeral Home was on the western outskirts of the town, a few hundred yards off K-56 down Acorn Drive. When Mort Thackeray's great-grandfather, Josiah Thackeray, began in 1892 what would eventually become a business, he simply provided other families with a coffin-making service from the barn of the family's farm over a quarter of a mile outside of the town limit. Back then, there was just one other building on the site, a ramshackle four room farmhouse where Josiah and his wife Ruth brought-up their eleven children, normally-surrounded by fields of wheat.

The drought of 1891 and the massive crop failure it caused in Kansas, forced Josiah to look for alternative income to supplement the failing crop at Acorn Farm. The coffin-making, using wood from the large copse of Bur Oaks behind the farmhouse that gave the farm its name, developed into assisting families with laying-out their loved ones. It was the great pandemic between 1917 and 1919 that brought the end of the farm due to the expansion of the undertaking business. During this short period Josiah's son, Matthew, expanded the outbuildings on the farm which were used as an isolation facility for treating infected townspeople. At the height of the pandemic, a furnace was added and this became the basis of the crematory on the site.

Over the years, the farmland disappeared as the town limits expanded to first reach, then eventually surround, the site, which had grown to accommodate a chapel and funeral home at the front facing the Y-shaped road junction that Chris McKinley was approaching in his car.

Charlie Watson had suggested that a more low-key visit might be better to this site, so McKinley had changed back into plain clothes when they returned to the Civic Center; Watson accompanied him, this time on the passenger side. They drove onto the forecourt and to the right into the smaller Chapel of Rest visitor car park, which was empty. There were no lights on in the Chapel to their left, behind which numerous industrial buildings were discretely hidden by rows of cypress trees. To their right, the family house sprawled around to meet the chapel forming a large, U-shaped building.

The front door opened as they pulled to a halt, revealing a small, dapper man in his early seventies, with impeccably groomed white hair and dressed in a perfectly-fitted morning suit. Mort Thackeray was expecting them, Charlie Watson having phoned-ahead while McKinley was changing, to ensure that there would be no bereaved parties at the Chapel when they arrived. By dint of their respective occupations, Mort and Charlie met regularly and Mort had a great respect for the current local Head of Police, who was by far the most thoughtful of all the senior policemen he had dealt with locally across the years.

Mort advanced towards them as they climbed out of the car, greeting Watson and shaking his hand warmly. McKinley walked around the car to be introduced by Watson. Mort offered his hand and McKinley took it gently, noticing the obvious arthritis inflicting the fingers that had spent more than fifty years preparing the deceased for their last meeting with their surviving relatives. Regardless of this, the handshake was still firm.

"Nice to meet you Detective McKinley and I am sorry for the reasons that bring you here for the first time." Mort's voice was calm and reassuring and McKinley could tell immediately why he was so right for his profession: "please come on into the house, we have some coffee and muffins for you." He turned to Watson: "your favourite raspberry peach ones Charlie."

Watson smiled and indicated for McKinley to follow Mort into the house. Watson took up the rear because he was already dreading what this visit may turn into. In such a small town a policeman got to know most every family, good or bad, not just through the job, but socially as well. Many of the good became friends and the Thackerays were in the category of really good friends of the Watsons. The main drawback, though, was that at times of difficulty the job demanded that those friendships be sorely tested. From what he had heard at Gladys Breitner's, plus the limited social contact he had over the years with Jake, Watson had reason to be concerned.

The initial chat in the parlour was pleasant-enough, over coffee and one of the most delicious muffins McKinley had ever tasted, baked by Mort's wife Mary. Mort proudly related the potted history of the family business that he had repeated many thousands of times throughout his career, but it was only delaying the inevitable change to the discussion of recent events that they all knew were the real agenda for this meeting. As a perfect host does, Mort made the necessary transition: "but I'm afraid, Detective McKinley, you haven't come all this way to hear about my forebears. You can only be here in relation to the awful revelations of the last week."

"Yes Mr Thackeray, I'm afraid we are. We understand that your son was a friend of Sean Shepherd's."

"Yes he is, sorry was, they were at school together and - what's the best way to put this? They were both on the fringe of school society, never in any groups or cliques that might form, kept themselves to themselves. I suppose you could say they were both loners in their own way, it often happens with only children."

"So Jake is your only son Mr Thackeray."

"Yes, Mary had much trouble. We lost a couple previously during pregnancy and I suppose Jake was our final attempt. I don't know how we might have been if we had lost him. When it turned-into such a difficult birth, I decided that I wasn't going to put Mary through any more - nearly lost them both, you know. Still, he's turned into a fine boy and a great blessing to us both."

"So, did they become friends at school?"

"Yes, they would look out for each other. Sean was, well, different and he attracted a lot of attention from the less savoury members of the class; so did Jake, but for different reasons. Jake was much more shy, but somehow the two of them together were able to avoid the worst effects and that made them both stronger individually."

"You say different. Were you aware of Sean's anatomical differences."

"No, not at all. He hid that completely and very successfully I have to say. But he did become somewhat effeminate as he got older, so we were never expecting that he would marry, if you understand what I'm saying."

"Did Jake know?"

"You will have to ask him that question, Detective. If he did, he certainly never told us - he is not one for keeping secrets from his parents."

"Did they keep up their friendship after school?"

"Oh yes, after Sean went away to university they would always get together when he came back home between semesters. Jake did not go on to college, he came straight into the business, as I'm sure Charlie would have told you." McKinley nodded in confirmation. "Of course, after Sean started working in California, they didn't see as much of each other, only when Sean came back to visit his Aunt."

"Did Jake ever visit Sean in California?"

"Oh no, Jake's not a good traveller; he even gets sick as a passenger in a car, which is why he just drives himself around most of the time. But they used to talk to each other on their computers."

McKinley flinched slightly at this information. For some reason, he hadn't thought of that: "you mean by e-mail?"

"Possibly, I couldn't really tell you, I'm not into any of that technology stuff. I like writing letters and hearing the replies fall on the mat by the door - I'm way too old to start changing my ways now. They used to chat to each other while they were playing those games. I think they called it Messenger, or something similar."

"So they were both into video games then?"

"Oh yes, played them for hours on end. They started with those Italians, what were they called? ah yes, the Marios. They tried to get me interested once. They seemed to know what I should be doing, but I couldn't really understand it all, so I used to watch them occasionally, their little thumbs flicking around so fast." He looked at his hands: "not much chance for me to play now, even if I wanted to, eh?"

"You said they communicated while playing. Did they play games on-line with each other?"

"Oh yes, regularly. They moved on to some science fiction game, 'Doom' I think it was called. It was all so dark and loud, guns and explosions and all that killing; I just couldn't be in the same room with it. I see enough death every day, I don't need it for a hobby as well. That's when we converted one of the sheds out back into a games room, so Jake could go out there. Soundproofed it an' all so we didn't have to hear any of it. Jake's very good, so I understand, has people all over the world calling him up, wanting to play against him you know. Plays all night sometimes, so we put a bed out there so he doesn't have to wake us up coming in during the night. I think the two of them even played in the same game sometimes, as a team; all this technology, what will they dream-up next?"

"And they also played out there when Sean came back for visits?"

"Yes, Susan doesn't have anything like that in the house, as you probably found out; not even a TV. I admire her for that, wish I could be so resolute."

"And how often would that have been?"

"Oh not so much in recent years, Sean came back maybe three or four times a year at most I suppose."

"And recently?"

"Let me think ... ah yes, we saw Sean about a month ago. Quite a surprise, Jake normally tells us when he's coming round, but I don't think he even knew Sean was back here that time."

"But not since."

"No, I certainly didn't know he was home again. Jake may have - again, you'll have to ask him that."

"Actually, that was going to be my next question - is he home?"

"He's working at the moment, out in the preparation room, but he's only tidying up. It's a bit slow at the moment, we don't have any jobs currently." He smiled as he continued: "good news for the people of Hillsboro is not necessarily good for our business."

"Maybe it would be better if we talked to him out there," Watson suggested.

"I think that would be preferable," Mort replied, "thank you." He turned to McKinley: "but go easy on him if you can, Jake never says very much, but I can tell he has taken all this business very badly."

"We will do our best Mr Thackeray, but you can appreciate that we are still trying to piece a lot of this together and your son appears to have been one of only two people who were in regular contact with Sean, so he may be able to fill some of the gaps we have."

Mort got to his feet gingerly, reminding the other two of his advanced age: "I understand, now if you'll follow me, I'll take you through."

One-Four-One

It had been ten minutes since Mackenzie had left the office. Morley had spent all of that time just staring at the back of the door that Mackenzie had departed through, folder under his arm containing the tapes that, at the very least, marked the end of Morley's tenure as the Head of Internal Affairs. They might even mark the end of an Internal Affairs Department in Wichita altogether.

Morley had been turning over the various options open to him. In fact, he had started turning those options over well before the interview session with Detective Holdsworth had finished. Once the interview had begun to focus on events during those early hours of the investigation, he recognised that he had made a serious error of judgement in relinquishing control of the session to Mackenzie, control he was never able to regain. His mind immediately began to punish him for that uncharacteristic lapse of judgement, one so simple it was difficult to come to terms with how serious its repercussions had been.

Once he had accepted the situation, and realised that subsequent analysis of each critical path came to a dead end, he began to surrender to despair. He kept telling himself that time was his ally and that any option that would buy him time was preferable, because anything could happen over time that would bring the game back to him, to reopen another option that led to a positive outcome. At the end, he realised that all of the plans to mop-up, to bury under the effects of disciplinary processes those within the Wichita Police Department that might be in a position to detect the diversions that had been undertaken in those early hours, were in tatters. The only remaining cards Morley held in his hand all had the word 'blackmail' writ large across them.

There were several individuals involved during those early hours who occupied higher perches, with further to fall than he; they could be susceptible to persuasion to assist in his, now lost, cause. But to play those cards from such a weak position could prove fatal. He had decided to take the metaphorical service revolver offered to him by Mackenzie.

He got up from his chair, walked to the door and, looking at his reflection in its glass, tidied his appearance. He took a deep breath, opened the door and walked away down the corridor.

One-Four-Two

Mort Thackeray led McKinley and Watson through an anonymous door at the side of the entrance hall of the house. It opened onto a blue-carpeted corridor that was lined by four doors, three to the right and one, at the far end, to the left. Light filled the clean white-painted walls, as it cascaded through high-level windows on the left, which faced west overlooking the small car park. The polished wooden doors on the right were for offices, each marked with a family name and position: 'Mordechai Thackeray - President'; 'Mary Thackeray - Vice President, Administration'; 'Jacob Thackeray - Vice President, Operations'. After passing these, Charlie Watson felt a tinge of guilt at not being aware of either Mort's or Jake's full first names. He had known the family for more than ten years, but had never bothered to consider the possibilities.

The final door on the left was to the Chapel of Rest and its own reception area. It was controlled by a keypad, as were the plain pale blue double doors, marked with the simple notice: 'Private - No Admittance', that the two policemen stood before at the end of the corridor. Mort punched-in a six-digit number; there was a loud click of acceptance as he pushed and held-open the right hand door for them to pass through into a square open area with whitewashed brick walls and a quarry-tiled floor. The temperature was noticeably lower than in the corridor, and the area was empty bar for half a dozen gleamingly-polished limber trolleys lined-up redundantly against the far wall.

There were three more sets of double doors. The one to the right of the limbers had small frosted windows through which the large black shape of the back of the company's panel van could just be discerned. As Mort led them towards the doors in the left hand wall, he gave them a brief description of the layout. The area they were in was the receiving area for the deceased, the second set of doors in the wall they had just come through were also for the chapel and those they were about to go through led to the preparation room.

Another keypad bleeped as the keys were pressed, its approval acknowledged by a deep clunk, followed by a whirring sound as the powered doors slowly opened towards them. They passed through into a much larger area, also whitewashed and bathed in natural light falling through the large skylights set between the exposed metal rafters supporting the high-pitched roof. The whole layout, including the six stainless-steel dished slabs arranged geometrically, reminded McKinley of the City Morgue, except that this area was less cramped.

At the far end a tall skeletal figure was hunched over one of the deep sinks, diligently scrubbing a stainless steel pail. He was wearing a red lumberjack shirt, blue jeans, rubber boots and a large green mortuary apron. Their entrance failed to distract his concentration from his current task.

Mort continued his potted overview of the facilities, pointing out the doors that led to the crematory, the cold-store and further storage areas: "it's a real rabbit-warren back there, some of the buildings go way back to Grandpa Matthew's time. We've even still got the coffin workshop, with all of the tools that he used. Of course we buy-in the coffins nowadays and we have a large stock that takes up a fair amount of the space. But if we had to, we could go back to making them on site I suppose, although it's more likely that, one day, it will all end up in some museum somewhere. I would show you, but you have more pressing matters - Jake!" He paused until he recognised that his call had registered with the figure at the sink: "could you leave that for a few moments?"

The figure pulled himself upright and turned to face them, picking-up a towel to dry his hands. His stoop concealed that he was probably around six-three. His mousey hair was straggly from the hard work he had been engaged on for several hours and his complexion was pallid, made more so by the expressionless face. He moved awkwardly towards them, somewhat flat-footed, as if his frame was bemoaning every muscular instruction. As he did so, his father completed the introductions: "you know Sergeant Watson, Jake. This is his colleague

Detective McKinley from the Wichita Police Department." McKinley offered his hand as Jake joined the group.

Jake shook McKinley's hand, but the grip was limp, the hand icy and moist from the cold water he had been using. McKinley felt a mild shiver pass down his spine, as if he were shaking hands with a corpse that had just arisen from one of the slabs. Then a bright smile completely transformed Jake's face, revealing for the first time the strong family resemblance to his father: "how'dya do Detective." Jake turned to Watson, acknowledging him with a slight nod: "Charlie, how're ya keepin'?"

"I'm fine Jake, thank you," Watson replied.

"Jake," Mort continued, "Detective McKinley would like to talk with you about Sean. They are trying to make some sense of it all and you probably knew him better than most. So please do all you can to help."

"Sure Pa," Jake responded turning to McKinley, "my office is a bit small for all of us, so we may as well go through here." He indicated towards the storage areas: "I've got a more comfortable area back there." Jake began to untie the waist ties of the mortuary apron, before pulling it over his head and depositing it on one of the slabs.

Mort offered his hand to McKinley: "in which case, you won't need me any more gentlemen." He shook the two visitors' hands in turn: "I still have a few chores to complete before I can finish for the day."

McKinley and Watson thanked him for his help and as Mort left them, Jake led them through the area to a door at the back.

One-Four-Three

Morley traversed the short length of corridor to the Chief's office, expecting to be able to walk straight in, as usual. This time, however, he was stopped by Stanton's secretary, who told him that her boss had left orders not to be disturbed. He could just make-out through the frosted glass that Stanton was at his desk and the red light on the top of the secretary's phone showed that he was on the line. Despite being advised that there was no chance of his being received, Morley decided to wait and took one of the seats opposite the secretary's desk. He focussed on the red light.

After around ten minutes, the light extinguished. Morley looked through the glazed divider but did not discern any movement; Stanton was obviously still at his desk. The intercom buzzed and Debbie pressed the button: "yes Chief."

"Debbie, I have to go out. I doubt I will be back today, so just tell anyone who calls that I will talk to them tomorrow."

Debbie looked across at Morley as she replied: "yes Chief, but I do have Captain Morley out here, he tells me it's urgent and that he only needs five minutes of your time."

"I'm afraid you will have to tell him that his five minutes must wait until the morning as well Debbie." The intercom clicked off.

"I'm sorry Captain," she sympathised, "but you heard that yourself."

Morley shrugged and got to his feet. Noticing Debbie had returned her attention to the computer screen and that there was still no movement in the office, he decided desperate times called for desperate measures. He moved quickly to the door, opened it and walked straight in.

Stanton was slumped at his desk, his head in his arms; he looked up, but did not react. This momentarily shocked Morley, who turned to look behind him seeing Debbie rapidly approaching around her desk. Morley raised his palm to stop her, which she did as she saw the dejected figure at the desk beyond him: "it's alright Debbie," Morley said calmly, nodding as he did so. She decided not to go any further and Morley closed the door behind him, leaving her standing outside.

He turned again to look at Stanton, who finally responded: "and what do you want that's so all-fired urgent?"

"You look like crap, Chief."

"What, you just came in here to tell me that did you? I think I already know that, seeing as it's how I feel right now. In fact, it looks like I could make the same comment to you, so as that means you probably ain't got nothin' to make me feel better, you may as well go straight back out that door."

"We've got a problem Chief."

Stanton focussed on Morley with a look of disdain: "really? No shit? In that case, 'we' will have to sort it out for ourselves. Now get out!"

"Mackenzie took over the interview of Holdsworth and he's figured-out the Tommy-Lee Thornton business."

Stanton sighed and replied with some disinterest: "what do you mean, he's figured it out? He's figured out how you screwed-up, or just that you screwed-up? If it's the latter, I think even the tea boy at KNKW sussed that out on the day, don't you?"

"I think he's figured-out why I screwed-up."

"In which case it's been nice knowin' you ex-Captain Morley. Close the door on your way out will ya." Stanton got to his feet and pulled on the jacket that had been draped across the back of his chair. He began to gather up a few small belongings from his desk, stuffing them into his pockets.

"I don't think you quite grasp the implications of this Chief," Morley continued with a hint of desperation, "if I go down for what happened that morning, I will only be the first domino in the sequence!"

Stanton looked at him and began to move, first around the desk, then directly towards him. Morley realised he was immediately between Stanton and the door; he had witnessed on several occasions how Stanton's lowered shoulder could painfully remove any physical obstacle to his progress. However, this time the gait was slow and lumbering, as if the weight of the world was on those massive shoulders. As Stanton drew level with him, he bent to bring his mouth within a couple of inches of Morley's right ear, then said in a slow, low voice: "now tell me, ex-Captain Morley, from what you have just witnessed, does your experience as a policeman inform you whether or not I actually give a fuck? Now, as I said, I have some business to take care of. I am going out and I will not be back for the rest of the day."

With that he continued to the door, opened it and walked away down the corridor, leaving the door open so that Morley could observe his entire departure.

One-Four-Four

Pete Baker had returned to the FBI Office in the Epic Center and had been briefing Sam Schneider on the content of his meeting with Chief Stanton. It was three-thirty p.m. and they were in the conference room, together with Chandler Clarke.

"So Pete," Schneider began, "am I right in assuming that you now believe that the targeting of Paul Kleberson wasn't just co-incidental?"

"In exactly the same way that I know that Tom Bonetti's death wasn't either," Baker responded. "The difference is that Shepherd was on the inside in Palm Springs. He set-up that whole scenario and controlled it himself, although I still can't figure out how he made Kryczek think it was him coming through that window. I guess that's something we will never know."

"It happens sometimes Pete."

"I know, but we're all guys who like to dot the i's and cross the t's aren't we? Otherwise why are we here?"

Schneider and Clarke nodded. Schneider continued: "but here was different - Shepherd was on the outside."

"Not all the time; he attempted to get inside by posing as Kryczek, but he was perhaps a bit too convincing, so you sidelined her ... him, although you didn't know that was what you were doing at the time."

"In the end that still worked, though - and in his favour."

"If that's the way you want to view it, that's up to you, but he couldn't have done so without help to set it all up. That help came from within the Wichita Police Department in the form of Chief Stanton."

"You're that sure?"

"You needed to be there, but yes. However, we have no evidence that's submissible in court, so we're going to have to get to the conspirators somehow. He is a crooked cop, but there was definitely somebody else between him and Shepherd pulling the strings."

"And there is only one family that fits that bill locally," Chandler Clarke intervened, "so we need to get to them somehow."

The Mantis Pact

"And quickly," Schneider observed. "Has anything come from the review of the computer files yet?"

"No," Baker responded, "and I'm also with you on that aspect Sam. We have to hope that there is solid evidence there, but we don't have the time to wait for it, because Stanton will be spooked now and there's only one place he's going to run for help with his predicament."

Just then, Schneider's cellphone rang. He looked at the screen and it reported the incoming call was from the Bureau phone assigned to Scott Holdsworth. He pressed the receive button: "yes Scott."

"Agent Schneider, something's happened, can you speak?"

"I am in the conference room with Baker and Clarke going over developments this afternoon, so yes Scott, go ahead."

"This has to be completely off the record and you won't be able to alert Chris, because I am under instruction from an IAD enquiry not to discuss it, so please bear that in mind."

"Understood. What have you got?"

Holdsworth quickly outlined the proceedings during his interview earlier at City Hall. Having heard them, Schneider asked one question: "where is Morley now?"

"I don't know. From what I gleaned from people on that floor, Mackenzie is drawing-up a report to submit to the Chief, but Morley beat him to it."

"You mean, he's resigned?"

"I don't think so. He went to see the Chief, but wasn't in the office for very long. It was the Chief that left his office first, then he also left the building and is not expected back today."

"Interesting. Do you know where Chris McKinley is?"

"He went out to Hillsboro this morning. He hasn't returned and his cell is off at the moment, so he must still be out there."

"Alright Scott, keep your ear to the ground and let us know any developments, particularly regarding where Captain Morley is. And Scott, thanks for all the risks you're taking."

"I don't think it will be risky for much longer Agent Schneider. I get the feeling this is all beginning to unravel within the department here."

Schneider hit the off button. "What was that all about?" Clarke enquired.

"Sounds like Stanton's on the run. He's left City Hall and he's not expected back today."

"Dammit," Baker cursed, "I knew I should have rung you to get a tail on him."

"Don't worry Pete, I think I know where he's headed." Schneider picked up the internal phone and punched Bill Johnson's extension: "Bill, get onto building security and get them to keep an eye on the CCTV. I want to know as soon as Stanton shows. Yeah, Chief Stanton. Thanks Bill."

"You think he's coming to see Friedmann?" Clarke asked.

"Makes sense, especially if we've got this right," Baker responded.

"There's more," Schneider added: "seems our young buck over there has flushed out Stanton's IAD poodle, Morley. Looks like he was under orders to stage that stunt with the arrest of the dog-fighter on day one."

"From who?" Baker asked.

"Not Stanton, apparently. Paul was convinced he knew nothing about it until it happened. So unless Stanton's suddenly become an Oscar-winning actor, we have another connection."

"To Shepherd?"

"No, to the Kendricks."

"But why would they run two guys in the same department separately?"

"I don't know. But I know who can tell us - Morley."

"Sounds like he's in enough trouble already, without putting himself in line for Federal charges as well."

"Morley's a little weasel. He's not going to go down quietly, but he will grab any lifeline he's thrown, especially if his security blanket, Stanton, is out of the game. For some reason, he thought he was exposed when Cochrane was murdered, so if he got that impression because he knows who is at the centre of all this, then he's unlikely to trust them any more."

"What you thinking of, immunity?" Clarke enquired.

"We can only do that from a Federal standpoint, but he's a minnow as far as we're concerned. So if we give him what he thinks is a free walk, creating a strategic chink in the Kendrick armour in return, then I think that's a good trade-off from where we stand right now."

"Do you want me to go and find him?"

"No Chandler - can you go Pete? We know Stanton's not there, so you can use an excuse of having forgotten to ask him something to get you in there again."

"I'm supposed to be flying back tonight."

"But do you really want to after this afternoon?"

"Not particularly."

"So cancel the flight and check back into the hotel."

One-Four-Five

Jake twisted the handle on the door at the back of the preparation room. It opened-up onto another corridor and, once through, McKinley and Watson followed Jake as it zigzagged its way through two more outbuildings. McKinley couldn't help wondering why Jake had made no comment on the revelations about his friend, or his activities, instead simply concurring with his father's request as if it were just another simple task within the day.

They arrived at a narrow door on their left, which Jake opened, initially revealing a completely lightless space. He flicked a switch inside the door and the neon tubes flickered into life revealing a windowless room probably twenty by fifteen, painted completely matt black. Against the far wall was a massive rear-projection screen, to each side of which were large equipment racks, the left appearing to carry Hi-Fi-style units, the right several PCs. There were four huge floor-standing speakers, one in each corner of the room, above which smaller units were mounted higher-up against the ceiling. All of the units, stands and speakers were also black, as were the fat looms of cables connecting them all together. Exactly in the centre of the room was a large reclining black leather chair, with an identical one pushed back against the left-hand wall. The right-hand wall was mainly covered by a full-height black curtain.

"Wow," McKinley said as he entered, "that's one hell of a set-up."

"Yeah," Jake responded, "I put it together when Ma 'n Pa got fed-up with all the crash-bangs late at night; only fair on them really." He turned the central chair to face the curtain, then dragged the other alongside it. He indicated to the chairs: "take the weight off, please." He then pulled the curtain open revealing a double bunk, set back into an alcove, alongside which was a shower cubicle and toilet. On the sidewall next to it was a full-height vanity unit containing a large sink; against the opposite wall was a matching wardrobe. Everything was black - furniture, tiles, bed linen, even the plumbing. Jake parked himself on the lower bunk facing the policemen: "so what can I tell you gentlemen?"

McKinley smiled: "I know it's not relevant, but what's with all the black?"

Jake laughed. His inner character seemed much lighter than his appearance suggested: "it's for the games, no reflections to distract me when I'm playing." He nodded at the screen: "that baby sure throws out plenty of rays when it's on, no need to have the lights on then."

"You play a lot?"

"Most nights. I'm not a great socialiser, I'm afraid. I tend to find the dead are in the more acceptable state for a human being, they don't have anything nasty to say and they can't tell you lies. I have hundreds of friends on-line though."

"So you contact other people, what, by e-mail?"

Jake laughed again: "hell no! we use Messenger mainly, we tap away on the keyboard in real time. But that will soon be obsolete since Microsoft introduced that baby." He pointed at one of the black boxes in the left-hand rack, which had several wires coming out of it, one of which terminated in a headset with earphones and a microphone. "Since they started the Xbox Live service, we can actually chat to each other as well. It's early days, so it's quite clunky, but it's the future once they get it sorted."

"But you said you didn't like socialising."

"No, that's right. When you go somewhere, you have no control over who you meet, or what they might want to say to you. With all this, I can use software to block-out the ones that annoy me. Anyone upsets me, they don't get to speak to me again."

"Mmm, I can see where that has its advantages. So these people you speak to, are they local?"

Find us some Felons

"Anything but! I could be talkin' to a guy in Carson City one minute, another in Tokyo the next, then one from Milan will join in. That's the great thing about it: la varietà è la spezia di vita." [1]

"È quello che cosa denominate varietà?" [2]

Jake smiled again: "I would have expected Gaelic from someone with the name McKinley."

"Irishmen from the Bronx often marry Italians. How many languages do you have?"

"Two fluently, Italian and Spanish. I can hold conversations in half a dozen more."

"But you didn't go to College?"

"Who needs college when you've got the wild wild web?"

"Isn't that worldwide web?"

"You obviously don't use it much!" Jake smiled again.

"So did you talk to Sean regularly? I understand he didn't get home that often."

"Most nights, unless he was away on business. We used to team up a lot on the games."

"What, you played each other on-line."

Jake smiled again: "you're really not up with this stuff are you Detective? With normal console games, the player will be the subject character and within the game there may be thousands of other characters that the subject interacts with, all generated by the game program, which makes them quite predictable. The on-line environment is all about multi-player games. As with the console version, the player is the subject character on his own screen, but the other characters are all controlled in real time by other players who are in the game as well. Each player will have selected his own characteristics, essentially creating his own personality within the game, which of course is far less predictable. Some of the games allow those characters to create alliances, so you can team-up with other players, hence the need to communicate with each other in real time."

"So you and Sean were a team."

"Not always. Sometimes he would create a new character to try and catch me out; didn't last for long though."

"You're a better player than he was?"

"I think so, but I don't think Sean would agree."

"Unfortunately, we can't ask him can we?" McKinley responded bluntly.

The response seemed to completely change Jake's demeanour for a few seconds, the light and airy countenance being replaced by the pallid expression they had seen initially in the preparation room. McKinley instantly recognised the potential signs of schizophrenia sitting in front of him and that he would need to go carefully if he was to retain contact for long enough to obtain the information he needed.

---

1 - *Variety is the spice of life*   2 - *Is that what you call variety?*

He quickly countered: "I'm sorry Jake, that was a bit insensitive of me."

The cheerful demeanour instantly returned: "oh that's OK, actually it will be good to talk about it. It's been quite a shock for us all, you know, small town, everyone knows everyone else so we all dance carefully around the subject, trying not to tread on each other's emotions, you understand Charlie, doncha?"

Watson nodded; he realised that he had to maintain the persona of a friend, having also picked-up the vibes. But unlike McKinley he had known Jake from a teenager. He may not have met him socially very much over the years, but he was aware of the background. He knew that, if they were to maintain conversation, the last thing they needed was Jake feeling that he was outnumbered.

Jake continued: "Pa hasn't tried to talk to me about it. He knows I'm hurtin' it's his profession. He just ain't as good with his own as he is with strangers."

McKinley restarted the questioning: "when did you last see Sean?"

"About a month ago. He rang me, which would have been unusual if he was at home." Jake hesitated, as if he was struggling to come to terms with his emotions.

McKinley decided to gently prompt him: "but he wasn't at home."

"No. He was here in Hillsboro, visiting his Aunt - not a normal visit."

"By not normal, you mean unexpected?"

"I suppose so." Jake went quiet.

"So you didn't know he was here a week or so ago."

"No."

"He hadn't told you he would be coming?"

"No."

The transition to monosyllabic responses was quite sudden. McKinley changed tack slightly: "when was the last time that you spoke to him?"

Jake seemed to be deep in thought, somewhat detached from proceedings, but he eventually responded: "about two weeks ago."

"Was that on-line?"

"Yes."

"In a game?"

"No."

"Did he contact you?"

"Yes."

"Was it a normal contact?"

"Yes."

"What did you talk about?"

"What?" Jake seemed to snap out of his detachment.

"When you spoke with Sean two weeks ago, what did you discuss."

"Oh, the usual - what we were playing that night, how useless I had been in the previous game, which I won incidentally, and so on."

Find us some Felons

"But he didn't tell you he was coming to Hillsboro."

"No; he said he would be away on business for a few days. That's why I don't understand what he was doing here."

"Maybe he was on business here."

Jake again went quiet, eventually answering softly, as if talking to himself: "yes, and he didn't want me involved."

"Did he involve you previously?"

"Sorry?" Again, Jake seemed to snap out of his thoughts as if he hadn't heard the question.

"Did you ever help him with his business?"

"Why would I do that?"

"I don't know, maybe he asked you for a favour occasionally."

Jake stared at McKinley, as though reviewing what he had said whilst simultaneously disbelieving the concept. He did not respond at all, so McKinley again decided to change tack: "you would play together here?" He paused for few seconds: "when he was home."

Jake still stared at him, almost in a tharn state. McKinley sensed he was dealing with a situation akin to questioning a dope fiend, consciously unaware of his recent actions, yet trying to focus on them. He knew instinctively, however, that Jake wasn't a user, so he offered a simple alternate question: "that's why there are two chairs."

"Two chairs?" Jake seemed not to be absorbing this new angle.

"The two chairs in this room ..." McKinley paused again, "one is your chair ..." another pause, "... the other was for Sean?"

Once again Jake seemed to shake-off the distance he had placed between them: "yes, that's right. Sean was the only other one who came here."

"And the twin bunks? Did he stay here as well?"

"When we had a long session, yes. That's why I put the extra bunk in. Sean would tuck his Aunt up in bed, then come over. She often turned-in early when she was real tired, before nine sometimes. Then he would give her a pill so she would sleep through. Sean wouldn't risk waking her by going home at three or four in the morning, so he would sleep here for a coupla hours, then go back so that he was there when she came around."

"So she had no idea that he had been out all night."

"No, none at all. Sean never wanted to worry her - she's a real worrier you know."

"I'm sure."

"So which bunk did he use?"

Jake looked up above him: "the top one."

"And you?"

Jake glared at him, but didn't answer.

McKinley pushed him a bit: "you always used the lower one?"

"Always."

"Did Sean ever use the lower one?"

"Never!" Jake was becoming agitated.

McKinley decided to keep the pressure on: "you never slept together?"

"NO! We weren't ..."

Jake paused as if trying to think of the right phrase: "... like that!"

"But you must have known that he was ..." McKinley took another pause for effect, "... different."

Jake stared at McKinley: "I don't know what you mean!"

"Oh I think you do Jake."

"We were friends, we had been friends since school. We played games. We didn't need ... that."

"You didn't; but maybe Sean did?"

Jake again gave McKinley an annoyed stare, but did not respond. McKinley knew he had pushed as far as he could in that direction, for the time being at least. He once again switched tack, looking at the equipment racks: "that right-hand rack over there, that's all computer equipment isn't it?"

Jake was taken a bit by surprise by this question but as the subject was a more familiar and acceptable one, he refocused quickly: "what? Oh yes, I have multiplexed servers, one handling the game in progress, duplexed to another identical one so that I can obtain an immediate recovery if anything goes wrong. Another controls the internet services so that I can maintain a constant connection and one more runs the real-time back-ups."

"You have more than one internet connection?"

"Three. The main one is via satellite, which has the greatest bandwidth as well as being the most reliable, unless we get real bad weather. Then I have a permanent terrestrial line, plus a dial-up that comes on line whenever one of the other two drops out."

"Impressive."

"Never lost a connection yet during a game."

"And the back-up. You say that's running all the time."

"Yes, I record all the games so that I can analyse anything that goes badly wrong, see where my tactics were at fault, so I can learn for the next time I get that scenario."

"So how long do you keep these recordings?"

"Oh, permanently. I have every game I've ever played in here."

"That's a lot of tapes."

Jake laughed again, seemingly having recovered his composure completely: "not tapes Detective - hard drives. These servers are what are known as RAID servers, they each have multiple removable hard drives. One drive can store a month of usage."

"And you've kept them all?"

"Yes."

"Sounds expensive."

"Not really. I don't drink, don't smoke, don't womanise, so I have nothing else to spend my money on. I just work in the day, play games at night."

"These recordings, do they include the on-line communications?"

"They include everything, even the game software that is downloaded locally - I need that to check which version we were playing and compare that to previous ones so that I can see whether program changes may have caused an error. Also lists of other players so I know who was involved - I run analysis against their previous performances as well. Plus the on-line comms in case something was said that caused a distraction."

"Do you store the disks here?"

"Yes, next door. I have a climate-controlled fireproof storeroom for them."

"Sounds to me that you have a better system than we have at City Hall!"

"Oh I expect so. City Hall will always cut corners, use cheap tapes, hire engineers that aren't good enough to hold down the same job in private industry. I bet there are a few criminals that have got away with their crimes because you've lost records. You can't cut corners with data storage, not if you ever want to go back to anything from the past."

McKinley immediately remembered a case of domestic assault that eventually ended in a death earlier in the year, where exactly that had happened: "tell me about it," he observed laconically. "And Sean? Did he run a similar system?"

"Not for his games. He wasn't interested in analysis, he seemed to be able to store it all up here." Jake tapped his right forefinger against his temple. "He would be able to wing it in a game, that's what made him such a strong opponent."

"But you beat him."

"Yeah, but I knew him - how he moved, how he thought."

"Really?"

"Game-wise, I mean. I analysed his tactics and they were predictable, most of the time."

"Most of the time. So not totally predictable then."

"No. He could create situations within situations without you realising it. Control your moves ahead so you basically walked into a trap. That was when you just had to shrug your shoulders and accept that the loss wasn't down to anything you could have done. You were doomed almost before you started."

"You said he didn't use a back-up system for the games. Did he use one for his business?"

"Oh yes, I set it up for him."

McKinley looked at him puzzled: "sorry, but I thought you had never visited him in California."

"No, I haven't. I designed it - he did all the hardware installation himself. He knew his way around computer systems well enough."

The Mantis Pact

"So it was the same as yours?"

"Pretty much, although he didn't have the storeroom."

"You mean he wasn't as thorough as you in that area."

"No, he didn't need one on site 'cos he used mine."

"You have his business system back-ups here in your store?"

"Yes, that's one of the reasons he made his normal visits, to swap his back-up disks around."

"Swap them around?"

"He kept one set of archives and three sets of current back-ups - one in his office, one in a bank vault and one here, along with the archives."

"So he would give them to you when he came here to visit his Aunt."

"No, he has his own passcode for the storeroom. I don't touch his rack in there."

"So when was the last time he swapped them around?"

"Three or four months ago."

"So not on either of his two recent visits."

"No. Like I said, it wasn't a normal visit a month ago and I didn't even know he was here this last time."

"So he couldn't have visited your store without you knowing."

Jake went quiet once more. McKinley didn't want to lose him again, so decided to prompt him quickly: "well could he or couldn't he?" Jake remained quiet. McKinley felt this was a crucial point: "Jake, did Sean have a key to this building?"

Jake didn't respond verbally, instead just nodding his head slowly in the affirmative. McKinley continued: "so, could Sean have visited your store here during that last visit without your knowledge?"

Jake continued to nod, but was mentally drifting away again. McKinley decided to risk jumping to the final question he had been working towards over the last ten minutes or so: "Jake, where is Kryczek?"

Jake stared at him, a puzzled look on his face: "Kryczek?" he asked.

"Kryczek. The woman whose body you collected in your van with Sean a month ago."

Charlie Watson, who had been sitting observing all of the interview throughout, turned to look at McKinley with some degree of disgust at the suggestion. All he saw was McKinley's profile, leant forward in the chair concentrating directly on Jake. Watson returned his view to Jake to see that there was a look of abject horror on his face.

Jake's jaw had dropped open and his eyes were filling with tears. He dropped off the edge of the bunk onto his knees, staring straight at McKinley as if he was about to crave forgiveness for some great misdeed. Instead, he buried his head in his hands and crumpled to the floor into a foetal position, his entire body convulsed by the sobbing that was emerging from him, along with a deep otherworldly groan akin to that of a cornered animal subsuming to its ultimate fate.

Find us some Felons

One-Four-Six

Sam Schneider was back in his office, going over a summary given to him by Jim Kowalski providing the initial analysis of the company details from the computer files recovered from the premises of Berger & Pastore in Palo Alto.

There were nearly three hundred business names on the list, but Kowalski had used a yellow highlighter on five of them: "those five companies all have obvious connections to the Kendricks, specifically the division that the son has overall responsibility for," Kowalski had announced in his usual matter-of-fact style. "I suspect, as we dig deeper, we will find more," he had appended as he departed Schneider's office a few minutes previously.

Schneider sat there just reviewing the list randomly, his spirits rising each time his eyes fell across one of the highlighted entries; his wall clock recorded the time - 16:34. Right at that point, he had nobody to share this new breakthrough with. McKinley had not responded to any voicemail messages all day and Baker was at City Hall on the trail of Morley. Clarke was in the Epic Center security office obtaining a copy of the CCTV that recorded the arrival of Chief Stanton at the building just before four p.m, then his progress to the twenty-eighth floor and the offices of Mulholland, White and Friedmann, where he was currently.

"We're getting closer to you," Schneider said quietly to himself. His whole being desired to have just sufficient probable cause to round-up the whole clan, together with their toadies and cohorts. He had even considered gatecrashing the top floor in a similar manner to the way Paul Kleberson had, what seemed like ages ago, although it was still only a matter of days, but he realised that a second such incident would jeopardise everything they were building together. In any case, Chandler Clarke had given the idea short shrift, which is why Clarke had taken the task of monitoring current movements.

That was when Schneider's cellphone rang. The screen read 'McKinley' and Schneider couldn't press the receive button quickly enough: "Chris, where've you been all day? We've got some news."

"So do I Sam and I need to brief you real quick. I've been called back to City Hall urgently; something's happening there, because I've been summoned directly by Deputy Chief Harper. If it's what I think, something from the IAD shit that Morley's puttin' together, I don't need to have my fingers anywhere near what I've found today. Have you heard anything?"

"A couple of things, but they may not be connected and from what you just said you don't need to know them right now."

"Sam, we've found the back-up store for Shepherd's records."

"That's fantastic Chris …"

"It is, but please don't talk Sam, because you need to get a handle on everything before anybody else grabs jurisdiction on it all. Just listen, OK?"

Schneider could detect the urgency in McKinley's voice. He tucked the phone between his chin and shoulder, then grabbed a pen to make notes: "understood Chris - go!"

"The store is in the Hillsboro Funeral Home on Acorn Drive. The owner's name is Mort Thackeray, but he has no involvement in this at all. His son, Jake, was Shepherd's closest friend and we've got all this from talking to him, but it looks as if he was likely duped by Shepherd as well. So at the moment, we haven't arrested anyone. They are both co-operating fully and Charlie Watson up at Hillsboro does not want any media flocking around their place like he's had to deal with at the aunt's house. You may not agree when you hear what else we've found, but you must trust me and Charlie on this Sam, otherwise it'll turn into a circus."

"We'll do whatever you say Chris, one hundred percent."

"Thanks Sam. Charlie is currently sitting on all of this for you, nobody knows bar him and me what we've got. Not even the Thackerays have the full story and they're not going to be saying anything to nobody, believe me! You need to get three Agents and a plain vehicle up here, but discretely, no lights or sirens. Use the gate at the side of the Funeral Home where the coffins are taken in and out; Mort Thackeray will be waiting to let you in. The contents of the storeroom are currently in the Funeral Home's panel van, which will be waiting there, ready for you to seize. One of your Agents needs to accompany Mort in that straight back to Wichita, another needs to secure the rear area of the Funeral Home. The other will then go to the Civic Center where Charlie has Jake Thackeray shut away in one of the interview rooms. Take Jake into custody and bring him back to your office - he will co-operate fully."

"Do I get to know why the cloak and dagger?"

"Charlie will fill-in the gaps for you; I assume you will be leading this?"

"If you say so Chris."

"I do, because what I haven't told you yet is that the van needs to make one stop en route, at the morgue. Because also in the back of the van, in one of Mort's transit coffins, is the body of Agent Kryczek."

"Jesus! And we ain't arresting these people?"

"No Sam, not yet. Not unless you want the politicians getting wind of what we have and muddying the waters as soon as they know; and certainly not until you've got all this under your jurisdiction. Charlie Watson will cover whatever story you want to spin around this. Like I told you, he's a good man and he has his own reasons for wanting it this way. We're also gonna need to get Mary Jourdain onside as well. Will you do that, or do you want me to?"

"I'll do it Chris, if she isn't happy I can just pull Federal jurisdiction."

"You shouldn't need to, I'm sure she won't be a problem. She's got a soft spot for Paul as well, so go easy on her - she's one of the good guys!"

Find us some Felons

One-Four-Seven

When McKinley returned to the Homicide Squad Room, it was empty, bar for Scott Holdsworth, who was quietly reviewing unsolved case logs - a bungled robbery on Grove, a drive-by in South Madison, a user in a dumpster in an alley back of Hydraulic. All meat and drink to the Squad during a normal period.

Nevertheless, the previous two years had not only shown a marked decrease in the number of unexplained deaths and murder cases investigated by the Squad, but also a significant increase in the percentage of cases closed by a successful conviction. This was mainly due to the reaction by City Hall to what the media had termed 'The Wichita Massacre' at the end of 2000, where five murders connected to a crime spree by two brothers, four during one home invasion, took the already-high count that year to the highest on record. In the aftermath, not only had policing of the worst areas been dramatically-increased, but far more emphasis had been given by the public prosecutor's office towards putting cases before a court. The first quarter of 2003 had hinted that the city may be headed towards having a murder rate below the national average for the third year running, until this recent trio had thrown the stats into turmoil.

Holdsworth looked-up as McKinley pulled his jacket off and went to drape it across the back of his chair: "progress?" he asked.

"Oh yes!" McKinley replied, quietly triumphant.

Holdsworth's spirits were raised by the response: "in that case, d'ya fancy a beer later?"

"Sounds like a plan."

"You know Harper wants to see you."

"Yeah, I got the message. What's that all about?"

"Can't reveal any details - orders from above - but something happened while you were out." He winked: "maybe Harper's gonna let you in on it."

McKinley stopped and looked closely at Holdsworth for a moment. There was a hint of cheshire cat in the grin on the young Detective's face: "now I'm intrigued," he replied, pulling his jacket back on, "guess I had better get along there right away." He looked at his watch as he left the room; it showed five-forty p.m. He paused in the doorway and turned to Holdsworth: "how about Murphy's around seven?"

"Works for me," came the reply. McKinley turned and walked away towards the administration area.

The door to Deputy Chief Harper's office was wide open and through it McKinley could see half a dozen senior officers gathered around the meeting table, poring over a large sheet of paper with various documents scattered around it, deep in discussion punctuated by much finger pointing towards what they were examining.

McKinley gingerly tapped the open door. Several of the faces snapped round to look at him, including Harper who smiled and beckoned: "ah, Sergeant McKinley, come on in."

Harper turned to the gathering: "boys, I need to talk with McKinley. I think we have reached a point where we can agree on the things we can move forward. Those we can't, at the moment that is, we can finalise after the Mayor's press conference in the morning."

There was a general consensus among the other officers. They all gathered-up their own papers and folders from the table and drifted from the room, one or two lingering to give Harper a friendly handshake before they did, along with which McKinley detected the odd word of congratulation. As the final one left, Harper closed the door behind them and indicated to McKinley to take a seat at the table, on the top of which he could see a large printed organisation chart, covered in red and blue marker pen alterations, some of which appeared to change names and lines of responsibility.

"Thanks for coming back in Sergeant." Harper smiled as he took the chair at the head of the table: "I know that you are busy at the moment trying to close up as many cases as you can prior to the re-organisation taking place, something that you must be finding a little tedious I suspect."

"All paperwork is tedious Sir, I'm sure you will agree, but it is a necessary part of our job."

"Quite." Harper wasn't sure if this was a statement of fact, or a subtle jibe. He knew that many of the men at the sharp-end resented his devotion to administrative matters and that he would need to overcome that in the weeks and months ahead: "that's what I really need to talk to you about."

McKinley was also taking a somewhat cautious approach, realising that the situation he had walked into wasn't the one he was expecting. His last remark might be accidentally interpreted two ways and, if this meeting was no longer likely to be adversarial, he immediately hoped the unintended meaning hadn't been taken. Harper continued: "I don't know if you have heard, but there are some major changes to this Police Department that will be publically-announced by the Mayor tomorrow morning. We have to put these in place as quickly as possible and I would ask you, as I have everybody else that has been in this office this afternoon, to please keep them close until that announcement is made."

"Of course Sir," McKinley responded, trying to conceal the complete puzzlement he felt.

"This afternoon, Chief Stanton tendered his resignation to the Mayor and I have been asked to take on that role with immediate effect."

"Congratulations Sir," was all that McKinley could, somewhat insincerely, manage as a kneejerk response, such was the shockwave that this news sent through his spine. He knew that he had to concentrate on what Harper was about to say, but his mind was working overtime trying to analyse the implications to his current investigation, most of which he knew Harper would be completely oblivious to, as his continued explanation confirmed.

"Obviously, we are already a few days into carrying-out the reorganisation that Chief Stanton implemented following the tragic incident involving Lieutenant Kleberson. Just within these four walls, Sergeant, you would not be aware how much I was opposed to certain aspects of those changes. Which brings me to your recent promotion."

McKinley's heart sank; the scenario he had expected was about to occur. The senior officer, sarcastically-christened 'Mr Charisma' by his peers, was about to reveal that he could playact just as well as the best among them. McKinley braced himself for the axe to fall, as Harper resumed: "I can assure you that there is nobody in this Department, at any level, who doesn't consider that promotion to be long-overdue. But would I be right in assuming that the reassignment that accompanied it would not be your first choice?"

McKinley could only shudder as the obsequious response came involuntarily from his own lips: "like everyone, Sir, I am happy to serve in whatever capacity I am asked." He would later reassure himself this was due to him not having full command of his emotions in the confused state he felt at the time. Quickly recovering, he concluded: "however, you are right, Sir. Having seen the inevitable consequences all too often, I am not looking forward to heading-up a Squad that is really only able to run a damage-limitation strategy."

"Good!" Harper replied enthusiastically, "because that makes my next question to you all the easier. My main objection to my predecessor's plans was the dismantling of the Homicide Squad. I intend to reverse that decision, although it will still be part of the new 'Crimes Against the Person' Division reporting to Lieutenant Van Allen, and it will not have the virtual autonomy it had under Lieutenant Kleberson. So, will you stay on to take charge of the Squad in those circumstances?"

McKinley couldn't believe it. His instincts were shouting for him to grab the opportunity before there was any chance of a mind-change on the part of the new Chief of Police, but also telling him that he was also in possession of a potentially-winning hand. This he needed to play quickly, but first he had a concern: "what about Lieutenant Kleberson, Sir?"

Harper displayed a relaxed smile: "your loyalty is commendable Sergeant, but there are two things that you need to be cogniscent of. First, officially, Lieutenant Kleberson is suspended. That will be rescinded as soon as it can be, but it has to be done by the numbers, otherwise it could have repercussions in other areas. I'm sorry if you find that difficult, but I don't make the rules."

'Whoa there!' McKinley thought to himself, 'I thought that was all you have done for the last five years.'

"Second," Harper continued, "I think you will agree, practically-speaking, right as we stand at this moment in time, Lieutenant Kleberson isn't returning to duty in the near-future. I know you're a friend as well as a colleague, and that you've seen him at the hospital, which I haven't, yet. So you will be able to tell me if I've got that wrong."

McKinley sighed quietly: "you've not got it wrong Sir, I'm sorry to say."

"I'm sorry Sergeant to have had to say that. I can imagine how you feel, but we are professionals and, from what I know of Lieutenant Kleberson, he would agree that, here in the department, we have to put our emotions to one side and get on with our jobs." McKinley nodded sadly. "In which case, we need a new Head of Homicide straight away, not at some presently-imperceptible time in the future. Rest-assured that the career interests of Lieutenant Kleberson will remain my first responsibility to him at all times. So, will you accept the position?"

McKinley waited a few seconds, as if pondering, then responded: "I will Sir - on two conditions."

Harper was not used to his underlings making bargains with him, so was a little taken-aback by the boldness of the response. Nevertheless, he was already recognising that this new role would make greater demands on his judgement than his undoubted organisational skills. He replied: "and they would be?"

"Detective Holdsworth remains as my Deputy."

"I wouldn't have it any other way; and Moreno?"

"He was never happy with our irregular hours, Sir. I'm sure he will be much more at home in Burglary."

"Fair enough, we can always discuss staffing levels at a later date. What is the other condition?"

"That I have sole authority to decide when a case is closed."

Harper smiled again. McKinley was already beginning to realise that this new top man was a far more amiable character than he had previously been aware: "I have no problem with that either, Sergeant - so do we have a deal?" He stood up and offered his hand.

McKinley also rose and took it. What he received was the firm handshake of a sincere man and, in that instant, McKinley realised that this marked a new beginning for Wichita Police Department, a feeling touched by a tinge of sadness that his good friend, Paul Kleberson, was not there to experience something he had quietly fought for years to achieve.

Harper retained his grasp: "I have one more request of you Sergeant. I want you to reopen the investigation into the attempted-murder of Lieutenant Kleberson."

McKinley could no longer conceal his disbelief at the developments. He just froze leaving his hand interlocked with that of his new boss, staring at Harper, who continued: "I know that the attacker was apprehended at the scene, but further information has come to light from the IAD enquiry that was commenced by Acting-Captain Morley. This may indicate that others were involved in that crime and I want you to find them and bring them to book. Incidentally, one of the other changes I am instituting is the closure of the IAD section. We are too small a department and, let's be fair here, too well run, to retain such a luxury. The savings in the budget can go towards more resources on the front line. In future any internal enquiries we may need can be conducted by an independent head of section. Lieutenant Mackenzie has taken over the responsibility for concluding that current enquiry and will liaise with you to hand over the appropriate evidence for your case files."

McKinley instinctively shook Harper's hand again: "thank you Sir. That means a lot to all of us in the Squad." He released Harper's hand: "just one question, if I may?"

"Fire away Sergeant."

"The attack on Paul, I mean Lieutenant Kleberson, was closely associated with the previous murders. We were co-operating with the Bureau before the cases were all closed and that co-operation was ended by the instruction of Chief Stanton. How do you want us to proceed with regard to any Federal implications in our reopening the case?"

"As I understand it, the local Bureau were sharing quite a lot of information with your Squad and that was of great assistance to us. We are all on the same side, Sergeant. I think that you should take your investigation wherever it needs to go and if that means obtaining the co-operation of another law enforcement agency, then so be it. All I would ask is that, if it should cause any jurisdictional problems, you bring them to me first so that I can help you to resolve them."

"I will Sir, thank you."

"You're welcome Sergeant - now go find us some felons to prosecute."

a breakthrough

One-Four-Eight

The operation in Hillsboro had gone without a hitch. Following McKinley's phone call, Sam Schneider had recalled Chandler Clarke from the Epic Center security office. They signed-out a Suburban from the car pool, which Clarke drove in convoy with Schneider's Crown Victoria over to City Hall, where they collected Pete Baker at the corner of Central and Main. He had failed to find any trace of Morley.

They continued out to the Crime Lab, where they were met by Mary Jourdain. Schneider had already given her the heads-up by telephone and, after recording the necessary objections with regard to security of crime scene, photographic evidence and so on, consistent with her public position, she agreed to await their return with the van's cargo as arranged. They left the Suburban in her car park, the three Agents continuing their journey in Schneider's Interceptor.

Once on I-135, Schneider filled-in what information he was able to, then called Charlie Watson on the car's hands-free, so that the other two in the car could hear the conversation. Some aspects of the briefing from Watson came as a surprise and revealed why he and McKinley had decided on the course of action taken. There was little more conversation on the last leg of the journey, other than the agreement on allocation of tasks once they reached Hillsboro.

Just before six, the car pulled onto Acorn Drive, taking the right-hand fork in front of the Funeral Home, then turning left into the open gateway that led to the loading bay behind the main building. They were met by Mort Thackeray, still dressed as he would be to receive any bereaved relative arriving at his premises. He operated the controls that brought the gate slowly and quietly sliding across to fill the entrance, closing the scene off from any prying eyes on the outside of the compound.

Also there to meet them was Sergeant Watson. After McKinley left, and in order to maintain as much secrecy as possible, Watson had decided not to remove Jake Thackeray to the Civic Center. His judgement was that Jake was not a flight risk and, sure enough, there, leant against one of the limbers to the back of the assembly area, was Jake, his stoop exaggerated by his solemn contemplation of the rubber boots he was still wearing.

As previously decided, Pete Baker climbed into the passenger side of the black panel van alongside Mort Thackeray, to accompany his Agent's body and the other cargo back to Wichita. Watson operated the gate release and Mort guided the van slowly from the yard, in no different a way to the many times he had done so previously, turning right towards K-56. The gate glided back shut behind them.

The attention then turned to Jake Thackeray. After a short discussion between himself and Chandler Clarke, it was confirmed that Clarke would take him directly back to the Wichita Agency in Schneider's car, where Jake would provide a statement then stay, voluntarily, until the Agents decided what to do with him. Because of Watson vouching for him, plus his obviously co-operative demeanour, it was agreed that he would ride, unhandcuffed, in the passenger seat alongside Clarke. Once everything was agreed, the two men got into the car, Watson again operated the gate controls and the Crown Victoria exited in a similar manner to the van ten minutes earlier.

Once again, the gate glided to a close, leaving Watson and Schneider alone in the complex. At Mort's suggestion, Mary Thackeray had earlier driven herself over to the Watsons, where she would await her husband's return later in the evening. The two men had important decisions to make as to how these discoveries should best be handled, but first, Schneider wanted to get more of an idea of the layout of the facility.

Watson first took him to the cold store area, where there were three double-height cabinets; one was closed and in operation, but sealed with police tape. Watson explained: "I decided to keep it running, just in case there was anything in there for the crime scene boys. The body had been in there for a few weeks."

"That's fine Sergeant, let's leave it like that for now. Where's the tape store?"

"It's way out back, I'll take you. You can call me Charlie if you like, we're quite relaxed on that sort of thing out here."

Schneider smiled: "OK Charlie, just as long as you call me Sam."

Watson led the way through the preparation area to the door and on down the corridor winding its way to the rear rooms. He stopped at the games room, the door of which was open with the light left on, with more police tape across the opening, which Watson pointed to: "I've done the same here, but I don't think there is anything in there of any use to us."

Schneider peered in, taking in the equipment and the layout. He let out a long whistle: "that's one hell of a set-up."

Watson continued: "the store's next door."

Schneider followed Watson down the corridor to the next door, which was closed. Above it, a green light glowed, showing the room air conditioning was operating. Watson flicked the light switch to the side of the door, then opened it. Once again there was police tape inside the door blocking the opening. Beyond it was a narrow room, probably twenty feet long, with racking down both sides. The racking to the left was full of boxes, all neatly labelled with numbers and date spans; the ones nearest to the door appeared to date from 1996. On the right racking, the boxes continued from the rear wall for about five feet; the remainder of the racking was empty.

Watson added a short explanation: "the boxes on the left hold hard drives dating from the mid nineties and all belong to Jake. They're all back-ups of his gaming systems. They continue around onto the racking at the far end. The closest box is dated last week."

"Do we not need these? I thought you said that Shepherd and Thackeray communicated by computer and that the communications were recorded?"

"Only the ones during games. Thackeray recorded the games, nothing else, so we took the judgement that there would be nothing on those that would mention anything pertinent to the investigation." Schneider nodded his agreement, then Watson continued: "the drives we have seized were all in boxes on this right hand side, just inside the door. The boxes weren't labelled, but the drives inside were."

"How many?"

"About a hundred I would think."

"That'll keep us busy for a few days. What were the dates?"

"About the same time span, from what I could see. Most of the older boxes were sealed, but the newest one was only half full. I saw one drive in there dated this month."

"I thought you said that Jake Thackeray hadn't met Shepherd during his last trip."

"He hadn't, but Shepherd had a key. It opened that door at the end of the corridor, which can be accessed from the laneway up behind the complex."

"So you think he came in when nobody was here."

"No, he would have set-off the alarm. I think he came in while Jake was working out there."

"Why would he do that?"

"Jake doesn't know. In fact, it was that thought that upset Jake as much as anything. Only thing I can offer is that he didn't want to involve Jake while he was on business."

"Didn't stop him when he needed Kryczek's body taking care of."

"I know. What's that going to do to him?"

"We'll have to see what he says in his statement. At the very least, he's an accessory to murder."

"But he didn't know it was a murder."

"He concealed the body of a Federal Agent for nearly a month; technically so did his father."

Watson looked shocked: "Mort had no idea ..."

Schneider cut him off: "Charlie, I'm giving it to you as it is. This is a Federal case and we aren't allowed the leeway of small-town logic. I'm sorry, I appreciate how close your two families are, but this is neither the place, nor the time frankly, for this discussion. First, I need to decide what else we need to do here, so close it up and let's go back out front."

A Breakthrough

One-Four-Nine

Chris McKinley had been in the Squad Room, alone, since his meeting with Harper more than an hour earlier. He had spent around twenty minutes thinking over what had transpired; the turnaround was so instant, and so complete, it took some absorbing. Having done that, he felt totally elated. Elated that his career was no longer under threat, elated that the Squad would continue and, mainly, elated that he would be able to continue the work of his good friend, Paul Kleberson.

The first call he made was to his wife. He was not sure what her reaction would be. She had been almost relieved when she heard that IAD were investigating the circumstances leading to the attack on Paul, even though it might end her husband's career. He knew that relief was not due in any way to his situation, but simply the thought that the family may be free of the constant fear that, one day, he may not return home; that every day, today could be that day. She had felt instantly guilty at expressing such emotions aloud, so when she heard the latest news she was immediately supportive of his decision to take the position. She realised that her husband was a cop through and through and, although he would take any job to keep the family financially secure, no other career could come close to giving him the fulfilment that being a detective did.

The next call was to Sam Schneider, who had just finished viewing the various rooms at Hillsboro Funeral Home. To McKinley, Schneider sounded exhausted as he tried to absorb the latest twists these cases had thrown up during the day. Nevertheless, Schneider wanted to call a full review later that evening back at his office in Wichita. The only problem was that he was in Hillsboro without transport, having expected Pete Baker to return and collect him, after dealing with the handover of Kryczek's body at the morgue and securing the delivery of the hard drives recovered from the Funeral Home.

In the end, Charlie Watson had solved the problem by offering to drive Schneider back to Wichita. This would mean that the premises would have to remain closed until a decision had been made, but in the meantime the Thackerays would stay with the Watsons. It also gave time for Schneider to discuss the options with Watson during the drive to Wichita and for Pete Baker to telephone Kryczek's mother to break the news to her earlier rather than later. The review was, therefore, called for nine p.m.

Chris' final call was to Leanne Kleberson; as there was no answer all he was able to do was leave a voicemail message. He realised that the family were probably all at the hospital and that he would not be able to visit that evening because of the review meeting, but he wanted her to know what had developed, so that at least she would hear direct from him that he had taken over Paul's Squad, rather than from some lazy journalist looking for an impulse response that they could twist into another non-story.

It was just after seven when he wandered into Murphy's to find Scott Holdsworth occupying one of the stools in front of the bar, alongside an empty one, before which a large white-headed Guinness already stood. Scott knew why McKinley had favoured Murphy's; he was of Irish descent and this was the only bar in Wichita that had the original Liffey Water on draught. Holdsworth welcomed McKinley with the question he had been busting to ask for nearly two hours: "so what did Harper want?"

McKinley lifted his beer, but did not slide onto the stool alongside him. He raised the glass: "cheers!" he said, then continued, "there's a free booth at the back, let's take these down there." He led the way, Holdsworth following him with his half-empty Sam Adams. They slid into the booth, but McKinley just sat quietly, sipping at his glass.

Holdsworth was impatient: "so?"

"So," McKinley started followed by a slight pause as he looked at Holdsworth with a glum expression: "oh, I'm sorry, I thought you were about to propose a toast to the new Head of Homicide."

"What?"

"You heard."

"Alright, I get it, you're messing around. So tell me what really happened."

"OK, may I thank my new Deputy for that rousing expression of support for my recent appointment."

"You're kidding me?" Holdsworth waited for a response, but all he got were a pair of smiling eyes looking back at him over the rim of the glass that was dispensing black liquid into McKinley's mouth. "You're not kidding?" He paused as if not knowing what to believe: "come on, are you or aren't you?"

"Stanton resigned this afternoon, Harper has taken his place, unofficially with immediate effect, officially in the morning after a media briefing from the Mayor. Turns out, Harper was not in favour of dismantling Homicide, so he's asked me to stay and take charge instead of going to Narco."

"What about the Lieutenant?"

"Harper assured me that he would be looked after when he returns."

"So you accepted."

"After he agreed to my conditions ... Deputy."

"What conditions?"

"That was one of 'em ... Deputy"

"Stop winding me up."

"Rule one for a Squad Leader is that you don't wind-up your deputy; Deputy."

"You mean you asked ... and he agreed?"

"You seem to have made an impression Scott, and not just with Harper. I mean, I leave you alone for a day and when I come back not only do we have our Squad back, but we have a new Chief of Police and no IAD department. So what on earth happened at that interview this afternoon?"

"Seems I must have hit the nail on the head."

"I'll say so! Do you want to know what the other condition was?"

"We all get our salaries doubled?"

"You wish! Instead would you settle for full autonomy on deciding when cases are closed."

"No, but I guess if that's all you have ... really? He went with that?"

"It's early days, but I get the feeling that a lot of people may find they've misunderstood Harper, some to their detriment."

"Can't make a judgement on that; never really met the guy, but for briefings."

"So, that's the good news and the really good news. Do you want to hear the really really good news as well?"

"Do I need another beer first?" He held his empty glass towards McKinley.

"Probably." McKinley emptied his glass and caught the eye of a waitress, who came over to the table: "a draught Guinness and a Sam Adams please."

"Sure guys," she smiled, "can I get ya somethin' ta eat as well?"

"May as well," McKinley responded, "how about you Scott?" Holdsworth nodded. "OK, can you bring menus as well please."

"Sure thing!" She took their empty glasses, placed a new beer mat in front of each of them and scurried-off in the direction of the bar.

"So?" Holdsworth craned forward in anticipation.

"We've been instructed to reopen the investigation into the attack on Paul."

Holdsworth slumped back into his chair, exhaling as he did so. All he could say was: "wow!"

"Plus, we have been given the green light to co-operate with the Bureau. I've got a meeting with Schneider at nine - an official meeting - you coming?"

"Try and keep me away!"

The waitress returned with the beers and the menus. Both men opened them and started to peruse while she waited for the order. McKinley continued: "better order a big platter Scott, I've got more to tell you."

"There's more?" Scott responded with surprise.

"Oh yes," McKinley said somewhat triumphantly, "I haven't told you about Hillsboro yet, have I?"

One-Fifty

McKinley and Holdsworth were the last to enter the conference room in the FBI suite at the Epic Center; it was just before nine p.m. Awaiting them with the three Agents was Charlie Watson. McKinley expressed surprise as he shook Watson's hand once more, introducing Scott Holdsworth as he did so.

Schneider had asked Watson to be involved in the first part of the briefing, because of the need to resolve the situation in Hillsboro while they still had it locked-down with respect to the local media. They had been monitoring news broadcasts on and off during the evening; thus far there had not been a ripple on the calm surface of the media pond with regard to their operation that evening.

Schneider began the meeting: "thank you all for staying with this to such a late hour, I don't intend to extend our day much longer as we will all need a good rest so that we can take full advantage tomorrow of the gains we have made. Therefore, I just want us to review what we have and allocate ourselves initial tasks for tomorrow morning so that we can hit the ground running. First though, I want to give my personal congratulations to the new Head of the Homicide Squad over at City Hall and to welcome him and his new Deputy back to these briefings, officially this time!" There was a general accord around the table and repeated congratulations from the other participants.

Schneider left sufficient space for this, then moved on briskly: "next, I want to resolve the situation that Sergeant Watson here is keeping a lid on for us up in Hillsboro, involving the Thackerays and what we discovered today. Chandler, you have taken a statement from Jake Thackeray, what are your thoughts?"

"Frankly Sam," Clarke began, "having spoken to him all the way back from Hillsboro, then taken the formal statement, I can only concur with Sergeant Watson's original assessment that the man has been duped by an old friend into believing that he was doing his public duty. Jake is a strange one; a loner, highly-intelligent with a particular obsession, all things we would look for in assessing a potential suspect. However, he plainly is an honest man, a result of a very good upbringing and of his religion. He has been fully co-operative, right from square one, and I have no reason to believe that this is in any way an act or form of clever deception. Sean Shepherd was his long-time best friend, quite possibly his only friend outside of his family, so when that friend decided to take advantage of that trust, Jake just swallowed the story he was given, hook, line and sinker."

McKinley interrupted: "but he did know that Shepherd was an hermaphrodite. He couldn't hide that when we were in his games room, could he Charlie?"

Watson shook his head sadly: "no, I can't dispute that Chris."

Clarke took over again: "I spent a deal of time on that Chris. Eventually he gave it all up, but not because he was complicit in anything - he is totally ashamed of what happened. Shepherd was a complete predator, not just in destroying lives, but sexually as well. One night, a couple of years ago after an all-night gaming sessions, they were led on their bunks chatting in the dark like they often did, when Shepherd switched the subject to sex, something Jake had always been scared of - still is frankly. But he found himself comfortable with discussing it with such a close friend. After a while Shepherd made a move. He got down from his top bunk and tried to get in the lower one with Jake. He was naked and Jake completely freaked-out. He pushed Shepherd to the floor, got free from the bunk and turned on the lights. His description of what he saw was 'like something out of one of the games they played'; there was his best friend buck naked, with a body that was entirely female at the top and male at the bottom, complete with erection. Jake tried to escape the room, but Shepherd stopped him. Jake says for a fleeting moment he thought he was going to die."

A Breakthrough

"So why didn't he?" Holdsworth asked.

"Seems that Shepherd had completely misjudged the situation. He just kept saying he was sorry and eventually managed to persuade Jake that he was telling the truth. For one of the few times in his life, he probably was, because the two were like brothers really - Jake said several times in the interview that he loved Sean, but not 'like that'. So they sat and talked about it, for several hours it seems. Sean even explained the difficulties his body gave him. It was deep stuff, but I suppose all the fascination with the games just made it easier for Jake to accept the improbability of what he was hearing and seeing. I doubt there are many others who could have had that conversation with Shepherd."

"Not and survived it!" Schneider observed, somewhat abruptly.

"Probably not; Jake will probably be haunted by that thought for the rest of his life, because as a result Jake agreed to keep Sean's secret, provided that what had nearly happened between them never happened again. That was when Shepherd asked him if he could keep another secret as well."

A perceptible shudder rippled through the room. Schneider was the first to react: "he told Jake what he really did for a living?"

"Not exactly. He told Jake the reason why he needed to keep his secret and his cover in the movie industry intact was that he really worked for the CIA, who had recruited him at university because of his peculiar circumstances, which allowed him to adopt whatever persona was needed for the particular operation he was engaged on. He likened it to a shape-shifter in their games, but assured Jake that he only ever used it for good purposes. Jake accepted that completely. He was unaware that, even at this time of soul-baring, Shepherd was setting-up yet another scenario he could use to his advantage if needed to in the future."

Baker sighed: "Kryczek."

"Exactly." Clarke went on: "we still have no idea what exactly happened when Kryczek tracked him down, but Shepherd obviously killed her then managed to rope Jake into aiding and abetting him to conceal the body."

McKinley butted in: "I can fill-in some gaps - Kryczek visited the aunt's house twice, about a month ago. The first time she spoke to Mrs Ferguson, posing as a friend from college. That brought him back for the second visit on twenty-fourth April. That time, all we know is that they drove off in Kryczek's car."

"After which," Clarke continued, "they ended-up in a seedy little motel outside of Peabody, because that's where Jake collected the body from later that night. Somehow, I doubt she was in that room voluntarily, or for the usual reasons."

"So why on earth did Jake get involved?" Schneider's lack of sleep was setting-in again and he was beginning to lose patience.

"Shepherd spun him the line that she was a connection into a biker gang under investigation for association with a terrorist plot. Shepherd was trying to infiltrate the gang and had managed to befriend her. She intended to give him some information that night, but when he turned-up to meet her, she was dead. There were pills all over the bed, looked like an overdose."

"There wouldn't be any reason for an undertaker to doubt that either," Pete Baker added: "from the very quick examination Mary Jourdain gave the body after we arrived at the morgue earlier, it looks like Shepherd used the needle on Kryczek as well. So it certainly wouldn't have looked like a violent death."

"On top of which," Clarke continued, "Shepherd told Jake that he couldn't be sure whether he had been sussed or not. So he needed to 'lose' the body for a few days until he could establish what the situation was. As soon as he knew, he would organise for the body to be collected and dealt with. Jake had the facilities and that was all Shepherd wanted."

"Beginning to sound like a bad episode of 'Alias'!" Holdsworth observed.

"Has there ever been a good one?" McKinley quipped.

"Think of it any way you want guys," Clarke responded, "but Jake believed him, possibly because he thought he was in a real version of a computer game. Only when all the media hype broke surrounding Shepherd being apprehended did he realise he had been duped."

"So why didn't he contact anybody?" Schneider was showing considerable irritation, "what about the father, surely he knew they had a spare body around?"

"Mort doesn't go back there any more," Watson intervened, "not since he handed full charge of the processing to Jake about eighteen months back. They hire a couple of casual assistants for when they're busy so he doesn't have to."

"So, why didn't one of them notice?"

"Last few weeks there's been very little business; what there has been, Jake's been handling on his own."

"That still doesn't excuse why he didn't report it. With all the media coverage he must have realised what he had back there. Or was he never going to?"

Chandler Clarke tried to bring the matter to a close: "look Sam, we're getting sidetracked again. Shepherd wove so many webs of deceit and he's still doing it even though he's been dead for a week. Why is Jake any different from any other naive idiot who got into something over his head, then got scared? We see this all the time, for goodness sake! Sure, we can charge him, throw the Federal book at him and his father for any number of reasons, but where does that get us? They get off on some technicality, such as our removing evidence without recording it?" He shrugged his shoulders.

Pete Baker added his thoughts: "in the meantime, we have to tell the whole world why we've closed-down the Hillsboro Funeral Home and alert our targets to exactly how close we are getting. Bottom line, for me, is that would be a real bad move to make right now."

Schneider sighed: "you're both right, I suppose." He pondered for a few moments, then turned to Watson: "alright Charlie, take your citizen home. But it is your responsibility to impress upon him and his father that if there is even the slightest hint of any leak of this from them, then they will be staring at the inside of a Federal Penitentiary for eternity. If you let us down, you can join 'em there as well!"

"I understand Sam," Watson responded, "and thank you!" He rose and shook Clarke's hand warmly, followed by everyone else, then made his leave.

As Watson opened the door, Schneider added: "we'll send CSI out tomorrow to check the scene and photograph everything for the files, so please leave those rooms as they are until they've finished." Watson nodded in affirmation as he left the room closing the door behind him.

"That was the right decision Sam," Pete Baker observed.

"I know, it's just a shame we can't mend some of the other families affected as easily. Let's take a five minute break, I need one of our dreadful cups of coffee if I'm going to have to make any more decisions tonight."

One-Five-One

Suitably equipped with mugs of fresh instant coffee and a plate of stale cookies discovered in one of the cupboards, the five men reassembled in the conference room. Schneider restarted the briefing: "OK, let's go around the table and all say what we have, plus where we want to take it tomorrow."

"I'll start," Baker volunteered, "because it follows-on from what we have just been discussing. I have spoken to Eleanor Kryczek and I'm having her flown-in early tomorrow. I will collect her from the airport and take her out to the morgue - we need her to do the formal identification."

"What have you told her?" Schneider enquired.

"Nothing, other than we have found the body - that was plenty enough for her to absorb in the circumstances. What I propose is that I tell her that the body has been laying in the morgue for several weeks as a Jane Doe. We can use the motel bit of Thackeray's statement for the discovery, but make it that she had no identification on her; Shepherd took that anyway, so it's plausible. Then we can tell her that nobody joined the dots immediately after we apprehended Shepherd because of all the other stuff, media circus and so on. We're sending CSI out to Hillsboro tomorrow, so let's get them to take some photographs at the Peabody motel as well, in case she needs to see anything for closure. We can photoshop it all together for the media if necessary."

"Oh what a tangled web ..." Schneider recited quietly. "Anyone see any problems with that?" All shook their heads. "You will need Mary Jourdain's co-operation," he continued.

"Already got it," Baker affirmed, "she's also agreed to delay the post mortem until Eleanor has seen the body."

"Won't Mrs Kryczek find that a bit unusual?"

"You or I might do, yes, but Eleanor isn't an Agent."

"In which case," Schneider responded, "that concludes the Hillsboro affair. Nothing on that goes out of this room until we decide if and how we release it all to the media, probably via your department Chris, is that agreed?" Again, there was no dissention. "Anything else Pete?"

"Yes. I don't want the Post Mortem carried-out here ..."

"Why on earth ...?" Schneider interjected, but Baker cut him off.

"Let me finish Sam. I want to go back to LA tomorrow with Kryczek's body and help organise the funeral; she was one of my Agents and we need to put some closure in place for her mother. It's been a month since the disappearance, she doesn't need more weeks going by while we pore over evidence of what? We know who killed her, where and, on a cursory examination by the local M.E, how. The why was most likely to silence her, so it will be nigh-impossible to tie-in to any conspiracy cases we can develop around the other murders. There are enough of those already for a capital sentence in this State."

"Can't argue with that logic - anything else?"

"Yes. I'll take the hard drives with me as well. That's what will happen eventually anyway; we've got better systems in LA than you have here and I've got more resources to load onto the analysis, including the IRS team. Plus, nobody outside this room knows we've got them, other than Watson and the Thackerays, and they sure as hell won't be talking about it. If I was to hang around, then in a few days suddenly head back to LA with a load of boxes, it somewhat highlights we've found something. But I'm going back with a body in a crate; what's to say that's all that's in it?"

"I like that Pete. But before you do, let us take a copy of the latest disk. I want Jim to see if there's anything on there to do with the murders here, particularly anything that we can use against the Kendricks. He can be doing that while you're in transit, then e-mail the analysis to you. It could give your guys a head start as well."

"Agreed. I'll make the arrangements in the morning before I go to the airport to collect Eleanor Kryczek."

Schneider turned to Clarke: "right - Chandler?"

"While you were getting coffee, I went round to the security office. Stanton left around a quarter before nine - with Friedmann."

"That's interesting. So he was here, what, five hours?"

"Pretty much."

"That's a lot of story."

"It is. Which is why I want to arrest him tomorrow morning."

"Stanton or Friedmann?"

"Stanton. He's got a storyline now, but he won't be fully au fait with it yet. The sooner we shake it out of him, the more chance we have of finding the holes."

"But if Friedmann is his lawyer, he will just turn up and spring him."

"Which gives us another confirmation of complicity. Come on Sam, Pete flushed him out pretty easily this afternoon, which was as near as dammit an admission of him setting-up Kleberson, or at least the circumstances for what happened. There ain't gonna be any written evidence of that anywhere, so it can only come from a confession. We're not gonna get that by letting him sit at home rehearsing his lines. You're the one that wanted to shake the tree - why have you stopped?"

"What do you think Chris?" Schneider enquired.

"Scott had his part in it as well by putting Morley in the frame. I have to collect the transcripts of that session from Lieutenant Mackenzie in the morning. They're going to mean that, at the very least, I need to interview Stanton about Morley's involvement. Strikes me, we have a common purpose there."

"What about Morley?" Holdsworth enquired.

"He seems to have dropped off the radar completely," Baker advised. "I spent an hour over at City Hall this afternoon and nobody seemed to know what had happened to him."

"So don't we need to find him?" Holdsworth queried, "he's gotta be easier to turn than Stanton, because he doesn't have the backing of the Kendricks via Friedmann. Far as we know, he thinks he's out on a limb on his own."

Clarke returned to his original thoughts: "Chris, do you reckon you could get Harper's blessing to arrest Stanton?"

"Not sure. He certainly was making the right noises this afternoon, but we don't know what the Mayor is going to announce tomorrow at the briefing. Nobody at City Hall seems to know exactly what reason is going to be given for Stanton's sudden departure, or if they do, they're not saying. Harper isn't going to risk upstaging the Mayor. Politically, he just ain't that brave."

"So Chris," Schneider asked, "does that mean you don't want to act until we know which way the wind's blowing?"

"No Sam, it means I don't want to give Harper any reason ahead of the media briefing to have second thoughts on my current terms of reference. His parting words to me this evening were 'go get me some felons' and I intend to obey them." He turned to Clarke: "as far as I can figure it, I'm expected to pick-up Mackenzie's file tomorrow morning, then go look for Morley, who sure as hell is going to make sure I don't find him. On the other hand, Stanton's expecting a visit from this office, having been flushed by Pete."

"I get it Chris," Clarke responded, "you want to swap those round."

"By the time I've read the IAD file, it's going to be time for the media briefing. Harper's going to be tied-up on that and other things for the rest of the morning, so as I'm gonna have a few questions for our ex-Chief, I might as well go and see him straight away. I can take Holdsworth with me and if we don't get the answers we want, we will just have to continue the interview back at City Hall."

"Meantime, I go find Morley. If he's already crapping himself at the thought of his department getting hold of him, he sure as hell won't want to see me."

"It's better than that Chandler," Schneider intervened, "he's never met you; he won't even know who you are. You can use any cover you want."

"What about Friedmann?" Baker enquired, "Stanton's gonna call him first."

Chandler responded: "I'll give you even money if he isn't at the conference, he'll be watching it, probably with the Kendricks. He's not going to be taking calls right at that time."

"That's it then," Schneider concluded, "I think we all know what we're doing in the morning."

"What about you Sam?" Clarke enquired.

"First I need to find out what's happening with Paul, having not been able to do so today. Then we need someone at the media briefing tomorrow, so I'll take that. I think that the Mayor and the new Chief of Police, maybe even some of our more prominent local members of society, will appreciate some reassurance that we're still involved, don't you?"

One-Five-Two

The night air was crisp when Schneider walked to his car; Chandler had left it in the surface car park when he returned to the Epic Center with Jake Thackeray. The fresh air gave his metabolism a lift; he looked at his watch to see it was not yet ten. He thought about going to the base hospital on his way home, so he rang Clara. She had looked after the two junior Klebersons for most of the day. She was exhausted and about to go to bed, so gave her blessing to the detour in return for his promise to try not to wake her when he finally got home.

The next call was to the base hospital, where Doctor Manderling was still on duty. He also gave Schneider a green light and said he would wait to give him an update on his arrival; the doctor assured that it would be a good update, which further lifted Sam's spirits. Half an hour later, having been briefed that the monitors were showing regular periods of consciousness, during which brain activity was fairly constant, Sam entered the hospital room.

The room was lit by several small, low level, red lights that allowed him to make out that his friend was on the bed, still surrounded by the equipment that had been set-up there on the previous Friday, most of which was no longer active. Paul was wearing the special goggles and headphones that the doctor had explained were being used to regulate the amount of input Paul was receiving. Paul's eyes had been opened earlier that day during one of his periods of unconsciousness, which allowed the goggles to be fitted. Doctor Manderling was in the room next door, having opened both sight and sound channels remotely, waiting to observe what would happen. Sam knew he would see no recognition of his arrival, as Paul was still paralysed.

The doctor had noticed, on analysing previous traces, that there was constant activity during all periods of consciousness, which heightened during visits. It was during Sam's previous visit that the greatest fluctuations had occurred and, from the brief discussion on Sam's arrival, the doctor had ascertained that Sam had talked to Paul about the investigation. He asked Sam to do the same this

A Breakthrough

time, which was not a problem as that was exactly what Sam had intended to do anyway. Doctor Manderling stayed to watch, with the nurse, for more unusual changes in the monitoring patterns.

Paul Kleberson had been piecing his situation together for more than a day, although he had no awareness that was what the timescale had been. Existence for him at that point was a series of conscious periods each ended by a feeling of fatigue which, he had already surmised, created periods of unconsciousness. After each of these, he would conduct a review of what he had amassed during his previous consciousness. It was just like conducting a murder enquiry and he used his alter ego, the invisible interrogator, to assess his progress. There were more images appearing during these interrogations, bringing him to conclude these were things that had happened at some time before - flashbacks.

Five or six awakenings ago, he became aware that he had some degree of sight, although what he could see was unfocussed and undefined; just shadows near to him. That had confirmed he was not in a box, but a room - a dark room. Although he did not know where this was, if medics had been involved at some point, it could be a hospital. His hearing had become more defined. He had worked-out that, if he was in a hospital, the rhythmic sound was likely to be medical machinery, which he concluded was keeping him alive. Paul had eventually concluded that he was definitely alive and in a hospital.

There were also other people in the room from time to time, because he could make out their voices, but could not define who they were, or if they were people he should know. There were a couple of voices that were more regularly in the room than anyone else. He concluded they were medics - the most common one must be in charge, a doctor.

There were also other voices. These would trigger different flashbacks, from which he got brief pictures of a number of different people, a mature man in uniform, a woman of similar age in a pinafore; two younger women, one blonde, one dark-haired, both very attractive. There were also two young children, a boy and a girl; their flashbacks often co-incided with the blonde woman. Then there were three men who appeared in separate flashbacks, one had darker skin, the other two were related somehow. He felt they must be contemporary in age with him, maybe they were detectives as well. The one with short hair was the one who gave him his name back; that one talked a lot when he was in the room. He had been in the room and was talking when this current consciousness began.

This had triggered three separate flashbacks in close succession, the one where this man gave Paul his name back, one where he was smiling and talking in a doorway and one where there was an argument and he knocked something over that contained liquid.

These commenced another interrogation: "do you know this man?"

'I must do.'

"He knows you."

'He knows my name.'

"He seems concerned when he says your name."
'Yes he does.'
"Where are you when he tells you your name?"
'I'm in a room.'
"Where's the room?"
'Don't know'
"Is it familiar?"
'I saw it in another flashback'
"Was anyone else there?"
'When he told me my name, yes there was, but I couldn't see them.'
"And the other time?"
'Yes, but I couldn't see who it was that time either. There were pictures of people.'
"Who were they?"
'Couldn't make them out.'
"Is he talking to you?"
'Yes'
"What's he saying?"
'Can't make it out'

The interrogator went quiet. The silence remained for a short while, then Paul heard mumbling. The mumbling became more defined and words started to materialise: "Chris ... Stanton ... Pete ... Morley ..."

'They're names - he's saying names. Why is he telling me names?' The interrogator was quiet, only the mumbling could be heard.

Sam was relating the events of the day, running through McKinley's visit to Hillsboro, Baker's meeting with Stanton and Holdsworth's IAD interview. He had got to McKinley and Watson at the Funeral Home talking to Jake Thackeray: "... so Chris decided to ask Jake about Kryczek and he broke down ..."

The nurse pointed to a spike on one set of traces: "what the hell caused that?" the doctor asked, "shut the channels down." The nurse leant forward and worked two faders which were on about half strength, bringing them slowly down to their zero positions. Doctor Manderling got out of his chair and walked towards Paul's room.

Paul was still trying to make out words, but all he was getting were more names: "McKinley ... Watson ... Jake ... Kryczek ..."

'Kryczek!'
"Who's Kryczek?"
'No!'
"Who's Kryczek?"
'No! ... NO!'
"What can you see?"
'The room.'
"Can you see the pictures?"

'Yes, they're on the dresser.'
"Do you recognise any of them?"
'They're all people in the flashbacks.'
"Family?"
'Maybe.'
"Your family?"
'Or his.'
"Is he there?"
'Who?'
"The man that knows your name."
'Sam?'
"Is that his name, Sam Kryczek?"
'No.'
"It must be, he's in the room, the pictures are his family."
'He's not there. What if it's my room?'
"Then the pictures are your family."
'But he's not in them.'
"Then he's not family, this Sam Kryczek."
'He's not Kryczek. He's Sam.'
"Then who's Kryczek, one of the pictures?"
'No!'
"So is he a friend?"
'Who?'
"Kryczek."
'No, not a friend, not Kryczek.'
"Then he's an enemy."
'She's there.'
"In the room; who?"
'The enemy.'
"Where, in the pictures?"
'No in front of them ... get away!'

Paul abandoned the flashback. He tried to refocus on the room he was in and the man talking to him, but the room was slowly going dark and the voice was fading away into the distance. He suddenly felt exhausted.

Doctor Manderling pushed quietly through the double doors into the room. Sam was still talking, slowly and in a low voice as instructed. He became aware of the door opening, so stopped and turned. The doctor said very quietly: "he's asleep now Agent Schneider, come out with me."

Sam turned to the bed and whispered: "sleep sound old buddy," then turned and followed the doctor out of the room.

When they were in the corridor, the doctor asked: "what were you talking about at the end there?"

"About a development in the case today."

"Can you tell me about it?"

"Not in specific terms - why?"

"I understand. But there was an interesting reaction while you were talking to him. Would he be familiar with anything you were talking about?"

"Not really, it's all fresh stuff really. Why, you think he heard me?"

"Oh undoubtedly. From what we are observing, he is becoming aware of what's going on around him and, from what I just saw then, he definitely heard something he recognised."

"Is that good or bad?"

"Good - definitely good from a progress point of view, the reaction was the first real indication we've had of some form of recognition. Problem is, we can only tell magnitude, not whether it was a positive or negative reaction. From what you were talking about, would you think you told him something that would excite him - raise his spirits."

"I wouldn't have thought so, we've had a breakthrough, but not what we would call a game-changer, not yet anyway."

"A name then, somebody he would want to see; other than you, of course."

"No, he would probably not know most of the people I've been talking about ."

"And you didn't mention his attacker?"

"No, you made it clear that was a no-no the other day."

"Then someone he would not wish to meet? Just before I came into the room."

"Kryczek, I mentioned Kryczek! Oh Lord, I'm sorry!"

"Who is Kryczek?"

"The person Shepherd was impersonating when he attacked Paul."

"Really?"

"I never even thought ..."

"Neither did I, Agent Schneider." Doctor Manderling appeared quite excited at this: "now that's really interesting. Tell me, at the time you found him in his apartment, would Lieutenant Kleberson still have thought he was attacked by Kryczek, or would he have known that it was Shepherd and not Kryczek?"

"He would have met who he thought was Kryczek, but by the time he was attacked he would definitely have known it was Shepherd."

"Then, Agent Schneider, we have made a breakthrough here as well. Not quite how I would have wanted to, and we will have to keep Lieutenant Kleberson under close observation again while we run some physical checks on him, but as long as they don't come up negative, which I don't think they will, then I think we may have a good chance of getting your friend back."

vacant possession

One-Five-Three

The media briefing had been called for nine-thirty a.m. It was being held in the council chamber, as the attendance was much lower than the more recent ones out front, when journalists had flocked to hang on every word. Following Monday's less-than-revealing session, the national anchors had instantly tired of Midwest hospitality and five minute slots alongside a draughty runway with nothing to report, so booked themselves on the first available flight back to base and, hopefully, a more juicy breaking story to get their fangs into.

All of the local media, TV, radio and newsprint, were in attendance, plus the usual scattering of freelancers with syndication contracts and the odd self-styled columnists representing niche interests. Pete Christensen held the first question slot for KNSZ, having wrested it from KNKW partly by dint of length of experience over his new adversary, Scott Adams, but mainly because KNKW had been slow in recognising Adams as their new main anchor, unsurprisingly considering the previous two had become news themselves within hours of each other.

Sam Schneider had wandered into the chamber just a couple of minutes before the briefing was due to start, taking an anonymous seat towards the rear. He was there, primarily, to get a handle on what had happened with Stanton because, unusually for City Hall in recent years, nothing was filtering out to give any clues; he also wanted to see what Harper's reaction would be to his presence. Schneider had not received a courtesy call from City Hall, as was customary in the event of there being a major change in management structure. In the short term, he was happy to conclude that Harper, being the stickler for convention he was, would need for the appointment to be announced officially before he made any such moves.

There had been a rustle of activity among the hacks when one of the female clerks came to the main microphone at spot-on nine-thirty, but the apologetic announcement was of a ten-minute delay, followed by her quickly scurrying off, stage-right, before any questions could be posed towards her.

Schneider took out his cellphone and turned it on. He thought that he may as well trawl his messages while he was waiting, having had little time earlier. The lack of sleep was still taking its toll and his wife had made two attempts to rouse him when the alarms went off, first at six-thirty and then seven. Neither had the slightest effect on him, so she decided to let him sleep through until eight before she literally pulled him out of bed and into the shower.

A quick check-in at the office allowed Carla to confirm that nothing urgent was happening, with everyone on their assigned tasks. This gave her enough time to pump a good-sized mug of black coffee down him, then point him in the general direction of City Hall. Having decided to walk, the fresh morning air combined with the caffeine to have Sam just about firing on all eight cylinders.

With his nose buried in the inbox list for a couple of minutes, he hadn't noticed the male figure approaching up the aisle between the ranks of seats. His first recognition was the voice: "Agent Schneider, so what brings you to such an unimportant media briefing?"

Schneider didn't look up from his phone: "Christensen, isn't it time they put you out to grass?"

"And it's so nice to see you again, after all this time," came the mildly effeminate response.

Schneider still didn't look away from his phone: "switch that fucking thing off, I'm here officially which means you don't get an interview without prior permission from the Bureau in triplicate."

It was a technique Schneider had picked-up at a seminar several years earlier, used by some high-profile celebrities who constantly swore at reporters in case they were trying to snatch a clandestine live sound-bite. This would send the director in the truck into apoplexy; Schneider had used it ever since, to great effect.

"Oh alright," Christensen flounced frustratedly, withdrawing the microphone towards his midriff as he demonstrably flicked the switch with his thumb. Schneider looked up. He glanced at Christensen, then at the microphone: "I fucking thought I fucking said to turn that fucking thing off!"

That was the second technique he had picked-up at the seminar - that a link-man will thrust a dead microphone at a celebrity which, when told to turn off, they actually turn on. Christensen winced as a separate flow of invective blasted through his earphone from the truck outside. He pushed the microphone under Schneider's nose, flicked the switch to off, then lowered it to his side. Pretending to have a mild hissy-fit, he asked his next question: "what - have they built some sort of magnetic flux detector into your cellphones now?"

"No Christensen, you shouldn't be so proud of those shiny buttons on your blazer - they reflect the LED like a searchlight."

"OK, off the record Agent Schneider, what are you doing here?"

"I just fancied a walk in the spring sunshine, noticed that something was going on over here at City Hall and, like any concerned local citizen, wandered in to see what it might be."

"That's the problem, we don't know. The whole place seems to have suddenly decided to imitate a duck's ass. Very unusual."

Schneider smiled at the link man's obvious discomfort at the prospect of having to actually earn his grain the proper way, by thinking on his feet with no prior preparation: "if someone as important as you isn't being let in on the secret, they're hardly likely to tell an organisation that 'leaks like an overfilled diaper' are they?"

"You're not still sulking over that are you? It was over three years ago."

"Well, you know what they say don't you - there are only three things that are certain in this life; death, taxes and the FBI never closing a file."

"So what's this, Pete Christensen's greatest hits? You have to admit, they are pretty good."

"That's a matter of taste - whether you have any, or not."

"Ooh, I like that! Mind if I use it one day?"

"As long as it's not on me - where shall I send the invoice?"

"So, now we have the pleasantries out of the way, a little bird tells me that Stanton's on his way."

"Really, there's a surprise. If it's true, you have got to be worried."

"Me? Why me?"

"Because everyone knows he runs rings round the local media at these things. Maybe a gamekeeper's going to turn poacher for a change."

"No chance. I've got the prime seat now and I'm not going to give it up to some ass-licking amateur."

"You're sure of that are you?"

"Course I am, why?"

"Because it looks to me as though they're just about to start and you're not in your prime seat."

Christensen snapped round to see that two figures were already taking their seats on the podium: "oh bollocks!" he hissed, as he turned and ran, in a somewhat ungainly fashion, back down the steps.

One-Five-Four

McKinley and Holdsworth had timed their departure from City Hall so that they would arrive at Stanton's house just after the scheduled start time for the media briefing.

The five-bedroomed house, on the outskirts of Andover, was in a fairly-exclusive development, less than ten minutes' drive from the Prairie Hills Golf Club, where Stanton was a member. The house was at the end of a cul-de-sac overlooking the entrance of the open-plan street, so it would not be possible for them to make any form of stealth-approach. They elected to drive straight onto the large forecourt in front of the garages.

As soon as they did, they realised they had a problem, because there in the corner of the manicured lawn was a large sign that read: 'Sold by Refined Realty - Your High-class Realtor for the Midwest'. It took just a few seconds for them to realise that not only had the property been sold, but also that the new owners had vacant possession.

The Mantis Pact

They got out of the car and took a look around; a quick squint through two windows confirmed that not a stick of furniture remained in the house. The neighbourhood was quiet, unsurprising midweek for a community made-up of professionals with growing families. There seemed little point in wasting time knocking doors, so as the address of the realtor on the sign was on North Rock, they decided to make that their next port of call. Ten minutes later, they pulled onto the vast forecourt in front of Best Buy and headed towards the low strip building along the left-hand edge that held the secondary businesses. Over the top of the third unit from the right was the bright red sign for Refined Realty.

Through the glazed door they could see an unimaginative layout of desks and chairs, typical for the type of business. Only one was inhabited, by a young blonde with tanned complexion and cheerleader features. As they entered, her unforced smile lit up the interior: "good mornin' gentlemen, what a lovely day."

"It is," McKinley responded, "I wonder if you could help us. I'm sorry, but we're not here to buy a property. We are police officers, I am Sergeant McKinley, this is Detective Holdsworth." They showed their badges.

Her smile remained, unfazed by the change of situation: "of course Sergeant, how can I help?"

"Thank you, Miss?"

"Walker - Melissa Walker."

"You have a property over in Andover, on Calluna Lake, Miss Walker?"

"Yes, but we sold it yesterday."

"Yes, we saw the sign. Can you tell us when the occupants moved out?"

A surprised look crossed her face: "they've moved out you say?"

"Yes the house is empty - you look surprised."

"Um … yes. We only did the viewing yesterday. The buyers confirmed their offer in the afternoon, which was accepted, but I don't think anything else has been processed yet. Let me get the file."

She got to her feet and walked to a bank of filing cabinets at the rear of the room, opened one of the drawers and started thumbing through. She stopped at a hanging file that was clearly empty, bar for a small slip of paper which she pulled out, examined, then replaced in the hanging file. She closed the drawer and walked to the rearmost desk on the right side of the room and began looking through the pile of files placed neatly on one corner. Not finding anything, she replaced the files then, with a look of concern, tried the deep filing drawer in the left hand pedestal; it was locked. She stood up and considered the top of the desk: "that's curious," she mumbled.

"What is?" McKinley prompted.

"The file. It's booked-out to the principal. Oh, sorry, that's Mike Walker, my boss - actually he's my Dad. But it doesn't seem to be here on his desk and his file drawer is locked, so I can't check that. If you can give me a few minutes, I can ring him."

"Of course."

She returned to her desk, picked-up the phone handset and hit a speed-dial button. The number was obviously ringing unanswered, because she looked at them and smiled a nervous smile as she waited. It eventually went to voicemail: "hi Dad, it's Melissa. I have two Police Officers in the office here, they are enquiring about Calluna Lake, but I can't seem to find the file. It's booked out to you, but it's not on your desk. Could you ring me back please."

She hung up: "I'm sorry, his cell's gone to voicemail. He must be on a view, he leaves it in the car when he is, so that he doesn't get disturbed."

"I must use you next time I want to buy a house," Holdsworth observed, "the last realtor we had never got off her phone talking to other clients during any of our views - hopeless!"

She smiled: "would you like to wait, or can I ring you?"

"Maybe you can give us the information we need."

"I'll certainly try."

"Has the property been on the market long?"

"No. Actually it might even be a new record for us for the quickest sale we've ever done."

"Really?"

"Yes. Dad took the instructions yesterday morning, so he went out and took the measurements, photos and so on. He hadn't been back in the office for more than ten minutes when we had a general enquiry for that sort of property. During the conversation, he mentioned it as a new instruction and the buyer arranged a view there and then. He met them about two thirty, was back just after four; they rang at four thirty to confirm."

"Wow, I bet you would like deals like that more often."

"Sure would! It happens occasionally with corporate clients, but I can't remember one that quick since I started here."

"You took instructions yesterday morning, can you remember the time?"

"Oh early, call came in soon after we opened."

McKinley looked at Holdsworth, then continued: "you say with corporate clients. Do you do a lot of business with corporates?"

"Oh yes, we specialise in the relocation market. We have a stock of suitable rental properties for immediate temporary accommodation for families of executives locating here; then we give them exclusive help with finding a permanent home. Probably two-thirds of our business is selling company-owned properties. The two markets work well together, because properties that have been suitable for one executive are often ideal for another."

"And the one in Calluna Lake, was that a company-owned property?"

"No, it's privately-owned. It has been purchased by a company though."

"A local company?"

"No, they're from Idaho I believe. They are setting-up a branch here in Wichita and will be using us for all of their housing needs for the senior staff moving here."

"So this isn't the first property you have found for them."

"Actually, it is. The phone call yesterday afternoon was the first contact we had with them. Let's hope all of the deals go as smoothly as this one!"

"Do you have many corporate clients that are local?"

"Oh yes, in fact our largest client is a subsidiary of The Kendrick Corporation; are you aware of them?"

"Yes. Actually I had the pleasure of meeting the younger Mr Kendrick recently. But I suppose that you would be dealing with one of their managers."

"Oh no, that Mr Kendrick often calls in to have a meeting with Dad; he likes to keep an eye on his properties. It's always nice to meet him, he is very charming. Always has a few words for everybody in the office, including me." She coloured-up slightly as she said this; McKinley and Holdsworth exchanged a knowing look.

"Getting back to Calluna Lake, do you know the name of the purchasing Company?"

"No, I haven't really spoken to Dad since the deal went through. It will be in the file, but I can't check that at the moment."

"When you find the file, perhaps you could look it up and ring me - here's my card."

She took the card and looked at it: "I'll do that Detective McKinley."

"One last thing - would you have a forwarding address for the vendors?"

"If we do, it will also be in the file; or you could try their lawyers - Mulholland, White and Friedmann."

"We'll do that, thank you."

The two policemen made their farewells and left the office. As they walked to the car, Holdsworth made an observation: "how often does a three-hundred-grand property sell within hours in the current market?"

"Only when the vendor's agent's main client is related to their lawyer. What's the bet that buyer is on one of those lists that Jim Kowalski is analysing?"

"So another dead end."

They reached the car and McKinley rested his arms on the roof over the driver's door. He looked across the roof towards Holdsworth who was standing on the passenger side: "yes, although it is interesting that the instruction came in first-thing yesterday."

"Stanton was on his way even before his meeting with Baker."

"Seems so. I suppose we could waste our time trying to find out how our ex-chief, his family and all of their possessions disappeared into the ether within the last twenty-four hours."

"Didn't you just work that one out?"

"Yes and they're running this game as well. Every time we think we might be getting near probable cause, they move another two steps ahead of us. Whether we like it or not, we're running out of options and they know it."

"There's still the disks from Hillsboro."

McKinley sighed: "that's the long game - we need something we can use now, not in six months time. We can only hope that Clarke's having more success with tracking-down Morley"

One-Five-Five

The two figures settled into their plush chairs behind the long counter that formed the dais in the Council chamber. The centre chair, beneath the City of Wichita logo, was occupied by Mayor Ramsey wearing his customary dark suit with the small gold republican lapel badge glinting in the temporary TV lights erected on their tripods to either side of the hall. To his right, between the City logo and the stars and stripes hanging limply from its wall bracket, Chief Harper sat in full dress uniform. The Mayor leaned towards the microphone in front of him: "good morning everyone and thank you for attending this unscheduled media briefing at such short notice. We would first like to make the following announcement."

He began reading from a sheet of paper: "it is with regret that I have to announce the resignation of Wichita Chief of Police Stanton for purely personal and family reasons. This came as a complete surprise when he tendered it to me personally just yesterday afternoon, when he also asked to be relieved of his duties with immediate effect. I accepted the resignation with great reluctance and sadness. I want to pay immediate tribute to the success he achieved and the manner in which he conducted himself throughout the seven years that he held this important post. The entire City Government thank him for his hard work in making Wichita a far safer city in which to live, than it was when he came into post. We send him our very best wishes for whatever the future may hold for him. Because of the crucial nature of the role, we have obviously had to move swiftly to appoint a replacement, and I am pleased to also announce that replacement will be Dick Harper, who accompanies me here this morning. Many of you will already know Dick, who has served as our Deputy Chief of Police for the last five years. He has been responsible for putting into action many of the initiatives evolved by his predecessor. This is a permanent appointment that provides both the City Government and the Police Department with the necessary continuity needed in such an unexpected transition. I will hand over to Chief Harper in a few moments so that he can give you details of the various operational changes he has already put in place since his appointment, following which he will take your questions. But first, I will take questions with regard to this announcement, stressing to you before I do so that I will not be taking any questions this morning with regard to Chief Stanton's reasons for his resignation, but assure everybody that it has not been submitted because of any connections with any operation currently or previously handled by his department; neither was it requested by myself."

As usual, the entire media pack all tried to shout their questions at once, but the Mayor was pointing at Christensen: "yes Pete."

"Pete Christensen, KNSZ - from what you have told us, Mr Mayor, this has obviously come out of the blue. So has something happened to Chief Stanton that we are unaware of?"

Mayor Ramsey's countenance darkened as he replied, barely concealing his annoyance: "I will give you the benefit of the doubt, Mister Christensen, that you were not paying full attention to the whole of my announcement. Now, do you have a question for me that I can answer, or not?"

"But the timing of this announcement could not be worse for you, so close to the recent murders and the events surrounding the attack on Lieutenant Kleberson. Are we really to believe that there is no connection whatsoever?"

Ramsey's voice took on an air of disdain: "I can only gauge from your response that the answer to my previous question is, therefore, no." He looked quickly around the room and pointed at a journalist from the Wichita Mail: "yes!"

The next few questions were fairly banal, Ramsey fielding them with his usual aplomb. Christensen was quietly fuming in his chair, while his director's voice in his earphone first chastised him for being so amateur, then gave him instructions so basic that even a rookie would be annoyed by them. He looked around the room for where Schneider was sitting, only to find the FBI man's contented smile of amusement focussed in his direction; this heightened Christensen's discomfort.

Seated alongside Christensen was Scott Adams, studying proceedings, having not yet asked anything, apparently keeping his powder dry for later in the session. Christensen leaned towards him and whispered: "do you not have a question Adams? Don't you think this is all a bit contrived?"

But Adams had learned a lot in the two weeks since he had been thrust into the role by Cochrane's absence: "sssh!" he whispered back, "I'm paying full attention." Christensen's demeanour was not improved by this, so he decided to sit still and smoulder until an opportunity arose for him to retrieve the situation.

After another round of questions from one of the radio stations, the momentum was slowing with regard to this part in the proceedings. Adams sensed that Ramsey was preparing to hand over to Harper for the operational detail, so he caught the Mayor's eye and got the customary barely-perceivable nod in return. After the latest supplementary had been handled on autopilot, the Mayor turned to Adams and pointed: "yes Scott."

"Scott Adams, KNKW - a question to both of you, if I may. We were told by Chief Stanton last week that all of the case files for the Vitruvio murders were closed following the death of Lieutenant Kleberson's attacker. Do you have any plans to reopen any of them?"

The hubbub in the room suddenly subsided; Sam Schneider craned forward in his seat. Ramsey took the immediate response: "I understand that action was taken because the cases have all been handed over to the FBI, who are conducting the wider enquiry into the various activities of Sean Shepherd, the perpetrator of those ghastly crimes." He turned to Harper: "is there anything you wish to add to that, Chief?"

"Yes Sir," he replied and addressed the media corps: "just that, in order to understand more fully what happened, Chief Stanton did institute an internal enquiry into the department proceedings leading-up to Lieutenant Kleberson's hospitalisation. That enquiry is still in progress. I have asked the Homicide Squad to take-over that enquiry and re-examine all of the evidence in conjunction with the enquiry submissions. On that task, they are now reporting directly to me."

Adams immediately asked a supplementary: "you mentioned the Homicide Squad, Chief Harper, but also in last week's session your predecessor advised that the Homicide Squad was being dismantled under the latest reorganisation."

Harper continued to take the responses: "that's right, he did. However, I intend to retain it and will be giving you more details of that, plus other changes in the Department, when we get to the operational briefing."

Adams looked at the Mayor and kept going: "one more, if I may?" He received the Mayor's assent: "we have received at KNKW this morning, from a reliable source, information that suggests that the Wichita Police Department, more specifically Chief Stanton, was provided with details of a meeting that took place between Hilary Nicholson and Agent Kryczek, the FBI Agent whose identity Sean Shepherd used to lure Lieutenant Kleberson to the situation where the attack took place. That meeting apparently occurred just two weeks prior to Ms Nicholson's murder. Can you confirm, Chief Harper, that this information is included within the files that the Homicide Squad are re-examining?"

The room went deathly quiet and Mayor Ramsey shot Harper a quick glance, to check whether his new Chief of Police was going to take the response, but also barely concealing the concern he was feeling as to what that response might be. He needn't have worried because Harper took it completely in his stride: "you appreciate, Mr Adams, that I cannot discuss specific details of an investigation while it is in progress. All I can assure you is that, if any information comes into the possession of my department at any time, regardless of who it is received by, it is immediately passed to the investigating officers responsible for the case it pertains to."

There was a brief lull in proceedings as the pack digested what they had just heard. Christensen was the first to react. He got to his feet and posed a follow-up question direct to Harper: "Pete Christensen, KNSZ - Chief Harper, are you able to give us any indication as to whether this information has any bearing on the continuing FBI investigations surrounding the Vitruvio murders?"

Once again, Harper did not flinch: "I am afraid that the FBI will have to provide you with that response. I did notice that the Head of their local Agency was here earlier, maybe you can ask him that question."

"Oh, rest assured Chief, we will!" Christensen turned smugly to face the seat occupied by Sam Schneider. To his intense annoyance, it was empty.

One-Five-Six

Schneider was walking briskly down Main towards his office at the Epic Center. He had already made two telephone calls since leaving City Hall. The first, to Chandler Clarke, had gone straight to voicemail, so he had left a message to ring him back immediately Clarke received it. The second had been to Chris McKinley.

Schneider's mood had not been lifted by the news of Stanton's vanishing trick. In fact, his cellphone nearly bore the brunt of his anger as he momentarily took aim, as if to hurl it at the adjacent parking lot. Thinking better of it, he concluded the conversation with McKinley by asking him to call into the FBI office before returning to City Hall. After hanging-up, he determinedly increased the pace at which he was walking.

As he crossed Third Street, his cell rang. It was Clarke: "hi Sam."

"Where are you Chandler?"

"I'm on North Broadway headed back to the office. I've completely drawn a blank at Morley's apartment."

"That figures. Where on Broadway?"

"Hang on ... I've just crossed Fourteenth."

"OK, go to the KNKW studios; they're on the corner of Thirteenth and Mosely. I'll fill you in when I meet you there in ten minutes."

"Sure thing Sam."

Schneider immediately speed-dialled Carla Courtney. She answered instantly: "hi Sam, enjoy the briefing?"

"For a while. Carla, ring Max Huberstein at KNKW and tell him I'm coming to see him in ten minutes' time. If he's not in his office, tell him to get there, unless he needs a Federal warrant swearing-out. And tell him I want Scott Adams in attendance also. I'm on my way to the studios now and Chandler's en route to meet me. Ring me back as soon as you have confirmation."

Five minutes later, Schneider's Crown Victoria had exited the Epic Center car park and swung left onto Main headed north. His cell rang. It was Carla: "all fixed Sam - he said he was expecting someone from WPD but you'll do fine."

"Did he? Cheeky bastard."

"Sam!"

"Sorry Carla, this morning's not starting well. Chris McKinley's on his way into you. He'll need some coffee then let him tie-up with Jim; we'll be back as soon as we can."

"Sure thing Sam."

Five minutes later, Schneider pulled-up behind Clarke's car alongside the converted parking lot at KNKW that housed three rows of satellite dishes pointing skywards. Together, they walked into the reception area, announced themselves and were immediately escorted by the receptionist along a short corridor to the burgundy-painted door at the end that bore the simple plaque: 'M Huberstein - Station Head'. She knocked, opened the door and ushered them in.

It was a modest office for someone with so much apparent power, overlooking an area where several outside broadcast trucks stood redundantly. There was a small desk covered by disjointed piles of papers and a computer; teed out of the desk was a conference table flanked by six metal-framed chairs. Max Huberstein was already standing waiting to welcome them. Introductions were exchanged, but pleasantries kept to a minimum, then the two Agents took seats at the table, while Huberstein resumed his behind his desk.

"Where's Adams?" Schneider commenced, somewhat brusquely.

"He's still at City Hall," Huberstein responded.

"I gave instructions for him to be here."

"Yes you did, Agent Schneider, but I ignored them. This country is not yet a police state."

Schneider folded his arms and leant forward on the table towards Huberstein, "I was at the back of the hall when Adams indicated that your station had received information about a meeting between Hilary Nicholson and Agent Kryczek. I would remind you that there is an ongoing Federal investigation into not only the recent events here in Wichita, but also a number of other murders across the country, at least one of which involves the death of a Federal Agent. So was it Mr Adams' intention to advise the Bureau of that information at some time, or was he just trying to advance his new career as quickly as possible?"

"I'll answer that Agent Schneider, but first, may I remind you that the first three victims here in Wichita all worked for this Station and that we are more interested in having some closure on their loss than scoring points off of anybody. I received the information and Scott was acting under my instructions, which were to find out if anybody within our law enforcement community was interested in such a piece of information. This was because, despite several telephone calls this morning, including one to your office I may add, I could find nobody who wanted to hear it."

Schneider relaxed his pose slightly: "Max, I'm sorry, but you probably recognise that these have not been the easiest cases to investigate. I'm talking off the record ..." he paused for acceptance, to which Huberstein nodded his head: "we are making progress, but really slowly because we are having to overcome some external interference and that is, as you have just seen, frustrating."

"As I assured Chief Stanton and Lieutenant Kleberson at the time this all started, we will co-operate completely. Even if that means at the end there is some exclusive that we miss-out on, it's a small price to pay for justice for our people. Everybody thinks that justice has been delivered by the death of Sean Shepherd, but my journalistic instincts tell me that was only partial justice and there will be more to come. Am I right?"

"Yes you are, but obtaining the rest of the evidence will be difficult and painful for us all. As you know, I have one of my best friends unresponsive in a hospital bed, so this is personal for me as well. But even I cannot guarantee success, I wish I could. So tell us, what is this information and where did it come from?"

"I had a call at eight a.m. from Madeleine Nicholson, Hilary's sister. She came to Wichita last week to make the preliminary arrangements to have her sister's body returned to Texas when it was eventually released. She also visited Chief Stanton - he thought it was just a meeting with a relative, but he soon found out that there was more to it."

"So why did she ring you?"

"The family has obviously been preoccupied with the funeral this last week, but they had also been watching for some news on developments in the case. When there had been none nationally, she rang us here to ask if it had just been covered locally. When I told her there had been no developments, she became very annoyed. She's a real old-fashioned southern lady - when they say jump, you don't get the chance to ask how high? She told me to go interview Stanton straight away; when I said we were attending a media briefing where we expected to hear he had resigned, she just went ape-shit."

"At which point, presumably, she said that she had told Stanton about this meeting between her sister and Agent Kryczek."

"Right."

"Anything else?"

"I managed to calm her down enough to get that out of her, but she will not give us any more - wants to speak to law enforcement. Or as she put it - law enforcement that ain't in someone's pocket. Believe me, if nobody calls her back this morning, you had all best watch out, because she's gonna be on the next plane here."

"Oh we'll do that, rest assured! You said you phoned-around this morning, who did you call?"

"Harper, but his secretary said he was too busy preparing for the briefing; she would get him to ring back, probably tomorrow. Ramsey ditto. Then your LA office. They said their head - Baker is it? - is down here; is that right?" Schneider nodded. "So I rang your office. Your secretary would not confirm that he was here, but would get a message through to him to ring me asap. Guess you train them not to give anything to the likes of us, although I'm surprised she didn't tell you I was looking for him."

"We're all big boys, don't need nursemaiding. Carla would have told Pete - you say he hasn't returned the call?"

"Not yet."

Schneider exchanged glances with Clarke, then continued: "he is on a task this morning. Rest assured, we will ring Madeleine Nicholson straight away; do you have the contact details?" Huberstein passed a slip of paper to Schneider, who looked at it and placed it in his wallet: "it will take us ten minutes to get back to my office, we'll ring her from there. If she calls again in the meantime, Max, impress on her to wait for that call. I don't want her up here tramplin' all over the corn before we get a chance to harvest it."

"Sure. But if that call comes in an hour's time and you haven't rung her, I'll help her with the trampling - is that understood?"

"It won't." Schneider rose from his seat and extended his hand towards Huberstein: "thanks Max."

Huberstein also rose and took Schneider's hand: "you're welcome, just nail 'em - whoever they are - all of 'em." He winked as he said it: "just one more thing. We rang Stanton for a quote - the phone's disconnected."

"We know, we're working on that as well. Talk to you later."

The two FBI Agents left the building and walked to their cars. Clarke posed the question: "what was all that about Stanton's phone being disconnected?"

Schneider turned as he reached his car: "McKinley and Holdsworth went out there this morning. He's gone."

"Gone? whad'ya mean gone?"

"Cleared out. House empty, no sign of anyone."

"Shit! Is that what he was doin' all that time with Friedmann yesterday?"

"Looks like it. What about Morley's place?"

"Oh, that looked like it had been ransacked."

"Ransacked?"

"Don't worry, janitor said he lives like a slob. He hasn't gone anywhere, but he hasn't been home either. Nobody's seen him since yesterday morning - not unusual apparently. Janitor's going to let us know when he turns up again."

"If he turns up. Let's get back to base; when we do, you ring Madeleine Nicholson." Schneider took the piece of paper from his wallet and handed it to Clarke: "I'll get the full details on Stanton from McKinley, then we'll decide what to do from there."

One-Five-Seven

It was just after eleven a.m. when the chartered Super King Air taxied to a halt on the concrete pan to the left of the small terminal building. Pete Baker had chosen the Colonel James Jabara Airport for two reasons - it was closer to the morgue and it was quiet. There were only a few scheduled flights each week from this smaller airport in the north-east corner of Wichita that was used primarily for executive aviation. This also meant they could drive the long wheelbase Chevy Suburban right up to the aircraft for loading.

At this time the vehicle had parked a little away from the aircraft, with Baker waiting nearby as the ground handler wheeled the shallow steps up to the door. They opened to reveal a diminutive grey-haired lady in her late fifties, wearing an understated, but stylish, black two-piece with a single inverted white lily pinned to the left breast. She looked remarkably fresh for someone that had just endured a near four-hour flight, longer than would have been preferred, but necessary as the slower King Air was the only aircraft with a cargo door available at such short notice. Baker stepped forward to help Eleanor Kryczek down the three steps to terra firma, welcomed her solemnly, then escorted her to the car.

He alone would take her to the morgue for the formal identification, after which they would wait for the body to be crated-up, then take it directly to the airfield. His Agent, who had flown down with her from El Monte Airport, would remain with the plane. Once loaded, they would all fly-out immediately.

Very little was said during the first couple of miles down Webb, other than the usual pleasantries, Baker enquiring about the flight, Eleanor remarking on the weather. Then, as they approached the junction with Twenty-First, Eleanor asked the first pertinent question: "did she suffer?"

"Not that we can see," Baker replied.

"I mean … oh dear!" Eleanor pulled her large handbag from beside her and opened it. Pulling out a dainty lace handkerchief, she gently dabbed her nose and eyes: "I'm so sorry," she sobbed softly.

"Nothing to be sorry about Mrs Kryczek, please take your time."

"Eleanor, please. I'm sorry, I told myself I wouldn't do this, but …" She went quiet again, turning to look away from Baker through the side window. Baker allowed her the space to recompose herself. Still looking through the side window, she eventually continued: "it's just that … all those horrible details on the news about the other victims … did he?"

Baker gave her a few seconds to finish the sentence, then helped her: "we can find no evidence of physical assault of any kind, not in this case. We believe that your daughter had been investigating him without telling me or anybody else in the office and once she identified him, decided to confront him on her own. I'm sorry, I had no idea …"

This time Eleanor Kryczek cut him off: "you mustn't blame yourself for anything, that would be typical Lesley - she had very little respect for authority."

"I noticed that," he replied laconically. Eleanor emitted a stuttered laugh, partly in response to the humour, partly in relief of the stress she was experiencing: "she was always a handful you know. Drove poor Roger to distraction when she was a teenager."

"Your husband?"

"Her father - rest his soul - been gone six years past."

"I'm sorry."

"No need. He never cared, had no time for death, just wanted to live every minute. Had no time for most conventions. We never married - he didn't believe in it."

"Did Kryczek, sorry I mean Lesley, know?"

"Oh yes and completely approved as well. When some of her so-called friends in sixth grade found out, they called her a bastard. Kids! They know everything and nothing at that age. She didn't even flinch, just ignored it - best thing to do really."

"I can't imagine the Lesley Kryczek that worked for me letting something like that pass by unpunished."

"Oh, I didn't say she forgot about it. Months later they were on a school outing to a local farm as part of a project they had. They got to the pigsty and while the teacher was explaining about pigs, Lesley crept up behind the girl who was the ring-leader, boosted her up and dumped her over the fence into the slurry. When they finally extracted the girl, crying her eyes out, Lesley just stood in front of her with her hands on her hips and said - now I'm a bastard!"

They both laughed: "that's the Lesley I knew," Baker observed.

But Eleanor's mood again turned sombre: "so how did she die?"

"We haven't done a post mortem yet; I wanted you to see her first."

"Oh! Thank you for that. That's so kind!" She began to lose composure again, but recovered quickly by putting her handkerchief to her nose once more.

Having again given her the time, Baker continued: "from the external examination we have done, we believe that he used the same injection that he used on the others. But that was it, he doesn't seem to have done anything else."

"So she wasn't shot?"

"No, definitely not."

"Oh, that's a blessing - it was what she feared most you know."

"No, I didn't. She seemed so - fearless."

"Oh yes, on the outside she was, but believe me, inside she was churning. Just wouldn't let it show to anyone, not even me. But mothers know these things. How was she found?"

"She was left in a motel room over in Peabody; the room service girl found her in the morning. She was just led on the bed. The girl thought she was asleep at first, but then when she realised …"

"So he just left her there?"

"That's it. This killer, Shepherd, was totally unpredictable, so much so that we are still trying to piece-together a lot of things."

"So why didn't you know it was her?"

"He took all her belongings - identity, cellphone, everything. That was how he managed to pose as her later on. To the local Police, she was a Jane Doe. Nobody came forward with a missing person report, so she just stayed in the morgue until we eventually joined the dots yesterday."

"I didn't think to …"

"Don't Eleanor. You said that she told you not to worry if you didn't hear from her."

"Yes, but …" Baker cut her off again.

"Stop now! If Lesley was here, what would she be telling you?"

"Not to be so damned stupid!" She immediately burst into tears.

Baker stopped talking, feeling completely guilty at what he had caused to happen, every soft sob prodding him in the ribs. He left her until the crying subsided: "we're almost there Eleanor. There's a vanity mirror behind the sunvisor if you want to use it."

She opened her handbag again and began digging for her cosmetic pouch. Her emotions had become more balanced: "I'm sorry, but I think I needed that."

"It must have been hard for you. Just take your time when we get there; the plane's not going anywhere until we all get back to the airport - we're on our own schedule today."

She pulled the sunvisor down and began to tidy her make-up: "funny," she observed, "I wouldn't have expected a vanity mirror in a Police car."

"We use it for surveillance."

"Of course, silly me."

Baker signalled right and began to slow: "here we are," he said.

Eleanor quickly packed her cosmetics away and was tucking the pouch back into her bag: "oh yes, nearly forgot." She pulled a small mailer from the bag: "Lesley sent this for you."

Baker pulled-up in one of the visitor slots in front of the building, applied the footbrake and turned off the ignition. He turned to see Eleanor holding the mailer towards him: "what is it?" he asked.

"I have no idea, it's sealed and it has your name on it."

"How did you get it?"

"She sent it to me, after she told me she was going to be under cover. It was one of her rituals; 'to be handed to my Lead Agent if I don't come back' was what she said the first time she gave one to me. Of course, she always did … until now."

"What happened to the others?"

"Oh they went into the trash - that was 'the procedure' as she called it."

Baker took the envelope. He could feel through the padding that it contained something thin and stiff - *'a disk'* was his first thought. He tucked it into his inside pocket. "Thank you," he said: "are you ready?"

"As I'll ever be," Eleanor replied, apprehensively.

the bird has flown

One-Five-Eight

When Schneider and Clarke returned to the FBI office, McKinley and Holdsworth were already awaiting them in the conference room. Clarke tied-up with Carla Courtney to arrange the telephone call with Madeleine Nicholson, who was waiting in her home on the island of St Lucia in the Caribbean. The island was just two hours ahead, so it was still only early afternoon there.

Schneider handed-over his office to Clarke for the call, collected a mug of coffee and went straight to the conference room, where McKinley and Holdsworth outlined the blanks they had drawn that morning in Andover and at the realtor. Schneider explained why he and Clarke had been delayed, then began to summarise what avenues were open to them next: "I think we can just forget about Stanton for now - the bird has flown and we have no idea where. Even when we find him, if we find him, there will be nothing documentation-wise that connects him with anything, he would have got rid of all that."

"What about this meeting with Ms Nicholson's sister? Maybe that will give us something," McKinley asked, more in hope than certainty.

"Maybe," Schneider replied, "but we will need for there to have been a document, something she handed to Stanton; and that it was a copy, not the original. If it was, that will have gone as well."

"What are we going to do about Morley?"

"I think you're the best placed to deal with him. The janitor at his apartment block will alert us when he surfaces, but there's little we can do unless he does."

"We have a meeting with Harper at two p.m. He wants a full briefing of what we have unearthed with regard to departmental staff."

"Guess he's looking to cover the department's back."

"Possibly, but I got the impression last night that he was taking a different stance to what I expected. He's always been the administrator, the guy who meticulously buries anything embarrassing, but he wasn't doing that last night."

"He certainly seemed every inch the politician on that podium in the media briefing this morning. I would counsel caution before making my mind up over exactly where he is placing himself in the grander scheme of things."

At that, the door opened and Chandler Clarke came into the room. He acknowledged the two city detectives, then settled down in a chair at the table.

"That was quick," Schneider observed.

"Yes," Clarke responded, "there's not an awful lot she could tell us, other than what she told Stanton."

"Which was?"

"That the last time she and Hilary spoke was in a regular weekly telephone call; during that call Hilary mentioned that she had recently met with a female FBI Agent. Madeleine thought about it as the rest of the events unfolded on the news and decided that she would come to Wichita in person to make the necessary arrangements, at the same time giving all the details she could remember from the call to the local police."

"Why Stanton?"

Clarke smiled as he replied: "she's a bit of an anachronism, like Huberstein said. When she says jump everyone else leaves the ground instantaneously - in her opinion anyway. She's a step-sister actually, well into her sixties so much the elder; Hilary was a product of her father's second marriage. Madeleine inherited everything when her father died, which just seems to have served to enhance her overinflated ego. She doesn't like travelling, but when she does everything is organised for her by her lawyers down to the finest detail."

"Must cost her a fortune."

"It does, but she can afford it and the law firm isn't complaining. So when she said she would only talk to the Chief of Police, that's what they arranged. Stanton wasn't likely to argue, what with all the high-profile media interest."

"So what did she tell him?"

"That she hadn't realised the significance of her sister mentioning the FBI Agent until the details emerged of the other murders. Then she began to wonder why a Federal Agent was meeting her sister and whether Hilary had been the only one visited. She told Stanton that this Agent might have actually been the murderer, maybe 'casing the joint before she bumped her off' as she put it." They all chuckled at the phraseology. Clarke continued: "you see what I mean."

"And when was this?"

"The phone conversation with her sister was about a week before Hilary died, so the meeting would have been during the week prior to that."

"That aligns with Kryczek visiting Mrs Ferguson's house in Hillsboro."

"It does. The meeting took place at the house in Derby, where the Agent outlined various things she had found out about an old university acquaintance of Hilary Nicholson's and that these may link somehow to her fiancé."

"Really? What things exactly?"

"Hilary didn't say because, apparently, she thought it was all a bit far-fetched. She said that she had answered a few questions, as best she could, because she hadn't seen the old university friend for nearly ten years and the Agent had gone away satisfied. Hilary did say, however, that the Agent could be making another visit, when she would bring with her copies of some documents."

"What documents?"

"Ms Nicholson didn't know. To me, Sam, this sounds like a pretty-standard first meeting. It was obviously Kryczek and she was both fishing and checking facts at the same time. She was keeping her options open, as well as leaving just enough clues to jog a few memories maybe down the line a bit."

"Yes you're probably right. Anything else?"

"Only that Hilary finished-off by saying that she might speak to him about it, to see whether there might be anything in it."

"Speak to who?"

"Kendrick I guess. If you remember, Kryczek did mention to Hilary that she thought there might be a connection to him."

"Not necessarily," Holdsworth interrupted. He had been listening quietly up to that point: "Shepherd was a he."

"Not when they met at USC - Norma Schaeffer, remember?"

"Yes, but Hilary Nicholson obviously knew of the dual sexuality."

"How?"

"Can't answer that, but she met a man at the airport didn't she? Remember the CCTV footage - that was no surprise visit by someone who'd had an unannounced sex-change since they last met."

The room went silent as all four considered this angle. McKinley was the first to respond: "so that would mean that Shepherd came to Wichita to silence her and that there was no connection to the Kendricks."

Schneider was quick to react: "hold on, let's not forget the main thrust of the investigation too quickly. Hilary Nicholson also told her sister that Kryczek had implicated her fiancé during the discussion, that's right isn't it Chandler?"

"It is Sam," Clarke responded.

"So Chris, we have Hilary Nicholson saying she's going to talk to him about it, him being Jackson Kendrick the Third. So the Kendricks are alerted to an FBI Agent sniffing around the activities of an associate, Shepherd, which starts the whole chain of events moving to sweep it all under the carpet. Having achieved that, the sister comes to Wichita, tells Stanton that Hilary said she was going to tell Kendrick about the meeting and the genie's out of the bottle again. We have Stanton and Morley running interference all over the investigation, Morley using his relationship with Cochrane to throw a false scent, the Kendricks' lawyer Friedmann meeting Stanton regularly, and Morley in Stanton's office during some of those meetings. If that's not a conspiracy, what is?"

"Yes, I agree Sam," McKinley replied, "we've been down that route already, several times, and satisfied ourselves of its clear potential. But it's all after the event, so we don't have anything yet to hang a prosecution on. Even if we think we do, any defence lawyer worth their salt is going to examine the line that Shepherd was the 'he' mentioned, if only to muddy the waters with a jury. If our main scenario is to stand-up, we must be able to discredit any other one."

"Chris is right Sam," Clarke added, "if the Kendricks ordered the deaths of Hilary Nicholson and her friends, there must have been a conspiracy that linked back to when Kryczek started poking around down here. If we can't find that, we cannot show conclusively that Shepherd was not acting on his own initiative, consequently we can't nail the Kendricks that way on anything other than circumstantial evidence."

"That's a depressing thought, bearing in mind what we already know."

"We can use it to our advantage though," Holdsworth observed.

"How?" Schneider snapped at him somewhat.

"We tell everybody we're examining that line of enquiry - lone killer working off own initiative, plus no survivors to argue against it, equals the Kendricks thinking they've thrown us off the scent. Doesn't mean we're not looking for something that links across to our main suspects, but maybe it stops them throwing rocks onto the road in front of us. That could buy us the space necessary to find what we need."

"So what are you suggesting?"

McKinley took over: "this information ties-in to Stanton, because it was given to him over a week ago. I have been directed to look into events in the department surrounding the attack on Paul and that currently revolves around Stanton and Morley. So this gives me probable cause for going through every piece of documentation that Stanton was involved with at that time."

"Can you persuade Harper to let you do that?"

"If he wasn't just blowing smoke last night, I shouldn't have to."

"I guess that will tell us whose side he's on. What about media release?"

"I'll advise Harper that we sit on it until we find anything concrete, otherwise the department's reputation is going to be publically-dragged through the gutter before we have any way of defending it should this all prove to be a conspiracy."

"So if anything leaks in the meantime, we know what channels to look at. Sounds good, let's go with it."

McKinley turned to Clarke: "do we know what day Madeleine Nicholson met Stanton?"

"May Twelfth," Clarke replied

"That's the day Paul was attacked," Schneider said quietly.

"So we have the nucleus of a timeline," McKinley continued, "eleven a.m, I'm with Paul out at Cochrane's, then we have a gap until he returned to the office at around one-fifteen. Half an hour later, Stanton marches-in, announces he's come from lunch with the Mayor and suspends Paul. We've been concentrating on finding-out what Paul was doing in those two hours; now we know that Stanton was meeting Madeleine Nicholson at that same time."

"We think Kleberson may have been out at the Kendrick estate that morning," Clarke added.

"Where did that come from?" Holdsworth asked.

"Something we were going over yesterday."

"Which you thought we shouldn't know?"

"Hold on Scott," Schneider interceded, "it was just a theory. It would fit the timescale, but we've got nothing else to back it up."

"Never mind," McKinley mused, "let's just go with that for a minute. If Paul went to the estate, he would have been there from around eleven-forty-five until maybe an hour later, because he was back here at one-fifteen. We don't know who he met, but assuming it was one or more of the Kendricks, they couldn't have started anything in motion until after he left, even by telephone. Stanton said he had lunch with the Mayor, who had been telephoned by the Governor. But he met Madeleine Nicholson at one. I'm assuming from what you said about her Chandler, she wouldn't have tolerated him not meeting her on time?"

"If he was late, she would undoubtedly have mentioned it."

"So when did he meet the Mayor? Let alone have lunch with him and receive the complaint from the Kendricks via the Governor. It's unravelling already."

Schneider leant forward with greater purpose: "right then Chris, you and Scott follow everything tying-in to City Hall and anywhere it takes you. Chandler, did we get anything else from the sister?"

"Not really," Clarke responded, "she said that she had looked for diaries at the Eastborough house that day she came back, but found nothing."

"Did you guys find anything out at Eastborough?" Schneider directed the question to the two city detectives, who looked at each other for an answer.

McKinley was the one to respond: "to be honest Sam, we can't answer that without having a look at the files. Moreno went over there, but I think he only interviewed the cleaner. I'm not sure to what level that house was searched."

Clarke jumped-in: "Madeleine Nicholson has given me her law firm contact here in Wichita. They are handling the practical end of the estate business and she has given me permission to talk to them."

"How kind of her!" Schneider added sarcastically.

"If making her feel important oils the wheels, why not use it?" Clarke responded. "Why don't I go see them and get them to let me in. Madeleine Nicholson is barely qualified to do a proper search, so it won't hurt going over the place again."

"Sounds good Chandler, you go on with that. I'm going to ring Pete and fill him in on this, so that he can see if Kryczek's mother can give him anything on those documents Madeleine Nicholson mentioned. Kryczek was on garden leave and working outside the system, so there would be nothing at the LA Field Office. If she had anything with her when she came here, we can assume that Shepherd took it after he killed her. I guess we can't rule out that he would have gone over her home when he got back to California afterwards, either. But she was a thorough Agent, maybe she kept copies somewhere else."

One-Five-Nine

The receptionist quickly summoned Mary Jourdain to meet the two visitors. When she arrived through the door marked 'No Admittance', Pete Baker quickly introduced the lady accompanying him. After entering the passcode to release the same door, Mary escorted them through to a long corridor that led down to the storage area.

Baker had taken Mrs Kryczek's arm after they had entered the corridor, and he was aware that the weight on it was getting heavier as they approached the double doors at the end. This was not an unusual phenomenon; it was as though the person being taken to view the corpse of their loved one was sub-consciously resisting the inevitable. However much someone told themselves that they could manage, the reality once those last doors were breached was always beyond any expectation.

He had lost count of the number of times he had performed this function during his career, yet it became no easier, particularly when the event was the final act of a hunt for a missing person, or the person fulfilling the identification function was a parent, particularly a mother. But the worst were both combined. In the natural scheme of things a mother should not survive their offspring, or lose contact with a child for more than a few days at a time. As they halted to await the door release, Baker looked at Eleanor and placed his free hand on the arm he was supporting as a further reassurance: "are you ready?" he asked. The response was a familiar rapid nod of the head that only confirmed to him that she was nothing like ready for what was about to happen.

Mary Jourdain rang the bell that would summon the attendant she had instructed a few minutes earlier to await them. This was a member of staff trained with dealing with the aftermath of the body-bag zip being opened, more than with actually operating the drawer or the zip. Those were functions that anyone could perform, but the manner of the outpouring of grief was a wholly different story, as it could manifest itself many different ways; for that, some psychological training was essential.

A few moments after the echo of the bell faded in the distance, there was a buzz followed by both doors being pulled open by pneumatic jacks to reveal a kindly-looking lady in her late thirties with blonde hair tied back in a pigtail that flowed from under her scrub cap and dangled over the collar of her green lab uniform. Mary ushered the pair through the doors, which shut behind them under the control of the air-dampers. The short corridor opened into a large clear area, off of which several open doorways led into smaller alcoves, the walls of which were filled with what looked like stainless steel filing cabinets.

Baker was pleased to see that, instead of being conducted into one of those, there was a solitary wheeled limber in the centre of the room covered with a green sheet, under which a shape, almost-distinguishable as a prone human form of diminutive size, was laying. Mary had decided that this should be the method of revelation in this case, as it was a kinder way than a swift tug on a large filing drawer followed by the rasp of the zip opening to reveal a pallid, but familiar, face. At least this way the shock was amortised over two acts, that of entering the room and perceiving an almost-familiar shape dampened the initial shock by providing a partial preview of what was about to be revealed. The subsequent act of gently lifting the cover only confirmed what had already become apparent.

The room they were in was also less claustrophobic than the storage areas, despite the obvious background smell of death and its associated chemicals.

The Bird has Flown

Baker conducted Eleanor to the side of the head end of the limber, where he stood to her left. The technician positioned herself to the right of Eleanor, half a pace behind her. Mary Jourdain went to the opposite side of the limber and grasped the end of the cover where it dangled from the edge of the limber. She looked across at Eleanor who was already beginning to tremble slightly: "are you ready Mrs Kryczek?" she asked gently. Eleanor again provided a rapid nod of the head and sucked in her lips slightly. Her grip on Baker's arm tightened and he steeled himself to absorb the reflex reaction that was coming next.

Mary had also done this too many times for comfort, but enough to know the best method. She pulled back the sheet quickly, but with a smooth action, to reveal the head and bare shoulders of a woman in her early-thirties, tousled mousy hair and fairly sharp features that bore a resemblance to the lady opposite, who was reacting with a short, but anguished cry. Eleanor's legs momentarily let go of their primary function, supporting her torso. At the same time Baker took most of her weight on his arm for sufficient time for the lab tech to wrap her arm under Eleanor's shoulder blades and help her back to her standing height.

"I'm sorry Mrs Kryczek," Mary said gently, "but I do have to ask you these questions now." Eleanor jerked another nod in acknowledgement, her eyes already filling with tears. Mary asked: "do you recognise this person?"

Eleanor nodded and forced a weak "yes" through her tightly pursed lips.

Mary Jourdain continued: "is this your daughter, Lesley Kryczek?" Eleanor repeated the previous response. Mary held the cover for a few moments, during which the weight on Baker's arm lessened as Eleanor began to recover her composure. Baker looked at the face and affirmed the confirmation in his own mind. Yes this was his employee, the one he had christened 'The Grinch' after the first Christmas she worked in his office, when she sabotaged the Secret Santa tradition, by telling everyone on the morning of the event what they were going to receive and from who.

The cover was gently replaced and the lab tech began to guide Mrs Kryczek away from the limber towards the doors, to an office beyond set aside for the completion of the associated paperwork over a cup of hot strong coffee. They all knew that she would ask to return, when she would be left alone with her daughter for as long as she needed, but would probably be no longer than five minutes or so.

Mary picked-up a clipboard from the side table, already loaded with the partially-completed forms: "this won't take too long," she reassured Eleanor as she was led away. She turned to Baker: "we have the crate ready out back, I will just need your confirmation that you have the body you require, plus a signature, before we secure it. Do you need one of our vehicles?"

"We have a Suburban out front. I would rather use that if we can."

"Should be OK, can you bring it around the side and back it right up to the roller-shutter."

"Sure - but first, have you a computer I can use? I need to send an e-mail to my office to confirm that we will be on our way, plus give an e-t-a for them to meet us at that end."

"No problem, you can use the one in my office. I'll take you through."

Mary Jourdain escorted Baker back down the corridor to a small office just to the right of the doors leading from reception. She logged-in to the system, then sat him down in front of a screen that was filled with a blank e-mail form: "there you go, just hit send when you're finished. There's no need to do anything else, it will log out on its own after about five minutes."

"Thanks," Baker said, and commenced typing into the form with two staccato fingers. He had never really mastered keyboard skills, despite having used a PC for many years. Mary left the room and disappeared down the corridor in the direction of the office where Mrs Kryczek was being comforted by the lab tech.

As soon as she had gone, Baker pulled the sealed mailer from his inside pocket and prised open the flap. He looked inside to see a single data CD, which he withdrew. He looked at the tower unit under the desk and saw, to his relief, that it had a CD drive. He pressed the button and when the drawer slid open, he slipped the disk in and closed it again. After a few seconds a blank dialogue box appeared on the screen, followed by a rotating hourglass; another fifteen or twenty seconds elapsed, then the dialogue box filled with a file list. From the file extensions, he could tell that these were a mixture of images and documents. Each was named with a familiar surname, followed by a number - 'Schaeffer_23', 'Nicholson_12', 'Kendrick_56' and so on.

He grabbed the mouse and double-clicked on a few photos. There was one of Shepherd getting into a car outside of the offices of Berger & Pastore in Palo Alto, Emil Friedmann talking to someone in the Epic Center car park, Hilary Nicholson and Jackson Kendrick III arriving at the Century II in full evening dress, the front of Mrs Ferguson's house in Hillsboro and more. He then took a look at a couple of scans. These were corporate filing documents and lists of directors; all the ones he looked at had the name Kendrick somewhere in the list. Finally the text files, which were surveillance reports, compiled in a distinctive style that he had seen many a time back at the office in LA. *'So,'* he thought, *'Kryczek had been surveilling these people for some time.'*

He closed the dialogue box and flipped the drive drawer open again, recovering the CD and pushing it back into the mailer, which he returned to his pocket. He completed the e-mail to his office, pressed send and, once the barber's pole progress box disappeared, got up and left the room. He looked down the corridor to see Mrs Kryczek disappearing back through the double doors to the viewing area with the lab tech. Mary Jourdain was approaching him with the clipboard.

"I'll let you out," she said with a smile: "turn left out of the car park, take the second left and you can't miss the shutter at the back. I'll meet you back there." Baker nodded; she punched in her passcode and the door obeyed the command.

The Bird has Flown

A couple of minutes later, Baker was backing the Suburban up to the shutter. Mary Jourdain appeared at the side door which she held open for him to enter.

The loading bay was quite large and there were all manner of boxes, crates and tables dotted around it. On one was a crate similar in size to a coffin, but slightly wider. She conducted him to it and pointed-out the slim compartment within, running the full length of one side, its covers already fixed in place.

"The disks are in here, as requested," she confirmed.

He nodded: "thank you."

"All a bit cloak and dagger isn't it?"

"We don't want anyone to know we have them - in fact we don't really want anyone to know they exist."

"You can trust my guys, they're sound. They see all sorts, they didn't even ask about it."

"Like I said, we really appreciate it - thank you."

"It's for Paul, there's no statute of limitations on him. Will it help nail them?"

"I can't tell you that till we get them back and analyse them, but if there's anything on there we can use, rest assured we will. You two were close?"

"Not in that way," she coloured-up slightly, "but I can confess to a stranger - I wouldn't have said no. Professionally, he is the best cop I've ever worked with, thorough, intelligent, remorseless - and fun! If he doesn't pull through ..." she forced back her emotions as she pressed the back of her hand against her lips.

Just then, the strip curtain at the edge of the loading bay flexed and parted as a limber passed through it carrying a body bag. The limber was being pushed by one male lab tech, with another walking behind him. They trundled their cargo up to the side of the table where the crate stood open, lifted the body bag off the limber and placed it in the crate. One wheeled the limber back through the curtain, while the other went to the back of the bay to recover the crate's lid, some screws and an electric screwdriver.

Mary proffered the clipboard: "you had better check the contents of the bag before we fasten the top down, don't want you getting all the way back to LA before you discover we've switched her on you!" She smiled as Baker took the clipboard, which he rested across one corner of the crate. He moved to the side, placing himself between Mary Jourdain and the crate, leant over and slowly unzipped the top end of the bag to reveal, once again, that familiar elven face. Then, in one swift action with his other hand, he whipped the mailer out of his pocket and placed it inside the bag. He then slowly zipped the bag back up. He picked-up the clipboard, signing the bottom of the form with a flourish before handing it back to her: "all present and correct," he announced.

"That's fine. If you would like to go out and open the back of your car, we'll get the top on and wheel her out to you." She turned to the lab tech: "OK Carlo, you can close it up now."

She looked towards the shutter and watched Baker until his back disappeared through the side door. She thought she had caught something out of the corner of her eye while he was at the crate, but couldn't be sure. She tried to tell herself she was imagining it, but her instincts rarely let her down. That's why she had become the youngest-ever M.E. for Sedgewick County.

Carlo was just about to place the lid on the crate, but she stopped him: "just a minute, I need to double-check something."

He smiled: "always the double-check," he commented, removing the lid again and standing with it vertically in front of him.

"That's me!" Mary replied with a theatrical shrug. She moved to the crate and examined the interior - nothing untoward. So she slowly unzipped the body bag to about two feet down. She glanced at the side door, to be sure that she was not being watched. It was all clear, so she gently lifted one lip of the rubber bag away from the body. There it was - a mailer: *'so he did put something in there,'* she thought.

She knew she couldn't risk pulling it out. Instead she rezipped the bag: "there you go Carlo, all correct."

"As it always is!" he replied with resignation.

"Help Agent Baker load up when you're finished, would you? Tell him I will bring Mrs Kryczek to the front door for him; he can pick her up there."

"Sure Mary," Carlo replied and began fixing the lid.

One-Sixty

Schneider returned to his office and began to take a cursory look at the various messages arranged neatly in their usual array of precedence, by Carla Courtney. It was one of the least important that caught his eye. It read: 'Ring Mr Friedmann's Secretary before four p.m - not urgent.' He pushed the button on the intercom.

As usual, Carla's voice responded instantly: "yes Sam?"

"This message to ring Friedmann's secretary?"

"Betty Wagner. She rang about half an hour ago, needs to speak to you, and you alone. Presumably, I'm not considered trustworthy enough to be allowed into her confidence!"

"She's not worth wasting your breath on, Carla, believe me. Paul wanted to arrest her you know."

"Really, what for?"

"Being Betty Wagner - unfortunately we had to tell him that wasn't a crime in its own right."

Carla chuckled: "he's sure given us more pleasant memories than that pompous ..."

Schneider interrupted her: "quite, so ring her back, give her a hard time for a few minutes, then put her though."

"It'll be a pleasure Sam."

The Bird has Flown

Schneider used the interval to review a few papers on his desk, then the phone rang. He picked it up and heard Carla's voice: "Ms Wagner for you." The self-imposed title was emphasised contemptuously.

"Thank you Carla."

The phone clicked and a different female voice emerged through the handset: "Mr Schneider, so I have finally got you?"

"You have Mrs Wagner, not that I was able to speak to you any earlier. I'm afraid that Federal lawbreakers do not work to timetables."

"Of course Mr Schneider, and it's Ms Wagner, incidentally. I presume that girl got it wrong."

"She didn't actually - and that would be Agent Schneider by the way."

Schneider imagined steam emitting from this overbearing woman's ears just a few floors above, but she continued regardless: "I have been asked by Mr Friedmann to extend an invitation to you personally. The Kendrick Foundation is holding a small, but exclusive, reception this evening at the Apeiron Estate, in aid of a local military charity. The family would be honoured if you could be able to attend, if only for a short time."

Schneider was quite taken-aback. He immediately realised that this was no social call, but on the other hand it was not an opportunity to throw-over. He bought himself a few moments of thinking time: "I don't think that should be too much of a problem, let me just check my diary - what time?"

"Six for six-thirty."

Schneider flicked a few pieces of paper as if opening a diary: "yes, I can make that, subject of course to nothing unexpected coming-up in the meantime."

"Of course. And could I impose on you for one more favour?"

"I suppose so."

"We understand that Agent Chandler Clarke is in Wichita at present. Your girl refused to confirm or deny that, which is frustrating because the family would like to invite him as well. He is an old friend of theirs, if you are not aware, so it would be unfortunate if we were unable to make the necessary contact."

Schneider felt his hand tighten on the handset, simulating his inner desire that it might be around this harridan's neck instead. He responded: "I am aware, and I will be happy to get the message to him for you although, of course, I have no idea whether he would be available or not this evening."

"I understand. So perhaps you could ask him to contact me to confirm by four this afternoon?"

"I cannot guarantee being able to get the message to him by then, but perhaps it would be best that he contact you only if he is unable to accept the invitation. That way there will be more time to make him aware of it. Unless, of course, you have an alternate you wish to invite in his place."

There was an audible splutter on the other end of the line, which brought a contented smile to Schneider's face. The voice resumed: "that is probably best, in the circumstances. Thank you Mr Schneider."

"You're welcome Mrs Wagner."

The line clicked off and Schneider settled back into his chair to contemplate what this actually meant. The first thing that struck him, as it had during the call, was that Emil Friedmann clearly knew that Chandler Clarke was in Wichita, despite their attempts to keep his visit low-key. Schneider had summoned Clarke to Wichita in a telephone call from his office after dinner at the Hyatt with the three English friends. At first, Chandler had been reluctant to assist, until Schneider revealed his visit to Clarke's step-mother in connection with the cases. Although Schneider had not intended to make a full revelation of the meeting in Friedmann's office until Clarke had made the journey to Kansas, the discussion evolved to a point where it no longer made sense not to. Schneider also secured Chandler's agreement to honour the commitment Schneider had given to Penny Clarke, that the details would only be disclosed to her step-son. In return, she promised never to place herself, or the Clarke family, in such a situation again, an undertaking she tearfully provided before fleeing to Washington, where she had remained, close to her husband, ever since.

Maybe the knowledge was accidental, Clarke being spotted entering the building by Friedmann at some time since he arrived; maybe there was a more sinister explanation. But Schneider had to dismiss such speculation in order to concentrate on the new potential provided by Madeleine Nicholson's information. He picked up his cellphone and dialled Baker. After a few rings, the other end picked-up, but the voice was almost drowned-out by background airport noise, specifically a jet aircraft taxiing nearby. The voice at the other end shouted a barely-audible commitment to ring back in a few minutes. There followed five minutes or so of peaceful paper-shuffling, suddenly punctuated by the sound of the cellphone's ringtone.

Schneider pressed the receive button and the voice emerged: "Sam, it's Pete."

There was still some muffled jet-noise in the background, but the voice was loud and clear. Schneider responded: "Pete, let me guess, you're at the airport."

"That's amazing Sam, can't imagine how you figured that out. Must be how you got to be such a successful Agent." They both laughed. "Yes, we're just loading-up - should be away in ten to fifteen minutes. Mrs Kryczek is in the rest room freshening herself up for the flight, so you have my undivided attention now that Gulfstream has parked itself up."

Schneider outlined the developments that morning, particularly the Madeleine Nicholson call. He finished with a question: "so we have this reference to documents, suggesting that Kryczek had assembled something that, presumably, she intended to show to Hilary Nicholson at some time afterwards. Kryczek wasn't keeping anything on your system, otherwise you would have found it. You knew her Pete, would I be right in assuming she wouldn't have kept everything just in her head?"

"You would, Sam. She was thorough in keeping paperwork, I only wish I could say that she was as thorough about its content. We used to call it the K-Files, like the X-Files but even less decipherable."

"But she would have kept something?"

"Sure - on a computer somewhere, probably. But we didn't find anything at her home. In fact, thinking about it, we found less than nothing. Not a whiff of any work."

"Unusual?"

"Hell yeah. Not the tidiest of people was Kryczek, you should have seen her desk in the office - like a war zone!"

"Could the apartment have been gone through before you got to it?"

"Seems probable now you mention it. Shepherd was based out there and he would have taken control of any possessions she brought down here. That would have been for a couple of weeks prior to our even realising she was possibly missing. Sorry Sam, the thought never crossed my mind, dammit!"

"That's academic now. But what about her mother? Did she leave anything with her mother?"

"Not that I'm aware. She hasn't said anything so far today."

"Can you ask her?"

"Sure. We have a three and a half hour flight ahead of us, it'll help to pass the time."

"If there is anything, anything at all, can you ring me on my cell before six. It might be useful information for the reception."

"Reception?"

"I've received a summons - to attend a reception this evening at the Kendrick Estate."

"When did you get that?"

"Just now."

"Sounds interesting, I'm beginning to regret not being available myself."

"Friedmann's secretary said it was exclusive Pete."

"I have no idea what you mean Sam." They laughed again. "Of course I will, and if there is something, I'll secure it as soon as I get back. Anything else?"

"No, that's it for now. If we don't speak later, let's do a conference call in the morning. I'll get Carla to set it up - have a good flight."

"Good flight, what, in a King Air across the Rockies? You gotta be kidding me! I'll leave the keys for the Suburban with the desk out here. Speak to you later."

One-Six-One

McKinley and Holdsworth had been outside of Chief Harper's office for around ten minutes. They had arrived just before two to be advised by his secretary that he was still at lunch with the Mayor. They took the option to wait.

Since arriving back at City Hall, McKinley had collected the IAD file from Mackenzie, a handover that had been accompanied by further indications that

The Mantis Pact

this new regime was going to be far harder on the more questionable elements in the department. Mackenzie offered the new Head of Homicide as many of his men as he deemed necessary to get to the bottom of what had really happened: "Kleberson's a good man," Mackenzie concluded, "the type we all want to work with. It's bad enough that we might lose him; it's even worse when we find out he was likely set-up by one of our own."

Holdsworth had checked with the janitor at Morley's apartment, but it was still empty. He had also obtained a key to Morley's office, which had been secured during the morning by building services. The two were discussing requisitioning a similar action for Stanton's, when Chief Harper strode down the corridor, still in his dress uniform.

"Sorry I'm late boys," he acknowledged as he opened the door and entered his office, leaving it open for the two to follow him in. "Thanks for waiting - coffee?"

"No thank you Sir," McKinley responded.

"I'm fine as well Sir," Holdsworth added as he closed the door behind them.

"Then let's get down to it shall we?" Harper directed them to sit at the conference table, took-off his jacket and put it on a hanger that he suspended from the coat rack, brushing-off the shoulders with his hand as he did so, before joining them at the table: "I understand there have been some developments."

McKinley outlined all that had happened that morning, Stanton's house, the realtor, Morley's apartment, KNKW, Madeleine Nicholson. Holdsworth added detail where necessary. All the time, Harper was leant forward, arms folded on the table top, listening intently without interruption by questions, despite the many he had. At the end, he leant back in his chair, arms still folded, considered everything for a few seconds in silence, then responded with a heavy sigh: "it doesn't get any better does it? Alright, what do you want to do?"

McKinley replied: "I want to go through every file that Chief Stanton dealt with, initially covering the last couple of months, but going back further if we find any probable cause. We will need to seal his office until I can get a team together to do that."

"Agreed. I'll requisition building services straight away and get them to give you the keys as soon as they've done it. I'll also talk to Debbie, his secretary; she will need to give you a statement. She's very loyal to him, but hopefully she will understand why she has to co-operate. If not, she can go on garden leave until we are finished. You're going to need manpower for all of that aren't you?"

"Lieutenant Mackenzie has offered me some resource."

"Good man Mackenzie, runs a tight ship. That will work, but if it's not enough, let me know and I'll find some more for you. What else?"

"Detective Holdsworth will take the investigation into Acting Captain Morley. As there is no sign of Morley at his home, we need to carry-out a similar exercise in his office as well."

"Only one thing there - let's refer to him as ex-Lieutenant Morley shall we?" The two men nodded, still somewhat surprised by the total contrast of Harper to his predecessor. Harper turned to Holdsworth: "do you think he will show?"

"Anything's possible," Holdsworth responded, "but realistically no. Having seen his reaction after he learned that Cochrane had been murdered, I would say that he's long gone. I hadn't met him much before these cases, but I would say he's not a brave man, so if he thought he was in the firing line back then, he sure as hell knows he is now."

"Not a bad appraisal, Detective, I can see why Sergeant McKinley here asked for you as his Deputy. Do you expect to find anything in his office?"

"If it's there, I'll find it Sir."

"Glad to hear it - anything else?"

"Just one more thing, Sir." McKinley took-up the dialogue again, hesitating slightly: "it could be delicate Sir."

"None of us are shrinking violets in here, Sergeant - shoot!"

"There is a problem with the timeline following the call with Madeleine Nicholson this morning. Prior to that, we were of the impression that Stanton had lunch with the Mayor prior to his suspending Paul, sorry, Lieutenant Kleberson. From the new information, he had a meeting with Madeleine Nicholson at around the same time as he should have been at that lunch."

"So you need to interview the Mayor, is that where you're going?"

"Yes Sir."

"OK, but make sure you have all the facts you need before you do. And check that I'm available to come with you when you're ready to do it; he'll not be able to stonewall you with his Chief of Police listening. Is that alright?"

McKinley took a deep breath: "it sure is!" He smiled with some relief.

"But there is one caveat - don't leave it too long. There's an election coming up in a few months, so if he is dirty as well, let's find out before rather than after. If the City has to pay for two elections, they'll punish the department responsible - so that's our budget gentlemen."

"Understood Sir," was all McKinley could muster in reply. Such was his disbelief at what he was hearing, that he almost wanted to pinch himself to make sure he wasn't actually just snatching forty winks at his desk.

"Is that it?" Harper enquired. The two men looked at each other, then nodded. "Good, in which case I have one more request of you Sergeant. I have had an invitation from the Kendrick family to visit their estate this evening for a reception. I assume they want to inspect the new incumbent. Well, I'm not a new horse for their stable and I have no interest in faffing-around at their beck and call like my predecessor. Instead I would like you to represent me, Sergeant. It's six for six-thirty - are you free?"

"I think so Sir," McKinley responded, a little shocked.

"Good! I will get my secretary to advise them of the change in arrangements." He winked: "good chance for you to gauge what we're up against, eh?"

because he could

One-Six-Two

The unexpected invitation had changed Sam's plans for the evening, which had been to go out to the base and spend some more time with Paul. He quickly concluded that there was nothing on his desk that needed urgent action, so he hit the intercom again; as ever, Carla answered instantly.

"I'm gonna take a coupla hours now Carla, go out and sit with Paul for a while. This invitation from the Kendricks means I won't be able to tonight."

Carla responded: "I was going to ask you, actually Sam - do you think I could get into the base and see him? If you're not going tonight, I could go instead."

Sam felt the guilt envelop him instantly; once again, he had overlooked the closeness of his secretary and his friend. He suddenly realised that Carla had not seen Paul since he was moved to the base hospital nearly four days earlier: "oh goodness Carla, absolutely! I'm so sorry, I ..."

"Don't worry Sam, I don't think I could have gone any earlier. It's taken me a few days to get past that last visit, seeing him so helpless - and all those pipes and things."

"Well, he's rid of most of those now."

"Yes, you said this morning. That's why I think I can visit again."

"What time would you like to go?"

"After work, say around seven?"

"I'll arrange it with the base."

"I don't want to be any trouble ..."

Sam cut her off: "you're anything but, Carla. I'll fix it."

"Thanks Sam. Don't tell him I'm coming, he likes surprises."

Sam found himself unable to respond; he just hit the off button.

Twenty minutes later, he walked through the base hospital door and made his way down the corridor. He noticed Doctor Manderling in the monitor room, so decided to check-in with him first. The doctor smiled as Sam walked through the door: "Agent Schneider - I wasn't expecting you back so soon."

"Something's come up for later, so I thought I would take the opportunity now. Is anyone with him?"

"Mrs Prabhakar."

"Oh. In that case, I can leave it."

"No, Agent Schneider, now might be a good time."

"I don't want to overload him again."

"Actually, I think last night had a really positive effect. We are getting some good patterns and the conscious periods are getting longer. As you were involved, I think we can try something else."

"Anything, if it's going to help."

"Thank you. Mrs Prabhakar has been in there around an hour and the readings have been showing activity throughout. I think Lieutenant Kleberson may be recognising her."

"Paul, doctor - please call him Paul."

"Of course, sorry, it's just my military training. Up to this point we have kept it to one visitor at a time, so now might be a good time to see how he responds to two. He's conscious at the moment, so we will be able to tell pretty-much as soon as you walk in. If it's a bad reaction, I will yank you straight back out."

"You say he's conscious?"

"Sorry, that's a relative term. Perhaps I should call it awareness rather than consciousness; he can't physically respond to anything. What I want to see, though, is how his readings react to you interacting with Mrs Prabhakar. Whether he is able to recognise that you know each other, as well as him."

"You think he recognises me?"

"Oh yes, and the rest of the family, but not the medical staff. The readings are completely different when we are alone with him. You and Mrs Prabhakar have produced the greatest activity, individually, so far."

"He can see us?"

"Maybe, vaguely - more likely he can hear you. You two talk to him all the time. So when you get in there, talk to each other please."

Sam could barely contain his feelings: "that's amazing!"

"Please Agent Schneider, don't let's get ahead of ourselves. We are talking about instinctive reactions, nothing we could prove is sentient - not yet. Like I keep saying, one step at a time. So, can we give my little experiment a try?"

"Of course! Oh, I nearly forgot, can you put another name on the permitted visitor list?"

"I'm not so sure that's such a good idea. Who might that be?"

"Her name's Carla Courtney - she's my secretary. She's also the nearest thing Paul currently has to a steady date; he's divorced remember."

"Oh, I didn't know. Sorry, not the divorce - that he had a current lady friend. That would be interesting. When does she want to come?"

"This evening, around seven."

"I will have to ask the family - Mrs Kleberson in particular."

"I doubt it will be a problem, they all know about Carla and she visited when he was in St Francis."

"Nevertheless …"

"Of course. Shall I go through?"

"Please."

One-Six-Three

Paul Kleberson's personal progress had been rapid since the revelation. He hadn't seen the person out of view, but he knew he didn't want to. So the flashback of the room he was in at that time, wherever it was, had been parked, as had his attempts to move. Somehow that seemed secondary to gathering his thoughts.

The recognition of Sam, however, had helped him to assemble other flashbacks, which he had come to recognise as memories - his memories. He had evolved to reasoning with little aid of the invisible interrogator, who was only asking questions if he hit an absolute dead-end. Even that hadn't been needed in his last two or three consciousnesses. He could also hear people more clearly when they talked to him. It was like a jigsaw. The visual pieces were appearing in isolation, prompted by the sounds, then a recognition of how they associated, first in pairs, then in small groups. Self-speculating how the groups may interact was beginning to produce other pieces. Two different sets of memories were being assembled. Sam - he couldn't remember yet what his other name might be - was acting as a common denominator because he fitted into both categories.

Just as this was beginning to make sense, another voice had brought a different name - Annie. As the jigsaw pieces featuring her began to proliferate, another thread came together, one not associated with Sam, because the two did not appear together in that set. Annie was currently talking to him constantly. He could also physically see her in outline - a bit like a silhouette. The silhouette matched the outline of the images of her. Annie was definitely there, in the room with him, and the memory pieces were all good. Then he heard another familiar voice.

One-Six-Four

The door opened and Sam walked through. Annie was seated to the side of the bed, holding Paul's hand, talking in a low, deliberate voice. She stopped and looked around as the door closed, a smile immediately breaking across her face. She gently let go of Paul's hand, got to her feet very slowly and walked across to where Sam was standing, just inside the door.

She threw her arms around Sam's shoulders and hugged him: "hi Sam, haven't seen you for a couple of days."

'It's Sam.' Paul registered the arrival and memory images began to appear. 'Annie and Sam. Together.'

"Yes," Sam replied fairly quietly, "busy day yesterday."

"I caught some of it on the news this morning."

"What, about Stanton?"

"Yes," Annie turned to look at the bed, "that's something I'm sure he would like to know."

'Stanton?' Paul recognised the name; an image flashed through his consciousness. A big man - shouting. He parked it almost instantly. It was replaced by another with lots of people in a large room together. They were all happy; Annie was hugging Sam. Another familiar face appeared closely in front of him. It was the blonde lady; she was wearing a flowing white dress.

"How does he seem?" Sam asked.

"Oh, nothing externally. Somehow, though, I get a feeling that he is here, when I hold his hand, you know? Something more than just a touch."

"I get the same - although I haven't tried holding his hand yet." Sam smiled; Annie responded likewise. She didn't feel guilty about the brevity, recognising that Paul would be making similar quips if he was in a condition to. She turned again to look at the motionless figure on the bed - who knows, maybe he was thinking of one right then. She hoped so.

Paul's image changed slightly. The blonde lady in the flowing white dress was alongside him and they were looking at a crowd, who were all applauding. At the front of the crowd there was Annie; alongside her, the man with the darker skin. Next to him was Sam, with his arm around another lady who Paul didn't recognise at all. He looked to his other side, away from the blonde lady; there was the older man in uniform with the older lady alongside him. They were both smiling at him and applauding as well.

"Has the doctor spoken to you about the monitoring?" Sam asked.

"Yes," Annie replied, "I so want what he says to be true, but …"

"I know Annie."

"I don't like talking about him, though, not in here. I talk to him about my memories - wonderful memories. Makes me feel so good."

"I talk about the case. It's amazing how it's helping, almost seems like Paul is throwing ideas at me."

"Is that good, do you think?"

"Doctor seems to think so."

"Actually, I have something to tell you about the case, I should have rung you, but …"

"Hey, we're all distracted."

"I'll wait outside and tell you after you've had some time with Paul."

"Actually, the doctor's asked us to talk in here. He wants to see what happens."

Annie laughed a nervous laugh: "really? What should we talk about?"

"How about telling me what you were going to say outside."

Annie bit her lip, then looked again at Paul on the bed: "I'm not sure that I'm comfortable with doing that."

"Why?"

"Because it's about that dreadful day."

"Go on."

"Are you sure?" Annie looked again at the bed.

"Yes, don't worry, the doctor's watching Paul."

"Well, you know that RP and I had lunch with Gloria Friedmann on Sunday?"

Gloria Friedmann.' Again Paul recognised the name. Another image appeared; he was near a lake, sitting at a table under a parasol. There was a lady sitting with him - not one he recognised from the other memories.

"Yes," Sam responded with anticipation.

"Paul visited her that day."

"In the morning!" Sam responded, somewhat excitedly.

"You knew?" Annie was puzzled.

"Not specifically. Paul was off the radar for a couple of hours. He hadn't said where he had been, then all the dominos started falling. We worked-out for ourselves that it was a possibility that he went out to Apeiron."

'Apeiron.' another name Paul recognised. Another image appeared of a grand house in a valley next to a lake. He connected the two images via the lake; the table was on a terrace between the lake and the house. The lady belonged to the house: *'Gloria Friedmann,'* he thought. *'Friedmann?'* That name produced another image of a man in an expensive suit, in a corridor. *'Is that one Friedmann as well?'* he asked himself.

"You didn't ask the Kendricks?" Annie asked, still puzzled.

"Not yet." Sam responded with some reserve; he wanted to say more, but was already aware of where the conversation might go. "I'm seeing them tonight, that's why I'm here this afternoon, I can't come later."

'Kendrick' yet another name Paul thought he recognised. The image of the smart-suited man in the corridor returned; he was stood in a doorway and looked annoyed. The door was open. Boots - he could see a pair of boots inside the room. Cowboy boots. *'Kendrick.'* Paul repeated the name: *'cowboy boots - Kendrick wears cowboy boots.'* The image refocused on the corridor; there were two other men in it. They were pointing something at him - guns. *'Guns!'* Paul parked the image. He was suddenly exhausted; the images all stopped. The room he was in began to go black again and the voices faded away.

The door opened behind them. It was Doctor Manderling: "can you both come out now," he asked.

Annie became agitated: "is everything OK?"

"Fine," the doctor said reassuringly, "you've sent him off to sleep."

Annie relaxed at the thought. She followed Sam and the doctor through the door into the corridor beyond.

"Did you get something?" Sam asked.

"Yes, a definite reaction to something just before he went off to sleep. What were you talking about?"

"About a visit Paul made on the morning he was attacked."

"Social or business?"

"Business."

"That may have been the intention," Annie interjected, "but the actual meeting became purely social."

"Really?" Both Sam and the doctor responded simultaneously. The doctor apologised to Sam, then continued: "was this someone you all knew?"

"She's an old friend of mine, lives here in Wichita. She would have met Paul once before, at my wedding, but she said that Paul had no recollection of meeting her previously."

"And you?" The doctor addressed the next question to Sam.

"No, I've never met her, but I have met her brother - his fiancé was the first victim in our murder cases here. Her husband's the family lawyer."

"We are talking of the Kendricks here, presumably."

"You know of them Doctor?" Sam responded.

"I watch the news, Agent Schneider. It's about all I get to do when I'm off duty at the moment. Did either of you mention that name?"

"I did," Annie replied.

"When during the conversation, can you remember?"

"Just before you came in."

"Thank you." Doctor Manderling turned towards the monitoring room.

"Wait, please," Annie appealed.

The doctor stopped and turned. He smiled as he replied: "the answer to your question is yes, Mrs Prabhakar."

One-Six-Five

On his return, Schneider had a session with Jim Kowalski on the progress of the analysis. He was keen to find out if anything from the newest RAID disk recovered from Hillsboro provided any insights into what had really brought Shepherd to Wichita on a professional basis. Unfortunately, Kowalski had not received a copy of the new disk contents from Pete Baker. Schneider concluded that, in all the activity of the previous evening, the process had been forgotten, so he would ask Baker to expedite it as a priority on his return to L.A. He sent an e-mail to that effect, in case there was no call from Baker that afternoon.

Clarke returned from Eastborough around four. He had conducted a thorough sweep of the large property and found no diaries or similar documentation. In fact, the house appeared little lived-in. All he found was a computer, which the lawyers released and he had turned over to Jim Kowalski on his return.

He had learned some more background on the Nicholson family, of how Hilary Nicholson had been virtually-excluded from her father's will with all of the major assets going to her elder step sister. This had been due, apparently, to a falling out between the father and his much younger second wife during Hilary's teens, resulting in a dramatic departure from the father's life by both mother and daughter. The father died within two years of that event, unreconciled. But when Madeleine discovered what her father had done with his will, it was she that challenged it, winning a substantial settlement for her step sister. When later asked by a reporter why she had done that, her reply was: "oh for goodness sake, there's only a certain amount of money that a middle-aged spinster can possibly spend."

Holdsworth had volunteered to write-up the day's notes for the case files, allowing McKinley the freedom to deal with the administration attached to sealing Stanton's office. It was no longer guarded by his ex-secretary who had, apparently, gone home unwell. The next task was the seconding of suitable officers from Patrol North, several of whom had passed their detective exams and were awaiting an opening. In between, McKinley had managed a phone call to Schneider to advise of his surprise assignment for the evening, the result of which was the agreement to meet in the Epic Center at around five-thirty to travel out to Apeiron together.

Around a quarter to six, Schneider's unmarked Interceptor pulled-out of the Epic Center garage and headed east on second, making the transition to Central via Market. The three men on board reviewed their days, concluding that Harper was making the right start in his new post and that, although the disappearances of Stanton and Morley were a frustration, at least the speed of their flight, and thus the ability to secure their offices, might salvage something in that area.

Schneider detailed the confirmation from Annie that Kleberson had visited Apeiron on the day of the attack, as they had suspected. They all agreed that this added to the interest in this evening's event, so the only disappointment was the apparent lack of anything coming from the visit of Eleanor Kryczek, plus the mild frustration felt by Schneider about the delay in getting the data from the disk recovered the previous night from Hillsboro. This aspect of his mood was about to be darkened when McKinley's cellphone rang.

It was Mary Jourdain, who had been struggling all afternoon with one aspect of the morning's transfer of Agent Kryczek's body. She outlined her concerns to Chris McKinley, who was the only one able to hear them. When she finished, McKinley made a proposal: "Mary, I'm in a car with Agents Schneider and Clarke and I would like them to hear what you've just told me. I think it would be better coming directly from you, so can we ring you back on the hands-free?" She agreed, so McKinley hung-up.

"What was that all about?" Schneider enquired.

"You need to hear this first hand Sam. Have you got Mary on speed dial?"

"I have." Schneider pressed the address book button, scrolled down to Mary Jourdain's name, then pressed the dial button. The phone rang briefly, followed by Mary Jourdain's voice announcing herself. Schneider responded: "hi Mary, it's Sam Schneider."

"Hello Sam - did Chris tell you why I rang?"

"No Mary, but he's here in the car with me, as is Chandler Clarke, who I don't believe you have met; Chandler's out of our Mississippi Field Office. If you don't mind, for Chandler's and my benefit can you start again?"

"Sure Sam. I may be making something out of nothing here, but this has been bothering me all day, and my I.T. guy out here has just found something that hasn't made me any less uncomfortable."

"Don't worry, we're listening. Let us decide whether it's important or not."

"It was something Agent Baker did this morning, just before he took charge of the body. We had done all the identification and paperwork, my guys had brought the body out to the loading bay and put it in the crate. I gave Agent Baker the forms to sign off and asked him to check that we had given him the correct body - standard procedure. So he unzipped the body bag to check and that's when I thought I saw him do it."

"Do what?"

"Put something in the body bag."

The two FBI Agents looked at each other; McKinley already knew what was coming. Schneider asked the obvious question: "what did he put in the bag?"

"A mailer envelope. I didn't see it go in, I just thought I saw an unusual movement. So when he went out while we nailed the lid on, to prepare his vehicle for us to put the crate in, I had a quick look in the bag. That's when I saw the mailer, shoved down the side of the body. It can't have been put there by us, only by him."

"How big was it?

"About six inches square, maybe slightly more."

"Did you look in the mailer?"

"No I didn't, I'm sorry. I know I should have done. It was just so difficult - if we hadn't nailed the top on, he could have come back in ..."

"Slow down Mary, you did the right thing in the circumstances. You're a medical examiner, not a police officer. So the mailer was still in the body bag when the top was nailed on the crate?"

"Yes, I zipped the bag back up."

"Alright, thank you. Leave it with us now."

"But there's more Sam."

McKinley intervened: "you need to hear this as well Sam," he insisted.

"OK Mary, we're still here," Schneider prompted her.

"Beforehand, while I was completing the paperwork with Mrs Kryczek, Agent Baker asked if he could send an e-mail. I let him use the computer in my office."

"Who was he e-mailing, did he say?"

"His office to advise them of his e-t-a back in L.A. I checked the e-mail he sent and that's exactly what it said."

"So he used your computer to send an e-mail to his office. What's the problem?"

"I don't know how these things work, so I got my I.T. guy to check it out for me. He found that the e-mail had been blind-copied to another address - helpdesk at psalm twenty three funeral dot com."

Schneider glanced across at Clarke, who was obviously still digesting this information: "anything else Mary?"

"Yes. We looked at the history for the computer for today and around the same time the e-mail was sent several files had been viewed. But they weren't on my hard drive, they were on the CD drive. They were text and graphic files, some were possibly photographs. Some of the filenames were familiar Sam. They were names - Nicholson and Kendrick among others"

"Do you have the e-mail address for my office Mary?"

"No I don't Sam; I have your phone number, but nothing else, sorry."

"That's OK. Is your I.T. guy still there?"

"Yes he is."

"OK ring my office, speak to Carla Courtney, she should still be there. Tell her we've had this discussion and ask her to get hold of Jim Kowalski and for Jim to ring your guy, what's his name?"

"Matt, Matt Randall."

"Can Matt stay there until Jim speaks to him?"

"Not a problem."

"Get Matt to explain everything to Jim. He will need to come over, so please don't do anything else on that computer until he gets there."

"We won't Sam."

"Thank you Mary, that's really helpful."

"OK; bye Sam."

Schneider pushed the disconnect button on the hands-free, then thumped the steering wheel as he exclaimed: "what the fuck!"

"The mailer contained the CD, it's the right size," McKinley observed.

"And he got it from Eleanor Kryczek, looked at it, then hid it." Schneider hit the wheel again, harder this time: "MotherFucker! Is there nobody outside of this car these people do not have their talons into?"

"Hold on," Clarke said, "let's not get carried away. We've got other stuff hidden in that crate. We don't want anyone here in Wichita to know what we've got, so he acted on his initiative."

Schneider glared at him: "and the e-mail?"

"Sorry, but I don't see how Pete sending an e-mail to his office, copied to a funeral home, about the e-t-a of a body is anything to get steamed-up about."

"Except," McKinley interjected, "he blind copied it. Why would he not just c.c. it if he needed to? And in any case, surely the local morgue will be collecting the body, for the post mortem - right? Not a funeral home."

"And certainly not a funeral home with a name like that!" Schneider added.

"Sorry Sam, what am I missing there?" Clarke asked, still sounding puzzled.

Schneider looked at him, his eyes full of rage: "recite Psalm Twenty Three Chandler!"

Clarke began: "The Lord is my Sh ... oh no, it can't be!"

"Exactly! And here's the clincher Chandler. I spoke to Baker at the airfield just before he flew out, while that crate was being loaded onto the plane. I asked him if Eleanor Kryczek knew anything about those documents Madeleine Nicholson mentioned, if her daughter had given her anything? He said no, Chandler! He said he would ask her on the flight back! Tell me - why would one FBI Agent need to tell another FBI Agent a barefaced lie, huh?"

"You know I can't answer that Sam."

"But we know a man who can!" Schneider pushed the address book button again, selected Baker's number and punched the dial button. After a short pause, the ring tone emerged from the speakers. The car went deathly quiet, but for the hum of the engine and the rasp of the ringtone. After what seemed an interminable number of rings, there was an answer: "this is Baker, I'm not available at the moment. Please leave a message."

The message was curt: "Pete - Sam - Ring Me!" Schneider punched the disconnect button so hard with his index finger, it must have left an impression of the logo on his fingerprint.

One-Six-Six

The car was well north on Webb nearing the junction with I-96. The silence had lasted a few minutes, as Schneider smouldered behind the wheel. McKinley was the first to break it: "Sam, we're less than ten minutes from Apeiron. We've got to focus on what we're doing here, otherwise we may miss a golden opportunity."

Clarke chipped-in: "Chris is right Sam, there's nothing we can do until you've spoken to Pete. It could be a complete misunderstanding. He's been a good Agent for longer than both of us, we can't jump to conclusions, not yet."

Schneider didn't reply immediately. After another, shorter silence, he finally responded, with more his usual calm demeanour: "I know what you're saying, but Jesus ..." He wrestled again with his anger for a little longer, then took a deep breath: "sorry guys, you're both right, so let's concentrate on this evening. Chandler, you've been to these things before, what should we expect?"

"It's for Mrs Kendrick's Foundation, so there will be a good crowd, probably fifty to sixty, all comfortably rich, enough to donate up to a six-figure sum each, to whatever good cause she has chosen to sponsor, without blinking."

"What the hell are we doing here then?" McKinley enquired.

"Not for a donation, that's for sure," Schneider responded.

"They want us to see their good side," Clarke explained: "this is what we do, this is who we know, this is why we're an asset to your community."

"This is why you shouldn't slap the irons on our son and cart him off to the hoosegow!" Schneider observed cynically.

"Not too far off the mark actually Sam, but underneath they want us to see what we're up against if we do that. This is about how much power they can wield if they have to. They want us to be impressed, but also to be overawed."

"Will you be?" Schneider enquired of Clarke.

"You want the truth, Sam?"

"What do you think Chandler?"

"I always have been. It's difficult not to be, as you will discover. 'The Turd' is not typical of the family, in fact he's the closest thing a family like that gets to a black sheep."

Schneider stared at him: "I hope that was a slip of the tongue!"

Clarke decided to semi-ignore him: "you need to go in with an open mind and you need to be alert to the bear traps they will lay for you. They may not contain deadly spikes, but they will make you a captive if you're not careful. You mustn't be aggressive, they will simply dismiss you if you are."

"Why would they care?"

"Because what they really want out of tonight is to see what they're up against. They're going to examine you, test you, then dissect you until they decide what to do with you. If you play it right, they will open up to you. Not in a way that a perp will when you have him cornered in the interrogation room, but in a way that they hope might assimilate you. So you need to use that against them, only then will you find out what you're looking for."

"And if I choose not to play their games?"

"Then you're no opposition, just another oaf, unworthy of their attention, somebody they can squash like a pesky fly if they need to - and we know that they can, don't we?"

"So how do I respond to them?"

"Politely, thoughtfully, deferentially when necessary and - most important - intelligently."

"Should be a breeze!"

"We're here," McKinley observed from the back seat.

The car rolled up behind two others, a Mercedes S Class and a Cadillac Escalade ESV, both current models. The security guard stood next to the Mercedes was carrying a clipboard, on which he was checking-off the visitors as they arrived. Once he had released the two cars, Schneider pulled forward alongside him.

"Good evening gentlemen, your names please."

"Schneider, Clarke and McKinley."

"Thank you." He checked down the list, ticking off two names as he did so. "I don't appear to have you on the list, Mr McKinley."

"I'm a late replacement, for Chief of Police Harper."

The goon rechecked the list: "ah yes, I have you now Sir." He popped his head close to the lowered window and looked around the inside of the car: "thank you gentlemen, go ahead please - and have a nice evening."

He signalled to another goon who was standing by the left gate pillar and Schneider pulled ahead. As they passed through the gate and onto the drive, Schneider glanced in his mirror. The second goon had grabbed his lapel and was speaking into a concealed microphone: "well, they know we're here," he said to the other occupants of the car.

The drive wound through the trees before emerging into a park area, from where they could see it descending to a large white house by a lake. "OK, I'm impressed," Schneider commented: "where do I join?" The others smiled, partially at the humour, but mainly because Schneider was obviously back in the zone.

Schneider's car pulled up on the forecourt, behind the Mercedes and Cadillac, from which other guests were emerging. A line of valets, all identically uniformed, were waiting for the cars. As they came to a halt, the foremost valet leapt forward and opened the doors on the driver's side: "welcome gentlemen," she said, "please leave your keys in the ignition, I will park the car for you. When you are ready to leave, just give your registration to the butler, Woodhouse, and he will radio for your car to be brought forward for you. Please take these steps to the top, you will be directed from there."

She indicated to a large flight of stone steps leading up to a terrace at the ground floor level of the house. No sooner had the three men started towards the steps than the girl had entered the car, started it and shot off across the forecourt in the same direction that the others had gone, towards a holding area concealed from view of the house by a row of sturdy pines. *'Obviously a piecework job,'* Schneider thought to himself.

At the top of the steps they were greeted by an impeccably liveried servant: "good evening gentlemen, welcome to Apeiron. My name is Woodhouse and my staff and I are here to ensure that you have everything you need during your visit here with us, so please ask any of us for assistance should you need it. If you would like to follow this terrace along to the end and around to the left, you will see a footman waiting by a large glazed entrance to direct you to the reception area." He indicated with his left hand in the direction he had mentioned.

The three men thanked him and moved off as directed, leaving him to recite the same short speech, verbatim, to the next set of guests reaching the top of the steps. Once they had moved out of earshot, McKinley turned to Clarke: "a butler called Woodhouse, you've got to be kidding me!"

Clarke responded: "he's a new one on me, but I haven't been here for a few years. It's typical Estelle though - that's Mrs Kendrick. You'll understand when you meet her."

They traversed the terrace, rounded the corner and spotted the next liveried servant by an open door in what appeared to be a vast glazed wall that soared to the top of the house. They walked across the next length of terracing, the house to their left, to their right terraced gardens leading down to the lake. On reaching the door, the next servant welcomed them: "good evening gentlemen, please go through into the reception area. There are a selection of aperitifs available for you, just help yourselves. The facilities are towards the back, to your right. You have around twenty minutes before your hosts welcome you."

Again they mouthed their thanks and passed through the double glass doors into a large foyer, whilst behind them his next recitation commenced. There were around fifty people standing in small groups in an area that would easily take a couple of hundred, but well spaced apart due to the usual initial coyness when arriving at a gathering where guests have not yet been introduced. "Know anyone?" Clarke enquired of the other two.

"That's the Mayor over there," McKinley observed, nodding slightly towards Clarke's left, "no surprise he's here."

"Huberstein's over there," Schneider nodded to Clarke's right, "you met him this morning. Other than that, no. How about you?"

"A few Washington faces, mainly retired politicians, presumably with their wives, but nobody who stands out yet." At that, one of the waitresses arrived with a tray of drinks. The three each selected their choice and she glided on to the next new group that had arrived.

"So what do we do?" Schneider enquired, "go and beard someone?"

"No, just stay put and chat idly. If they need to, someone will find us."

One-Six-Seven

The double doors at the end of the glazed reception area were swung open by two liveried servants to reveal a third, the same impeccably uniformed man who had greeted the guests as they arrived. He clapped his gloved hands twice and announced in a friendly, but firm, voice: "Ladies and Gentlemen - your hosts will receive you in the Red Drawing Room."

He swept to one side, extending his right arm in a summoning gesture to reveal a magnificent vista through the doors. The room was at least sixty feet long, probably two-thirds that in width and decorated throughout in a Regency style, using the most lavish fabrics in every shade of scarlet and crimson, trimmed in gold threads and braids. Surrounding the room were a number of pieces of furniture, plus tables and chairs, all of gilded wood with upholstery matching the walls and curtains. The ceiling soared above, brilliant white with gilded plasterwork decoration, from the centre of which hung a huge crystal chandelier, flanked by two smaller imitations.

At the far end, frozen in time against a large marble fireplace, like a formal photograph of a titled family, stood five smiling figures perfectly choreographed and looking straight towards the door as if down the lens of a camera. In the centre, Estelle Kendrick wearing a exquisitely tailored navy blue silk cocktail dress, with restrained beaded decoration to set-off her 24-carat gold matching jewellery, set with the finest diamonds.

To her right, facing her, was her husband Jackson Kendrick Junior, in a charcoal grey Saville-Row suit, white shirt and plain tie of the same material as his wife's dress. To her left and facing the same direction as Estelle, her daughter Gloria Friedmann, wearing a simple, but elegant, black dress above which her necklace of the whitest pearls radiated in the concealed spotlighting that lit the scene from behind the cornices above them. On the outside of the group, next to his father, was their son, Jackson Kendrick III and the opposite end next to his wife, their son-in-law Emil Friedmann. Both of the younger men wore virtually-matching navy blue double-breasted blazers over cream chinos, white shirts and burgundy ties.

Their guests entered the room, taking-in the magnificence of the surroundings as they filtered towards the posed group, to stand admiring them. A ripple of applause began, which was acknowledged by the hosts with broad smiles and mildly-patronising nods of the head. As if by the signal of some invisible director, when the final guests passed through the portico, Estelle stepped forward raising her hands to politely quell the applause: "Thank You," she said once, waiting just the correct amount of time before repeating, "Thank You" accompanied by a mildly more demonstrative movement of the hands to indicate that really was enough applause - for now.

As the final ripples died away, the smile broadened and she began her welcome: "Thank you all so much for coming this evening to our little soiree in support of our Foundation and in particular one of the most important charities that it helps to maintain, on which our daughter Gloria will have a few words to say in a moment." She turned to Gloria, who acknowledged the reference, just in case some of the audience were not aware of the relationship.

"Now I know some of you have been to our little gatherings here at Apeiron previously, but not all will be familiar with this room, which we do not use as often as perhaps we ought to. So for them and for those whose first visit this is, I would like to give you a brief history of how it came to be here, because the original acquisition of this room demonstrates why you don't necessarily need money to buy the very best things."

She smiled knowingly as she paused for the effect to filter the room, before continuing: "When England finally defeated Napoleon in eighteen-fifteen, their country was bankrupt, their King was mad and they were ruled by his profligate son, the Prince Regent. The government brought in harsh economic measures to clear their debts, attempting to cut back on everything, including the Royal Household. Faced with this, what do you think the Regent did?" Another pause, just long enough for the gathering to digest how ignorant they were not to be able to answer: "he built the grandest house the country had ever seen, right in the centre of London, just off Piccadilly. It was called Carlton House and this ..." she swept her hand in an arc in front of her "... was one of its rooms."

She paused once more for this to be absorbed, before continuing: "he decorated and furnished it with the help of his architect, John Nash, with the finest materials and works of art available. No expense was spared and, of course, the poor government just had to stump up for it. When he became King, five years later, he moved to Buckingham Palace, which wasn't then the fine building it now is. His father had been a frugal man, maintaining quite a small household, so the son set about spending more government money turning that house into a palace suitable to his tastes. Having done so, he became bored with Carlton House, so what do you think he did with it?" She cocked her head, as if waiting, in vain, for the reply: "he knocked it down! But why? Well, because he could - why else?"

A chorus of polite laughter rippled through the room. Most of the audience were staunch Republicans, so there was little need for political correctness here, not that Estelle would have worried either way, she already had the audience hanging on her every word. "So how did this room survive? Ah, that's the good bit! It was not unusual in those days for complete rooms to change hands between the rich and powerful. You see, the decorations are mainly hangings and panels, a bit like a film set, they were made that way so that an entire area could be transformed almost overnight. Decorators' ladders and the constant smell of paint were not the thing for the Georgians."

She paused for more laughter: "that's where Sir Humphrey Chesterman comes into the story. He was what we would call 'new money'. He had made his fortune buying up bankrupt estates and selling off the separate parts for more than the cost of the whole; our more radical press might term him an asset-stripper. One of his main customers was the Prince Regent. Chesterman became a millionaire and was given a Baronetcy, which gave him a seat in the House of Lords where he was known as the 'Penny Peer', because of his reputation for taking-over an embarrassed person's debts in return for all of their property, for which he paid them one penny. He even had some special pennies minted for the purpose. He had been a regular guest at Carlton House and apparently adored this room. One night he was at a dinner at Buckingham Palace when the King announced that he was demolishing Carlton House. He then turned to Sir Humphrey and said he was aware of his love of this Red Room, so if he were able, would he like to buy it for one of his famous pennies. Sir Humphrey jumped at the opportunity, but the King was really having some sport with him; he was actually offering - a wager." On the last two words, her voice conveyed an air of mystery, as if reading from a children's thriller.

"The King said that Sir Humphrey could have the room, but the final price would depend upon on the spin of one of his pennies. If Sir Humphrey won, then indeed the King would keep just that penny; but if he lost, then the King would receive a million of the pennies instead. That's around half a million dollars in today's money, although you might agree with me if I said that it still sounds cheap for what you get." She paused to allow the general consensus of nodding heads to subside before continuing: "Sir Humphrey took the wager - and won! He quickly removed the room, before the King could change his mind, to his stately home in Suffolk where he built a new wing especially to house it. The penny is still in the Royal Collection, apparently."

"So how did the room get all the way from Suffolk to here? Well, that was down to my mother-in-law. When she and Jackson's Father were building this house in the 'fifties, they heard of a baronial family in Suffolk, England, that had fallen on hard times and needed to sell their estate. Already having a mind to own property overseas, they took a boat across to see it. Jackson's mother fell immediately in love with the house, so they bought it. But when they realised it had been so neglected it was about to fall down, they decided not to spend money on it and sold it off again - at a profit, of course." Another ripple of laughter circumnavigated the room: "apart, that is, for this room which they brought over here, maintaining the tradition, so to speak. No doubt one day, when this house is falling down, the room will move on again. Because as we all know, wealth is temporary, but class is permanent."

The room deferred into polite applause, just as may have been heard nearly two hundred years earlier in its first location. Having let it die-down again, Estelle concluded: "and now, to explain how we intend tonight to make some of your current wealth even more temporary, I will hand-over to Gloria."

One-Six-Eight

More applause travelled around the room as mother made way for daughter. Gloria stood momentarily to wait for it to abate, then began: "Thank you all for attending tonight at such short notice. You probably heard on the news, last week a number of soldiers out of Fort Riley were killed in a helicopter crash in Iraq. Our thoughts are with their families, as they are with all our brave boys and girls serving overseas. As you will know, my mother's Foundation supports a number of military charities, and tonight we are staging a short auction of some works of art, the proceeds from which will be used to create a support fund for those soldiers' families."

She waited while another sprinkling of applause died away: "on display at the back of the room, are four paintings by Clinton Wallis, depicting our troops in action in Iraq and Afghanistan." She extended her hand gesturing toward the doors at the opposite end of the room, that had been closed to be framed by the two liveried servants. The entire audience turned to see that the area they had walked through but minutes earlier was filled by four easels that had appeared as if by magic. Each held a framed painting approximately four feet by three, of an action scene involving soldiers in camouflage uniforms, on foot or in vehicles.

Gloria continued: "For those of you who do not know him, Clinton is a Captain in the Twenty-Fourth Infantry Division out of Fort Riley who has had several tours in theatre over the last two years. In fact he would have been with us tonight, except that he is back out there again. He uses his down time to record, in these amazing paintings, what he sees on a daily basis. He does not sell any of them, but donates them all to military charities to be reproduced, or sold, for the benefit of his fallen comrades." The applause this time was noticeably more approving. Gloria allowed it to continue to its natural conclusion.

"So these are original paintings, they are completely unique and have not been used for any print runs. This will be the only chance anyone will have to purchase them. We are running a silent auction on them, so please bid generously. Whatever the winning bids are, the Kendrick Foundation will match that bid on each painting." There were nods of approval throughout the room: "so you will have the pleasure tonight of not only spending some of your money, but also some of ours as well."

The laughter during the pause this time was less restrained, allowing Gloria to smile winningly as she concluded: "bidding will close at eight p.m, so don't be shy or you'll lose this unique opportunity not only to own a piece of this country's history, but more importantly to help the relatives of those who, sadly, did not survive the making of it. Thank You."

The applause again rippled around the room as the group of five exchanged a few 'well dones' and began to spot individuals in the crowd who they acknowledged, each heading towards a group they had selected as their first port of call for the evening.

One-Six-Nine

As the family group broke up, the three policemen became aware that Estelle Kendrick and Gloria Friedmann were making a beeline towards them. Their progress was interrupted momentarily, several times, by individuals making their own introductions, but the resolve was determined and they traversed the distance relatively quickly. As she reached them, Estelle extended her hand towards Chandler Clarke: "Chandler, how lovely to see you!"

Clarke took her hand: "and you Mrs Kendrick, it's been some time."

"I know dear and I am sorry for that. I do miss your mother so, she was such fun whenever we were working together on one of the charities; but then you already know that don't you. How is your Father? I don't think I've seen him since he found that new wife of his. She seems a lovely girl, but we've never met; must move in different circles now - we're not much for that old Hollywood scene."

As she came up for air, Clarke managed to pop-off a couple of answers: "he's fine, thank you and, yes, they seem very happy together."

"It must feel strange to have a step-mother your own age though?"

"Oh, the Old Man has always made it easy, made her role such that she's more like a sister, so an auntie for the kids rather than a new grandmother."

"Eminently sensible your Father. Always has been, shame there aren't more like him in Washington! But then, I mustn't get into politics tonight, Jackson'll tell me off if he hears me. Are you going to introduce us?"

"Of course, this is Sam Schneider from our local Agency and Chris McKinley from the Wichita Police Department."

"How do you do, gentlemen." She took their hands gently in turn, but didn't shake them: "this is my daughter Gloria." Gloria followed likewise, but added a gentle kiss to Clarke's cheek when she reached him. Estelle continued, speaking to the others: "as you can see, these two already know each other."

"More than twenty years I think," Gloria added.

Clarke nodded: "guess it must be - at least that."

Estelle grasped Gloria's elbow and broke-in in a low tone: "Gloria dear, can I leave you to look after Chandler and his colleagues. The Connollys have just caught my eye again and if I don't go over, they're just going to follow me round all evening like a pair of loyal Labradors." She turned to all the men: "it's been lovely to meet you - especially you Chandler, you do look well you know. Gloria will look after you all." She turned to Gloria: "make sure they get some food won't you dear, before the locusts clear it all." With that, she was off, towards a distinguished-looking couple in their seventies who were hanging-off just out of earshot. Their faces lit up with excitement as she approached them.

"She doesn't change," Clarke observed.

"No," Gloria observed somewhat wistfully, "I'm convinced that when old man time finally knocks on her door, she'll open it, express her dismay at how he looks like he hasn't had a square meal in days, grab him by the arm and march him to the kitchen, where she will instruct cook to feed him, tell him she'll be back for him a bit later, then promptly forget all about him."

"I know what you mean, I think even he would give up trying to nail her down. Easier to go off and find someone else."

"Just as long as he doesn't take cook instead - Mom would be totally lost without her! But, that's not the best subject for us to be talking about, is it? I assume you're up here on that ghastly business of a couple of weeks ago."

"Yes, looks like it may link into something I have open back in Mississippi."

She turned to Schneider and McKinley: "were you both colleagues of Paul Kleberson?"

"We are still colleagues," McKinley answered sharply.

"And friends," Schneider responded.

"I'm so sorry, that was very clumsy of me. He is such a lovely man, and we have a common friend, Annie Fraser. Well Annie Prabhakar as she is now - they were at Cambridge together."

"I know, Annie gave me the history when we had dinner last week," Schneider replied.

"How is Lieutenant Kleberson? I would have visited, but he was moved before I was able to."

"No change."

"Oh, I thought he had been brought out of the coma."

"Yes, he is supporting himself, but there is no physical change. No sign of movement or perception that we are in the room with him."

"So tragic. Annie tried to appear upbeat about it when we had lunch on Sunday, but I wondered how much she was holding back."

"She hides her feelings very well."

"That's Brits for you. You know that everybody expected her and Paul to marry don't you?"

"I knew they were close, but no, I didn't realise they were that close. So you met Paul often?"

"We only met twice. The first time was at Annie's wedding. He was Rashid's best man, fabulous speech, so funny, I just love that British sense of humour. He didn't remember me though, when we met the second time - the morning of the day he was attacked."

"I didn't realise he was coming specifically to see you," McKinley responded, feigning slight confusion.

"Oh he didn't, no. He was really looking for one of the boys, maybe even Pops, but they were all away that day; and Mom. I was here on my own - I doubt he would have got in if any of the others had taken the call from the gatehouse."

"What did you talk about?"

"Everything really - money and marriage, Greek philosophy, private schooling, England, Annie."

"Not the murders."

"Only in passing, couldn't not in the circumstances. I gave him a bit of family history; I just got the impression he was looking for background, something to explain why he disliked my brother and my husband so much. I can understand the situation with my brother, who outside of this family doesn't dislike him? But Emil? I don't know what it was between those two, he really got under Emil's skin you know - not many manage that."

"But nothing about the cases."

She raised her right hand as if taking a mock oath: "I swear, officer, so help me God." She smiled to break some of the ice that had formed: "now, let's change the subject shall we - I'm supposed to be entertaining our guests." She looked across at the paintings: "so - are any of you going to bid?"

Schneider responded first: "not on my salary. I have to say they're not my thing really, I prefer the portraits around this room."

"Yes they are magnificent aren't they? Mind you, I don't think I could afford them on my salary either!" The group all laughed. "That one there is a Gainsborough," she pointed at a full length portrait of a bewigged gentleman in the robes of a Knight of the Garter: "the last Gainsborough to sell at auction made over five million dollars." She pointed at a religious scene: "that one's by

Hoare, a contemporary of Gainsborough, although not as well known. I have to say, I think he was a better artist, but then what would I know?" she added self-deprecatingly. "There are a couple of Lawrences here as well," she added.

"They are magnificent," Schneider replied, you are lucky to own them."

"Oh I don't know so much about that. We're custodians really. Yes we may have paid money for them, but you never actually own eighteenth century artwork like this, you just look after it for the next generations. But even that's a nightmare, because they have such history and provenance. Every art critic, particularly those with an expensive pen but no money for the ink in it, wants to know why they are not being exhibited publically, that they are being cared for properly, or wants to have them x-rayed to find-out what the artist was originally thinking. Worse still, someone always wants to challenge their authenticity, and every time they do, we have to move them to satisfy these demands, after which the insurance broker is able to order a new Ferrari or move to an even bigger house."

"It just goes to show, the other man's grass is not necessarily as green as you might expect."

"How true!" She turned to Clarke: "but as I remember, Chandler, you're more into modern art aren't you?"

"You have a good memory Gloria, we must have both still been at school when we had that discussion."

"So have your tastes changed then?"

"Not at all."

"In that case, come with me." She grabbed his hand like a naughty schoolgirl taking a friend to show them a secret and started to move off towards the doors, before stopping suddenly and turning back to the other two: "oh, I'm sorry, you can come as well. There's a room I want to show you that's a bit less formal than this one - come on!"

She turned and hauled Clarke off; the others followed in their wake.

crossing the divide

One-Seventy

Gloria led them across the glazed reception area and into another room that couldn't be a greater contrast to the one they had previously left. The walls were all plain and painted brilliant white, as was the high ceiling. The large frieze that ran all around the top of the walls looked like a reproduction of scenes from a Mesopotamian victory stele, but was probably composed of genuine marbles looted at some time in antiquity. The floor was highly-polished rosewood and the only furniture, bar for several floor installations, were a series of low-back sofas, some long, some circular, placed on perfectly-symmetrical Persian rugs.

The walls were covered in modern art of all shapes, sizes and colours, but although, on first entry, this room appeared to have all the immediate charisma of just another Chelsea loft, it quickly evolved into a warm and friendly space that welcomed its guests to stay and enjoy each other's company as well as the decoration. One other person was in the room when they arrived, wearing a blazer and slumped on one of the long sofas. Gloria addressed him somewhat offhandedly: "ah, brother dear, surely you haven't had enough already?"

The happy welcoming aura displayed to the assembled throng no more than twenty minutes earlier had been replaced by an ominous presence, almost malevolently draining the sweet air from the room: "if ah has ta listen to another old granny blathering on about how she knew me when ah was knee-high to a cricket, ah swear ah'll bid a million each for those damned paintin's out there just ta be rid of 'em all before seven-thirty."

Gloria walked straight to the sofa, bent over and threw her arms around the moribund figure: "sold! to the man in the blazer with the miserable chequebook," she said, as she planted a gentle kiss on his cheek.

It seemed to have little effect: "an' that's another thing, why am ah all done up like a fairground barker. Ya knows why ah don't wear no tie, less ah has to. The starch in this collar is playin' hell with ma skin allergies, ah won't be able ta shave fer a month!"

"You rarely shave more than once in a month anyway," came her slightly-exasperated response. The previously-condescending tone then changed to almost that of a kindergarten teacher: "look, we're doing this for Mother. You know how she likes to keep up appearances at these affairs, so come on. It's another couple of hours tops, then you'll probably be off the hook for the rest of the summer. Anyway, we have an old friend here who you haven't met for many a year."

He looked up, past her shoulder towards the three men stood just inside the door; he squinted as if his vision was out of focus. The first person he recognised was Schneider. He slumped back into the sofa: "if ya' means tha one on tha right, he ain't no friend'a mine, or of this family!"

Gloria looked over her shoulder and, realising who he was referring to, appeared to have her composure slightly disturbed. She stood up and folded her arms, slightly frustratedly, then turned to Schneider: "please accept my apologies for my brother's rudeness, he's obviously mistaken you for someone else." The final single syllable word was accompanied by a sharp tap of her Gucci kitten heel on her brother's shin.

Jackson Kendrick III shot to his feet, quickly straightening his jacket to face the group of men, and his voice changed instantaneously to an almost-refined New England accent: "of course, Agent Schneider, how nice to see you again."

"And you, Mr Kendrick," Schneider responded.

Jackson Kendrick III was still trying to focus on the other two as he continued: "but Sis, I don't believe I've had the pleasure of being introduced to these other two gentlemen."

"Maybe not the one in the middle. This is Sergeant McKinley from the Wichita Police Department." McKinley walked over and shook her brother's hand. Gloria continued: "but you must remember Chandler Clarke, surely?"

For more than just a split second, the projected aura shattered around Jackson Kendrick III. The look on his face was almost that of sheer terror, like a nine-year-old caught red-handed behind the counter with his hand in the sweet jar. Although Schneider had attempted to keep Clarke's presence in Wichita low key for just this moment, having wanted to see just how barefaced 'The Turd' could be, what interested him even more was that, apparently, no attempt had been made to prewarn her brother of this potential meeting. Had this been through total innocence of the circumstances, or because someone in the family had decided to disturb his equilibrium for some reason?

In the time it took for Clarke to traverse the distance between them, the confident aura had snapped back around the younger Kendrick. But Clarke had also spotted the disturbance in the force field and knew that he had the upper hand, whatever he did. He extended his hand in a totally friendly manner: "it's been a long time Johnson."

Another barely-perceptible ripple swept across the calm pool of his target's face at the mention of his family nickname, another indication that he was far from comfortable in the presence of someone who knew more about him than he would be happy to admit. He took Clarke's hand and shook it fairly coldly: "oh, I haven't used that nickname for many years Chandler."

"It's been many years since we last met Johnson ..." the name echoed through Kendrick's mind as if it was a nail being struck with a hammer: "... so what would you prefer?"

He shrugged: "it doesn't matter - what's in a name anyway?"

"What indeed?" There was an air of menace in those two words that was deliberately put there by the dispatcher and received loud and clear by the addressee. Clarke's tone lightened: "may I say how sorry we were to hear of your recent loss."

"Why, that's very kind of you Chandler; it was indeed a heavy blow to bear."

"Yes, I wouldn't imagine it would be easy to find a woman both ready and able to take on the responsibilities attached to being part of your future ..." he paused as he looked deep into Kendrick's eyes, as if he was probing for the existence of a soul, "... what with having to look after all of this while you're away most of the time on 'business'."

Gloria had clearly picked-up the undercurrent and stepped in to diffuse the immediate situation: "losing Hilary has been a huge shock for the entire family, Chandler, but Johnson will still have the support of the rest of us when the time comes for him to assume his full role."

Clarke decided to back-off, just a bit: "this certainly is one interesting collection you have here. But I never got the impression when we were younger that this was really your bag Johnson."

A deeper, older voice came from behind them: "oh, there's little point in asking him about any of this, he's really never got into art and design that much, unless it's been on the back of a pack of cards, isn't that right Johnson?"

"If you say so Pops," came the somewhat indifferent reply.

Clarke turned to see Jackson Kendrick Junior walking purposefully towards him, hand outstretched in welcome: "Chandler, m'boy, how the hell are you?"

The handshake was warm and friendly from both parties: "I'm very well Sir, and you?"

"Nothing a sizeable cheque to a specialist wouldn't cure." He kept hold of Clarke's hand and placed his free hand on top of both: "I was so sorry to hear of your Mother's passing. Such a wonderful woman; we were so upset that we couldn't be at the funeral. We were over in some Godforsaken corner of Eastern Europe when we heard the news and as it had taken a few days to get to us, all of the formalities were already over."

"That's OK Sir, we understood; thank you for the kind words in your letter. But you have also had a sad loss to bear recently."

"Yes, poor Hilary. Lovely girl, would have done Johnson here proud - no would have done us all proud. Terrible business," he shook his head, "no doubt that is what has brought you all the way up here from Mississippi."

"It is Sir."

"And these two gentlemen as well?"

"Oh sorry Sir, may I introduce Sam Schneider from the Agency here in Wichita."

Schneider stepped forward and shook hands with Junior: "nice to meet you Mr Kendrick."

"And I you. You were there when Lieutenant Kleberson was attacked?"

"I was."

"I could never do your job, y'know," Junior shook his head again, "the things you have to deal with. And you have been a regular visitor at the hospital, I understand."

"Yes, we have been close friends since he first came to live in Wichita."

"Any news?"

"Not really. I think the official communiqué says that he is stable, but all that really means is he is just laying there."

"What a tragedy; and how has Annie taken it all? You know that her family are close friends who knew him well when he was in England."

"I do, and she has taken it as well as could be expected. She was with Paul when I visited earlier this afternoon. His family are looking after her and her husband while they're over here."

"Yes, great girl Annie." Junior turned back to Clarke: "and your other colleague?"

While they were talking, McKinley had wandered over to a large piece of art on the rear wall, which he was studying closely. The circular canvas, around eight feet in diameter and entirely black in colour, was the solitary occupant of the wall. It was framed in an entirely circular minimalist frame, made from ebony which offered an interesting complement to the semi-gloss finish of the painting itself. Clarke announced him: "this is Sergeant Chris McKinley, he is Lieutenant Kleberson's right hand man."

Junior strode over towards where McKinley was standing: "and I see he is admiring my pride and joy."

The two men shook hands warmly. McKinley responded: "I am Sir. I was going to ask you if it is a Malevich."

"Ah, you have an appreciation, but are not sure - I'm impressed."

"I read some years ago that there were some lost works that he left behind in Germany when he exhibited there in the nineteen-twenties. Apparently, he knew that his country would turn against modernist art after Lenin's influence waned. He was right, of course, which I always thought somewhat ironic - Stalin banning Suprematism that is."

"My my! I had no idea that City Hall recruited art graduates."

"They don't Sir, it's a private passion. Not the sort of thing we discuss regularly over donuts during a break in the caseload, I'm afraid."

"So you'll have no problems with these then?" Junior swept his hand towards three large abstract canvases on the adjacent wall.

"No Sir," McKinley smiled, but Junior put his hand up to prevent him from continuing.

"You have a colleague here who shares your passion, isn't that right Chandler?" Junior turned to Clarke who acknowledged with a nod and a smile.

Junior continued: "so Agent Schneider, is this a new trait in law enforcement? Can you tell us who these three are by?"

"I'm afraid not, Mr Kendrick, my tastes are more towards the room we have just come from."

"Pity. Sergeant, I'll let you enlighten him shall I?"

"They're Pollocks," McKinley responded.

"You know, I was thinking that myself," Schneider observed with a smile. A snort of suppressed laughter came from the sofa where Junior's son was still lounging, which brought a reactive glare from his father.

"But it isn't a Malevich, is it Mr Kendrick?" The fresh question came from McKinley, who had returned to studying the circular black painting.

"Very astute of you, Sergeant, so why do you not think it's by him?"

"Because it's not minimal. There's a dot in the centre, plus a hint of some geometrical patterns."

"Excellent! Although we don't know for certain that Malevich was not involved at some time. My Father purchased it in nineteen-sixty-three, just before he died, from a Swedish collector who had owned it for nearly twenty years. It was made by a German professor named Friederhoffer. Like many scientists in Germany in the 'twenties and 'thirties he was breaking down age-old boundaries and scientific dogma to make exciting new discoveries. His field was micro-imaging and he worked with Goldberg on microdots; it was during that time we believe that he met Malevich. After Krystalnacht, Goldberg fled Germany, but like many contemporaries, Friederhoffer continued his work thinking the Nazi party was just a temporary aberration, until it was too late and he found himself enslaved by the State. But Hitler knew the value of his scientists, so during the war they were given every comfort and assistance to develop their techniques, but obviously not for the good purposes they originally envisaged. You can imagine the value Hitler saw in micro-imaging. Late in nineteen-forty-four, Friederhoffer realised that it was all going to end in tears and that the area where his establishment was located, near Greifswald on the Baltic Coast, was likely to be overrun by the Soviets, as a result of which he would probably fall into their hands. He couldn't escape, he was too high-profile, but he organised for a lot of his personal items, including his art collection, to be transported to Sweden, a neutral country where he had scientific contacts. He hoped that he could follow them later. He never did."

"It's just amazing. But what is the technique?"

"Most of his papers were either captured by the Soviets, or destroyed by the German soldiers guarding his facility. From what we've pieced-together, he was working on perceptive techniques associated with micro-imaging, a way of hiding things in plain sight. Not everybody can see the patterns. For example my daughter can, but my son here can't."

There was a snort of disgust from the sofa. Junior continued: "Friederhoffer was working on whether this ability was built-in to everybody's brain, or just into certain individuals - you can imagine how easy it was for him to obtain funding from his government on that type of research. Believe it or not, what you are perceiving is on the microdot in the centre. It's a similar response to that found in the recent scientific work that has demonstrated how we can read a sentence comprising a load of jumbled-up words, as long as the first and last letters are in the correct place in each word."

"How do you know I am seeing what you think I am?"

"You see a square whose corners are touching the edge of the canvas, within that a circle that touches each side of the square and within that an equilateral triangle whose corners touch the circle, with the dot exactly central to it."

"Is that all?"

"You tell me."

"The triangle is upside down and there are the beginnings of squares formed from each side."

"Are the squares complete?

"No, they form a hexagon at the limits of the canvas." McKinley stepped forward to examine the canvas more closely, only to discover that it was entirely plain black paint other than for the microdot mounted in the centre, the contents of which were completely indecipherable to the naked eye. "That's incredible," he whispered, "how did he do that?"

"The real question, surely, is how did you do it? Do you understand the symbology?"

"I would imagine it's about dimensions. There are five geometrical shapes and that has to suggest the five dimensions."

"Very good! Obviously you understand the shapes and you can see the four dimensions, they are on the microdot. But what of the fifth?"

"That's the frame, the limit of the work."

"But is it? Have you ever seen the old TV series 'The Twilight Zone'?"

"There is a fifth dimension, beyond that which is known to man."

"Ah you have - good! So what if I tell you that the microdot does not contain the hexagon? That your mind has drawn that because it cannot conceive the lines emanating from the sides of the triangle escaping the frame, because it does not understand that extra dimension."

"So am I seeing a black hole?"

"Maybe. The circle is the most unusual shape, as it is made up of a single line that creates a two dimensional form that, when it's three-dimensional solid is viewed by the human eye, is identical in every plane to the two-dimensional version. But because it is perfectly curved, you may be seeing the outside surface or the inside surface."

"Which presumably has a meaning."

"Yes. Because the single line is always unbroken, the circle both contains and excludes. But because the line is infinite, it does so without separating what is inside from what is outside. So what is inside can see out and what is outside can see in. Which is what life is about - you know the various phrases, moving in different circles, meeting in the middle, on the outside looking in and so on."

"Crossing the divide."

"Exactly! We humans are only limited by our perceptions. So we may be on the outside looking in, wondering why we cannot be part of what we see, but there is nothing to stop us from crossing that barrier, because it is we who have erected it ourselves, in our own perception."

At that point Emil Friedmann entered the room: "ah Gloria, there you are. Your Mother is anxious that you are depriving our other guests of your knowledge of the paintings on sale, and their artist."

"Then leave us you must!" Junior declared. Gloria made her apologies and left the room. Her husband was about to follow her when Junior stopped him: "Emil, actually this is quite opportune. Come in and close the door. Have you met these gentlemen?"

Emil Friedmann dutifully obeyed and, as he turned back from the closed door, he acknowledged Schneider: "yes, I know Agent Schneider, he and I share a building downtown - how are you?" They nodded to each other. "Detective McKinley and I have crossed swords professionally a couple of times at City Hall - no hard feelings I hope? But I don't believe I know this gentleman." He wandered over to Clarke extending his hand in greeting.

Junior completed the introduction: "Chandler this is Gloria's husband Emil Friedmann. Chandler is an old friend of the family back to when he and your wife used to argue over balloons and chase each other around the pool and into it much of the time as well - Chandler is Senator Clarke's son."

Schneider could not see Friedmann's face, but was watching Junior closely. He seemed to detect a glint in Junior's eye, an almost boyish delight at the discomfort this introduction was obviously causing to the lawyer. Clarke could also see that discomfort at close hand, because he not only saw the colour drain from Friedmann's face, but felt the hand try to let go as if it had been stung by one of those toys that give a mild electric shock when the hand being shaken touches it.

'Strike two,' Clarke thought, as he deliberately held for a little longer the hand that was so desperately attempting escape; just long enough to force Friedmann's eyes to meet his and to see the look of determination on Clarke's face.

One-Seven-One

"Gentlemen," Junior began, "the opportunity seems to have presented itself that we are all together in the same room, and I'm sure you are aware that it is not a Kendrick trait to miss an opportunity. I have some unanswered questions, as I'm sure that you gentlemen have as well, certainly from what I've picked-up just from the chemistry, or lack of it, in this room at the moment. Agent Schneider, I presume that you have taken-over heading-up the investigation, so as long as you don't believe it would have any negative effect on your situation, why don't we all have a seat and get ourselves some answers?"

He sat on the long sofa near to his son, who had readopted the slumped couldn't-give-a-damn pose from when they first entered the room. The others elected to remain standing, creating an interesting dynamic.

"I have no objection to that Mr Kendrick," Schneider responded, posing the question by gestures to Clarke and McKinley, who both shook their heads in assent.

Junior took the initiative: "I know that my son and son-in-law have been kept in the loop with regard to the events of the last few weeks, but I have to say that I have been somewhat on the periphery. Not that I have a problem with that, Hilary wasn't my fiancé, but she was as good as a member of this family. Then there is Lieutenant Kleberson, not somebody I know personally, but a very close friend of a very close friend's family, and highly thought-of by them. I take a great deal of interest in my family. I also take a very great interest in my friends, as I'm sure Chandler will be happy to affirm."

"I would Sir," Clarke replied, "but, with all due respect, we were of the impression that the family had been kept fully informed through official channels from City Hall."

"If you're referring to that buffoon Stanton then I can understand how your colleagues may have formed that opinion Chandler." He turned to Schneider: "the problem with powerful families like this one, Agent Schneider, is that, similar to any large body, their gravitational pull is sufficient to drag all sorts of debris into their orbit. There is no choice about its arrival; once there it is not easy to dislodge, but it retains a degree of independence. That's not a problem, necessarily, unless it decides to use that independence to ingratiate itself with the host body. That can cause all manner of problems and misunderstandings."

"So are you saying that Chief Stanton did not give you important details regarding the continued conduct of the case?"

"No, he did exactly that - whether I wanted him to or not! However, most of the time it was what he thought we should know. That in itself could have compromised this family's position, as we tried to inform him subtly."

"You are aware that he has resigned."

"Yes, and just as well. I hope that Ramsey's made the right choice as a replacement. From what I've picked-up, it sounds like more of the same."

"And that Stanton has disappeared."

Junior shot a look at both Friedmann and his son. The former had chosen to stand near one wall and was not moved by the question; the latter looked at the back of his hand in boredom. Junior responded: "no, I didn't - nothing sinister I hope."

"Not unless you find it difficult to understand how someone sells up and moves their family and belongings out, lock, stock and barrel, within twenty-four hours without leaving a forwarding address."

Junior shrugged: "stranger things have happened. I don't see what bearing it has on this discussion."

"Your son-in-law's company handled the transaction," Schneider added, matter-of-factly.

Friedmann responded unemotionally: "my company handles thousands of transactions each year. I can't possibly have knowledge of them all."

"So you didn't see Stanton at all yesterday?"

"Don't recall it."

"Not during the five hours or so he was in your offices?"

"We have three floors of offices Agent Schneider."

"Or while you were driving him away from them yesterday evening?"

Junior interjected: "gentlemen, if you want to interrogate my son-in-law, then you can take him in after our guests have gone. He's a big boy, and I'm sure he has a good lawyer." A cynical grin washed onto Friedmann's face and his brother-in-law emitted a quiet grunt of approval. "But, if I remember our discussion from a few moments ago, it was you who were agreeing to answer my questions." Junior looked at all three visitors in turn and saw no disagreement: "good - so, Agent Schneider, this Shepherd character, what on earth was he?"

"The truthful answer Mr Kendrick is we still don't really know. We pretty much know his life history and how that shaped the individual. The shrinks will no doubt spend years studying the mental profile, but we're not really interested in that. It's how he became what he was - a very effective killing machine - that we are concentrating on. But that's not proving easy because every time we get close to a break, it seems to be snatched away from us. It's as though there is somebody in the shadows running interference for him, even though he's dead." The final sentence was delivered looking directly at Friedmann. Junior was watching that interaction closely.

"Have you any idea why he chose Hilary for a victim?" This question brought the first sign of any reaction from his son, who looked at his father for quite a few seconds after it was finished.

"We have several ideas, which probably illustrates perfectly why these cases are so difficult to get a handle on. You are aware that the two were at least acquaintances at USC."

Junior looked distinctly shaken by this piece of information; his son shot a concerned look at Friedmann, who remained unfazed. Junior responded: "no, I didn't - how?" Chandler Clarke mentally noted the singular in the answer.

"Shepherd went through college as a woman. It appears she was attacked on campus."

Junior laughed: "I bet the attacker got a shock!"

"He did, a week later. When he had an 'accident'"

Junior's humour subsided: "serious?"

"Terminal."

"Dear God! - and you think it wasn't a co-incidence."

"Not now. Campus Police didn't make a link because Shepherd refused to give details of the attacker - for obvious reasons."

"An examination would reveal her secret. But how does Hilary figure in this?"

"She came across Shepherd just after the attack. It was Hilary who took him, sorry her, to the police and tried to persuade her to give up the attacker's details. After that, it seems Hilary took Shepherd under her wing."

"That figures. Just the thing I would expect her to do - always collecting waifs and strays." Junior looked at his son as he shook his head sadly: "what a loss." He paused in a moment's reflection, then continued: "so do you think she knew about him/her?"

"Definitely. When Ms Nicholson picked Shepherd up from the airport, he was no longer a she."

"Hilary met him? At Mid-Continent?"

"On the day she died, yes. You didn't know?"

"No, I didn't." Junior bolted looks at the other two family members: "did you?" he asked them. His son wouldn't look at him, so Friedmann was forced to respond, but only got three words out: "we didn't want …"

Junior jumped to his feet and faced his son-in-law: "what else didn't you want me to know? Well?"

"It wasn't about you, Sir, it was for Estelle. She was already grief-stricken by it all and she would have wanted the details. That's why we got Stanton to feed everything through me."

Junior was furious. He shouted at Friedmann: "and you think I got where I am today by not knowing when to build Chinese walls round my family when I needed to? You're an idiot Emil! I am thoroughly disappointed in you." He turned to the slumped figure of his son: "both of you."

He rounded on Schneider, but subsumed his anger before asking: "you kept this out of the media - why?"

"We've kept a lot out of the media, Mr Kendrick, they were having enough of a feeding-frenzy as it was. If we had let them have too much information, they would have trampled all over the evidence. Remember, this only began to emerge the day we finally apprehended Shepherd. We didn't even know who he was before that point."

Junior calmed down: "of course, forgive me for the outburst. I suppose everybody thought they were doing everything they did for the best." He walked over to his son and placed a fatherly hand on his shoulder. He looked at Schneider: "so if Hilary knew about him, does that mean he killed her simply to keep her quiet?"

"It's a possibility."

"And the other two, they were at the same university weren't they? They would have known, presumably, so he had to get rid of them as well."

"That would be nice and tidy, Mr Kendrick, but I'm afraid it isn't that simple. I'm satisfied that the other two didn't know about Shepherd's sexuality, certainly not when they were at USC. Ms Nicholson had kept the secret for many years; we are not aware of any reason why that should have changed."

"Damned if I can see any other explanation, but then I suppose there's still an awful lot more you know that you're not going to tell us. And where does this Kryczek figure in it all. She was an Agent of yours wasn't she?"

"Not mine directly, she was out of LA."

"And this Shepherd, how did he come to impersonate her?"

"We think she confronted him at some point."

"So do you know where she is now?"

"She's most likely dead."

Junior shook his head: "I don't know, what a business."

"We also know that she met Ms Nicholson sometime in the month before she died."

The son shot a shocked look at Friedmann, who again didn't flinch. Junior's antenna picked-up on this instantly: "seems like something you didn't know this time, huh son?" He glared again at his son-in-law: "so your Ma and Pa aren't the only ones being protected here either."

Schneider and Clarke both noticed this surprising revelation. Schneider decided that this would be a good time to try and drive a wedge between the three Kendrick men: "may I ask, Mr Kendrick, were you privy to the details of the pre-nup agreement between your son and Ms Nicholson?"

Friedmann reacted this time: "now just a minute Agent Schneider, we had an agreement …"

Schneider cut him off: "any agreement we may have made, Mr Friedmann, was surrounding making any details public, which we haven't - yet. This is not a public forum and, as the Kendrick family were subject to the document, it would be helpful to establish exactly how many were aware of its contents."

"And as the family lawyer, I have to advise you that you have not only exceeded any remit you may have had to be here, but you have also gone well beyond the realms of respect for your hosts. Therefore this informal discussion is at an end."

"Emil," Junior said quietly and somewhat exasperatedly, "let's not get into areas of exceeding one's remit, because that can lead to embarrassment for all concerned, including family lawyers. I shouldn't have to remind you that you are not in your twenty-eighth-storey palace downtown, you are in my house and, while it remains my house, I will decide when a guest, however closely associated, has outlived their welcome." He lifted his eyebrows to accentuate the final words.

"I'm sorry Sir," Friedmann apologised, quite humbly.

Junior turned to Schneider: "and in answer to your question, Agent Schneider, no I didn't. Neither do I wish to, or would have wanted to at the time it was prepared. Agreements like that are decided between the parties concerned, with whatever legal assistance they need, because it is they who will need to live by the consequences for the rest of their lives."

"Even if those consequences affect the family business?"

"I gave you an answer, Agent Schneider, I should not need to qualify it. But for the sake of clarity, nothing my children can sign could have any consequence on any of the family businesses during my lifetime, and I doubt I will be in any position to care afterwards. So that's the end of the matter."

Junior looked at Clarke, changing the subject: "so Chandler, why are you here? Not at Apeiron, you're always welcome here, you know that - I mean in Wichita."

"My office is handling some similar cases from down in Memphis last year. There is a very strong connection."

"I thought you were on a large corruption case." He paused as he watched Clarke for a reaction, but not getting one he continued: "your Father told me last month when I bumped into him in Washington - and that lovely new young wife of his. He's going to have to keep her close, especially in Washington - all those young bucks chasing around." He cast a swift glance at his son, who was looking back at him, this time with a look of some concern.

"You must hear plenty of rumours up in Washington, Sir. Most of them don't make it to the Delta."

Junior continued to look at his son: "oh, the jungle drums are beating all the time in the capital. Politicians in and out of each other's beds, and not just politically." He turned to McKinley: "and Sergeant, what are you doing here? No disrespect, but I'm sure my wife wouldn't have invited someone of your pay grade to a charity auction where we are hoping for five-figure bids, not unless you have family connections that would allow you to take part at that level."

"No offence taken Sir. Chief Harper asked me to represent him as he was unable to come himself."

"Interesting. Maybe I've made too hasty a judgement of your new boss."

At that point the door opened and Estelle Kendrick breezed into the room: "ah! so this is where you all are. Emil, Gloria has someone that she wants you to meet dear, it's probably worth a few dollars on the bidding, so run along quickly would you?" She turned away from her son-in-law, having completed his summary dismissal from the room; Friedmann obediently strode out, heading for the Red Drawing Room. She turned to McKinley with a broad smile: "now, Sergeant, I've come to rescue you as well. My dear friend Mary Brewster has just finished reading the latest Harry Bosch - have you read it?"

"The one with the boy's body discovered after twenty years?"

"You have! Oh that's wonderful! Come with me dear," she grabbed his arm and tucked hers around it, taking him off in the same direction, continuing as they walked: "now, we have a disagreement over some of the forensic evidence and you are the perfect person to resolve it, being a professional that is."

"I'll certainly try Ma'am," were the parting words the others heard as the pair passed through the doorway.

"Now, there's a brave man," Junior observed, "getting between those two when they're arguing over the plot from a whodunit, eh Chandler?"

Clarke nodded: "do you think he'll survive it, Sir?"

"Oh, I should think so, but he may have to bear the scars for a while!" They both laughed. "Now, Agent Schneider, seeing as this little gathering has been broken up by my wife, I have something I would like to show you. Would you step out with me onto the terrace?"

Schneider acceded to the request and Junior opened a pair of French doors leading outside. The two men passed though with Junior closing the doors behind him, leaving his son and Chandler Clarke alone in the room.

One-Seven-Two

You could cut the atmosphere in the large airy room with a knife. The two men remaining were not looking at each other, neither having any intention of making the first move. Nevertheless, they both knew that there was no escape from the situation; the elephant in that room was going nowhere until one of them took hold of the rope to lead it. Clarke looked towards the sofa occupied by the younger Kendrick, slowly contemplating the slumped figure. His options, all initiated by the emotions coursing through his body, rattled through his mind.

Clarke could shoot him there and then. He was still carrying his service weapon, there having been minimal security applied at the gate. Result, total and instant revenge for his mother, followed by the pain caused to the rest of his family by his own incarceration and, still permissibly in this State, eventual execution. Not an option then, unfortunately, not because he personally feared the ultimate consequences, but due to his father, in particular, having suffered enough already from the actions of this oversexed imbecile. It would also turn a fool into a martyr and, although his nefarious activities would finally be publicised for all to know, he would never have to face up to them as he should.

Exposure then? Jackson Kendrick III's face emblazoned across every evening news programme in the country, and probably many more around the world, hounded by the packs of media hyenas wherever he went, doorstepped at every property he owned and discussed ad infinitum at society gatherings. But what of the collateral damage? Clarke's own family name dragged through the dirt and, even though there would be immense sympathy for his father having been cuckolded twice in short succession by the same serial adulterer, the Senator was no longer a young man. Such revelations would weigh heavier on his shoulders than those of a younger man, especially one dispossessed of all conscience.

Perhaps he should just stroll across and deliver a single, devastating right hook to the jaw. Clarke had been school middleweight boxing champion back East, at the same school where his adversary had avoided all possible physical activity by dint of a co-operative doctor who diagnosed him with whatever infirmities he needed, whenever he needed them; that doctor had driven Bentleys ever since. Neither had the younger Kendrick suffered retribution for his various extra-curricular activities on and off campus, thanks to a bunch of sizeable cronies, some of whom still inhabited his inner circle of friends. They were supplemented, when necessary, by a combination of substantial cheques and tightly-drafted non-disclosure agreements. Unfortunately, Clarke knew that, once again, this would provide instant satisfaction followed by the numbing memory that Jackson Kendrick III would take such punishment as full and final settlement of any moral debt owed to the Clarke family, and thereafter be freed to continue as if nothing had happened.

No - the only option was to use his professional position on the building of evidence surrounding these cases, to nail his family's torturer on charges sufficiently serious to finish every single one of his activities once and for all. The world at large would not miss Jackson Kendrick III; his family might, but even that would probably be only for sufficient time for appearances to be satisfied. The truth was that, although the family ladies preferred there to be no cracks apparent in their beautifully-sculpted society facade, Junior had regretted conceding to their pleas to let the prodigal son return to the fold, almost from the day of reconciliation.

Clarke was rocked from his thoughts by some words filtering through them from across the room: "so what's it to be Chandler?" Clarke's focus returned to the figure on the sofa, who was sitting forward, hands interlocked between spread knees. Jackson Kendrick III had decided to take the initiative and was looking directly at him posing the question: "are you going to shoot me or call the National Enquirer?"

"I'm currently considering laying you out on these beautifully-polished boards," Clarke responded without hesitation.

Kendrick pushed out his jaw and pointed at it with his right index finger: "in which case, champ, can you hit this side. I need some expensive bridgework done here and it will be cheaper if they solve all the problems in one sitting."

The comment was designed to make Clarke do exactly that. Kendrick had decided to go for the martyr angle - heir to fortune attacked in own home by old family friend, who also happened to be an FBI Agent. The tabloids would love it, maybe even the broadsheets. The networks would lap it up too, at which point all manner of perfectly-timed revelations would create the breadcrumb-trail that would lead them all to the reason for the attack, and the collateral destruction of the Clarke family name. Nobody could argue that Jackson Kendrick III had not inherited the paternal line's opportunist genes.

"Yes, you would actually love that wouldn't you Johnson? A little pain in exchange for a full acquittal. Strange thing is, though, I do think there is some kernel of a conscience in there. If I'm right, then the best punishment for you is actually no punishment."

"Oh, I'm not going to dispute that! Not the last part anyway."

"Right now, maybe. But eventually, Johnson, we all have to be confronted by the man in the mirror and, when someone like you has to do that, it is probable that the experience will be enhanced by some illegal substance or another, which will do a far more effective job than even my seventy percent stoppage record could inflict."

"So you're going to leave me free to scratch whatever itch comes my way?"

"Not every one, Johnson, one in particular will not be creating any temptation again, having been fully apprised of your 'reputation'."

Kendrick shrugged arrogantly: "not a high price to pay. It has to be said that the replacement was no substitute for the original."

Clarke felt both his fists clench involuntarily as he fought every sinew in his legs, which were trying to propel him across the ten feet separating the two men. The comment made him realise that his estimation of the existence of even a miniscule trace of conscience had been hugely overgenerous. There was no point, during the rest of this exchange, in the avoidance of trampling on any potential feelings. As was the case with the majority of interrogation subjects, there simply weren't any to trample on.

He retaliated verbally: "you know, the one thing that really amazed me when I read that pre-nup document, was that it didn't contain a clause requiring Hilary and Marjoree to get it on for your entertainment on the honeymoon night."

To Clarke's amazement, Kendrick shot to his feet, traversed half the distance towards him before stopping, purple faced. His voice changed from the smooth East Coast society accent he had affected earlier to his usual Midwest drawl: "ah will not have tha memory of that fine lady sullied like that, particularly by a useless piece a crap like you. FBI Agent ma ass, ya couldn't find a trick in a whorehouse, even after it clamped its lips arahnd ya dick!"

Clarke greeted the outburst with slow, ironic applause: "what have we here? The plot for a new Hollywood blockbuster in which a devastated society beau defends the honour of the lesbian gold-digger that made him sign-away all his family's fortune to their future child-to-be? That would have been one hell of a price to pay for one roll in the hay with a dyke - must've been some high stakes at risk for you to take that bet."

"Ahm warnin' ya!"

"Oh really, what you gonna do Johnson - hit me? If you are, don't worry which side," he pointed at each cheek in turn, "both are capable of absorbing the light touch of a powder-puff without the need for reconstructive work!"

Clarke knew two things - he had turned the tables and there was no bookie that would give odds against Kendrick taking that shot. As anticipated, Kendrick turned away: "pah, you're not worth it!" He spat out the words with false disdain as he slumped back onto the sofa.

"Is that why she had to die? She changed her mind didn't she? And you couldn't afford that could you? What made her change her mind - that visit from Kryczek? What was it Kryczek told her about you, Johnson?"

Jackson Kendrick III was staring out of one of the windows, away from Clarke's gaze and into the middle distance. He began to speak, the society accent returning, along with an eloquence never previously experienced by the old family friend: "you have no idea what's going on here, no experience of what it is to be exiled by your own blood from everything you ever knew, or of how the loyalty of true friends can provide succour in that darkest hour. No idea of the forces in play or the factions bringing those forces to bear, of the hazards, the menaces, the perils of life at this stratospheric level - how could you?"

He turned to face Clarke, who was shocked to see the change in the young Kendrick's countenance, his face contorted as if possessed by a combination of anger and some unbelievable inner torture, his eyes reddening behind the moisture beginning to glisten within them: "how could you, Chandler Clarke, know of these things? You - the son of a Senator descended from old money, but of a family that no longer possesses any, yet still rides on the coat-tails of those able to afford that type of apparel and the lifestyle it heralds. The son that pretends to make a living as a professional investigator but can never see the wood for the trees; the friend of a family that has always sponsored that friendship. I despise you as much as you despise me, not from jealousy, but from the total contempt I have always felt for you and everything you stand for. Now get out of my sight, you pathetic little gumshoe."

"Johnson!" The embarrassed female voice came from the direction of the doorway behind Chandler Clarke. It belonged to Gloria Friedmann who had entered the room unnoticed by the two combatants, just as her brother had commenced his final tirade. She stood anchored to the spot, the shock on her face clearly exhibiting the extent to which her confident demeanour had been momentarily shattered by the unexpected scene she was witnessing. Her brother slowly turned away from both of them to resume his pose staring beyond the window at nothing in particular in the middle distance.

Clarke turned to Gloria and, immediately on seeing her concern, walked over to her, took her arm and gently turned her towards the open door: "it's alright Gloria," he reassured, "your brother and I were just finishing-up anyway. Why don't you show me those paintings you are auctioning?" He turned to send the last portion of his parting remark back into the room in the direction of the sofa: "my family may not be well-off enough to warrant the attention of some parts of, so-called, ordered society, but we still possess a heritage that has never shirked the support of a worthy cause."

With that Clarke led Gloria from the room, quietly quelling her attempts to apologise for her obvious discomfort. Only Jackson Kendrick III knew if he felt any similar shame at what he had just done, but as ever, that would remain a matter for his own counsel.

on the outside

One-Seven-Three

After leaving the gallery room, Junior had led his guest around the side terracing to the rear of the house, where it expanded to the vast area of formal gardens leading down four or five levels to the lake. The evening sun was beginning to throw shadows of the trees surrounding it onto the surface of the water, where the unshaded ripples glinted gently.

Junior paused to allow Schneider to take-in the vista, at the same time checking through the windows of the Red Drawing Room behind them that their presence outside was not attracting any undue attention from the assembled gathering.

"You're very lucky, Sir," Schneider observed.

"Lucky, Agent Schneider?" Junior queried

"To have such a wonderful view to look out on every day."

"Oh, there's no luck involved I assure you. Sixty years ago that lake was just a coupla hundred acres of worked-out Midwest farmland destined to become some unsuspecting descendant's lifetime millstone. That was until my Father relieved the particular family of their burden of responsibility and persuaded the appropriate authorities that it could be put to better use."

"You mean this is all man made?"

"Every last square inch of it, as far as the eye can see, plus more that it can't."

"That's amazing. Did your Father build it all?"

"He did all of the major engineering and landscape works then, when I inherited it all, my wife and I carried-on adding the various finishing touches over the last forty years."

"That sounds a very modest statement, if you don't mind my saying so."

"Not at all, but we did have some assistance from nature itself, you know. It's quite amazing looking back at those early photographs and comparing them, realising how easy it is to forget how much more barren it looked back then."

"How deep is it?"

"The lake? Oh mostly just a few feet - it's merely ornamental to cover what's underneath."

"Underneath?"

"My Father never paid for anything he didn't need to, so when somebody mentioned to him that they had a need for a facility in this area, he told them that he would rather like a lake in his grounds. The two projects kinda dovetailed together nicely."

"Facility? I'm not aware of any 'facility' on my doorstep."

"Oh I'm sorry, Agent Schneider, I appreciate that the FBI are guardians of certain aspects of our national security, but you can't do it all alone can you? I couldn't possibly reveal too many details, not unless I shot you afterwards and I don't think that would be appropriate, would it?" Junior chuckled at the thought. Schneider followed suit, slightly nervously due to this unexpected revelation. Junior continued: "I was born during the war, so I grew-up through the period when the cold war was at its height, when we were all worried about 'reds under the bed'."

"McCarthyism - we did a project on it at school. A blot on our historical landscape."

Junior guffawed at the trivial nature of the remark: "and no doubt your pinko-democrat teacher poured their heart out to all you impressionable youngsters about how free-thinking people were persecuted for having views unacceptable to the establishment of the time, and how we should fear the return of such un-American ideals - Land of the Free, Home of the Brave and all that?"

"Steady on Sir, I'm a Republican as well you know!"

"A Republican are you?" Junior chuckled: "they may still call themselves that but, like you my friend, most of 'em are all too young to have any idea of what it was like to have fought a war, then set-out to create the means of preventing it ever happening again. We developed the best defences in the world against every form of terrestrial or airborne atomic attack, then woke up one morning to hear the bleep-bleep of a Soviet satellite broadcast live on the radio as it made another pass just a hundred miles above our heads. Not only a quantum leap ahead of all of our advanced technology, but also out of range of anything we had even close to having a capability of destroying it, or its payload. Have you any idea how powerless that felt?"

Schneider took a deep breath at the thought before he responded, slightly agitated by the sentiments: "no Mr Kendrick, I confess that I don't."

"In which case, just imagine for a moment looking out on such a view as this," Junior swept his arm around the horizon, "then add the realisation that it could all disappear in a moment in one blinding flash that your government had no ability whatsoever to prevent, neither had they possessed the foresight to envisage that it could. Would that not spur you to some degree of independent action, had you the resources to take it?"

"But the cold war is long gone."

"Sure it is. Times change, people forget, governments become complacent - do you know we even have a piece of that damned Sputnik in the Smithsonian? And when they show it to the school kids of today, they all go 'wow! cool!' and take a picture of it with their little cameras to show their mom when they get home, a mom who replies 'that's nice dear' without even looking at the photo. I also go cool when I look at it, y'know? From the shudder it still sends down my spine - the reminder of our continued naivety."

There was a sound of voices behind them, accompanied by the clatter of high heels on the terrace. They turned to see Estelle Kendrick approaching, that seemingly irrepressible smile in full radiance as she chattered to a gentleman, in his late fifties and a good foot taller than she, whose arm she clasped in hers as she towed him to the spot where her husband and Schneider were standing.

Almost without breaking verbal stride, she turned to her husband: "Jackson dear, the Murdochs are in danger of making a scene if they don't have at least five minutes of your time to discuss their upcoming clambake back East at which, I warn you, they want you to be the keynote speaker." She turned to Schneider: "so Agent Schneider, I'm afraid I am going to have to take my husband back inside to disappoint them personally. However I have brought you a substitute." She looked up at her hostage who was smiling back at her: "a poor one I have to confess, but he does know a lot about the estate, having managed parts of it for the last twenty years, so I'm sure he can fill-in any gaps for you."

Junior shook hands with Schneider: "unfortunately Agent Schneider, it seems we have to end our discussion. It has been most interesting though."

With that, Estelle detached herself from the arriving captive, immediately reattaching to her husband, to lead him off back in the direction from which she had arrived.

One-Seven-Four

The tall gentleman offered his hand: "Agent Schneider, how do you do?"

Schneider took the hand, which engulfed his in a firm grip, and replied: "how do you do, Mr?"

"Sullivan. As Mrs Kendrick mentioned, I have the responsibility for some of the facilities here at Apeiron." He walked forward a few steps past Schneider, then turned-back to face the frontage of the house: "and behold there was a very stately palace before him, the name of which was Beautiful."

"Bunyan."

Sullivan appeared surprised at the response: "very good! I have always taken a great interest in the progress of pilgrims."

Schneider had already sensed that he was about to learn the real reason for tonight's invitation. If it was to be a coded message, he was not intending to provide the messenger with any comfort that the full meaning of it may, as the deliverer might hope, miss the mark: "and, no doubt, the successor to whom their sword would pass," he responded.

Sullivan surveyed the figure before him, a mildly quizzical look on his face: "for some reason, one does not expect to find too many scholars in your line of work."

"Or scholars who are also pilgrims?"

Sullivan once again surveyed his sparring partner for a few moments before responding: "I think that we can speak frankly, Agent Schneider?"

"That may be preferable, in the circumstances."

Sullivan's gaze moved to contemplate somewhere in the distance, as if assembling his thoughts before commencing a speech, then returned to look straight into Schneider's eyes: "assets are important in this unpredictable world, are they not?" He awaited a response, which was not forthcoming, so continued: "however much we may publically bemoan the concept, privately we value our assets above most everything. So when we find that an asset has been misappropriated, particularly a unique one, it causes us displeasure. Worse still, should such misappropriation result in the total loss of the asset, would we not seek compensation for the loss?"

"Compensation? Or retribution?"

"Maybe both, particularly should the loss cause us ..." he paused for effect, looking more intently at Schneider, "... concerns as to our, how should I put this ... continuity."

"Continuity is of importance to you?"

"It is of prime importance, particularly to a Facilities Manager."

"Facilities plural - so you manage more than just this one."

"We have more than one, yes."

"And where might those facilities be?"

"Here and there."

"Let me guess - Savannah, Memphis, Denver, Palm Springs."

"Among others, maybe."

"Palo Alto, La Crescenta-Montrose, San Diego, Strasbourg, Naples, Grand Cayman?"

"I believe some of those facilities may have closed recently."

"So, facilities close when they lose their manager?"

"Or when they lose their main asset."

"But assets are replaceable."

"Not in the case of unique ones."

"That could be reassuring to some."

"Not to us."

"You mentioned that assets may occasionally be misappropriated - would this be internally or externally?"

"That is for us to know."

"So you deal with all misappropriation internally?"

"We are generally capable of resolving our own problems, yes. But we do occasionally call for external assistance."

"In what circumstances?"

"When the misappropriation has become troublesome."

"To do so must cause tensions."

"Tensions?"

"Between privacy and disclosure."

"Neatly put. We find signposting is the best solution for tension."

"Signposting?"

"Most of our activities do not appear on any radar, that is how we like it to be. Those that do are signposts."

"Something out of the ordinary."

"Exactly."

"And for how long would these 'signposts' be displayed?"

"For long enough for those we select to notice them."

"And where do they lead?"

"To the terminus we have signposted."

"And if that terminus is difficult to find for those selected?"

"Termini are transient, they ultimately have to disappear."

"And the signposts?"

"They become redundant, the lettering fades in time."

"But what of those still following them?"

"They become marooned."

The two men stood in silence, watching each other closely, Schneider considering his next option, Sullivan awaiting it. After a few moments Schneider continued: "so, do you manage many assets?"

"Just enough to sustain our needs."

"And those needs are?"

"As I said before, we value continuity above all else."

"And 'we' are what? CIA? NSC?"

"Let's just say that we are what we are."

At that point, more voices could be heard approaching along the terrace. The conversation paused and shortly afterwards Chris McKinley appeared around the end of the building accompanied by Emil Friedmann; they approached Schneider and Sullivan. As they did, Friedmann greeted the taller man: "Mr Sullivan, I didn't know you were here this evening. Nice to see you again Sir."

He turned to McKinley: "it appears that I have brought you out here at an opportune time, Sergeant. Mr Sullivan here knows as much about Apeiron as anybody, far more than I do in any case. We don't get to see him out here as much these days as we might like." He turned to Sullivan: "I was about to try to give McKinley here a brief history of the estate, but perhaps I could leave him in your capable hands instead?"

"It would be a pleasure," Sullivan replied, pseudo-deferentially.

"In that case, if you will excuse me gentlemen, I will get back inside to our other guests." He acknowledged Sullivan briefly, then turned and disappeared around the corner.

"I thought you managed this facility, Mr Sullivan," Schneider queried sarcastically.

"Some facilities manage themselves, Agent Schneider, when properly evolved."

He turned to McKinley, rapidly changing the subject: "and did you have a bid on any of the paintings?"

McKinley laughed: "a bit out of my league I'm afraid." He turned to Schneider: "one of them already has a half-mil on it Sam, that wasn't you was it?"

"Sounds like it might be mine," Sullivan intervened, "was it the one with the bomb disposal group?"

"It was," McKinley responded.

"I particularly liked the tension in that one, it shows that despite the weight of inevitability, some men still have the inner-confidence to challenge the odds head-on." He turned to Schneider: "I am sure, Agent Schneider, that we all know of someone who, at some time, experienced the futility of taking-on something that was pre-ordained to failure. Wasn't it Bunyan who also said: 'better to be despised for too anxious apprehensions than ruined by too confident a security'?"

"It was," Schneider replied, "and he also said 'know, prudent cautious self-control is wisdom's root,' but that 'there is a limit at which forbearance ceases to be a virtue'." There was a silence, as Sullivan viewed Schneider with a look of almost mild admiration.

The silence was quickly broken by the sound of yet more voices approaching, this time from the opposite direction. Gloria Friedmann was walking across the top level of the formal gardens, with Chandler Clarke on her arm. As they reached the group, she spoke to Clarke: "here they all are, admiring the view no doubt." She released Clarke and addressed the others: "Chandler here has seen it all before of course, he knows all the little nooks and crannies from when we used to play hide and seek here as kids - but not as many as I did."

"She always won in the end," Clarke replied, "I was convinced that someone had built her new ones every time I came." The group all laughed politely.

Gloria moved over to Sullivan and hugged his arm fondly, looking-up at his face that was already projecting a warm smile back in her direction: "that would have been you, wouldn't it?" she asked him.

"Guilty as charged m'Lady," he responded, the smile widening into a satisfied grin as he looked at Chandler Clarke. "I could never bear the thought of this little one losing-out to a younger man, especially when she was intellectually his superior."

"Hey, steady-on!" Clarke complained, theatrically.

"Oh, my apologies Agent Clarke, that wasn't a reference to you," Sullivan replied. He then turned to Schneider: "but you see, sometimes traditions do not always serve the status quo when rigorously-applied, such as in the matter of paternal succession. Best person for the job, male or female, is a far better concept, don't you think?"

Gloria interrupted before the question could be answered: "now that's enough of your subversion, Gilbert! Mother has sent me out to fetch you in there ..." she nodded towards the Red Drawing Room beyond its window that overlooked them, "... for when the auction results are announced, because it looks like you may have a chance of being one of the successful bidders. So I hope that you have your chequebook with you!" She turned to address the other three: "I am whisking him away from you now, I hope you don't mind. Thank you so much for coming, I hope you had a good evening - and you Chandler, don't leave it so long next time!"

All three expressed their thanks for her hospitality and with that she walked the tall man off into the house; they watched in silence until the two figures disappeared. McKinley was the first to make a comment: "Gilbert Sullivan?" he said with a degree of derision, "not seriously?"

Schneider nodded as he mused: "that may not have been quite a comic opera tonight, but the performance and choreography were impeccable."

"This family has always been big on ulterior motives," Clarke observed.

"You think this evening was just about us, Chandler?"

"I know it was," Clarke responded, "there was nothing spontaneous about any of it, we have been shuffled around by an expert director to play our part in each separate scene, to recite our lines and receive individually the message of the author, before being reunited at curtain-fall outside of the theatre to discuss the merits of the performance."

"So," McKinley asked: "what exactly was it all about?"

It was Schneider who gave the answer: "it was about showing us how far we will be out of our league if we continue on our current path - but I think we've already sussed that. It was about suggesting how wrong we might be and about why, even if we are right, which we probably are, we will always be behind the game. It was about telling us that they have circled the wagons to enclose what needs to be protected. That there will always be those who will protect whatever it is, by whatever means they choose."

Schneider turned and looked through the window. Inside the room, the results of the auction were being announced by Estelle Kendrick. Somebody in the room was getting the good, or bad, news dependent on how closely attached they felt to their bank balance.

But the group outside could not see any of the expectant faces, only the side view of Estelle making the pronouncements from a slip of paper in her right hand. Alongside her, but half a pace behind, stood her husband, constant as ever, surveying the room ready to provide all of the support she might need. To his right, a little distance removed and facing the window, Emil Friedmann stood alongside his wife. He was completely absorbed in what Estelle was saying, admiring her every word. Gloria Friedmann looked straight through the window at Schneider; there was a contented expression on her face, which did not change. She was looking straight into his eyes. There was no sign of Jackson Kendrick III.

Schneider looked long and hard at Gloria. As he did he completed his summary: "we are being told that the circle will always remain unbroken."

"That we will always be on the outside, looking in?" McKinley asked.

"Exactly that. We may see the truth, but we will have no access to it."

"Or to gain access to it, we must risk being absorbed by the force surrounding the black hole it resides in."

"Now hold on!" Chandler Clarke interjected, his mood turning dark: "I hope you're not saying what I think you are."

Schneider turned to Clarke and in a subdued voice replied: "and what do you think Chandler? What is it we are saying?"

"That you are about to drop the cases. That they will get away with it again!"

"Get away with what, Chandler?" he replied with a heavy air. "Having a fiancé that met a killer at university before he turned into one? Or having a lawyer that moves heaven and earth to protect the family he became part of?"

"With murder, Sam! Oh no, not with pulling the trigger, or squeezing the windpipe. But by playing God and deciding when and where people's lives on this planet should end. Many people Sam, dozens, maybe even hundreds. Business rivals, inconvenient officials, your friend - almost!"

"Your Mother?"

Chandler Clarke looked at Schneider with an expression somewhere between disbelief and desperation. He could not reply, because the synaptic channel between his mind and his mouth was temporarily off-line.

Schneider continued in a calm tone: "so do we know any of that for certain? Or could Junior's expedient theory be nearer the truth - that Kryczek met Hilary Nicholson and gave her a theory, hoping that she would make a connection and turn on the family she was about to marry-into. But instead, Ms Nicholson rang her old friend and told him about Kryczek, so he came down here to silence her, plus everyone else in that group that knew him back then. As Chris said earlier, we have to disprove that, and any other explanations that may conveniently fall in our laps, before we can prove the rest"

"No!" Clarke almost moaned the response.

"Oh, rest-assured Chandler, we are not dropping these cases, not until our last options have evaporated. But evaporate they will, because the signposts to them are already fading, some through neglect, but most through assistance - assistance from even those we might expect to be on the same side as we are. We would not need those signposts had we asked the right questions while we had the window of opportunity to do so, but we didn't and now those windows are closed to us - Ms Nicholson, Ms Rolles, Cochrane, Bonetti, Kryczek, Shepherd himself, Stanton and Morley maybe - all of them beyond answering that crucial question that we would want to ask them with the hindsight we now have. Even your Mother, Chandler."

"Sam," McKinley said in a low tone. Schneider looked towards McKinley, who sloped his head to his right, indicating towards the side terrace.

There, just out of earshot was the servant Woodhouse, who, having gained Schneider's attention, swept his arm towards the main steps leading down to the forecourt: "your car has been brought around for you gentlemen."

Schneider looked through the window again. The scene was almost identical, except that Estelle was shaking someone's hand, someone that appeared to be very happy at handing her a cheque for what was probably an obscene amount for the canvas they had acquired. Her son-in-law was still one-hundred-percent focussed on her

Gloria Friedmann was concentrating on the window, as before, as was her father, also looking directly into Sam Schneider's eyes. Schneider turned away, walking towards the direction indicated by Woodhouse, followed by McKinley and, finally, a somewhat dejected Chandler Clarke.

As Clarke moved off, he cast one final look towards the house, momentarily catching Junior Kendrick's eye as he did so. It was Junior who turned away this time, back to surveying the room, a broad smile emerging on his face as someone within, but beyond external sight, caught his eye.

Chandler Clarke shook his head, then quietly under his breath concluded: "on the outside looking in."

epilogue

"This is KNKW evening news on Wednesday thirtieth July, two-thousand-and-three. It's eight p.m. and I'm Scott Adams. Today's headlines:

In Washington, The President calls for action on the thirty-eighth anniversary of the creation of Medicare.

On Wall Street, bond yields pulled back from yesterday's year-highs, soothing fears that the recent rapid rise in rates may lure some investors out of stocks.

And in sport, the Yankees cut Mondesi following his outburst after Sunday's game in Boston.

But first, today's top local news stories here in Wichita:

There was a large turnout at the funeral service for Jackson Kendrick the Third, which was held this morning at St Gregory's Church. Leading the mourners were Mr Kendrick's parents, his sister and her two young sons, along with the Governor of Kansas, State Senators and hundreds of national and local dignitaries. The lesson was read by Mr Kendrick's father, the widely-respected local businessman Jackson Kendrick Junior.

Jackson Kendrick the Third died just over a week ago when his Cessna Citation crashed in the Arizona desert, shortly after take-off from Las Vegas. He was piloting the aircraft himself and there were no other passengers on board. Initial investigations, which have not revealed any obvious mechanical failure, are concentrating on the probability that the accident was caused by pilot error.

Mr Kendrick had become CEO of a number of companies within the Kendrick business empire following his reconciliation with his family after a high-profile separation during the latter part of the nineteen-nineties, caused by serious personal problems including drug and alcohol addiction. Mr Kendrick's reformation was partly due to his romantic association with the well-known local businesswoman, Hilary Nicholson, to whom he had announced his engagement less than a year ago.

But in May this year, she became the first Wichita victim of the serial killer Sean Shepherd, whose sensational apprehension left Wichita Police Lieutenant Paul Kleberson laying in a coma in intensive care.

It had been anticipated by many market observers that Jackson Kendrick the Third would take over as President of the Kendrick Corporation sometime in the next couple of years, when his father eventually announced his long-anticipated retirement. However, recent persistent rumours linking several companies within the division of the Corporation already under the younger Mr Kendrick's control, and possibly even Jackson Kendrick the Third himself, to an ongoing investigation by the FBI and IRS into international money laundering and tax evasion, had brought those plans into some question.

In a connected story, Jackson Kendrick Junior and his daughter, Mrs Gloria Friedmann, attended the Wichita Coroner's Court later this afternoon to hear a verdict of accidental death recorded on Mrs Friedmann's husband, the leading Wichita lawyer Emil Friedmann. Mr Friedmann died in June when his Mercedes SUV left Highway Ninety-Six near Haven and crashed into a culvert. Mr Friedmann was travelling home from a business meeting in Hutchinson during the early hours of the morning.

Initial reports that his car had been seen earlier travelling at high speed near Yoder, closely followed by another vehicle containing two men, proved to be unfounded."

———— ◊ ————

Junior leaned forward in his leather armchair, picked-up the remote and hit the mute button. He sighed: "it's amazing how these TV news channels can condense such a difficult day into just a few short paragraphs."

"Would you prefer a 'Sixty-Minutes' exposé on it instead?" The question came from Sullivan, seated in an identical chair across the room.

"Of course not. As well as difficult, it's also been a long day - would you like a nightcap before you go?"

Sullivan nodded: "do you still have some of that Woodford Reserve?"

Junior got to his feet and smiled back: "is the Pope Catholic?"

"Tee-Total last I heard."

"Just as well, saves me having to send him a case with my plea for absolution." He turned to the sofa where his daughter was occupying one end: "how 'bout you Gloria?"

"I need to get the boys to bed Pops, it's way past their bedtime."

"I'll see to them," Estelle Kendrick intervened, gingerly getting-up from the same sofa: "I'm about ready to turn-in myself to be honest. By the time I've sorted them out, that'll be it for me. You stay Gloria, your Father looks like he's in the mood for talking the night away."

Estelle forced a weak smile as she ushered the boys from the corner where they were playing and, after the usual initial protestations, made sure they said goodnight to everyone, finishing with them throwing themselves into their mother's arms, who hugged them both while planting a long kiss on each of their heads in turn. Gloria watched as they left the room with her mother, who had rapidly become a pale shadow of her former self. The three deaths in as many months weighed heavily on her, now frail-looking, frame.

Gloria wiped away a small tear from her eye as the door closed behind them: "guess I'll have that nightcap after all Pops," she sighed as Junior wandered across to the cadenza. He opened it and took out a bottle and three glasses.

Epilogue

"They're fine boys," observed Sullivan, "the organisation will ultimately be in good hands."

"Yes," Junior replied somewhat deflatedly, "but not for another ten to fifteen years." He carried the bottle and all three glasses as he walked across to Sullivan, placing one glass on the table by his chair before pouring it about a quarter full.

"You'll be nearly eighty by then," Sullivan observed.

"What has that to do with anything?" Junior snapped back at him.

"Come on Mr Sullivan," Gloria tried to raise the mood, "Pops is as fit as a fiddle and you know it." Junior placed the next glass on her side table and repeated the dosage. With his back to Sullivan, he gave her a private, but approving, nod.

"I'm not so concerned about the strategic side," Sullivan continued, "it's whether Junior has the stamina for staying in the game for that length of time. He had already begun to ease-off, you know."

Junior shot Gloria another glance, raising his eyebrows disapprovingly, then wandered back across to his chair, placing the final glass on the table in front of it, into which he poured a substantially larger measure from the bottle. Placing the bottle well within reach, he picked-up the glass and relaxed back into the familiar soft leather. As he sipped the tawny liquid, he responded: "we have to cope with the hand we're dealt, but I accept that I had never bargained on having to lose the next generation within weeks."

"You haven't Junior," Sullivan observed, "not entirely."

"How many times have we had this discussion?" He looked across at Sullivan: "all three of us. I know my daughter is more than capable, always has been." He raised his glass to her, which she acknowledged likewise. "But the conservative world in which we conduct business still ain't ready to have the glazing in it's ceilings busted - and you know Gloria has always accepted that."

"Sure," Sullivan responded, "I know the chauvinists we have to deal with, but we also have to face facts here. I'm right about your stamina, and you're not gonna need that just until one of those boys reaches majority; you're gonna need it for a few more years until they get established. We could be talking about you still at the helm way past eighty you know. That's too much of a risk."

"I was only twenty-three when I had to take the helm, hadn't been in the business more than a twelve-month - and I didn't get any handover."

"But you would have if your father had lived longer. That was needs-must in a different time in a different world. We can't rely on good fortune any more, not in the twenty-first century on an ever-shrinking planet."

"He's right Pops," Gloria added, "the subject was a bit of fun for you to banter over while there was never a question of it happening, but that was before circumstance placed us in the situation we now find ourselves in."

Junior glared at her: "circumstance and your damned-fool husband's over-ambition."

"Pops!"

"I'm sorry Gloria, but how many times did we tell him not to cut Johnson any slack - both of us. But no, the great Emil thought he could control the uncontrollable."

"Well he could!" Gloria snapped.

"Johnson maybe, but not those evil so-called friends of his, as Emil found out to his ultimate cost when it was too damned late! Should never have let you talk me into bringing Johnson back into the fold."

"This is going nowhere Junior," Sullivan interceded, "that's all history. Can't change what's done - Johnson went completely out of control. We need to be looking forward now, there's only one future I can see and she's sat right there."

"I don't even need to be visible, Pops, I can work just as effectively in the background. I know the plan, heck I even helped you put it in motion. So you don't have to start again from scratch, I'm already up to speed."

"Look Gloria, I know it's the only alternative - OK? But there are other factors."

"Such as?"

"Such as you're now the most eligible widow in the country. What do we do with husband number two when he arrives in our lives?"

"He won't!" She scowled in her father's direction at the suggestion, continuing: "I don't know why you still can't accept that Emil was the love of my life. I need to move on as well you know, but it won't be into the arms of another man." Her eyes showed a mixture of grief and determination: "that aspect of life is done with, not that it was ever that important to either Emil or I once we were married, other then the wonderful results we've just said goodnight to. We gave you the heir and the spare you needed and, as far as sex is concerned, that's it for me."

"Can't say fairer than that, Junior," Sullivan observed.

"Alright, Alright," Junior held up his hands in surrender, "but if we're going that way, Sullivan, then you need to have your end of things nailed down tight - and keep it that way."

"It is Junior," Sullivan said with his usual quiet-confidence.

"No loose ends?"

"Not after today."

"What about Schneider?"

"There's nothing left for him to work on."

"He's never going to give up, you know - he's made promises."

"Promises?" Sullivan laughed dismissively.

"Yes, promises," Gloria interceded, "and he's a man of his word, just like his old friend is. Paul Kleberson's special, not something that you can say about too many people you meet. I can't help wondering how dangerous he is even in the state he's in, let alone if he ever recovers."

Epilogue

"That's unlikely, you know that. Anyway, we've overcome far greater adversaries, ones that were fully-functioning. I don't see what danger promises pose - they're an abstract concept."

"It's not what they are, Mr Sullivan, it's who they're made to. You've never met Annie Fleming have you? There's someone I would never have wanted as an enemy, but she has recently become just that, even though she doesn't know it. If I'm going to do this, I need your word she will never know."

"You need not doubt that you have it," Sullivan responded. He turned to Junior: "I will keep a special eye on Agent Schneider's activities. And on Lazarus, should he ever rise."

"In that case," Junior stood up, lifted the bottle from the table and carried it across to the other two: "a toast."

Gloria and Sullivan rose to meet him and he recharged all three glasses. He raised his in their direction: "To the future."

They chinked their glasses against his and chorused: "The future!"

———— ◊ ————

Schneider leaned across and turned-off the small portable TV. It had been allowed in Paul Kleberson's hospital room for the last month, following an apparent stalling of the recovery process. The doctors had decided by the end of June that Paul was conscious and were optimistic that he would soon demonstrate the restoration of some degree of movement. The physical tests seemed to confirm there was no permanent loss of muscular action, but there had been no further progress since.

Following a conference with other neurological experts, it was decided to allow all forms of sensory stimulation. So the goggles and headphones were removed and some equipment brought from his home, hence the small Hi-Fi from his kitchen and a pile of his favourite CDs which were played to him by visitors, accompanied by their recollections of memories associated with the tracks he heard. The television was used similarly, but was also sometimes left on during daytime periods when no visitors were present, tuned to one of the local news networks. Doctor Manderling was convinced that some spur was needed, some memory to respark the recovery; all they needed to do was find it.

Paul had pieced a lot of memories together over the two months since he had started to come around. Although he was able to face-up to what had happened, he still quickly switched-off the really bad parts. He had reached the stage, however, where he recognised that he would have to face those at some time.

Having established who he was and why he was where he was, he had started to attempt to move, but found that he could not. His arms, legs and neck all resolutely disobeyed the commands his brain was sending; a constant stream of commands went from his mind, but nothing responded. The most frustrating of these aspects were his eyes which, although able to focus automatically on anything placed in front of them, were still immobile; he could not move his eyeballs, nor open or shut his eyelids. Sleep was still being achieved courtesy of the medical staff, who placed a blindfold in place at times they considered suitable. These did not necessarily align with when Paul himself wanted to sleep, but he had no way of communicating such information.

The family had settled to a rotation routine, with one 'on duty' at McConnell, as Walter termed it, while the other two ran 'The Commune' in California. They kept the kids' routines as normal as possible, except for the fortnightly visits they would make to their father during weekend changeovers, when they would chatter constantly to his motionless form about all they had been doing in between. Paul loved the banality of those reports, it was so refreshing to have these inconsequential new events relayed to him with such enthusiasm that only a child can engender.

Sam had arrived at the base hospital just before eight p.m. that evening. When he entered the room, Annie was already there. She had flown-in the previous day to attend the funeral of Jackson Kendrick III, representing her family; she would be staying a week. She and RP had been similarly alternating their visits for nearly two months, one would visit for a week, then they would have a week at home together with their kids, then the other would visit. She had been due in Wichita at the end of that week, but the funeral had brought the visit forward a few days.

Annie had been telling Paul about the funeral. Had she been able to hear his reactions, she may have been shocked at his animosity towards the deceased. Sam had managed to shield Annie from most of the sordid details of how the FBI investigation had been developing. He had not been so reticent with Paul, who had not agreed with all of the conclusions Sam's team were reaching: *'if only I could speak,'* would be a constant mantra running through Paul's mind for hours after Sam left the room. It continually failed to work.

The reference to the investigation in the news bulletin brought a question from Annie: "is that your investigation they are referring to, Sam?"

'Come on Sam,' Paul prompted in his thoughts, *'it's about time you told Annie what's been going on.'*

"You know I can't discuss that with you Annie," Sam responded.

'But you do with me Sam, all the time,' Paul shouted back, silently.

"Not details Sam, just in general. They said money laundering and tax fraud; so was that Johnson alone, or the whole family?"

'The whole family Annie,' Paul tried to speak; he felt the frustration welling within him.

"I can't Annie, it's …"

"Is my Father's company implicated?"

"Annie …"

'No it isn't, Annie. Come on Sam, at least tell her that.'

Epilogue

"If my Dad is a crook, I'm the one who will have to deal with the fallout. Mummy's not the strongest, so am I looking at yet more grief from this monster?"

"Not that we are aware, Annie. But that's as far as I am prepared to go, and you are not to repeat that to anyone, is that clear?"

'Good man.' Paul thought, *'she's suffering enough heartache right now without all that anguish on top.'*

"Thank you Sam, at least I can concentrate on Paul here without those fears." She turned back to the figure on the bed and took his hand in hers once again.

Paul's mind registered a strange feeling, but couldn't figure-out what it was. He focussed on this in order to identify what it might be - months of nothing working, other than his brain, had made him acutely aware of anything unusual. Annie and Sam were talking, but Paul wasn't following what they were saying. Eventually he abandoned the attempt to identify what he had felt and refocused on the conversation.

Annie was speaking: "I will try and see Gloria before I go back this time, but I won't be going out to Apeiron. I don't really like the rest of the family to be honest Sam, they've always been, how can I put it? Distant."

"Did that include the son?" Sam enquired. Paul realised they must be talking about the funeral.

"Oh, I only met him a couple of times, but yes - in a different way, though. We were teenagers. Gloria was older; only a few years, but when you're that young it may as well have been two decades. I got on with her fine, but it seemed he was never interested in anything - certainly not me. I think our parents might have harboured some vague hope that we may have hit it off, like some long-time friends do, but there was never even the slightest spark. I thought he was a spoilt brat, to be honest; he probably thought I was a stuffy old Brit."

"That's something I can be glad of, and I suspect Paul would agree if he could."

'Damned right!' Paul found the prospect of Annie being swept up unknowingly into that circle quite abhorrent, then consoled himself: *'at least now I know the man was definitely stupid, or mad - or both.'* He felt another unusual occurrence, but again could not pin it down.

"Gloria found Paul fascinating you know," Annie replied.

'Really?' Paul hadn't even computed that one: *'actually Annie, I thought she was playing games with me.'*

"Rumour has it that she will take over from her brother," Sam responded, "did you get any indication of that today?"

'Really?' Paul hadn't computed that either.

"It was a funeral, Sam," Annie responded slightly miffed at the question, "I was a mourner - one of hundreds. Do you really think I went over to her in her widow's weeds and enquired what her meeting diary looked like for tomorrow?"

'Nice one Annie, that was unusually dumb of you Sam,' Paul thought.

The Mantis Pact

"I didn't mean …" Sam's attempt at recovery failed before it had started.

Annie glowered at him: "perhaps you forgot, Sam, that she was wearing black for two reasons - first, it was her only brother's funeral, and second she was going on afterwards to her husband's inquest. So if I am able to see her this week, before I go back, it will be to console an old friend at a very difficult time, not to act as some sort of conduit for an FBI enquiry. Is that understood?"

Paul felt something again. He tried to focus on it, but it was gone as soon as it started.

"I'm sorry Annie," Sam responded meekly, "that wasn't what I meant by the question." The room went silent.

Paul waited for the next part of the conversation to commence, but nothing happened: *'well, come on you two,'* he urged in his mind, *'you're supposed to be visiting me - you know, talking to me. Hello?'*

He felt something else. This time it had a familiarity - like a twinge, but he couldn't identify where it was coming from. The silence continued as the two visitors each tried to think of a new subject to change to.

But Paul was no longer thinking about other subjects, he was analysing this new data: *'so, you think that Gloria's taking over do you Sam? That may mean that Junior wasn't in full control of what was happening and this is a way of re-establishing that control; through a doting daughter who will do what she is told in order for her sons to inherit. But that's not what she was saying to me at Apeiron, she was as interwoven with everything as anybody else in that family.'*

Annie finally broke the silence: "I'm sorry too Sam, it was unfair of me to make assumptions like that."

"I'm an FBI Agent Annie, I'm never really off a case until someone's locked-up."

'Good you two,' Paul approved and felt another twinge, this time stronger. He quickly reasoned all of this was connected and his mind became excited by the prospect.

"Perhaps we should change the subject, "Annie concluded.

'No!' Paul's mind responded instantly, causing another twinge: *'start talking about the case again. Please! I need more info from you - both of you.'*

"Is that what you really want?" Sam's response was not wholly that of a friend. This time it was from an experienced interrogator who had sensed something that his subject wanted to talk about.

'Come on Annie,' Paul prompted silently, *'he's left the door open for you. Ask your question.'* This time the twinge was really strong and Paul thought it was on the right side of his body somewhere.

Annie did not respond immediately, wondering if it was really her place to ask an FBI Agent the question that had been gnawing at her ever since her father had relayed to her the news of the plane crash a week before.

Eventually she replied: "I suppose not."

Epilogue

She took a deep breath, then asked: "two accidents in a month, Sam. I'm not saying that's impossible, tragedy strikes families all the time. But it's got to be long odds that it should happen in such a way so soon after what occurred back in May."

"Is that your question Annie?"

'Oh, come on Sam!' Paul felt frustration that his friend was being too much the FBI Agent: *'this ain't evidence gathering, give the girl a break.'* Another twinge shot through his body; this time it was definitely on his right side. He also felt a temperature change - something warm.

"My question is, are these incidents all connected?"

'And if you even think you're going to bat that one off with any form of no comment, Sam, I'll jump out of this bed and thump you!' Paul was very agitated. He was processing two streams of thought, the conversation and the twinges, the latter of which were transforming into a constant warm feeling on his right side.

"Jackson Kendrick the Third's plane crashed in the desert just across the Arizona border, about twenty minutes after taking-off from Vegas. He was alone, he was a good pilot, he had made all normal radio communications during the flight and there were no Maydays. The post mortem did not show up any medical issues. The NTSB has found nothing obviously wrong with the plane, it was well-maintained, everything seems to have been working normally all the way to the point where the trace dropped off the radar screens. As there are no cockpit or flight recorders on that type of aircraft, all they can do is keep looking through the wreckage; we won't know the outcome of that for months. The Kendrick Corporation are paying for a full investigation, so they obviously want to know what happened as well."

'Or they want to make it look like they want to know what happened,' Paul's scepticism was one of the first things that had returned to him: *'they already know what really happened.'*

"What about Emil - what happened there?" Annie asked.

'He was murdered Annie,' Paul's response was instant: *'maybe by the family, more likely by his brother-in-law. Whoever it was, he had either become a liability or had outlived his usefulness.'*

"He just ran off the road into a culvert," Sam replied. "Again, the vehicle examiner found nothing wrong mechanically, and there was no sign of impact damage other than what would have been caused by the accident itself. He was on his own driving home, early hours of the morning. By all accounts he was not a reckless driver, certainly had no tickets to his name. Coroner concluded he fell asleep at the wheel."

Paul was trying again to communicate: *'tell her about the impact speed, Sam - estimated at ninety-plus you told me. And the cruise control was off - people who fall asleep at the wheel at that time of the morning more often than not are in cruise control, you know that.'* The warm feeling on his right side was growing. Paul was beginning to wonder if it was his arm he was feeling.

"Yes," Annie replied, "I had a telephone conversation with Gloria a couple of weeks after it happened; she said that was what it was looking like. I only met him occasionally, but he struck me as a really steady guy, not the type to fall asleep at the wheel. He didn't drink either."

"No, post mortem showed no alcohol in his system, but he had eaten well - he had been at a business function. Also, Gloria told the coroner he had been having trouble sleeping in the weeks leading-up to the accident."

'Did she now?' Another revelation raising Paul's suspicions. As he absorbed it, the feeling in his right arm became warmer, and he was aware that it was originating from the end of the arm - in his hand maybe.

His thoughts continued: *'why should she say that? To influence the coroner? Who was it? Truman I bet, especially if it was involving the Kendricks; he's in their pockets. Even if he isn't, he couldn't spot a barn door if it fell off it's hinges on top of him. Assuming it's true, why would someone who couldn't sleep, fall asleep at such a conveniently inconvenient moment - doing ninety down a dead straight deserted piece of road with his foot hard on the throttle?'*

"But, what about this other car?" Annie asked.

'Yes Sam, what about this other car?' Paul repeated the question in his mind, *'you were convinced it was connected when you told me about it.'* Paul felt a tingle at the end of his arm; his attention was diverted momentarily. Was that his fingers? Could he feel something touching his fingers?

"That came from a farmhand who was returning home from helping out at a neighbour's place when his old truck had overheated, not for the first time. So he pulled off the road for a while to let it cool before continuing home. He had nodded off for a few minutes, when the truck was rocked by a vehicle going past at high speed. As he woke up, he thought a second vehicle had gone by at the same high speed. He also thought he saw two sets of rear lights going off down the road, but he couldn't be sure. In fact he wasn't even called to give evidence, because the coroner thought his statement was too unreliable - he had been drinking."

"So he could have seen what he thought he saw," Annie added.

'Of course he could,' Paul was desperate to join in the conversation. The tingling was getting stronger; it was in the fingers of his right hand - he could feel them now. He could also feel what was touching them - another hand! He couldn't see either visitor, so quickly orientated the voices. Sam was to his left, Annie to his right. It had to be Annie's hand, and the more he thought of that, the more the memory began to return of what her hand felt like in his. Yes, it was Annie's hand. He had to let her know he could feel it, but his fingers refused to obey the commands. He was becoming frustrated.

"We found nothing to back it up Annie."

"But, if someone ran him off the road ... " Sam cut her off.

"If you're thinking murder Annie, or a hit, then they would have stopped to see if they were successful. We combed both sides of the road for half a mile in

Epilogue

either direction, looking for some sign the other vehicle may have stopped, or turned around. Nothing."

'They didn't stop,' Paul was responding as if he was doing case analysis with Sam. *'What if it was meant as a warning? If that was the case, it wouldn't have mattered to them whether Friedmann was alive or dead.'*

Paul could feel Annie's hand gripping his.

"Look at me Sam." Annie's voice was determined. Sam was still standing-up beside the bed. He looked straight across the bed at Annie, sitting on the other side holding Paul's right hand. She was looking Sam straight in the eye: "are you telling me, Sam Schneider Head of the Wichita FBI, that both of those cases are closed?" Paul felt Annie's grip tighten as she said the words. He tried to respond, but again nothing happened.

"Yes - officially," Sam responded sheepishly, "unless something untoward comes out of the NTSB investigation."

'That's very selective of you Sam,' Paul's annoyance was rising, both with his old FBI friend and at the feelings he was struggling to identify. *'The truth, Annie, is that they cannot be closed until all the rest of the investigation has panned-out, and that won't be allowed to happen. Why? That's the question you would ask me if you could and, if I physically could, I would certainly give you the answer! Tell you about the connections between Shepherd's companies and too many subsidiaries in the Kendrick empire to be a co-incidence. About the bent members of the Wichita Police Department who ran interference throughout for the Kendrick family until they conveniently "disappeared", and the FBI Agent who also did a disappearing act with some disks. But don't be too hard on Sam, Annie, because he knows instinctively what's been happening, he just can't prove it. If he voices his concerns too early, it will be Sam that's off the case, leaving the Kendricks home and hosed. So Sam pretends not to push too hard, running two investigation logs, just like I had to. If only I could get up out of this damned bed to help him!'*

Annie was looking at Paul led on the bed; it was as if she was receiving the knowledge he was sharing with his mind. The silence went on for what seemed like an age until she eventually turned to look Sam straight in the eye again: "and unofficially?"

Sam sighed: "of course not. You asked me to give you a promise back in May, and I did. I'm still keeping that promise Annie, and I will continue to keep it until I can face you and tell you, officially, what you asked me to."

"So you don't think that the people responsible for doing this to Paul are dead, is that what you're telling me?" Annie asked.

"Some are." Sam responded.

"But not all." Annie was pushing him now. Sam didn't respond.

"Sam, if some are still alive, then that means you know who they are ..."

"Annie, I can't ..."

Annie ignored him: "... which can only mean one thing."

Paul was no longer really taking this in. Instead he was focussing all of his efforts on the muscles of his right hand, trying to make them work.

Again Sam did not respond, but he maintained eye-contact with Annie. He wasn't going to tell her, not verbally, but he wasn't going to lie to her either. Annie had got her answer, unspoken though it was.

She looked at Paul's motionless form on the bed, completely unaware of the invisible inner turmoil this conversation was causing him. After a few moments, she turned back to Sam. He was still looking straight at her.

She resumed eye-contact once more: "Sam, does Paul know it was the Kendricks that did this to him?"

Sam stood motionless. Annie's eyes implored him for an answer.

Then, suddenly, she jumped to her feet and looked at Paul with a shocked expression. She was still holding his hand: "Oh my God!"

"What?" Sam responded, but Annie ignored him.

"Paul? Was that you?" she gasped.

Sam looked at the bed, then back at Annie: "What? What is it Annie?"

"Do it again!" Annie shouted at the form on the bed, almost hysterically, as she sat back down as close to Paul's side as she could.

Adding her other hand to the grip, she shouted again: "Paul, can you hear me? Do it again!"

Sam was transfixed to the spot, he wanted to move to his friend's side, but he feared that doing so would lose the moment.

Then Annie shouted to him: "get the doctor, Sam!"

She didn't take her eyes from the figure on the bed, her expression a mixture of joy and trepidation as she concluded: "Paul's just squeezed my hand again!"